SECURITY

By
SUSAN HODDY

Second Edition published September 2019

Cataloguing-in-Publication details are available from the National Library of Australia.

ISBN: 978-0-6480857-9-9

Website: https://www.susanhoddy.com

OTHER BOOKS BY SUSAN HODDY

The Lepidoptera Vampire Series

Attraction
Awakened
Affirmation

Grow Old Along With Me

THE BEST IS YET TO BE

~Robert Browning~

PROLOGUE

"Rebecca Landers," called the doctor, standing in the doorway to his office, looking around the sterile hospital waiting room for his patient.

Hearing her named called, Rebecca looked up from the book she was reading, quickly placed it into her handbag and followed the doctor into his office, nervously smiling as she entered.

"Take a seat, Rebecca," said Dr Ness, gesturing to the chair in front of his desk. "How are you feeling today?"

"Good, thanks," said Rebecca, politely smiling, and sitting on the chair and placing her bag on the ground. "So… what do the last MRI results show?"

"Good question. Let's have a look," said Dr Ness, as he manipulated the mouse on the desk to bring up the results on his computer screen.

Rebecca waited patiently, and watched him compare the new MRI to the last one done eight months ago in October.

Turning the screen around to show her the results, Dr Ness said, "I am afraid I don't have good news. It seems the tumour has returned." Manipulating the mouse's pointer on the screen he outlined where it was located on the scan in her brain. "There is also a cyst which is growing on top of the tumour as well."

"Oh, right," said Rebecca, as she tried to hold back just how scared and anxious she felt. "So that means another operation then?"

1

"Yes, I'm afraid so, Rebecca," said Dr Ness, watching the disappointment in his patient's face. "And by the looks of how big this has grown in such a little time frame, the sooner we do the surgery the better."

Rebecca's nodded and her eyes closed briefly, as she took a deep breath and exhaled it slowly. Staring straight ahead, she remembered how she felt weak and sick for days in hospital after the first brain tumour was removed. It had taken her three months to fully recover and most of those days were spent convalescing in bed or on the lounge at home, whilst her husband, Jackson and daughter, Paige, looked after her and tended to her every need. She certainly wasn't looking forward to the next lot of surgery, let alone having no smell or taste for two months as her nasal passages recovered from the invasive surgery, or the time frame it took for her anxiety to subside and her brain to recover.

"So, we will go up through the nose again to take the tumour and cyst out. Hmm… I may even see if I can get can the same ear, nose, throat doctor as well. You know, Dr Gossford," said Dr Ness, watching no emotion come from Rebecca. "You Ok, Rebecca?" He stepped out from behind his desk and sat in the chair next to Rebecca.

Rebecca blinked once slowly and her heart hammered in her chest. She hadn't heard a word he said about the next surgical procedure

CHAPTER ONE

Terrific… peak hour traffic; don't you just love it, thought Rebecca, as her car approached the overhead bridge. Frustrated, that once again, she had to sit in traffic that was bumper to bumper like a car park, she sighed. *I can't wait for them to finish the road works here. Humph, another couple of months… Note to self: Must find an alternate route from work to home on Fridays.*

Rolling her shoulders backwards to try and release the ache from the stressful day she had been subjected to at the mining company she worked for, Rebecca thought, *Not sure I like this new manager. Already I am sick and tired of him looking over my shoulder every minute of the day. Talk about impatient.* Picturing her husband, Jackson, and his soothing hands, she couldn't wait to get home, as she knew he would be able to massage out the knots in her shoulders.

With the traffic at a standstill, Rebecca thought about the plans that she, Jackson and Paige had. She always loved the weekends, as this meant catching up with family and friends, and relaxing.

Hearing a song on the radio, which she loved, she turned up the volume. Luckily, it was a hot day and she had the air conditioner on and windows up, as heads would be turning, because the speakers were thump, thumping. Singing along and tapping the steering wheel to one of her favourite songs, 'Burn It To The Ground' by Nickelback, she noticed in her rear vision mirror an ambulance and police car approaching from behind, so she turned down her radio and pulled over to the left hand side of the road to let them pass through.

Unnerved by seeing the ambulance and police pass by her car, because usually it meant that there had been some sort of accident, it dawned on her that maybe that's why the traffic was so bad today.

Hmm, maybe it's not just the normal peak hour traffic jam on a Friday and the road works. I hope whoever it is will be Ok and go home safely to their family, thought Rebecca.

As Rebecca stopped at the first set of traffic lights, which were on the overhead bridge, she could see blue and red lights flashing up ahead. The police were re-directing traffic around the area of the accident, and everyone was driving watchfully around the accident site.

It only looks like one car has been involved, thought Rebecca, craning her neck.

The traffic lights turned green and Rebecca moved forward slowly. As she approached the accident site, she could see a white work ute, which had smashed into the metal guard rail on the bridge. Looking at the damage as she drove by, she noticed the fire brigade had been called out to try and cut the person out of the car, but couldn't see much else as they had a tarp around the ute and person, so that passers-by couldn't see what was happening.

Hmm... that ute is very similar to Jackson's. Rebecca craned her neck to see if she could get a better look at the car. *Can't see anything.* Rebecca shook her head and dismissed any other thoughts of the what-ifs and maybes that were entering her mind for consideration. Frustrated, she watched as every driver, including herself, was gawking at the car crash and going slower than expected, as the police were directing traffic around the crash site.

Passing by the accident, Rebecca felt anxious, and her body started to quiver all over. Looking down at her arm, she noticed goose bumps appearing on her skin. Wincing, as she felt a sudden wave of sickness in her stomach, she thought to herself, *Poor bugger, I hope they'll be all right.*

After passing the accident, she pulled up to the next set of traffic lights and was glad to be away from the accident scene and on her way home. Waiting for the lights to turn green, she started thinking about all the things she and Jackson could do that weekend.

Might see if Jackson wants to go out for a few drinks tonight or grab some takeaway. Maybe we could go for a swim too. That should relax me. Just need to drop Paige at her friend's house for their sleepover tonight and we have the house all to ourselves, thought Rebecca.

The traffic lights seemed to be taking a long time to turn green, so Rebecca decided to ring Jackson to see what time he would be home this afternoon from work.

Instead of answering, his mobile didn't pick up and she got his recorded phone message, "Hi you have called Jackson, leave a message."

As the message did its usual beep, she said, "Hi babe, I am stuck in traffic, and just wondering what time you will be home today? I was thinking we could get some takeaway for dinner or head out for some drinks. Let me know what you think? Give me a ring when you get this message. Love you. Bye." Pressing the end button on her mobile, she noticed the traffic lights turn green and slowly moved forward in her car and watched the traffic start to dissipate.

The letterbox was overflowing with mail when Rebecca pulled the car into the driveway. As she stepped out of her car to retrieve the mail, she noticed a moving van had pulled up at number eight in her street. *Looks like the old Thomas family house has finally been rented out again. I wonder who is moving in. I must introduce myself when they get settled in.*

Looking through her mail as she walked into the kitchen, Rebecca was met by her daughter, Paige, who had been eagerly waiting for her to arrive home.

"Mum, can you drop me off at Sydney's house soon? I promised her I would come over straight after you got home," said Paige, impatiently.

"Sure, sweetheart," said Rebecca, placing her handbag and the mail on the counter. "Do you have all of your stuff packed and ready to go?" She ran through a list of things she would need for a two-day sleep over.

"Yes… I have everything, Mum," said Paige, rolling her eyes.

"Ok… give me ten minutes, sweetie. I just want to get changed into something more comfortable and get a drink," said Rebecca.

"Oh, Ok," said Paige, taking her phone out of the back pocket of her denim jeans and messaging her friend what time she would be arriving.

Pulling into their driveway, Rebecca remembered how she first met Sydney's parents many years previous. Both their daughters had started Year One together at the same school and eventually became good friends. She remembered the two girls having sleepovers at each other's houses, and Paige telling her that they always treated her like their own daughter. Over the years Rebecca and Jackson had become close with Doreen and Steve and had always enjoyed their friendship.

"Come in," said Doreen, opening the front flywire door. "Haven't seen you for a while. How have you both been?"

"I've been good thanks, Doreen. And you?" said Rebecca, giving her a warm hug.

"We've both been well," said Steve, walking towards Rebecca and Paige.

"Yep. I'm good," said Paige to Steve and Doreen, noticing her friend, Sydney, walking towards the doorway. "Sydney... hi, how's it going?" She rushed over and gave her a hug.

"Good. Better now you're here," said Sydney, smiling and giving Paige a hug back. "Hi, Mrs Landers."

"Hello, Sydney. Good to see you, love," said Rebecca, smiling.

"Thanks. It's nice to see you too. Been way too long," said Sydney, smiling. Turning to Paige and taking her by the hand, she said, "Come on... I have something to show you in my room. Let's go..."

"Come on in. I'll make you a cuppa," gestured Steve, watching the two girls quickly walk towards Sydney's bedroom.

"Thanks, Steve. That will be great," said Rebecca, following him into the house.

Looking at her watch, Rebecca couldn't believe how fast the time had gone since she had arrived at Doreen and Steve's house. She had already been there for an hour. "Well... I had better head off. Jackson is probably at home waiting for me. We can catch up some more when we see you both on Sunday around five o'clock to collect Paige," said

Rebecca, standing and placing her handbag on her shoulder. "Thanks for the cuppa."

"No probs. It's been nice catching up. Hey, did you want to come for a barbeque on Sunday?" said Doreen, standing.

"I will talk it over with Jackson and let you know, if that's Ok," said Rebecca, taking the car keys out of her handbag.

"Sure, no probs," said Doreen, leaning in to give Rebecca a hug.

"Drive safely, and we will catch you on Sunday," said Steve, giving her a hug goodbye.

"I will," said Rebecca, hugging him back.

Entering the hallway as Rebecca got near the front door, Paige said, "See ya, Mum."

"Bye, sweetheart. See you Sunday around five o'clock," said Rebecca, giving Paige a warm hug.

"Will do," said Paige, hugging her back. "Love you, Mum."

"Love you too, sweetie," said Rebecca. "Bye."

Pulling away from the driveway, waving goodbye, Rebecca thought, *I haven't heard from Jackson yet. It's not like him to not ring me back. Maybe he left his phone in his car and hasn't got my message yet.* Shrugging it off, she continued to drive home.

Finally turning into her street, Rebecca was distracted by her thoughts of the many things Jackson and she could do tonight. Glancing into the rear view mirror, she noticed a police car following her. As she pulled into her driveway and pressed the garage door remote, which was on her sun visor, she noticed the police car, in her rear view mirror, had pulled into her driveway too.

I know I haven't done anything wrong, so I wonder what they want, thought Rebecca. Anxiously, she pulled the car into the carport, put the car in park and turned off the engine. Getting out her car, she watched the two police officers walk towards her.

"Mrs Landers, is it?" said Officer Fuddin, in her Irish accent.

"Yes," Rebecca said, apprehensively. "What can I do for you?"

"Can we go inside and talk for a moment?" said Officer Lough, in his Scottish accent.

"Sure," said Rebecca, taking the door keys out of her bag. *I wonder what they want.*

Opening the front door, she heard the alarm beep, and entered the code to turn it off. "Come in, officers," gestured Rebecca, holding the door open.

Proceeding inside to the kitchen, the two officers followed her, but they were not saying a word.

"Can we sit down here, Mrs Landers?" said Officer Fuddin, pointing to the kitchen table and chairs.

"Yes… but what is this all about? I didn't break any traffic rules, did I?" asked Rebecca, walking over to the table.

"It's not about your driving ma'am. It's your husband, Jackson," said Officer Lough, sitting down at the table with the other officer.

"What about Jackson?" said Rebecca, taking a seat at the table.

"I am so sorry to tell you this, Mrs Landers, but your husband has been in a car accident and… well… I have some bad news," said Officer Fuddin, as she reached for Rebecca's hand. "He passed away on the bridge near your house this afternoon."

At first Rebecca's body felt like someone had knocked the wind out of it and her mind was numb from the shock. As she looked into the female officer's eyes, the tears started to flow freely down her cheeks. Sobbing uncontrollably, she asked, "Are you sure?"

Officer Fuddin nodded slowly.

"No… Jackson… I can't believe it," screamed Rebecca, as she placed her hands over her face and cried uncontrollably.

Without emotion and staring aimlessly out the window of the police car, Rebecca watched other cars whizz by. The next thing she knew was they were pulling up outside the Royal Perth Hospital.

"Mrs Landers, would you like us to call anyone for you, for some support?" asked Officer Fuddin, sitting next to her in the back seat.

"Sorry… what are we doing here again?" asked Rebecca, with a furrowed brow. She couldn't comprehend what was happening.

"I asked if you would like us to ring someone to help you with the identification of Jackson's body," said Officer Fuddin, placing her hand on Rebecca's.

Rebecca's eyes widened and tears filled her blood-shot eyes as realisation hit her like a bag of cement coming to land directly on her chest. Light-headed and confused as to why this had happened, her body weakened, slumped on the back seat of the patrol car and she fell unconscious.

Disoriented, Rebecca woke to find herself in a hospital bed. With her eyes searching the dimly lit room, but not remembering why she was there, she spotted the female police officer, whom she recognised from earlier today at her home, sitting on a beige, vinyl chair next to the bed.

"How are you feeling?" asked Officer Fuddin, sitting up straight, when she noticed Rebecca was awake.

"I'm a bit light headed. But I am Ok," said Rebecca, touching her head.

"Do you remember anything we have told you today?" asked Officer Fuddin.

The instant the officer asked the question, Rebecca remembered.

Your husband, Jackson has crashed his car on the bridge near to your home. We believe he died of a heart attack, but won't know for sure until they do an autopsy.

Nodding to the police officer, the tears started to form in Rebecca's eyes as she took the blanket off her body and moved to the side of the bed, dangling her legs over the side. "Are you sure it was my Jackson?" asked Rebecca, her heart pounding in her chest, hoping the officer was mistaken.

"We are certain it is Jackson, ma'am. We pulled his identification out of his car at the scene of the accident," said Officer Fuddin.

"No... No... please don't let this be true," she screamed. She couldn't believe that her loving husband had been taken so soon from her.

With sympathetic eyes, the female officer rose from her chair, placed her hand on Rebecca's back and rubbed it slowly. Handing her a tissue, she said, "Is there anyone I can call for you?"

Looking blankly at the officer, Rebecca blinked slowly and said, "Umm... eh...yes. Did I bring my mobile phone with me or my handbag?" Rebecca couldn't even remember leaving home, let alone what she took with her.

Officer Fuddin bent down next to the bed and picked Rebecca's handbag up off the floor and handed it to her.

"Thank you," said Rebecca, her hands shaking, as she took the bag from the officer and opened the zipper to find her mobile. Pressing 'M' on her contacts list, Rebecca flicked through the list to find her mum and dad's number. But she then remembered that they were away on a caravanning holiday around Australia.

Oh Mum, Dad, I wish you were here. I just need a cuddle and to know everything will be all right again, thought Rebecca, as she scanned through her phone again for someone else to call, trying to hold back her heaving sobs.

"Could you please call this number and explain what's happened and ask her to come and help me?" said Rebecca, handing her mobile phone to Officer Fuddin.

"Yes, ma'am. I will ring Penny for you now," said Officer Fuddin, looking at the name on the screen to ring. As she held the phone to her ear, the officer listened to the phone ring and then finally ring out. "She's not answering, ma'am. Would you like me to ring someone else for you?"

"No. She is probably busy... can you try again?" asked Rebecca.

"Yes ma'am," said Officer Fuddin, dialling the number again.

The female officer tried Penny's number a few more times, but there was still no answer. "Sorry ma'am, it keeps ringing out."

"Umm... maybe Mitch. He is my neighbour," said Rebecca, wiping her runny nose and the tears from her face.

"Ok. I will give him a ring," said Officer Fuddin, looking through the phone contacts list on Rebecca's mobile.

Staring into space, Rebecca's body heaved, as she sobbed and tried to hold back the tears. *Why has this happened now? We were so happy. This isn't fair.*

Rebecca listened to the female police officer talk to Mitch on her phone, and then noticed a tall, black-haired man in a grey suit enter the room. As he approached Rebecca, who was sitting on the side of the bed, he said, "Hello, I'm Doctor Simons. How are you feeling?"

"Numb… I… I just can't believe it," said Rebecca, sobbing.

He nodded and said, "That's completely understandable. I would like you to take one of these sedatives, dear. It will help to calm your nerves."

"Oh, Ok," said Rebecca, blankly reaching out to take the tablet out of his hand. After she took the sedative with some water, Rebecca lay down in a foetal position on the bed and closed her blood-shot eyes. With her chest aching from the heartbreak she had endured, the sedative started to work and she soon fell asleep.

A few hours later, Rebecca woke to find a blanket had been placed on her and the room in darkness. The only light coming into the room was the light from under the doorway. Looking over to the window she realised it was dark outside and wondered how long she had been asleep for. As she looked around the room with her tightened, tear-stained face, she noticed a figure sitting next to her bed on the vinyl chair. At first she though it was the female officer until he spoke.

"Hello Rebecca," said Mitch, standing up and switching on the dim light in the room, next to her bed. "I am very sorry for your loss. I can't believe Jackson is gone." His voice was low and sincere.

"Me neither," said Rebecca, squinting her eyes from the light. Sitting up, she noticing he looked wretched.

"What can I do to help you?" asked Mitch, as he sat down on the edge of the bed and placed his hand on hers.

"I know it's a lot to ask, but could you please come with me to the morgue to identify Jackson's body. I… I don't think I can handle this on my own," said Rebecca, as the tears spilled over onto her cheeks.

Mitch's heart was heavy as he looked at her with tears welling in his eyes. "Sure," he said, trying to hold back his croaky voice. He wanted to be strong for his good friend and neighbour, but at the same time, he was gutted that one of his friends had passed away.

Swinging her legs over the side of the bed, Rebecca tried to stand, but her legs seemed to give way.

"Are you all right?" asked Mitch, catching her from falling and placing her back on the bed. "Would you like me to get you anything?"

She shook her head slowly, with a furrowed brow and said, "I don't need anything. I just want to go and say goodbye to Jackson."

Mitch put his arm around Rebecca's waist to help her get off of the bed. "Do you think you can walk?"

Taking a deep breath, Rebecca said, "I don't think so. Can you take me over to that wheelchair in the corner?" She was weak and she knew she wasn't going to be able to walk without the assistance of a wheelchair.

As they approached the doors to the morgue, Rebecca swallowed hard and tried to compose her breathing. Blinking slowly, her hands shaking as she wiped her tear-stained face, she felt her stomach temporarily become nauseated, and wondered if she was going to vomit. "Can we stay here for a minute...? I don't feel too good."

"Sure..." said Mitch, coming to stand in front of her, looking at her pale face. "Why don't I go and get us both a hot drink? It may help your nerves, Bec. Ok?"

Staring blankly ahead, she nodded.

Returning a few minutes later with a tea from the vendor machine, Mitch knelt on the floor in front of Rebecca and placed the cup into her trembling hands. "Drink this... it will make you feel better. Ok?"

As her gloomy eyes adjusted from the staring at the floor to Mitch's face, she nodded in appreciation. Taking her first sip, Rebecca's nauseated stomach started to settle a bit and by the time she had finished her tea, she was feeling brave enough to see Jackson. "I am ready to go in now. Can you please wheel me in?"

"Ok," said Mitch, taking her empty cup and placing it in the bin.

Mitch pressed the button on the wall for the double doors to open inwards to the morgue. When they opened, a distinct cold, sterile smell came gushing his way and into his nostrils. Pushing Rebecca into the white, vinyl-covered floor room, the wheelchair's wheels squeaked until they stopped in front of a morgue attendant.

"Hello... would you like some time alone with him?" asked the attendant, gesturing to Jackson, who was behind him.

She nodded and said, "Yes, please."

"I will be right outside those doors when you are ready to leave. Take as much time as you need," said the attendant, with his hand on her shoulder.

"Thank you," said Rebecca, in a soft voice.

Mitch pushed Rebecca over to the side of the room, where Jackson's lifeless body was. Holding back the tears as he stood next to his friend, Mitch placed his hand on Rebecca's shoulder and said, "I'll wait outside too. There is no rush. Take your time."

"Thanks, Mitch," said Rebecca, as she pulled herself up out of the wheelchair and stood next to Jackson, who was lying on a metal table with a white sheet pulled up to his chin. She didn't even notice Mitch leaving the room and wiping the tears from his eyes.

You look peaceful; like you're asleep, my sweet man, thought Rebecca, as she lightly stroked his hair. Studying every inch of his face, her tears flowed over onto her cheeks and she started to weep.

With his ghostly, slitted open eyes looking back at her, she placed her head on Jackson's chest and wrapped her arms around him, as best she could.

I wonder why your heart gave up? You were healthy. I don't understand what happened.

After a few minutes she kissed his forehead and then his lips. His lips were cold and not at all what she had expected. As she stood there looking at his lifeless, hospital-gowned body, she placed his hand in hers and held it firmly, wondering if they would ever meet again, one day, in the afterlife.

"I am going to miss you so much, Jackson… God, how I love you… What am I going to do without you?" She had so many questions, but there were no answers to be heard from her loving husband, only silence.

Two hours had passed since Rebecca entered the morgue to say her goodbyes to Jackson. When the doors swung open and the morgue attendant entered the room, he found Rebecca resting on Jackson's chest, with tears streaming down her face.

"Sorry to disturb you Mrs Landers, but the police are here for the formal identification. Are you ready?"

"Yes…" she said, sitting back down in the wheel chair and wiping her tear-stained face. "Send them in."

"Yes, ma'am," said the morgue attendant, as he gestured to the two police officers, who were standing at the doorway, to come in.

The same two police officers who came to Rebecca's house to let her know of Jackson death, were the ones that came in for the identification. They just asked her one question.

"Mrs Landers… can you please let us know if this is your husband Jackson Landers?" said Officer Lough, standing next to the table.

She nodded, wiped her nose with a tissue and said, "Yes… this is Jackson Landers."

"Thank you, Mrs Landers" said Officer Lough.

Rebecca nodded and wiped her overflowing tears away with the same tissue.

"Would you like us to give you a ride home?" said Officer Fuddin, standing next to Rebecca.

"No, thanks. I will take Rebecca home," said Mitch, from the back of the room, as he watched the male officer tagging Jackson's body for identification purposes. "We live across the road from each other."

"Right. Ok. Well… we will be off then. If there are any questions you need answered, Mrs Landers, please don't hesitate to ring. Here is my card," said Officer Fuddin, handing her a business card.

"Thank you," said Rebecca, numbly staring at the officer.

As the police left the room, the morgue attendant approached Rebecca and said, "Mrs Landers… I am sorry for your loss… here are your husband's personal items."

Looking at the clear plastic zip lock bag that the attendant was handing her, Rebecca noticed that Jackson's wedding ring, wallet, phone, and jewellery were in the bag.

"Thank you," said Rebecca, taking them from the attendant and placing them into her own handbag.

"Would you like to stay longer?" said Mitch, standing behind her, as he put his hand on her shoulder.

At first she hesitated. She didn't want to leave Jackson, but she knew there was nothing more she could do.

"Can you take me home?"

"Sure," said Mitch, nodding. His tear-stained face felt tight and his heart was heavy as he took once last glance at his friend, Jackson.

"Goodbye, Jackson. Until we meet again…" sobbed Rebecca.

Mitch opened the passenger door to his black Holden ute, and helped Rebecca get in. Buckling her seat belt, he said, "Is there anything I can get you?"

Staring straight ahead out the car windscreen, Rebecca shook her head. She felt numb, and her mind was drained. The shock of Jackson's death and having to say goodbye had taken its toll on her.

Rebecca knew then, that her life had changed, and she was about to be taken on a different path. One she hadn't even thought about, or wanted.

Chapter Two

The next morning, Rebecca's eyes squinted as she woke to the bright sunlight that was shining in through her bedroom window. Looking over at her bedside digital clock, she noticed it displayed the time of eight o'clock. Blinking slowly, she sat up in bed, her head felt foggy and her stomach started to churn from being empty. Swallowing her saliva back down, she felt like she was going to vomit. Rebecca jumped out of bed and quickly ran to the bathroom, throwing up in the toilet.

Washing her face with the basin water, she then looked into the mirror, and remembered the events of yesterday. As she grabbed a towel to dry her face, it dawned on her that she had to go and pick up Paige and tell her that her wonderful daddy had passed away.

As she stood there looking in the mirror at her red, swollen eyes, she started to sob uncontrollably into the towel. Her husband was dead and she didn't know how she was going to get through not only today, but any day without him. Let alone tell Paige that she wouldn't see Jackson again. Feeling anxious, she left her bathroom dressed in her PJs and headed out to the kitchen, as she thought making a cup of tea might calm her nerves.

Entering the lounge room, she was stopped in her tracks when she noticed Mitch sleeping on the couch. He looked uncomfortable, with his long legs hanging over the lounge chair arm and his head positioned to the side from using a cushion as a pillow. He had stayed last night after he brought Rebecca home. Not that she even remembered coming home last night, let alone being put to bed.

When she approached him, he opened his eyes and sat up quickly. "Can I get you something?" said Mitch, wiping the sleep from his blue eyes.

"No, that's Ok, Mitch… I was going to make a cup of tea; would you like one?" said Rebecca.

"I would love a cup of coffee. But I will make it. You sit down at the breakfast bar," he ordered.

Mitch placed a mug of tea and some toast in front of Rebecca.

"I don't want anything to eat," she said, feeling nauseous from the smell of the toast.

"Eat up. You will need your strength for Paige," said Mitch, pulling Rebecca's face up to meet his.

Nodding, the tears flowed from her eyes freely. Pulling away from Mitch's hand, she placed her elbows on the breakfast bar and as she cried into her hands, her long brown hair falling all around her face.

Shit… thought Mitch.

"I'm sorry. I didn't mean to upset you. But you need to keep your strength up… and the only way you will get through this is to eat. You need to take care of yourself. Paige is going to need you too," said Mitch, as he came around the side of the breakfast bar and gave her a hug for reassurance.

As she placed her head and shoulders onto his broad chest and leant into him for support, Rebecca said, "Thank you, Mitch. I don't know what I would do if you weren't here to help me. You are such a good friend." Her eyes stung from the tears filled with salt.

"You're welcome… now, you need to eat your toast and drink that tea down," said Mitch, pulling away slowly and moving the breakfast closer to Rebecca.

She nodded once and ate the toast, which he had put Vegemite on.

Taking her plate and cup and placing them in the sink for washing, Mitch said, "Now that you have finished your breakfast, you need to get yourself in the shower, dressed and then I will take you to where Paige is."

She nodded. "This is going to be the hardest things I have ever had to do, telling Paige about her father's death," said Rebecca, her stomach churning. "God give me strength." She looked up at the ceiling.

"It sure will. If there is anything I can do, please don't hesitate to ask," said Mitch, whole-heartedly.

"Thank you," said Rebecca, standing.

After her shower, Rebecca retrieved her denim jeans and a grey and white windcheater out of the wardrobe. As she shut the door to the wardrobe, the smell of her husband's cologne wafted passed her.

"Jackson…" whispered Rebecca, with a furrowed brow, as she looked around her bedroom.

But there was no answer, only the lingering smell of his cologne.

Shaking her head, she wondered if his spirit was in the house or whether it was just his clothes in the wardrobe that she could smell with his cologne on them.

I sure do miss you, my sweet man, thought Rebecca, as she was dressing herself. Walking into the bathroom to brush her teeth, her thoughts were of Jackson. *Life won't be the same without you.*

Her puffy eyes and chalky reflection in the mirror said it all as she brushed her teeth and rehearsed in her mind what she was going to say to Paige. She wasn't looking forward to the fact that she had to tell her teenage daughter that it was only them two now.

Taking a deep breath in then out, Rebecca thought, *I need to ring Doreen and Steve on the way and let them know about Jackson, so they can prepare themselves for my visit. God they are going to be devastated.* She reached for a tissue to wipe her runny nose as the tears slowly rolled down her face.

Mitch pulled up in front of a brick wall outside Doreen and Steven's house. Turning the car engine off, he looked over at Rebecca and said, "I will stay in the car… I think this is something personal between you and Paige, and you don't need me hovering."

Nodding, she said, "Thanks Mitch." Swallowing hard, and taking a deep breath, she stepped out of the car slowly and walked towards the front door.

She didn't even make it to the front door, before Doreen and Steve came rushing outside to greet her. With tear-stained faces, they both gave Rebecca a hug together and their condolences. The four of them had been friends for many years, and they were shattered by the news of Jackson's death.

Upon entering their house with Doreen and Steve, Rebecca spotted Paige coming out of the bathroom. "Hi sweetie." Her voice was distressed.

"Hi Mum. What are you doing here? I thought you were picking me up on Sunday." She then took a look at her mum's face and frowned. "Have you been crying? You look pale…" A sickened feeling hit her, and she knew something was wrong.

"Come sit in the lounge room, sweetheart. I have some bad news," said Rebecca, as she gulped and tried to hold back the tears that had welled in her eyes.

"What is it, Mum?" said Paige anxiously, as she sat down on the lounge.

"I don't know how to tell you this Paige, but here goes… your father… he passed away last night from a heart attack," sobbed Rebecca.

"What… NO!" Paige screamed.

The tears formed in Rebecca's eyes as she placed her arms around Paige and tried to console her, whilst Paige cried uncontrollably into Rebecca's chest.

"I can't believe that I won't be able to see him again, ever. It's just not fair, Mum," said Paige, through the tears streaming down her face.

"I know sweetheart. I feel the same way. I don't understand why he has been taken from us so soon. We all still had so much we wanted to do," said Rebecca. She wiped her runny nose on her sweater sleeve.

As they continued to comfort each other on the lounge, they discussed Jackson's death, his funeral, and what they would do, now it was only the two of them. They both knew that life sure was going to be different.

"Can you please pack your things up sweetheart, and then we can go home. Mitch is waiting for us out in the car to take us," said Rebecca, looking into her daughter's big blue eyes and handing her another tissue.

"Ok, Mum," Paige said, numbly.

Mitch's ute pulled into their street and as soon as he pulled into the drive way of their house, Paige started to cry uncontrollably.

"He's not there," sobbed Paige. It had occurred to her that previously when she came home, Jackson was always waiting for her on the veranda. But now he wasn't there, harsh reality set in.

"Come on, sweetheart, let's get you inside," said Rebecca, pushing her daughter's mousy blonde hair away from her face and placing her arm around her shoulder, and helping her out the car.

"I will go back home and leave you two to have some time alone. But if you need anything please don't hesitate to ask. I am only across the road for help or support. Ok?" said Mitch, as he took Paige's bag out the back of the ute.

"Thanks, Mitch. I appreciate everything you have done for us," said Rebecca.

Placing Paige's bag on the front veranda, Mitch gave them both a hug. "Don't forget I am here if you need me," repeated Mitch, stepping off the veranda and walking towards his house.

Rebecca and Paige both nodded. The loss and sadness was apparent in their eyes.

Rebecca opened the door to Paige's bedroom and placed her bag next to the wardrobe. Watching Paige, with a forlorn face, slump down hard on the side of the bed tore at her inner core. "Lie down, sweetheart... I'll go and get you a sedative so you can sleep for a while."

Nodding, Paige didn't say a word. Instead she pulled back the covers of her bed and hopped in.

Returning seconds later, Rebecca handed Paige the sedative and watched her take the tablet with some water.

"Can you stay with me, Mum?" asked Paige.

"Yes... sure, sweetheart," said Rebecca. Lying on the bed, she cuddled Paige and listened to her sob, until she quietened and finally fell asleep.

Rebecca lay on Paige's bed staring at the ceiling as a single teardrop escaped from her eye. As reality set in, she soon realised that she needed to make some phone calls to both sides of the family and friends to give them the bad news.

God… give me strength, thought Rebecca.

The next couple of days were a blur for Rebecca. Organising the funeral. Finding out what embalming entailed. People coming over to offer support and food. Flowers being delivered. Phone calls of condolence. Paperwork to fill in and mail being delivered, which she would have to deal with at a later date when she was up to it. Even everyday living was hard to deal with too. She just wanted it all to go away and return to normal. But sadly, she knew that wasn't going to happen.

The day of the funeral was much the same: a blur for both Rebecca and Paige. Overwhelmed with grief, which Rebecca dealt with privately; she was like a robot as she greeted family and friends and tried to appear brave for her daughter. With the wake at her house, Rebecca rushed around making sure everyone had a drink and something to eat, all the while listening to them talk about Jackson and the lovely things he had done for each person, whilst Paige sat quietly, with a numb expression, and listened to everyone talk about her dad.

After the funeral, the days and nights seemed to blend into one another and the feeling of numbness and depression took its toll on Rebecca and Paige. They were lucky though, to have a good neighbour and friend, Mitch, and long-time friend Penny, who came by daily to check on them and make sure they ate and took care of themselves. But what surprised Rebecca the most was that a lot of their friends and some of Jackson's family stopped coming around to check up on them, as they couldn't deal with the fact that Jackson was no longer at the house when they visited.

* * *

Mitch pulled into his driveway, which was across the road from the Landers' house, and spotted Rebecca sitting on the front veranda, in the dark.

Hmm… she doesn't look too happy. Better go and see if she is all right, thought Mitch, as he alighted from the car and walked towards Rebecca.

"Hello… what are you doing out here?" asked Mitch, as he walked up the two steps of the veranda and sat in the cane chair next to Rebecca.

"Just thinking… it's been four weeks today since Jackson passed away."

"I know. Time goes by quickly, doesn't it?" said Mitch. He too missed his friend.

"What am I going to do with myself, Mitch? What with Jackson's death and me still trying to recover from my brain tumour operation six months ago, I just… well… don't seem to be coping too well," said Rebecca, as the tears formed in her eyes and she pulled her legs up to her chest.

Placing a hand on hers, Mitch said, "I think it's time for you to go back to work, Rebecca. Sitting around here isn't doing you much good, nor Paige. You need to try and get back to some sort of normality. And Paige… well… she needs to be back at school. To be around her friends… listen… tell me to shut up if you want, but I know how grief affects people… and… I am sure your health is just about back to normal now."

"Wow… way to shock me back into reality…" said Rebecca, pulling her hand away quickly.

"Sorry… but as your friend, I see what you are doing to yourself. Tormenting yourself all the time. And what you don't realise is that is rubbing off on Paige. Listen, I know you are both still grieving, and believe me I know about grief, but the only way to move forward and for things to get better for you both, is to take baby steps. Go back to work and Paige can go back to school. Just take it a day at a time. If you feel like going one day but not the next, so be it. But at least try. I am sure Jackson would not like to see you both like this."

Rebecca looked at Mitch, and said, "I know he wouldn't be happy at all. But how am I meant to pick up the pieces and move on with life, when I still feel his presence in the house?"

"Do you?" asked Mitch, with a creased brow.

"Yes… only some of the time though. He seems to be there when I need him the most," said Rebecca, looking Mitch in the eyes.

"Right…well… have you thought about getting some counselling?" asked Mitch.

Hmm, not sure I am ready for that or even want to speak to someone about my private life. But maybe he's right, thought Rebecca, hugging her legs and resting her head on them.

With a furrowed brow, Rebecca looked at Mitch and said, "Actually, you are not the first person to suggest that to me. My mum and dad came by yesterday before they returned to their caravanning holiday and told me that I need to seek professional help. And Penny, she came by yesterday and said the same thing. But I don't know… I don't usually believe in that type of thing."

"Well, your parents and two of your best friends can't be wrong, can they? Try it. And hey, if it doesn't work, at least you have given it a go," said Mitch, shrugging.

"I'll think about it… in the meantime, I think you are right about going back to work. I will give my boss a ring later and tell him I will be back tomorrow. And like you said, I can take it one day at a time," said Rebecca, placing her feet on the ground.

"Good on you, Bec. What about Paige?" said Mitch.

"I'll talk with her later and see if she is ready to go back to school yet," said Rebecca. "Maybe I should see if she is ready to go back to work too."

"Good idea. And between you and me, we can give Paige lifts to and from work. It will all work out. Don't worry," said Mitch.

"Thanks, Mitch. I don't know what I would do without you. You're such a good friend," said Rebecca. "I might go make a cuppa. Would you like one?"

"Nah…thanks anyway, but I am off to get some zeds. Been a long day at work. I just thought I'd pop over and see how you are doing first before I head to bed," said Mitch.

"Oh, Ok. Thanks for coming over and checking on us," said Rebecca, standing.

"Well… I will catch you tomorrow," said Mitch, standing and giving her a hug. "Oh, and let me know how you go when you see the counsellor."

"I will," said Rebecca, smiling politely. *Yeah, not likely gonna see one. Sorry, Mitch.*

CHAPTER THREE

Eleven Months Later...

Startled from her dreams of happier times, Rebecca was woken by her clock radio alarm blaring in her ears.

6am... Is it that time already? Just seems like I went to sleep, thought Rebecca, as she thought about reaching for the snooze button on her alarm clock. *Where did the weekend go? Wish I didn't have to go to work... I hate Mondays, and I don't feel like getting out of bed yet.*

Rolling her eyes, Rebecca thought, *Oh how appropriate, the song on the radio is, 'I don't like Mondays', by the Boomtown Rats.* Staring at the ceiling, she wiped the sleep from her eyes and listened to the end of the song playing.

After a few minutes the radio announcer said it was 6.08, and Rebecca jumped out of bed for her daily routine on the treadmill for thirty minutes, some sit ups and then a well-earned shower.

Sitting on the black leather bar stool at the kitchen bench whilst she ate her breakfast, Rebecca heard Paige's bedroom door open and watched her walk into the kitchen.

"Good morning, sleepy head."

Paige grunted and walked sleepily over to the toaster. After making her breakfast she said, "What time are you getting home from work today, Mum?"

"About four o'clock, sweetie. What do you have going on today?" said Rebecca, picking up her coffee cup.

"I have my last driving lesson today at three o'clock, and then I am going for my actual licence at four-thirty. I probably won't be home until six o'clock," said Paige, spreading Nutella on her toast.

"Oh, I forgot about that. Good luck, sweetie. I hope you get your licence today; in fact, I know you will pass as you are a great driver," said. Rebecca, smiling.

"Thanks, Mum. When I get back home from my driver's test, can you drop me at work tonight at seven-thirty?" said Paige, setting her breakfast down on the bench and sitting next to her mum.

"Sure. What time do you finish work tonight, sweetie?" said Rebecca.
"Around 12.30am."

"Hmm… that's a bit too late for me to pick you up, Paige, as I have work tomorrow. Did you want me to ask Mitch if he can organise one of his security guys to pick you up or are you getting a lift with someone else?"

"If you could please ask Mitch for me that would be great, Mum," said Paige.

"Ok. I will give him a ring later on to organise that for you. Well, I have to go to work now, so I will see you tonight. Have a good day," said Rebecca, placing her dishes in the dishwasher and collecting her bag from the kitchen bench.

"Bye Mum," said Paige, standing and giving Rebecca a hug goodbye. "You have a good day too."

"Thanks… and good luck," said Rebecca, giving her a hug back.

When Rebecca arrived at work, her boss straight away approached her desk. "Good morning… we are having a meeting in the conference room in ten minutes."

"Morning… oh, Ok. Do I need to bring a notepad?" asked Rebecca.

"No. Just bring yourself," said her boss, smiling.

Nodding, Rebecca made her way to the staff kitchen out the back and made herself a hot cup of tea and then continued on to the conference room to get a good seat.

"Our meeting this morning is about profit and loss of the company and how we are going forward for the next six months," said the boss, standing at the front of the room, next to the projector.

Oh, how boring, thought Rebecca, as she placed her hand over her mouth and silently yawned.

"But before I talk about that, I have a bit of other news. I am going to be implementing a new computer system in the next couple of months and the training is going to be done in Seattle, USA," said the boss, looking in Rebecca's direction to see the reaction on her face.

This didn't affect anyone else in the room except for Rebecca, as she was the only one, besides the boss, that used the MYOB computer program for all of her office payroll and accounts work.

Rebecca listened eagerly as the boss discussed the new program in detail.

I am going to Seattle. Cool. How exciting, thought Rebecca, grinning from ear to ear. She didn't hear anything else her boss said in the morning meeting.

Rebecca followed like a sheep the crowd of workers walking out the conference room, and headed for her desk. As she neared her desk, the boss approached Rebecca and asked, "So… when is a good time for you to be off to Seattle for the training?"

"Umm, can I let you know tomorrow? It's just that I will have to organise someone to look after my daughter whilst I am away," said Rebecca, turning her computer screen on.

"No problem," he said.

"Will you be coming along with me to learn the new program?" asked Rebecca.

"No. We are too busy for me to go at this stage. So I was thinking that I would get you to train me when you come back," said the boss, as his mobile rang.

"Oh. Ok. Sure," said Rebecca, watching him walk into his office to take the call.

Settling into her heavy workload for the day, she couldn't help but have a Cheshire Cat smile on her face. With the prospect of not only learning a new computer program, but also going to Seattle, she felt privileged to be going. Rebecca had never travelled outside of Australia before, and even though she was feeling a bit anxious about travelling by herself, she was also looking forward to having some fun for a change and meeting new people.

Looking at the time on her computer screen, Rebecca hadn't realised how fast the day was going. It was lunchtime already and she had just remembered that she needed to ring Mitch to organise Paige's ride home tonight after work.

"I'm just gonna take a break, boss," said Rebecca, standing in her manager's office doorway.

"No problem. I'll watch the phones," said her boss, turning around. "Are you all right?"

"Yeah… I do have a bit of headache at the moment, but otherwise I am feeling good. Why do you ask?" said Rebecca, frowning as she rubbed her temples.

"You look pale, that's all," said her boss, standing. "How is your health these days? I have been so busy lately that I haven't even asked you how you're going?"

"I have my good days and bad. The doctor did say that it would at least take twelve months for me to completely recover and for the headaches to stop. Since my last operation, I have had two MRIs done and they have both come back all clear, which is good," said Rebecca, remembering the two brain tumour operations she had been through in the last eight months.

"Well, that is good news. You sure have been through the wringer since Jackson passed away, hey?" said her boss.

Rebecca nodded. "It sure has been one hell of a ride. But I can now see the light at the end of the tunnel… and… well… thank you for being so patient with me since I have returned to work."

"You're welcome. And anyway, we couldn't do without you here. You are such a great asset to this company, Rebecca. How do you think you will go travelling and learning the new modules?" said her boss.

"Oh, that is so nice of you to say. Thank you… yeah, I think I will be all right travelling and with the training. I know sometimes I have some blank moments, but I think I will be fine," said Rebecca.

"That's good. Well… you go and have that break," said her boss, as the office phone rang.

Rebecca smiled and said, "Ok."

Taking a seat outside in the back barbeque area, Rebecca took her mobile out of her bag and she dialled Mitch's number.

"Hi… how's it going?" said Rebecca, when he picked up her call.

"Hello. Not bad for a Monday. And you?" said Mitch.

"Good, for a change. I actually rang you for a favour. I was wondering if it was possible to have one of your security guys pick Paige up from her work tonight?" said Rebecca.

"Umm… yeah, that shouldn't be a problem, kiddo. What time?" says Mitch, looking in his diary.

"Around 12.30."

"Leave it with me. I will have someone there on time to collect her," said Mitch, writing it in his diary.

"Thanks, Mitch. You're a lifesaver. How much will I give you for that?" said Rebecca.

"No money needed… umm, maybe you can cook me a meal sometime," said Mitch, cheekily.

"Are you sure? I feel guilty not giving you any money for this," said Rebecca.

"Yes, I am sure. What are friends for anyway? Like I said, maybe you can cook me a meal sometime," said Mitch.

"Ok. Thanks heaps, hey. You are too kind," said Rebecca.

"In fact, what are you doing tonight? I have the night off, so I can come over," said Mitch, tapping the pen on his desk.

"Umm… Ok. How does say, eight o'clock sound?" said Rebecca, trying to think of what she could cook.

"Sounds good. See you then. I will bring some drinks. Ok?" said Mitch.

"Great. See you at eight. Bye for now," said Rebecca, hanging up the phone.

He has always been really nice to Paige and me. I don't know what I would do without his friendship. Actually, when I think about it, besides my best friend Penny, Mitch and his housemates are the only ones who have stuck by Paige and me, since Jackson passed away last year. It's funny how a lot of my friends and family have dwindled away, thought Rebecca, placing her phone back in her handbag.

Arriving home from work, Rebecca placed her handbag, keys and mail on the counter and decided to make a start on dinner.

Hmm, I could make a Beef Stroganoff and rice, she thought as she stood in front of the freezer deciding what meat to get out. *Yep, that sounds good.* Placing the tray of beef in the microwave to defrost, she retrieved all the other ingredients she needed to cook the meal with from the pantry and fridge.

With the meal simmering in the fry pan, Rebecca had a final taste test. *Mmm, that's perfect.* Placing the meals on three separate plates, she then retrieved the cling wrap from the pantry and covered each meal. She knew this would work best as later on when she got back from taking Paige to work, she could reheat hers and Mitch's up in the microwave. That way, Paige could have hers before she went to work too. She then stacked the dishes into the dishwasher and went to have a well-deserved shower.

With her palms resting on the tiled shower wall and the water cascading over her head, neck and shoulders, Rebecca sensed the tension of her busy work day fade away. As she washed her body with the apricot and rose scented body wash, she felt rejuvenated and was ready for the evening. Turning the faucet off and stepping out of the shower onto a black and white fluffy bath mat, she collected her towel from the rack. Noticing that there were two bath towels on the rack, she wondered if she would eventually remember that she only needed one towel now. She still, after twelve months, couldn't get used to having one towel on the rack. Rebecca still had a lot of adjustment to deal with, when it came to things around the house.

I can't wait for Paige to get home, to see if she passed her driver's test. I hope she did, thought Rebecca, as she towelled dry her hair.

Standing in the kitchen, Rebecca heard a car door shut and Paige screaming in excitement. "I got my driver's licence!"

By the time she had got inside, she had a grin from ear to ear. Showing Rebecca her actual driver's license, which had her photo on it, Paige twirled herself around the room in excitement.

"Well done, sweetie. I am proud of you," said Rebecca, giving her a hug. "We will have to go out and celebrate this tomorrow. What do you think?"

"Sounds good, Mum. Can we go to my favourite restaurant?" said Paige, releasing her hold.

"Sure… I will book it tomorrow for us," said Rebecca, smiling. She was glad of her daughter's achievements. "Actually… I have some good news of my own. My boss told me today that he wants me to go to Seattle to do a computer training course."

"Really… how cool is that, Mum? You lucky thing," said Paige.

"I just have to let my boss know when I can go and he is going to book it. I am bit worried about leaving you though, Paige. Did you want to stay with someone or stay here at home with someone? I wasn't sure what you wanted to do," said Rebecca.

"What about if I go stay at Doreen and Steve's house? They are always good to me," said Paige.

"Hmm, Ok… I'll give them a ring tomorrow and see if you can stay with them. But are you sure you are going to be all right with me gone for a week?" said Rebecca.

"I will be all right Mum, and you are only a phone call away. But I will miss you, though," said Paige, giving Rebecca a hug. They had become really close since Jackson had died and so far hadn't been apart for more than a day.

"Now that is all sorted, are you hungry? Because I have made dinner already for you. Thought you might like to have it before you go to work," said Rebecca, pointing to the plates near the stove top.

"I'm famished. Can you please heat it up for me?" said Paige, eyeing what was on the plates.

"Sure," said Rebecca, opening the microwave door.

"Hey… there are three plates. Who is coming over later for dinner?" asked Paige.

"Well… when I rang Mitch today to ask him if he could organise one of his security guys to pick you up from work tonight, he wouldn't take any money from me for their time or fuel. So I said to him that I would make him dinner to say thank you instead," said Rebecca, placing her finger near the reheat button on the microwave.

"Right," said Paige, nodding, with a smirk on her face. "I might go have a shower and get ready for work."

"Ok, sweetheart. I will wait till you get out the shower and then warm your dinner up for you."

"Thanks, Mum," said Paige.

Rebecca pulled her car to a stop at the back of Paige's work, in the parking lot. "I will see you tomorrow. Have a good night, sweetie," said Rebecca, reaching over to the front passenger's seat to give Paige a hug.

"Thanks for the lift, Mum," said Paige, giving her a hug. "Have a good night."

"No probs. Well I had better get going. It's a long drive home and I don't want to keep Mitch waiting," said Rebecca, pulling away from their embrace.

"Yeah, hopefully I should have enough money saved soon for my own car so that you don't have to give me a lift," said Paige, unbuckling her seat belt.

"Honestly, I don't mind driving you sweetie. And I know you love working here at this restaurant, so I don't mind the forty-five minute drive. You had better go in hey, otherwise you will be late," said Rebecca, looking at the digital clock on her dashboard.

"Ok. Bye, Mum," said Paige, as she opened the door.

"Bye, sweetie," said Rebecca, watching her alight from the car. Rebecca waved to Paige as she watched her enter the restaurant.

Rebecca turned the engine off and noticed Mitch waiting for her on the front veranda. Locking the car door, she heard his footsteps as he approached the car.

"Hi… did you just drop Paige off at work?" asked Mitch.

"Yeah… sorry I'm late. It took me a bit longer than usual to get back home as there was lots of traffic tonight. Come inside," said Rebecca, walking towards the front door, with her handbag over her shoulder.

"No problem. I only arrived a few minutes ago," said Mitch, following Rebecca to the front door. "I was running late from work, anyway."

"Ah, Ok." Unlocking the door, and walking inside, Rebecca noticed that Mitch had drinks in his hand. "Did you want to put them in the fridge?"

"Sure," said Mitch, walking over to the fridge.

"Are you hungry yet?" asked Rebecca, placing her bag on the kitchen benchtop.

"Starving… I didn't get time for lunch today," said Mitch, noticing the plates on the benchtop.

With the microwave dinging, Rebecca retrieved the oven mittens and took the first hot plate out the microwave and placed it on the bench.

"Mmm… that smells good. What is it?" asked Mitch, sniffing the air.

"It's Beef Stroganoff," said Rebecca, as she placed the next plate of food into the microwave. Waiting for the next plate to warm up, Rebecca got out the cutlery and set the table. "Can you pour the drinks for us?"

Mitch nodded. "Sure… glasses… where do you keep them?" asked Mitch, opening the usual cupboard door in the kitchen and found they had been moved.

"Oh, sorry. They're in the centre cupboard now. I have been doing a bit of reshuffling of things in the kitchen. Thought they would be more accessible in that cupboard," said Rebecca, pointing to the cupboard.

"Ok. No problem," said Mitch, closing the cupboard door.

Sitting next to each other at the dining table, eating their dinner, Rebecca took a sip of her drink. "Mmm... this is really nice wine. Fruity...thanks for buying that," said Rebecca, placing the glass on the table.

"You're welcome. Thanks for dinner. You're a good cook," said Mitch, placing the last mouthful in his mouth.

"I should be the one saying thanks, as you have organised someone to collect Paige from work for me. I really appreciate you doing that for us," said Rebecca.

"Hey... that's what mates are for," said Mitch, smiling.

"Did you want to hear my good news? I have been dying to tell you," said Rebecca, with her eyebrows raised.

"Whatever it is, you look really excited," said Mitch.

"I am... I am... at work today, my boss asked me if I wouldn't mind going to Seattle to do some training on a new computer program they are implementing," said Rebecca.

Surprised when she said Seattle, Mitch said, "You're joking. Wow, aren't you lucky? Have you been to the USA before?"

"No. I have never been outside of Australia. I am so excited. Apparently it's only for one week," said Rebecca, placing her knife and fork down on her plate.

"I was actually born and raised in Seattle. My family still live there," said Mitch, looking from his plate to his glass and then to Rebecca.

"Really... unbelievable... I didn't know you were from Seattle. And you don't even have an American accent either. You sound Aussie. I would never have guessed. So how long have you lived in Australia for?" said Rebecca.

"I moved to Perth about five years ago. Actually, I had my own security business in Seattle as well. But I needed a change. So Dad and I looked into me coming to Australia to see if I could make a go of it here. As it turned out, it was a sound investment because most of the artists here needed security guards," said Mitch.

"Right. So... do you still have your security business in Seattle?" asked Rebecca.

"Yeah. My Dad and my brother run it for me at the moment," said

Mitch.

"You know, I have learnt more about you in the last few minutes than in the whole time I have known you. So… you have a brother? Do you have any other brothers and sisters?" asked Rebecca.

"I have two younger brothers who still live in Seattle, and there is Mom and Dad of course," said Mitch.

"Oh right… I will have to pick your brains about what sight-seeing I should do whilst I am there," said Rebecca.

"I'll write you a list of things to see and do. That way you can have a look on the internet before you go and make some plans on what you will have time for," said Mitch. "By the way, clothes shopping in Seattle is to die for, so I have been told. But don't forget to take some warm clothes, because even though it'll be summer, Seattle can be a cold, windy place in July."

"Thanks Mitch. Good to know. Hmm… I hadn't even contemplated doing some clothes shopping," said Rebecca. *I can't believe Mitch is from Seattle. The things you don't know about your friends.*

"Don't all women like to shop?" snickered Mitch.

Rebecca laughed and slapped his arm lightly.

"Can I use your toilet?" asked Mitch.

"Yeah sure. You know where it is… you don't have to ask, you know," said Rebecca.

"Oh, Ok. Be back in a minute," said Mitch, standing.

Whilst Mitch was gone, Rebecca decided to take the dishes into the kitchen and stack them into the dishwasher.

"Well… I suppose I had better get going, Bec. I have an early shift in the morning," said Mitch, looking at his watch as he entered the kitchen.

"Already…"

'Yeah, sorry. Thank you, once again, for dinner. We will have to do this again soon."

"Yeah… for sure. I would like that. I have enjoyed tonight. It's a pity you have to leave," said Rebecca, with a furrowed brow.

"I have enjoyed the night too," said Mitch, walking towards the front doorway. "Catch you soon." He leant into to hug Rebecca. *I wish she would see me. Don't push it Mitch, it's way too soon.*

Giving him a friendly hug goodbye at the front door and lingering, Rebecca thought, *Mmm, he smells nice tonight. Maybe it's the wine. I have had way too much.* As he pulled away slowly and their cheeks brushed against each other, Rebecca looked into his eyes for the very first time. *So good looking… stop… Mitch is only a friend.* Embarrassed, she pulled away from their embrace quickly.

"Night, Rebecca," said Mitch, realising what had just happened.

Ever since Jackson had passed away Mitch had grown fond of Rebecca and their friendship. He had secretly liked her from afar, but had never acted on his feelings, because he didn't want to lose their friendship. And he knew she wasn't ready to move on previously either. But tonight he caught a glimpse of maybe what could happen in the future between them.

"Yeah, night," said Rebecca, as her heartbeat quickened and her cheeks turned crimson red. Watching Mitch walk away from her front veranda, Rebecca sighed heavily, and shut the front door. *What was I thinking…?*

Staring at the ceiling of her darkened room for what seemed like eternity, Rebecca went over and over the conversations she had with Mitch tonight. Knowing he had stirred some feelings in her which weren't of friendship puzzled Rebecca. She had only previously thought of Mitch as a good friend and nothing else. But tonight she realised that she may want something else.

That night she dreamt about Mitch.

Waking the next morning with a startle, Rebecca reached over and hit the alarm button, to stop it from beeping continually. Yawning, she stretched her arms out towards the ceiling and wondered what the day would bring. Pulling back the covers, Rebecca decided to do her usual morning ritual of walking three kilometres on the treadmill and some sit ups.

Showered, dressed and ready for her day at work, Rebecca decided to check in on Paige, only to find her sleeping soundly. Standing in the doorway of Paige's bedroom, Rebecca watched her sleep and smiled as she realised her beautiful daughter was growing up fast and had come a long way in twelve months, since Jackson's death.

Time sure is a good healer, thought Rebecca, as she walked towards the front door with a spring in her step.

Placing her bag on the desk at work, Rebecca watched her boss make his way over to her. "Good morning."

"Morning, Rebecca. Have you made a decision on the training in Seattle?"

"Yes… I can go Friday, this week. When does the training start over there?" said Rebecca.

"Oh good, that will work out well because I received an e-mail this morning telling me that the training is starting on Monday, next week. So are you Ok with me to book your flights for Friday and coming back at the end of the week after?" he said.

"Yes, that would be good… actually… I wanted to do some sight-seeing whilst I am there. So if you can book me to come back on the Sunday night, would be better," said Rebecca.

"Ok," he said. "Leave it with me and I will organise the flights and accommodation now. You excited about going?"

"Sure am. Not only am I looking forward to the shopping and sight-seeing, but also I am looking forward to learning the new program," said Rebecca, eagerly. She always liked to keep her skills up to date with what was currently being used in the workplace.

"That's great. I am sure you will be able to pick up the new program in no time at all. You know… I have been to Seattle many years ago and I am sure you will love it," he said.

"Yeah. Actually a friend of mine who used to live there is going to give me some sight-seeing tips. So looking forward to checking out what I can see and do on the internet too," said Rebecca, hearing the work phone ring.

"I'll chat with you later," said her boss quietly, as he walked back into his office.

With her stomach grumbling, Rebecca checked the screen on her computer for the time, and realised that it was morning tea time. She had been busy all morning and hadn't realised where the time had gone. Taking a piece of fruit out of her handbag, she sat at her desk and ate her mandarin, and continued to work through.

"Would you like a cup of tea, Rebecca?" asked her boss, as he walked past her desk.

"Umm… no thanks. I have a bottle of water here to drink. But thanks for asking anyway," said Rebecca, smiling politely.

"You're welcome," said her boss.

As she continued to work, Rebecca's mobile phone rang. Taking a peek at the screen she saw it was Mitch. "Hello, Mitch. How's it going?"

"Hi, Rebecca. Yeah, I am good. Hey… I wanted to ask you something."

"I am all ears. What is it?"

"Would you like to stay with my family whilst you were in Seattle? They have a huge house and can take you to your training course and sight-seeing if you like," said Mitch.

"That's nice of you to offer, but my work has already booked the accommodation. The hotel I am staying at is the same place as where the training will be held. Thanks anyway. Maybe I can meet up with your family for lunch or dinner whilst I am there. That would be nice," said Rebecca.

"Oh, Ok…." Disappointment in his voice. "Rebecca… what about if I come with you to Seattle? I could show you around the place myself. I haven't seen my family for over five years, so it would be nice to see them again," said Mitch, eagerly hoping she would say yes.

"Mitch, as much as I would love for you to come with me, I can't ask you to do that for me," said Rebecca, as she then wondered why he would be offering to come with her.

"Why not? I would love to come and keep you company and show you around. I wouldn't offer if I didn't want to, Rebecca," said Mitch, strumming his fingers on his leg as he moved it up and down quickly.

The phone call went silent as Rebecca sat there for a few seconds thinking whether to say yes or no. Secretly, she did want Mitch to come with her, but she wasn't sure if there were any strings attached, especially after what happened last night. It was something she was not prepared for.

"Mitch, I don't know how to say this, so I am going to just say it… I would love for you to come with me as we always seem to get along good together and I do always enjoy myself when I am with you, but I don't want you thinking that it will be any more than just friends," said Rebecca, feeling her cheeks turn crimson red from embarrassment and her heartbeat quickening. *This is not a conversation I feel happy to discuss, but I need him to know where we stand. Friends… Anyway…*

Her thoughts were interrupted by Mitch.

"Humph… what… Rebecca… come on, I don't think that way about you. Yes, we do get along good together and enjoy each other's company, but to me you are just a great friend and I do have respect for Jackson as well," said Mitch, trying to sound convincing. "In fact, when we get to Seattle, there is someone I would like you to meet. You will then know for sure that I only want to be friends."

"Oh… Ok. Sorry… now I feel silly, hey," said Rebecca, wondering if it was just her that felt the awkward moment between them last night and now wishing she had never mentioned it. "But I am not sure what you mean by that last comment about someone you want me to meet. Anyway, yes, I would love for you to come with me. I can't wait to go. I am really excited. Actually, my boss has booked me to fly out on Friday's flight."

"Friday… I can't see that being a problem. Could put me through to your boss so that I can confirm the flight details with him? That way you and I can catch the same flight," said Mitch, looking in his diary for his client appointments to be carried out whilst he was away.

"Ok. Give me a sec and I will go and get him for you. Hey… why don't you come over tonight and we can discuss our trip some more," said Rebecca, excited.

"Sure… I won't be able to make it until around 8.30 though, as I have to work late," said Mitch.

"That's no problem. See you then. I will hand the phone to my boss now," said Rebecca, as she walked into her boss's office and explained the situation to him.

Heading back to her desk, Rebecca's head was in the clouds as she thought about her trip to Seattle and Mitch coming with her. Was she totally wrong about last night? Shaking her head, she thought, *Anyway, what would everyone think if I moved on this early? Jackson hasn't even been gone long…and Paige…OMG, what would she think. And Jackson… well… I love him way too much to even think about being with another man. Nope… it's just friends.*

The rest of the week seemed to go by slowly for Rebecca, even though she was busy. What with organising her passport, working full time, and making sure things were all sorted at home, she barely had a moment to herself, but still she thought Friday was never going to come.

She had never been out of Australia before and was feeling anxious about going, but was also looking forward to flying out to Seattle. And now that she had dropped Paige off at Doreen and Steve's house, all she needed to do was finish packing her suitcase.

I wonder if I am flying economy or business class seats? I forgot to ask the boss, thought Rebecca.

CHAPTER FOUR

Rebecca just about jumped through the roof as her alarm clock started to beep loudly. Pressing the snooze button, she couldn't believe it was 3am already.

Only just feels like I went to bed, thought Rebecca, as she turned her bedside light on.

Sitting on the side of the bed, Rebecca wiped the sleep from her eyes and tried to get her bearings. With her mind starting to race, knowing what she still needed to do prior to leaving the house, she jumped out of bed. Placed neatly on a chair were her clothes she was going to wear to the airport that she had picked out the night previous. Scooping them up, she quickly headed for the shower.

With the water cascading over her body as she washed herself with the body wash, Rebecca thought, *cab is booked for 4am to collect Mitch and me from my house, and our flight is at 6am to Sydney. We are only in Sydney for two hours and then we fly to LA. From there we get on a domestic flight to Seattle. God, I am going to be absolutely buggered by the time we get there. I hope I can sleep on the plane. Note to self: need to pack my deodorant in my hand luggage.*

Dressed, Rebecca yawned as she headed for the kitchen to make herself a cup of tea. Hearing a horn beep out the front of her house, Rebecca thought, *Looks like I won't have time for a cuppa. I think the taxi is here already.* Opening the front wooden door, she noticed the taxi had pulled into her driveway and was idling his car with the head lights on, waiting for her to come out with her suitcase, which were already parked in the lounge room, near the front door.

"You ready to go?" asked Mitch, who was already waiting on the front veranda with his suitcase.

"Yep," said Rebecca, checking her handbag for her passport and flight details.

"I'll go put these in the taxi, whilst you lock up," said Mitch, taking the two suitcases.

"Ok, thanks," said Rebecca, as her mind went through her check list to see if she had everything for the trip, whilst putting her key into the lock.

As the cab driver pulled onto Roe Highway, Rebecca leant forward to the front seat and asked Mitch, "Do you have your passport and plane tickets?"

"Yes. Got all that sorted already," said Mitch, looking back at her and smiling.

"Wow… you're organised," said Rebecca, as she sat back in her seat and looked out the window. *For a man, that is!*

On arrival at the Perth domestic airport, Rebecca's stomach started doing somersaults. She had never flown over seas before and was anxious about the trip. Stepping out of the taxi, whilst Mitch paid the driver, she fidgeted in her handbag for her plane ticket and passport.

"You Ok?" said Mitch, from behind her.

"A bit nervous. But I will be all right," said Rebecca, turning around, and watching him take the suitcases out of the boot of the taxi.

"Come on… let's go get these bags checked in and then we can go and have some breakfast. How does that sound?" said Mitch.

"Sounds good. I wouldn't mind a nice cup of tea," said Rebecca, as she watched Mitch take control of their bags. She then followed him into the building and over to the check in counter.

"Now that's done, why don't we go and get some money changed from Australian to US and then we can go and have some breakfast," said Mitch, as they walked towards the escalators.

"Lucky you are on the ball. I totally forgot about the currency exchange," said Rebecca.

After breakfast they decided to check out the duty free shops, and then stopped off at a newsagency to buy themselves something to read and eat on the plane trip.

Mitch selected a newspaper to read and asked Rebecca, "Did you want any magazines to read?"

"No thanks," said Rebecca, as she took a book out of her handbag, showing him the one she was going to read.

He smirked and said, "Hmm... Fifty Shades. I have read the three of them books. It's different, but I liked it."

"I can't say I know too many guys who have read the books. But so far I like Book One," said Rebecca, with raised eyebrows. She felt her face redden slightly.

"Tell me what you think once you finish the first one," said Mitch, paying for his newspaper at the counter.

She nodded and placed the book back in her bag. *Hmm... another thing I have just learnt about Mitch. Full of surprises...*

Whilst walking to their gate number with their carry-on luggage, Rebecca and Mitch heard over the PA system a boarding call for their flight number being called. As they neared the flight attendant at the boarding counter and Mitch gave her the boarding pass, Rebecca noticed the seats were in economy.

Cattle class. Oh well suppose you can't have everything. I should be grateful that I am going to Seattle at all, thought Rebecca.

Once they boarded the plane and found their seat allocation, Mitch placed their hand luggage into the overhead baggage compartment and took his seat next to Rebecca.

"How's the nerves?" asked Mitch.

"Yeah, not bad. I'm a bit tired, though," said Rebecca.

"Yeah, me too. I might try and get some sleep on this flight," said Mitch.

"Not a bad idea," said Rebecca, fastening her seat belt.

Rebecca's head jolted forward as the plane's wheels screeched onto the tarmac and the plane reversed its engines to slowly stop the movement forward. Approaching the terminal, the captain said over the PA, "Ladies and gentleman, we have arrived into Sydney domestic airport."

"That went quick… I can't believe that I have slept all the way," said Rebecca, trying to stretch her legs and arms out front in a cramped space.

"You must have needed it," said Mitch. Yawning he placed his newspaper in the seat pocket in front of him and undid his seat belt.

"What time is it?" asked Rebecca.

"A little after 1pm Sydney time."

"Ok. Do you know how we get from the domestic to the international airport?" asked Rebecca, taking her seat belt off.

"Yeah. There is a bus that will take us there for nothing. Don't worry, I will show you when we get off," said Mitch.

Arriving at the international airport book in counter, Mitch handed the lady their passports.

"Hmm, it seems you have been upgraded to first class Ms Landers," said the attendant, looking at the computer screen.

Rebecca looked from the booking attendant to Mitch and said, "Cool. I wonder who paid for the upgrade?"

"The name on the upgrade is actually the person you are flying with today," stated the booking attendant.

"You paid for the upgrade?" said Rebecca, with raised eyebrows as she smiled at Mitch.

"Yes," said Mitch. "It's no big deal."

"You didn't have to do that. I will pay you back for the upgrade," said Rebecca.

"No need to pay me back; that's not necessary," said Mitch, waving his hand.

"Thank you. You are too kind," said Rebecca, glad to be able to travel by first class. Taking their boarding passes and customs paperwork from the booking attendant Mitch and Rebecca proceeded to go through customs.

As they retrieved their hand luggage and valuables from the x-ray scanner conveyer belt and placed their shoes back on, Mitch noticed on the computer screens, which hung from the ceiling at the airport, that their flight had changed its boarding time and gate number.

"Shit. We are going to have to make a run for it, Rebecca. It looks like our boarding time is now and gate number has changed. You Ok to do that?" said Mitch, watching her place her shoes back on.

"Yep. Give me a second to put my shoes on and I am ready to make a dash for it," said Rebecca.

Taking her hand in his, Mitch said, "Come on. Let's go." He pulled her towards their gate, which was at the other end of the building.

As they ran throughout the airport, ducking and weaving through the crowds of people everywhere, Mitch heard over the PA system a boarding call for their flight. When they neared their gate number and saw the long line of people waiting to board, they both stopped suddenly and tried to regain their breath.

"We made it," said Rebecca. She couldn't help but laugh as she shook her head.

"Thank God," said Mitch, noticing he was still holding her hand, as he laughed too.

Over the airport intercom Rebecca heard the steward call the seat allocation for boarding. "That's us… let's go," said Rebecca, realising she was still holding Mitch's hand, quickly letting go.

Mitch gestured to Rebecca to walk in front of the line of people to board first, as the steward was calling for first class passenger seating allocation only. "Ok. Come on," said Mitch, handing the boarding pass to Rebecca.

Mitch smiled as he watched the excitement on Rebecca's face. He knew she was looking forward to checking out the first class seats and the flight.

Stepping onto the plane, the stewardess took Mitch and Rebecca's boarding passes and showed them to first class. As they take their seats across the aisle from each other, Rebecca said, "Wow… this is nice.

These seats are huge and it looks like they actually lay down too. We even have our own TVs."

Mitch silently laughed to himself as he buckled his seat belt. He'd never seen someone so excited about flying first class before.

"I can't believe how lucky I am to be able to travel in first class. Thank you again, Mitch," said Rebecca, as she fiddled with the TV remote.

"You're welcome," said Mitch.

"Have you flown first class before?" asked Rebecca, buckling her seat belt.

Mitch nodded. "I don't fly any other way."

"It's all right for some!" stated Rebecca, with raised eyebrows.

When the plane started to move backwards, Mitch looked across the aisle at Rebecca and noticed her looking at a photo. "Are you Ok?"

"Yeah. Just thinking about Paige. I miss her already," said Rebecca, looking up from the photo. "We haven't been apart since Jackson's death and I am feeling guilty for leaving her behind."

"Oh, right... I am sure she will be all right. You know Steve and Doreen will look after her. What about if I order a drink for you? It may help settle your nerves," said Mitch, trying to gauge her reaction.

"Sure." Rebecca sighed. Looking out her window she watched the buildings rush by fast as the plane taxied down the run way.

At 18,000 feet, the seat belt sign had been turned off by the captain. Mitch watched the stewardess get up off her seat and start to prepare the meals. Taking his own seat belt off, he decided to go and see the stewardess and order some drinks.

"I'll be back in a minute," said Mitch to Rebecca.

She looked at Mitch, nodded and then continued to watch the TV screen.

Placing a clear plastic cup with a small bottle of pineapple flavoured Midori on Rebecca's tray, Mitch said, "Here you go. Try this and see if you like it."

"Wow... thanks Mitch," said Rebecca, pouring the drink into the cup full of ice. Taking a sip of her drink Rebecca's taste buds came alive in her mouth. "Mmm, this is really nice."

"Thought you would like it," said Mitch.

"Where's yours?" asked Rebecca.

"It's coming. Just waiting for the stewardess to make it," said Mitch, as he sat back down in his seat and pulled the tray down.

"Oh. Ok. So how much do I owe you for the drink?" asked Rebecca, as she started to get her purse out of her bag.

"Nothing. Drinks like that are free in first class," said Mitch.

"Oh, right," said Rebecca, watching the steel food and drink trolley being wheeled toward them. "Maybe I might have another one then when I finish this one."

Mitch smiled and nodded.

"Thank you," said Mitch to the stewardess, dropping off his drink.

As the trolley stopped in between Mitch and Rebecca and the steward rolled off the menu for tonight, they both selected their meals. Rebecca couldn't believe the fantastic choice of food they had to choose from.

After their restaurant cooked meals were finished and the trays had been collected by the air stewardess, Rebecca decided to settle back in her chair and read her book. Out the corner of her eye, she realised that Mitch was watching her read and he seemed to be observing her reactions.

"What are you smirking at?" she asked him, smiling.

"What do you think of the book so far?" asked Mitch.

"At first I didn't like it. But after reading some more; yeah... it's not bad. I wouldn't mind being the female in this book, though," said Rebecca, smirking. *Oops... did I just say that out loud?*

Mitch laughed and said, "That good, hey?" with a grin on his face.

"I can't wait to buy the second book to see what it's like," said Rebecca.

"Maybe we can visit a bookstore in Seattle and buy the next book?" stated Mitch.

"Sounds good," said Rebecca.

A few hours later into the flight from Sydney to LA, Rebecca finished reading the entire book. As she placed it in her handbag, which was under the front seat, she looked over at Mitch and noticed he had laid down and from his light snoring had gone to sleep.

God, he's even cuter when he is asleep. Then again, maybe it's the alcoholic drinks I have had. You really need to get a hold of yourself girl. Mentally she slapped herself. *No… he is off limits. You are just good friends and you don't want to spoil that; do you?*

Rebecca struggled with her new-found emotions for Mitch as she took the remote out of its holder which was on the arm of her chair. Since Jackson had passed away twelve month previous, she had never looked at or thought about another man in the way she was now thinking about Mitch. The turmoil inside of her ate her up, as she struggled to contemplate another man in her life. Pushing the thoughts she was having to the back of her mind, Rebecca turned on her TV to find a suitable movie to watch to distract her thoughts. As the movie she selected started, she yawned and decided to press the button on the side of her seat for it to collapse and start to resemble a bed. Placing a blanket over her body, she continued to watch the movie, until her eyes became heavy and she fell asleep.

"Rebecca… Rebecca," she heard a voice say.

Opening her eyes, Rebecca heard Mitch calling out her name again.

"Yep, I'm awake," said Rebecca.

"Breakfast is being served. Would you like some?" asked Mitch.

"Hmm… sure," said Rebecca. Yawning, she watched the steward wheeling the steel trolley towards them.

"Did you get much sleep overnight?" asked Mitch.

"Slept like a log. I reckon I would have gotten around eight hours' sleep. I don't feel too bad, hey. Thank you for upgrading me to first class. What about you; did you get much sleep?" said Rebecca, as she pressed the button on her chair to sit up straight again.

"Probably about six hours. But that's enough for me as I don't need much sleep. Looking forward to getting off the plane though," said Mitch, stretching his arms out front.

"Me too. Actually, before they drop off breakfast, I might go to the loo," said Rebecca, standing up and stretching.

By the time she waited in line for the toilets and arrived back at her seat, breakfast had already been dropped off. It was scrambled eggs, bacon and pancakes on the side.

"I ordered you a cup of tea instead of coffee," said Mitch.

"Thanks," she said, taking her seat. *He is always so thoughtful.*

"Actually Bec, there is something that I wanted to speak with you about before we get off the plane in the LA airport," said Mitch, anxiously.

"What is it? You look worried. What's wrong?" said Rebecca, with a creased brow, swallowing hard.

"Well… we may find that there are a lot of magazine and TV reporters at the airport and they will probably be coming over to me and asking for an interview," said Mitch, watching her reaction.

Rebecca looked at Mitch dumbfounded and said, "Yeah right. You are always the kidder."

"I am serious, Bec. I come from a very well known, wealthy family and when I used to live in USA, I used to get hounded by the reporters all the time. They called me USA's most eligible bachelor," said Mitch, laughing.

Not believing him, she started to laugh, and said, "Yeah right… that is hilarious."

"Yeah I know, stupid and ridiculous," he said in a monotone voice. "But in all seriousness I am telling you the truth. I haven't been to the USA for over five years, so they may not recognise me. But if they do, we will get hounded, I can tell you."

He is telling the truth, shit. "So… if you are from a wealthy family, what do your parents do for a living?" said Rebecca, trying to absorb what he had told her.

"We are all in the security business. My family actually do security for most of the popular stars here," said Mitch, seriously.

"You're kidding. Really. So why did you leave Seattle then?" asked Rebecca.

"It's a long story, and not one I want to talk about right now," said Mitch.

"Hmm, Ok. So does that mean that I live across the road from not only an eligible bachelor, but also a multi-millionaire?" she said, teasing him.

He nodded and laughed.

"I would never have guessed that. You are so...well... normal. Sorry... I just have always thought that people who have lots of money would be, you know, stuck up and wouldn't talk with people like me," said Rebecca.

"What do you mean people like you?" asked Mitch.

"You know, poor and not as sophisticated like the rich," she said.

"Rebecca, you shouldn't put yourself down like that. You are such a lovely, kind person, with a heart of gold, and I think a lot of you," said Mitch.

"Wow, thanks. I didn't know you felt that way," said Rebecca, raising her eyebrows.

"Anyway, we will just have to take it as it comes at the airport. Just don't tell them your name or anything about yourself. Nothing... don't even talk to them, as they will take what you say out of context and you will be all over the news," said Mitch, matter-of-factly.

She frowned at Mitch in bewilderment and made a zipping of her lip motion with her fingers. "No problem. Will it be all right if I walk next to you?"

"Don't be silly, Bec. Of course you can walk next to me... I'm sorry, I probably sound like a bit of a jerk. But you will see what it's like when we get inside the terminal, especially if they recognise me. I am just hoping that they have forgotten all about me," said Mitch, nervously. He hated the attention the media gave him.

Before they knew it, the plane was landing and they were taxiing along the runway to the terminal. When the plane finally stopped and the seat belt sign had been turned off, Mitch stood up and took their hand luggage out of the overhead lockers.

"Thanks for getting my bag for me, Mitch," said Rebecca, standing.

"You're welcome," said Mitch, as he handed Rebecca's bag to her and watched the stewardess walk towards them.

"Hope you enjoyed your flight with us. You can now disembark from the plane, when you are both ready," said the stewardess, standing between Mitch and Rebecca.

"Thank you," they both said together.

With their hand luggage trailing behind them, Mitch and Rebecca disembarked and headed on into the terminal to collect their bags from the carousel.

"This trolley seems to have a mind of its own," said Mitch, as they walked over to the carousel to collect their bags. Watching the bags continually go around on the steel carousel, Mitch noticed a reporter, whom he remembered from the past, looking over in his direction. Taking a peaked cap out of his hand luggage, he turned away from the reporter and placed it on his head, in the hope that she didn't recognise him.

"Mitchell... Mitchell Portellico, is that you?" said the reporter, as she made a bee-line for him.

"Oh, God. Here she comes," said Mitch to Rebecca. "Don't say anything, Ok?"

Rebecca nodded and nervously took a deep breath.

As she neared them, the reporter, who had a tape recorder in her hand, says, "Mitchell... please, can I get an exclusive interview?"

Knowing she was not going to give up, Mitch turns to her and said, "I will give you an exclusive. But not here at the airport. Too many reporters around. What about later on today?"

"Sure, that would be great. But where have you been for these years, I haven't seen you around?" said the reporter.

"I will talk to you later, Claudia," said Mitch, authoritatively.

"Ok. Here is my card. Ring me later for a time and place."

"Sure," said Mitch, taking the card. Watching her walk away, he realised that she was the only one so far that had recognised him.

He knows her first name. That's impressive, Rebecca thought to herself.

"That was Claudia, and she is from TGM. And if I didn't say I would give her an exclusive, then she would have hounded us and all the other reporters would come over too. So I just agreed to the exclusive interview to get rid of her," said Mitch, as he saw their bags approaching on the carousel. "Sorry Rebecca."

"Hey, don't be sorry. It's Ok. It's not your fault you are so gorgeous," teased Rebecca, smiling.

"Oh you are just so funny... not," said Mitch, taking their bags off the carousel and placing them on the trolley. "Once we go through customs, we need to head to the departure lounge, for Seattle. Thank God no reporters are allowed in there."

"Yeah, I know," said Rebecca, looking at her watch. "We only have about an hour before our next flight." *I can't wait to get to my hotel to freshen up. I need a shower badly.*

"Did you want a drink, Rebecca?" asked Mitch, as they entered the departure lounge.

"I will have a bottle of water, thanks Mitch," said Rebecca, taking the money out of her purse.

"I don't want any money for a water. Put that back in your purse. The drink's on me," said Mitch, waving his hand at her, as he walked off to get the drinks.

Waiting for Mitch to return, Rebecca took her phone out her handbag and sent a text message to Paige and a few other people, letting them know she had landed safely in LA. As she looked up from her texting, Mitch had already returned and was sitting next to her.

"Thanks for buying me a drink," said Rebecca, as she took the water from him. "Oh and sorry I doubted you about the reporters too. That was too intense out there,"

"No problem, kiddo. But we aren't over the worst of it yet. There will be some at the Seattle airport as well. I have organised for the family driver to collect us from the Seattle airport," said Mitch.

"You have a driver? Talk about spoilt," said Rebecca, her eyebrows raised.

Mitch looked at her and laughed. "It's funny you know, I have just grown up with this sort of wealthy lifestyle. But to you it must seem unbelievable," said Mitch, unscrewing the lid to his drink.

"What's not to like? Besides the reporters hounding you, you must have had one great life growing up? You are so lucky. Whereas me, I have had to work for everything I have. Life sure is strange!" said Rebecca.

He nodded and said, "Let's go. They are calling us to board the plane now."

Once they were up in the air, Mitch and Rebecca went over what they were going to see and do for the next couple of days prior to Rebecca starting the course. The five hour flight didn't seem to take long and before they knew it they were landing at Seattle airport.

As they entered the terminal, it was like a frenzy. The reporters were everywhere. Taking photos and video. Calling Mitch's name and asking questions. But he just took it in his stride and didn't say a thing.

I wonder, how did they know he was going to be here? thought Rebecca, as she walked alongside him, staring straight ahead.

Once they retrieved their bags from the carousel, Mitch took Rebecca's hand and said, "Come on. The driver is waiting for us just outside those doors, over there."

Walking quickly to the double glass sliding door which took them outside, Mitch spotted their driver waiting by the car with the back door open for them. Hurrying over, he left the luggage with the driver and they hopped into the black, stretch limousine.

"Sorry about all that back there," said Mitch, settling into his seat.

"It's Ok…. I have never been in a limo before, Mitch," said Rebecca, looking around in awe and soaking up the moment. As the driver took his seat and they pulled away from the terminal, Rebecca craned her neck to watch the surroundings outside through her window. So far she was enjoying each and every moment of this trip.

"God… you think after five years of being away, that they would have given up and forgotten about me, Dad. But it was just like when I lived here. Frenzy of reporters everywhere as soon as we entered the terminal. I am sure that the TGM reporter from LA probably tipped them off. Unbelievable… bloody bastards. I think that they probably scared Rebecca a bit too, as she has been quiet since we got in the car," said Mitch, talking with his Dad on the phone and looking at Rebecca.

Rebecca shook her head, and mouthed the word, 'No'.

"I am going to drop Rebecca off at her hotel and get her settled in and then I will be home, Ok… looking forward to seeing you all. I have missed you all so much," said Mitch, eager to see his family.

"Are you staying with your family, whilst you are here?" asked Rebecca, once Mitch was off the phone.

"Yeah, looking forward to it, too. And they also asked if you would like to stay there as well… but I told them that the course you are taking is at the hotel you are staying at. So it will make it easier during the week to attend the course," said Mitch.

"That was nice of them to ask," said Rebecca.

"My family are a lot like me, Rebecca. They are just normal people," said Mitch.

"Oh, Ok. You will have to see if maybe I can take them out for lunch or dinner whilst I am here. It would be nice to meet them," said Rebecca.

"I will ask them later on and let you know," said Mitch, excited at the prospect of Rebecca meeting his parents.

The hotel Rebecca was staying at was about a forty-five minute drive from the airport and on the outskirts of the Seattle city centre. When the car pulled up out the front of the hotel, Rebecca's eyes lit up as she couldn't believe how luxurious it looked, with its cream and brown colours shaded into the marble walls, and gold surroundings door frames. There was even a doorman.

I will have to thank my boss for booking me into somewhere so elegant, Rebecca thought to herself. She truly felt spoilt.

Rebecca watched the doorman approach the car, open the door and stand to one side. She turned to Mitch and said, "You don't need to come in. I will be all right. You go and see your family."

"Oh, Ok. But I will help you get your bag out the boot of the car," said Mitch.

"Thanks." Alighting from the car, Rebecca stood there in

wonderment, taking in all the sights.

"Are you sure you will be all right booking in at the reception?" asked Mitch, as he placed Rebecca's bag in front of her on the ground.

Waving her hand, she said, "Yeah, I will be Ok. You go and I will see you later on this afternoon. You have my number so just give me a ring when you are ready."

"All right. See you later on," said Mitch, hugging her goodbye.

"See you. Take care," said Rebecca, as she pulled away from their embrace, picked up her luggage and walked inside.

CHAPTER FIVE

With her eyes darting all around as she walked into the hotel, Rebecca was welcomed by a magnificent foyer. The marble floor tiling was a rich and creamy, rustic colour, with a shiny surface and the walls were painted in cream and black, with artwork hanging here and there. In the middle of the foyer was a beautiful majestic water fountain and to the right of the fountain was a lounge area. Spotting the black marble reception desk on the left, Rebecca approached the assistant and introduced herself to book into her room.

"Hello, Ms Landers. Welcome to the Hyatt," said the receptionist, as she took the paperwork from Rebecca and looked into her computer for Rebecca's room number. "The room we had booked for you isn't available at the moment, so we have booked you into the executive suite instead for the duration of your stay. I am sure you will like this room a lot better anyway ma'am. Here are your keys to the room. Can I ask you if you could sign here on the accommodation paperwork, ma'am?"

She placed the paperwork on the counter for Rebecca to sign.

"No problem. Thank you," said Rebecca, signing the paperwork.

'I will ask a bellboy to take your bags up to your room and he will show you how everything works in the room as well," said the receptionist, gesturing for the bellboy to come over to the desk.

"Thank you," said Rebecca.

If the lobby is any indication of what the whole hotel is like, then I can't wait to see my room, thought Rebecca.

The bellboy approached Rebecca and took her bags. "Come this way ma'am. I will show you to your room."

Wow, are all hotel staff and service this good? I feel like I am royalty, thought Rebecca.

They arrived at the elevators, which were located to the left of the reception and stepped in; the bellboy pressed the seventy-second floor button.

OMG. I'm on the seventy-second floor. I can't believe it. I bet the view is to die for. I am so excited, thought Rebecca, smiling.

When they arrived at the room the bellboy took the swipe card from Rebecca and opened the door. "After you ma'am. Go in and make yourself comfortable."

Entering the antique white painted room, the smell was one of newness. It had several luxurious furnishings, a flat screen TV, bar fridge, two queen beds, which had white linen, with a rustic colouring comforter lying on the end. The charcoal and white coloured bathroom, which had a spa was extravagant and she noticed on the vanity that it had some body wash and toiletries for Rebecca to use.

Wow, I feel like I have died and gone to heaven, thought Rebecca.

As the bellboy showed her how to work things in the room, he asked, "Where are you from, ma'am?"

"I'm from Perth, in Australia," said Rebecca.

"Wow. You are a long way from home. Are you here for business or pleasure?" said the bellboy. His Southern American accent was pleasing to the ear.

"Both," she said.

"Well… I hope you enjoy your stay with us, ma'am," said the bellboy, walking toward the doorway.

"Thank you," she said, following him. Reaching into her purse, Rebecca remembered to get some money out for a tip. She had read that if you get great service you should tip.

"Thank you," said the bellboy, taking the money from Rebecca's hand.

"You're welcome," said Rebecca, smiling.

"If you need anything else Ms Landers, please don't hesitate to ask reception," said the bellboy.

"Thank you."

The door closed and Rebecca walked over to the bed and fell onto it and hugged herself. Her mind was racing as she stared at the ceiling and then around the room. Never before had she ever felt so grateful to be given the opportunity of having such a lovely room.

Hmm, what to do… maybe a shower is what I need, thought Rebecca as she sniffed her underarm.

After her shower, Rebecca put her hair up in a towel, so that it would dry quicker. Once she was dressed, she decided to ring Mitch.

"Hello… you miss me already?" teased Mitch when he answered.

"Well… I have had my shower and washed my hair and now I am dressed and not knowing what to do with myself. Can we meet for lunch or do you have something you need to do?" said Rebecca, hoping he was free.

"Umm… what about if I pick you up out the front in say thirty minutes and we can go somewhere?" said Mitch.

"Sounds good. See you in about thirty then," said Rebecca.

"Ok. Bye."

Hanging up the phone, Rebecca returned to the bathroom and dried her hair off. Once done she applied some mascara and lip gloss. Looking in the mirror, she said, "Hmm, not bad."

As the elevator doors opened, Rebecca headed towards the front doors of the hotel. Spotting Mitch, who was waiting for her near the entrance, she waved.

"Hello," said Mitch, as he reached Rebecca and gave her a hug.

"Hi… thank God you're here. I was starting to get bored," said Rebecca, pulling away from their embrace slowly.

"Well, we will have to do something about that," said Mitch, excited to see her. "But first I wanted to take you somewhere that is very special to me. It's not the most greatest place, but like I said, it's special to me."

"Ok. Sounds intriguing," said Rebecca, with her eyebrows raised.

As they walked outside, Rebecca was looking around for the limo, but she couldn't see it anywhere. She just assumed Mitch would still be in the limo.

"This is my car, over here," said Mitch, pointing to a black sports car.

"This is your car? Nice ride," said Rebecca, admiring how sleek it was.

"Thanks," said Mitch, as he opened the door for her to get in.

Pulling away from the hotel, Rebecca said, "Wow… this is very nice to ride in, Mitch. Does it have an iPod or CD player?"

"Yes. What would you like to listen to?" asked Mitch.

"I don't mind. You pick something," said Rebecca. She watched him press a button on the dash and it belted out AC/DC. "One of my favourite bands."

"Yeah, I know. Me too," said Mitch, turning up the volume and tapping the steering wheel.

They had been driving for about twenty minutes out of the city, when Mitch took a turn off the main highway, which pulled the car directly into a cemetery. Frowning, Rebecca looked over at Mitch apprehensively and waited for him to say something, but he kept quiet.

"Why are we here?" asked Rebecca, with a furrowed brow.

"You'll see," said Mitch. Parking the car, Mitch got out and then came around to open the door for Rebecca.

When she stepped out of the car, Mitch took her hand and led Rebecca to a grave site. Once she saw the name on the grave, 'Christine Portellico', a warm realisation hit her.

"This is a special place for me. This was my wife Christine. She died about five and a half years ago now," said Mitch, looking down at the gravestone.

"Oh, I'm so sorry, Mitch," said Rebecca sadly, placing her hand on his shoulder. "I didn't even know you were married, let alone a widower. God, you must miss her so much. Especially as you can't visit that often, whilst living in Australia."

"This lovely lady was the love of my life and yes, I do miss her so much, every day. Just like you do with Jackson," said Mitch, looking into her tearful eyes.

"So is this why you left Seattle?" asked Rebecca.

"One of the reasons," said Mitch.

"Oh, Ok. Can we go and buy some fresh flowers so that I can put them on her grave and talk with her, if that's Ok with you?" said Rebecca, wholeheartedly.

Mitch looked at her surprised and said, "Oh, that is nice of you. You don't even know her and you want to talk with her. This is what I meant about you Rebecca, when I said you were a lovely person with a good heart; because you are."

"Well... you may not believe this, but since my Jackson passed away I have always felt like I can feel his presence when I visit his grave each week and I somehow feel a comfort in knowing he might still be there listening to me, even if he can't communicate with me. So I figure that Christine may be here too, and I am sure she would love some fresh flowers on her grave."

"That's good you still feel his presence. It does feel good knowing they are still here... let's go and I will take you to the shop that is at the entrance to the cemetery," said Mitch, gesturing to the car.

I wonder how Rebecca would react if she knew that I could actually see Christine and speak with her when I visit her gravesite? I still don't understand it myself how I can see and speak with Christine, but it sure does make me feel good, thought Mitch, as he turned his head back around quickly and smiled at his wife, who was shimmering near the headstone, as he and Rebecca walked towards the car.

After Rebecca bought a bouquet of flowers and they drove back to the cemetery, she asked Mitch, "Would you mind if I could talk to Christine by myself for a while?"

He nodded and said, "Sure... I will sit in the car. Let me know when you are ready."

Rebecca sat on the green grass next to Christine's grave and laid the flowers at the head of her headstone.

"Hello, Christine... I am sorry for your loss. Mitch is such a lovely person. You must miss him so much. Life just isn't fair sometimes, is it? I have just lost my husband too about twelve months ago and I still miss him a real lot. I don't think I will ever find another person like him. Not that I would let anyone into my heart again either; I just can't."

Rebecca's heart was heavy as she realised the pain Mitch must have been through when Christine died. But she felt comforted at Christine's gravesite knowing she would be glad he had returned to see her. She talked to Christine for about twenty minutes and then said her goodbyes. As Rebecca was about to step away from the grave she heard someone whisper Mitch's name. But when she turned around, there was not a soul in sight. Shaking her head, she frowned, until she heard the voice again.

'Thank you.'

With her eyes darting from side to side, looking all around, she gulped and took a deep breath inwards. But again there was no one in sight. Looking back at Christine's gravestone, she thought, *Am I hearing things? Maybe it is just the wind.* Shaking her head, she chuckled to herself and then returned to the car.

Approaching the car, she noticed Mitch had his seat laid back and was relaxed listening to music. When she opened the door he turned the music down and said, "Everything good?"

"Yeah," said Rebecca, smiling politely as she took a seat next to Mitch. She didn't feel the need to mention anything about what she thought she may have heard down at the gravesite.

"Do you mind if I go and talk with Christine now?"

"Go for it. I will wait here and listen to some music," said Rebecca.

"Thank you," said Mitch, placing his seat in an upright position, leaning in and kissing her cheek.

CHAPTER SIX

Guilt ridden, Mitch approached the grave site nervously because he hadn't been to see Christine in five years, since he had moved to Perth. Sheepishly smiling, he wasn't quite sure of the reception he would get when he saw her shimmering next to her grave. But as he got closer to the headstone, she smiled back at him with her ghostly blue eyes. Christine's long brown hair seem to be blowing in the wind and he could tell from the smile on her face she was excited to see him. Whenever he had visited her grave previously, it had brought him contentment from the many conversations they had.

"Hello, my love," said Mitch, with a furrowed brow, tracing every inch of her features with his eyes.

Christine smiled and said, "Hello."

"I have missed you so much. I am sorry I haven't been to visit you in a while. When you died, I couldn't bear to be here in Seattle without you anymore, so… I just ran as far as I could. I have moved to Australia. I am sorry, my love," said Mitch, dropping to his knees next to the headstone, with tears running down his cheeks.

"I understand, my love," said Christine. She was always so patient with him. "What was her name, the lovely girl who put flowers on my grave and sat with me?"

"Her name is Rebecca and we live across the road from each other, where I live in Australia," said Mitch, looking up at Christine.

"I don't know whether she could see me or not, but she is the first person besides yourself that actually talked to me. She is so nice, Mitch and has a really good heart. Do you like her?" said Christine.

"We are just good friends, my love," said Mitch.

"I get the feeling she likes you a lot. But can't commit herself because she only, not long ago, lost her husband. She feels guilty for even thinking about you," said Christine.

"Really… I do like her, Christine, but you are the only woman that I ever want to be with; you know that. Anyway Bec has told me that she only wants to be good friends, so I won't pursue it," said Mitch, standing up.

"Mitch I am dead and you are alive. I do give you my blessing, you know, to find someone else and eventually marry them… I know you have a successful business, as Rebecca told me all about it. But that is not enough in life. You need to have someone you can come home to and love. You know, like what we had when I was alive," said Christine, placing her ghostly hand on his shoulder.

"I don't know if I can do that Christine. Losing you was the hardest thing I have ever had to endure," said Mitch, looking into her adoring eyes.

"As much as I love you, Mitch, I have been told that I won't be here for too much longer and that I will be passing onto heaven soon. So I want to make sure you are looked after. I don't want you moping here for me every day," said Christine.

She knew Mitch wouldn't move on, unless she gave him her blessing.

Mitch's brow was creased as he looked at Christine with tears in his eyes and said, "They are taking you that soon. I will miss not being able to see you all the time, my love. Can't you stay longer? I need you here."

"Sorry, my love; any day now I will be passing on. So I just wanted to say goodbye and to tell you to get on with your love life. Don't hold back," said Christine.

"I won't ever forget you, Christine. I love you," said Mitch, wiping the tears from his face with the back of his hand.

"I love you too, baby. I have to go now. Take care of yourself and live life to the fullest," said Christine, as she vanished into thin air. Her visits were never too long.

In Mitch's mind he knew he would see Christine again before he went back to Australia. But he also knew that next time could be the last time and he wasn't prepared for that.

CHAPTER SEVEN

Mitch's car was only parked metres away from Christine's grave site. Looking out the window, over to her left, Rebecca watched Mitch standing next to the headstone wiping the tears from his face and he seemed to be sobbing, so she decided that she would go over and see if there was anything she could do to console him.

"Are you Ok?" said Rebecca, approaching him from behind and placing a hand on his shoulder.

Turning around slowly, Mitch said, "Not really." Wiping his runny nose on the back of his sleeve, he tried to avert his eyes downwards. His tear-stained face was apparent to Rebecca, as his body heaved with grief.

Rebecca leant in and placed her arms around Mitch for a heartfelt hug. "Shhh, everything will be all right,' said Rebecca, rubbing his back as she tried to soothe his pain, which she knew all too well.

"Thanks Bec. I needed that... I will be Ok," said Mitch, pulling away slowly and wiping his eyes.

"Come on, why don't we get out of here and go have a drink somewhere," said Rebecca, placing her hand on his upper arm.

He nodded and said, "Sounds like a good idea." Mitch knew where a bar was nearby where they could have lunch. He had drowned his sorrows there many a time before, when Christine had first passed away.

Placing an arm around his shoulders, Rebecca walked back to the car with Mitch.

Rebecca acquired a seat on a silver framed, black leather bar stool at the long wooden bar next to Mitch. "It's my shout… what would you like?" asked Rebecca, as she looked around the empty place.

"Umm…" said Mitch, looking at the mirrored wall behind the bar, trying to decide what he wanted. "I might have a Jacks and Coke. Make it a double."

"Right… I will have a Vodka and Pineapple, with some Sprite, bartender," said Rebecca, watching the bartender take the Jack Daniels off the shelf behind him.

"Will you be ordering something to eat as well?" asked the bartender to Mitch.

Looking at the black board on the left hand side of the bar, which had the lunch time menu, Mitch said, "I'll have the steak burger and fries. What would you like for lunch, Rebecca?"

"I might have the same," said Rebecca, looking from Mitch to the bartender.

"No problem. I will bring it out to you if you want to take a seat in one of our booths," said the bartender, gesturing to where the booths were om the left hand side of the room.

Collecting their drinks from the bar, Mitch and Rebecca headed over to one of the booths and sat across from one another.

"Would you like to listen to some music?" asked Rebecca. "Looks like they have a jukebox over in the corner."

"Sure," said Mitch. "Maybe some country and western."

"Ok. Leave it with me," said Rebecca, stepping out the booth. As she stood in front of the jukebox, Rebecca placed the coins in the slot, flicked through the selection of albums and found a selection of songs she thought Mitch might like. Upon returning to the booth, Rebecca also noticed that the bar had a pool table, which was located in the back corner. *Hmm… after lunch I might see if Mitch is up for a game or two. Might take his mind off things.*

The afternoon went by fast and by the time they had eaten their lunch, played a few games of pool and were ready to go, they were both a bit too intoxicated to drive Mitch's car. So Mitch organised with the bar owner, whom he knew well, to park his car safely in his locked garage until he could come back and get it later. Then he called a cab to take Rebecca and himself back to her hotel.

As the cab pulled up at the front of the hotel Rebecca said, "Would you like to come and see my room? It's so luxurious. I can't even believe it's my room."

"Nah, that's Ok. I might get going," said Mitch. He knew it was not right to enter a lady's hotel room, especially when he was intoxicated.

"Come on. I have to show someone. Come on…" pleaded Rebecca, paying the cab driver.

"Hmm.. oh, all right then. But just for a minute," said Mitch, smiling politely.

As they entered the hotel foyer Mitch said, "Hmm… nice."

"My room is on the seventy-second floor," said Rebecca, as they walked into the elevator. "Wait till you see my room. It's even better."

"I bet the view is really good," said Mitch, watching her press the button.

Opening the door to her room, Rebecca said, "Quick, go have a look." She was excited to show Mitch her room.

"Wow… this is luxurious. Must have cost your boss a fortune to stay in this room," said Mitch, as he finished looking around and the sat on the bed. "And you were right; the view is awesome… actually Rebecca, would you mind if I lie down for a minute? I have a splitting headache and just need to rest for a few minutes."

"No problem, Mitch. Would you like something for your headache?" said Rebecca.

"Yes please," said Mitch, laying on the bed with his eyes closed.

"No problem. I am sure I have some headache medication in my luggage," said Rebecca walking toward the wardrobe.

"I still also need to go and see my family, but I don't want to turn up feeling like this," said Mitch, rubbing his temples.

"Oh, right. I thought you had already been home when you turned up in a different car," said Rebecca.

"Yeah I did go home, but they weren't at home when I arrived, so I picked up my car and was on the way to the cemetery when you rang," said Mitch

"Oh, right," said Rebecca, searching through her suitcase for the headache tablets. "Here we go." When she returned to give Mitch the medication and glass of water, he was asleep.

Best I let him get some rest. He looks peaceful sleeping, thought Rebecca, placing a blanket over him which she found in the hotel wardrobe.

It occurred to Rebecca whilst Mitch was resting that maybe his family might be worried that he hadn't turned up yet, so she decided to ring them and let them know where he was. Finding their number in Mitch's mobile, which she pulled out of the inside pocket on his jacket, she decided to ring his mom.

As the phone rang, Rebecca became a bit nervous, until his mom answered.

"Hello… my name is Rebecca. I am a friend of Mitch's."

"Oh, hello Rebecca. Mitch has told us all about you. Did you have a good trip over from Australia?" said his mom. She had a strong American accent.

"The trip was really good. Long, but good. Mitch was so nice to me, he got my seats upgraded from economy to first class and that made all the difference on the long trip. He is really thoughtful," said Rebecca.

"That's my boy, always so thoughtful. Are you coming over for dinner tonight, dear?" said his mom.

"Thanks, that would be lovely. Is it dressy or jeans type of dinner?" Rebecca said, anxiously.

"It's a dressy type of dinner," said his mom.

"Ok," said Rebecca.

Rebecca found Mitch's mom really easy to talk with and they seemed to talk for a while, until Rebecca remembered why she called in the first place.

"Well, it's been lovely talking with you, but the main reason I rang you is to let you know that Mitch has fallen asleep in my hotel room. I didn't want to wake him because he has had a terribly upsetting morning.

You see, he took me to meet Christine and from there he got a bit tiddly and has now fallen asleep. Anyway I didn't want you to worry about why he hadn't turned up, so that is why I rang. When he wakes up we will come over to your house," said Rebecca.

"That was very thoughtful of you, dear. Thank you, I appreciate the call," she said.

"You're welcome. Would you like me to bring anything tonight? Maybe something nice to drink or some dessert?" asked Rebecca.

"No, dear. Just bring yourself, and oh, my son of course! Thank God he has you to look after him today," she said.

"You know in all the confusion, I forgot to ask your name, I don't want to call you Mitch's mom," said Rebecca.

"It's Helen, dear, and I am so happy you are here with Mitch. Well, we will see you around 7.30pm then for dinner," said Helen.

"Yes ma'am. And thank you for the invite."

As Rebecca hung up and placed Mitch's mobile back in his jacket pocket, she thought, *what am I going to wear? I didn't bring anything really nice with me to wear at a dinner party. Hmm…*

Looking around the room, she spotted the telephone next to her bed and decided to ring the hotel reception to see what shops were close by for a dress to wear tonight.

"Good afternoon, Ms Landers. What can I do for you?" said the receptionist.

"Can you tell me if there is a dress shop close by to the hotel that I can walk to?" asked Rebecca.

"Well actually, we do have a dress shop in the hotel ma'am," said the receptionist. "It's on the second floor and reasonably priced as well."

"Oh, right. Thanks… bye," said Rebecca, hanging up the phone.

Checking on Mitch, who was lightly snoring, she figured he would be asleep for a while, so she left a note to tell him where she had gone and quickly went down to the shop in search of something nice to wear.

As soon as she walked into the shop, Rebecca spotted a stunning dinner dress on the first rack. It was a knee length, green, opal coloured dress, with spaghetti straps and a love-heart shaped neck line. Rebecca knew she had shoes that she brought with her in her suitcase that would go perfectly with it. She had also brought with her from home a bit of dress jewellery as well that she thought would go nice with the dress.

When she arrived back to her hotel room, Mitch was still asleep. So she just let him rest as he obviously needed the sleep.

Chapter Eight

About four-thirty Mitch woke to find Rebecca sitting on the bed opposite to him watching TV.

As he sat up she said, "Hi gorgeous. How you feeling now?"

"Gorgeous, now that's new. And yes, I am feeling better. Thanks for letting me take a nap here. I certainly needed it," said Mitch, placing his feet on the floor.

"That's Ok. I hope you don't mind, but I rang and spoke with your mom to let her know you were all right and for her not to worry," said Rebecca.

"Thanks Bec. That was nice of you." said Mitch, wiping the sleep from his eyes.

"Your mom actually invited me over for dinner tonight. She said we had to be there about 7.30," said Rebecca, excited at the fact of wearing her new dress and meeting Mitch's family.

"Oh, right. Hey… I might go and get my car and if you don't mind, could I have a shower and get ready here?" asked Mitch.

"No problem. Are you going to be able to drive, though?" said Rebecca.

"Yeah, all good, Bec. I shouldn't be too long," said Mitch, placing his jacket on.

"Oh, Ok. I'll go get you the key to the elevator and my room, so you can get back in when you return," said Rebecca, walking over to her handbag.

"Thanks," said Mitch.

Whilst Mitch was gone, Rebecca had a shower and put on her new dress and shoes. Once she had done her hair, makeup and jewellery, she took a look in the long mirror in the bathroom to see if she looked Ok. It was then that she heard the door open to her room. It was Mitch returning.

"Where are you?" Mitch called out.

"I'm in the bathroom," said Rebecca.

When he came into the bathroom, his mouth dropped open and a huge grin came over his face.

"Wow… don't you look beautiful in that dress. Is that new? It's just… well, I haven't seen you wear a lovely dress like that ever before," said Mitch, raising his eyebrows.

"Your mom told me it was a dressy dinner party. So I went down to the shop they have here at the hotel and found it. What do you think? Do I pass the test?" said Rebecca, twirling around.

"You look really nice and yes, it does looks great on you." said Mitch, eyeing her up and down.

"Thanks. What are you going to wear?" said Rebecca, as felt her cheeks warming. She hadn't had a compliment like that in a while. Especially not from a man.

"I popped into the store downstairs just now and bought these," said Mitch, holding up a white plastic bag with a shirt and trousers inside. "But I just need to iron them."

"You go and have a shower and I will iron them for you, Ok," said Rebecca.

"Thanks gorgeous," said Mitch, teasing her.

She laughed at him and said, "Hey, was your car all right?"

"Yeah, all good. The bar owner looked after it for me," said Mitch, taking his clothes out of his suitcase, and handing them to Rebecca to iron. "I won't be long in the shower. You sure you don't mind ironing them for me?"

Rebecca waved her hand at him and said, "No problem. Take your time."

Placing the ironing board and iron back into the cupboard, Rebecca looked up to see Mitch coming out of the bathroom with wet hair and a towel wrapped around his bottom half.

Don't look… don't look at his muscular body. Just look straight at this face, thought Rebecca, her heart beating fast.

"Mmm, you smell nice. Did you use the berry shower wash?" said Rebecca, handing him his ironed clothes.

"It does smell nice, doesn't it? Thank you for ironing my clothes," said Mitch, taking his clothes from her. He returned to the bathroom to get dressed.

Mmm… delicious. I would like to kiss that body all over. God… mind out of the gutter, Bec. Remember he is only your friend, thought Rebecca, staring out the window of the hotel room.

Her thoughts were broken when Mitch came back into the room and flicked her with a wet towel.

"Ouch!" said Rebecca, touching her leg.

"What were you just thinking about? You looked like you were a million miles away," said Mitch, with a smirk on his face.

"That's for me to know and you to find out," teased Rebecca.

He laughed and said, "Are you nearly ready to go? It's a bit of a drive to Mom and Dad's house in Hunts Point."

"Five minutes and I will be ready."

On the drive to Mitch's parents' house, Rebecca sat quietly in the leather upholstered seat staring out the window, taking in the view.

"Seattle sure is a beautiful place, Mitch," said Rebecca.

"I can tell you like it here by the smile on your face and how much you are enjoying yourself," said Mitch.

"Seattle reminds me of Perth in many ways, but at least the weather here is a tad warmer than Perth at the moment," said Rebecca. "I believe that the wind chill factor here can get pretty cold in winter?"

"I can't say that I miss the weather here in winter, as it can get bitterly cold. But funny you should say that Seattle is like Perth, as that is exactly why I love living in Perth, because it reminds me of Seattle. I do miss being home," said Mitch, watching the road and glancing at Rebecca.

"Great minds think alike," said Rebecca.

He smiled and said, "Yeah… it's not far now, just around the bend here."

The car slowed as it rounded the bend in the road and Mitch pulled into a driveway which had a high limestone brick fence that had an electric wire fencing surrounding the top of the limestone. There were signs signalling it was live.

Wondering what was behind the wrought iron gates, Rebecca watched Mitch carefully key in the code on the keypad located outside. As the gates opened, he drove in, along a winding cream brick paved driveway, with manicured green lawn, pencil pines and colourful gardens on both sides. When the mansion came into view, to say it looked magnificent was an understatement. It had cream rendered brick walls, with accentuated white windows with wrought iron balconies and white door frames, white pillars and a light grey gabled roof. Excited, Rebecca couldn't wait to see inside, as she guessed it would be just as spectacular. Like something that might be seen in the magazines for the rich and famous.

"OMG Mitch, is this where you grew up? That is the most beautiful house I have ever seen. Look at the garden, that is so lovely. Your family is so lucky," stated Rebecca, looking around in bewilderment. As the car pulled up to the front door, she noticed there was a doorman who was waiting for them.

"Good evening, ma'am," said the doorman, as he opened her door.

"Good evening… thank you," she said, surprised by the formality.

He smiled and nodded at her politely.

"You ready?" said Mitch, standing next to Rebecca and indicating that they needed to go inside.

"Yes," said Rebecca, standing next to the car apprehensively.

"Come on," said Mitch, taking her by the hand.

As they stepped inside his parents' house, Rebecca stood there in wonderment, and couldn't believe how absolutely beautiful the house was inside. The foyer had a long glass chandelier hanging from the ceiling, which glistened brightly, next to a white marble staircase which was off to the left.

I can tell rich people live here, Rebecca thought to herself.

"It's not too intimidating is it for you?" said Mitch, watching her reaction.

"Sure is. I'm not used to seeing this type of housing. But I wouldn't call this a house. It's a mansion," said Rebecca, looking around.

"You'll be all right," said Mitch smiling, taking Rebecca by the hand and leading her into the sitting room where his family was.

Walking in, Rebecca felt nervous, but as soon as Mitch introduced his mom and dad to her, her nerves ceased. His dad, Grayson, was tall and was distinguished-looking with his grey hair. She then realised that Mitch's looks came from his dad's side of the family.

"Nice to meet you, Rebecca," said Grayson, shaking her hand.

"Thanks. It's nice to meet you too," said Rebecca.

"Welcome dear. It's so nice to finally meet you," said Helen, as she gave Rebecca a tight motherly hug.

She was actually the same as Rebecca had pictured her. Brown hair, blue eyes and had a beautiful figure for someone her age.

"Hello… it's nice to meet you too," she said, smiling.

Mitch then introduced her to his two younger brothers, Nick and Michael, who gave Rebecca a hug and made her feel welcome.

"Nice to meet you. I have heard lots about you from Mitch," said Nick.

Rebecca looked at Mitch and frowned, not knowing what he had said or even why he was talking about her.

"I am sorry, but I don't know much about you both at all. Clambake here doesn't tell ya much. I didn't even know Mitch grew up here until a few days ago. But I am sure you both can enlighten me," said Rebecca, looking from one brother to another.

Mitch looked at Rebecca and smirked.

"That is typical of Mitchell. He never has given much away about people... except for you. He has spoken of you a lot lately when he rings," said Nick, looking from Rebecca to Mitch and smirking.

"Shut up Nick," said Mitch, his cheeks red.

"What would you both like to drink?" said Grayson, interrupting.

Rebecca let Mitch go first as she didn't know what to order for a drink.

"I'll have a white wine, Dad," said Mitch.

"I'll have the same thanks, Mr Portellico," said Rebecca, smiling politely.

"Call me Grayson, dear," he said. He then went to the bar in the corner of the room and poured their drinks.

"Here we go," said Grayson, handing them their drinks.

"This wine is really nice. It's not something I have had ever before. What is it, Mr Port-, I mean, Grayson?" said Rebecca, after she took a sip.

"It's just a plain white wine, dear. I am not sure of the brand or label name. I can find out from our staff and let you know later, if you like," said Grayson.

"Yes, thanks. I wouldn't mind taking a bottle back home with me to Australia," said Rebecca.

"No problem, dear," said Grayson.

"Dinner is being served in the dining room everyone," said Helen, interrupting.

Rebecca followed Mitch into the dining room and they took their seats at a long wooden table, which was set up with white lace placemats, and fine bone china plates and silver cutlery, with a long colourful flower arrangement in the middle of the table. Sitting at the table next to Mitch, Rebecca looked down at her place setting and realised there was so much cutlery that she didn't know which one to use first. She had only ever had one knife and fork or spoon at any dinner party she had previously attended.

Oh well... I will just have to wing it, she thought to herself.

As the family happily chatted away, a waitress came into the room and announced to everyone that there was a buffet dinner tonight and gestured to the side buffet counter set up, which had a bain-marie of food to eat. It all sounded delicious to Rebecca. She didn't realise how hungry she was until she smelt the aromas coming off the food, as her stomach rumbled.

Standing at the bain-maries spooning her food onto her plate, Rebecca noticed Mitch's brother Nick lean in close to her and he said, "You know he is smitten with you, don't you? He just won't say anything to jeopardise your friendship, that's all."

"What…who?" asked Rebecca, frowning.

"Mitch," said Nick.

"No… I didn't know that, Nick and now I feel uncomfortable. I wish you hadn't told me," said Rebecca, feeling her face turn crimson red.

"Sorry, Rebecca. I just assumed you liked Mitch. I can see from your body language that you do," said Nick, matter-of-factly.

"I do like Mitch, Nick. It's just… well… I am a bit scared to move on so soon after my husband's death. I feel a bit guilty, you know," said Rebecca, with a furrowed brow. "And I really don't want to wreck our friendship."

"Well… you don't want to wait forever. A man can only wait for so long before he loses interest, you know," said Nick, joking.

Rebecca pursed her lips sideways at Nick and walked away from the bain-maries. Returning to her seat, Rebecca wasn't quite sure how she felt about what Nick had said. *I wasn't even aware that Mitch liked me, let alone that he was smitten with me.* Sitting quietly eating her food, she was interrupted by Mitch.

"You are quiet… are you Ok?" said Mitch, quietly as he leant into her side.

She looked into Mitch's eyes and discovered his concerned for her. For the first time Rebecca actually noticed how handsome he really was and wondered why she hadn't realised this before.

Placing her hand on his, she said, "Yeah, I'm Ok. It's just a bit overwhelming that's all. And to top it off, Nick has a big mouth, hey. He told me the way you feel."

"Oh, shit, I'm sorry, Rebecca," said Mitch quietly, when he realised what she was talking about. With his cheeks red from embarrassment, he took a deep breath in. "My family means well. It's just that they want to see me happy, that's all. Don't take what Nick said to you the wrong way. I know that you only want to be friends and that's fine with me."

"That's the problem, Mitch. I'm not sure that I just want to be friends. I am scared of what I might be feeling, especially when Jackson hasn't been gone long. I would really like to take our friendship further, but…" She trailed off as he interrupted her.

"I feel the same way as you do. I have true feelings for you," said Mitch. Leaning in, he kissed her lips tenderly.

Rebecca's heartbeat quickened as her mind sensed his warm and caring lips and she kissed him back gently. As she pulled away slowly, her face heated when she felt all eyes on them around the table.

"Does anyone want some more food before the waitress takes it away?" asked Helen, trying to take the attention away from her oldest boy.

Everyone went up for second helping of food, except for Mitch and Rebecca.

"Actually… we might go for a walk outside, Mom, if that's Ok? We won't be long. I need to talk to Rebecca about something," said Mitch, standing with Rebecca.

"Take your time, dears," said Helen, from the bain-maries.

Walking outside into the Seattle cool night air, Mitch took Rebecca's hand in his and asked her, "Would you like to stay here tonight? I can ask the maid to make up a room for you. It's just that it's a long way back to the hotel and…"

His voice trailed off and she didn't hear what he was saying. Rebecca's heart was beating loudly, and she felt anxious, as she contemplated saying yes or no to his question.

Looking into his eyes, she thought, *This gorgeous multi billionaire has asked you to stay the night and you are just standing here not knowing what to say. Awkward…*

He leant in and kissed her tender lips again.

With a warm feeling in her heart, she couldn't help herself, she kissed him back fervently and her breathing became rapid as her hands roamed over him.

Pulling away from his lips, Rebecca said, "I don't have any other clothes here, Mitch." It was just an excuse because she was nervous. Her mind was saying one thing and her body was saying another.

"That's Ok. I can ring the hotel and ask them to bring your suitcase here if you want," said Mitch.

"You can do that?" she said, surprised.

"Yes, it won't be any trouble. And tomorrow I can take you back to the hotel so that you are there for your course on Monday. What do you think?" said Mitch, almost begging her to stay the night.

Rebecca stood there for a few moments, thinking.

What am I going to do? Her breathing was rapid.

All of a sudden a voice from nowhere seemed to say, "Just say yes. What do you have to lose?"

Looking up at Mitch, who was waiting for her to answer, she said, "Ok. But could you please organise for my clothes and toiletries as well from the hotel?"

"You mean it? You'll stay here?" said Mitch, smiling.

"Yes," Rebecca said, nodding quickly. But she was unsure if she was doing the right thing and what signals she was giving.

"I am so glad. That way we can spend a bit more time getting to know each other. Don't worry, my family won't annoy us," said Mitch, excited. In all his wildest dreams he never thought this day would come. He always thought that they would be only good friends.

"I am not worried about your family. I am more worried about you and I. You have to understand Mitch, I have never been with or even kissed anyone else besides Jackson. We were childhood sweethearts," said Rebecca, nervously fidgeting with her hands.

"Well, if it makes you feel any better, I haven't kissed or slept with anyone since Christine passed away. So what you are feeling, I am feeling it too. But I don't want to let you slip through my fingers, Rebecca. I would like to try to see what will happen for us as we get to know each other better," said Mitch, sincerely, with his brow creased.

Mitch pulled her in close and placed his arms around her waist. As their lips met for the third time, Rebecca felt a fire ignite in her stomach. His kiss was passionate and she could feel herself falling for him.

"What will your parents think of me staying the night?" asked Rebecca.

"Actually, do you remember they asked me if you wanted to stay before we even left Australia? So I am sure they won't mind for one night," said Mitch.

"Oh, that's right."

"I suppose the next question is… do you want to stay in my room or have your own room for tonight?" said Mitch, anxiously watching her reaction. He wasn't sure she was ready for the next step, so soon.

Rebecca's stomach was now doing back flips and she felt her face heat up. She opened her mouth and quickly closed it, not knowing what to say. Twice.

"Can I decide later?" she said, nervously.

He nodded, kissed her on her forehead and said, "No problem."

Chapter Nine

Walking back inside, Mitch had his arm around Rebecca's shoulder. "Everything will be Ok," said Mitch.

Rebecca smiled and nodded.

"You cats sorted everything out?" said Nick, as he approached them in the hallway.

"I suppose we should be saying thank you to you, Nick. Because if you didn't say anything to either of us, well… we probably wouldn't have pursued it," said Mitch, as he looked from Nick to Rebecca.

"I could see the chemistry and body language between you two. But nothing was happening and I couldn't let that happen. And you are welcome," said Nick, smirking. "Actually, Mom asked me to come and get you both as dessert is being served."

"I don't have any room left for dessert. Do you feel like dessert, Mitch?" said Rebecca.

"No. I am full," said Mitch, rubbing his stomach.

Walking back into the dining room, Mitch said, "We don't want any dessert, Mom. We are both full from dinner. But thanks anyway."

"Oh, Ok… well sit down anyway, sweetheart. We haven't seen you for over five years and just want to talk with you a bit more before you go anywhere," said Helen. She had missed him whilst he was living in Australia.

"I am not going anywhere, Mom, and you will see me for the next week before I leave," said Mitch, giving his mom a tight hug.

Sitting at the table, Mitch's family started to talk about what they had been doing lately. Rebecca really loved the banter between the brothers as well.

He sure is lucky to have such a really nice family.

"Would you like another drink of white wine, my dear?" Grayson asked Rebecca.

All too quickly she said, "Yes, please." Rebecca's nerves were shot and she needed a drink to calm herself. Especially as Mitch was rubbing her thigh up and down under the table. She hadn't had a man touch her like that in a long while and it was really turning her on.

Rebecca leant in and whispered into Mitch's ear. "Stop that. I won't be able to control myself soon." She tried to push his hand away, but he was persistent.

He smirked at her and whispered in her ear, "That's the plan, beautiful."

By the time Grayson came back with her drink, Rebecca was quietly panting, and felt heated from Mitch's teasing touch under the table.

"Thank you," said Rebecca to Grayson, smiling. She drank her glass of wine down fast to calm herself.

"Feeling a bit tense are we?" said Mitch quietly, with a raised eyebrow.

"I think I might go to bed. I am feeling a bit tired. Can you show me where my room is?" Rebecca asked Mitch.

Helen overheard what Rebecca had said to Mitch.

"I would say that you may feel a wee bit jet lagged for a few days, my dear. I have had the maid make up a room for you. Mitch will show you where it is."

I hadn't even realised that Mitch had asked Helen and Grayson for a room to be made up for me. I wonder if he had asked or whether they just surmised that I would stay. Oh well, thought Rebecca.

"Thanks Helen and thanks for letting me sleep over here tonight. I do appreciate all the trouble you have gone to," said Rebecca, standing.

"No trouble at all, my dear. See you in the morning," said Helen.

"Good night all," said Rebecca, looking around the room.

Mitch gave his mom a kiss good night on the cheek and shook his dad's hand.

"Good night. See you all in the morning," said Mitch, looking around the room.

Nick and Michael said good night to Mitch and Rebecca as well.

Walking up the marble staircase together, hand in hand, Mitch directed Rebecca to his room, which was over to the right of the stairs. Entering his bedroom, he pulled her quickly into the room and shut the door behind them. Gently pushing her up against the wall, he impatiently kissed her neck, whilst caressing Rebecca's body with his hands. When his teeth brushed over her left earlobe, Rebecca's body trembled all over. With her mind racing and her body quivering as his touch awakened her libido, she moaned as their lips met again and he opened her mouth with his sensual kiss. Their tongues met for the first time, searching, wanting, drinking up the flavours of each other's mouths. Breathless, she couldn't deny her feelings for Mitch any longer as their bodies fused together.

"Take your shirt off," she said, dominantly. He did as she asked and placed it on the floor quickly. In the dim light of the moonlit bedroom, Rebecca stood there looking at his body in amazement, soaking up how gorgeous he was. But in her greed she needed to see more.

"Take your trousers off," said Rebecca, reaching down to undo his top button.

He shook his head. "You take something off first."

"Can you unzip my dress?" said Rebecca, turning around.

Mitch unzipped her dress and Rebecca's dress fell to the floor and she was left standing there in her black bra and panties, with high heels on.

"You are so beautiful, Bec," said Mitch, looking at her in admiration. Pulling her in close so that their bodies were touching, his hand journeyed up to her supple right breast. Through the material of her lacy bra he felt her nipple harden and she was lost to his touch.

Rebecca's breathing increased as she undid his trouser zipper. Pushing them off his hips, they fell to the ground and he stepped out of them, kicking them away.

Impatiently Mitch picked her up in his arms and placed her on his king size bed. They lay on the bed kissing and their tongues searched each other's mouths, wanting and knowing what would come next. When she reached down, his shaft was hard through his briefs and she couldn't handle this teasing anymore. Before she knew it, her hunger for him took over and she pulled his briefs off quickly and started to suck his elongated cock. As she swirled her tongue around the head of it, he groaned in unmistakable pleasure. Glancing up at him, she noticed he was enjoying every moment of it, especially when she placed her teeth onto his shaft and sucked it harder.

"Rebecca you need to stop before I come in your mouth," said Mitch, breathlessly trying to push her away.

Her breath was staggered as she slowly worked her way up his chest, kissing him gently as she went and when she got to his lips, she heard him moan in her mouth.

Pushing Rebecca onto the bed gently, he said, "My turn." Slowly he kissed her neck and bit her earlobe. His hot breath on her neck excited Rebecca and she could feel her body was ready for him. He reached for her bra clip and undid it hastily and discarded it to the floor. His hot mouth sucked and bit her nipples one by one and she was tipped over the edge as her body had its first orgasm.

"Mmm... you are excited, aren't you?" said Mitch, as he felt her wet clitoris.

Making his way down to her pelvis, he kissed her navel. With her body tingling and feeling like it was on fire, she was reeling in pure delight by the time he took her black panties down.

"God, you taste good too," said Mitch, as he sucked and lapped at her clitoris.

Panting, Rebecca was in seventh heaven, floating, and once again she had an orgasm.

Feeling slightly out of breath, she pleaded with Mitch. "Please... stop teasing me. I can't take much more."

"All in good time, my love. It won't be long now," said Mitch.

Reaching for a condom from his suitcase, which was still lying on the bed, he asked her to put it on. Rebecca tore it out of the packet fast and then slid it over his shaft.

"Are you sure you want to do this?" Mitch asked Rebecca.

"Yes…" she whimpered breathlessly.

Pulling her knees up on either side of him, he leant down and put his hardened cock into her vagina. Slowly he pulled his throbbing, hot molten cock in and out of her so she could adjust to the size of him. Feeling her settle, he started to fuck her fast and hard.

Rebecca called out, "Faster." She was enjoying this much more than she would ever have imagined.

Pulling his cock out of her vagina quickly, Mitch said, "Turn over."

Breathless, she did as she was told, with no hesitation. With her face in the mattress and in the kneeling position, Mitch thrust his shaft into her vagina from behind.

"Oh God… that… feels… so… good. Please… don't stop," she said, panting, as he fucked her lustfully. Feeling another orgasm coming, she tried to stop it, but it had a mind of its own. As she orgasmed Rebecca heard him groan as he came inside her.

Lying across the bed sideways, Mitch put his arm out for Rebecca to cuddle into his chest and he kissed her forehead. Out of breath and both exhausted, it was a minute or so before they could speak.

"That was what I call great sex," said Rebecca, looking up at him. She couldn't believe how much she needed that and how good it felt.

"Oh, it was better than great. It was pure hot molten pleasure and I can't wait to do that again," said Mitch, smirking.

She laughed and said, "Yeah, you're right."

As they lay there massaging each other slowly, Rebecca reached down and could feel his penis getting hard again.

"You ready for round two?" asked Mitch.

With raised eyebrows, she smiled and nodded.

Rebecca lost count how many times they made love. But after a while they were both totally spent and fell asleep in each other's arms.

The sunlight shone in through the window onto Rebecca's face and she opened her eyes to see Mitch asleep next to her. Looking over at the bedside clock she noticed it was already eight thirty.

As she turned around in bed to hop out, Mitch roused and said, "Good morning, beautiful."

Smiling, Rebecca said "Good morning yourself, gorgeous."

He put his arm out for her to snuggle into him. As she cuddled into the nook of his shoulder and placed her leg over his muscular body, Rebecca thought about how she felt content to lay there and how she felt safe with his arms wrapped around her.

"I have my own bathroom just through that door there. Would you like to have a shower with me?" said Mitch, indicating to the bathroom doorway.

"You don't have to ask me twice," she said, jumping out of bed, pulling him into the bathroom with her.

His bathroom had been painted antique white with light grey and silver-patterned wallpaper and a black-tiled floor. The white-tiled, clear screen shower was so big that it would fit at least five people in it. There was also a large white, claw-foot bath tub and a long dark grey vanity cupboard with a large mirror on the wall. To say it was enormous was an understatement.

"Nice bathroom," said Rebecca, looking around the large room.

"Yeah, it's not bad," said Mitch, shrugging his shoulders.

"Can we have a bath instead of a shower?" she asked, smirking.

"Sure. Anything for you, beautiful," said Mitch. Running the bath, Mitch squirted some bath oils in, which created some bubbles. As the bath started to fill, Mitch took his pyjama bottoms and jocks off.

Standing naked in front of her, his muscular body excited Rebecca. *Oh that arse; OMG... I am wet already.*

"What did I do to deserve a wonderful guy like you, Mitch?" said Rebecca, realising how lucky she was to have found love again.

"I was just thinking the same thing about you, Rebecca," said Mitch, as he walked towards her.

"You are so good to me and I think I am falling for you in a big way," said Rebecca, looking into his beautiful blue eyes.

There has always been a connection between us since Jackson passed away and now I know why, she thought to herself.

"I feel the same way. I am glad we have had a chance to get to know each other. I have liked you from the first day I met you and I can't believe how terribly lucky I am," said Mitch, pulling her into his chest for a cuddle and kissing her forehead.

His muscular arms around Rebecca made her feel safe and loved, like nothing else mattered. As she looked up into his loving eyes, he kissed her passionately. His lips were soft and Rebecca's heart skipped a beat as his tongue entered her mouth.

Their lips parted and he undressed her with carnal eyes. Carrying her over to the bath, which was now three quarters full, she snuggled into his neck and drank in his scent.

Mitch placed Rebecca onto the bath ledge and she stepped into the hot water. Feeling the heat from the water on her skin as she slowly sat down, her senses came alive from the bath oil's perfume, which Mitch had squirted into the water previously. As her body settled in the water, Rebecca's skin felt tingly and alive all at the same time.

Mitch stepped into the bath and sat resting his back up against one end, with his legs stretched out nearly touching the other end. Sitting between his legs, Rebecca pressed herself up against him and laid her head on his left shoulder.

"I have waited so long for you to notice me, Bec. I never thought that this day would eventuate," said Mitch, wrapping his arms around her.

"You are so sweet," she said, turning around to face him.

Leaning in, Mitch kissed her tender ruby lips.

Rebecca melted in his arms and wondered in that moment if life could get any better.

God, I really adore this man and how he makes me feel. I hope I don't wake to find this a dream, Rebecca thought to herself.

Lying in the bath enjoying the moment in each other's arms, Rebecca noticed that the heater pump had come on, which helped keep the water warm for them. The swirling motion of the water was stimulating and awakened her every sense in her body and she was ready, once again, for him to ravage her mind and body. Turning around she sat up straight in the bath, then slowly lowered herself over his enormous hardened penis and felt the sensation of it entering her wet vagina. Hastily moving up and down whilst holding onto his shoulders, she watched Mitch to see if he was enjoying this just as much as she was. With his head back against the bath and his lips making the letter 'O', his breath quickened as he moaned in unadulterated pleasure.

Whilst holding onto her hip with one hand and gently pulling her head towards him with the other hand, he kissed her soft lips ever so tenderly. Rebecca could actually feel the need in his lips to own her mouth.

"I can't seem to get enough of you, Mitch. You are driving me crazy," said Rebecca, breathlessly.

"Get up. I want to fuck you from behind," Mitch said, forcefully.

She rose off him and turned over in the hot foaming bath, ready for him. He put his cock into her sex, slowly teasing her, and then he started to fuck her faster. In and out, in and out.

Oh god, I am about to explode, thought Rebecca.

"Please… faster. I need you to go faster," she pleaded.

When her orgasm finally came, she was spent, but continued to enjoy the pounding Mitch gave her as he fucked her hard and fast, until he came. As he stilled over her, kissed her back, he said, "How good was that?"

Sitting back down in the bath, Rebecca rested in between Mitch's legs and snuggled into his chest, and listened to his fast heartbeat as he enveloped her in his muscular arms. In that moment she was so happy and in awe of this man. Tears of happiness welled up into her eyes and she couldn't seem to stop them from overflowing onto her cheeks.

Hearing Rebecca sniff back the tears, Mitch sat up straight and asks with a furrowed brow, "What's wrong? Why are you crying, Bec?"

"This is just so perfect… in fact you are perfect, Mitch. I am scared I am going to wake up from a dream and this won't be real. I love you so much, and hope you never want to leave me," said Rebecca, looking up at him with tears in her eyes. She never thought in her life that she would be saying "I love you" to another man so quickly either.

He gently wiped her tears away and said, "This is not a dream, beautiful. It's real and I will always be here for you, sweetheart. You obviously don't know how much you mean to me yet. But I will show you how much I need and want you, babe. You know even though we have only just connected two days ago, I feel like we have been together for ages," said Mitch, smiling.

They lay there cuddling in the bath for a few minutes more and then Mitch said, "Come on beautiful, why don't we get out, get dressed and go downstairs for breakfast?"

"Good idea. I am famished. So breakfast sounds great," said Rebecca, looking back at him.

Mitch stood and helped her out of the bath, handed Rebecca a towel to dry herself off, and he did the same.

After they were dressed they headed downstairs.

Chapter Ten

Walking into the dining room, Rebecca noticed that all of Mitch's family were seated at the long table, eating breakfast. All eyes were on them as they entered the room and approached the table, and Rebecca started to wonder if his family knew they had slept in the same room last night. She felt like a naughty schoolgirl again, shy, and embarrassed. Mitch didn't seem to mind, he looked at ease.

"Good morning," said Helen, as Mitch and Rebecca sat down at the table. "There are eggs, bacon, tomatoes, pancakes, cereal for breakfast in the bain-maries, oh and coffee and tea. Just make yourself welcome and choose what you want, dears."

"Thanks Helen," said Rebecca, nodding. She was overwhelmed by the spread they had for breakfast. Usually at home she would have toast or cereal, with a cup of tea.

"Thanks Mom," said Mitch, looking over at the bain-maries.

Mitch and Rebecca wandered over to the buffet and chose their breakfast.

"Hungry are we?" asked Mitch, with raised eyebrows and smirking.

Rebecca whispered into his ear, "Only for your hot body." She was ravenous from all their love-making.

Mitch smirked and carried on getting his breakfast.

"Would you like a coffee?" said Rebecca to Mitch.

"Yes please. White, with two sugars," said Mitch.

Rebecca made a tea for herself and a coffee for Mitch and they sat down at the table.

"What have you both got planned for today, then?" asked Grayson.

"I was thinking about taking Rebecca on some sight-seeing and then maybe a picnic lunch somewhere," said Mitch, looking from Grayson to Rebecca.

"That sounds great, son," said Grayson, cutting his food.

Rebecca placed her hand on Mitch's and mouthed, "Thank you." Leaning in, she kissed him ever so tenderly on his right cheek.

Eating her breakfast, Rebecca sat there listening to Mitch and his family chat about life, amongst other things, and thought to herself, *these are such normal, wonderful people. And here I was thinking that all rich people are snobs. I sure got that wrong.* Taking a sip of her tea, the maid came over to Rebecca and said, "Ma'am, a package has just arrived for you at the front door."

Rebecca looked at Mitch and he shrugged his shoulders at her.

"I wonder what it is," said Rebecca, looking at around the table. "Maybe it's my toiletries from the hotel. They sent my clothing but not the toiletries, so I rang them this morning and requested a delivery,"

"The only way you are going to find out is to go and see what it is," said Mitch. "Come on, I will go with you."

hen they entered the foyer, where her package was supposedly waiting, Rebecca just about fell over backwards. She had to look twice.

"Paige…!" screamed Rebecca. "Oh my god. What are you doing here? Oh, how I have missed you, sweetie." She threw her arms around her daughter and gave her a tight hug.

"Hi Mum. Surprise….. Mitch thought it might be nice for me to come and visit you whilst you were in Seattle. I missed you too, Mum," said Paige, hugging her back.

"I can't believe you are here, sweetheart," said Rebecca, standing back and taking a look at her.

It seemed as if she hadn't seen her for years instead of days, the way she was acting.

"What about your job?" said Rebecca, worried.

"Well, I asked my boss if I could come to Seattle to see you and he said yes. I couldn't believe it when he told me I could have the time off. But he did want me to go to some restaurants here to check out the food and report back. He is thinking about changing our menu at work and would like some feedback on some new dishes," said Paige, smiling.

"Oh, right. I still can't believe you are here," said Rebecca to Paige, shaking her head.

Mitch walked over to where they were standing and put his arms around Rebecca from behind and said, "Hi Paige. How was your trip?"

"It was good thanks. Thanks for the first class seat. It was awesome... I see you have finally talked Mum around," said Paige, looking from Mitch to Rebecca.

Rebecca looked at Paige and then to Mitch and said, "What are you two not telling me?"

"Mum, Mitch asked me about maybe four months ago now, how I felt about him taking you out on a date and maybe one day getting together. I told him I was happy for you both... but I did warn him that you were a bit of an ice queen," said Paige, snickering.

"Humph. So you are not angry that Mitch and I have become closer?" said Rebecca.

"No, not at all, Mum. I just want to see you happy," said Paige.

Rebecca gave Paige a hug and said, "Thanks, sweetheart." Rebecca always thought that if she did find another partner one day that surely, Paige would have a problem with this. She was surprised that Paige was taking it that well. But she wasn't about to complain.

As Rebecca looked around, she noticed that Michael, Mitch's brother, had joined them in the foyer. "Welcome Paige," said Michael, as he leant in and hugged her.

"Michael, it's so nice to finally meet you. Thanks for the tips on what clothing to bring for the holiday. Made it a lot easier to pack," said Paige, hugging him back.

"You two know each other then, how?" said Rebecca.

"Well, I have been talking with Michael on Skype the last couple of days. But when I have been over at Mitch's house, Mitch has actually been talking with Michael and his family on Skype. So I have known Michael for probably about six months now. Sometimes we even just Skype to each other… you know, only to find out if you two were an item or not yet," said Paige, smirking.

Rebecca laughed and shook her head at what had been happening without her even knowing it.

"Why don't we go and introduce Paige to the rest of the family," said Michael.

"Good idea," said Mitch.

Michael grabbed Paige's hand and said, "Come on," pulling her towards the dining room.

Walking back into the dining room, Rebecca proudly said, "Everyone… this is my daughter, Paige."

Helen, Grayson and Nick got out of their seats and came over and greeted Paige.

"It's so nice to finally meet you, dear. It's been good chatting with you on Skype though. You are even more beautiful in person," said Helen, giving her a warm hug.

"Mom, don't make the girl feel embarrassed," said Mitch.

"Come. Sit down and join us, dear," said Grayson.

"Have you eaten on the plane?" said Helen, sitting next to her husband again.

"Yes, thanks, Mrs Portellico," said Paige, sitting at the table.

"Would you like a drink, Paige?" asked Michael.

"Yes, please. I'll have a cup of tea; white with two sugars," said Paige, watching him walk over to the bain-maries.

"Did you have a good flight?" asked Helen.

"Yes, it was really awesome. In first class, I could actually lie down for the long flight from Sydney to LA. I slept like a log. By the time I arrived into LA I felt really refreshed. And the breakfast they served us was nice too," said Paige, excited.

"That's great, dear. So what would you like to do today?" said Helen.

Michael placed Paige's cup of tea in front of her and said, "If it's Ok, I was going to take Paige sight-seeing with Mitch and Rebecca."

"That sounds awesome," said Paige. "Thanks."

"I can't even believe you are here, Paige," said Rebecca, as she gave her another hug. "Thanks Mitch for organising all this. You are such a wonderful man. And thank you both Helen and Grayson for allowing Paige to stay here at your beautiful home."

Mitch put his arm around Rebecca and gave her a kiss on her cheek and smiled.

"Yes, thank you Mr and Mrs Portellico for letting me stay in your beautiful house," said Paige, looking around.

Rebecca could tell that Paige was overwhelmed with the enormity of the house and how magnificent it was to be there, as she felt the same.

"You're welcome, dears. We are happy you are all here," said Helen, smiling.

Once I am done with the training, this is going to be the most wonderful holiday ever, thought Rebecca, smiling.

Looking across the table, Rebecca secretly observed Michael and Paige eyeing each other off and getting on really well. Too well, in fact, for her liking.

I think that these two might have a connection. I had better keep an eye on them. Michael is one year older than Paige, but he seems like a really nice guy though, thought Rebecca.

Rebecca leant in and whispered into Mitch's ear, "Mitch… do you think there is anything going on between Michael and Paige?"

Mitch looked sheepishly at them both and saw exactly what Rebecca had seen. Eye contact and body language.

He nodded. "Hmm… I will put a stop to it, but only if you want me to," said Mitch, with a furrowed brow.

"I don't want Paige getting hurt, that's all," said Rebecca, quietly.

"I think they have become close since they have been chatting on Skype a lot lately," said Mitch, leaning into Rebecca.

"I see… I want to keep an eye on them for the moment. It may only be friendship, but their body language doesn't say that," said Rebecca, concerned.

"Right," said Mitch, watching Paige and Michael.

CHAPTER ELEVEN

Before they knew it, the morning had disappeared and the four of them were off sight-seeing. Mitch had organised for his family chauffeur to drive them around in a black limousine which was owned by his parents.

Talk about spoilt. I feel so fortunate. We have seen the Space Needle, the Museum of History and Industry, the Art Museum, the Waterpark Front and many more interesting monuments. Seattle sure is a lovely place to visit, thought Rebecca, as she held Mitch's hand and looked out the window, enjoying all the sights of Seattle.

"Well, it's nearly one o'clock," said Mitch, looking at his watch. "What about if we stop somewhere nice for a picnic lunch? I asked the cook to make us up a hamper of food and drinks this morning before we left, which are in the boot."

"Sounds great, Mitch," said Rebecca, amazed at how organised he was.

Michael and Paige nodded in agreeance.

"Thanks for taking me sight-seeing this morning, Mitch. I really like Seattle," said Paige, smiling.

"You're welcome. We have only just seen the tip of the iceberg today. We will have to take you both out and show you some more another day," said Mitch.

"Sounds great," said Paige.

Mitch instructed the driver to take them to a nice grassy area that overlooked the ocean, which was called Matthews Beach Park.

As they were setting up the two picnic blankets and food on the green grass, Rebecca said, "Thank you for organising all of this, Mitch. It's a beautiful spot."

"You're welcome. Maybe next week on Saturday, when you have finished your course, we can do this by ourselves," said Mitch, leaning down to kiss her.

"Come on you two… this is just too mushy," teased Paige.

Mitch and Rebecca grinned as they slowly pulled away from each other.

"Would you like to go for a walk down along the ocean for a while? We can leave the love birds here," said Michael to Paige

"Sure… that would be nice, Michael. Is that all right with you, Mum?" said Paige.

"Yes sweetheart, but please be careful," said Rebecca, taking a seat on the blanket.

"Mum, I am nearly twenty-one years old. I am sure I will be all right and careful," said Paige, in an annoyed voice.

"Sorry… it's just that we are not at home now and I worry for you. That's all," said Rebecca.

"I know you can't help it. But I will be Ok. I have Michael with me anyway," said Paige, as she slowly walked towards the water with Michael.

"Have a look at that. They are holding hands," said Rebecca to Mitch, as she watched them walk away.

Mitch looked up and said, "Michael is a very touchy, feely type person. So it might not be anything." Just as Mitch said that, he saw Michael quickly kiss Paige on the lips.

"Still think they're just friends, do you?" asked Rebecca, with a raised eyebrow.

"No, I don't… I will have a word to Michael when we get back home, on the quiet, Bec. I am not happy about this either. It would be different if Michael and Paige lived in the same country. But they don't. I can see Paige getting hurt because long distance relationships don't always work out."

"Thanks Mitch. You know they will probably tell us both to mind our own business, don't you? I just... well... I don't want to see Paige upset, that's all," stated Rebecca.

"In the meantime, let's not worry ourselves about it. Today, I want to have a great time with my beautiful girlfriend," said Mitch, on his knees setting up the food hamper on the blanket.

Rebecca looked at him in surprise. "Girlfriend... is that how you see me? I am honoured to be your girlfriend," said Rebecca, leaning over, closing her eyes and kissing him passionately.

Slowly, Mitch pulled away from her indulgent lips, looked into her eyes and said, "You are lucky we have company and are out in the open. Because I just want you and that sexy body of yours wrapped around me in my bed. I want you so much, it's driving me crazy."

"I feel the same way. I can't get enough of you... but there is something I did want to ask you though," said Rebecca, looking down at her hands in her lap.

"What is it?" asked Mitch, frowning.

"What is going to happen with us when we get back home?"

He lifted her chin up and kissed her lips gently, and said, "A lot more of what has been happening here. Don't over think it, Bec... I will still come and see you each day. Oh, and have hot sex with you." He laughed. "But most of all, I just want to be a normal couple. You know, enjoying each other's company and doing things together. Maybe down the track we might even move in together, who knows," said Mitch, watching her reaction.

"You really want to do all those things with me?" said Rebecca, astonished at what he had just said to her.

"Yes, I do. I love you," said Mitch, looking deeply into her eyes. "I have watched you from afar for too long Rebecca and I want to make my feelings clear."

Rebecca placed her arms around Mitch, and said, "I love you too, my sweet man. I am starting to feel like my life is going to be perfect with you in it when we get back home."

Mitch smiled and kissed her lips with so much body heat, that

Rebecca felt her heart warm and her body relax.

She had only ever felt like this about one man previously.

Rebecca watched the bubbles form in the glass as Mitch poured her a glass of white wine. Sitting upright, with her legs to the side, she took a few items off the grazing plate Mitch had graciously organised and considered their surroundings.

"Here you go," said Mitch, placing the glass in her hand.

"Thanks."

"What would you like to do tonight?"

"I don't know... what about if we all go out to dinner with your family and then take it from there?"

"Hmm... that sounds like a good idea. I might give Mom and Dad a ring now to confirm with them first," said Mitch, taking his phone out of his pocket.

Rebecca nodded, as she chewed on a mouthful of food.

When Mitch finished his call, he said, "As it happens, everyone is free tonight. Mom actually suggested that we go to a new restaurant that has just opened up called, 'Grayson's'. She said she will book it for us for about seven o'clock. Does that sound all right?"

"Sure, sounds good. The restaurant... it's called after your dad? Does he own it or is it just a coincidence?" said Rebecca.

"Well it's a long story. But the short of it is that the owner named the restaurant after Dad because my father saved the owner's life last year," said Mitch, humbly.

"Wow... you must be proud of your dad," said Rebecca, with raised eyebrows.

"I sure am," said Mitch, sitting closer to her and placing his arm around her shoulder.

"I am looking forward to dinner tonight. Can't wait to see what's on the menu," said Rebecca.

As they were talking Paige and Michael returned from their walk.

"Looks like you are going to get one restaurant out the way, Paige. We are going to a new restaurant tonight and seeing that the owner knows their dad, maybe he might let you go out into the kitchen to see what they are cooking," said Rebecca.

"Cool," said Paige, excited.

"How was your walk, you two?" asked Rebecca.

"It was nice, Mum. With the sand under my feet and the wind on my face, it was really relaxing."

"Oh, that's good sweetheart. Would you two like some lunch now?" said Rebecca.

"Actually I'm not that hungry, Mum. I am starting to feel a little bit jet lagged. Do you mind if I go back to the Portellico family home? I just want to get a few hours' sleep before we go out tonight," said Paige.

"Yeah, I am not that hungry either," said Michael.

"Oh, Ok. That's no problem. How about you help me pack up and then we can go?" said Rebecca, looking from Paige to Mitch, to see if this was Ok with him.

Mitch just nodded and smiled politely.

On the road back to the Portellico family home, Paige's head became heavy on Michael's shoulder as her eyes shut from exhaustion.

"She must be tired. Hope you don't mind her sleeping on your shoulder, Michael," said Rebecca, with her eyebrows raised.

"It's Ok… I am sure you know or have guessed that we like each other anyway. So I don't mind her sleeping on my shoulder," said Michael.

"Thanks, Michael. I do appreciate you being honest about how you are feeling. But do you think it's fair on Paige if she falls for you and then when we go home, you stay here? I just don't want to see her hurt," said Rebecca.

"To tell you the truth Rebecca, we have already fallen for each other. I think it happened when we were talking each night via Skype. Then finally meeting each other today in person, made it so real. I don't want to hurt Paige, but I don't want to let her go either. What we have so far is well worth exploring. I know long distant relationships don't work, but maybe it won't come to that. Can we just see where it goes over the next week and then decide?" pleaded Michael.

Hmm, he has a very mature attitude, thought Rebecca.

When Rebecca listened to what Michael had to say and could see how serious he was about how much he liked Paige, she said, "I suppose so, Michael. You are both old enough to make your own decisions anyway. Just keep in mind, if you hurt my daughter, you will have me to answer to." The look on Rebecca's face of determination said it all to Michael.

Michael looked at Mitch and then Rebecca and gulped.

"You can't say that you haven't been warned, bro. So you had better get it right," said Mitch, with a raised eyebrow and smirk on his face.

The drive home was a long one and as they pulled up to the house, Paige woke.

"Hello, sleepy head," said Michael to Paige.

"Michael would you mind taking Paige inside and up to her room, as I want to take Bec somewhere?" said Mitch.

"Sure. No problem, bro. See you both later on," said Michael, as he stepped out of the car and waited for Paige.

Paige gave her mum a kiss on the cheek and said, "See you both later." She followed Michael inside.

"Where are we going Mitch?" asked Rebecca.

"You'll see," said Mitch, helping her out of the limousine.

Walking arm in arm around the side of the house, Rebecca's face lit up when she saw the beautiful orange and pink sunset over a smooth black lake at the back of the house.

"Isn't it beautiful?" said Mitch.

"Wow… that is jaw-droppingly astonishing. The sunset looks like it's going into the lake. Can we sit out here for a while?" said Rebecca, thankful he had shown her. Her gaze was overwhelmed by its magnificence.

"Sure. I'll go and get a blanket to wrap around us and some drinks. Take a seat… I won't be long," said Mitch, gesturing to a comfortable three-seater, beige outdoor lounge, with brown striped throw cushions and a table.

"Ok," said Rebecca, sitting down under the open, beige painted, wooden slatted patio, and watching the sun continuing to set in amazement.

"Thanks for the blanket. It's starting to get cold out here," said Rebecca, goosebumps forming on her body as she took the blanket from Mitch.

"You're welcome. Seattle can get extremely cold at certain times of the year," said Mitch, pouring a glass of white wine for her. "Here you go."

"Thank you," said Rebecca, looking from the glass of wine on the table in front of her to Mitch and then at the sunset.

Cuddled together, with the blanket around them, watching the sun finally set, Rebecca looked up at Mitch and noticed he was looking at her adoring eyes.

"What."

"God, you're beautiful. Life sure is great at the moment," said Mitch, beaming.

"Back at ya, gorgeous," said Rebecca.

He leant in and kissed her lips wantonly, his tongue searching her mouth for release.

Her breathing became rapid. "Let's go upstairs," she said, tempting him.

Mitch looked at his watch. "I would love to, but we actually don't have time. We need to get ready for dinner."

"Shit… I had forgotten about dinner. Come on. I need to get ready," said Rebecca, standing.

Chapter Twelve

As their car approached the restaurant, Mitch instructed the driver to go around the back of the restaurant, so that the reporters didn't see them. Grayson's was in the middle of Seattle city, where there were plenty of paparazzi hanging around, just waiting to snap a photo or trying to get an interview with the rich and famous.

With the driver stopping the limousine across from the back door entrance into the restaurant, they quickly departed from the vehicle and were escorted by the restaurant manager to a private dining room on the tenth floor, where other celebrities were dining.

Stepping out of the elevator, the first thing Rebecca noticed was the view of Seattle city skyline, through the roof to floor windows.

Wow...it's like many coloured jewels shining brightly all at once. Beautiful, thought Rebecca.

The private dining room was painted a charcoal colour with ambient lighting, except for the glass chandelier hanging in the middle of the room and all the marble tables were set with white linen table cloths, sparkling glasses and silver cutlery. At the end of the long room was a gas log fire burning brightly, which kept the room warm. And over on the left hand side of the room was a fully stocked bar with two barmen serving drinks.

The waitress who greeted them at the door, recognised the Portellico family and they were shown to their long table and seated. Handing around to each of them the menus for the food and drinks, she advised them of what was on special tonight whilst another waiter filled their glasses with water, leaving a few carafes on the table to consume during their dinner. As she placed their white napkins on each of their laps, the waitress took their drink orders, punching them into her small computer tablet, and then headed for the bar.

Paige sat next to Mitch at the table and Rebecca smiled when she heard Mitch giving Paige the spiel about not talking to the reporters at all and the reasons why. She remembered how she thought Mitch was joking when he initially told her on the plane.

Paige nodded at Mitch and said, "You have my word. I will not talk to them, Mitch."

"No wonder you left here, Mitch. These intrusive reporters would drive you mad, hey. I mean, it's not too bad some of the time. But to hound you all the time, then that would drive even me mad," said Rebecca, looking around the restaurant to see if she recognised any of the celebrities already seated at their tables.

"I was extremely happy that they didn't follow me to Australia. At least there I was unknown and it also meant that I could live out in the suburbs and not get hounded by reporters," said Mitch.

Helen, who was sitting next to Rebecca, placed her hand over Rebecca's and said, "Rebecca, I wanted to thank you for making my eldest boy happy. You know for a lengthy time there, we didn't think he was going to pull through the death of his wife, Christine. Ever since he has met you and now you are finally together, he is happy and seems back to normal again. Whatever you are doing my dear, please keep doing it, as we haven't seen him this happy for a long time."

Rebecca smiled. "Thanks, Helen. That's nice of you to say. I really do love your son. I don't know what I am doing, besides being myself to keep Mitch happy, but I can tell you the feelings are mutual. I adore him, and he makes me feel alive again, which in turn keeps me happy," said Rebecca, realising how fortunate she was to be part of a loving family.

"I was a mess when my husband died. But you know when I think back now, from day one Mitch has always been there for me. I just thought he was such a great friend. But little did I know there was more to it… you know I have been leaning on Mitch for a long time and he has always been good to me and Paige. I wish I had realised earlier how much I did need Mitch in my life."

"You weren't ready, dear, and anyway all good things come to those who wait. My mom taught me that," said Helen, patting Rebecca's hand.

Rebecca smiled at her and said, "It should be me thanking you, anyway. For not only letting Paige and me stay at your lovely home, but also for bringing Mitch up to be such the wonderful, caring person that he is."

"Thank you, dear. Only a mother would think that. Your daughter is so lovely and you have done a wonderful job with her as well," said Helen.

Rebecca leant over and gave Helen a hug and said, "Thank you."

"What are you two talking about?" said Mitch, looking from Helen to Rebecca.

"Secret mothers' business. You don't need to know, dear," said Helen, smiling.

Mitch snickered, nodded and smiled.

Mitch leant in and kissed Rebecca's neck softly. Looking into her eyes he placed his hand over hers and squeezed it gently.

"I love you," she mouthed to him.

He smiled and mouthed back, "I love you, too."

Grayson came over between Helen and Rebecca and said, "Looks like I have another son smitten with a girl from Australia? They sure breed you well over there." He was indicating to Michael and Paige.

Helen slapped him on the arm, and said, "Don't be crass, Grayson."

"Actually Rebecca, Michael has asked me if he can move to Australia to live with Mitch and help Mitch with his security business there. But I wanted to talk with you first about this. I know you are not blind and can see that Michael and Paige have feelings for each other. But I wanted to know if you were happy with them being together. I told Michael that

I would talk with you first and then I would give him an answer," said Grayson.

"Grayson, before I give you my answer, I want to see how they go over the next week first. You see my daughter has not lost her innocence yet, if you know what I mean, and has a good job to go back to and well, there are so many things to think about. Do you mind if we talk about this, say… next Friday night? Maybe the four of us can go for a coffee and discuss it a bit further," said Rebecca.

"Yes, dear. That sounds like a good idea," said Grayson, patting her on the shoulder. "We will talk then." He sat back down next to Helen.

Oh my, I can't believe what I just saw. Grayson put his hand on Helen's leg and giving her a passionate kiss. How nice is that? I have always secretly wished that my marriage would be like that when I was older. Still as fresh as the first day we met, thought Rebecca, feeling warm and fuzzy.

Mitch tapped Rebecca on the shoulder and smiled. "It's not polite to stare."

"I can't believe your parents are still so much in love after all this time they have been together," said Rebecca, turning to Mitch.

"Great role models, hey," said Mitch.

She nodded, "Yes."

"So… have you had a chance to look at the menu yet?" asked Mitch.

"No, but I will now. I am famished. I need to keep my strength up for 'laters babe'," said Rebecca, smirking.

Looking down the table, Rebecca spotted Michael and Paige holding hands and talking to each other. She smiled at Paige and mouthed, "Happy for you."

Paige mouthed back, "Thank you."

When she looked up Mitch was shaking his head at her. "God, you're beautiful." He leant in and kissed her passionately.

When she came up for breath, Rebecca said, "You're not too bad yourself, Mr Portellico." She then made her selection from the menu for dinner.

"Would you like a white wine with your dinner?" said Mitch.

"Umm, I might have a White Russian, if that's Ok," said Rebecca.

"I forgot you like that drink," said Mitch. He called the waiter over to order some more drinks.

"Grayson... I wanted to ask a favour. Could you ask the owner if it would be Ok for Paige to go into the kitchen and have a look around a bit?" said Rebecca, leaning over the table towards Grayson.

"Here he comes now. I will ask him for you," said Grayson. Standing he welcomed and shook the owner's hand.

The owner of the restaurant said, "Hello, my friend. Everything good with you?"

"Yes, good, my friend. Everything is really good, thanks. George, I was wondering if I could ask you a favour," said Grayson.

"Anything for you, my friend," said George.

"My son's friend, Paige, is an apprentice chef in Australia and she would like to know if she could have a look in your kitchen and ask you for some information on your menu. Would that be all right?" said Grayson.

"Of course, my friend. I am only too happy to help an up and coming chef," said George. "Which one of you is Paige?" asked George, in his Italian accent.

Paige stood up and said, "That's me."

"Come with me," said George, as he walked over to her and put his arm around her shoulder. He took Paige out to the kitchen. They were gone for about thirty minutes, before Paige returned.

"Wow... that was so good Mum. I learnt a lot in the short time I was in there," said Paige, smiling with excitement, as she sat back down at the table.

"I'm glad, sweetie," said Rebecca. "You'll have to tell me all about it later."

Paige stood up and walked over to Grayson and gave him a hug and said, "Thank you for organising that for me. I appreciate it very much."

"You're welcome, dear," said Grayson, sincerely.

With their meals starting to be delivered to the table, Rebecca was looking forward to getting her pasta carbonara and a garden salad. Mitch had ordered fresh oysters for entrée and steak, salad and chips for his main meal.

"Have you tried oysters before, Bec?" asked Mitch, eyeing off his plate.

"No, I have never had them," said Rebecca, watching Mitch squeeze a bit of lemon juice on one oyster. "But I wouldn't mind trying one though."

"Open wide and let it slide down your throat. Don't chew it, just swallow, Ok?" said Mitch, holding the shell up to her lips.

"Mmm... they're nice. Can I have another one?" said Rebecca, appreciating the taste.

"Sure," said Mitch, as he put another shell to her lips again.

As she sat there smiling, Mitch said, "What are you thinking about?"

"You really want to know?" said Rebecca, smirking.

He nods, smiles and said, "Yes."

"I was thinking about the part in the book *Fifty Shades*, where they are at that restaurant and they were eating oysters and talking about the contract," said Rebecca, smirking.

Mitch laughed and said, "So was I. There are so many parts in those three books that sound good. I can't wait for you to read the other two books."

She smiled, and raised her eyebrow at Mitch and whispered in his ear, "So you like a bit of kinky fuckery do you?"

"Sure do. What I would like to do with you at the moment is certainly kinky... eat your food up, Rebecca. I don't like it when you leave your food," whispered Mitch.

She laughed, because she knew it was a line in the books. As Rebecca looked into Mitch's adoring eyes, she noticed that he was smirking at her and she started to eat her food.

"Are you smirking at me, Mr Portellico?" ask Rebecca.

"I wouldn't do that, Ms Landers," he whispered and then laughed. *Another line in the book.*

Rebecca put her hand on his leg, just near his balls. He tensed and said in her ear, "You are such a bad girl."

"You haven't seen anything yet, Sir," teased Rebecca.

Mitch laughed as he knew that the word 'Sir' was from the book as well.

After their main meal Mitch and Rebecca ordered warm apple pie and cream, which they shared. When the waitress put the dessert plate in front of them, Rebecca licked her lips and put a spoonful of the cream in her mouth and kissed Mitch's mouth, whilst licking the cream off.

Nick, who was watching from across the table, leant across the table and said quietly, "Get a room you two."

Both Mitch and Rebecca laughed, looked at each other and were thinking the same thing. Rebecca had a room at the hotel she was staying at and they could go there.

"Michael… could I ask you if you would take care of Paige for me and take her home after dinner?" asked Rebecca.

"Yes, ma'am. I will make sure she gets home in one piece," said Michael.

"Paige… Mitch and I are going back to my hotel for the night, so I will see you tomorrow afternoon after my course, Ok?" said Rebecca, standing.

"Ok, Mum. Have fun. I will see you tomorrow," said Paige, coming around to give her mum a kiss goodnight.

"Mom, Dad, I'll see you tomorrow," said Mitch, standing between their chairs.

"No problem, son. See you tomorrow," said Grayson, standing and giving Mitch a handshake.

"Night, my boy. See you both tomorrow," said Helen, standing and giving both Mitch and Rebecca a hug goodbye. "Don't worry dear, we will take both Michael and Paige home with us."

"Thank you, Helen. Goodnight everyone," said Rebecca, taking Mitch's hand.

Mitch and Rebecca then excused themselves.

Mitch pushed opened the door, which led them outside, at the back of the restaurant. "Come on," said Mitch, pulling Rebecca by the hand, gesturing to where the driver had parked the limousine near the laneway across from them. Thinking that the paparazzi were still out the front of the restaurant, Mitch wanted to get Rebecca and himself in the car before they even got a glimpse of them both.

Little did they know that there was one photographer who was tucked in behind a dumpster bin, and had already snapped a photo of them together as they rushed out the back door entrance of the restaurant, holding hands.

Hopping quickly into the unlocked limousine, Mitch reached over into the front seat and handed the driver the address of the hotel. "Can you please take us to this hotel?"

"Yes, sir," said the driver, turning around to retrieve the piece of paper that had the address on it. Turning the key to the ignition, he placed the car in drive and they drove out of the laneway and onto the street, all the while watching the paparazzi and their flashing cameras try to get a picture of who may or may not be in the limousine.

"Are you sure you like kinky fuckery?" whispered Mitch to Rebecca, as they drove along.

She nodded. "It sounds good in the book and I would like to try it."

Mitch took her hand in his and started to rub his thumb slowly over the top of her hand. Rebecca's heart skipped a beat from his touch and instantly she became excited. Jumping onto his lap, she wanted him, there and then.

Mitch watched the driver's expression in the rear view mirror and then pressed the button to position the divider up between the driver and his passengers.

"You need to get back in your seat and put your seatbelt on, Rebecca," said Mitch, dominantly.

Rebecca laughed and Mitch smiled. By the time they reached the hotel, Rebecca was wet and she could feel that Mitch had an erection through his trousers.

This should be interesting, Rebecca thought to herself.

CHAPTER THIRTEEN

The elevator doors shut slowly behind them and Rebecca pushed the seventy-second floor button. Luckily there was no one in the elevator with them, as Mitch turned to her and pushed her back against the wall of the elevator. Slowly he kissed her lips and when his mouth reached her neck and then her earlobe, she was panting with the sheer delight he was offering. His hands wandered up under her dress and up her legs, into her panties. His fingers entered Rebecca's sex and he pulled them in and out slowly, teasing her.

She cried out, "Stop… this is way too much."

"Shhh…" said Mitch, trying to compose her excitement. He hoped the hotel didn't have cameras in the elevator.

The elevator dinged and came to a stop at the seventy-second floor and they quickly straightened their clothes, but their breathing was rapid. Luckily no one was getting on as elevator doors opened.

Walking quickly to her room, Rebecca took the key to the door out of her bag. Placing the card in the door, Mitch picked Rebecca up in his muscular arms and carried her into the room, shutting and latching the door as they went.

"Take all your clothes and shoes off, except for your bra and panties," ordered Mitch.

She did as she was told and noticed over in the corner of the room, that her luggage had been returned to her room from the Portellico family home.

Mitch took off his clothes and shoes and left only his boxer jocks on.

"Get onto the bed and lay down on your back," said Mitch.

She did as she was told without saying a word.

He took the handcuffs out of the bag of toys that they bought from the adult shop on the way to the hotel and wrapped them around her wrists and then handcuffed her to the bed. Next he tied her ankles to the bed posts with some rope. Her legs were spread wide apart.

"I think you have seen enough," said Mitch, standing next to the bed, as he slid the face mask over her eyes.

Rebecca's heartbeat quickened in anticipation of what he would do next.

Quivering, she felt something soft, like a feather, touch her clitoris through her panties.

Biting her bottom lip, Rebecca's body felt like it was on fire as she tried to lap up the sensation of him teasing her.

Mitch undid her bra straps and her soft, supple breasts sprang free.

At first she felt the tip of his rough tongue slide around the edge of her nipple and then the warmth of his mouth as he sucked it vigorously. He couldn't seem to get enough of her breast as he groaned in delight and then blew on it with his warm breath. Her nipple went hard and lengthened and she arched her body off the bed in enjoyment. Mitch did the same to the right nipple.

My oh my. She couldn't take much more.

"Lift up," said Mitch.

She did as he instructed and felt him slide her panties down towards the ankle restraints, which he had to unfasten and then put them back on. Once again her legs were wide apart. He took the feather again and brushed it up against her bare clitoris and her navel area. Watching her tense and pull on the restraints with every sensation, he placed his two fingers into her vagina and moved them in and out and in and out, slowly teasing her until she called out, "Please… no more," as she had an orgasm.

When Mitch eventually lifted off the blindfold and took the handcuffs and ankle restraints off, she was spent; too many orgasms.

Rebecca was glad when he took the handcuffs and ankle restraints off her limbs as they were starting to ache. Looking at her wrists and ankles, Mitch realised from the red marks they left, that they looked a bit tender and started to massage them gently for her.

"Thank you," said Rebecca. His touch was overwhelming to her senses and even though her breathing was rapid, Rebecca's vagina would welcome any release he could give her.

Lying on the bed together, Mitch asks, "How was that, beautiful?"

"Too good. I am totally spent," she said, yawning.

"I'm not boring you, am I, Rebecca?" teased Mitch.

"No, Sir," said Rebecca, as she rolled her eyes at him.

"Rebecca, you just rolled your eyes at me and you know what that does to me," said Mitch, roleplaying in the dim light of the room.

Her eyes went wide and she knew what he was going to do next. He sat on the side of the bed and pulled Rebecca over his knee and spanked her with his hand. It was not pleasant, in fact it hurt, no matter how hard she tried to enjoy it.

"No more," she pleaded.

Pulling Rebecca off his lap, he quickly sat her back down on the bed. "Sorry my love… did I hurt you?" said Mitch. The look on his face was one of shame.

"Yes. It hurt too much, Sir. Can you please rub it better for me?" said Rebecca, teasing him.

"Cheeky girl. I'm not done with you yet," said Mitch, rolling her on her back again. "Turn on your front, with your bum up in the air." Mitch demanded.

She did as she was told.

Leaning over her, he eased his cock into Rebecca's wet vagina and started to fuck her slowly. As he fucked her faster, she panted in anticipation of yet another orgasm.

"Oh Mitch… that… feels… so good. Please… don't stop," said Rebecca, breathlessly. She was excited way beyond her control and her thermostat was about to blow.

Oh god, I can't stop it. Neither can I hold it back, thought Rebecca, trying to hold the walls of her vagina inwards.

After a few minutes Mitch came inside her and they were left sated and exhausted.

Rolling onto one side, next to her, Mitch says, "So how was that? Close to some things in the book hey?"

"I knew it would be good. But not that good, Mitch. God, can we do some kinky fuckery all the time?" said Rebecca, looking up at the ceiling as she panted.

He laughed and said, "Whatever you want babe, I am happy to give."

Lying on top of the bed feeling content, they cuddled into each other's arms. Feeling her body relax, within minutes Rebecca fell asleep, naked and satisfied.

Rebecca woke, startled, the next morning to the alarm going off at six o'clock.

I don't remember setting the alarm. Mitch must have set it for me, thought Rebecca. Fearing Mitch might wake, she quickly pressed the button to switch it off.

Today was the first day of her computer course and she needed to hop out of bed, get showered, dressed and breakfast eaten by seven-fifty, as the course started at eight o'clock in the conference room downstairs on the fourth floor.

When she stepped out the shower and was drying her hair with a towel, Mitch came into the bathroom wearing only his boxer shorts.

With one eyebrow raised, she licked her lips, and thought, *mmm, he looks delicious. If I didn't have to go to the training today, I reckon I would have had my way with him.*

"Morning, beautiful… sleep well?" said Mitch, yawning.

"Morning, sweet man. I slept like a log, thanks to your kinky hands last night," said Rebecca, watching him in the mirror washing his hands at the basin and drying them off with the hand towel. Her eyes wandered down to his tight boxer shorts, where she could see every inch of him.

Placing her brush down on the bench, Rebecca's knees went weak as he came around the back of her and pulled her hair back, only to graze her ear with his teeth. As he kissed her neck, she felt her body relax and the world she knew shift. Turning Rebecca around, Mitch kissed her fervently and she felt his need for release when his hardened shaft touched her inner leg.

Realising that she was going to be late and gathering her thoughts, Rebecca slowly pulled away from his soft lips. "Sorry, sweet man, but I will have to leave soon. Can I take a rain check...?"

The look of shock on his face was priceless, as he pulled away gritting his teeth and rolling his eyes.

"I have ordered some breakfast for us, Mitch. It should be here any minute now and then I have to go," said Rebecca, standing in front of the mirror as she unzipped her makeup bag and applied her mascara.

"I wish it was still Sunday," said Mitch, as he sighed and pursed his lips. "But I do need to get going soon myself as well. I have a meeting this morning."

Hearing a knock at the door, Rebecca said, "I think that may be our breakfast."

"You finish getting ready. I will get the door," said Mitch, walking out of the bathroom.

"Thanks."

Mitch looked through the peep hole and observed the waiter, who was wearing the hotel uniform, on the other side of the door. Opening the room's door, he said, "Come in."

"Thank you, sir," said the waiter, wheeling the breakfast in on a trolley. Taking the cloche off each plate, he asked, "Is that everything, sir?"

"Yes, I think so."

"Can I be of any further service this morning, sir?" asked the waiter, walking towards the doorway and politely waiting for a tip.

"No, that is all for this morning. Thank you," said Mitch, handing over a tip.

"Thank you, sir. You are very kind." said the waiter, noticing the one hundred dollar bill, pocketing the tip and leaving them to enjoy their food, closing the door behind him.

"Mmm, this looks yummy," said Rebecca, entering the room and noticing the breakfast.

"Sure does. Thank you for ordering this for us," gestured Mitch, as he walked over to Rebecca and gave her a loving cuddle. "I will sure miss you today, beautiful. Will be lonely without you with me."

"I am sure you have plenty to do to keep yourself busy until I finish at four o'clock. Why don't I meet you in my room at five o'clock," said Rebecca, cuddling into his chest.

"Sounds like a plan."

"Come on, let's get stuck into this breakfast. I need to leave in about ten minutes," said Rebecca.

By the time she had finished her breakfast and applied her lipstick, it was time for Rebecca to leave for the course. Entering the bedroom, she found Mitch sitting on the bed, reading the newspaper.

"See you, gorgeous. I love you," said Rebecca, standing in front of Mitch.

Mitch jumped off the bed, placed his arms around Rebecca and kissed her passionately goodbye.

"See you laters babe," said Mitch, teasing her.

Rebecca laughed as she pulled away slowly from his loving embrace.

"Bye." Picking up her handbag, she walked towards the doorway.

CHAPTER FOURTEEN

Rebecca reached the fourth floor in no time at all. Walking out of the elevator she noticed a white signage board indicating which way the room was for the training she was undertaking today.

The conference room was full of other men and women as she walked in and Rebecca noticed that there were long, white tables and chairs, in five rows diagonally, with computers on each of them. Counting the chairs she realised there were fifteen other people besides her doing this course. Making her way over to the table, which was located at the side of the room in a corner where the tea and coffee was, she introduced herself to the other participants, who were standing around drinking their hot drinks and chatting.

"Ok everyone, please take your seats," said the grey, curly-headed, male course instructor, who was now standing at the front of the room, near the projector.

Rebecca carried her hot cup of tea over to the first desk and retrieved her note pad and pen out of her bag. She was eager to start and feeling motivated to learn the new program.

"Right… first things first. I want to introduce myself. My name is Warren Gift and I will be teaching you all this computer program for the next five days," said the instructor, pointing to the screen up on the wall that had his name typed in bold. "Today, we will be going over each of the functions the program has, amongst other things. But for now, I would like each of you to tell the class your name and the company you work for and a bit about yourself. We will start at the front here and work our way around to the last person at the back of the room." He pointed to Rebecca. "Ok… if you could go first and stand when you are speaking."

Nervous, but in full control, Rebecca pushed her chair backwards, stood up and faced her peers, who were now all looking in her direction. "Good Morning… umm, my name is Rebecca Landers and I work full time for an oil company in Perth, Western Australia. Besides my boss, I am the only one in the office who will be using this program. My job entails anything from receptionist to accounts to payroll, to taxes. I'm what you may call a multitasker or Jill of all trades." Everyone in the class laughed when she referred herself as Jill of all trades. "I currently use this program, but came here today to learn what is new so that I can implement it when I get back to work next week. Being a multitasker, I am hoping this new information will be able to make my job a lot easier and less time consuming… thank you." Rebecca took her seat and turned to the person sitting next to her.

After listening to each participant take their turn to speak about themselves, the course instructor, who was now standing at the side of the room said, "Wow… it would seem that we have a big diversified list of companies here and I can see each of you would use this program differently. Very interesting…" He then walked back to the front of the room, with all eyes following him. "Ok. Let's get started." He retrieved his laser pointer from his trouser pocket and pointed to the projector screen, which now had the first slide up and started explaining about the new functions of the program.

At ten o'clock Rebecca, along with all her classmates, had a well-deserved morning tea break. The morning had gone by fast and so far Rebecca was confident that she already knew most of what the instructor was training them on. There was tea, coffee to drink and an assortment of pastries for everyone to eat, which was set up at the back of the room.

Sitting back at her desk, Rebecca quickly ate her pastry she had chosen and then checked her mobile for messages. There was one text message from Mitch.

'Missed you this morning. Can't wait for tonight. I have yet another surprise for you. Laters babe.'

Rebecca sat at her desk grinning. *What a wonderful man. Surprise… wonder what it is?*

She then texted him back.

'Dear Sir, you really need to stop texting me whilst I am working. It's very distracting you know. Yes, I can't wait to see you tonight as well. ILU. Looking forward to my surprise. Laters babe.'

Of course this was from the book as well. Rebecca sat there grinning like a Cheshire cat until she heard the course instructor informing them that they were starting again.

Before she could blink, the course instructor was letting them know it was lunch time and that a buffet lunch was provided in the restaurant at the hotel. Rebecca was famished and couldn't wait to see what was included in the buffet.

Taking the elevator to the restaurant, the class all chatted about their morning so far. When the elevator door opened, they all walked into a room that was a deep blue and gold in colour which had a bar to the left hand side of the room. There were lots of tables with white linen table cloths, sparkling glasses, silver cutlery and a spray of colourful flowers in a small clear vase on each table. In the middle of the carpeted room were two hot and cold bain-maries in glass stands, which had an assortment of food in them. The waitress, who was situated at a black stand next to the elevator doors approached them as they stepped into the restaurant and took them to their long table. Once everyone was seated she informed them about the food and what was provided with the course they were partaking in.

Yum… this all sounds so good, thought Rebecca, as she listened to the waitress talk about the buffet.

As Rebecca was selecting her food from the bain-maries, the course instructor stood beside her with his plate in hand. "This all looks good," said Warren, leaning into her.

"Sure does," said Rebecca, placing some garden salad on her plate.

"Oh, can I have some of that," said Warren, indicating for Rebecca to place some of the garden salad on his plate.

"Sure," said Rebecca, her brow creased. *Humph…get your own.* She placed a small amount on his plate and then repositioned the tongs back into the salad. Moving away from him to select some lasagne, which was already cut into square pieces for ease of serving, from the bain-marie, she felt his presence once again.

"Mmm… that smells divine. Would you mind serving me a piece of that?" said Warren, as he made her aware of his presence by standing close to Rebecca and leaning into the side of her body.

Looking up at him, Rebecca said, "Umm… I am going to sit down and eat my lunch. You're a big boy, I'm sure you can get some yourself." She smiled politely at him and walked back to her table. *Lazy shit.*

"Right," he called after her. Squinting his eyes, he scrutinized the way her clothes hugged her body and smiled as he watched her sit back down in her seat. Serving the lasagne onto his plate, he thought, *Cheeky thing.*

Rebecca sat across the table from two other ladies who smiled at her when she looked over at them. "He's a bit of a sleaze," said the blonde-headed woman, gesturing to the course instructor.

"Hmm, that sure was weird how close he stood next to me. And the audacity of him… he asked me to serve him food from the bain-maries," said Rebecca in a low voice, her brow creased as she looked over to where the instructor was sitting at the next table.

"Yeah… he tried it on me too, this morning at morning tea time," said the blonde woman in a German accent. "I soon put him in his place."

"And he got me to make him a coffee this morning before the class started and yeah, he stood too close to me too. We were the only ones in the room at that stage. I felt a bit intimidated," said the other woman, with a South American accent. "I didn't know what to do."

"Do you think he needs reporting to someone, or maybe he is just a touchy feely type person?" asked Rebecca. "Maybe we should give him the benefit of the doubt, before we do anything, ladies."

"Let's just wait and see if he hits on anyone else," said the German accented woman.

Both the South American woman and Rebecca nodded in agreeance.

As Rebecca ate her lunch, her phone, which was on the table, buzzed. It was another text message from Mitch.

'How is your lunch, my beautiful lady? ILU as well.'

She text him back straight away.

'My lunch is really nice. Buffet… How is your day?'

She received a text message straight back from him.

'I am in a meeting with the managers of my security business here in Seattle. Very dry and ho-hum. My day is a bit boring without you in it. Looking forward to seeing you tonight.'

Rebecca smiled to herself and was excited about tonight.

Once lunch had finished, they all headed back up to the conference room.

Taking some mints and a bottle of water from the table at the back of the room, Rebecca headed back to her designated seat and wondered what the afternoon would be like. As she typed in her password for the computer, she covered her mouth with her hand as she silently yawned and tried to look interested. Looking over at the instructor, who was getting the projector ready with the next lot of slides, she questioned in her mind what had happened at lunch and shook it off as his personality.

"Right… let's log onto our computers and keep going," said Warren, looking around the room.

Before Rebecca knew it, it was four o'clock and the course had finished for the day. After she said her goodbyes to the other course participants, she headed for the elevator. As she waited for the doors to open, she felt a presence standing behind her.

"What did you think of the course today, Rebecca?" asked Warren.

Rebecca turned to see him standing directly behind her. Smiling politely, she said, "I am enjoying it so far, Mr Gift."

"Call me, Warren. Mr Gift is way too formal… I am glad you are enjoying it. So… any plans for tonight?"

"Yes, actually… I am meeting up with my boyfriend," said Rebecca, her heart pounding in her chest.

"Right… well… he's a lucky man then," said Warren, surprised. Brushing past her gently, he moved towards the elevator button, which was already lit.

When the doors opened and he walked in ahead of her, Rebecca knew it was only going to be the two of them. Thinking quickly she said, "Oops, I have left my phone in the conference room."

Holding the doors open with his right hand he said, "I'll come with you to find it."

Holding her hand up, she said, "Nah, that's Ok. I will be all right to find it by myself. See you tomorrow." Rebecca swallowed hard and walked off in the direction of the conference room. Hearing the elevator doors close, she didn't dare look behind her in fear of that he may be following her. As she reached the conference room, she spotted the German accented woman, who she spoke with at lunch.

"Are you all right?" asked the German woman, who noticed Rebecca's rapid breathing and pale complexion.

"Yeah, I am now. Mr Creepy… I don't know what it is about him, but his creepy presence disturbs me. I didn't want to get in the elevator with him by myself, so I made an excuse that I had left my phone in here," said Rebecca. "Would you mind catching the elevator with me?"

"I think we are safer in numbers, don't you?" said the German woman, with her hands on her hips. "I think if he plays this card again tomorrow, we will report him. What do you think?"

"Yeah, I think that might be a good idea," said Rebecca, hoping she was wrong.

"Come on. Let's go," said the German woman.

With her heart hammering, Rebecca quickly pushed the door shut to her hotel room. As she slid down the door and sat on the carpeted floor, Rebecca felt safe again. Had her mind been playing tricks on her when she thought she heard someone following her down the hallway from the elevator? She wasn't sure.

"Mitch... you here?" Rebecca called out.

There was no answer.

Picking herself up off the floor, Rebecca walked towards the bedroom to see if Mitch was there, but there was no sign of Mitch. *He must still be busy with work.*

Placing her bag and course folder on the bed, she noticed there was a small parcel wrapped in brown paper with her name on it, waiting for her on the end of the bed. Sitting down on the bed she speculated what it was as she eagerly opened it up.

Wow... Mitch has bought me the last two books of 'Fifty Shades, thought Rebecca, excited.

There was a card inside the parcel as well from Mitch, which says, "Hope you enjoy these two books just as much as I have. I have marked out in the books some of the wording and scenarios that maybe we can try. That's if you want to. Sir wants to. Laters babe."

Rebecca laughed a little to herself as she flicked through the books to see what Mitch had marked out in the pages and thought, *He really like to role play. Life sure is not going to be dull with this man around. Hmm... should be interesting tonight.*

Startled from her thoughts of Mitch, she heard someone knocking at her door. Walking over to the door, she looked through the peep hole in the middle, top part of the door, only to see a bellboy standing there with a parcel in his hands. Breathing a sigh of relief, because she thought it may be the course instructor, Warren Gift, she opened the door.

Handing her a long, white parcel the bellboy said, "I have been instructed to tell you that inside this parcel is some clothing. Mr Portellico wants you wear them tonight and to meet him in the dining room on the 50th floor at six o'clock ma'am."

"Oh, Ok. Thank you," said Rebecca, as she pulled some loose change out of her pocket for the bellboy.

"Thank you ma'am," said the bellboy, handing over the long parcel, slightly bowing his head and walking away.

Excited, Rebecca shut the door, rushed over to the bed and unzipped the long white bag. Inside was a floor length strapless, silver satin dress, metallic high heeled sandals, a grey strapless bra and panties. She stood there in shock looking at the items he had bought her.

Wonder how he knows my size, let alone if the colour will suit me, Rebecca thought to herself. *Shit, six o'clock. What time is it now?* She retrieved her phone from her bag and looked at the time. *I had better start getting ready.*

Mmm, that's better… the hot shower is soothing my aching shoulders, thought Rebecca, as she took a few more moments in the shower than usual, rounding her shoulders over and over, as the water cascaded over them.

Eventually turning off the faucet, Rebecca stepped out of the shower and onto a soft, white floor mat. Taking the towel off the rack to dry herself she thought, *I must find out where to buy this fruity smelling berry body wash, because it makes me feel rejuvenated.*

The room was quiet as Rebecca walked into the low lit bedroom naked. Trying on the bra and panties Mitch had bought her, she looked down at her body and realised that they fit her well and made her feel sexy. Stepping into her new dress and fastening the side zip up, she decided to see what it looked like in front of the long mirror in the bedroom. Twirling around, she couldn't believe how good the dress looked on her, as it wasn't something she would have picked out from a rack, at all. Walking back over to the bed, she took a seat and tried on her metallic sandals. Fastening the buckle on her sandals, she returned to the mirror to see what they looked like with the dress.

Wow… they look really nice with this dress. Now for my makeup and hair, thought Rebecca as she lifted her long brown hair up off her shoulders, to see if her hair would look good up or down with the strapless dress.

Hmm… I might put it up in a half up and half down style, with a few curls around the front to soften my face.

Once she had styled her hair, she applied her silver-toned make-up and sprayed on her favourite perfume, Britney Spears, *Fantasy.* Taking another look in the long mirror located in the bathroom and twirling around to see if she looked all right, she smiled at herself and was nearly ready to go.

I can't believe how good this dress looks on me. It fits in all the right places and accentuates my curves… oh and I think I have just the right diamond necklace and earrings to wear with it too, thought Rebecca, walking back into the bedroom and checking her suitcase for the jewellery and a black, soft leather clutch bag she was going to use tonight.

Taking one last look in the mirror, she was now ready for her date with Mitch.

Rebecca pushed the 50th floor button in the elevator and watched the golden doors shut. Looking at her reflection in the smoked glass mirrors, she felt nervous but excited at the same time that she was seeing Mitch, as she had missed him during the day. When the elevator arrived at the 50th floor and the doors opened, she was greeted by a room that had full length windows all around the outside of the restaurant, with sparkling chandeliers hanging opulently here and there from the roof. The tables were beautifully set up all around the outer side of the room with white linen table cloths, sparkling glassware and silver cutlery, with the kitchen and fully stocked bar located in the middle of the room. Taking in the lavishness of the room, her eyes didn't know where to look first. She then noticed a black reception counter, with two waitresses eyeing her off and waiting for her to approach them.

"Good evening ma'am. Who are you dining with tonight?" asked the blonde headed waitress.

"Hello… I am with Mitch Portellico," said Rebecca, smiling politely.

The waitress nodded and said, "Come this way ma'am."

Rebecca's eyes were darting around the room as she followed the waitress into the restaurant. Spotting Mitch near the bar with his back to her, she also noticed his brothers were there as well. She politely pointed and said to the waitress, "There is my man. I will join him at the bar."

She acknowledged Rebecca with a nod and turned to go back to her desk at the elevator.

The three Portellico brothers were all dressed in black suits and looked truly handsome. The rest of his family and her daughter, Paige were at a round table to the right of the bar. Paige noticed her mum as she walked in and waved. Rebecca smiled and waved back.

Secretly, Rebecca was disappointed that it wasn't just her and Mitch having a romantic dinner together, but she was glad to be having dinner with her daughter and Mitch's family as well.

Walking towards the bar, Nick and Michael saw her first. With their eyebrows raised and smiling, they both nodded in her direction.

"Bec is here," said Nick to Mitch.

"Oh, Ok. Thanks," said Mitch, as he turned around to see Rebecca walking towards him. His face lit up as soon as he saw how gorgeous she looked in the dress he had bought her.

Without hesitation, he walked over to her and said, "Wow…you look stunning in that dress. I can't believe how beautiful you are."

She smiled and melted into his arms as he gave her a sensual kiss and hugged her tight.

"Thank you, kind Sir. And thank you for the dress, etc. That was really nice of you to buy them for me," said Rebecca, smiling and pulling back gently. "You don't look too shabby yourself in that suit." Her eyes were all over his body.

"Thank you… would you like something to drink, beautiful?" asked Mitch, gesturing towards the bar.

"Yes please. Can I have a white wine?" said Rebecca, walking over to the bar with Mitch to greet Nick and Michael.

"Sure," said Mitch, placing his hand in hers.

"Hello guys," said Rebecca, looking from Nick to Michael.

"Hello Rebecca," said Michael.

"Whoa woman, don't you look nice? You are one lucky man, bro," said Nick, bumping Mitch on the arm.

Rebecca felt her face blush, and said, "Thanks, Nick. You don't look too bad yourself."

"Paige and the rest of the family are over there at the table," said Mitch, indicating to where they were sitting in the restaurant.

"Yeah, I saw them when I walked in," said Rebecca, looking into his blue eyes.

Taking her seat at the table, Rebecca said, "Hi everyone."

They all greeted her, as she sat next to Paige and smiled at her daughter.

"How are you, sweetheart? What did you do today?" asked Rebecca, giving her a hug.

"Michael and a couple of his friends took me to a theme park. We were there most of the day. I had such a ball, Mum," said Paige, remembering all the rides she went on and the fairy floss she ate.

"Awesome... I am glad you are enjoying yourself, sweetheart," said Rebecca.

Paige knew that her mum liked theme park rides too and was secretly hoping that they might be able to go together before they left Seattle at the end of the week.

"Do you like my new dress Mitch bought me today?" said Paige, standing to show her mum.

"Wow... that is lovely, sweetheart, and it looks really nice on you too," said Rebecca, smiling.

"Thank you for buying Paige that beautiful dress. It was really nice of you to do that," said Rebecca, leaning into Mitch, who was now sitting beside her.

"There was method in my madness today. I told Paige if she helped me pick out an evening dress and shoes for you then I would buy her something as well for tonight," said Mitch.

"Ah, right... you are too kind, Mitch. Oh and thank you for the two books. I can't wait to read them already," said Rebecca.

"You're welcome," said Mitch, smirking.

"So what is the occasion for coming to this lovely restaurant tonight?" said Rebecca to Mitch.

"Nick scored a really big contract today with Pink. His team are now going to be her security for the next year," said Mitch.

Rebecca looked across the table at Nick and said, "Congratulations, man. That is wonderful news on getting the contract for Pink."

"Thanks, Bec," said Nick, smiling.

Out the corner of her eye, Rebecca could feel Mitch staring at her. As she turned around to face him, she whispered, "Does Sir like what I am wearing?"

"Yes, Sir likes what you are wearing, very much. Sir would like to undress you as well and have his way with you," said Mitch, with his eyebrow raised and smirking.

Rebecca giggled and her face felt warm, as she looked around the table to see if anyone had overheard their conversation. Luckily for her, no one had.

"How was the course today?" asked Mitch.

"It was really good. The instructor is a bit strange though. Very touchy feely type of person. Makes me feel uneasy."

"Hmm, that's not good. He better keep his hands to himself, otherwise he will have me to deal with," said Mitch, his brow creased.

"Yeah, me and two other ladies are gonna make a complaint if he doesn't," said Rebecca, remembering her conversation with the two ladies today at lunch. "Actually, I have been trained on this type of program before at another place I used to work. So it's pretty easy for me. And the instructor did say to me today that I wouldn't have to do the whole week because I knew most of it already. He told me that he would see how I was going tomorrow and if he could see that I didn't need any more training then I didn't have to go back the rest of the week. He said he would just pass me and give me my certificate," said Rebecca. "How good will that be?"

"Wow, that's great Rebecca. Maybe we can then spend some more time together," said Mitch.

"That would be nice… Mitch I wanted to ask you something and I hope you don't take this the wrong way," said Rebecca.

"What is it, beautiful?" said Mitch, puzzled.

"I would really like to spend a day with Paige whilst we are here in Seattle and maybe even your mom, too. I was thinking that I could do some shopping with them both, or have a morning tea or something. What do you think?" said Rebecca, hoping he would be Ok with her plans.

"Why would I take you spending time on your holiday with my mom and your daughter the wrong way? I think that is nice of you to even want to spend time with Mom. Most girls don't want a bar of the boyfriend's mom, let alone spend time with them," said Mitch.

"Your mom is a nice lady, Mitch, and I hope one day to be half the person she is," said Rebecca, sincerely.

"Where did you come from? And what did I do to deserve you, beautiful?" said Mitch, looking into her eyes lovingly.

She smiled at him and he kissed her wantonly. As she pulled away from their kiss, Rebecca said, "I feel the same way. I love you, sweet man."

With their meals being placed in front of them, Rebecca watched and listened to the band playing music near the dance floor. "Can you dance?"

"Yes… it's something my mother made us do growing up. We took dance lessons each week. I haven't danced in a while though, so I would be pretty rusty," said Mitch, picking up his knife and fork.

"After dinner, did you want to dance with me?" asked Rebecca, hopeful.

He smiled and said, "I would be honoured."

Throughout dinner, Paige spoke about some of the rides she went on during the day at the theme park and Michael gave running commentary on what Paige was like when she was getting off each ride.

Rebecca looked at Michael and mouthed to him, "Thank you."

He mouthed back, "Welcome."

He is such a great boy. My daughter is lucky, that's for sure, thought Rebecca, watching them recall their day.

Mitch placed his hand over Rebecca's and said, "Would you like to dance, beautiful?"

"Sure… never thought you would ask. Let's go," said Rebecca, standing up.

When they reached the dance floor, Mitch took Rebecca in his arms and they danced slowly to the music.

With her head on his shoulder, whilst they swayed to the music, she thought, c*an life get any better than in this moment?* She was falling for Mitch and in a big way.

"Can I sleep over tonight?" whispered Mitch in her ear.

She smiled up at him and said, "I just assumed you would. Does Sir have something in mind?"

"Just to see you and be with you by myself will be all this Sir needs tonight. I have missed you today, Bec," said Mitch, lovingly as he held her in his arms.

Rebecca placed her head back on his shoulder and said, "I love you, sweet man." Content they continued to dance for another three songs.

Mitch felt a tap on his shoulder. When he pulled away from Rebecca and turned around he realised Helen was standing behind him.

"We are all going on home now. Don't worry, I will look after Paige for you, Rebecca. We will see you tomorrow night for dinner at our house. It's a barbeque, so jeans will be fine."

"Ok. Thanks, Helen," said Rebecca. "See you tomorrow night."

Rebecca gave Helen a hug goodbye.

"Thanks, Mom. Not sure if I will be home tonight, so I will see you tomorrow for breakfast," said Mitch, as he leant in to give her a kiss on the cheek.

"Have a wonderful time," said Helen, looking from Mitch and Rebecca. Walking back over to Grayson, who was standing at the table with the waitress, she watched him pay for the night's meals and drinks.

Mitch followed his mother back to the table to say his goodbyes to everyone, with Rebecca.

"Have a good day tomorrow, sweetie," said Rebecca to Paige, who was standing with Michael, Nick and Grayson.

"Thanks Mum, I will," said Paige, giving her mum a hug. "You too. Enjoy yourself tonight."

"I will," said Rebecca, hugging her daughter back.

Mitch and Rebecca then said their goodbyes to the rest of the family, before heading to the elevator.

Rebecca placed the magnetic card in the slot of the door to gain access to her hotel room. As the light changed from red to green on the slot, she opened the door and walked in with Mitch. Placing her black leather clutch bag on the desk she heard Mitch from behind her say, "Turn around so I can unzip your dress."

Rebecca did as she was told.

Unzipping it, her dress fell to the floor and she was left standing there in her new strapless bra and panties Mitch had bought her earlier today. Turning her around in the low lit room, Mitch picked Rebecca up in his arms and carried her into the bedroom, placing her down on the edge of the bed. Kneeling down next to the bed, he took Rebecca's shoes off and started to massage her feet.

"Mmm… feels wonderful. I have sore feet from the new shoes." Her head tipped back with her eyes closed as she welcomed the attention he was giving her feet.

Once he was finished, he stood back up and stripped off his jacket. As he was about to take off the rest of his clothes, Rebecca stood up and said, "I'll do it."

With her eyebrows raised and a smirk on her face, she looked into his blue eyes and then smiled.

Mitch smirked and let her take charge.

Undoing the buttons to his white collared shirt, Rebecca first noticed his muscular chest and abdomen.

Oh my, those washboard abs. I just want to eat them, thought Rebecca, rubbing her thumb over her bottom lip. *This man is all mine. I am one lucky girl.*

He looks down at her with carnal eyes and sees Rebecca smiling and says, "Penny for your thoughts."

"I was just thinking about how gorgeous you are and I still can't believe you are all mine, to do with what I want," said Rebecca, teasing him, with a smirk on her face.

Mitch takes her in his arms and kisses her lips vigorously. His tongue searched the inside of her mouth, drinking in the flavours of it. They were all hands and saliva, heady. Breathless, she hurriedly pulled off his white shirt and threw it on the ground. Leaning into him she could already feel his hardened cock through the material of his trousers.

"Mmm… is that for me, Sir?" she teased.

His eyebrow raised on one side and a smile came over his face.

Rebecca conveniently brushed over his hardened shaft with her hand, as she undid his fly. Pushing his trousers down over his hips, they fell to the ground and he stepped out of them, pulling off his shoes in the process.

Pushing her down gently onto the bed, Mitch lay next to her. His strong hands worked their magic as he massaged her body. Slowly he took her panties and strapless bra off, nipping at her right nipple. As he pulled it gently with his teeth she felt the pain and pleasure all at once. His warm mouth was her undoing as he forcibly pulled her breast into his mouth further. As she arched her back off the bed, Rebecca had her first orgasm.

Oh God, I am in ecstasy, take me.... she thought to herself.

When Mitch was finished with her left nipple, he made his way down her stomach, kissing and taunting her. Nearing her pubic hair, he opens her legs, and sucks on her clitoris.

Oh my, I feel like I have died and gone to heaven, thought Rebecca. Overwhelmed, she orgasmed again.

"Mmm... you taste mighty fine," said Mitch, looking up at her.

The teasing was relentless, as he took two fingers and inserted them into her vagina, pulling them in and out until she couldn't take it any longer.

"Please, Mitch... no more teasing. I can't take much more of this," pleaded Rebecca.

"All good things, my dear. All good things," said Mitch, enjoying every moment.

Rebecca watched as Mitch retrieved a condom out of his wallet and slid it onto his elongated penis. The anticipation of it all excited her. Looking into his eyes, she realised in that moment that she would do just about anything to please this man. Leaning over her on the bed, Mitch put his hardened cock into her wet vagina. At first he took it slow with Rebecca and as she got more comfortable, he started to fuck her hard and faster. Her body was on fire and was in the need to be put out, as she kept up with his fast paced rhythm. Within minutes Rebecca felt her orgasm coming. She tried to stop it, but to no avail and as she orgasmed, Mitch stilled over her as he too reached his climax inside her. Breathing heavily, he leant down and kissed her forehead.

"Now that is what I have been looking forward to all night," said Mitch, as he lay next to Rebecca and looked into her blue eyes.

"Mmm, me too," said Rebecca, breathlessly, as she snuggled into the crook of his shoulder.

They lay there naked until they recovered their exhausted bodies.

"Would you like to have a bath with me?" asked Rebecca.

He nodded, pulling his body away from her gently. She watched him get up slowly and walk to the bathroom.

Hearing the faucet being turned on and water running into the bath, Rebecca smelled the delightful perfumed aroma of rose.

Without saying a word Mitch returned from the bathroom, picked her up in his broad arms, carried Rebecca into the bathroom and placed her in the warm foam filled bath.

Stepping into the bath, he lay with his back to one end of the bath, stretching out his legs in front of him, leaving only enough room for her to slip in between his legs and lie back on his chest.

As she cuddled into him, Rebecca thought to herself, *I am so lucky. He could have picked someone else, someone from the same background as him to be his partner. But he chose me. I feel like the most luckiest girl in the world at the moment.* She grinned to herself and snuggled into him tighter, whilst listening to his heart beat fast.

The last thing she remembered was Mitch kissing her hair, as she fell asleep in his arms.

CHAPTER FIFTEEN

The next morning, Rebecca made it to the course just as everyone was taking their seats to start. Breathing heavily from running all the way from the elevator, she took her seat at the front of the class, turned her mobile on silent and opened the training folder to where they left off from the previous day. As she settled into her seat, she noticed a woman, in a grey toned business suit, standing at the front of the room, next to the projector.

"Good morning, everyone. I suppose you are wondering where Mr Gift is today. Well... he will not be teaching this course any longer. I am replacing him for the rest of the week. My name is Clarissa O'Dett. Can anyone tell me where Mr Gift left off yesterday afternoon?"

Rebecca, and the German woman looked over at each other, their eyebrows raised.

"I believe he finished at the purchasing module," said the German woman, looking over at Clarissa.

"Awesome..." said Clarissa, looking through the contents page on her open folder. "Right... let's open our folders to page fifty-six and start there today."

Hmm... I wonder what happened with Warren Gift. Rebecca placed her folder in front of her and checked she was open at the right page number. Looking up at the projector, she listened carefully to Clarissa's conversation about the next module they were learning.

By the time morning tea time had come around, Rebecca's stomach was ravenous. As she made her cup of tea to have with her extra piece of pastry, the course instructor approached Rebecca and said, "I see from the notes Mr Gift left and from what I can see from today that you are doing really well in this course. So what I propose is that you probably won't need to come the rest of the week. I will need to run through with you only this afternoon, some of the finer points that your company will need and then that will be it. I can have your certificate of completion ready for you this afternoon as well. Would you be happy with that?"

"Yes, that will be Ok. Thank you. I look forward to learning something different this afternoon," said Rebecca.

"Great," said Clarissa. "Five more minutes people and we will start again," she said out loud and then headed back to the front of her class with her cup of tea.

"Hey, I wonder what happened to Mr Gift?" said the German woman, as she come to stand next to Rebecca.

"Not sure. But I have noticed that the other lady, can't remember her name, you know the one with the southern accent at lunch yesterday, well, she is not here today. Makes me think something happened between her and Mr Gift. Maybe management found out and that's why we have Clarissa," said Rebecca, shrugging her shoulders.

"Yeah, you could be right. Good riddance to him, anyway," said the German woman. "Looks like she is about to start again so we had better go back to our seats."

Rebecca looked to the front of the class and nodded.

Sitting back at her desk, Rebecca felt her phone vibrating. When she looked at the screen, she realised that it was a text message from Mitch.

'Hi beautiful. Miss you already. How is your day?'

Rebecca texted him straight back.

'Hi babe... I am finishing my course today. So I will be able to spend more time getting to know your body a lot better tomorrow. lol... ILU.'

Within seconds he texted her back.

'LOL. ILU as well. See you at five o'clock, beautiful.

Reading his text, she smiled knowing it wouldn't be long before she could see this wonderful man of hers. Placing her phone back on the desk, she listened attentively whilst Clarissa started chatting about the accounts module.

The afternoon went slow, but Rebecca welcomed learning some new sections of the computer program which would make her job back home more fulfilling. As the course was finishing the instructor handed Rebecca her certificate.

"Here you go," said Clarissa, smiling politely.

Rebecca took the certificate from Clarissa and said, "Thanks." She looked it over and read the wording. "So… can I ask what happened to Warren Gift?"

Clarissa frowned and said, "Let's put it this way… his inappropriate overtures were noted and dealt with by not only the hotel management, but the authorities too. That is all I can say."

"Right… well it's not as if he didn't get what he deserved, then," said Rebecca, remembering how he made her feel. "He sure made a few of us women feel uneasy."

Clarissa nodded and smiled politely, bidding Rebecca a goodbye, as she walked towards the front of the room.

Placing her certificate into the training folder, Rebecca then said her goodbyes to everyone in the course and made her way to the elevator.

As the elevator went up to the seventy second floor, she thought to herself, *I don't have a course tomorrow, so I wonder what we can do. Maybe I can even move to Mitch's parents' home instead of staying here. Either way, I am happy to be spending more time on holidays with everyone.*

Reaching her floor, the elevator dinged and the doors opened. Rebecca walked down to her room and opened the door. Pushing the heavy wooden door shut, she rested her back against it and thought to herself, *I will have a shower to freshen up. Mmm, a barbeque at Mitch's parents' house tonight sounds just the treat. Oh and I can finally wear my new jeans I bought just before I left Perth.*

Entering the bedroom, Rebecca was surprised to see Mitch lying on the bed and he was fast asleep. She quietly put down her things and sat next to him and watched him sleep.

God he is even more gorgeous when he is sleeping… Is that possible? I can't help myself, I have to touch him.

She run a hand through his hair, and his eyes opened.

"Hello, babe," said Rebecca, smiling.

"Hello, beautiful. It's so good to see you," said Mitch, wiping the sleep from his eyes.

She leant down and gave him a tender kiss on his lips. "Are you tired?" she asked.

"Mmm, it's been a hectic few days for me. I lay down here and before I knew it I was asleep," said Mitch, yawning.

"We don't have to be at your parents' until seven o'clock, so why don't you stay there and rest. I need to go and have a shower to freshen up, anyway," said Rebecca.

"Sounds good," said Mitch, as he turned over and closed his eyes.

The water was extremely hot and made her body tingle all over.

I love having hot showers as they always make me feel rejuvenated, especially my shoulders and neck.

With the clear glass shower steamed up from the hot water and her eyes closed, Rebecca finished up washing the conditioner out of her hair. When she heard the shower door open, she opened one eye and saw Mitch through the steam, stepping into the shower.

"Does Sir want to play already?" teased Rebecca, opening both eyes.

"Sir has wants too, you know and you always know how to please me," said Mitch, pulling her in close to his muscular body.

She smiled at him sheepishly and placed her arms around his waist, only to feel his hardened penis touch her clitoris. Her teeth grazed his right ear, and Mitch's breathing became rapid. With warm lips, she kissed his neck, tormenting him as she lapped and sucked it firmly. Continuing down his body, she kissed and sucked every inch, until she was down on her knees in front of him. Looking up into his carnal eyes, she smiled and hurriedly took his cock in her mouth. Placing his back against the tiles, he positioned his hands on her shoulders as she relentlessly sucked his penis and swirled the head of it around in her mouth, sucking and teasing him as she went.

"God, woman... that... feels... too... good," stammered Mitch, as he pulled his cock vigorously in and out of her mouth. When he couldn't take the pleasure anymore, Mitch pulled his cock out of her mouth. Looking down at her dominantly, he said. "Stand up."

As the water cascaded over her head, Rebecca did as she was told.

Picking her up in his arms, he turned off the faucet and carried her into the bedroom. Gently placing her wet body down on the queen bed, he pulled her close to the edge, opened her legs and enjoyed the pleasures of her vagina with his tongue.

Arching her back off the bed, Rebecca moaned with sheer delight as she gave in to her first orgasm.

Leaning on the bed, Mitch pulled himself up into a standing position, the blood was rushing through his penis as it pulsated and elongated, wishing for him to give it release. With carnal eyes on her well-toned body, he said, "Turn over."

Rebecca did as she was instructed.

Mitch took a condom out of the drawer, which was next to the bed, ripped it open and rolled it onto his hardened penis. As Rebecca knelt on the bed and pushed her bum into the air, Mitch thrust his penis into her wet, hot vagina. She moaned as the fullness of his cock filled her and penetrated in and out of her vagina over and over. With him filling her every need, in ways a lover should, Rebecca was overwhelmed as she felt him still over her and she orgasmed.

Panting, but not fulfilled, she anticipated what Mitch would do next, as she felt her saturated vagina pulsate for more reward. His breathing was rapid, as his hands slowly teased her breasts and massaged her body.

Feeling his penis, once again, extend in length inside her, Mitch asked, "Ready for round two?"

"I'm on fire, sweet man. I need to be put out," said Rebecca, as she wiped the beaded sweat from her upper lip.

"Humph," smirked Mitch, as he grabbed hold of her hips and pounded her flesh.

When their love-making was finally over, they lay naked on the bed panting, with sweat dripping off their bodies.

With the sated breathing of exhausted lovers, they eventually fell asleep in each other's arms.

When Rebecca woke, the room was dark, with only a silhouette of light coming in from around the edge of the closed curtains. Checking the clock on the bedside cupboard, she notices that it is six o'clock already. *Shit.* Waking Mitch, they hopped quickly out of bed, got showered, dressed and on their way in Mitch's sports car.

Smirking, Mitch says, "Now that was a fun afternoon."

"Humph, fun... man, I would call that hot," said Rebecca, remembering their molten hot sex they had. "Hey, you had better call your parents and let them know we will be late."

"Hmm... good idea," said Mitch, pressing the buttons on his dash to dial their number, so he could let them know they would be there about seven-thirty.

When Rebecca and Mitch arrived, everyone was around the back of Mitch's parents' house enjoying a few drinks. Grayson was cooking the meat on the barbeque and there was quite a spread of salads on the table for everyone to eat.

"Here they are. About time you got here, you two," goaded Nick.

"Sorry everyone that we are late. We both fell asleep on the bed at the hotel," said Mitch, with his arm around Rebecca's waist.

"Yeah, likely story," said Nick, laughing as Mitch and Rebecca walked past the barbeque.

Mitch's pursed his lips and his nostrils flared, as he gave Nick a look that said, 'shut your mouth', as they sat down at the table.

"Would you like a drink?" asked Mitch.

"Yes, please. You choose," said Rebecca, as she sat next to Paige.

"Hi, Mum," said Paige, giving her a hug.

"Hello, sweetheart," said Rebecca, hugging her back. "What did you do today, sweetie?"

"Michael took me to a beautiful park today and we had a picnic. It was really nice, Mum. After that we went horse riding. They have horses down the back of the property here," said Paige, excitedly.

"Sounds like you had a really good day, sweetie," said Rebecca. "Actually, I have some good news. I have finished the course and I can spend the rest of the week finally holidaying. Maybe we can do some shopping or something together tomorrow. What do you think?"

"I would love to, Mum," said Paige, eagerly.

Reaching across the table, Rebecca said, "Helen… I was wondering if you would like to come with Paige and me tomorrow. Maybe we can do morning tea and some shopping. What do you think?"

"Have you finished your course?" asked Helen.

"Yep," said Rebecca, smiling.

"Oh wow… that would be lovely, dear. I wouldn't miss it for the world. It will be nice to spend the morning with you both. I have to be back by one-thirty though, as I have an appointment at two-thirty. But I am really looking forward spending time with you both," said Helen, smiling. *Such a lovely girl.*

"Michael… you don't mind if I steal Paige away for the morning do you?" asked Rebecca.

"No, that's Ok. I have to work tomorrow anyway, so that will work out good," said Michael, looking from Rebecca to Paige.

"So what about if we leave around nine-thirty, girls? This will give us plenty of time for shopping and morning tea," said Rebecca, looking from Helen to Paige.

Paige and Helen both nodded and Paige said, "Yep, sounds good."

"We can take the limo tomorrow. That should make it easier to get in and out of places quicker. And I know of some really great places to take you both shopping. You'll love it," said Helen, excited to be spending the day with them.

"I am looking forward to going out with you tomorrow, Helen and Paige. Should be lots of fun," said Rebecca, smiling.

Mitch sat next to Rebecca and positioned her drink on the table in front of her. Placing his hand over hers, squeezing it, he leant in and whispered in her ear, "I love you."

She smiled and kissed his lips tenderly.

"Ah… what time do the theme parks close tomorrow?" asked

Rebecca to Mitch.

"Around eight o'clock, Bec," said Michael, overhearing the question.

"How do you feel about taking Paige and me to a theme park tomorrow afternoon?" asked Rebecca to Mitch.

"I would love to, beautiful. I have a meeting in the morning, but I can meet you here, say around two o'clock," said Mitch.

"Sounds great," said Rebecca.

"Cool... can't wait to go on some of the rides with you, Mum," said Paige, listening to the conversation.

"Yeah, me too," said Rebecca.

"Meat's ready, everyone," interrupted Grayson. "Come and dig in before it goes cold."

What a wonderful family this is to be a part of. They are all so close and are very welcoming. I am starting to really feel a part of this family. I will miss them all when we go back home, thought Rebecca, as she finished her dinner and looked around the table, remembering conversations with each of them.

Looking over at her daughter, Rebecca said, "You look tired, sweetheart."

"Yeah, I am feeling tired. I might go to bed, Mum. I will see you tomorrow at breakfast." She gave Rebecca a kiss on her cheek.

"Good night, sweetie. Sleep well," said Rebecca, hugging Paige. *Jet lag.*

"Night, Paige," said Mitch. "See you tomorrow afternoon."

"For sure... night, Mitch," said Paige. "Night everyone."

"Would you like to watch a movie in the theatre room?" asked Mitch.

"Sure," said Rebecca, enthusiastically. "Thank you for a lovely meal, Grayson and Helen. I thoroughly enjoyed myself."

"You're welcome," said Grayson.

"Bec and I are going to watch a movie in the theatre room, so we will see you all in the morning," said Mitch.

"Ok. Good night, dears," said Helen, giving them both a hug. "I think we may head off to bed ourselves."

"Sounds like a good idea, Mother," said Grayson.

Nick and Michael bid them good night as well.

"What movie are we going to watch?" said Rebecca, walking inside.

"Have you seen *Battleship* yet?" asked Mitch.

"No, I haven't seen that one yet. But I have heard it's meant to be a good movie," said Rebecca.

"Good, then that's what we are watching," said Mitch, placing his arm around her shoulder.

When Mitch opened the door of the theatre room Rebecca's eyes darted around the room in amazement. It actually looked like a movie theatre. Big screen at the front of the room, with lots of comfortable charcoal coloured velvet reclining armchairs, and long red drapes all around the grey painted room.

"Wow, this is nice, Mitch. Are there two seats together so I can cuddle up to you?" said Rebecca.

"Sure are," said Mitch, pointing to where they would be sitting at the back of the room.

"You go and make yourself comfortable over there and I will put the movie on." When he returned he had some popcorn with him, which he had retrieved from a black cupboard on the left of the room. "What's a movie without popcorn, hey?" said Mitch, sitting down next to Rebecca.

"My thoughts exactly," she said.

Humph... even though I have been gone for five years, mom and dad still keep the popcorn in the same cupboard. Talk about creatures of habit. It is nice to come home to familiarity though, thought Mitch.

Once the movie started, Rebecca snuggled into Mitch's side. Content, she couldn't take her eyes off the screen. As it ended, she said to Mitch, "That was a good movie. The special effects were done beautifully. I could watch that again one day."

"Sure was," said Mitch, as he turned off the movie credits with the remote.

"Would you like a cup of tea before we go to bed?" asked Mitch.

"That would be lovely. Thanks, Mitch."

Sitting on the stools in the kitchen at the island bench, they discussed the movie at length. Sipping her tea Rebecca was surprised to see Nick walk in.

"What you guys up to?" asked Nick.

"We're just having a hot drink and then we are off to bed, bro," said Mitch, looking over at Nick.

"Ok... hey Rebecca... do you and Paige like Pink's music?" asked Nick.

"We love her music. I have all her music back home," said Rebecca.

"Would you like to go to one of her concerts on Thursday night?" said Nick, getting a cold drink of water out of the fridge.

"Oh man that would be awesome. Is she playing in Seattle?" said Rebecca.

"Yes. She is doing two concerts here and has asked me if I would like some tickets," said Nick, sitting next to Rebecca at the island bench.

"I would love to go, Nick. And I am sure Paige would like to go, too," said Rebecca, eagerly.

"It's settled then. I will get enough tickets for all of us to go," said Nick.

"Thanks, Nick," said Mitch.

"Yeah, thanks Nick. Can't wait to go," said Rebecca.

"No problem. Well... I am off to bed. Got a big day tomorrow," said Nick, standing. "Night."

"Night," said Mitch and Rebecca together, as they watched him walk towards the doorway.

"That was nice of him to get tickets for the Pink concert for us."

"Sure is. I know he can be a pain sometimes, but his heart is always in the right place," said Mitch.

"Yeah... he does have a good heart," said Rebecca, as she yawned. "Actually, I am getting a bit tired myself. Let's go to bed."

"Sounds like a good idea," said Mitch, taking their mugs and placing them in the dishwasher.

CHAPTER SIXTEEN

Opening her eyes and reaching across the bed for Mitch, Rebecca realised he was not next to her and wondered where he was. Looking at the bedside clock, it said seven-thirty and she remembered Mitch had an early meeting today. Gathering her thoughts, she heard the water running in the shower and hopped out of bed. Entering the bathroom, she found Mitch in the shower.

"Good morning, gorgeous," said Rebecca, opening the glass door to the shower.

"Morning, beautiful," said Mitch, as he washed his hair.

"It's a pity you have a meeting to go to, because I am horny as hell this morning," teased Rebecca.

"Sorry babe… but there is always later on tonight," said Mitch, turning the water off. "Can you hand me a towel?"

"Sure," said Rebecca.

Playfully she swatted his gorgeous arse with the towel as he bent over to pick up his clothes to wear for the day.

With raised eyebrows he flinched and said, "Sir likes that very much."

Rebecca smiled and said, "You had better get out of here before I come undone, teaser."

He smirked at her and continued on into the bedroom to get

dressed, whilst Rebecca welcomed a toilet break.

When she entered the bedroom, Mitch was already dressed and ready to leave. "See you this afternoon, beautiful." He gave her a loving kiss goodbye, and slapped her on the bum as he walked off towards the door.

"Have a good day… I love you," said Rebecca, as she watched him walk out the door. *Could he get anymore handsome in that suit?*

Rebecca walked into the dining room, noticing Helen and Paige were already having their breakfast and decided to join them.

"Morning," said Rebecca.

Helen and Paige said, "Good morning," to her at the same time.

"Make yourself some breakfast, dear," said Helen, indicating to the bain-maries.

"Thank you," said Rebecca, looking from Helen to the bain-maries. She was famished, as usual, this morning. *Hmm… I might have some scrambled eggs on toast, with a side of tomato. Oh, and a nice mug of tea.*

"We have about half an hour before the limo will arrive at the front door for us," said Helen, watching Rebecca sit next to her.

"Ok, thanks, Helen," said Rebecca, placing her plate on the table. "How are you this morning, sweetie?"

"Good… I slept like a log last night, Mum. I think I am probably over the jet lag, finally," said Paige.

"That's great, love," said Rebecca.

"You both ready for some serious shopping today?" asked Helen, as she placed her knife and fork down together in the middle of her plate.

"Can't wait," said Paige, smiling.

"Sure am," said Rebecca, cutting up her tomato.

After Helen, Rebecca and Paige had finished their breakfast, Rebecca excused herself and ran up the stairs to Mitch's room to retrieve her purse, phone and a jacket. They had all planned to meet in the foyer in five minutes. Taking one last look in the long mirror in Mitch's bathroom, Rebecca applied her lipstick, smiled and headed down to the foyer.

"Ok… are we ready to go?" asked Helen, with her handbag hanging over her forearm.

Rebecca and Paige nodded and smiled.

The family limousine was parked near the front doors of the house, and as they approached the driver, he helped them step into the back of the black, leather seated car.

Placing her purse on the seat next to her and fastening her seat belt, Rebecca watched through the side window, as the house with its magnificent gardens disappear from view. *Stunning.*

As the limousine arrived at the shopping centre, east side entrance, Helen instructed the driver where to pick them up from once they were finished shopping. "I will ring you when we are ready," said Helen, looking in the rear view mirror at the driver.

"Yes ma'am," said the driver, quickly hopping out of the car, opening their door and holding it open.

Rebecca's eyebrows rose and her jaw dropped as she entered the shopping centre through the double glass sliding doors, with Helen and Paige. She couldn't get over the enormity of the two storey facility and the amount of shops they had to choose from as they continued to walk through.

"Follow me ladies, and I will take you to some of my favourite stores first," said Helen, enthusiastically.

Rebecca and Paige looked at each other and smiled as they followed Helen into the first shop.

Helen, Paige and Rebecca searched throughout the racks, selecting clothing items they liked the most, whilst the shop assistant took the garments from the ladies and placed them into the change rooms for them to try on when they were ready.

Paige ended up trying on some nice clothes, but only decided she wanted to purchase a black dress and a dressy black jacket.

Rebecca found herself a beautiful opal blue dress and shoes to match. She also bought a couple of tailored blouses for work and some floral tops for wearing with either a skirt, shorts or jeans.

Hmmm… doesn't this look good? I am sure Mitch would agree, thought

Rebecca, as she twirled from front to back and looked at her toned body in front of the mirror, at the lacy black lingerie outfit she was contemplating on buying. *I might buy Mitch a nice grey tie from the men's department that I saw in the back section of this shop.*

Helen ended up trying on and buying herself a lovely knee length dress and elegant jewellery to match.

About two hours later, they left the shopping centre and the driver was instructed to take them to a shopping mall nearby, which Helen had been to previously, that had designer clothes.

Not knowing what to expect, Rebecca thought to herself as she climbed back into the car, *Humph… this is going to be interesting. If the designer clothes here are the same as back home, then it will just be window shopping for Paige and me, as I really can't afford them.*

Walking through the mall Helen said, "Ladies… I want you to pick out anything you want in this mall and I will pay for it. I don't want you looking at the price tag, just pick something that looks stunning and something you really like."

She then saw the stunned look on their faces.

"Helen, we don't expect you to do that," said Rebecca, with raised eyebrows.

"No arguments… I won't take no for an answer," said Helen, smiling. "It's my pleasure, anyway."

"Oh, thank you," said Rebecca, smiling politely. "You're very generous."

"Really… thank you," said Paige, smiling.

Rebecca and Paige gave Helen a hug and kiss on the cheek at the same time. They couldn't believe how fortunate they were.

"Come on. Let's go in here," said Helen, gesturing to a women's designer store she liked.

Paige could tell by looking through each fully stocked rack in the store that the well-made designer clothing was of excellent quality. She had always dreamed as a teenager to be able to not only shop in this type of shop but also to afford this type of exquisite clothing as well.

The three women selected a few clothes off the rack and headed for the change room to try them on.

At the counter, Paige handed over to the shop assistant a designer, one-off floral dress that was knee length. Rebecca handed over a designer, one-off blue and white patterned dress that was knee length and Helen also bought herself a beautiful floral print dress.

As the shop assistant passed their bags over to each of them, with their new dresses in them, Paige and Rebecca gave Helen a big hug and said at the same time, "Thank you."

"You are truly welcome, dears," said Helen, hugging them back.

As she they approached the car, Rebecca felt content with her purchases for the morning and the gift Helen had bought her. "What about if we have some morning tea now? I don't know about you two but I am really thirsty after all that shopping."

"Mmm… sounds like a good idea. I know of a great place around the corner we can go to. They have the most mouth-watering pastries and cakes, and oh, the coffee is to die for," said Helen, walking towards the car.

"Yum. Looking forward to that," said Rebecca.

Paige nodded and smiled.

"The car is just parked over there," gestured Helen, pointing across the street. "We can give our bags to the driver and then walk to the coffee shop, which is just down the block."

"Sure," said Rebecca, as she watched the driver alight from the limousine and open the boot.

The glass cabinet at the café had an array of not only savoury treats and sandwiches, but also cream filled cakes and muffins. Rebecca felt overwhelmed with such a large selection and wasn't sure what she was going to choose.

"This treat is on me. So order what you want." said Rebecca to Paige and Helen, who were still deciding.

Helen smiled and said, "Thank you, dear."

Paige's face lit up and she said, "Awesome… thanks, Mum."

Once they had placed their orders and Rebecca had paid, Helen said, "Let's go sit outside. It's too lovely of a day to be sitting in here."

Rebecca and Paige looked through the clear front window of the café and spotted a round table with four chairs, which was vacant, and agreed.

When their morning tea arrived at the table and Helen tipped the waitress for her good service, she said, "It's a pity you girls are going back to Australia on Sunday. You know… you certainly make my boys happy, and as a mother that is all I care about: that my boys are happy and have lovely girls like yourselves."

"Aww, thanks, Helen. That is nice of you to say. We sure are going to miss you as well when we go back home. The way that you have made us feel so welcome in your home; I couldn't thank you more. Do you think you may come and visit us in Australia one day?" said Rebecca, placing her hand on top of Helen's.

"I would love to, my dear. I will talk it over with Grayson and see if we can come over soon," said Helen, as she patted the top of Rebecca's hand and smiled.

The next hour passed by quickly as they sat at the coffee shop chatting and laughing about different things that had happened in their lives, whilst getting to know each other at the same time.

"Well, as much I would love to sit here and chat all day long with you lovely ladies, we will have to go now as I have an appointment to go to soon," said Helen, placing her coffee cup on the saucer.

"Thank you for a lovely day Helen and Paige. I haven't laughed like this in a while and have thoroughly enjoyed myself." said Rebecca, looking from Helen to Paige.

"Yeah… me too, Mum. I can't wait to get back to the Portellico home to try on my new clothes again," said Paige, excited.

"I too have enjoyed myself today and I must say, I have enjoyed getting to know you both a bit more," said Helen, standing.

"Us too," said Rebecca, standing with Paige.

The limousine pulled up at the front door of the Portellico home and the driver came around to the right-hand, back door and opened it for the three women to alight.

"Well, that was a really great day, ladies. Thank you for inviting me. I had the best time. I will see you later on then," said Helen, taking her shopping bags from the boot of the car.

"Me too," said Paige, as she took her and Rebecca's shopping bags from the boot.

"Yes, it was a good morning. See you later on, Helen," said Rebecca, giving Helen a hug.

Rebecca and Paige walked inside and towards the marble staircase with their shopping bags in hand. Taking each step one at a time and holding onto the rail with her left hand, Rebecca said, "Mitch will be here in about thirty minutes. Can you please be ready to go by then?"

"Sure, Mum. I'm just going to have a quick shower and get my jeans on for the park rides. You will love the rides, they are so much fun," said Paige, remembering the theme park she had been to with Michael.

"Ok. That's actually a good idea; I might have a shower to freshen up too. Well, I will see you soon," said Rebecca, standing at the top of the stairs with Paige.

Rebecca stood in front of the long mirror in the bathroom and turned from side to side, checking out whether her comfy jeans and blouse looked all right with her Converse shoes. Giving herself the thumbs up motion, she turned off the bathroom light and headed for the stairs.

Walking down the stairs, she spotted Mitch coming up the stairs. "Hello, gorgeous man of mine," said Rebecca.

"Hi there, beautiful lady," said Mitch.

Leaning in, he kissed her lips passionately.

As she pulled away from him, she frowned and asked, "Are you Ok?"

He looked at her puzzled and said, "How do you know something is even wrong?"

"Well, I am starting to get in tune with you and your body, so I can tell you are upset about something," said. Rebecca, as she brushed her hand through his hair.

"I have had a shit of a morning, that's all," said Mitch, his brow furrowed. "But seeing you just now has made my day start to get a lot better. Let me go and get ready and I will be back down in a few minutes."

"Oh, Ok. Take your time. There is no rush," said Rebecca, watching him walk towards his bedroom.

As he entered his bedroom and shut the door behind him, Rebecca thought, *I might leave him to get ready and go see how Paige is doing.*

Knocking on Paige's bedroom door, Rebecca called out, "Paige?"

"Won't be a sec, Mum. Just getting dressed," said Paige, through the door. Within seconds she opened the door. "What's up?"

"I wanted to let you know that we won't be going to the theme park for probably another hour. Sorry sweetheart," said Rebecca, noticing Paige's wet, messy hair and realising she probably wasn't ready to go yet either.

"That's Ok, Mum. I'm not ready anyway and this will give me a chance to try on everything that I got at shopping this morning," said Paige, smiling. She was excited at the prospect of trying on her new clothes and seeing how good they looked in the mirror. "Everything all right?"

"Yeah… everything's Ok. Just wanted to give Mitch a bit more time to get ready, that's all," said Rebecca.

"Ok. Well, I will wait in my room until you come by and pick me up," said Paige.

'Ok. See you later then. I'm looking forward to going on the rides with you," said Rebecca, as she walked towards Mitch's bedroom doorway.

"Me too," Paige called out after her.

The door clicked closed as Rebecca entered Mitch's bedroom. "Hello," said Rebecca, as she watched Mitch retrieve his denim jeans and white T-shirt out of the wardrobe, placing them down on the bed.

Looking up, Mitch watched her walk towards him. "Hello… I won't be long."

"That's Ok. Sit down on the bed and I will massage your shoulders," said Rebecca

"Aww, thank you. That sounds great. Just what the doctor ordered," said Mitch, smiling as he sat on the bed.

"Back in a second," said Rebecca, walking towards the bathroom doorway.

Opening the vanity, she looked through the shelving and found some Deep Heat cream and then returned to Mitch who was now lying on the bed with his eyes closed.

As she stood beside Mitch, Rebecca thought, *he looks drained. Poor thing.*

"Sit up, babe," instructed Rebecca, squeezing some of the cream into her hands and rubbing them together vigorously. She then sat behind Mitch on the bed and started to rub his shoulders and arms slowly.

"Mmm… that feels nice," said Mitch, briefly closing his eyes as he felt the tension leave his body. "Thank you, Bec. I am enjoying your massage."

"Shhh… just put your head down and relax and I will do the rest. Ok," said Rebecca.

He nodded and did as instructed.

Rebecca continued to knead out the knots in his shoulders and neck and once finished, she instructed Mitch to lie face down on the bed so she could massage his back.

"A guy could get used to all this attention," said Mitch, feeling her tireless hands massage his back.

When she finished massaging his back, Rebecca said, "Ok, I have finished. Now you need to go and have a hot shower. As hot as you can stand it. This should refresh you."

Turning around, lying flat on his back, with one hand under his head, Mitch said, "What would I do without you? Come here." He pulled her towards him and their lips intertwined.

Coming up for a breath, Rebecca looked into his carnal eyes and said, "We can play later. Go get in the shower, you teaser."

Mitch smiled, jumped off the bed, patted her tight arse and walked towards his bathroom.

After Mitch had his shower and was drying himself off, he noticed Rebecca standing in the doorway to the bathroom. "So… how do you feel?" asked Rebecca.

"Actually… I feel pretty damn good and my body feels totally refreshed. How did you know that would work?" said Mitch.

"I used to do that for Jackson when he had a shit day at work too. I actually did a course on relaxation techniques a few years ago now," said Rebecca, walking over to Mitch.

"Well, you're truly good at it. Thank you, beautiful," said Mitch, placing his arms around her waist and kissing her neck.

"Hmm…I love when you take advantage of my neck," said Rebecca, closing her eyes, as she reached down towards his penis. Taking a deep breath to steady herself, she moaned when his fingers played with her right nipple through her blouse. She was on fire and needed some relief from all this tension. "Does Sir want to play?"

Mitch didn't answer. Instead he picked Rebecca up in his muscular arms and carried her over to his bed, where they made love.

Mitch pulled his car into the theme park car park and drove to the underground parking lot, where they had security parking for the expensive cars. This firm not only looked after the cars, but they also kept the paparazzi away from them as well.

"Wow… look at all those lovely cars," said Rebecca, as she rubber-necked through the passenger window at all the cars parked side by side in the underground parking lot.

Mitch smiled as he reversed his car into a parking bay and the car came to a stop in front of the escalators. Turning the car off, he said, "Right… everyone ready to go? We'll take the escalators up to the theme park, Ok?" He pointed to the escalators in front of them.

"Ready when you are, bro," said Michael, pulling on the door handle to open the door.

The steel turnstile rotated easily when Mitch placed the tickets in the slot on top of the machine. Once he was through, Mitch gestured for everyone else to follow his lead.

Rebecca walked through the turnstile and noticed a white, wooden stand that had pamphlets on it, which showed what rides, events and things there were to do at the theme park. "Paige, come look at this."

Paige rushed over to her mum and they looked through the pamphlet together, pointing to events and rides that they both would like to do together. "Looks awesome, Mum," said Paige, pointing to a roller coast ride called the 'Duelling Dragons'.

"Yeah, can't wait," said Rebecca, excited.

"Madam… would you like some photos?" said the theme park photographer, who had a camera with a long lens in his hand.

It was apparent to Rebecca from looking at his blue and white collared shirt that he worked for the theme park and was willing to help them make their day memorable.

"Sure. Can we get a group one with the theme park signage in the background?" asked Rebecca.

"Yes ma'am. As many as you want. The way it works is you get photos taken all over the park whilst you are here and at the end of your day or night then you collect them from the photo store just before you leave. Sound Ok?" said the photographer, taking a card from his shirt pocket.

"Sounds great," said Rebecca.

"Great… once I take your photos then I will give you this card," said the photographer, holding it out front of him. "Then every time you want photos taken around the park, all you need to do is give them this card and they will place your photos on it. That way when you are about to leave the park, you just hand this into the photo store and they can download all your photos, for you to choose which ones you would like to get printed."

"Sounds easy enough," said Rebecca. "Come on guys, let's get our first photo done," said Rebecca, grabbing Mitch and standing next to Paige and Michael.

"Ok. Now that they are done, let's go," said Mitch to everyone, as he placed his hand in Rebecca's.

Pointing to their first ride as she watched the TV monitor, which was placed outside the ride so that customers could see if it suited them or not, Paige said, "Let's go on this one first." Smiling, she pulled Michael towards the ride and gestured for Mitch and Rebecca to follow. As they had purchased tickets at the front gate that took them to the front of the line for each ride, the four of them were able to go on each and every ride a lot quicker than others at the amusement park.

The whole afternoon flew by quickly and before they knew it, the day had turned into night and it was time to go home as the theme park was closing.

Paige looked around the room, as she stood in line with her mum at the photo store. "Mmm… look Mum, fairy floss. You want some?" gestured Paige, as she looked at the front counter where the cotton candy was stacked on a shelf.

Smiling, Rebecca said, "Yum, sure do. One of each colour."

"Piggy… it looks like they have three colours. Mind if I share?" said Paige.

"Yeah, that's Ok, sweetheart. Oh, and looks like they have some souvenirs too. I saw some throughout the theme park, that I wouldn't mind getting." said Rebecca, as they moved along in the line toward the registers.

Rebecca smiled as she couldn't remember having this much fun in a long time.

On the drive home they all talked about what rides they liked the best and the ride that was the scariest; along with what were the funniest things they saw and did. As laughter filled the car, Rebecca enjoyed watching her daughter's happiness, but most of all she loved spending time with her as she hadn't done that, or seen this side of Paige in a while. She also found out another thing about Mitch that she didn't know: that he liked theme park rides and how well he interacted with Paige. For a mother who was beginning a new romance in her life, Rebecca had been not only confused, but worried with how Mitch would fit into their life, once they arrived back in Perth. But from watching them both interact today, her concerns were not warranted.

With one hand on the steering wheel and the other hand holding Rebecca's, Mitch said to Rebecca, "Would you like to go out for diner tomorrow night? I know an amazing restaurant we can go to and I want to take you out and spoil you for the night."

"I would love to," said Rebecca, looking at Mitch with excitement.

"I have to work for a while in the morning, but after that we have the rest of the day and night to ourselves." Looking in the rear view mirror, Mitch said, "I know Michael is not working tomorrow Paige, so maybe you two can do something together."

"Maybe we can go for a drive and you can meet some of my friends?" said Michael.

"Great," said Paige, snuggling into Michael's side.

It was nine o'clock when they all arrived at the Portellico mansion and everyone was feeling tired from the day's excitement. Walking up the stairs they all said their goodnights and headed for their bedrooms.

When Mitch opened the door to his room and Rebecca walked on in, she said, "Why, thank you Mr Portellico." Smirking, she remembered that she had bought Mitch a gift today, but that she hadn't given it to him yet.

Walking over to her suitcase, Rebecca said, "Oh, I just remembered... I have a surprise for you. Sit on the bed and I will get it for you."

Mitch looked at her and smiled. "What is it?"

Luckily she had already wrapped it up before they went out, so that he couldn't see what it was when she gave it to him.

"You'll have to open it to see what it is," said Rebecca, playfully. Retrieving the item from her suitcase, she then walked over to Mitch and sat next to him on the bed.

Excited, Mitch ripped open the box quickly. Pushing the tissue paper to one side, his eyes lit up when he realised what she had bought him. "Wow... this is a fine-looking tie. I love it." His adoring smile melted her soul. He leant in and kissed her lips passionately. Pulling away slowly, he looked into her eyes, smiled and caressed the side of her face with his hand. "Thank you."

"You are welcome. Would Sir like to tie me up?" said Rebecca, mischievously.

He looked at Rebecca with a smirk on his face and said, "Yes, Sir would love to tie you up. But what I would really like to do tonight is just to cuddle up to you and savour our moments together."

"That sounds good too… you look tired, my sweet man," said Rebecca, sympathetically, as she brushed her hand through his hair.

"Yeah, I don't know if I am coming down with something, but I feel like my body has been zapped of its strength," said Mitch.

"Maybe after a good night's sleep you will feel better in the morning," said Rebecca, feeling his forehead. "I might go and have a shower before I go to bed."

"That sounds like a good idea. I will have one after you," said Mitch.

Dressed in her silk nighty, after having a long, hot shower, Rebecca turned the light off in the bathroom and headed for the bedroom. "It's all yours, sweet man," she called out, as she walked into a lamp-lit room.

With his back to her and curled up in a foetal position, Rebecca found Mitch under the covers of the bed asleep. His breathing was slow, and he was quietly snoring. Smiling, as she watched him sleep, Rebecca walked around to her side of the bed and hopped in. Turning off the bedside lamp, she cuddled into Mitch and closed her eyes. Finally relaxing after her fun-filled day of excitement, it didn't take her long and she was asleep too.

As the sunlight hit her face, Rebecca woke to find Mitch cuddled into her chest. *I am one lucky woman to have such a wonderful guy like this in my life*, thought Rebecca, studying his face.

As she continued to watch him sleep, Mitch stirred and his eyes opened. Looking at her smiling face, he smiled. "Morning, beautiful," said Mitch.

"Good morning yourself, gorgeous," said Rebecca. She kissed his lips with desire.

"Mmm you taste good," said Mitch. But he had a look of someone who had forgotten something. "Shit… what time is it?"

"It's six-thirty," said Rebecca, looking over at the digital clock on the bedside table.

He sat up quickly. "I have a meeting this morning at seven-thirty. I need to get moving. Sorry beautiful. I would love to stick around and have my way with you. But I can't."

"Are you sure I can't tempt you?" teased Rebecca.

Mitch shook his head and said, "Sorry… no."

She pouted, and watched him get out of bed.

He was showered and dressed in no time at all.

"Mmm, you smell nice. Yummy enough to eat," said Rebecca, watching him put his tie on.

"Sorry, babe. I have to go. See you later on today. Love you," said Mitch, as he walked over to the bed and gave her a quick kiss on her forehead goodbye and was gone out the door.

This has been such a good holiday so far. And Mitch… I couldn't have asked for a more wonderful man. Even his family are so nice. I sure feel lucky, thought Rebecca, who was lying flat on her back, looking at the ceiling. Looking over at the digital clock next to the bed, Rebecca decided to send a text message to Mitch, as she knew he wasn't driving this morning and would be able to answer her.

'I miss you already… don't be long, gorgeous. I love you too.'

She received one back straight away.

'Sorry we didn't spend time this morning together. I miss you already too, beautiful. By the way, I love my new tie. Thank you, it looks nice. See you around one-thirty and hopefully I can make up for rushing off this morning. Look forward to seeing you later.'

Smiling, she sent one back.

'Can't wait. ILU. See you later.'

Mitch smiled as he looked at his phone screen and then looked out the car window. *Can't believe I have this lovely lady in my life.*

What am I going to do today whilst Mitch is working? Paige has gone out on a picnic with Michael and everyone else is either working or had appointments to keep this morning, thought Rebecca, taking a sip of her tea, as she sat by herself at the large dining room table, looking outside. *Hmm, maybe I might go and get in some exercise. The Portellico grounds are huge, so maybe a run is what I need to burn off some of this energy.*

With her grey track pants, white tank top and running shoes on, Rebecca headed down the marble stairs, two at a time and out the front door, to go for a run around the property. Feeling the bitter cold wind hit her body and face, she decided to brave it and make a quick dash for the front gates to get herself warmed up.

As she reached the front gates and then headed back towards the house, Rebecca had the strangest feeling, like she was being watched. Looking over her shoulder and scanning the property from side to side as she continued to run, she couldn't see anyone and wondered if it was all in her mind, because she was alone at the enormous Portellico property. When she reached the front door step, Rebecca jogged on the spot for a few more minutes and then stopped for a much needed break. Turning around, she looked towards the front gates and its surrounding fence line as she leant forward to try and catch her breath. Smiling, she shook her head and walked inside; feeling silly for even entertaining the idea of someone watching her. Totally exhausted from her run and in need of a shower, Rebecca wandered upstairs to Mitch's bedroom to pamper herself.

The hot water felt wonderful on her skin and as always, made her feel refreshed and rejuvenated, as Rebecca stood under the square shower head, with her head down, letting it cascade over her shoulders and back. Once she had washed the conditioner out of her hair, Rebecca turned off the faucet and stepped out the shower onto a thick, black bathmat. Retrieving two white towels from the under cupboard of the vanity, she continued to dry herself and wrap her hair up in a towel.

Dressed in her lacy, black and opal green bra and panties, Rebecca walked out of the bathroom towards the wardrobe, where her clothes that she had purchased the day previous were hanging. Taking her new jeans and colourful blouse off the hangers, she decided to try them on in front of the mirror.

Hmm, these look nice on me, thought Rebecca, as she paraded around in front of the mirror.

With the sun now shining in through the large, double door windows into the bedroom, Rebecca sat on a armchair which was placed near the doors and felt the sun warming her back, as she bent over and placed her shoes on. With her hair brushed, but still wet from the shower, she decided to return to the bathroom and dry it off. But as she stood up, Rebecca once again had the feeling that someone was watching her. Knowing that she was the only one in the house besides some of the staff, she starting to feel a bit uneasy. Swallowing hard, she picked up her mobile from the bedside drawer and decided to ring Mitch.

"Hello, beautiful," said Mitch. "What you up to?"

"Hi… this may sound a bit strange and it might be because I am in a big house and no one is home, but I feel like I am being watched. I physically can't see anyone, but I felt it as well when I was taking a run this morning around the property. I am not sure what to do, as I don't usually scare this easy," said Rebecca, sitting on the bed, her breathing uneasy.

"Babe, you say you are alone in the house," said Mitch, wondering what could be going on at the house.

"Yes," said Rebecca, anxiously.

"In the top drawer of my bedside table there is a pair of binoculars. I want you to get them out and then go to the window and have a look around. If someone is out there, you will be able to see them. Will you be all right to do that?" said Mitch.

"Yes, Mitch. But you are scaring me," said Rebecca, as she kept Mitch on the phone and retrieved the binoculars. Standing next to the window, she scanned the front yard through the binoculars. "I don't see anyone, Mitch."

"Keep looking, babe," said Mitch, strumming his fingers on his desk.

When Rebecca looked further out near the property fence line, she saw a black SUV parked outside the property with a guy pointing what looked like a camera in her direction. Gulping, she became nervous. "Mitch, I think I know why I am feeling like I am being watched. There is a black van parked outside the property and this guy has a camera and I can see him watching the house. What do you think he is up to?"

"He's probably a photographer babe, that's all. He possibly photographed you running around the property this morning and is looking to get some more photos of anything that is happening at the house for the magazine he works for. Bloody bastards, they never give up. Don't worry, Bec. What I want you to do is, go out into the house and find a staff member and tell them. They will get rid of the photographer. I shouldn't be too much longer here and I will be home soon. If you get nervous, just hang around the staff and that should make you feel safer. Ok?" said Mitch.

"Ok. Thanks, Mitch. I feel silly ringing you, but I didn't know what else to do," said Rebecca, sitting on the chair next to the window.

"Hey, don't ever feel silly ringing me, about anything. Anyway I love hearing your voice, beautiful. How are you feeling now?" said Mitch.

"Yeah, I'm Ok. I will let you get back to your work. See you soon," said Rebecca, standing.

"Laters babe," said Mitch and he hung up.

Rebecca placed the binoculars back in the drawer and headed for the doorway. As she approached the marble staircase, she spotted one of the housemaids coming up the stairs with a feather duster in her hand, dusting the balustrade as she walked up.

"Good morning," said the maid.

"Hello... umm, I was wondering if you could please help me," said Rebecca, now standing on the same step as the maid. "I think there may be a photographer at the front gate who is snapping photos of me. Is it possible for someone to go and get rid of him?"

"Of course, ma'am. I will go and let the security guards know, and they can deal with the photographer."

"Thank you, so much," said Rebecca, breathing a sigh of relief.

"You are welcome ma'am," said the maid, smiling and briefly touching Rebecca's arm. She then turned and walked down the stairs.

Rebecca decided to return to the bathroom so that she could dry her hair. As she stood in front of the mirror with the hair dryer, she thought, *I can't believe the audacity of that photographer this morning. Cheeky bastard... I don't think I could handle that sort of intrusiveness in my life all the time.*

After drying her hair, Rebecca wandered downstairs and into the kitchen. *Might make a cuppa.*

"Good morning ma'am," said the male chef. "Is there anything I can get you this morning?"

"No thank you. I might make a cup of tea, if that's Ok?" said Rebecca.

"Yes ma'am, that is Ok. There are some cupcakes in the container on the bench, over there," said the male chef, gesturing to the bench where the coffee machine was set up over to the left of the room.

"Mmm, sounds good," said Rebecca, walking over to the side bench. Lifting the lid off the container she chose two small cupcakes and placed them on a plate, which she retrieved from the underneath cupboard. Placing them into the microwave to warm them up, she then made herself a cup of tea.

"It's a beautiful day outside today, ma'am," said the chef, hearing the microwave bell ding. "I can bring your morning tea out to the sunroom if you would like?"

"Oh, that would be nice. Thank you," said Rebecca, smiling. She wasn't used to this type of service.

As she leant back on the long sofa with her feet up and soaked in the rays of the sun, Rebecca thought about the events of the morning and her man, whilst she looked out to the lake and sipped on her tea. Shaking off how uneasy she felt from the presence of the photographer, she placed her mug down on the small table, which the chef had placed beside her, and picked up her book that Mitch had bought her. Scanning through the pages, she yawned and eventually her eyes became heavy as she became more comfortable.

The next thing she knew, someone was stroking her hair gently and saying, "Wake up, sleepy head."

When she opened her eyes, she smiled as Mitch's face came into her view.

"Hello," said Rebecca, sleepily.

"Hi, beautiful… I see you are reading the second book," said Mitch, pointing to the open book.

Rebecca look down at the book which was lying next to her, open at the last page she was reading. "Mmm… after what happened this morning, I thought I would come out to the sun room to get some rays, and I started reading it. I must have fallen asleep. What time is it Mitch?" said Rebecca, sitting up and placing her feet on the ground.

"It's three-thirty," said Mitch, sitting next to her.

"You had to work back?" asked Rebecca.

"Yes. Sorry… I did try to ring you on your mobile, but you didn't answer. So I rang the house and they told me you were out here asleep. So I told them not to disturb you," said Mitch, stroking her hair and looking at her lovingly.

"Ok. How was your day, anyway?" asked Rebecca, placing her hand on his left leg.

"Pretty hectic. I sure could do with another one of your massages though," said Mitch, rounding his shoulders backwards.

"Turn around, my sweet man," said Rebecca, smiling.

"Thanks." Mitch turned his back to her and she started his massage. His shoulders and neck had so many knots that it took her a while to knead them away.

Once she finished his massage, Rebecca asked, "Does that feel better?"

"Sure does. You have magic hands. I don't feel so tight anymore," said Mitch, shrugging his shoulders and turning back around. "My head is still pounding though. So I think I might go and get some headache medication and have a lie down, if that is Ok with you?"

Looking at his face and demeanour, she could see he was tired from his long day at work. "What about if we go to bed for a couple of hours' sleep? You look tired," said Rebecca, brushing her hand through his hair.

"Just what the doctor ordered. Sounds great," said Mitch. "Let's go." He stood up and placed his hand out front for her stand up.

With her head resting on the pillow, Rebecca watched Mitch take small, deep breaths and lightly snore as he fell into a deep sleep. Not tired, she slipped quietly out of the bed, trying not to wake him and made her way back down to the sun room to retrieve her book. She then visited the kitchen for a hot cup of tea, which she decided to take back to Mitch's bedroom. Once back in his bedroom, Rebecca sat down on the bed next to Mitch and continued to read her book, whilst she sipped on her much needed cup of tea.

CHAPTER SEVENTEEN

Rebecca heard a soft tapping sound at the door. Quickly she hopped off the bed and opened the door.

"Hi Mum. Are you busy?" said Paige.

"Shhh… Mitch is asleep," whispered Rebecca, closing the door. "What can I do for you?"

"Oh, sorry. I wanted to ask you if it would be all right if I go out to dinner tonight with Michael?" said Paige, excited.

"Umm… I can't see that being a problem. Are you chauffeur driven tonight?" said Rebecca, with a creased brow.

"Yes," said Paige.

"Ok. Do you know where he is taking you?" asked Rebecca.

"No. He said it was going to be a surprise. I'm a bit nervous, though," said Paige.

"If I know these Portellico men, then you will have a great time and the restaurant will be fantastic as well. Michael is such a nice young man," said Rebecca.

"He sure is. I think I might be falling for him, Mum," said Paige, enthusiastically.

"Just be careful, Paige. You know we are leaving on Sunday and how will you both deal with a long distance relationship?" said Rebecca, with a furrowed brow.

"Yeah I know. That's what I am concerned about too, Mum. I am just taking it one day at a time at the moment," said Paige.

"Anyway, I'm sure you know what you are doing. Well, enjoy yourself tonight, sweetie. Don't over think it," said Rebecca, as she gave Paige a hug.

"Thanks, Mum. I will see you tomorrow," said Paige, hugging her back.

Opening the door to the bedroom, Rebecca said in a low voice, "See ya, sweetie."

Entering the bedroom, Rebecca noticed that Mitch had woken and was sitting up in bed.

"Did you sleep well?" said Rebecca, as she approached the bed.

"Like a log. I feel much better now… hey I forgot to tell you; I have booked a nice romantic night for us at great restaurant tonight. It's booked for eight pm," said Mitch, looking up at her, as she stood beside the bed.

"Have you?" says Rebecca, excitedly.

"You will need to wear something dressy as it's that type of place," said Mitch.

"Ok. I had better start getting ready, as it is six-forty-five now," said Rebecca, looking at her watch.

By seven-thirty she was ready to go. Wearing her new blue opal dress with some grey strappy high heel shoes and her hair which was half up with a really pretty clip and the other half down, with some curls to soften her face, she twirled in front of the long mirror. Not one for much makeup, she put on a little bit of blush, mascara, and lip gloss.

When Rebecca finally stepped out of the bathroom to tell Mitch she was ready to go he said, "Wow… you look really nice in that dress. Is it new?" as he eyeballed her from head to toe.

"Thanks… I bought it the other day when I went shopping with your mom," said Rebecca, smiling. "You don't look too bad yourself, Mr Portellico," said Rebecca, noticing how handsome Mitch looked wearing some black trousers with a long sleeve white shirt.

"Why, thank you, Ms Landers," said Mitch, smiling. "Are you ready to go, as I have organised for the chauffeur to take us to a restaurant tonight?"

"That will be nice. I am looking forward to it," said Rebecca. "I just need to get my bag and I am ready to go."

"Great," said Mitch, placing his phone in his trouser pocket.

Snuggled up in each other's arms in the back seat of the limo, Mitch looked in the rear view mirror and instructed the chauffeur to go around to the back of the restaurant to drop them off, as the paparazzi were out the front, as usual. When the car came to a stop the driver came around to Rebecca's door and opened it for her, whilst Mitch got out the other door. Making their way from the car to the back door of the restaurant, a photographer was waiting in the wings, near a dumpster bin and he snapped their photo.

"Bloody bastards. They are getting so bold these days. They seem to know where we are," said Mitch, annoyed. Taking her hand, he pulled Rebecca forward into the restaurant to get away from the photographer.

"Hey... don't let that parasite wreck our night out," said Rebecca.

"You are right, Bec. Let's just forget about them and have a good night," said Mitch, placing his arm around her shoulders. Making their way through the kitchen and restaurant, to the front door, they were approached by the doorman.

"Good evening, Mr Portellico. Your table is ready for you and your lovely lady. Come this way," said the doorman. He nodded and indicated to Mitch and Rebecca's waiter to show them over to their table.

Following the waiter through the carpeted restaurant, Rebecca noticed that the restaurant was painted in a deep purple, with gold curtains and extravagant crystal lighting fixtures. The waiter seated them at a table for two near a floor length window, in a quiet part of the room, which was finished with fine white linen table clothes, and silver cutlery. He proceeded to let them know what the house specials were tonight and gently placed their napkins in their laps and waited patiently for them to make their selection.

The menu had a large variety of different dishes to choose from and whilst the waiter waited for them to make their selection, he organised some water for their table and poured out two glasses for them. Once Rebecca and Mitch decided on their drink and food orders, the waiter left them so he could organise their drinks.

"You look beautiful tonight, Bec," said Mitch, placing his hand on hers and looking into her eyes.

"Thank you," said Rebecca, leaning into him, as she smiled and kissed his warm lips.

It wasn't long before the waiter brought their drinks and entrée over to them. Mitch picked up the first piece of bruschetta and put it in front of Rebecca's mouth. Smiling, she took a bite and savoured the taste and Mitch did the same. Her heartbeat quickened as their rhythm was quite sensual. Her mind was no longer on food. Mitch reached over and held her hand again; his touch made her shiver with excitement. Rebecca felt like she could skip dinner and go home to relieve her sexual tensions.

"What are you thinking about?" asked Mitch, brushing the hair away from her face.

"About you, actually. And how much you have brought to my life. I can't believe how happy I am right now. I never want it to end," said Rebecca, looking into his blue eyes.

He smiled at her and says, "I feel the same way. You were on my mind all day. I hope it never ends either, as I love you so much." He leant in and kissed her lips tenderly.

"Excuse me, sir, madam, dinner is served," said the red-faced waiter, as he interrupted their affectionate moment.

Startled, Mitch and Rebecca looked up at the waiter and wondered how long he had been standing there.

Swallowing hard, the waiter said, "For madam, chicken marsala, with a garden salad." He placed the plate in front of Rebecca. "For sir, steak, medium rare, on a bed of mashed potatoes, with mushroom sauce, green asparagus, and baby carrots." He placed the plate in front of Mitch. "Would you like some ground pepper on your meals?"

"No, thanks," said Rebecca.

"Yes, please," said Mitch. He watched the waiter take the metre long pepper shaker and grind some pepper on his food. "Thank you."

"Enjoy," said the waiter, as he walked away.

Rebecca noticed that Mitch had a glazed expression about him as he looked out the full length window and chewed his food.

"You're quiet... what are you thinking about?" asked Rebecca.

He placed his hand over hers, smiled and said, "Umm... I do have something on my mind that I wanted to talk with you about. It's... well... I am not sure how you will feel, that's all."

Rebecca looked at Mitch with a furrowed brow and a puzzled smile, and said, "What is it? You can ask me anything or tell me anything, you know."

Mitch looked into her adoring eyes, thought about it for a few seconds longer and swallowed hard. *Here goes.* "Will you marry me... one day soon? I know we have only been together for nearly a week, but I have loved you from afar for at least one year."

Rebecca's eyes opened wide and she pulled her hand away from Mitch quickly. She wasn't expecting 'Will you marry me?' Not sure how to answer, she said. "Will you excuse me...? I need to go to the ladies." Standing, she could hear her heart pounding in her ears and feel the blood rushing to her face.

"Don't go... please," pleaded Mitch, standing.

Hesitant, she sat down. Taking a deep breath in and out, she fiddled with her hands in her lap.

Mitch pulled his chair back in and sat next to her, and taking her hand in his, he said almost pleadingly, "Tell me what you are thinking?"

Wavering for a few seconds, she answered. "I am not sure what to think, Mitch. I know we love each other; but it's only early days. We haven't even lived together yet and you may not like living with me as I can be difficult when I don't get my own way. There are so many things we don't even know about each other yet. I'm sorry.... I am just a bit shocked, that's all. Yes, I do want to get married again one day; but not soon. I want to get to know you better first. You know since we have been together, you are all I think about. I live, eat and dream Mitch Portellico at the moment. Sorry, I know I am rambling, but you did ask me what I was thinking," said Rebecca, looking into his eyes. Her brow creased inwards.

He looked at her for a minute and said, "So you would consider it one day?"

She nodded and said, "Of course I will. I do love you, Mitch. But I want to enjoy and explore what we have together first."

"Thank you for being so honest with me, Bec. I think what you are saying makes sense. So I will hold what I have in my pocket for a day when we have been together for a while and know each other more," said Mitch, touching his jacket pocket.

He now had her intrigued.

What does he have in his pocket? Rebecca thought to herself.

"That's not fair. You have just told me that you have something in your pocket for me and now I can't see it,"

"You want to have a look?" asked Mitch, raising his eyebrows and smirking.

She nodded in excitement. He pulled out a dark blue velvet box that looked like it might have jewellery in it. When he opened it, inside was the most beautiful ring Rebecca had ever seen: an oval shaped diamond on an 18 carat gold band. As she reached towards the ring, he shut the box quickly and put it in his jacket pocket.

She gulped and said, "You bought that for me?" *So beautiful. Wow, he has good taste. How lucky am I that this gorgeous ring might be on my finger one day.*

He nodded and said, "It says how I feel about you, Bec. And if you didn't know by now, I am in love with you."

Rebecca leant over and kissed him passionately and said, "I love you too."

"Would you like some dessert?" said Mitch, trying to change the subject away from something she clearly was not ready for yet.

"Ok... but only if I can have you with whipped cream all over," teased Rebecca.

He looked at her with a smirk on his face and said, "Did you want to go back home or maybe a nice hotel for the night?"

"Your parents' house is like a hotel anyway to me, so I don't mind. I will let you choose where we go," said Rebecca, shrugging her shoulders.

Mitch nodded, took his mobile phone out of his pocket and called the driver.

Summoning the waiter over, Mitch gave his credit card to him for their meals and drinks. Once Mitch had signed the credit card slip, they quickly left by walking through the back door of the restaurant and stepping straight into the waiting limo again.

"Thank you for a lovely dinner," said Rebecca, leaning into his body and kissing his cheek.

"You are welcome, beautiful," said Mitch, kissing her forehead.

As the limousine pulled away from the restaurant, Mitch pushed the button to place the screen up between the driver and them. Placing his hand on her knee, he slid his hand down Rebecca's right leg, near her vagina.

"Your skin is so soft and I want to take you here," said Mitch, as his teeth grazed her earlobe.

Rebecca's mind was racing as they caressed each other in ways that tormented their inner souls. His tongue and lips felt sensual and Rebecca felt her heart hammering as he sucked and kissed her neck wantonly.

Mmm, Seventh Heaven..., thought Rebecca, closing her eyes, as he continued to have his way with her.

She didn't know it yet, but Mitch had instructed the driver to take them to a hotel for the night.

"Sir... we are nearly here," stated the driver, through the car intercom.

Straightening their clothes, Rebecca and Mitch watched the Hilton hotel come into view. As the driver alighted from the car and came around to her door, Rebecca took a deep breath and tried to shake off how physically excited she was.

Stepping out of the limousine, Mitch said to the driver, "You can return home as we won't be needing you for the rest of the night. Oh, and I will give you a ring tomorrow when we need collecting."

"Yes, sir." The driver nodded and closed the limousine car door behind them.

Ushering her over to the left elevator, which was open, Mitch indicated for Rebecca to walk in. Pressing the button to the eleventh floor, the doors closed and they were the only two in the floor to ceiling mirrored elevator.

The sexual tension between them was electric and Rebecca's libido had just hit full throttle.

I want him… badly, thought Rebecca, as she stood beside Mitch, held his hand and looked into his hungry, carnal eyes and beamed.

Not caring who would see them on the elevator cameras, Mitch pulled Rebecca into his muscular body and kissed her lips wantonly. Within seconds she pushed him up against the elevator wall and enjoyed the flavours of his mouth, as their tongues intertwined. Their breathing, heavy, Mitch teased her right ear with his teeth and continued down to her neck, sucking and kissing as he went, whilst caressing her left breast with his hand. Pulling her left thigh up to his hip, he leant into her and she felt his hardened shaft on her inner thigh. Taking a deep breath inwards, Rebecca moaned as she continued to enjoy his mischievous torture.

They arrived at the eleventh floor, the elevator pinged and the doors opened. Dusting himself off, Mitch picked Rebecca up in his arms and stepped out of the elevator, knowing the room he had booked was not too far away. Rebecca cuddled into Mitch's chest and placed her head on his shoulder as he carried her to their room.

When they reached the doorway, Mitch said, "Can you get the key card out of my jacket pocket?"

She nodded and placed her hand into his jacket side pocket. Retrieving the key, she held it out in front of her and placed it into the red flashing door slot.

The room was dimly lit as they entered and straight away Rebecca noticed the red rose petals all over the white linen bed.

"Wow, this is beautiful. Did you do this today?" said Rebecca, scanning the room.

Mitch nodded, dropped their overnight bag he packed previously on the beige, L-shaped lounge and carried her into the candle-lit bathroom, where a foaming, hot steamy bath had been run. Placing her on the white tiled floor in a standing position, Mitch undressed Rebecca, without taking his eyes off her and she did the same to him. Once they were both undressed, he picked her up in his arms and they stepped into the bath.

As Mitch lowered her body into the water, Rebecca's skin developed goosebumps as she sensed the water was hot. As her body adjusted to the temperature of the water, she cuddled into the crook of Mitch's neck and saturated her awareness with the smell of his cologne, whilst Mitch got comfortable leaning back against the end of the long white bath and savoured their intimacy.

The enjoyment of being held by his strong arms was overwhelming for Rebecca. Relaxing, she closed her eyes briefly and said, "You are so good to me. Thank you for the rose petals and this lovely room... I'm sorry I didn't say 'yes' to your proposal tonight; but that won't last forever, as I know I do love you."

"You are most welcome and I know you love me. But, the only thing I don't know is when you will say yes. But I am prepared to wait," said Mitch, holding her tight in his arms. "Would you like some wine, Bec?"

"Sounds like a good idea," said Rebecca, slowly sitting up. She watched his soapy backside as he stepped out of the bath and poured them a drink of the chilled white wine he had ordered previously, which was standing in a bucket of ice next to the vanity.

"Thank you," said Rebecca, taking the two glasses from Mitch as he stepped back into the bath and leant back into position with his legs out front. Handing him his glass, Rebecca smiled and leant into his chest. They lay there for a few minutes in the foamy water, soaking up the ambience of the room and each other whilst they sipped their drinks.

"Sir would like to tie you up," said Mitch, smirking and wondering how far he could take this.

"At the moment... all I want to do is have hot sex with my man," said Rebecca, sitting up.

"Hmm... let me see... I think Sir can accommodate that request," said Mitch, taking the glass out of her hand and placing it on the tiles with his.

Mitch picked Rebecca up in his arms and stepped out of the bath onto the bath mat. Collecting a fluffy towel from the rack on the way, he carried her into the bedroom. As she lay naked on the side of the bed, Mitch leisurely dried her body off; slowly kissing and teasing every inch of her body as he dried her. Standing, Mitch walked over to their overnight bag, where he took out the tie she had bought for him and a blindfold as well.

Hmm… he has come prepared, thought Rebecca, her eyebrows raised as she placed her head on the pillow.

With a smirk on his face, he approached her in silence. Reaching the bed, he placed the tie on the bedside table, looked into her eyes briefly, and then placed the blindfold over her eyes.

"Mitch," said Rebecca. Her world was now in complete darkness.

He placed his pointer finger over her lips and said, "Shhh."

She lay there waiting for him to do something, but nothing was happening.

Sitting beside her on the bed, he leant in for a kiss.

She felt the sensation of his cold but tasty lips touch hers.

"Open your mouth," said Mitch, slowly pulling away, but watching her reactions.

Rebecca swallowed hard and does as she was told and parted her lips.

Mitch placed a glass near her lips and gently poured the wine into her mouth.

The sweet flavour of wine intrigued her as it hit her taste buds and slowly slid down the back of her throat. "Mmm."

Mitch smiled as he watched her enjoyment. Placing his pointer finger into the glass of wine, he then dripped some of the wine down onto her breasts. As the droplets ran off the side of her nipple, he lapped and sucked them, one by one, teasing her.

Panting, Rebecca thrust her heels upwards and arched her back off the bed when Mitch kneeled on the floor and lapped at her exposed clitoris. When he finished his relentless pleasure, he slowly placed two fingers into her vagina and started to pull them in and out. With her chin tilted towards the ceiling and the letter 'O' formed on her mouth, Rebecca moaned with pleasure as Mitch continued to watch her and become aroused, she gave into whatever her body desires.

"Please… no more," pleaded Rebecca. She was panting from his relentless torture.

"All in good time, my sweet lady," said Mitch, looking up at her. By the time he was finished, Rebecca was extremely wet and she relished the thought of him being inside her. Lying next to her, he took her blindfold off, kissed her lips wantonly and gently bit her bottom lip, pulling it towards him.

Breathless, Rebecca wiped the beading sweat from her top lip and watched him hop off the bed and open the bedside drawer, only to take out a condom. As she watched him roll the condom on his cock, she licked her lips with anticipation. She was ready.

At first they made love in rhythm with each other, slowly and sure of their love for one another. Eventually quickening his pace, she whimpered with delight and could feel that she was about to come. As her orgasm sprouted its wings, Rebecca's body grew goosebumps and she tried to catch her breath and contain her excitement when he continued to pound her vagina.

Without warning, Mitch pulled his cock out of her quickly and turned Rebecca over onto all fours. Kneeling behind her, he fucked her vigorously from behind, whilst holding onto her hips. It didn't take Mitch long before he came and they were breathless.

Slipping his limp penis out of her engorged vagina, he took his condom off and discarded it into the bin next to the bed.

"How was that?"

"Just what the doctor ordered," joked Rebecca.

Mitch laughed, and lay on the bed next to Rebecca. Wiping the sweat from his forehead, he placed his arm out for her to cuddle into his chest.

As they lay in each other's arms cuddling, Rebecca felt a sense of happiness and belonging. Smiling to herself, she wondered if she would ever feel this content as she did in this moment.

Exhausted, they cuddled into each other on top of the bed with the rose petals all around them and eventually fell asleep.

Subconsciously, Rebecca could hear Mitch's voice. With the room still in darkness, and only the moonlight seeping in through an opening in the curtains, Rebecca's eyes opened. Still naked, but now under the duvet, she felt for Mitch and realised he was no longer next to her. Looking over at the bedside digital clock, which was displaying a time of five-twelve in the morning, she heard Mitch talking to someone. As she wiped the sleep from her tired eyes she heard him say, "Bastards... they just can't help themselves. Why can't they just leave us alone?" There was a pause in his voice and then he said, "No, I haven't told her yet. She is asleep. I don't reckon she will be too happy, either." Wondering what was going on, Rebecca hopped out of bed and placed her satin dressing gown on, which was still in the overnight bag.

Walking into the room, her eyes met his.

He smiled briefly at her and said to whom he was talking, "I have to go. I will talk with you later."

"Hello gorgeous... you're up early," said Rebecca, her brow creased. Placing her hand over her mouth as she walked towards him, she silently yawned.

"Morning," said Mitch, standing. "Sorry... did I wake you?"

"Yep... but that's Ok. Everything all right?" wondered Rebecca.

"You're not going to like this, Bec... we have made the front page of the TGM magazine. They have photos of you and me at the restaurant last night and they also have photos of us at the airport and of you at the house when you were jogging. Sorry, you must be annoyed at me," said Mitch, knowing Rebecca liked her privacy.

With her eyebrows raised, Rebecca said, "Unbelievable. They don't miss a trick, do they?" It hadn't even dawned on her yet what this would mean for their relationship or their privacy.

"Any chance they get, they take it, I can tell you," said Mitch, frustration across his face.

Rebecca yawned and walked over to him. "Come here... give me a hug," said Rebecca, pulling him in close and placing her arms around his waist. "I am not annoyed at you and this is not your fault. Don't worry, it's only pictures and idle gossip. The most important thing is that we know what's true or false in what they write in that magazine. Come back to bed and let's cuddle up and go back to sleep."

Pulling away from her slowly, Mitch looked at Rebecca with a furrowed brow. "You're not mad at me for what has happened then?"

"No… why would I be mad at you? You can't control what the paparazzi do," said Rebecca, frowning.

"God, you are one special lady… so forgiving." His blue eyes searching her unperturbed face.

"What's there to forgive?" said Rebecca, looking into his adoring eyes.

Tracing his right hand down the side of her face, he looked into her eyes and said, "I love you so much, my sweet lady. And I know my timing wasn't right last night when I asked you to marry me, but I do wish you would marry me soon. I feel we are meant to be together."

"It's funny you should bring that up, you know, getting married," said Rebecca, remembering her dream. "Just before I woke up this morning, I was dreaming of what our wedding would be like and when I woke up I remember smiling and feeling so happy and content."

Mitch smiled at her and said, "Come on, let's go back to bed. I want to cuddle up to your beautiful body."

Lying on her side facing Mitch, with her hand propping her head up off the bed, Rebecca gazed into his blue eyes and said, "Yes," and then kissed his lips passionately.

He looked at her, puzzled, and asked, "What are you saying 'yes' to?"

"I am saying 'yes' to marrying you soon," said Rebecca, smiling.

Mitch sat up quickly. "Am I dreaming? I thought you just said, 'yes' to marrying me," said Mitch, with raised eyebrows, smiling.

Rebecca kissed him again and said, "You're not dreaming, my gorgeous man. I love you and yes, I want to marry you."

"Are you sure?" asked Mitch, his brow furrowed. "I don't want to push you into something you are not ready to do. What changed your mind?"

"Well… when I woke from my dream of marrying you, I felt like the most luckiest woman alive. It just felt right. Hard to explain, but in that moment I reckon I knew that I wanted to marry you," said Rebecca.

Without a word, Mitch jumped out of bed and ran into the lounge room. When he returned he had the ring box in his hand. Turning the light on, he got down on one knee next to the bed. "Will you marry me?"

Rebecca sat up quickly and with a grin from ear to ear, she said, "Yes."

Taking the ring out of the box and placing it on her finger, Mitch looked into her loving eyes and then kissed her lips fervently. As Rebecca pulled away slowly from his pleasurable touch, she looked down at the ring on her finger and smiled.

"It's beautiful and it fits perfectly," said Rebecca, looking into his excited eyes. Moving her hand left then right to see how the ring looked on her finger and the way it sparkled, she knew that even though they had only just become acquainted, she had made the right decision. *Why do I need to wait? Trying to justify it doesn't make sense.*

"Beautiful… just like the lady wearing it," said Mitch, watching her excitement.

Rebecca smiled and clutched her hand to her chest. "I love you, Mitch Portellico. Come to bed and we can celebrate."

Turning off the lights and discarding his clothes to the floor, a naked Mitch hopped back into bed. Leaning over his fiancé, who had stripped naked and was lying on the pillow, he stroked the hair away from her face and kissed her eyelids, one by one, wantonly. Rebecca moaned with desire as he kissed, then sucked her ear and neck, giving her a satisfying orgasm. As they made love to celebrate their engagement to each other, they both wondered in that moment, if life could get any better.

CHAPTER EIGHTEEN

Rebecca's eyes fluttered open slowly and she tried to adjust to the light coming in from the mid-morning sun through a large glass window next to her bed. Lying flat on her back, her eyes darted from one side of the sterile smelling room to another as she realised she had something lodged in her throat which was making it hard to swallow. Gagging, she reached for the tube hanging out of her mouth and tried to pull it out.

"Mrs Landers… it's Ok," said Nurse Hazel, standing next to the bed, moving Rebecca's hand away from the tube. "You're in hospital. Wait one moment and I will take the tube out." She pressed the emergency button behind the bed.

Rebecca's large black pupils filled her wide frightened eyes and her breathing became rapid as she tried to ascertain what was going on.

Within seconds, the door burst open quickly to Rebecca's single room, and an older nurse came rushing over to the bed. "Good… you're awake. Let's see if we can get this tube out of your mouth and make you a bit more comfortable."

Rebecca looked into the older, reassuring nurse's eyes and tried to calm her anxiety as she gagged.

"Let's turn off the ventilation machine and disconnect it from the tube," said Nurse Charlotte, reaching over to the ventilation machine behind her and pressing the blue button. Taking a suction hose from the wall at the back of the bed, the grey headed nurse placed it down the ventilation tube and sucked out any sputum that might be left in the tube and Rebecca's mouth.

"It's Ok, Rebecca. We are nearly done," said Nurse Hazel, looking into Rebecca's worried eyes.

"Ok… let's get this tube out," said Nurse Charlotte, as she fastened the suction hose onto the back wall. Peeling the tape off Rebecca's face, which was holding the tube in place, she leant over Rebecca and said, "Cough."

Rebecca did as she was told.

"It's Ok," said Nurse Hazel, watching Rebecca's eyes widen as she gagged on the tube the other nurse was pulling out quickly.

"That better?" asked Nurse Charlotte to Rebecca.

Rebecca nodded.

"Right… do you know where you are?" asked Nurse Charlotte.

"Hos…hospital?" questioned Rebecca, in a hoarse voice.

"Yes that's correct. How is your pain level from one to ten? One being good and ten being bad," asked the Nurse Charlotte.

Rebecca held up five fingers.

"Five…so bearable then?" said Nurse Charlotte.

Rebecca nodded.

"Ok. Let's see if we can sit you up a bit," said Nurse Charlotte, pressing the button on the side of the bed to elevate Rebecca's upper half of her body. "How does that feel?"

Rebecca gave her the thumbs up signal.

"Can you go and get a jug of water and a cup with a straw for Mrs Landers?" said Nurse Charlotte to the Nurse Hazel.

"Yes ma'am," said Nurse Hazel, walking towards the doorway.

"How's the throat?" said Nurse Charlotte to Rebecca.

"Sore," said Rebecca, with a hoarse voice.

"Hmm, let's see if this water will help you," said Nurse Charlotte, watching Nurse Hazel walk back into the room with the water jug.

Rebecca watched Nurse Hazel pour her a cup of water and place it near Rebecca's lips with a straw. "Take a sip, slowly."

As Rebecca took a small sip of the water and let it slide down the back of her throat, she gagged a bit and said, "Can I have some more?" Taking another sip from the straw, and then another, Rebecca's throat soon felt a little bit better.

"Better?" asked Nurse Hazel.

Rebecca nodded. "Yes." As she swallowed and the saliva hit the back of her throat, she cringed at the razor blade-like pain that hit her throat.

"Sore?" said Nurse Hazel.

Rebecca nodded.

"We can rectify that. We'll get you some Panadol for the pain," said Nurse Hazel.

"Right... we might get some obs done on you, Mrs Landers," said Nurse Charlotte, pulling the heart rate monitor machine closer to the bed and placing the cuff on Rebecca's right arm.

Nurse Hazel then placed a pulse oximetry on Rebecca's pointer finger to measure Rebecca's oxygen levels at the same time.

"That all looks good," said Nurse Charlotte, checking the machine for a reading.

"I am just going to check your temperature," said Nurse Hazel, pressing the ear thermometer tip into Rebecca's left ear. "Hmm... that's good too."

Rebecca smiled as she looked over at the young, dark skinned nurse and noticed her name badge, which was pinned to her shirt. *Hazel Mahoney*.

Nurse Charlotte looked up at the stand which held a bag of saline that was attached to Rebecca's cannula in her arm. "Can you get another bag of saline for Mrs Landers, oh and some Panadol as well?"

"Yes ma'am," said Nurse Hazel.

"Are you hungry at all Mrs Landers?" asked Nurse Charlotte.

Rebecca nodded. 'Yes." *Charlotte Wilson*, thought Rebecca, noticing her name badge.

"We'll see about getting you something to eat," said Nurse Charlotte, checking her watch and smiling.

"I believe someone is awake... how's it all going in here?" asked the attending doctor, as he walked into the room.

"We've just done some obs on Mrs Landers and she is looking good," said Nurse Charlotte, handing over Rebecca's hospital notes to the doctor.

"Nice to see you awake, Rebecca. I'm Doctor Smitt." He stood at the foot of her bed.

Rebecca smiled.

"How's the head?" asked Doctor Smitt.

Rebecca frowned and caught a glimpse of herself in the television monitor. Touching her head, she felt the bandage that was around her skull.

"I am assuming from the look on your face you are not quite sure what I am talking about?" said Doctor Smitt.

Rebecca shook her head sideways. "No." Her heart rate accelerated.

"Do you remember having a brain tumour operation?" asked Doctor Smitt.

"Yes."

"Good. Do you know what day or date it is?" asked Doctor Smitt.

"Saturday…?" said Rebecca, her voice hoarse. She wasn't really sure.

"Right," said Doctor Smitt, looking from Rebecca to the older nurse. "When is the neurosurgeon due to come in and see Mrs Landers?"

"Umm…" said the older nurse, taking the medical notes from the attending doctor. "It looks like Dr Ness will be visiting today sometime." She pointed to the chart alerting the attending doctor to notes Dr Ness had left previously.

"Ok… Rebecca, I might let you get some rest now and I will come back later and see you," said Doctor Smitt.

"Ok," said Rebecca, frowning. She watched him walk towards the doorway with Nurse Charlotte. As they reached the corridor to her room, Rebecca heard them discussing her case but couldn't quite hear what they were saying.

"How are you going?" asked Nurse Hazel, as she entered the room.

"Yeah… Ok," said Rebecca, watching the nurse hang a bag of saline and another bag for pain relief on the stand.

"Would you like to watch some television? Or maybe I can get you something to read?" asked Nurse Hazel.

"Maybe television," said Rebecca, looking at the TV on the wall in front of her bed.

"Here's the remote. You just press the green button to turn it on and press the arrow buttons to change channels" said Nurse Hazel, indicating to the buttons on the remote.

"Ok. Thanks," said Rebecca, pressing the button to turn the TV on. It was automatically on low sound.

"I believe someone is hungry?" said the kitchen delivery attendant, as she carried a tray of food into Rebecca's room.

Rebecca looked at the food on the tray as it was placed on her table and wheeled in front of her. "Mmm… looks yummy."

"Enjoy," said the kitchen delivery attendant, smiling.

Rebecca smiled. "Thank you."

"Here… I will help you to sit upright a bit further," said Nurse Hazel, pressing the button on Rebecca's bed.

"Thank you."

"Is there anything you need help with?" said Nurse Hazel.

"Umm… Ok," said Rebecca, watching the nurse take the plastic cover off the plate of bacon carbonara and placing it down on the table. "Actually, can I ask if you can call my partner and daughter? I would love to see them." Rebecca's voice was low and hoarse.

"Sure. I am certain Mr Landers is still here. He only went down to get a coffee just before you woke today," said Nurse Hazel, looking over at the chair he had been sleeping in the night previous, which had a white cotton blanket sprawled across it. "I will give him a ring. I'll be back in a moment."

"Thank you," said Rebecca, as she slowly tried to cut up her pasta. Her hands seemed to feel weak, but she assumed it was because of the operation.

As she waited for the nurse to return, Rebecca became full from only a couple of mouthfuls of food and wondered why every time she swallowed, her throat felt like swallowing razor blades. Placing her fork down on the plate and pushing the mobile tray away from her, she yawned. Feeling a bit dizzy, she closed her eyes, and decided to take the opportunity for some rest.

Opening her eyes, Rebecca heard the sound of gushing air and realised from touching her nose, that the nurse had placed a nasal cannula up her nose. She remembered waking briefly at one stage during the afternoon when the nurse was checking her obs, but then went straight back to sleep.

Hmm… maybe my breathing wasn't quite right, so that is why I have the air tube up my nose, thought Rebecca, as she felt the plastic tubing around her ears.

Turning on her left side, she looked out the large window of her darkened room and seen the street lights on. With cars parking in the car park across from the hospital, she watched hospital staff hurrying across the car park to avoid the rain.

Night time already. I must have been asleep for a while. Humph… my head is aching. Where is the buzzer to call the nurse? thought Rebecca, as she rubbed her forehead.

"Hello," said a familiar voice from the right hand side of the room.

Sitting up quickly, she turned to see the shadow of a person sitting in a chair next to her bed. Even though the voice was familiar, she couldn't quite see who it was. Pressing the light button on her remote, the room became lit and she stared in bewilderment at who was sitting before her. With her heart hammering, Rebecca's eyes widened and her breathing became rapid. Pulling the blanket up to her chin, she started to shake.

Jackson… am I dreaming? thought Rebecca.

"Sorry… did I scare you?" said Jackson, watching the alarmed look on his wife's face.

"What… but… how. How are you here?" said Rebecca, confused.

"Are you Ok, Rebecca?" asked Jackson, as he stood beside the bed and placed his hand on her hand.

She quickly pulled her hand away from under his and moved back against the beds headboard. "How come I can see you?"

"What are you talking about, Rebecca?" said Jackson, worried that his wife had lost her mind.

Rebecca blinked slowly in bewilderment. "Jackson, I hate to tell you this, but I buried you over twelve months ago. You had a heart attack and passed away. But… but I don't understand how you are here." *Ghost…*

"Rebecca... that is ridiculous. I think we might call the nurse," said Jackson, walking towards the doorway.

Jackson walked towards the nurse's station, which was located at the end of the corridor. "Excuse me," said Jackson.

"Yes, sir," said the Irish, male nurse.

"My wife... Rebecca Landers... she seems to be disoriented," said Jackson, leaning on the counter.

"What do you mean?" said Nurse O'Farrell.

"She seems to think that I passed away. I don't understand why she is thinking that," said Jackson, with a furrowed brow.

"That is strange. Let's go and see her," said Nurse O'Farrell, placing his stethoscope around his neck.

"Knock, knock, Mrs Landers," said Nurse O'Farrell, as he continued to walk into the room.

"Come in," said Rebecca, who was still sitting up in bed with the blanket pulled up to her chin.

"How are you feeling? Any pain?" said Nurse O'Farrell, as he approached Rebecca's bed.

Jackson walked in behind him, but didn't say a word.

"No, I'm not in pain," lied Rebecca, as she looked around him to where Jackson was standing.

"We might just check your obs, Rebecca," said Nurse O'Farrell.

"Can you see him?" whispered Rebecca to Nurse O'Farrell, as he placed the pulse oximetry on her pointer finger.

"You mean your partner, Jackson?"

Rebecca nodded.

"Yes," said Nurse O'Farrell.

"But I buried him over twelve months ago. So how can he be here?" questioned Rebecca.

"What year is it, Rebecca?" asked Nurse O'Farrell, as he pulled the heart monitor towards Rebecca.

"It's 2014. What does that have to do with Jackson?" said Rebecca, with a creased brow. The tears started to well in her eyes.

Hmm... she does seem to be disoriented. Considering its only 2012, thought Nurse O'Farrell.

"Nothing, Mrs Landers," said Nurse O'Farrell, as he looked at the heart monitor read-out. "Hmm… your heart rate is high. We might go get you some medication."

"Ok," said Rebecca, lying down on the bed. *What is going on?* thought Rebecca, her eyes darting from side to side and then to Jackson.

"I will be back in a few minutes Mrs Landers," said Nurse O'Farrell, indicating to Jackson to follow him out of the room with a nod of his head.

"Follow me," mouthed Nurse O'Farrell to Jackson.

"You see what I mean?" stated Jackson.

"Yes…I'm not sure what is going on. I think I will get her a sedative and try to get her back to sleep. That may help. Considering she has been in coma for two weeks, this may have played with her mind. After I have gotten her settled for the night I will call her neurosurgeon and see what he has to say. Maybe he can shed some light on what is going on," said Nurse O'Farrell. "But in the meantime, I think it might be a good idea for you to stay out of her room. Your presence seems to be upsetting her."

"Right…" said Jackson, shaking his head. His heart was breaking for the love of his life. "If there is nothing I can do here and it frightens her to see me, I think I might as well go home for the night. What do you think?"

"I think that would be a good idea Mr Landers. Come back in the morning. By then the neurosurgeon would have been in and I would say that we might be able to make sense of all this," said Nurse O'Farrell. "Don't worry, we will take good care of her."

"Thank you," said Jackson, shaking his hand. "Are you here tomorrow?"

"Yes. I will be here tomorrow night. When you come in the morning there will be another nurse on. But don't worry, I will write up some notes on what has transpired here tonight," said Nurse O'Farrell.

"Great. Well, I will be off," said Jackson, taking his parking ticket out of his back pocket. "See you tomorrow night then." He hadn't slept in his own bed since Rebecca had been in a coma.

"Drive safely, Mr Landers," said Nurse O'Farrell.

"Knock, knock, Mrs Landers," said Nurse O'Farrell.

"Come in," said Rebecca, through her tears.

"Here is some medication for you Mrs Landers. Take this tablet and we will get you settled in for the night hey," said Nurse O'Farrell, handing over the tablet in a small clear container.

"Thank you," said Rebecca, sitting up to take the tablet and drink some water. "What is going on?"

"I think all will reveal itself in the morning ma'am," said Nurse O'Farrell. "Let's get you more comfortable." He placed her bed in a semi flat position and repositioned her pillow and the sheet and blanket on her bed. Pulling up the rail on both sides of the bed, he then positioned the call button remote above her head. "The call button remote is above you, dear. Please don't hesitate to ring during the night if you need me." He then turned off her light switch at the head of the bed.

"Thank you," said Rebecca, closing her eyes.

Nurse O'Farrell walked towards the lit corridor and closed the door behind him.

CHAPTER NINETEEN

"Good morning, Rebecca," said Dr Ness, as he entered the room and found Rebecca eating her breakfast. "I hear you had an interesting night. How are you this morning?" He sat in the chair next to her bed.

"Hello. Much better, thank you," said Rebecca, placing her spoon down on the tray.

"So… what year is it Rebecca?" asked Dr Ness.

"It's 2014. Why do you ask?" said Rebecca. She was tired of the same questions.

"Rebecca… I think you may be experiencing some sort of brain trauma. And considering you have been in a coma for two weeks, this may explain why you think it's 2014, when in fact it's only 2012," said Dr Ness, watching her every reaction.

"What… I don't understand. I was in a coma for two weeks. What, since my surgery?" asked Rebecca, with a furrowed brow.

"Yes, I am afraid so. When I operated on you two weeks ago, the surgery went fine. But you didn't want to wake when we got you into recovery," said Dr Ness.

"Oh, right. So if I have been sleeping for two weeks, or in a coma as you put it, why do I now think it's 2014?" asked Rebecca. "Doesn't make sense."

"I can't answer that one. Do you feel like you have been dreaming, possibly?" asked Dr Ness.

"Maybe. I don't know. But what I do know is that Jackson is alive. I saw him last night," said Rebecca.

"What makes you think Mr Landers had died?" said Dr Ness, looking at his patient's folder notes.

"I remember it as plain as day. His death, the funeral, my daughter Paige and I upset. And I think the most upsetting memory now is that after Jackson passed away, I had moved on with another man. These memories all seem real to me Dr Ness," said Rebecca, rubbing her temples.

"Hmm...I don't know what to say," said Dr Ness, standing. "Let's get an MRI done this morning and see what's going on in there."

"Ok. So when will you be back to see me?" asked Rebecca.

"I will come by this afternoon and we can then chat about your MRI results," said Dr Ness.

"Ok. Thanks" said Rebecca, anxiously.

Dr Ness walked towards the doorway, stopping to chat with the Nurse Hazel in the doorway. "I will be back this afternoon. Can you please organise for an MRI to be done for Mrs Landers."

"Yes," said Nurse Hazel, taking Rebecca's notes from the doctor. "I will ring the fourth floor now for an appointment." She continued to follow the doctor out to the nurse's station.

"Thank you," said Dr Ness, as he walked towards the elevator.

Rebecca pressed the TV remote button. As the morning Sunrise show came on the screen and they reiterated that it was indeed 2012, the tea lady popped her head in the doorway.

"Cup of tea or coffee this morning ma'am?" asked the curly headed tea lady.

"Yes, please. A cup of tea, white with one sugar, would be great. Thanks," said Rebecca.

Pouring her cup of tea, the tea lady said, "Beautiful day outside today."

Rebecca looked over at the window and noticed the clear blue sky outside. "Sure is. Thank you for the tea," said Rebecca, as she watched the tea lady place it on her tray.

"You're welcome," said the tea lady, as she walked towards the doorway.

"How are you going with your breakfast this morning?" said Nurse Hazel, as she entered the room.

"Yeah, Ok," said Rebecca, looking down at the tray.

"Would you like some help with spreading the vegemite and butter on your toast, Mrs Landers?" asked Nurse Hazel.

"Yes, please," said Rebecca. Her hands were still having trouble with some actions. It seemed like her brain didn't want to tell her hands what to do sometimes. As she watched the nurse manipulate the blunt knife she thought, *humph… she makes it look all so easy.*

"Here we go," said Nurse Hazel, as she placed the toast in front of Rebecca.

"Thanks," said Rebecca, picking it up and taking a small bite. *Hmm, my throat is not so sore this morning. Thank goodness.*

"How would you feel about getting out of bed this morning and maybe even having a shower?" asked Nurse Hazel.

"I'll try," said Rebecca. Even though she was feeling weak, she was looking forward to getting off the hard mattress. Her body felt sore from lying down for so long.

Out of breath and feeling weary from her shower, Rebecca hopped back into her bed. With her teeth brushed and her hair towel dried, she lay upright in the bed and watched the TV, nodding on and off until lunch was served.

The kitchen attendant carried in her lunch and placed it on the tray in front of Rebecca. Sitting upright in bed, she said, "Thank you."

"You're welcome," said the attendant, walking towards the door. "You have a chicken and salad sandwich."

"Great," said Rebecca, as she looked from the kitchen attendant to the TV that was now displaying the midday movie. As she unwrapped her sandwich, she thought, *I don't feel like eating this.*

As she took the first bite of her sandwich, the door opened to her room and a male nurse with a wheelchair walked in. "Hello, Mrs

Landers. I'm Eddy… are you ready to go have your MRI done?"

"Umm… yeah, I suppose."

"Don't worry, your lunch will be there when you get back," said the nurse.

"Oh, good. Can you help me get out of bed?" said Rebecca, still feeling weak.

"Yes ma'am," said Nurse Eddy, pulling her blankets off and helping her to the wheelchair.

Rebecca then noticed that the catheter had been taken out whilst she was asleep, because it was no longer attached to her. *You think I would have woken up when they took it out. Humph, maybe it's something to do with the coma why I didn't wake.* Frowning she wondered what else had been going on around her whilst she slept, considering she was usually a light sleeper.

"Ok. Off we go," said Nurse Eddy, wheeling her through the doorway.

"Is Rebecca Landers all right to have visitors?" asked Mitch, as he stood at the nurse's station overlooking the counter. Jackson had seen Mitch the previous night and had spoken to him about Rebecca being awake, amongst other things. Mitch had two hours to spare from work, so he thought he would pop into to see his friend and neighbour.

"Yes, sir. But she is having an MRI at the moment. She should be back in about ten minutes though, if you care to wait," said the nurse, looking up the patient records on the computer.

"Oh, Ok. What room is she in?" asked Mitch, looking at the time on his mobile phone.

"104, just over on the right hand side, sir," said the nurse, pointing to where the room was located down the corridor.

"Thanks. I am assuming it will be Ok for me to wait in Rebecca's room?" stated Mitch.

"Yes, sir," said the nurse, looking from the computer to Mitch.

"Thank you," said Mitch, making his way to her room. Entering Rebecca's room, Mitch made his way over to the window and stood there for a few seconds looking out and into the clear blue sky. When he heard voices from behind him, he turned to see a male nurse wheeling Rebecca into the room.

Mitch smiled and said, "Hello, Rebecca."

Rebecca's face lit up as soon as she saw Mitch. "Hello."

Mitch waited for the male nurse to help Rebecca back into her bed and leave the room. Watching her get comfortable, he said, "How are you?"

"I'm good. A bit weak, but good," said Rebecca. Her heart was beating a million miles a minute.

Mitch leant in and gave her a hug.

Hugging him back, Rebecca lingered a bit too long as she caught the scent of his cologne. Even though this didn't make sense, the feelings she had towards Mitch, she couldn't help but feel some connection to him from her dreams, she was assuming.

"I bought you some flowers to cheer you up," said Mitch, pulling away and gesturing to the assortment of flowers in a brightly coloured yellow cardboard box, that he had placed on the window ledge.

"Oh… thank you. That's nice of you," said Rebecca, smiling. "They're beautiful."

"You're welcome. So… it looks like you haven't finished your lunch," said Mitch, looking at the food on her tray.

"Yeah, they came and got me before I could finish it. Take a seat, Mitch," said Rebecca, gesturing to the chair. "I'm not hungry now. Might have some more later."

"Ok. Thanks," said Mitch, sitting on the leather chair. "So, have you been able to walk yet?"

"Not really. Only to the shower so far. But now that they have taken the catheter out, maybe they might get me up walking some more. My legs feel heavy though," said Rebecca, looking from Mitch to her legs. "I'm just glad to be alive, anyway."

"Yeah, I bet. I know Jackson and Paige were worried about you when you were in a coma. Do the doctors know what has caused it yet?" said Mitch.

"No… that's why I had the MRI done this arvo. The neurosurgeon said he would pop by later on this afternoon and let me know the results," said Rebecca.

"Oh, that's good," said Mitch. "Bit of a worry, hey?"

"You're not wrong... I even thought it was 2014," said Rebecca, shaking her head as she remembered her thoughts and dreams from when she was in a coma. She still wasn't quite sure how to process it all yet. It all felt so real to her, especially now Mitch was standing in front of her.

"What made you think it was the year 2014?" asked Mitch, with a furrowed brow.

"I don't know... it... it all felt so real, you know. One minute I was a widow and the next thing I knew was when I woke up, Jackson was sitting beside me. Strange..." said Rebecca, shaking her head. "Like I said, it all felt so real. I am still trying to come to terms with what is reality and what was, I think, a long dream. You were even in my dreams."

"That is weird, hey," said Mitch, frowning. "Me, in your dreams. Well, that must have been a nightmare?" He laughed.

Rebecca smirked. *Humph... if he only knew.*

"So, how long are they keeping you in here for?" asked Mitch.

"Not sure. I suppose I will find out this arvo from the neurosurgeon."

"Right. Where is Jackson today? I was a bit surprised to not find him here," said Mitch.

"I'm not sure," said Rebecca, her brow furrowed. "I might have frightened him off."

"Frightened him off... I don't think so. Why do you say that?" asked Mitch.

Rebecca twitched her mouth from side to side. "Well, one of my supposed dreams was that Jackson had died. You've got no idea what it was like waking up and seeing him sitting next to me when I thought in my mind he was dead. I even remember going to his funeral and how miserable Paige and I felt. It certainly was weird," said Rebecca, rubbing her forehead.

"Really... you dreamt Jackson was dead? God, that is weird. I wonder what is going on in that little pea sized brain of yours?" joked Mitch.

Rebecca laughed. "Thanks, Mitch. I needed to have a laugh. I have missed the banter we usually have," said Rebecca, smiling. "You're such a good friend." *Friend… humph.*

"Yeah… I have missed our playful banter too. Anyway, I'm just glad you are awake, hey." Looking down at his mobile phone, Mitch said, "Well, I had better get going. By the time I walk down to my car and drive over to Morley to meet with a client, I will just make it in time."

"Ok. Thanks for coming, Mitch. And thanks for the flowers too," said Rebecca, smiling, wishing he would have been able to stay longer.

Mitch leant in and gave her a quick kiss on the cheek and hug goodbye. Rebecca enjoyed his touch way too much.

"You're welcome. Glad you liked them," said Mitch, as she pulled away and walked towards the doorway. "I will give you a ring tomorrow to see how you are going. See you soon. Take care."

"Yep, I will. See ya," said Rebecca. By the time he had left Rebecca's heart was racing.

Gazing aimlessly out the window of her room, Rebecca wondered when the doctor would arrive. Yawning, she decided to have a rest whilst she waited for him to come in with the test results.

"Knock, knock," said Dr Ness, who walked into the room with the nurse currently looking after Rebecca's needs. "Hello, Rebecca."

"Hi, Dr Ness," said Rebecca, as she watched him walk into her room. She turned off her TV and placed her bed in an upright position.

Looking at the chart in her folder, he said, "I have had a look at your latest MRI scan… and, well… everything looks fine."

"Humph… Ok," said Rebecca, frowning.

"In fact, if all your vitals and test results come back good today, we may send you home tomorrow," said Dr Ness, hoping Rebecca was happy to be hearing she could go home.

"Home… right. So why do I still think it's 2014?" asked Rebecca, frowning.

"I can't answer that, Rebecca. It's strange what the brain can do or think sometimes… now, when you go home tomorrow, I want complete bed rest. You are to take it easy for at least the first couple of weeks.

Then I want you to come and see me in a fortnight's time," said Dr Ness, placing the folder back in its holder at the foot of her bed.

Rebecca nodded, "Ok." She had been hoping he had some answers for her.

"I will write out some prescriptions for medication I want you to take when you are at home and leave them with the nurse. If you have any questions or don't feel well when you get home, please don't hesitate to call me," said Dr Ness.

"Right. Ok," said Rebecca, looking from the doctor to the nurse.

"Ok… so I will see you in a fortnight," said Dr Ness, holding his hand out to shake hers.

"Ok. Thank you," said Rebecca, shaking his hand. She watched him then walk toward the doorway.

When Rebecca looked towards the doorway she saw Jackson leaning against the metal frame with his arms folded across his chest. His shabby clothing, messy hair and unshaven look made him look exhausted.

"I will be back in a few minutes, Mrs Landers," said the nurse, following the doctor out the room.

"Ok," said Rebecca. She gulped hard when she saw Jackson walking towards her bed.

"Hello," said Jackson, as he leant in to give his wife a hug.

"Hello… you look how I feel," said Rebecca, hugging him back.

"Yeah… I didn't get much sleep last night. How are you?" said Jackson, sitting on the bed.

"I'm Ok. Dr Ness said that if all goes well I can go home tomorrow morning," said Rebecca, looking over his tired facial features.

"Oh, that's good," said Jackson, hoping she had wanted to even return home, considering what had transpired between them the previous night. "It will be nice to finally have you home."

"Yeah, I am looking forward to getting out of here. How is Paige?" said Rebecca, wondering why she hadn't seen Paige yet and trying to change the subject.

"She has university and work today. She told me this morning that she will ring you in her break. But to answer your question, she is ecstatic that you are awake and can't wait to see you… wait till she finds out you might be coming home tomorrow, she will be so happy. She has missed you, my love," said Jackson, as he sat on the leather chair next to Rebecca's bed and placed his hand in hers. "And so have I."

Looking into his loving eyes, she nodded, gulped, but wasn't quite sure what to say. Taking her hand away from his, she pointed to the window and said, "Can you please move my table back over."

"Sure." Jackson stood up and walked over to the window. As he wheeled the table in front of her, he said, "Is there anything I can get you?"

Shaking her head, Rebecca said, "No, thanks."

"Is everything all right between us?" asked Jackson, nervously. "It's just… well… you don't seem too happy to see me."

"I am happy to see you. It's… I am nervous about going home. At the moment, I can't walk or shower myself or do much for that matter of fact. And I don't want to be a burden to you." *God, what am I going to do? This doesn't seem real. One minute I am with Mitch and have become his fiancée and the next minute I am waking up to Jackson being alive and still married to him. I am so confused…*

"For better or worse. In sickness and health, no matter what, I am here for you, my love. It's going to be Ok. We can sort everything out when we get back home. You'll see. And you're not a burden," said Jackson, sitting on the bed. Leaning in, he placed his arms around Rebecca's shoulders and gave her a loving hug.

Rebecca placed her head on his shoulder and closed her tear-filled eyes. Even though she felt confused, she felt safe in his muscular arms that enveloped her and that's all she could ask for at this stage.

"Here we go, Mrs Landers," said Nurse Charlotte, as she entered the room and placed the prescriptions down on Rebecca's table. "Dr Ness said on your way home you can get these filled at your local chemist."

"Oh, right. Thank you," said Rebecca, pulling away from Jackson and sitting up straight.

Making her way to the foot of the bed, she picked up the folder which held Rebecca's medical condition and her stay at the hospital and said, "Actually, Dr Ness said if you are feeling up to it, you can go home tonight if you want to. Isn't that good news?"

Rebecca gulped hard, looked at Jackson and then at the nurse. "I can't walk or shower myself yet. Would it be Ok if I stay tonight at least?"

Looking at Rebecca over her glasses, Nurse Charlotte said in an English accent, "Well, we will have to do something about that, won't we? Once your husband has gone and you have had your dinner, we can get you out of bed and get you walking these corridors ma'am. Got to strengthen those muscles again, my dear."

Rebecca nodded and looked down. Sniffing back the tears forming in her eyes, she pressed the beds arrow button to lay down, and pulled herself into a foetal position on the bed.

"Mr Landers, might I suggest that you take an early mark, so that Mrs Landers can get some rest," said the nurse, watching the anxiety of her patient.

"Umm... sure," said Jackson, looking at the nurse. "I can see you need your rest, my love. I will come back tomorrow morning." Giving Rebecca a quick peck on her cheek, he patted her arm and said, "Bye, my love."

"Bye," said Rebecca, smiling briefly. She then turned over, faced the window and pulled the blanket up to her chin.

As Nurse Charlotte watched him walk out of the room, she stood in front of the window and said, "Are you all right, Mrs Landers?"

"No... not really," said Rebecca, her brow creased.

"What's the matter, my dear?" said Nurse Charlotte, taking a seat next to Rebecca's bed.

Rebecca explained about Jackson and Mitch and the events that had taken place in her dream.

"Well, I'll be damned, my dear. That is a bit of a pickle you have yourself in," said Nurse Charlotte, taking her glasses off and placing them on her lap. "I suppose the only bit of advice I can give you is to be honest with not only yourself but these two lovely men as well."

Nodding, Rebecca said, "Yeah, I know. But until I do sort this out, I am not looking forward to going home."

"Well, unfortunately my dear, you do have to go home tomorrow.

So why don't we get you up and see if we can get those legs of yours moving freely. Come on," said Nurse Charlotte, taking the blanket off Rebecca.

'Ok," said Rebecca, sitting up and shifting her legs to the side of the bed.

The night seemed to go on forever for Rebecca, who had tossed and turned most of the night, thinking about Jackson and Mitch. Lying on her side with the blanket pulled up to her chin, she watched through the window the morning sun rising, and wondered how she was going to get through the day. She was going home today and that was making her feel apprehensive. With her eyes feeling like they had grit in them, she pressed the bed remote arrow to sit up. As her body came up into a sitting position, she swung her legs over the side of the bed and reached for the walking frame the nurse had placed beside her bed the night previous, after they had taken many walks down the corridors. Standing, Rebecca slowly walked into the bathroom for a toilet break.

As she stood in front of the bathroom mirror, washing her hands, Rebecca looked at her drained facial features and watched the tears form in her eyes. *Oh God. What am I going to do? Please help me.* Wiping the tears that had fallen onto her cheeks away, she decided to get some of her clothes out of her hospital stay bag and have a shower. *Maybe this might make me feel better.*

Being an Aquarian, the water always seemed to make her feel alive.

As she lay in bed, the morning seemed to go by fast. With the nurse coming in for observations to be done, breakfast delivered and enjoyed, the tea lady joining her for a cuppa, and then the final paperwork prepared for her release, Rebecca was packed and ready to go home.

Slowly walking the corridors to keep her strength up, for the last time before she was collected by Jackson, she walked by many hospital room doorways glancing in for only seconds at other patients.

Humph… when I see how sick these poor people are… well, I have nothing to complain about, thought Rebecca, shaking her head in disappointment of herself and her thoughts. *Just appreciate what you have, girl.*

"Mum." Rebecca heard someone call out. Looking up, she smiled when she spotted Paige walking towards her with Jackson.

"Mum…. I have missed you," said Paige, reaching Rebecca and placing her arms around her for a warm hug.

"I have missed you too, sweetheart. It's so good to see you," said Rebecca, hugging her daughter back, as the tears formed in her eyes and spilled onto her cheeks. Pulling away slowly, she wiped her cheeks and sniffed back her runny nose. Taking in Paige's youthful appearance, Rebecca pulled her in close again and hugged her tight, only letting go when Paige released her hold. "Let me look at you… my, you have grown."

Rebecca instantly felt her anxiety disappear.

Jackson stood behind Paige and watched, with happiness, as his wife and daughter bonded. Clearing his throat, he said, "Hello, my love. How are you today?"

Looking up at his face, she smiled. "I'm a bit weak, but I will be Ok in time. I get to take this monstrosity home with me, so at least I will be able to move around by myself until I get my strength back." She pointed to the walking frame.

"You're a strong lady, so I am thinking that you won't need the walker for long," said Jackson, coming to stand beside to her. Looking into her eyes, he smiled, placed his arms around her waist and pulled her in close. "I have missed you," he whispered.

Taking in the smell of his cologne as she cuddled into his tanned skinned, muscular chest, Rebecca said, "I have missed you too." This was a familiar place for her that she knew all too well.

"Come on you two love birds. Let's get Mum's things and blow this joint," said Paige, smiling.

Rebecca smiled and said, "I'm all packed and ready to go." Turning her walker around, they all headed for her room.

With her eyebrows raised, and a smile from ear to ear, Rebecca noticed the 'Welcome Home' banner which was hanging over the front porch, as soon as the car pulled into the driveway of their Thornlie home.

"Aww, thank you. I love it," said Rebecca, turning to Paige and

Jackson. "I have missed being home."

"You like it?" asked Paige, smiling.

"Like it? It's awesome," said Rebecca, taking her seat belt off. Excited and at the same time apprehensive about being home, she placed her hand on the door handle and pulled it inwards, the door sprung open and she swung her legs around to alight from the car. *What am I doing... I need my walker to assist me.* Taking a deep breath inwards and then out, she realised Jackson was standing in front of her with his arms out in front.

"Come on... I will help you inside," said Jackson, taking charge and picking her up from the seat. As he carried Rebecca towards the front porch he looked over his shoulder and said to Paige, "Can you get Mum's bags and walker for me?"

"Done," said Paige, already carrying the bag and walker. "Here... give the key to me and I will unlock the front door."

"Thanks, sweetheart," said Jackson, only now realising he would find it difficult open the door, considering he had Rebecca in his arms.

Rebecca smiled as she watched Paige unlock the door and open it wide for Jackson and her to walk through. "Thanks sweetie."

Paige smiled at her mum. "That's Ok."

Placing Rebecca down on a chair next to the dining table, Jackson looked into Rebecca's eyes and said, "Can I get you anything?"

"Umm... no, I think I am right," said Rebecca, as she adjusted herself in the chair.

"Here you go, Mum," said Paige, placing the walker in front of Rebecca. "I'll put your bag in your bedroom. I can help you unpack it later, Ok?"

"Thanks sweetie," said Rebecca, watching her walk towards the bedroom that she shared with Jackson. *Bedroom... humph, that's going to be interesting.*

"Would you like to have a rest, Bec, or did you want to go outside?" asked Jackson, as he sat next to Rebecca at the table.

"I would love some fresh air. How about the front porch...it feels like I have been cooped up in that hospital room for ages," said Rebecca.

"Would you like me to carry you outside or are you happy to try your walker?" asked Jackson, standing.

"Umm… let me see if I can manage it first by myself," said Rebecca. With her hands holding onto the handles of the walker, she pushed herself upwards. Standing in front of the walker, she tried to balance herself to stand up straight and then she moved slowly towards the front door. *Slowly Rebecca. One foot in front of the other.*

Jackson watched on in anticipation, hands ready, as his wife slowly took one step at a time. When she finally reached the front doorway, he watched her hesitate for a moment and then push the walker over the doorstep and onto the wooden floor boards on the front porch.

Taking her seat in one of the black wicker chairs, Rebecca breathed a sigh of relief. "Well that was harder than it looked. But I did it."

"Well done, my love," said Jackson, standing in front of her. "Did you want me to leave the walker in front of you, or would you like it pushed over to the side?"

"It's Ok in front of me, for now," said Rebecca. "Jackson… could I trouble you for a cup of tea?"

"No trouble, my love. Do you still like it white with one sugar?" said Jackson.

"Umm… yeah I think so," said Rebecca, frowning as she wondered why she couldn't remember a simple thing like how she preferred her cup of tea made. As she watched Jackson walk back inside, Rebecca looked across the road at the brown brick house, where Mitch lived. Craning her neck, she couldn't see any movement at the house. *His black ute is gone, so he must be still at work.* Thinking back to what she thought was reality and the year 2014, she remembered Mitch's sweet, tender touch and how he had asked her to marry him. Shaking her head, Rebecca wondered if she would ever eventually stop thinking about something that had never happened. *Oh God, what am I going to do… my focus should be on my loving husband, Jackson. How am I going…?*

Her thoughts were interrupted by Jackson placing a mug of tea next to Rebecca on a side table. "Penny for your thoughts."

Rebecca blinked slowly, holding back the tears forming in her eyes. "Hmm… umm… just glad to be home." She smiled and said, "Thank you for the cuppa."

"You're welcome. How you feeling?" said Jackson, looking at Rebecca's drained appearance.

"A bit tired. I might just drink this down and go have a rest," said Rebecca, picking up the mug.

"Ok," said Jackson, sitting on the chair next to Rebecca. "So… what would you like for dinner tonight, my love?"

"Don't go to too much trouble, Jackson. Just make something easy. Maybe a spaghetti bolognaise; that will do," said Rebecca. "I'm not eating much these days anyway."

"Spag Bol it is then," said Jackson. "I might go and get the mince and sauce from Coles now. Will you be Ok on your own?"

"Yeah, I will be Ok. Paige is here and anyway I am sure she will look after me," said Rebecca.

"Right… well I won't be long," said Jackson, standing and bending over to give Rebecca a fond, reassuring kiss.

Rebecca quickly placed her right cheek in the path of his lips.

With a creased brow, Jackson averted his eyes downwards, let a short puff of air escape his nostrils and pulled away slowly. "Everything all right?" said Jackson, looking up and searching her face for answers.

"Yep. All good," lied Rebecca. She couldn't look him in the eyes. She wasn't sure how she felt about any sort of intimacy with Jackson yet. Even if it was just a quick kiss goodbye. "See you when you get back."

Jackson nodded and walked down the step, towards his car parked in the drive way.

Rebecca watched Jackson pull away from the house and shook her head. *I keep thinking about Mitch and what we had in what was supposedly a dream.* Frowning, she rubbed the side of her head in desperation. *What am I doing? I need to give my marriage a chance. Poor Jackson.* As she looked off into the distance thinking about Jackson and Mitch, Paige came and sat next to Rebecca.

"Mum… Mum," said Paige, waving her hand in front of Rebecca's face.

"Hmm…" said Rebecca, with a furrowed brow, looking in Paige's direction. "Oh, sorry sweetheart. I was off with the pixies. Didn't even hear you come out here. Everything all right?"

"Yeah, yeah, I'm all good. Where did Dad go?" said Paige, sitting back in her chair, with her bare feet on the seat and her knees up to her chest.

"He went to get some food from Coles for dinner."

"Oh right. How you feeling, Mum?"

"I'm Ok. Might go have a lay down, as I am a bit tired," said Rebecca, standing slowly.

Standing, Paige stood in front of the walker and held it tight, to kept it stable for her mum.

"Thanks sweetie. I will be Ok," said Rebecca, taking a step forward.

Paige smiled and nodded. Standing back, she watched her mum walk towards the doorway inside.

"I might have a nap on the lounge. Would you mind getting me a pillow and a blanket?"

"Sure," said Paige, walking past Rebecca inside and retrieving the pillow and blanket.

Rebecca slowly walked into the lounge room and strolled over towards the L-shaped, charcoal lounge. Turning the walker around, she placed her backside onto the lounge and took a seat. Yawning, she watched Paige walk towards her.

"Here you go," said Paige, placing the pillow and rug on the lounge.

"Thanks, sweetheart," said Rebecca, placing her head on the pillow.

"Would you like the TV on?"

"Yes please," said Rebecca, pulling the blanket up to her chin, as she watched her daughter walk towards the TV.

"Here's the remote," said Paige, placing the remote on the coffee table in front of her.

"Thanks. What are you going to do this afternoon?"

"I have some washing to do. And then I have work tonight," said Paige.

Rebecca yawned. "Ok... what time do you start and finish work tonight?"

"I start at five-thirty and finish at twelve," said Paige. "Oh, that reminds me... I will need to ask Dad to pick me up from work."

Rebecca frowned. *That's right, you don't have your licence yet. It was all a dream.*

"Well… I will leave you to rest up," said Paige, walking towards her bedroom. "If you need anything, just yell."

"I will. Thanks sweetheart," said Rebecca, picking up the remote. *Hmm, I wonder what's on.* Rebecca yawned and flicked through the channels, until she came across a show she liked. Snuggling into the blanket, her eyelids eventually became heavy and she fell asleep.

CHAPTER TWENTY

Rebecca's eyes opened slowly, and to her surprise she found Mitch sleeping soundly beside her. Confused, she frowned and took a deep breath in and then out. As she studied his facial features and listened to him lightly snore, she smiled and breathed a sigh of relief.

Thank God that was just a dream. But it felt so real. I am glad I woke up, thought Rebecca, anxiously rubbing the side of her left temple. *I don't know what is going on, but my brain doesn't seem to work the same way since my last operation and lately I always seem to have these types of weird dreams. I wonder if this dream has anything to do with the second tumour I had removed. Oh, don't be ridiculous, Rebecca… God, who knows…*

With her heart racing and her mind emotionally exhausted, Rebecca lay on her back, staring at the ceiling of the hotel room, wondering what had caused her to have a dream that felt so real, about Jackson and Mitch. She also remembered back to the day when she was told by the neurosurgeon that her brain tumour had returned and that she was to have a second operation to remove it again and how long it took for her to recover.

I must remember to ask my neurosurgeon about these dreams. Since Jackson has passed away, I seem to be having more and more of them. Frightens the crap out of me. Humph… cramp, thought Rebecca, screwing her face up. Quietly, she slipped out of bed and headed for the bathroom, taking her knickers and satin nightgown from the overnight bag on the way.

Staring straight ahead, she sat instinctively on the toilet and thought about their previous night and Mitch's proposal.

Have I done the right thing by saying 'yes'? I know I love him… but am I rushing into a new life with Mitch? Is that why I dreamt Jackson was still alive? thought Rebecca. Her pulse quickened as doubt crept into her mind. *I wonder what Paige will say, let alone, how anyone else will react to our news.*

Her large, blue-eyed, distressed reflection in the mirror, as she stood in front of the vanity washing her hands, was not of a woman who should have been happy and over the moon about accepting Mitch's proposal, but one of a troubled woman with doubts. Taking a deep breath, she placed her knickers and satin nightgown on and headed towards the lounge room.

Might ring room service to see if I can get some breakfast delivered to our room, thought Rebecca, walking towards the phone.

Placing the desk phone back on the receiver, she quietly headed back into the bedroom to see if Mitch was awake yet.

"Where have you been beautiful? I missed you," said Mitch, as he sat up and yawned, when she walked into the room.

"Morning gorgeous fiancé of mine. I have ordered some breakfast for us," said Rebecca, smiling as she walked towards him.

"Come back to bed," said Mitch, holding out his arms to her.

"You don't have to ask me twice," said Rebecca, pulling back the duvet. Hopping back in bed, she snuggled into Mitch's chest and closed her eyes. As her racing mind calmed itself and she felt his warm, loving, reassuring touch, she breathed a sigh of relief, if only for a minute before the doubt crept back in again.

Hearing a knock at the door, Mitch said, "Must be our breakfast."

"That was quick," said Rebecca, sitting up.

Mitch jumped out of bed and placed his bathrobe on. "I'll get the door," said Mitch, walking towards the doorway.

Rebecca nodded and jumped out of bed quickly to straighten her nightgown.

Looking through the peep hole Mitch spotted the waiter on the other side and opened the door.

"Morning, sir," said the waiter, who was dressed in a white coat and black trousers. "You ordered breakfast."

"Yes. Thank you. Come in," said Mitch, as he caught a whiff of the coffee aroma.

The metal trolley clinked as the waiter pushed it through the doorway and into the lounge room.

"Mr Portellico... I... I thought you might like to know about this," said the waiter, pointing to a picture in the newspaper and the TGM magazine.

"Thank you... we already know about it," said Mitch, as he tipped the waiter.

He nodded and left them to enjoy their breakfast.

"Mmm... smells good," said Rebecca, walking over to the trolley.

"Sure does," said Mitch, taking each plate, which had a cloche over them to keep them warm, and placing it on the small, low, rectangular lounge room table. "Have a look at this." Mitch handed Rebecca the magazine.

Taking the magazine from his hand, Rebecca walked over to the window, which was dressed with white sheer curtains, and sat on the corner of the beige chaise lounge chair.

The front of the TGM magazine said, 'Has Mitch, Seattle's Most Eligible Bachelor, Found Love Again?' There was a picture of Mitch and Rebecca at the restaurant from the previous night as well.

Rebecca frowned as she read the headline and then realised that there was more, when she read the fine print on the front of the magazine that said, 'More pictures on page five.' With a creased brow, she quickly turned to page five inside the magazine. There in all its glory was a three page lift out of Rebecca jogging around Mitch's parents' grounds yesterday, Mitch and her at the airport when they arrived into LA and a picture of Mitch holding her hand and pulling her into the restaurant last night. The article that was written on these pages was about how Mitch lost his wife Christine and how he hadn't been seen for the past five years. They wondered where he had been living. They also talked about how Mitch was one of Seattle's most eligible bachelors and wondered where Mitch and Rebecca met. They didn't know her name yet, or where she lived, but had asked readers to write in and tell them about her.

Mitch watched her reaction to the article and sighed.

When Rebecca finished reading the article, she looked up at Mitch and said, "These people sure are nosy aren't they. Fancy asking readers to write in and let them know who I was. I know this sort of information is gossip and readers enjoy it, but this is downright rude."

"Very intrusive aren't they? This is what I was trying to tell you about. They just can't help themselves. Bloody bastards. Anything for a story," said Mitch, irritated.

"How will we get away from them at the Pink concert tonight, Mitch?" said Rebecca, worried. "I would just prefer not to go if they are going to follow us all night long for some more pictures."

"Nick has already organised for us to have four security guards tonight. He has also organised for us to go in via the back door and then find our seats. We should be Ok. But they will probably get some more photos. Sorry babe, there is no getting away from these parasites," said Mitch, placing the coffee pot on the table.

"I hate to say this, because I like being here in Seattle, but I can't wait to go home to get away from these fuckers," said Rebecca, walking over to Mitch.

"You know that's why I said to you, not to talk to them. Because if they work out your accent, then they will work out that we are in Australia and will eventually find us. I know how relentless these bastards can be to get a story," said Mitch, pulling her in close for a hug.

"Thank God you told me, Mitch. Otherwise our life would be miserable," said Rebecca, resting her head on his shoulder and holding him tight.

Pulling away slowly, Mitch said with a furrowed brow, "Are you sure you are going to be all right? Especially as you have now said you will marry me. I will understand if you want to back out. I won't like it; but I will understand. I have had to put up with the paparazzi most of my life, so I know what to expect. But you haven't, so I do understand." His tormented face said it all.

"I must admit... I am a bit worried that I said yes to your proposal too soon. We haven't been together long and that is a real concern to me, Mitch. But you can't get rid of me that easily. I love you too much to ever want to leave you because of paparazzi," said Rebecca, with a creased brow.

"I love you too, Rebecca and I want to spend my life with you. But if you are still unsure, I can wait," said Mitch, saddened at how quickly life could change for him because of his status.

"What about if we have a long engagement? Say a year... what do you think?" said Rebecca, looking into his blue eyes.

"I don't mind waiting that long," said Mitch, hopeful.

"Great. I am glad we have sorted that all out," said Rebecca, as she cuddled into Mitch's chest.

After all, she had only known Mitch as a friend previously and really needed to get to know him better before she made the biggest commitment of her life.

"How about we eat this lovely breakfast you ordered for us? It looks awesome. Thank you," said Mitch, pulling away from her slowly.

"Good idea," said Rebecca, sitting on the lounge with Mitch. "We will have to ring my parents and tell them we are engaged. Not sure how they are gonna take the news."

Mitch looked at Rebecca sheepishly and said, "Ah... I already asked your mum and dad for their permission to marry you... so they already know."

"Bit of a forgone conclusion, was I?" said Rebecca, smiling.

He shook his head and said, "No, not really. I wasn't sure you would say 'Yes'. But I wanted to ask them for their permission first and to reassure them that I wasn't rushing you into this."

"I suppose at the restaurant last night when I said 'No', that would have put a spanner in the works," smirked Rebecca.

"It sure did. But I was not about to rush into something you were not ready to do either, Rebecca," said Mitch, his brow creased.

"What did I ever do to deserve you?" said Rebecca.

"It should be me saying that to you," said Mitch. He pulled her in close for a sensual kiss.

As their car pulled away from the kerb, Rebecca placed her hand on Mitch's and said, "Thank you for the great night out and the hotel room. I have been thoroughly spoilt and I loved every minute of it. Especially as I got to spend it with you."

He smiled and kissed her lips tenderly. Pulling away slowly he looked into her eyes and said, "You're welcome. I enjoy spoiling you." They relaxed in each other's arms and enjoyed the ride home to the Portellico mansion.

Their bodies jostled together as the car ran over the rough pavers out the front of Mitch's parents' house.

"Does anyone else know that you proposed to me last night and that I accepted?" asked Rebecca.

"No. But I would like to tell them all now, if that's Ok with you," said Mitch.

She nodded at him excitedly. "I can't wait to tell everyone. But I am still worried about their reaction."

"Don't worry, my love. It will all work out. Let's go," said Mitch, taking her by the hand and alighting from the car.

Walking into the house, not knowing where everyone was, they heard voices coming from the back of the house. "Where is everyone?" shouted Mitch.

"In here, love," shouted Helen.

"Come on," said Mitch, pulling Rebecca by the hand towards the dining room.

"Hello… would you both like some lunch?" asked Helen, as she stood to give them a hug when they entered the room.

"Yes please," they both said in unison, hugging her back.

Before Mitch sat down he spotted their waitress standing near the side board. Smiling, Mitch approached her and asked "Could you go and get us some glasses of champagne?"

"Yes, sir," said the waitress, bowing her head slightly.

"What's the occasion for the champagne, son?" said Grayson, as he stood up to shake his son's hand and watched the waitress walk into the dining room carrying a tray of glasses filled with champagne.

Mitch smiled and stood tall. "Everyone... I... we have something to tell you all... I have asked Rebecca if she would do me the honour of being my wife and she has said 'yes'."

"Woo hoot," shouted Nick, standing. He walked over and gave them both a warm hug. "Congratulations."

"Oh, wow. Congratulations," said Helen, giving them both another hug and peck on their cheeks.

Grayson shook his son's hand and gave Rebecca a warm hug. "Congrats."

Rebecca looked over at Paige and watched her walk towards them with a big grin on her face. As she ran into her mum's arms she said, "I am so happy for you, Mum."

"Thank you sweetie," said Rebecca, hugging her daughter back.

As the waitress stood in front of each of them with the tray and they all took their glass of champagne, Grayson lifted his glass into the air and said, "To Mitch and Rebecca."

They all chanted, "To Mitch and Rebecca."

Taking a sip of her champagne, Rebecca couldn't believe how happy she was in that moment.

"Let's see the ring," said Helen, smiling.

Rebecca held her left hand out front and revealed the ring. As she watched it sparkle, she said, "I am the luckiest girl in the world to have found such a loving man, like your son."

"I am sure he feels the same way about you, my dear," said Helen looking from Rebecca to Mitch. "I am so over the moon about your news. So... when are you planning to get married?"

Mitch and Rebecca looked at each other and smiled. "We haven't set a date yet. We are hoping it won't be too far away," said Rebecca.

"Will you get married in Seattle or Australia?" asked Helen.

"We're not sure of any details yet, Mom. We still need to sit down and talk about it. But we will let you know when we have made a decision," said Mitch.

"You are welcome to have the ceremony and reception here at

home if you want to. But I will leave it up to you of course," offered Helen. She was just content to see her oldest boy happy again.

"Not changing the subject Mitch, but have you seen this morning's newspaper?" said Michael.

Mitch nodded and said, "Yeah we've seen it. Bloody parasites. That's another reason why we are not sure at this stage whether to have it in Seattle or Australia. I don't want to subject Rebecca or Paige to the paparazzi any more than they have to." He looked from Rebecca to Paige and then his family.

"We understand dears. We can talk about this later. Let's sit down and eat our lunch," said Helen, gesturing to the dining room table. "There is plenty of food to go round."

"Another round of champagne, Greta," indicated Grayson, to the waitress.

Greta slightly bowed her head and walk towards the doorway, whilst Mitch and Rebecca made their selection of food from the bain-maries.

Rebecca sat at the table, looking off into the distance.

"Penny for your thoughts," said Helen, as she sat next to Rebecca and placed her hand over Rebecca's.

"Hmm…" said Rebecca, hearing Helen's voice and realising that she had sat next to her. "Umm, I was just thinking about all the wedding arrangements."

But what she was really remembering was her first wedding to Jackson. The dress she wore, the vows she made and the reception. It all only seemed like yesterday to Rebecca. *Jackson…*, thought Rebecca, remembering just how much she loved him.

"If you need any help with planning the wedding dear, I am only too happy to help out. I know of a great wedding dress designer as well."

She is so thoughtful, thought Rebecca, smiling.

"Oh, thank you, Helen, that is lovely of you to offer. I sure will need your help and advice when it comes to planning the wedding," said Rebecca, appreciative.

"You're welcome, dear."

Nick leant across the table and said, "Hey guys… the Pink concert is tonight and I have organised tight security for us all. Michael and Paige, you will go in one car with a driver, Mitch and Rebecca you will go in another car with a driver. We will have security following both vehicles and once you all arrive at the venue, the security will escort you all through the back doors and to your seats. You will still come across the paparazzi, but at least they won't be able to get too close to you all. Then after the concert, the security team will escort you back to your waiting cars, which will take you back home."

"Thanks for organising the security for us Nick, much appreciated," said Mitch, shaking Nick's hand.

"No problem bro. It should be a great concert. You ladies looking forward to going?" said Nick, looking from Mitch to Paige and Rebecca.

"I can't wait for tonight. Pink's music is lit and she is so amazing," said Paige, smiling.

"I'm looking forward to the concert too. I can't thank you enough for organising tickets and security for us, Nick. That was so considerate of you," said Rebecca.

"Hey, that's no problem at all," said Nick.

"Actually… I'll have to go and see what I have to wear for tonight. Would you like to help me Paige?" said Rebecca.

"Sure," said Paige.

"Babe, you go spend some time with Paige. I have some business to attend to anyway. I will see you later on," said Mitch.

"Ok, my fiancée," said Rebecca, as she leant in and gave him a hug. "Come on Paige; let's go figure out what we are going to wear tonight and how we are doing our hair and make-up."

Paige nodded and stood up.

Rebecca sat on Paige's bed and watched her daughter sort through her clothes for the concert. "Paige, I wanted to ask you something."

"What is it, Mum?"

"How do you feel about me marrying Mitch?" asked Rebecca.

"Mitch is a wonderful, caring guy and I know he has wanted to be with you for a while now, and I can see when you two are together that he makes you happy. As long as you are happy, that's all that matters to me.

There is one thing that is bothering me though," said Paige, frowning.

"What's that sweetie?"

"Don't be mad at me… but when you are married to Mitch, I don't have to call him Dad, do I? It's just that I only have one Dad and I don't ever want to call anyone else that. It doesn't seem right, if you know what I mean," said Paige, her brow creased.

"Sweetheart, I would never expect you to call Mitch 'Dad'. I would expect you to call him by his name. Truthfully I don't know what's going to happen when we get back home anyway. We haven't actually lived together yet. I haven't said anything to Mitch yet, but I don't know how I am going to feel living with Mitch in the same house as your father and I lived in. It just doesn't feel like the right thing to do. I don't know how to explain it. I think I am going to take it as it comes. Maybe it might come down to the fact that we move to a different house. I don't know Paige. I'm rambling aren't I?" said Rebecca.

"Mum, you do tend to overthink things a bit and then it clouds your judgement," said Paige, sitting next to Rebecca on the bed. "Just remember, Mitch loves you and he is willing to do whatever it takes to keep you. I know this, because he told me. You just need to tell him how you are feeling when you get back home."

"When did you become so old and wise, my sweet girl?" said Rebecca, placing her hand on Paige's upper arm. "I wanted to ask you something else, Paige. Would you like to be my bridesmaid at our wedding?"

With a grin from ear to ear, Paige hugged her mum and said, "Yes. Of course I would love to be your bridesmaid. I can't wait to start helping you plan it out. I have so many ideas."

"Cool… I am so excited," said Rebecca, hugging her daughter back. "So… are you and Michael serious about each other?" Rebecca searched Paige's face for a reaction.

"He's the first guy I have ever truly liked, Mum. Most of the guys back home are immature at his age, but not Michael. He's such a gentleman and he knows what he wants in life too. I shouldn't be telling you this Mum, but I feel I can… he hasn't even pressured me to have sex with him yet. I know from my girlfriends back home, that their boyfriends pressured them and so most of them gave in," said Paige.

"So you are still a virgin then?" asked Rebecca, surprised at how the conversation had turned.

"Yes, Mum, and I would like to keep it that way until someone comes along that I really love. I feel that losing my virginity to someone is very special, so I want to at least know and love this guy very much. In saying all this though, and to answer your question, I feel we are serious about each other. But the only thing is, he lives in Seattle and I live in Perth and usually long distance relationships don't work," said Paige.

"Did you know he has asked his parents if he can move in with Mitch when we go back home?"

"No, I didn't know that. Have his parents agreed to it?" said Paige, eagerly.

"We are all going to sit down on Saturday and discuss it. I think for me, I was just seeing how you were both getting along here first and then I was going to decide. This is the reason I have asked you if you are serious or not. I don't think it's fair to string a boy along if you are not serious about him, especially as he is thinking of uprooting his life and going halfway around the world to be with you in Perth,"

"I really do like him a lot, Mum. So please give us some consideration on Saturday," said Paige.

"You know Paige, after what you have just told me I think I already know that the answer is going to be 'yes' from me. I can't believe he hasn't even pressured you for sex yet. You know that is a true gentleman and he obviously cares for you. You don't find many guys like him these days," said Rebecca.

Paige hugged Rebecca and said, "Aww, thanks, Mum."

"You mean the world to me sweetie, and your happiness is all I want for you in this life," said Rebecca, hugging Paige. "Now… let's find some clothes to wear for the concert tonight. Are you excited about going?"

"Yeah, I can't wait."

Paige and Rebecca spent most of the afternoon trying on and picking out their clothes, talking about hair styles and their make-up. It sure was one satisfying day for them both to spend some time together.

"Knock, knock," said Mitch, opening the door and popping his head through the opening. "Sorry, I hope I'm not interrupting something?"

"No, you're not interrupting anything. Come in... could you help us decide on whether to wear flat shoes or high heels tonight?" said Rebecca.

"Either will be all right. Knowing how long women take to get dressed, I would say you both had better start getting ready. We only have one and a half hours before we have to go," said Mitch.

"Oh right. Well, I think we are all sorted now anyway," said Rebecca, looking at her phone for the time. "See you in a little while, sweetie."

"Ok, Mum," said Paige, watching Rebecca walk towards the door.

"What are you wearing tonight?" said Rebecca to Mitch, as they walked into their room.

"Denim jeans and a shirt, converse shoes. What about yourself, beautiful?" said Mitch.

"Denim jeans and a green camisole and a jacket," said Rebecca.

"Mmm, your cute arse always looks great in tight jeans. I look forward to seeing that," teased Mitch.

"Does Sir think we have time for a bit of play before we go?" said Rebecca, with raised eyebrows.

He looked at her with a huge smile on his face and said, "You are so incorrigible Ms Landers. Get in the shower." She smiled. He swatted her arse as he walked over to the wardrobe.

"Well, a girl can only but try," said Rebecca, laughing.

CHAPTER TWENTY ONE

As the driver braked to a stop at the lights across the road from the concert venue, Rebecca noticed through the window that there were thousands of screaming fans, some dressed in Pink attire, waiting in line to get inside once the doors opened to the Pink concert. With the lights turning green, the driver moved forward and pulled into the parking lot. Noticing the paparazzi were out in full force tonight, he made a bee-line for the back of the venue, so that Mitch and Rebecca could go in via the back entrance to the concert.

The car came to a stop in front of a long, silver-handled, grey door and their car door opened for them to alight. Mitch recognised two security guards in uniform waiting for them as they hopped out of their car to quickly escort them inside. Looking around, Mitch smiled as he noticed Michael and Paige's car was parked behind his and they were walking towards them.

"Come on," gestured Mitch to Michael and Paige, to hurry up and get inside.

With two security guards in front of them and two at the back, Mitch, Rebecca, Michael and Paige walked throughout the cream walled, burgundy carpeted corridor of the back stage area. As they rounded a bend in the corridor, Mitch spotted Pink coming out of her dressing room and watched her walk towards them with two security guards in tow.

"Hello, you must be Mitch, Rebecca, Michael and Paige," said Pink, smiling and shaking each of their hands. "I'm Alecia. Welcome to my show. I hope you enjoy the concert." Nick had shown her a photo of them previously.

"Hi, it's nice to meet you. Do you believe how crazy it is outside? Looks like you will have a full house tonight," said Mitch, shaking her hand. "Oh yeah, and the paparazzi are everywhere tonight."

"Yeah, them bastards never give up. They are relentless. Looks like they have you in their sights at the moment though, Mitch and Rebecca. But don't let them get you down, they will move onto someone else soon, they always do," said Alecia.

"Thanks Alecia. I just can't believe the lengths these creeps go to, to get a photo," said Rebecca, frowning.

"You're not wrong. The bastards even tried getting a photo of me the other day swimming at the hotel. Hey… your accent… are you from Australia?" said Alecia.

Rebecca looked at Mitch for his permission and he nodded.

"Yes, I am from Perth, Western Australia and this is my daughter Paige. We are trying at the moment to keep it from the paparazzi, so that we don't get hassled when we go back home. So far so good."

"No problem. My lips are sealed. Actually I have some friends in Perth. They live in a suburb called Joondalup. I picked your accent straight away, as you sound like they do. When I play concerts in Perth I usually stay with them. I don't seem to get pestered there by the paparazzi," said Alecia.

As they were chatting, Pink's stage manager came over and said, "Excuse me, Alecia, but we need to go over some of the songs and performances tonight, so you will have to wrap it up."

"Ok, no problem," said Alecia to her manager. "Hey, if you guys are around later after the concert, maybe we can catch up."

"We would love to. I will have to check with our security first though," said Mitch, smiling.

"Ok, let me know," said Alecia, as she walked off with her stage manager.

"How amazing was that?" said Paige, excited. "I can't believe I just met Pink… Sydney is going to be so jealous."

Seated in the front row, close to the stage, Paige looked behind her at the darkened room that was semi-lit in pink, at all the people who were waiting for the concert to begin. *Unbelievable*, thought Paige, as she took a video with her mobile phone. She had never seen this many people at a concert before.

Rebecca smiled as she watched her daughter's face beam with happiness.

After about an hour of waiting and people chanting Pink's name, the band started to play the music and then Pink came on stage. Dressed in a long sleeved leather dress that was black and pink striped, she put the microphone up to her lips and spoke briefly to the crowd. Once Pink started to sing her first song, everyone stood up out of their seats and moved to the rhythm of the music. The whole show and her performance was world class.

Paige and Rebecca knew every song she sang and they danced in the aisles, whilst singing along to her songs. Mitch and Michael also sang and danced along with them, whilst the security guards kept watch.

"I can't remember having this much fun at a concert before. It's one I won't forget in a hurry," screamed Paige to Rebecca over the loud music. "This is awesome."

"Sure is," said Rebecca, leaning into her daughter's ear.

As the last song was being sung by Pink, Rebecca noticed Mitch looking around and he nodded to her to look to her right. Looking over her right shoulder, she saw some paparazzi, who were constantly taking photos of them all.

Thank God the security guards Nick hired are here. That way those scum photographers can't get too close to us, thought Rebecca.

"Are we going to be able to stay around after the concert to speak with Alecia again?" asked Rebecca, leaning into Mitch and speaking into his ear.

"Probably not babe, as we need to get away from the reporters. We don't want them hearing your accent," said Mitch.

Disappointed, Rebecca said, "That's a shame."

"Maybe we can ask Alecia if she would like to come over tomorrow night to my parents' place for a late supper and drinks after her concert," said Mitch.

"Sounds good. Can you get Nick to ask her for us?" said Rebecca. Mitch nodded yes.

As everyone was shouting 'one more song' for Pink to come back on stage, Mitch, Rebecca, Michael and Paige headed out to the back stage area again. The paparazzi who were inside the venue tried to follow them but Nick's security guards stopped them in their tracks.

Nearing the back doors of the venue, Rebecca said to Paige and Michael, "See you both back at home. Maybe we can watch a movie or something."

Paige gave Rebecca a hug and said, "Sounds great. See ya back there then." Their security team escorted them outside to their car which was already waiting for them. Rebecca and Mitch stood at the door entrance and waved them goodbye and then their security team escorted them to their waiting car as well.

In the car Mitch and Rebecca cuddled up to each other. "My ears are still ringing from the loud music at the concert," said Rebecca.

"Yeah, mine too," said Mitch, rubbing his left ear.

"That was such an amazing concert. She was lovely to talk with as well," said Rebecca.

"Yeah, for sure. I had a great time tonight. But my favourite part was dancing with you," said Mitch, as he leant down and kissed her lips.

Their moment of passion was disturbed by the driver as he lowered the divider between the driver and Mitch and Rebecca. Looking in his rear view mirror at them, the driver said, "Sir, looks like there has been an accident up ahead. We might be here for a while."

Both Mitch and Rebecca looked out the front window of the car and could see a black car had smashed into another car and an ambulance and police were there attending to the injured.

Rebecca sat up straight and craned her neck to get a better look at the accident. *That black car looks exactly like the one Michael and Paige drove off in.* Rebecca's body formed goose bumps as she tried to tell herself it wasn't their car.

"Shit…. it's Michael and Paige's car," said Mitch, opening the car door, jumping out of the car and running towards them. Rebecca followed him out of the door.

As Mitch and Rebecca reached the accident they were stopped in their tracks by the police placing yellow tape around the accident site. "Sorry, we can't let you near the accident. There is a fuel leak and we fear the cars could ignite," said the curly haired police officer, who stood in front of Mitch and Rebecca and stopped them from entering the scene.

"That is my daughter and her boyfriend in the black car. Can you please at least tell us if they are all right?" said Rebecca, with a tear-stained face.

"Sorry, Miss. As soon as the site is safe, we will let you know. What's your daughter's name?" said the police officer, getting his small pad and pen out of his top pocket.

"Paige… Paige Landers. Michael Portellico is also in there with her. Please… can you go and find out," said Rebecca, as she grabbed Mitch's hand and held it tight.

"Yes, ma'am," said the police officer, writing the names down on his small lined pad.

With tears streaming down her face, Rebecca stood at the edge of the yellow tape waiting, searching for any sign that Michael and Paige were going to be all right.

"God, what is taking so long?" said Mitch out loud. As Mitch said this, he noticed the two security guards that were following Michael and Paige, running towards him and away from the accident.

When they reached Mitch and Rebecca, the tallest of the two guards said, "Mitch, the bloody paparazzi, they caused this accident. They drove next to Michael and Paige's car trying to get a photo, but when the road narrowed they didn't stop; instead they ended up smashing into Michael and Paige's car and when they hit the car, Michael and Paige car ended up spinning upside down and then it smashed into the tunnel wall."

He pointed towards the accident and the tunnel wall.

"Fuckers… they are going to pay for this. Please go and tell the police what you have just told me. I want your statement on record for when this goes to court." said Mitch, calmly.

"Yes, sir," said the guard.

As Rebecca looked from the security guards to the accident scene again, she noticed that paramedics had both Michael and Paige on stretchers and were wheeling them towards the ambulance. With her eyes open wide, and shock starting to set in, she pulled on Mitch's arm to make him see what was happening, because she couldn't seem to get any words out of her mouth. She then pointed in the direction of the accident.

"Excuse me, officer, which hospital is the ambulance taking Michael and Paige to?" asked Mitch.

"It's the 'Virginia Mason Medical Centre', sir," said the officer.

"Is the driver still in the car? Is he Ok?" asked Mitch.

The police officer swallowed hard and said, "Sorry sir, the driver died on impact. They couldn't revive him. The firefighters are trying to cut him out of the wreckage now."

Closing his eyes and running his hands through his hair, Mitch said to Rebecca, "I have known the driver, Sawyer, since I was a kid, I can't believe it. He was such a great bloke." Tears welled in Mitch's eyes and overflowed onto his cheeks. Giving Mitch a hug, Rebecca tried to console him.

Pulling away from her, Mitch indicated to Michael and Paige's security guards to come over to see him.

"I want you both to stay here with the accident. You need to inform me of events and keep me up to date during the night on what is happening. Do you understand what I am asking you?" said Mitch, his nostrils flared.

"Yes sir," both guards said in unison.

Grabbing Rebecca's hand, Mitch said, "Let's go to the hospital and see how Michael and Paige are going."

On the drive to the hospital Mitch rang his parents and informed them of what had happened. They told Mitch that they would ring

Sawyer's family and let them know that he had passed away and then they would come to the hospital themselves.

All the street lights, signs and cars seem to fade away as Rebecca eyes glazed over, out the window of the car. Not knowing what to say, but praying to herself that both Paige and Michael would be all right, the tears welled in her eyes and ran down her cheeks and she started to sob.

"Come on, they will both be all right. You have to think positive," said Mitch, placing his arm around Rebecca and kissing her forehead.

Rebecca cuddled into Mitch not saying a word, but hoping he was right, as she wiped her tear-stained face with the back of her jacket sleeve.

By the time they arrived at the hospital and were standing at the emergency room reception, Paige and Michael had already been taken into the treatment rooms. Taking their seats next to each other in the waiting room, Mitch and Rebecca stared blankly ahead as they waited for the doctor to come and see them.

After what seemed like hours, finally a nurse appeared in the doorway of the waiting room. "Portellico?" called the nurse.

"Yes," said Mitch, standing up and walking towards the nurse, his stomach in knots. "Michael is my brother."

"Come with me and I will take you to see your brother, if you like. We have attended to his injuries, but he hasn't woken up yet," said the nurse, looking at Mitch.

Mitch swallowed hard as a cold chill ran down his spine. "Why hasn't he woken yet?"

"We are not sure yet. Come on, follow me," gestured the nurse.

"Wait… what about Paige Landers," said Rebecca, stopping the nurse in her tracks.

The nurse looked at her clipboard and read the notes on Paige. "Paige is in surgery."

"What is she being operated on for" asked Mitch.

"Her spleen was ruptured and there was a lot of bleeding. She has a broken arm, fractured skull and the scans are showing she has head trauma, with swelling to the brain. She is in a bad way, but the doctors are doing all they can to get her stable," said the nurse, looking from Rebecca to Mitch.

"Oh God," said Rebecca, holding onto Mitch for support. "Will you let us know when she is out of surgery?"

"Yes. Are you family?" said the nurse.

"Yes, I am Paige's mother," said Rebecca, tears forming in her eyes.

"Right. She is a fighter, Ms Landers. We are doing everything possible to help her at the moment," said the nurse.

"Thank you," said Rebecca, wiping her runny nose on the sleeve of her jacket.

"Follow me and I will take you both to Michael's room," said the nurse.

Mitch held Rebecca's hand tight as they walked down the sterile passage way to Michael's private room.

When the nurse reached the doorway to Michael's room, she gestured for Mitch and Rebecca to go in to see Michael. "Go on in. I will be in the back of the room if you need anything."

Mitch and Rebecca nodded and walked into the room.

Rebecca took a deep breath through her nostrils and placed her hand over her mouth when she first saw Michael lying in the bed with his head bandaged. "Oh my God… Michael…" said Rebecca, her breath stammered. "What are his injuries, nurse?"

The nurse walked towards Michael's bed and stopped at the foot of the bed to pick up the information folder. As she read his medical information, she said, "He has a deep cut on his forehead that required stitches, this is why his head his bandaged. He also had a broken left arm and three broken ribs." She watched their saddened eyes, which were searching for answers, move towards the machine next to the bed. "The ventilation mask is to help him breathe." Placing the white folder back in the wire holder, she walked around to the side of the bed and checked the flow on Michael's intravenous drip in his right arm.

With her brow creased and a heavy heart, Rebecca briefly closed and opened her eyes slowly. As she came to stand by the bed, watching his every breath, she leant over and gently kissed his forehead.

"Please wake up, Michael," said Rebecca, as the tears formed in her eyes.

Mitch retrieved a chair from the back of the room and took a seat next to Michael's bed. As he watched his brother's chest move up and down, he searched every inch of Michael's face. Placing his hand over Michael's, he said through weakened breath and tears, "Come on bro, time to wake up. We need you here with us... I love you bro."

Within seconds of Mitch saying this, Michael said in a muffled voice through the mask, "Please... no mushy stuff, bro." Opening his eyes, it took him a few seconds to focus.

"Are you in any pain?" asked the nurse.

"Yes. My head feels like someone has bashed me," said Michael, as he felt his bandaged head. Looking down at his left arm, he noticed the cast. "Looks like I have a broken arm?" Taking a breath inwards he wondered why his chest hurt. "My chest hurts too." Michael closed his eyes and screwed his face up.

"On a scale of 1-10 how bad is the pain?" asked the nurse.

"It's a nine," said Michael, pushing his mask off.

"Right... give me a minute and I will get you some pain relief," said the nurse, walking toward the doorway. Within seconds she returned to the room. Tearing open the sterile wipe sachet, she wiped it over his upper right arm, then took the syringe with the pain relief inside of it, out of its packet, and administered it into Michael's arm.

"Ouch," said Michael, as the needle entered his arm.

"How is your pain now, Michael?" said the nurse after a moment.

"It's about a four, not too bad," said Michael, breathing easy. As Michael looked from the nurse to Rebecca, he realised someone was missing from the room. "Where is Paige?"

Rebecca looked over at Mitch and gulped.

"She is in surgery, Michael. She has some pretty bad injuries. We still don't know if she is going to be all right," said Mitch, his voice breaking and the tears forming in his eyes as he said it out loud.

"No.... I don't want to lose her now. Please dear God, no." snivelled Michael.

"I think it would be best if you leave Michael to get some rest," said the nurse, watching his vitals on the machine.

Mitch nodded. "Ok. We will wait out in the corridor," said Mitch, watching his brother's sadness.

They both gave Michael a kiss on his forehead and left the room.

With her head on Mitch's shoulder, Rebecca watched as nurses walked towards them and then walk past.

How much longer do we have to wait. God… please, please, I need Paige to be all right, thought Rebecca, swallowing hard, trying to hold back the tears.

Sitting forward, Rebecca positioned her elbows on her thighs and placed her hands either side of her face. Sighing, her eyes averted towards the white tiled floor, the tears overflowed freely onto her cheeks as realisation hit her that she might lose her daughter.

Mitch rubbed her back and said, "Shhh… Paige will be Ok. You'll see."

The torment of losing her husband last year and now the thought of not knowing if she was going to lose her daughter as well was distressing. Feeling powerless, Rebecca started to sob uncontrollably.

"Shhh… come on," said Mitch, holding his arm out for Rebecca.

Rebecca cuddled into the crook of his shoulder for support as her body heaved with every breath she took.

"Ma'am, are you Ok?" said the small framed nurse, as she came to a standstill in front of them.

Rebecca nodded. "I… just… want…my Paige," stammered Rebecca, as she sat up straight and wiped her nose on the sleeve of her jacket.

"How about we get you settled somewhere, whilst you wait for Paige… is it?" said the nurse, as she placed her hand on Rebecca's right arm.

Rebecca nodded and wiped her tear-stained face with her hands.

"Can we sit with my brother in his room? His name is Michael Portellico," said Mitch, indicating to Michael's room across the corridor from where they were sitting.

"I can't see that being a problem, but I will have to check with his nurse first. I will be back in a minute." said the nurse.

Mitch nodded and watched her walk into Michael's room. Through the half glass wall, Mitch and Rebecca watched the two nurses chatting and gesturing towards them.

As the small framed nurse returned, she said, "After speaking with the other nurse, we have come up with an idea. She is happy for you both to sit in Michael's room as long as you keep quiet. She has given him a sedative to sleep and doesn't want him getting distressed whilst he recuperates."

"We can do that," said Mitch, standing with Rebecca.

"There is actually a laydown type seat in Michael's room, so we were thinking that maybe you could rest up there whilst you are waiting for your daughter to come out of surgery," said the nurse.

"Oh, thank you. That's thoughtful of you. But I am not sure I will be able to sleep," said Rebecca, with a creased brow.

"What about if I see the doctor on duty and find out if we can get you a sedative?" asked the nurse, as she placed her hand on Rebecca's right upper arm.

"Nah, I don't need one of those. I will be Ok," said Rebecca, looking from the nurse to Mitch.

The nurse nodded. "Ok. Well… don't hesitate to ask, if you change your mind."

"Thanks," said Rebecca.

"Why don't we get you both settled in Michael's room," said the nurse.

When Mitch and Rebecca walked back into Michael's room, they noticed that two cream leather chairs had now been placed next to Michael's bed. One had a square back and base and the other had a longer base, with a lever on the side to place it into a bed position.

"Thank you," said Mitch to the nurse who was looking after his brother.

"You're welcome."

Mitch sat in the square backed chair next to Michael's bed and watched his brother sleep peacefully. "You sit there, my love," whispered Mitch to Rebecca.

"Ok," said Rebecca, sitting in the chair.

Pulling the lever on Rebecca's chair downwards, Mitch said, "That a bit more comfortable?"

"Yeah… thanks" said Rebecca, now lying flat on the bed.

"Here you go ma'am," said the nurse, handing Rebecca a pillow.

"Thank you," said Rebecca, taking the pillow and placing it under her head.

Chapter Twenty Two

Rebecca heard someone calling her name and felt a hand rubbing her arm. Opening her eyes she noticed Mitch looking down at her and then realised she was still in the hospital.

"What time is it?" asked Rebecca, sitting up quickly.

"Shhh… you will wake Michael. It's three-fifteen. You have been asleep for about three hours," said Mitch, looking at his phone for the time. "Paige is out of surgery and in recovery."

"Can I see her yet?"

"Yes. Come on, I will take you to where she is," said Mitch, holding his hand out.

The steel door frame felt cold as Rebecca leant against it in the doorway of Paige's hospital room. She was overwhelmed by the sight of all the machines Paige had hooked up to her pale, lifeless body. There was a ventilator which was helping her breathe, drips in both arms, heart rate and pulse monitors. She also had a bandage down the left hand side of her forehead. Rebecca couldn't see if there were any other injuries, as she had a blanket pulled up over her unconscious body.

Her legs felt heavy and her mind was faint, as she walked towards the single bed, which had rails up on either side. As she stood at the side of the bed, willing Paige's eyes to open, Rebecca watched the ventilation machine breathe air into and out of the lungs of her sweet little girl.

Placing her hand over Paige's, Rebecca leant forward, closed her eyes and kissed her daughter's forehead, lingering for only a second to take in her scent. When her eyes opened and she stood up straight, the low lit room was a bit hazy. Holding onto the bed railing with one hand for support, she looked at Mitch, who was standing beside her, and grasped his hand.

"You all right?" asked Mitch, as he placed an arm around her back, supporting her weight on him.

"I'm feeling a bit light headed. Can you get me a chair?" said Rebecca, rubbing the side of her head.

Looking around the room, Mitch spotted a chair on the other side of Paige's bed. "Hold onto the railing. I'll get that one," said Mitch, indicating to the chair.

Rebecca nodded, and tried to fight the urge to faint, as she watched Mitch obtain the chair and place it behind her.

From the back of the hospital room, a nurse approached them and stood at the foot of the bed. "Are you Paige's relative?"

"Yes. I am her mother," said Rebecca, as she looked from Paige to the nurse.

With a calm and heartfelt look on her face the nurse said, "I will be stationed in the room tonight and will be looking after your daughter."

Rebecca looked at the nurse's light blue uniform and noticed her name badge. "Bronwyn, is she going to be all right?"

"She is one brave girl. Her surgery certainly went well. They took out her ruptured spleen, so she does have a few stiiches in her stomach. Also we have set her broken left arm in a cast. The only thing the doctor is concerned about at the moment is the swelling on her brain. It hasn't come back to normal yet. Apparently sometimes it can take a few days or even weeks for that to happen. So we will need keep an eye on it. The reason she has a tube down her throat is because she is not breathing on her own yet. That will stay there until she wakes up. She will probably sleep for a while because she has just come out of surgery," said Bronwyn.

"When will we know more?" asked Mitch.

"At the moment all we can do is wait. The rest is up to Paige. I will be closely monitoring her throughout the night and keeping her comfortable. The doctor should be in to see Paige in the morning, so if you need to go home for some rest, I can get the hospital to ring you if you like," said Bronwyn, looking from Rebecca to Mitch.

"No… I won't be leaving the hospital until she wakes. Is it possible to organise for me to have a laydown seat next to her bed whilst I am here?" said Rebecca.

"Yes ma'am. I will have one organised for you," said Bronwyn. She returned to her desk at the back of the room and made a call about the seat.

"I can't believe my sweet little girl is here like this. God, I hope she is going to be all right," said Rebecca, staring at Paige and holding her hand. The tears formed in her eyes and overflowed onto her cheeks.

"She is going to be Ok, Bec. Try to stay positive," said Mitch, placing his arm around her and kissing her forehead.

"I hope so," said Rebecca, through the tears, as she placed her head on his shoulder.

Mitch and Rebecca sat next to Paige's bed, one on either side of Paige, each holding a hand and watching her for any sign of movement. Looking up at the clock, which was situated near the door, Rebecca noticed that one hour had passed by, and still Paige hadn't woken. As she listened to the whooshing sound of the ventilator and the beeping sounds of the vitals machine, Rebecca looked up at the information on the screen at the back of Paige's bed which was displaying her vitals.

Hmm… she seems to be all right, thought Rebecca, watching Paige's heart rate.

Turning to Mitch, Rebecca said, "You don't have to stay with me, I will be fine. Go and see how Michael is doing."

"Are you sure?" said Mitch, worried she might collapse.

"Yes I am sure. I can lie down here if I want, anyway," said Rebecca, indicating to the seat.

"Is there anything I can get you?" said Mitch, walking around the other side of the bed.

"Umm… on your way back can you please get me a drink of

something?" said Rebecca, standing. "Tell Michael I love him and get better soon."

"Ok. I will. I won't be long. If you need me, ring and I will come back, Ok," said Mitch. He gave her a kiss on her forehead and a hug. "I love you."

As Mitch walked into Michael's room, he found his parents and Nick were there sitting at his bedside.

Helen rushed over and gave Mitch a hug. "How is Paige going?"

"She is still unconscious. But stable at this stage," said Mitch.

Grayson gave Mitch a hug and said, "How is Rebecca holding up?"

"She's a mess and worried," said Mitch.

"That's understandable," said Grayson.

"Is there anything we can do, Mitch? Like donate some blood or anything at all? I just feel useless sitting here doing nothing," said Nick.

"No there is nothing anyone can do. The nurse told us that it is up to Paige now to pull herself through and wake up. Thanks for asking anyway," said Mitch, as the tears welled in his eyes.

Nick walked over to Mitch and gave him a warm hug. "We are here for you, bro."

"Thanks," said Mitch, wiping his eyes.

"Is there anything we can do or get for you, son?" asked Grayson.

"No thanks, dad. Just some prayers would be good," said Mitch. Noticing Michael was awake, Mitch walked over to his bed. "How are you feeling, Michael?"

"Pretty damn sore and sorry for myself, bro. If it wasn't for the medication I would be in a world of a pain. Hey… could you please give Paige a kiss for me when you go back to her room. I wish I could go and see her, but they won't let me out of bed until tomorrow. I just want to go and sit with her and hold her hand. God, I hope she is going to be all right," said Michael, with a creased brow.

"No sweat bro, I can do that for you. Should I tell her you love her, maybe that might bring her around?" said Mitch, with a smirk on his face.

"No… I will do that myself once I can get out of this bed," said

Michael.

"Michael… I wanted to ask you; do you remember anything of what happened tonight at the car accident?" said Mitch.

"I don't remember much, bro. Just that the paparazzi caused the accident. They were chasing us and trying to get pictures, when the road narrowed and they crashed into us. That's all I remember. I have given a statement to the police as well… I just can't believe Sawyer is dead, man. That guy was so good to us as we grew up and he didn't deserve to die like that. I will surely miss him," said Michael, with tears welling up in his eyes.

"Me too, bro. We had so many good times with him over the years," said Mitch.

"That reminds me; I must go and pay my respects to his family. I told them I would see them tonight sometime. Will you be Ok here, my dear?" said Grayson.

"Yes, my love. You go and I will see you later. Give Sawyer's family my love. Ring me and let me know what you're doing, Ok?" said Helen.

Grayson nodded, kissed Helen on the forehead and then said goodbye to his sons and left the room.

"Would you like some magazines from the shop?" said Mitch to Michael.

"Mom's going to go down soon and get me some, but thanks anyway, bro," said Michael.

"Well… I might get back to Bec and keep her company. I will come by and see you later on," said Mitch, shaking Michael's hand. "And I will see you tomorrow sometime, Mom." He gave his mom a hug.

"Take care, my dear," said Helen, hugging Mitch back.

On his way back to ICU, Mitch found Rebecca standing alone in front of a vending machine.

"Hello babe," said Mitch, coming to stand next to her.

"Hi," said Rebecca, giving him a hug.

"Is there any change in Paige?" said Mitch, pulling away slowly, searching her eyes for answers.

"No… I thought I would stretch my legs and get some potato

chips," said Rebecca, pressing the button on the vendor machine. "How is Michael going?"

"Michael is doing fine," said Mitch.

"That's good," said Rebecca, politely smiling. "Mitch, could you please do me a favour?"

"What would you like?" said Mitch.

"I don't know how long it will be before Paige gets better, so I was thinking I should cancel our flights back home. I was wondering if you could organise that for me?" said Rebecca.

"Sure, no problem at all. Would you like me to ring your and Paige's work as well?" said Mitch.

"Oh, I hadn't thought of that. Yes, please. That would be great, thanks," said Rebecca, her eyebrows raised.

"Is there anything else you would like me to do for you?" asked Mitch.

"Umm… could you give my mum and dad a ring and let them know? It's just… I don't think I am quite up to ringing anyone at the moment. My mind is a bit fuzzy" said Rebecca, wiping her hands over her face and sighing. "My head hurts a bit though. I just need to keep myself calm, hey."

"No problem, I can ring them first. I will tell your mum and dad that you will ring them later, when you know more, hey? Can I get you a Panadol?" said Mitch.

"Thanks Mitch. Nah, I don't need a Panadol. It's not that type of pain. Since my brain operation, I seem to get this type of pain if I am stressed or have high anxiety. But thanks for offering anyway," said Rebecca, rubbing the side of her head.

"That's Ok. If you think of anything, just let me know. I'll go and make some calls now and meet you back inside Paige's room soon," said Mitch, leaning into to give his fiancé a tight hug.

"Thanks, Mitch," said Rebecca, placing her head on his chest and hugging him. "Don't worry about me, I will be fine."

With his body and mind starting to give way to fatigue, Mitch leant against the metal door frame and watched Rebecca sitting on the square backed chair, as she held Paige's hand and chatted to her. Yawning as he walked into the room, Mitch noticed Rebecca had a photo in her hand and was looking from the photo to Paige.

"Would you like me to come back later?" said Mitch, coming to stand behind her. He noticed the photo she was looking at was of Jackson, Paige and Rebecca in happier times.

Patting the chair beside her, Rebecca said, "Come sit with me."

Mitch sat in the seat next to her.

Placing the photo back in her wallet, Rebecca said, "I hope you don't mind me looking at or even having this photo with me."

"Don't ever think I would mind, Rebecca. If this is what makes you happy, then you look at it. Infact, I too have a photo of Christine in my wallet. I don't ever think I will take it out. When I look at the photo it reminds me of happier times with her," said Mitch, opening his black leather wallet to show her.

"Thank you," said Rebecca, as she looked at the photo Mitch had. "Wow… that's a nice photo of you two together."

"Yeah. It was the day I proposed to her," said Mitch, looking at the photo and remembering that day.

Rebecca nodded.

Mitch closed his wallet and placed it back in his jeans pocket. "Would you like a drink of something?"

"No thanks. I am starting to feel drained. I might get some more sleep, whilst I can. What about you?" said Rebecca, standing.

"Yeah, me too. I might lay down there with you," said Mitch, standing and walking over to the laydown bed with Rebecca that had been set up in Paige's room.

As they relaxed in the chair in each other's arms, with a small white blanket over them, Mitch and Rebecca both fell asleep from the exhaustion.

Woken from a dream of happier times, Mitch could hear someone calling his name. "Hey, sleepyhead." said Rebecca, gently rubbing his arm. "The doctor is here and he wants to talk with us."

"Huh… Ok… right," said Mitch, sitting up and rubbing his hands over his face. The sleep deprivation still apparent on his face. "Good morning, doc."

"Good morning, I am Dr Cameron," said the doctor, holding his hand out front to shake Mitch's hand.

"How is she going, doc?" asked Mitch, standing and shaking his hand.

"I'm afraid there has been no change overnight or this morning so far. Paige's brain swelling has gone down a little bit, but we are still concerned as to why she hasn't woken up yet. The problem with head injuries is that it's a waiting game. It may take days, weeks, months even before she gets better and wakes up. We just have to stay positive. The best thing I can suggest for you for today, is to go home and get some rest and eat some food. You are going to need your strength for the coming days."

"So besides her head injury, she is all right?" asked Rebecca, concern in her voice.

"Yes. That is correct," said Dr Cameron, placing Paige's chart back on the nurse's desk. "Well, I will be back later on this afternoon to check in on Paige. If anything happens in the meantime the nurse will contact me."

"Ok. Thank you, Dr Cameron," said Rebecca, watching him walk towards the doorway.

"Excuse me..." said Rebecca, looking to the back of the room where the nurse was seated. "Mitch and I are gonna head home for a while to get some rest. If there are any changes in Paige's condition, will you please ring me?"

"Yes ma'am. Don't worry, we will take good care of Paige," said the nurse, checking her paperwork to make sure she had Rebecca's mobile number on file.

"Thank you," said Rebecca, noticing for the first time this morning that Paige had a new nurse. Her name tag said 'Gwen'.

With the machines still making their usual sounds, Rebecca leant over her daughter and kissed her on her forehead. "See you later on, sweetie. I love you." She searched every inch of her daughter's face for signs that she may understand, but there was no movement.

"Don't worry, my love, she will still be here when we get back," said Mitch, placing his arm around Rebecca's shoulder.

"God, I hope so. I feel guilty leaving even for a minute," said Rebecca, leaning into Mitch.

"Come on, let's get you home for some rest," said Mitch. "See you later on, Paige." *Don't even think about leaving us, Paige. Keep strong, little lady.* Looking down at her he smiled briefly as the tears formed in his eyes.

The hot water gushed over Rebecca's skin releasing her knotted shoulders and aching back. Placing her head under the large square-shaped shower head to wash her hair made Rebecca feel relaxed.

"You Ok in there?" called Mitch, as he opened the shower glass screen door.

"Yeah, I'm all right. This hot water feels nice on my skin," said Rebecca, closing her eyes.

"You've been in there a while. I was starting to get worried," said Mitch.

"I'm getting out now," said Rebecca, turning off the faucet.

Mitch handed Rebecca a towel, as she stepped out onto the bathroom mat.

"I was thinking of making something for us to eat. Would you like it in our room or downstairs, Bec?"

"Could we have something up here, Mitch? I am exhausted and all I want to do is shower, eat and sleep," said Rebecca, placing her knickers on.

"That's no problem. I won't be long downstairs," said Mitch.

"Thank you," said Rebecca, leaning in for a hug.

Whilst Mitch was downstairs in the kitchen, Rebecca finished getting dressed. Walking into the bedroom, she headed for the window to see what sort of day it was outside. As she stood at the window looking out across the paddock, there was a knock at the door.

"Can I come in, dear?" asked Helen.

"Yes of course you can," said Rebecca, indicating to come in.

"How are you my dear?"

The tears welled up in Rebecca's eyes and before she knew it, they were overflowing onto her cheeks. Sobbing she said, "Sorry."

"Don't be sorry. Let it out, dear. That's what mothers are for, to help you get through it," said Helen, hugging her and rubbing her back.

Rebecca pulled away slowly and looked at Helen through her tears. "Thank you for being so kind. You are such a lovely mother. Thank you for the hug too; I needed that. I am so worried about Paige. I don't want to lose her too, Helen. I don't think I could handle if the doctors said she wasn't going to be all right."

"Listen dear… you must have faith and stay positive. I know that is easy to say, but it does work. Would you like to come to the church with us this afternoon? We are all going to say a prayer for Paige and Michael and Sawyer," said Helen.

"That would be lovely Helen. Thank you," said Rebecca, giving her another hug. "Sawyer… I am so sorry about Sawyer. His poor family; what they must be going through."

"Thank you, dear. I can't believe it myself. He has been a valuable employee and friend for years," said Helen, pulling away from their hug slowly. "His family sure have some tough times ahead. But we have told them that we are here for them always."

"Oh, that's nice," said Rebecca.

"I believe Mitchell is getting you some food," said Helen.

"Yes. He is really good to me. I love him so much. You have such a wonderful son. He is probably tired himself, but instead he is looking after me," said Rebecca, wiping her wet face.

"He will be fine, dear. He is a pretty strong man. Best thing for you both to do is to have some food and then have a sleep for a while. You will feel much better. Then we can go to the church later, Ok?" said Helen.

"Sounds good… thank you, Helen."

"Here we go," said Mitch, walking into the room with a tray full of food and drinks.

"Well… I will leave you both to your lunch. See you later on, Ok?" said Helen, standing.

"Thanks, Mom," said Mitch, placing the tray down on the bed and then giving her a hug.

"Thanks Helen," said Rebecca, watching her walk towards the door and close it behind her.

Mitch patted the bed and said, "I have made us some chicken and vegetable soup, with some French bread stick and a glass of wine."

"Thank you Mitch. This looks like just what the doctor ordered," said Rebecca, sitting across from him on the bed.

"You're welcome, beautiful," said Mitch, handing her a glass of wine.

After Mitch and Rebecca had finished their soup, they laid down on the bed and cuddled into each other. It didn't take them too long and they were fast asleep.

Waking from her dreams of Paige as a baby, Rebecca smiled and felt warm all over. As she looked over at Mitch to see if he was awake, she found him lying on his pillow with his eyes wide open, gazing at her.

"Hello beautiful. How do you feel?" said Mitch, looking into her eyes.

"I feel better, thanks babe. What time is it?" said Rebecca.

"It's six-thirty," said Mitch, looking over at his bedside clock.

"Far out… I have been asleep for five hours. But I do feel better for it," said Rebecca, yawning.

"Did you want to get up and go downstairs for some dinner and then we can go to the church with everyone?" asked Mitch, pulling himself up onto his elbow.

"Sure. Give me a minute, I just need to freshen up and then we can go down together," said Rebecca, getting off the bed.

"No problem. I will go have a shower whilst you are getting ready," said Mitch, hopping off the bed.

Rebecca pushed her food from one side of the plate to another, as she wondered if Paige was going be Ok. Looking around the dining room table at the Portellico family she noticed everyone's quiet demeanour as they ate their roast lamb, vegetables and gravy for dinner.

"Everyone… in about twenty minutes we have a couple of cars going to take us to the church. We will meet you all at the front door," said Grayson.

They all nodded and pushed their half-eaten plates to one side.

Rebecca snuggled up next to Mitch in the back seat of the car and placed her head on his shoulder. He held her hand firmly as they leant on each other for strength and stared straight ahead.

When the cars pulled up out front of the rustic, red brick, West Seattle church, Rebecca noticed that a priest, dressed in a cream coloured vestment, was waiting for everyone at the top of the steps. He knew they were coming because Grayson and Helen had planned a lovely service for tonight. They both were great believers in the Lord.

"Good evening," said the priest, as everyone walked by him and through the wooden doors.

Wow... what a beautiful Catholic church. Cream walls, with rustic colour pillars, and wooden pews. Really lovely, thought Rebecca, her eyebrows raised as she walked down the beige coloured tiled aisle, towards the front of the church. With her eyes darting from one side of the church to another, taking in the magnificent gold architraves and the wonderful rounded glass ceiling, Rebecca made a sign of the cross on her chest as she approached the altar. Turning to her right, Rebecca noticed the devotional area. She hadn't been to a church since Jackson had passed away and sought comfort in saying a prayer and taking a turn at lighting a white prayer candle, which symbolised light for Paige, and Michael and Sawyer and their families.

Once all the family members took their seats in the wooden pews, near the front of the church, the parish priest stood on the steps of the altar and looked at each of the faces that sat before him and started his service. He talked about Sawyer and how the world had lost a great soul and that God would take good care of him. He also talked about Michael and his road to recovery. He then said a prayer for Paige and asked God to help Paige heal and to watch over her. Finally he prayed for everyone, to help them through their tough and sad times ahead. The service brought comfort and strength to everyone who attended.

When the service ended and everyone was saying their goodbyes, Rebecca approached the priest and said, "Thank you, Father. That was a lovely service you gave tonight. You have given me the strength to carry on now."

"You are most welcome, my dear. If there is anything I can do to help you through your daughter's recovery, please don't hesitate to ask. I am here for you always," said the father.

"Thank you," said Rebecca, leaning in to hug him.

As she pulled away, he smiled at her. "May God be with you, my child," said the father.

"Thank you," said Rebecca, as she walked towards Mitch, who was waiting at the car.

The father nodded politely.

"So… you ready to go?" said Mitch to Rebecca.

"Yes," said Rebecca, placing her hand in his.

"Are you off to see Paige, dears?" asked Helen, overhearing that they were leaving.

"Yes," said Mitch.

"Is she still in ICU at the moment?" asked Grayson, as he stood next to Helen.

"Yes and unfortunately she can't have any visitors yet," said Rebecca, looking from Grayson to Helen. "Are you going to see Michael tonight?"

"No, not tonight. We promised Sawyer's wife and children that we would come by tonight and discuss the funeral arrangements, amongst other things," said Grayson, as he looked over Rebecca's shoulder to see Sawyer's wife and children getting into their car.

"Ok… well, we might head off to the hospital. See you all tomorrow," said Mitch, shaking his Dad's hand.

"Let us know how Paige is doing, dears," said Helen, as she gave Rebecca and Mitch a hug goodbye. "Give Michael a hug from Dad and I."

"We will," said Mitch.

"Give me a ring if you need anything, bro," said Nick, shaking Michael's hand. "Give Paige my regards."

"Thanks, Nick," said Michael, shaking his hand back.

"Thanks, Nick," said Rebecca, as she hugged him.

"Why don't we go and get a coffee and come back later," whispered Rebecca to Mitch, as they stood in the doorway to Paige's hospital room and watched Michael sitting by her bed, holding her hand and talking to an unconscious Paige.

"Good idea. I have heard that they make a nice latte in the hospital cafeteria," said Mitch, quietly.

"Great... I think the cafeteria is on the fifth floor. Let's go," whispered Rebecca.

"I can see now that Michael really does love Paige, you know. In fact after what Paige told me yesterday, I am liking your brother even more," said Rebecca, placing both cups of coffee on the table and taking a seat.

"What did she tell you yesterday, Bec?" said Mitch, ripping open the sugar sachet and emptying it into his cup.

"She said that Michael hadn't even asked her to have sex yet and that he was a true gentleman," said Rebecca, stirring her latte.

"For real; she told you this?" said Mitch, taken back. "The old Michael I knew would never had been like this. He must truly like Paige to be holding back like that." Mitch smiled and raised his eyebrows.

"You mean he wasn't like this with other girls?" asked Rebecca.

"No. He has never been like that. But you know from the moment I introduced them on Skype, I could tell that he liked her for her personality, not for what he could get out of her. He just seemed different when they were talking that's all. I put it down to me being away for five years and thought he had matured. But obviously it's because he is smitten with your daughter," said Mitch, picking up his cup.

"When I was talking with Paige yesterday, she told me she really liked Michael and hoped he would be able to move to Perth with you. God... now look at her. Lying there in a bed, not knowing if she will be all right; it breaks my heart, Mitch," said Rebecca, with tears filling her eyes and her voice wavering.

Mitch placed his hands over Rebecca's and said, "Come on, think positive, not negative. Why don't you go and sit with Paige for a while and I can keep Michael company in his room. Ok?"

"Ok. Thank you, babe," said Rebecca, nodding as she wiped her eyes with the back of her hands.

Michael looked up to see Mitch and Rebecca standing in the doorway listening to him read to Paige. Smiling, he shut the book quickly and placed it in his lap.

"Hey guys," said Michael, placing the book on the window ledge.

"Hi, Michael. Thank you for being here with her. I'm sure if she was awake, Paige would tell you herself that she enjoyed you reading to her," said Rebecca, walking over to him and giving him a hug.

"You're welcome. I didn't want to leave her alone. She means a lot to me, Bec," said Michael, looking over at Paige.

"I know she does, Michael. She likes you as well. She told me so yesterday. She also told me that you have been really good to her. If your parents agree to it, I can't wait for you to move over to Perth with us," said Rebecca.

"Thanks, Bec," said Michael. "I just hope Mom and Dad agree."

"Have the nurse or doctors said anything about Paige's condition today?" asked Rebecca, now standing next to the bed and looking at her daughter.

"No, they haven't said anything to me," said Michael.

"I might go and see them to find out if there are any updates on her condition," said Rebecca, walking towards the doorway. Just as Rebecca was about to leave, the nurse returned to the room.

"Good evening," said the nurse, with an English accent.

"Hello… could you please give me an update on my daughter's condition?" queried Rebecca.

"Her condition hasn't changed. Once she wakes up, we will know more," said the nurse.

"Oh, Ok. Thank you," said Rebecca, nodding.

The nurse returned to her desk at the back of the room.

"How are you feeling today, bro?" asked Mitch.

"Still feel really sore, man. But the Doc said if I am well enough, I can go home tomorrow. I would rather stay here though. I want to be here when Paige wakes up," said Michael, wholehearted.

"I am sure you do. But your health comes first. You are no good to

Paige if you are ill when she wakes up," said Mitch.

"I know you are right. I was thinking that maybe I could do the morning shift and Bec could do the afternoon/night shift of sitting with Paige, whilst she recovers. What do you think?" said Michael.

"Only if you are well enough bro, and you need to talk it over with Bec," said Mitch, looking over at Rebecca.

"What do you think, Bec?" queried Michael.

"Michael, that is lovely of you to offer, but we have to think about your health first. Only if you are well enough, would I agree to that," said Rebecca, standing back at Paige's bed.

"Sounds fair enough" said Michael, sadly.

"Well… I think I will take you back to your room, Michael. Rebecca wants to spend some time alone with Paige for a while," said Mitch.

"Oh, Ok," said Michael, smiling. Leaning over Paige he gave her a kiss on her forehead. "Good night, Paige. See you in the morning."

"Night, Michael. See you tomorrow," said Rebecca.

"Yeah, night. See you tomorrow, Bec," said Michael.

"See you when you get back, babe."

"Ok," said Mitch, pushing Michael in the wheelchair towards the doorway.

Rebecca placed her handbag down next to the window and then took a seat next to Paige's bed. Looking at the monitor behind Paige's bed, which displayed information on her health, she thought, *When are you going to wake up, sweetie?*

"Hello Paige… it's Mum. But I guess you already know that if you can hear me. Where are you, sweetie?" said Rebecca, holding her hand and looking over her daughter's lifeless facial expression. "Come back to me, *please*."

There was no movement from Paige, only the sound of the ventilator and the other machines hooked up to her, which were keeping her alive.

I wish there was something I could do to wake you up, thought Rebecca, as she watched Paige's eyeballs move from side to side under her eyelids.

"The Portellico family and I all went to a church service tonight, sweetie. Yeah, I can hear you now: 'Wow Mum, you haven't been to church in a while,"' said Rebecca, with a creased brow. "I went to pray for you, my sweet girl. God, how I love you so much." Rebecca picked up Paige's hand and placed a lingering kiss on the top of it. Placing it back down on the bed, she leant forward and rested her forehead on her forearms on the side of the bed and prayed some more. Within minutes of resting her head, her eyes closed and Rebecca dreamt of happier times with Jackson, Paige and herself.

Chapter Twenty Three

It had been two weeks since the accident and Paige's motionless body still lay unconscious in hospital. The doctor had taken the ventilation machine off of her because she was now breathing on her own and had transferred her out of the ICU and into a normal ward. All of her injuries had healed nicely and even her brain swelling had finally come down. The doctors had assured Rebecca that Paige should wake up any day.

Rebecca smiled as she leant against the doorway of Paige's room, watching and listening to Michael talking to Paige about things they had in common.

"Hey Paige, you had better wake up soon because you are going to miss out on meeting Bella, Edward and Jacob from Twilight. Nick has organised for you to actually meet them at the movie premiere of 'Breaking Dawn Part 2'," teased Michael, as he held her hand. He knew she loved the Twilight characters and how much she wanted to meet them, so he had hoped if he teased her enough about something that she really liked, then she would wake up.

But to his disappointment, she never woke.

"Hello Michael. You are doing a good job there," said Rebecca, walking into the room. "I am sure she can hear you."

"Hi Rebecca. I wish Paige would open her eyes. The doctors and nurses all say, keep talking and reading to Paige as she can hear us and that's what I have been doing. But she isn't waking," said Michael, tears welling in his eyes. His voice was frustrated.

She leant down and gave him a hug.

"Yeah, I know. I am starting to wonder if she will ever wake up," said Rebecca, with a creased brow. "What are you up to tonight Michael?"

"Nothing actually. I am hoping that I might be able to get an early night because I haven't slept well since the accident. And today my back seems to be aching more than usual, from the kidney infection I have… humph. I just want to get better and for Paige to wake up so we can do things together," said Michael, as his shoulders slumped and the tears came streaming down his cheeks. The fatigue and fear of the unknown had taken its toll on Michael. Letting go of Paige's hand to wipe his tears from his face, Michael felt Paige try to grasp his hand. It took him a few seconds to register what had happened.

"Paige…" said Michael, squeezing her hand. "Paige… are you able to open your eyes?" He leant over her and watched her eyes move from side to side under her eyelids.

Rebecca stood beside the bed and waited as Michael talk to Paige. She seemed to recognise his voice.

"Mmmichael, I… hear… you," said Paige, slowly.

He kissed her lips and said, "I love you Paige Landers. Open your eyes."

"Trying…can't," said Paige, her speech delayed.

Rebecca looked on in amazement and called out "Nurse… nurse, she's awake."

Hearing her mum's voice Paige said, "Mum."

"Yes… I am here sweetie," said Rebecca, looking down at Paige.

"Can't… see… you," said Paige.

"It's Ok, Paige," said the nurse, coming to stand on the other side of the bed. "How's your pain level?"

Paige put her thumb in the air.

"Good. So… first things first. Do you know where you are?" asked the nurse.

Paige shook her head.

"You are in hospital. You were in a car accident," said the nurse, looking from Paige to Rebecca and Michael.

"Ok," said Paige, weakly.

"I'm just going to check your vitals," said the nurse, looking up at the machines attached to Paige. "Well, it's looking good. Can you open your eyes, Paige?"

Paige's eyes fluttered open and then closed. "What's... wrong?" asked Paige, with a creased brow.

"Paige... you have been in a coma for two weeks. It may take a few hours, but usually you will regain your speech and the eyes will follow. It's just the brain's way of waking up. This is quite normal."

Paige nodded, as a tear escaped down the side of face.

Rebecca breathed a sigh of relief, knowing her daughter was going to be Ok.

"Twilight... I... hear... you," said Paige.

Michael laughed at her and said, "It took that to wake you up. I have tried everything possible of teasing you and this worked. Unbelievable."

"Mum... where... Mum?" asked Paige.

"I am right here, sweetie. I am so glad you have woken up," said Rebecca, holding her hand as the tears formed in her eyes.

"I saw Dad. He ask me... to stay with him. Lonely," said Paige, her mouth dry.

"That explains why you didn't want to wake up. Was Dad all right when you left?" said Rebecca.

She put her thumb up and said, "He found his brother. He was happy I was there," said Paige slowly. As Paige's eyes moved from side to side under her eyelids, all of a sudden they opened and she tried to focus. "I see you. Bit blurry, but Ok now." She tried to wipe her eyes with her hand.

"Sounds like your speech is getting better too, sweetie," said Rebecca, smiling.

"Yeah... I feel strange," said Paige, as she tried to sit up. "Humph, feel dizzy." Closing her eyes, she laid back down again.

"You will probably feel like that for a few days, Paige. But we will help you with that and eventually you will be able to sit up and walk too," said the nurse. "You need to realise you have been through a big ordeal and it will take time to get you back to normal. Let me try adjusting your bed and see how you feel." She pressed the bed elevation button and slowly brought Paige up into a semi sitting position.

Taking a deep breath, Paige said, "That's better."

Rebecca and Michael smiled.

"Right. I will leave you three to chat, but don't wear her out," said the nurse, looking from Rebecca to Michael.

They both nodded.

"We won't," said Rebecca.

"I need to go and fill out some paperwork and alert the doctor that you have woken up," said the nurse to Paige.

"Ok. Thank you," said Paige, watching the nurse walk towards the doorway.

"How are you feeling, sweetheart?" asked Rebecca.

"Humph, my head hurts a little bit," said Paige, feeling the left hand side of her head and realising there was a small square bandage on her temple. She then noticed a white cast on her left forearm. "Must have been one hell of an accident. What happened?"

"Let's not talk about that now. We just need you to get better. So…" said Rebecca.

"Mum…" interrupted Paige. "I want to know."

"The paparazzi caused the accident. They got too close to the car. Don't you remember?" said Michael.

Paige rubbed her head again and frowned. "No, I don't remember much at all."

Rebecca looked up at the vitals machine and watched Paige's heart rate accelerate. "Sweetheart, you need to try and calm yourself down. We can talk about this more when you are fully recovered, but until then let's change the subject."

"Yeah, I think your mum's right, Paige," said Michael, his brow furrowed as he looked from the vitals machine to Rebecca and then Paige. "Are you comfortable there?"

"Yeah, I'm all right. Maybe… can you move some of the pillows for me," said Paige, leaning forward. "Humph, dizzy hey."

"Sure," said Michael, stacking the three pillows behind Paige.

"Thank you," said Paige, as she leant back into the pillows.

"Hopefully the dizziness will go soon," said Rebecca, as she leant forward and gave Paige a kiss on her forehead. "Can we get you anything?"

"Am I allowed to have a drink of water? My mouth is so dry," said Paige.

"I think we may have to wait for the doctor to come in first before you can have anything to drink or eat. It's usually standard procedure at hospitals when a patient has first woken up," said Rebecca. "I am sure the doctor won't be long now." Rebecca looked from Paige to the room's doorway, searching to see if the nurse was on her way back.

Paige nodded slowly.

After they had all talked together quietly for a while, Paige heard Michael's stomach rumble. "That sounds like it needs feeding?" said Paige, smiling.

"Yeah, I am a bit hungry," said Michael, rubbing his stomach.

"Why don't you go and get something to eat, Michael?" said Rebecca. "I will stay here with Paige."

"Sounds like a good idea. Would you like anything, Rebecca?" said Michael, as he stood up.

"No, thanks. I'm fine," said Rebecca, watching him walk towards the doorway.

"Ok. Well, I'll see you in a little while guys. I won't be long," said Michael, who was off to the cafeteria to purchase some dinner for himself.

"You know, I heard everything you all said to me when I was asleep. It's true what they say. I could hear you, but I couldn't seem to find my way back. And when I found Dad and he looked so unhappy, I felt that I couldn't leave him. Not until he found his brother, anyway. Then I knew he would be all right if I left... he told me to tell you that he loves you, Mum. He also said that you need to marry Mitch and that he is happy that you have found someone else," said Paige, with a creased brow, watching Rebecca's reaction.

Rebecca looked into Paige's eyes and saw she was serious about what Jackson had told her. As the tears welled in her eyes for the loss of her husband, she gave Paige a hug and said, "Thank you, sweetie. I sure am glad you found your way back and are awake. I have missed you and your beautiful smile."

Walking through the doorway the doctor said, "Knock, knock... well now, haven't you made a speedy recovery, Paige?" Reaching her bed, he looked up at the monitor to check her vitals. "I am sure there are a few people who will be glad you are awake. If all goes well with your scans and tests that I will organise today, then maybe we can let you go home in a few days."

"Really?" said Paige, smiling.

"I can't see why not. The brain sure is a fascinating thing, with the way it works," said the doctor, taking the white folder off the table and writing some notes. "Let me have a look at your eyes, dear. Watch my finger and follow it." Placing his pointer finger in front of Paige's eyes he moved it from left to right and watched her eyes follow his finger. "Good... now, what day is it?"

"It's Sunday, I think," said Paige, looking at Rebecca for some acknowledgement that she was right.

'Ok. Good," said the doctor, taking his pen light out of his pocket. "Let me have a look in your eyes. Look up. Now down. Yes, that is good. I need you to wiggle your toes for me." He lifted the blanket to watch her move. "Lift your legs, one at a time, off the bed and then raise your arms above your head."

Paige did as instructed with ease.

"Good... well, it looks like you are recovering fine. But we will know more from the tests. I will come back in the morning and see you. Ok?" said the doctor, placing the white folder into its holder at the end of the bed.

"Thank you, doctor. Is Paige allowed to eat or drink anything?" said Rebecca. "It's just she has complained about being thirsty."

"She can have water only, until tomorrow. The drip will stay in so she won't get dehydrated or hungry. You can have some ice to suck on. I will let the nurse know on the way out. Well, it's good to see you awake,

Paige. I will see you tomorrow," said the doctor, walking towards the doorway to continue his rounds.

"Thank you," said Paige, as she watched the doctor pass Michael in the doorway.

"That was quick. How was your dinner?" asked Rebecca, as Michael walked towards her.

"Yeah, it was Ok. You know what cafeteria food is like," said Michael, sitting next to the bed.

"Humph... sure do," said Rebecca, nodding.

"What did the doctor say?" asked Michael.

"He said that I may be able to go home in a few days, all going well with my next lot of tests," said Paige, excited at the prospect of going home.

"Wow... that is good news. So he must be happy with your progress so far?" said Michael, smiling. He placed his hand over Paige's and gently squeezed it.

Rebecca sat on the windowsill observing the conversation and body language between Paige and Michael. As she watched her daughter smile and laugh, she thought, *I haven't actually realised how close these two are.*

"Would you two like some time alone?" asked Rebecca, as she looked from Paige to Michael.

Michael and Paige nodded and said, "Yes."

"No problem. I might go get something to eat from the cafeteria. Just ring me if you need me and I will come back. Ok?" said Rebecca, standing next to Paige's bed. She leant in and gave Paige a hug.

"Thanks Mum," said Paige, hugging her back.

Michael smiled and said, "Thanks Rebecca."

The elevator pinged and the steel doors opened up at the cafeteria which was on the fifth floor of the hospital. As Rebecca stepped out she spotted a small black melamine table with a couple of metal looking chairs which she could sit at. Taking her phone out of her handbag, she rang the Portellico home and took her seat at the table.

"Hello," said Grayson.

"Oh, hello, Grayson. It's Rebecca. I have some wonderful news...

Paige has woken up."

"That is the best news I have had all day," said Grayson, smiling. He turned to his wife, "Helen… Paige has woken up."

"Oh my God, really? Give me the phone," said Helen, smiling and grabbing the phone from Grayson. "Rebecca, it's Helen. Is she allowed visitors?"

"Yes."

"And so the doctor has said Paige is all right then?" asked Helen, nervously.

"Yes. They are going to run some more tests and if they all come back with good results then she might be able to leave hospital in a few days. I just can't believe my little girl is awake." Tears of joy sprang to her eyes.

"We are so happy for you, my dear," said Helen. "Tell Paige we will come and visit later on tonight."

"I will. Can you let everyone else know about Paige for me?" said Rebecca.

"Yes, dear," said Helen.

"Thanks, Helen. Well… I might go and give Mitch and my parents a ring," said Rebecca, who was looking out the tinted window and watching people walking in and out of the hospital grounds.

"Ok. We will see you soon. Give Paige our love. Bye," said Helen, placing the home phone back on the cradle.

Rebecca pressed the red end button on her mobile and then located Mitch's number in her phone.

"Hello babe. How's everything going?" asked Mitch.

"She's awake… Paige is awake!" said Rebecca, excitedly.

"That is great news, babe. Actually, I am only minutes away," said Mitch.

"Cool. I am in the cafeteria. I am giving Michael and Paige some time alone."

"I'll meet you there," said Mitch.

"Ok. See you soon," said Rebecca. Hanging up the phone she then located her parents' number and rang them to give them the good news.

With her purse in her hand, Rebecca stood in line at the cafeteria to purchase a hot drink. Feeling someone's arms position themselves around her waist, she turned around to find Mitch standing behind her, smiling.

"Hi beautiful. Can you get me a coffee as well?" said Mitch. He gave her a quick peck on the cheek.

"Hi babe. No problem. My things are over there," indicated Rebecca, to the table she had been sitting at previously. "I will bring the drinks over."

"Ok. Thanks," said Mitch, looking over to the table near the window. It had been a few weeks since Mitch and Rebecca had spent any time together. He had been busy with his business and she had spent most of her waking hours with Paige at the hospital.

"Here we go," said Rebecca, placing the hot drinks on the table.

Mitch stood and gave Rebecca a warm hug. "Good news about Paige, hey. I am glad she is going to be all right."

"Yeah… humph, I can't believe it took Michael teasing her about the next Twilight film for her to wake up," said Rebecca, smiling.

"Unbelievable. But sometimes that's all it takes," said Mitch, placing his hand in hers.

"Mitch… I want to tell you something," said Rebecca. She wasn't sure how he was going to take the news.

"What is it?" said Mitch, with a creased brow.

"Well… it's something Paige told me. Umm… when she was sleeping she said that she saw Jackson," said Rebecca, watching his reaction. "He said to tell me that I should marry you and that he was happy for us."

Mitch looked at Rebecca with raised eyebrows and said, "You're joking! That is unbelievable. He must still be around and can see that we are happy. He sure was a really nice guy."

"I know. It really spooked me out when Paige told me," said Rebecca.

"Yeah. Well now we know why Paige didn't wake up. She must miss him terribly," said Mitch. "How is she anyway?"

"Was scary when she first woke up. She couldn't open her eyes, or speak properly. But you would never know that now. She still has a few tests to do and is still feeling a bit dizzy, but otherwise she is better. Can't wait to take her home though."

"Yeah, me too. I am looking forward to going home. I mean Perth that is," said Mitch.

"Perth… God I haven't even thought about home for a while. It sure will be interesting getting Paige settled back in Perth, especially as Michael and her have become so close. I just didn't realise how close they are until tonight when I was watching them chat. That was one of the reasons I thought I would give them some time alone."

"Ever the romantic," said Mitch.

Rebecca smiled. "I wanted to give them a bit of time to talk, cuddle and catch up without anyone else being there. They needed some privacy, you know."

"Yeah, for sure. So how long before she can come home?" asked Mitch.

"I don't know yet. I suppose it depends on her recovery," said Rebecca, shrugging her shoulders.

"It's good news anyway. You must feel like a weight has been taken off your shoulders now?" said Mitch.

"Sure do. Once she is better, then we can all go home. I miss being in my own house," said Rebecca.

"Yeah I miss being in Perth too. But I will miss here as well," said Mitch. He had enjoyed living in Seattle with his parents and family again.

After about an hour of waiting in the cafeteria, Mitch and Rebecca caught the lift back down to Paige's room. Walking in, they found Paige and Michael snuggled up to each other, watching TV on Paige's hospital bed. Paige's face lit up when Mitch and Rebecca came into the room.

"Hello Paige. Good to see you awake finally. You must have been having one hell of a good time in your sleep," said Mitch, smiling.

"How did you guess?" said Paige, as she laughed.

He then gave her a warm hug.

"Hello, sweetie. How are you feeling now?" said Rebecca, leaning in to kiss her forehead.

"I feel really good actually. Michael has been making me laugh with all the news for the past two weeks," said Paige.

"I am glad, sweetheart. Has the doctor been back in to see you yet" said Rebecca.

"No. He will be back first thing in the morning, remember?" said Paige.

"Oh, that's right. Sorry I forgot," said Rebecca, rubbing her right temple.

"So how many nights have you two had together since I have been in here?" asked Paige.

"None sweetheart. But that doesn't matter. You were all I could think about and I didn't want to leave you," said Rebecca.

"Well why don't you both have a night out tonight and do something special. Michael said he wants to stay with me anyway. So I will have someone keeping me company," said Paige.

"Are you sure, Michael? You have been here since early morning. You must be tired," said Rebecca, worried for his health.

"I was, but now that Paige is awake, I am not leaving her," said Michael, looking at Paige adoringly. "The only thing I really would like is a decent meal. I have a laydown bed here anyway if I get tired. You too go and enjoy yourselves and we will see you tomorrow."

"Ok. But we will bring you back something good to eat, all right?" said Rebecca.

He nodded and said, "Thanks, Bec."

Rebecca leant in and kissed Paige on the cheek. "I am *so* glad you are awake, my sweetheart. I love you very much and have missed you. If you need anything, ring me and I will bring it in. Otherwise I will see you tomorrow."

"Thanks Mum. See you tomorrow," said Paige, hugging her tight.

"Hopefully you might have some more good news tomorrow. You two have a good night," said Mitch, giving Paige a kiss on the cheek and then shaking Michael's hand.

"Bye, sweetie," said Rebecca, kissing her own palm and then throwing it in Paige's direction. "See you, Michael."

"Bye," said Michael.

"See ya," said Paige, pretending to catch her kiss.

"Come on… the car's over here," said Mitch, pulling Rebecca by the hand, across the pathway to his black chauffeur driven limo, which had been waiting for them. Mitch opened the door for her and they both hopped into the car. "What would you like to do?"

"Are you tired from work today?" asked Rebecca, as she snuggled into his side and lay her head on his shoulder.

"No, I'm not tired. But I would like to take you out to dinner somewhere nice," said Mitch, holding her hand.

"That sounds nice. How about we go home first and I can get something nice to wear on and then we can have dinner?"

"Sounds good to me. I want to have a shower anyway and put on some fresh clothes. Whilst you are getting ready I will book something for us," said Mitch. Mitch instructed the driver to take them home and told him that we would be dining out later, so he would be needed for that as well.

He also organised for a local restaurant to bring Michael some food and something nice to drink at the hospital.

On the way to the restaurant Mitch said, "I have booked at table for us at a restaurant down at Pier 67, called the 'Six Seven Restaurant'. I have heard it's really good food and great service, with spectacular views."

"By the water, sounds nice. Can't wait to see what they have on the menu," said Rebecca, excited.

As the limo pulled into the restaurant car park, which was attached to the Edgewater Hotel, Rebecca said, "Wow… look at that gas fireplace, which is out in the open. I have never seen anything like that before. With the chimney stack made of cream and cement coloured cobble stones and the flame burning bright, it looks beautiful on that roundabout. Doesn't it?"

"Sure is beautiful; just like you, Rebecca," said Mitch, as he looked into her eyes.

She smiled and kissed him passionately on his lips and said, "Thank you."

Mitch alighted from the car first and place his hand out front for Rebecca to steady herself as she stepped out of the car. As they approached the glass and wood doors to the hotel, a lady approached them and said, "Do you have a reservation, sir?"

"Yes. Under Portellico," said Mitch, taking Rebecca's hand in his.

Looking at her list, the attendant said, "Ah, yes sir, we have your table ready. Come this way." She held the wooden and glass door open for them to continue on through.

When Rebecca walked into the restaurant she was stopped in her tracks by the impressive view of the calm dark blue water overlooking the Seattle city jewelled lights, through the full length glass windows. But what struck her attention the most was the opulence of the place. Besides having the same design of fireplaces inside the restaurant as outside, it also had wood patterned hard tiled floors, with lookalike tree trunks and bare branches touching the wooden boat decking ceiling. The dimly lit room, which seemed to have a safari theme, had lavish furniture and its cushions were all either brown, cream or a cheetah coloured. Even the lighting had look-alike reindeer antlers hanging from them in an adjacent room. Looking around at the other patrons at their tables, Rebecca noticed that their menus were illuminated for ease of reading, because of the room's darkness.

Once they were seated at their table, which was situated next to a clear glass window overlooking the water, Mitch ordered a bottle of 'Bollinger Grande Année Rosé 1999'.

Hmm, that sounds familiar, thought Rebecca, trying to remember where she had heard that wine name from.

When the waitress returned with their wine, she opened it with precision and poured a mouthful into Mitch's glass. Mitch took a sip and said, "Mmm, nice." The waitress poured a glass for them both and then placed the bottle in an ice bucket next to their table.

Tasting the pink coloured wine Rebecca said, "Mmm, this is nice wine, Mitch."

"Sure is a sweet drop. Like you are, Rebecca," said Mitch.

"You sure are full of compliments tonight," said Rebecca.

"I never grow tired of looking at your lovely face and I will always be here to tell you how much I love you," said Mitch, holding her hand as he looked into her blue eyes.

Kissing him tenderly on his lips, she ran the back of her hand down the side of Mitch's face. Looking into his eyes, she said, "I love you too, my gorgeous man. My life has not been the same since I met you. You're always complimenting me. I am looking forward to our married life together."

"When do you think you will be ready? I could marry you today, but I don't want to rush you. Though it sure would be good if we could at least set a date," said Mitch, with a creased brow.

"It's June now, what about in August. I believe the weather here will be much warmer then," said Rebecca, watching the reaction on his face.

Mitch's eyes lit up and with his smile from ear to ear. "That's only two months away and you want to get married here, in Seattle?"

Rebecca nodded and said, "Yes. I know August is not far away, but I bet we could organise a really nice wedding and reception in two months. Especially as your mom has offered me her help. I want to get married in Seattle, because this is where I fell in love with you and I want this to be our city of romance for us."

"I can't believe you want to get married so soon and here, in my home town. God… I feel like the most luckiest man alive at the moment," said Mitch, smiling. Leaning in, he kissed her so passionately that she could feel her stomach doing somersaults again.

As their lips parted Rebecca said, "I don't see the point in waiting. We both know we love each other and from a personal point of view, I just know that you are the person I want to spend the rest of my life with."

"I feel the same about you too, Bec and I can't wait to marry you," said Mitch.

"So now I have picked the month, what date would you like to choose?" asked Rebecca.

Mitch reached into his jacket pocket and took his mobile phone out to look up the calendar and see what dates fell on a Saturday in August. "What about the 12th of August? We can make it an afternoon ceremony and a night time reception."

"Sounds perfect. How do you feel about having the reception at your Mom and Dad's house?" asked Rebecca.

"Are you kidding… I would love to have the reception there and I am sure Mom and Dad would too," said Mitch. "Wow… I can't believe how easy that was. I certainly wasn't expecting to pick out a date for our wedding so soon."

Rebecca noticed the waitress waiting in the background waiting to take their order. "You know, we had better have a look at the menu before the waitress comes back. At least once we have ordered, she will leave us alone so we can talk more about the wedding," said Rebecca, picking up her menu.

"Good idea," said Mitch, looking in the same direction as Rebecca at the waitress.

"Are you both ready to place your orders?" said the waitress, standing next to their table as she poured them another glass of wine.

"Yes. I will have a 10 ounce sirloin steak with a garden salad," said Rebecca, looking from the menu to the waitress.

"And I will have the cedar plank salmon with vegetables," said Mitch, handing his menu to the waitress.

"Both good choices. Is there anything else?" said the waitress, looking from the iPad screen to Mitch and Rebecca.

"Not for me, thanks," said Rebecca.

"No thank you," said Mitch.

"Ok, thank you," said the waitress, closing the order on the screen and walking towards the bar area.

"Here we go, ma'am," said the waitress, placing Rebecca's meal in front of her.

"Thank you."

"And for you, sir," said the waitress, placing Mitch's meal in front of him.

"Thank you."

"Can I get you anything else?" asked the waitress.

"No, thank you," said Mitch.

"Enjoy your meals," said the waitress, smiling.

As they ate their dinner, Mitch and Rebecca chatted and went over some more ideas and thoughts about their wedding ceremony and reception. With the excitement of planning it within two months, they didn't even notice the time or that all the customers had gone and the restaurant was closing, until the manager approached them.

"Sorry… but we are closing in about ten minutes. Would sir or ma'am like to take some dessert with you and maybe some more wine? Or just the bill?" He handed them a dessert menu.

Mitch nodded and took the dessert menu from the manager. "Ah… we will take another bottle of Bollinger Grande Année Rosé 1999 and also for dessert we will have a Crème Brule and a pumpkin cheesecake, with some whipped cream as well. Can you please put both the wine and the dessert in some ice trays as we have a long travel home?" said Mitch, handing the menu back to the manager.

The manager nodded and said, "Yes, sir. Give me five minutes and we will have all this ready to go for you." Mitch gave him his credit card to pay for the dinner, wine and dessert.

"Thank you, sir," said the manager, as he took the card from Mitch's hand and walked towards the counter.

Raising an eyebrow at Mitch and smiling, Rebecca said, "Thank you… mmm, yum, the dessert sounds really nice. Can I eat mine off of you?" She snickered.

He laughed and said, "All in good time, my dear."

They chuckled together.

Mitch instructed the driver to take them to the Hilton Hotel and pushed the button to put the divider up between the driver and them.

"So what does Sir have planned for us at the Hilton?"

"Now that would be telling," teased Mitch. Kissing her neck, he sent tingling shivers up her spine. By the time they arrived at the hotel, Rebecca's libido had kicked in and all she needed was Mitch inside her.

Anticipation was high for both Mitch and Rebecca as they watched the lift doors open slowly and stepped in. It had been two weeks since they had had any type of sexual interaction, or had been alone together.

Mitch pushed the button to the floor they were on and stepped to the back of the elevator with Rebecca. Smirking, he watched her suggestive reflection in the mirrored walls as the doors closed.

As the elevator took them up to the 11th floor, Rebecca's heart was racing with enthusiasm when she eventually noticed him looking at her in the mirrored walls. Smiling, she raised one eyebrow and brushed her hand over his hardened penis, which she could see protruding through his trousers. With one eyebrow raised, Mitch quickly pulled Rebecca into his arms and kissed her luscious lips, searching for her tongue as she opened her mouth. Their hands were all over each other. Panting, she couldn't get enough, as he teased her neck with a sensual kiss. When the elevator pinged and the doors opened at their floor, Mitch picked Rebecca up in his arms and carried her to their room.

Cuddled into his chest as they entered the dimly lit room, Rebecca noticed that it was set up with white tea candles placed randomly throughout the room and had a passionate feel to it. She smiled as he carried her through the lounge room and into the bathroom. Placing her on the floor, Rebecca realised the effort Mitch had gone to when she saw the huge white bath in front of her was filled already with hot steamy water and a lovely berry smelling bath bubble solution. The bathroom had small white candles everywhere and next to the bath was an ice bucket with a bottle of wine for them to drink. On the ledge of the bath were two sparkling crystal glasses. She looked up at Mitch and smiled, feeling like she was the luckiest woman in the world to have such a thoughtful and romantic man like Mitch in her life.

As Mitch pulled her quickly into his arms, Rebecca's heart accelerated. "Turn around."

She smirked and did as she was told.

"You won't be needing these," said Mitch, unzipping her dress, unfastening her bra and pulling her knickers down. Stepping out of her knickers, her toned body was left standing there naked, panting.

"God, you have such a beautiful body, Rebecca. I can't get enough of you.....I want you here and now," said Mitch, taking his clothes off.

Rebecca looked down and saw his huge erection. Smirking, she couldn't help herself, but to touch it tenderly as she licked her lips. *Mmm, I want that inside me.*

Mitch looks into her carnal eyes and says, "Sir is waiting for your next move."

Rebecca directed him into the bedroom.

Gently she pushed him down onto the bed and lay next to him. She started with his neck, sucking it, then grazing his earlobe with her teeth as she went. Moving down his body, she felt him quiver as she gently sucked and kissed his abdomen. His breathing became heavy as she took hold of his elongated cock and sucked it hard, whilst twirling her tongue around its head.

Oh my, he tastes so good…..smells so divine……and I can't get enough of him, thought Rebecca, as she continued to enjoy him.

Rebecca heard Mitch moan and watched him press his head back into the bed quilt, as she continued to suck his penis.

"Please… stop… Rebecca… I am on the precipice," pleaded Mitch. His body was about to explode.

She looked up and stopped. Kissing his abdomen, then his chest, she teased his nipples with her teeth. When she reached his earlobe, she sensually caressed it with her tongue and lips.

"Oh God woman, you are damn good at this," said Mitch, his breathing heavy.

She whispered into his ear, "Does Sir want to beg some more, or have you had enough?"

Mitch smirked, rolled over and gently pushed Rebecca onto her back. "Sir has not had enough."

Sitting up, he then opened the side drawer next to the bed and took out a condom. Closing the drawer, he smiled at her carnal eyes and then ripped the packet open with his teeth. Taking the condom out of its packet, he slid it over his cock and pushed her legs open, feeling her clitoris.

Hmm, nice and wet, thought Mitch, as he leant down into her to have his fill.

Rebecca quickly adjusted to the fullness of his penis. Mitch pulled in and out of her agonisingly slow, teasing her.

"Faster… please," pleaded Rebecca. Her breathing was heavy.

But he didn't. Instead he pulled out of her and turned her over.

Once he was inside her again, he started to fuck her fast and hard. Their rhythm was immeasurable.

Oh God, I can feel I am going to orgasm, thought Rebecca, as she quivered all over. *No… I can feel it coming…no… no. Too late. Humph.* Her breathing heavy.

But Mitch hadn't had his fill yet. "Oh baby, you feel too good. I could fuck you all night," he whispered breathlessly in her ear.

Just as Rebecca was about to have her second orgasm, Mitch came and stilled over her.

Exhausted and sweaty from their lovemaking, Mitch leant in and kissed Rebecca's forehead. "You sure know how to please a man, woman." Picking her up in his arms, he carried her into the bathroom and they stepped into the hot bath.

As she cuddled into his body, Rebecca felt a calmness envelope her. "I could stay here all night with you like this, cuddling into your gorgeous body. I never want this night to end."

"It does feel pretty darn good, doesn't it," said Mitch, wrapping his arms around her. "Would you like a glass of wine?"

"Yes, please." Rebecca watched him pour two glasses for them both.

"Here you go," said Mitch, handing her a glass.

Taking a sip, she says "Mmm, that's nice."

"Bit thirsty, hey," said Mitch, watching her drink the last drop.

"Only for you," teased Rebecca, with one eyebrow raised.

Mitch smiled and drank the rest of his wine. *Mischievous.*

"What was that? Is someone at the door?" asked Rebecca, as she pulled away from Mitch's chest.

"I will get it," said Mitch, hearing another knock at the door.

Mitch hopped out of the bath and spotted a bathrobe on the back of the bathroom door and placed it on.

The bellboy was standing on the other side of the door, as Mitch looked through the peep hole.

"Come in," said Mitch, opening the door fully.

The bellboy nodded and wheeled the metal trolley into the lounge room. "Everything as you requested, sir," said the bellboy, indicating to the dessert from the restaurant and some hot drinks.

"Thank you," said Mitch, reaching on the floor for his trousers for some money. "Here you go."

The bellboy nodded once and said "Why, thank you, sir." Mitch had given him a considerable tip. "Will there by anything else?"

"No, thank you," said Mitch, walking towards the doorway.

"Good night, sir," said the bellboy, as he pulled the door closed behind him.

"Who was that?" asked Rebecca, as she stood in the doorway of the lounge room with her bathrobe on.

Mitch gestured to the table he had now set up with the dessert and drinks on.

"Oh, wow. You organised all this? I had forgotten about the dessert from the restaurant," said Rebecca, looking at the table next to the window which gave a beautiful view of the harbour. "I feel spoilt. Thank you, Mitch."

"You're welcome. Come and sit down and we can enjoy our dessert. There is tea and coffee here too," said Mitch, standing next to her chair.

Rebecca walked over and gave him a peck on the cheek. Smiling she took her seat and looked over the table. "Mmm, looks good."

Mitch smiled and sat across from her.

Could this night get any better? Rebecca thought to herself.

Chapter Twenty Four

Rebecca woke to the sunlight shining in through the sheer curtain windows of the hotel room.

Seems early... I wonder what time it is? she thought. Rubbing the sleep from her eyes, she looked over at the digital clock on bedside table. *Hmm, 7.03am.*

Slipping out of bed, trying not to wake Mitch, she headed for the bathroom for a much needed toilet break. As she sat on the toilet, she thought, *Today we are going to find out when Paige can leave hospital and possibly fly back to Perth. As much as I have loved spending time in Seattle and getting to know Mitch's family, I do miss my home and can't wait to get back to some sort of normality. Even though I have been able to log into the computer system and do some of my work, I am sure my boss will be glad to know when I will be returning too. Lucky to have a job, I suppose.* Shrugging her shoulders, she flushed the toilet and then stepped into the shower.

With her hands resting on the tiles, she held her head under the large shower head and soaked up the heat from the water. As it cascaded off Rebecca's head and down her back, she heard the shower screen open.

"Morning," said Mitch, holding the glass door open. "You are up early."

"Yeah, I couldn't sleep. The room was too bright. We forgot to close the curtains last night," said Rebecca, looking around at Mitch.

"Yeah, I forgot all about that. Was too busy enjoying myself. Hey… you hungry? I might order some breakfast," said Mitch, yawning.

"Sounds good," said Rebecca.

"Would you like anything in particular?" asked Mitch. "For breakfast that is." The smirk on his face apparent.

Rebecca laughed. "I don't mind. Surprise me."

"Oh, Ok," said Mitch, smiling. "After breakfast, did you want to head over to the hospital to see Paige?"

"Yes, please. Hopefully she will be released from hospital today," said Rebecca, as she washed her body with the berry body wash and scrubber.

"Right. I will organise for the chauffeur to collect us at say, around 10am," said Mitch.

Rebecca nodded.

Mitch closed the glass door and headed for the lounge room to make his calls.

The traffic was pretty much like a car park that morning as the chauffeur drove Mitch and Rebecca to the hospital to see Paige.

"I can't wait to tell everyone today what date we are getting married. I bet Mom and Dad will be over the moon when I tell them that we want to have the reception at home," said Mitch, holding Rebecca's hand.

"Yeah, I am excited about telling everyone, too," said Rebecca, placing her head on Mitch's shoulder as she gazed out the front windscreen of the car.

Rebecca's thoughts started to drift to what Paige had told her the previous day, about seeing Jackson, and it haunted her. Even watching the traffic going slow at first and then disperse, it reminded her of the day Jackson died. She had started to wonder if she would ever not feel guilty about being with another man.

"Penny for your thoughts," said Mitch, looking down at her.

"Just taking in the scenery," lied Rebecca. She wasn't about to explain that she was having second thoughts and feeling guilty to Mitch.

He smiled and pulled her in tight to his body.

As they walked past the half glass partition of Paige's room and into her doorway, Rebecca and Mitch noticed the doctor had already arrived and was standing next to Michael. When he saw them walking into the room, he said, "Now that is good timing. I have some news for Paige, but I didn't want to tell her until you were here."

"Morning," said Rebecca, as she came to stand beside the bed and give Paige a kiss on the cheek. "Hello Michael."

"Hi Bec, Mitch," said Michael. He shook Mitch's hand and gave Rebecca a hug.

"Hello, doc," said Mitch. "How's our favourite patient this morning?"

"She seems to be doing really well today and if this continues I will release her tomorrow to go home," said the doctor.

"That's great. But how long before she can fly? We need to take her home to Australia," said Rebecca.

"At the moment… I would give it another week or two. Paige will need to come in every second day so we can see how she is going. Then as she gets better, we can let you know when she will be able to fly," said the doctor.

"Oh, Ok. Thanks doctor. Will she need physio, medication or anything when she goes home?" said Rebecca.

"At this stage, no. She just needs to take it one day at a time. Only time tells with these types of injuries," said the doctor, placing Paige's chart back on the end of the bed frame. "Ok Paige, I am pleased with how you are going today, but I will make a decision tomorrow on if you can go home. So I will see you tomorrow morning." He shook their hands and left to go and see his other patients.

"Wow, that is good news, sweetheart. We may be able to go home in two weeks," said Rebecca, feeling positive.

Paige looked at Rebecca with sadness in her eyes and said in a not so convincing voice, "Yeah… that's great, Mum."

"What's the matter, Paige? I thought you would be glad to be out of the hospital and going home to Perth," said Rebecca, confused.

"The problem is, Mum, I don't want to go home to Perth. I am happy living here. I want to be with Michael and he wants to be with me," said Paige, holding Michael's hand.

Rebecca looked from Paige to Michael in shock.

"You are not even twenty-one yet, Paige and you have no way of supporting yourself here. And if you did want to stay here there is also the paperwork to be done and submitted to the government to apply to be a permanent resident. Trust me, that could be rejected. At the moment we are here on a holiday visa and it lasts for three months. So once the three months is up you will have to leave," said Rebecca, matter-of-factly.

"Either way, Mum, whether I live here in Seattle with Michael, or Michael comes back home and lives with Mitch, I will be happy. But we are not sure if Michael's parents are going to agree to either. One thing we are sure of though is that we have both made up our minds, we don't want to live a million miles away from each other," said Paige, looking from Rebecca to Michael.

"I can see that you two care for each other. I will talk with Michael's parents today for you and see what I can do. I can't promise anything, but I will try on both your behalves," said Rebecca.

"Thank you, Mum. I really appreciate anything you can do for us," said Paige, holding her hands out for a hug.

"Thank you, Rebecca," said Michael.

"Actually Michael, why don't you come home with us and get yourself showered, changed and maybe even some rest. We can bring you back later to stay with Paige, if you like," said Mitch.

"Ok, bro. Sounds like a good idea, as I probably don't smell the best at the moment," said Michael, smelling his armpits. "I will see you later on this afternoon, Paige. Don't miss me too much." He leant in and gave her a hug and chuckled.

"Can't wait for you to return," whispered Paige, as she hugged him back.

"Will you be Ok here by yourself for a few hours, sweetheart, whilst I go and talk with Michael's parents?" asked Rebecca.

"Yes, Mum. I need to get some rest anyway," said Paige.

"Ok," said Rebecca, giving her a kiss on her forehead.

"Bye, Paige," said Mitch.

"Yeah, see you later on, Mitch," said Paige.

Arriving home to the Portellico house, Michael went upstairs to have a shower and to get some rest for a couple of hours, before they went back to the hospital, whilst Mitch and Rebecca went and spoke with Helen and Grayson.

Walking through the house to the backyard, they found Helen and Grayson sitting outside, under the gazebo in the back gardens.

"Hello Grayson and Helen. Do you both have a few minutes to have a chat?" said Rebecca, walking toward them.

"Yes dear," said Helen, placing her book down.

"Have you had a chance to think about Michael moving to Perth with Mitch yet?" asked Rebecca, taking a seat next to Helen.

"Yes we have, dear. We don't think it's a good idea. Michael has so much going for him here and we are not sure he is doing the right thing by moving to Perth. What are your thoughts, Rebecca?" said Helen.

"We have just come from the hospital and both Michael and Paige have told us today that if Michael is not allowed to move to Perth, then Paige wants to move to Seattle. You see, they don't want to be apart. I have tried talking them out of this but they have their minds set on being together. Now, I'm not sure what the answer is," said Rebecca, with a furrowed brow.

"Hmm, that's a tough one. How would Paige support herself if she moved here?" said Grayson.

"Well, I could pay some money. But I don't earn a hell of a lot of money to be supporting her financially, until she finds a full time job. And who's to say that the US government will allow her to stay here permanently, anyway? What I can see is if we all don't come to some arrangement today, then I think they will do just about anything to stay together and God knows what they might do. I am seriously worried about this situation," said Rebecca.

"We could support Paige if she lived here. But she would have to get a job. Maybe we could ask some of the restaurant owners we know and see if they could take her on as a junior chef or something. But do you really want your daughter moving here, away from you? Knowing how much you love her, it would be the hardest thing for you to do, letting her move to Seattle," said Helen.

"I know I wouldn't like it, Helen. I would miss her terribly. But if my daughter was happier here than with me, I don't want to stop her happiness. I think what worries me is that she won't have any family here and if Michael and Paige split up, what will happen then? It's such a big gamble," said Rebecca. Her mind was racing.

"I think what we need to do is sit down with Michael and Paige and discuss this with them. You know, letting them hear our concerns and asking them some serious questions as well," said Helen.

"Sounds like a good plan, Helen. Paige may be getting out of hospital in the next couple of days, so we can sit down with them both then. What do you think?" said Rebecca.

"Good idea. Don't worry too much, my dear, things always seem to sort themselves out eventually," said Helen, patting Rebecca's hand.

"I hope so," said Rebecca.

"Well… after that heavy discussion, we would like to tell you both something," said Mitch, beaming with excitement.

"What is it, son?" asked Grayson.

"Rebecca and I have set a date for our wedding. It's the 12th of August and we would like to ask you both, if we could have the reception here at home," said Mitch, smiling.

Helen and Grayson both stood up and hugged Rebecca and Mitch.

"Congratulations, we are so happy for you both. Of course you can have the reception here," said Helen, excited. "Oh my… that's only two months away. You certainly have a lot to plan for a wedding that close. I can help with some arrangements if you want, dear. But I am also thinking, you are going to be going home soon, so how are you going to plan it whilst you are in Perth. We sure are going to be on Skype a lot."

"Mitch and I have discussed it and we thought that the major things we could plan before we leave Seattle. Then the minor things, if we could ask you for your help, would be great. And you are right, we would probably use Skype a lot," said Rebecca, smiling.

"Let me know, dear, what I can do and I am only too happy to help out," said Helen, excited.

Giving Helen a hug, Rebecca said, "Thank you. I really appreciate everything."

"I think we should toast to this exciting piece of news. How about I organise some drinks to celebrate the occasion?" said Grayson, excited.

"Awesome," said Mitch.

After a delightful afternoon of celebrations with Helen and Grayson, Mitch organised for the chauffeur to drive Rebecca and himself back to the hospital with Michael.

The corridors were quiet as Rebecca, Mitch and Michael stepped out of the lift and headed for Paige's room. As they neared Paige's room, they heard voices and wondered who would be visiting her.

"Hello Nick," said Michael, smiling as he walked through the doorway.

"Hello," said Nick, looking up and seeing his family walk through the door. He shook Michael and Mitch's hands when they reached Paige's bed.

"Hi Nick. How are you?" said Rebecca, giving him a quick hug.

"I'm doing all right," said Nick.

"How are you sweetheart?" said Rebecca, leaning over Paige and giving her hug.

"Really good thanks, Mum. Nick has been keeping me company for a while. He is so funny," said Paige, smiling.

"That was nice of you to come and visit, Paige," said Rebecca, turning to Nick.

"I have just finished work and was in the area. Thought I'd come and cheer her up," said Nick.

"Cheer me up. I don't think I have laughed so much for a long time," said Paige smiling.

"I'm just glad to see you awake and smiling. And I am sure Michael is too," said Nick, looking from Paige to Michael.

"How are you, my girl?" said Michael, standing on the other side of her bed.

"Better now you're here," said Paige, looking into his eyes.

"When does the doctor think that you might be able to go home to Perth," asked Nick.

"If all goes well, probably about two weeks. But he said to take it day by day; so it could be sooner," said Rebecca.

"Right… so… I was wanting to ask you a favour," said Nick.

"What is it?" said Rebecca.

"I have taken on a security job to watch Pink whilst she is in Perth soon and I was wondering if you are not home, could I stay at your house? Or if you are all back, then maybe I could stay with Mitch?" said Nick.

"Sure… that's no problem with me. We have plenty of room even if we are back. You are welcome to stay as long as you like," said Rebecca, welcomingly.

"Thanks. It's always good to stay with someone else, rather than a lonely hotel," said Nick.

"For sure. Just to give you a heads up…. the house we live in is rented and it's not like your parents' house. It's very basic, but we love it," said Rebecca.

"I know where you live Bec, as I looked it up on Google Earth. I needed to see how far away I would be from where Pink is staying. I think your house is great. So all good there," said Nick.

"At least I can make you some home cooked meals, whilst you stay with us. That's if we are back of course," said Rebecca.

"I will definitely take you up on home cooked meals. Thanks Bec," said Nick.

"No problem," said Rebecca. Smirking and looking off into the distance, she thought to herself, W*ouldn't it be funny if Nick found a girlfriend whilst living in Australia. That would be three brothers that had Australian partners.*

"So, Mum… what happened with Michael's parents today? Did they agree to anything?" asked Paige.

Rebecca didn't answer.

"Mum."

"Huh… sorry I wasn't listening," said Rebecca, coming back to reality, after thinking about who she knew was single and could introduce to Nick.. "What did you say, sweetie?"

"I asked what happed with Michael's parents today?" said Paige.

"Ah… we haven't come to an agreement on anything as yet, sweetheart. They are still considering what they want for Michael. So when you get out of here, we are all going to sit down and discuss this further and come up with a solution. Hopefully one that will make you both happy," said Rebecca, looking from Paige to Michael.

"Oh, Ok," said Paige, her voice full of sadness. *Humph, I bet they say no.*

"Don't worry. It will all work out, I am sure of it," said Michael. Paige smiled at Michael and squeezed his hand tight.

"Michael's right, sweetheart. No need to worry about anything yet. On another note, Mitch and I have some really good news," said Rebecca.

"What is it? Come on, spit it out," said Nick.

"Mitch and I have set a date for our wedding. It's the 12th of August and it's going to be here in Seattle," said Rebecca.

"Wow… that soon, Mum. How are you and Mitch going to plan everything so quickly?" said Paige.

"Well Mitch and I are going to plan the major things, you know like venue, church, food, photographer, etc., whilst we are still here. But the minor things we can take care of once we are back in Perth. And Helen said she would help me as well with anything," said Rebecca.

"Sounds like you both have got it all sorted out already," said Paige.

"We still have a lot to do, but it will come together nicely," said Rebecca.

"I am so happy for you, Mum. You deserve some happiness again," said Paige, holding her hands out in front for a hug.

"Aww, thank you," said Rebecca, hugging her back

"Congratulations guys… the 12th of August, I will have to write that in my diary. Looking forward to it," said Nick, shaking Mitch's hand and then giving Rebecca a hug. "Well… I had better hit the road. Need to get some shut-eye. I am glad you are going to be Ok, Paige. Will see you back at home when you get out of hospital." He gave Paige a hug.

"Yep, you sure will," said Paige, hugging him back.

"See you at home, bro," said Nick to Michael.

"Yeah… I will be home tomorrow," said Michael, shaking Nick's hand.

"Night all," said Nick, as he walked towards the doorway.

"So… did you want us to stay for a while, sweetie or would you prefer to spend some time with Michael by yourself tonight?" asked Rebecca.

"I hope you don't mind, but I would like to spend some time with Michael by myself, if that's all right?" said Paige.

"That's Ok, sweetheart. I can come and see you tomorrow anyway. Hopefully the doctor will say you can go home tomorrow," said Rebecca.

"So are you sleeping here tonight Michael, or do you need a lift home later on?" asked Mitch.

"I will sleep here in the laydown bed. I want to spend as much time with Paige as possible," said Michael.

"Right," said Mitch. "I will swing by and collect you in the morning." He shook Michael's hand. "See you tomorrow."

"Thanks. Night, bro," said Michael. "Night, Bec." He leant in and gave her a hug.

"Night. See you tomorrow," said Rebecca, hugging him back. "Take care of my girl."

"Yeah I will."

"Night, sweetheart. Will see you in the morning," said Rebecca, giving Paige a hug.

"Night, Mum. Hopefully I can go home tomorrow," said Paige, hugging her mum back.

"So… what are we going to do tonight?" said Rebecca to Mitch, as they walked out of the elevator on the ground floor of the hospital.

He thought about it for a few seconds and said, "What about if we go to the movies and then get a bite to eat somewhere casual?"

"Sounds good to me. I haven't been to the movies in ages," said Rebecca, smiling.

Mitch pulled out his mobile phone from his pocket to see what movies were showing and where. "What about, *The Expendables 2*?"

"Yeah, I'd love to see that. The first one was not too bad," said

Rebecca.

"Cool… it's starting in about forty-five minutes. We should make it in time," said Mitch, looking at his mobile phone for the time. I'll get the driver to drop us off. We can decide on where to eat after the movie, if that's Ok."

"Sounds like a plan," said Rebecca, leaning into him as they walked along toward the car.

Finding their seats in the theatre, Rebecca and Mitch cuddled up next to each other to watch the movie.

As the lights dimmed and the curtains moved back to increase the screen size, Rebecca turned to see if Mitch was enjoying the popcorn and found him smiling at her. Leaning into her, he whispered, "You look so beautiful just sitting there. I couldn't help but to stare at you. I feel so lucky."

She smiled and kissed his lips. "Thank you. I hope you feel like this after we get married. I hope these feelings you have for me never wear thin. I never grow tired of you saying how much you love me and want me."

"My love for you will never end, beautiful. I will never grow tired of you either. I am in awe of you," said Mitch, looking into her eyes. He kissed her passionately on the lips.

Chapter Twenty Five

"Morning," said Mitch and Rebecca to the doctor as they walked into Paige's hospital room with Michael.

"Good morning… that was good timing, as I need to discuss Paige's release. She seems to be going really well this morning and improving all the time, so I am going to let her go home today," said the doctor looking from Mitch to Rebecca. "She can only go home if she stays in bed for at least the next week. I mean she can sit outside, as the fresh air and sun will be good for her, otherwise it's rest and relax." He looked back at Paige.

"Really… oh thank you, doctor. I can't wait to go home," said Paige, smiling from ear to ear.

"Now… what I would like you to do is come and visit me at my practice every second day, so I can keep an eye on your recovery. Then once you are well enough, you can fly back home to Perth," said the doctor.

"Yes, sir," said Paige.

"I will fill in the paperwork so that you can be discharged from the hospital this morning. I will also leave my practice address and phone number so that you can come and see me every second day. You will need to ring and make the appointments though," said the doctor, filling in Paige's hospital chart.

"Thank you, doctor," said Rebecca, placing her hand out in front to shake his hand.

"If she starts to feel sick, or has any headaches or anything else., don't hesitate to ring me or come back into the hospital. Well... I will see you in a couple of days, Paige." He left to finish his rounds.

"Wow... that is such good news, Paige. Will be nice to have you back home again. Here are your clothes I brought in from home. Would you like some help getting dressed or are you Ok?" said Rebecca, handing Paige the bag of clothes.

"I'll be fine, Mum," said Paige, looking through the bag of clothes.

"Whilst you are getting dressed, we will get your things together and then we can go home," said Rebecca.

Michael helped Paige get out of bed and over to the bathroom.

"She is still a bit weak," said Michael, with a creased brow, as he shut the door to the bathroom and walked towards Rebecca.

"Yeah. She will probably be like that for a while because she spent two weeks asleep. It takes the body a bit of time to recover. But she will be Ok," said Rebecca, watching his worried expression and rubbing Michael's arm.

"Oh, right. That's good to know," said Michael, nodding.

Paige smiled as she watched the Portellico house come into view through the front windscreen of the car as she sat next to Michael on the back seat. "Feels like I haven't been here for ages. Mum, don't you reckon their house is like something out of the magazines? It's just *so* beautiful."

"Sure is, sweetheart. We have been very lucky to be able to stay here. Grayson and Helen have been really good to us and I wish I knew how I could repay their kindness," said Rebecca, turning around in the front seat to look at Paige.

"You don't have to repay anything, Bec. Mom and Dad are glad you are both staying with us. In fact, they adore you both and think of you as their daughters," said Mitch, quickly glancing at Rebecca and concentrating on his driving.

"Aww, that's sweet. You know you two are lucky to have good

parents. I just hope you appreciate them for everything they do for you both," said Rebecca, looking at Mitch and turning around to Michael.

"We know we are lucky, Bec and yes, we do appreciate our parents," said Mitch.

Mitch parked the car near the front door of his parents' house, so that Paige didn't have too much of a walk to the door. She was still feeling sore from her operation and needed to take it slow. Whilst Michael and Rebecca helped Paige walk slowly inside to a bedroom that Helen had organised for her downstairs, Mitch carried her bag.

Rebecca pulled back the doona and top sheet and stacked three pillows against the headboard on the bed. "Here, sweetheart. Get in," said Rebecca, patting the sheet.

"Thanks, Mum," said Paige, as she sat on the edge of the bed.

Knocking on the door as she walked in, Helen placed her arms out in front and rushed over to Paige. "Welcome home, dear. Can I get anything for you? Are you hungry or thirsty?"

"No, I am Ok for the moment. Thank you for organising this room for me. That was very thoughtful of you," said Paige, welcoming her warm hug. "Actually, I am a little bit hungry. What time is lunch? I was thinking I could sit in the dining room with everyone else, if that's Ok."

"Lunch will be served in about thirty minutes, dear. Are you sure you will be Ok sitting with all of us? Wouldn't you prefer to sit quietly?" said Helen, concerned.

"I have had way too much time by myself in hospital, Mrs Portellico. So I would really love to sit in the dining room with everyone else," said Paige, leaning back on the pillows and placing her feet up onto the bed.

"Ok, dear. I am sure Michael can help you walk to the dining room when lunch is ready. After lunch, would you be up for a talk?" said Helen.

"Sure," said Paige, looking from Helen to Michael.

"Great," said Helen.

"Mmm… whatever the cook is making for lunch smells good," said Paige, sniffing the air. "The hospital food was so bland, so I am looking forward to an enjoyable meal."

"Well… we might all just let you get settled in, dear. It's nice to have you back home," said Helen, giving Paige another hug.

"Thanks, Mrs Portellico," said Paige, smiling politely.

Once lunch was finished and the dishes had been taken away from the table, Grayson stood up from the table and said, "Let's all go into the sitting room. It's a bit more comfortable in there for a chat."

Helen, Michael, Paige, Rebecca and Mitch all nodded in agreeance.

Michael helped Paige out of her chair and walked slowly to the back of the house.

As they all took their seats in the sitting room, Rebecca looked over at Paige and Michael and watched them sit close together and hold hands.

"So… I understand you and Paige would like to be together in Perth," said Grayson, looking from Michael to Paige.

"Yes…" said Paige, her voice wavering.

Michael swallowed hard.

"Your mother and I have talked about this and have come to a decision… we don't want you leaving Seattle to live and work with Mitch. We feel that you are still too young, Michael, and you need time to see what you want to do with your life first. Now, whether or not that includes you, Paige, time will tell. So in saying this, it is our decision to say 'no' to Michael living in Perth," said Grayson, looking from Michael to Paige, watching their reaction.

Paige took a deep breath and tears formed in her eyes, as she heard the decision.

Michael gripped Paige's hand tight. "But Dad, Mom…"

"Let me finish first… we think we may have come up with a solution, though. What about if you stay with us for six months Paige, here in Seattle. You can live here with us, but you must get a full time job. As you will probably need at least two week recovery before you can fly home, we thought that in the next two weeks we could help you to sort out your residency application to the US government. If that is approved and we can see in the next six months that you and Michael are committed to each other, then, we will review the situation. Maybe –

and this is a big maybe – then Michael can go and live with Mitch for six months in Perth. What do you think about this decision Rebecca, as this affects you as well?" said Grayson, as he looked from Paige, to Michael then Rebecca.

Paige looked at Rebecca and said, "Before you answer, Mum, there is something I want to say." Turning to Grayson and Helen. "Firstly, thank you Helen and Grayson for such a gracious, lovely idea. But I am not sure I would be able to survive here in Seattle without my mum. I would miss her too much. I don't want to sound ungrateful and don't think I don't want to stay here and see what Michael and I have. It's just… well… that I am not sure I want to leave my mum, let alone my home yet. She is all I have. If Mum says yes, can I have a couple of days to think this over?"

"Yes, dear. You can have as much time as you like," said Helen, looking from Paige to Rebecca.

"Rebecca, what do you think about all this?" asked Grayson.

With raised eyebrows, Rebecca took a deep breath. "I know Paige would be well looked after here and I do thank you both for your kind offer; but I really don't want to leave my daughter here for six months. Since Jackson passed away, we only have each other. I know that sounds stupid, because I am about to be married to Mitch and Paige is starting a relationship with Michael, but I am like Paige: not sure."

Mitch placed his hand over Rebecca's and said, "What about if the time frame is shorter? Say two months at a time."

Grayson and Helen looked at each other and nodded and Helen said, "That sounds acceptable to us."

Rebecca looked at Paige and said, "What do you think sweetheart? Would you be happy with two months? It's Ok with me, but I still would miss you. We could always Skype once a week or more if you like. I know it's not the same, but we could try it and see how you and I go."

"Umm…that does sound better. Oh, all right…. I will try it for two months. But what if I don't want to stay after a couple of weeks because I miss you too much? Then we would be in the same boat as now, which is that Michael and I would be apart," said Paige, her voice heavy with sadness.

"Put it this way, if Mitch and I go home next week and you stay here, by the time we come back in six weeks for the wedding, you would probably know if you would like to stay here or not. Actually, it would be good you being here, because you would be able to help Helen with some of the things we need done for the wedding," said Rebecca.

"Ok. I will give it a go," said Paige.

"Are you both happy with that, Grayson and Helen?" asked Rebecca.

"Yes, that sounds good. But we will hold off on the residency application for the moment. Just in case you change your mind and don't want to stay. We will have to get your current visa extended though, Paige. But we can organise that next week. So how do you feel about all this Michael?" said Helen.

"At the moment, that sounds good. I am worried though. If Paige doesn't want to stay in Seattle and she has to return home… well… then I won't be able to go with her," said Michael.

"Only time will tell, Michael and really it's not worth worrying about something that might not happen. Paige may love it here and be happy talking to her mom via Skype, you never know. And once Rebecca has married Mitch, maybe they will come visit more often. Things always seem to work out. So for the moment, just think positive," said Helen.

"I suppose you are right, Mom. I just can't believe you are going to live here with us, Paige. I am so excited! You won't regret your decision. Thank you everyone," said Michael, looking at each of them.

"How are you feeling, sweetie?" Rebecca said to Paige.

"A bit tired, Mum. So if you all don't mind, I think I will go have a sleep for a while," said Paige, standing up.

"Ok. You go and rest up, sweetheart. We will see you later for dinner," said Rebecca.

Michael helped Paige back to her room and once she was settled, Michael returned to the sitting room, where Helen, Grayson, Mitch and Rebecca were still situated.

"Michael… I wanted to ask you something that is a bit personal," said Rebecca.

"I think I probably know what you are going to ask me. I do plan on being a complete gentleman to Paige," said Michael, feeling the blood rush to his face.

"Thank you, Michael. I appreciate your honesty and I do appreciate that men have needs too. But my daughter is still innocent and I would really feel better knowing that you intend to keep your word about being a gentleman until she is ready," said Rebecca, with a creased brow.

Rebecca could see Helen, Grayson and Mitch out the corner of her eye looking at her and not believing that she even broached the subject.

"Sorry, but when it comes to my Paige, I am not backwards in coming forward. She is my world and I don't want to see her hurt in any way," stated Rebecca, out loud to everyone in the room.

"Don't worry, my dear, we will keep an eye on them both," said Helen.

"Thank you, Helen," said Rebecca.

"Now that we have all of this sorted out, when did you want to go back home, Bec?" asked Mitch.

"I would like to see how Paige goes over the next couple of days and if she is well, then maybe we can book a flight back home for say, Friday?" said Rebecca.

"Sounds good to me. I need to get back to Perth for my business," said Mitch.

"I am sorry Mitch; with everything that has been going on with Paige, I completely forgot that you do have a business to run in Perth. If you need to go back now, don't wait for me. I can always fly back by myself. Your business is more important," said Rebecca, sincerely.

"I am sure the business will be fine for another couple of days, but I do have to go back to Perth soon though. Anyway you can't get rid of me that easily," said Mitch, smirking.

She leant in and kissed his cheek, and said, "I love you."

"I love you too. Oh, yeah… sorry, I forgot to tell you that I will be working tonight with Nick. He rang me earlier and asked me if I could work, as one of his security guys is sick. I told him I could work for him. I hope you don't mind," said Mitch.

"That's Ok, babe. I am sure I can find plenty to do. Anyway I need to sit down with Helen to discuss some of the wedding arrangements.

Plus I would like to spend some time with Paige before I go back home. What time do you have to leave?" said Rebecca.

"About another hour and a half. I have to be there by 6pm. Actually, there was something that I wanted to talk to you about, concerning the wedding arrangements," said Mitch. He then pulled her up off the seat and said to his m0m and dad, "We will catch you later. Thanks for today."

"Yes, thanks Grayson and Helen. I really do appreciate everything," said Rebecca.

"You're welcome, dear. We will see you later for dinner," said Helen.

"Ok," said Rebecca, as she walked towards the doorway with Mitch. They left the sitting room and went up to Mitch's bedroom.

Mitch closed the door behind them and locked it. "Sir would like to play. Are you ready?"

"Yes," said Rebecca, raising her eyebrows. She giggled.

"Yes, what," stated Mitch.

"Yes, Sir. I am ready and willing," said Rebecca, smirking at him.

"Take your clothes off and lie on the rug," said Mitch, pointing to the long haired, grey rug beside his bed. He then undid his shirt buttons.

She did as he instructed.

Lying on the plush rug naked, Rebecca said nothing as she watched him place a blindfold over her eyes. With all her senses heightened, she heard Mitch take off his clothes and felt him lie beside her. His hot breath caressed her nipples and slowly he kissed her from the neck to her pubic hair, nipping and teasing her along the way. Rebecca's body arched off the floor in anticipation of what he would do next. Pulling her legs apart, he gently massaged her clitoris, whilst his tongue enjoyed the flavours of her mouth. The delightful torment continued when he placed his finger inside her vagina, pulling it in and out, teasing her even further. She moaned as she felt his hard shaft graze her leg. Rebecca pressed herself into it, wanting, needing him so badly, but he had not finished teasing her yet. Just when Rebecca thought she couldn't take much more, she felt his tongue lick, then suck her clitoris.

I am in seventh heaven, oh…have lost my way. Breathless, she orgasmed.

Finally he whispered into her ear, "Are you ready for Sir now?"

She eagerly nodded. Her body was overstimulated from all his teasing.

Impatient, Mitch positioned himself between her open legs and placed his cock inside her wet vagina.

Oh, feels so good. Just what this fella needed, thought Mitch, his rhythm relentless as he pulled it in and out of her slowly, still teasing her, as she panted.

Within seconds his eyes grew wide. *Condom... shit... forgot... humph, she is on the pill. Thank God*, thought Mitch, breathing a sigh of relief.

"Please, Mitch, no more teasing," pleaded Rebecca. Her voice brought him back to reality.

His pace quickened and finally they were one. With the blood rushing to his cock, he fucked her faster and faster, harder and faster until she was ready to come. As he released over her, both of them were sated, breathless and exhausted.

Taking his cock slowly out of her vagina, Mitch lays next to Rebecca on the rug, takes the blindfold off her and props himself up on his elbow. "How was that?"

"Sir sure knows how to show a lady a good time, and with so much pleasure as well," said Rebecca, pushing herself up onto her elbows. Smirking, she leant in and kissed his lips.

Slowly he pulled away from her inviting lips. "We sure do make great sex together. I love being inside you." He stretched out his arm for Rebecca to cuddle into his chest.

"Wake up, sleepyhead," said Mitch, tapping Rebecca on the arm.

"Hmm... what time is it?" said Rebecca, trying to open her eyes and adjust to the light. Rubbing her eyes she thought, *God, I don't even remember falling asleep, let alone getting into bed.*

"It's nearly time for me to leave. I wanted to come and kiss you goodbye before I go to work," said Mitch, sitting next to her.

Rebecca pulled herself up into a sitting position and placed her arms around him. "Mmm, you smell good. Can't you come back to bed?"

"Sorry, beautiful, I can't, not today. I promised Nick I would be there at 6pm," said Mitch.

"What time will you be finished tonight?" asked Rebecca.

"I should be home around 1.30 – 2.30am, babe," said Mitch.

"So I won't see you until tomorrow morning?" Rebecca pouted.

"You will have me all to yourself tomorrow, I promise" said Mitch, smiling at her.

"Ok. Please take care of yourself at work tonight. It's just that I worry," said Rebecca.

"I will," said Mitch. Leaning in, he kissed her passionately on the lips. "See you later, beautiful." Standing, he walked towards the doorway.

"Bye, babe. Take care, hey," said Rebecca, watching him shut the door behind him.

Rebecca yawned, turned over and went back to sleep.

"Hello, Rebecca, I was just coming to see if you wanted some dinner," said Helen, as she met Rebecca on the staircase later.

"Thanks, Helen. I would love to," said Rebecca, graciously smiling. "But I might just go and check on Paige first."

'I'll come with you," said Helen, as she walked with Rebecca down the stairs.

Rebecca nodded and smiled.

"Knock, knock," said Rebecca, as she tapped on Paige's open door.

Looking up, Paige smiled and said, "Come in."

"Hello, sweetie. How you feeling?" said Rebecca, as she walked into the room with Helen.

"Bit sore. But otherwise I'm Ok," said Paige, looking from Rebecca to Helen.

"Anything we can get you, dear?" asked Helen, standing next to Paige's bed.

"Umm… no, that's Ok," said Paige.

"We are about to start dinner in the dining room. Are you hungry?" asked Helen.

"Yes, starving. But would it be Ok if I eat my dinner in here tonight?" said Paige.

"No problem at all, dear. I will have the chef organise to bring you some dinner in soon," said Helen.

"Aww, thanks Mrs Portellico."

"Well, we might head into the dining room. See you later, sweetie," said Rebecca, leaning in to give her a kiss on the forehead. "Let us know if you need anything."

"I will. Thanks Mum and Helen," said Paige.

"Bye, dear," said Helen, rubbing the side of Paige's arm.

"You're quiet, dear. What's the matter?" queried Helen, as they headed towards the dining room.

"Besides worrying about Paige, I miss Mitch not being here, as well. I'm feeling a bit lost," said Rebecca, her brow creased.

Helen slowed and placed her arm around Rebecca and said, "We can always go over some wedding arrangements after dinner, if you like. That will keep your mind off things. But let's go and get some dinner first."

"Thanks, Helen. Sounds great," said Rebecca, hugging her.

That night after dinner, as promised, Helen sat with Rebecca in the home office and they went over the wedding arrangements.

"Right, here's your list, and mine," said Rebecca, handing Helen her handwritten list of things Helen was to organise for the wedding.

"Invitations, yes; but you will need to give me a list of your wedding guest names. Menu and alcohol, yes; I know what you both like in the way of food, so this should be easy. Marquee, yes; I can organise that. Oh, you know what we have forgotten?" said Helen, going through the list.

"What?" asked Rebecca.

"What about the table and chairs for the reception in the marquee?" said Helen, typing in "wedding table and chairs set up" into the search engine of her computer. "What about this type of set up?" She pointed to the computer screen.

"Hmm, I not sure I like that type. What about something with white linen table cloths on round tables and the chairs to have like a white linen cover, but with a bow in the same colour as the bridesmaids' dresses, tied at the back of the chair?" said Rebecca, clicking onto a design on the computer screen. "Like that one."

"Ah, yes, that design is better. Love it," said Helen, now adding the table and chairs design to her list of things to organise for the wedding. "Oh and I will give my designer friend a ring in the morning to discuss an appointment time, whilst you are still here, for your wedding dress and the bridesmaids' dresses as well."

Rebecca had thoroughly enjoyed going over the wedding arrangements with Helen. Making up lists of who was organising what and looking over so many websites on wedding dress styles, bridesmaids' dress styles and colour, flowers and table arrangements, how she wanted the marquee set up, etc., all made Rebecca feel enthusiastic about having it all sorted out before she left to go back home to Perth.

As Rebecca started to yawn, Helen said, "You look tired dear; why don't you go up to bed?"

"Yeah, it's been a long day. Would you mind if I made myself a hot drink in the kitchen before I go up?" said Rebecca, placing the pen down on the desk.

"Sure dear. Make yourself at home. Actually, what is the time anyway?" said Helen, as she looked at her wrist watch. "It's nearly 1.30! I was having so much fun helping you organise some things for the wedding, that I didn't realise what time it was. I think I will go to bed myself," said Helen. "Good night. Sweet dreams."

"Good night, Helen and thank you for helping me with the wedding arrangements tonight. I really enjoyed spending time with you as well," said Rebecca, leaning in to give her a hug.

"Oh, you are welcome, dear," said Helen, hugging her back. "Night."

Walking towards the kitchen, to her surprise, the back door opened inwards. Mitch and Nick were returning home from work. "Hello," said Rebecca, smiling.

"Hi Rebecca," said Nick, closing the door. "Night… I'm beat, I'm off to bed."

"Oh, Ok. Night, Nick," said Rebecca.

"Catch you tomorrow, bro," said Mitch.

Nick went upstairs to bed.

"What are you doing up so late? I didn't expect to see you up this time of morning," said Mitch, as he held Rebecca in his arms and kissed her tenderly.

"I was doing some wedding planning with your mom tonight and the time just got away from us. We got a lot done though. Actually, I was going to make myself a hot drink, before I head off to bed. Would you like one?" said Rebecca.

"Mmm, sounds good. I would love one," said Mitch. He followed her into the kitchen.

"Tea or coffee?" asked Rebecca, as she felt Mitch's arms envelope her from behind, then kiss her neck.

"Hmm… I might have a hot chocolate, actually," said Mitch.

"Ok. How was work, babe?" asked Rebecca, as she stirred the hot drinks.

He proceeded to tell her all about his night and how they were security for Pink whilst she was out at dinner etc.

"Sounds like you had a busy night?" said Rebecca.

"Sure was. But you know what the best thing of the night was?" said Mitch.

"What's that?"

"Being able to come home to a beautiful, lovely woman and tell her how my night was. On the way home in the car, you were all I could think of, actually," said Mitch.

"I missed you too. Let's take our hot drinks upstairs and we can talk more about your night," said Rebecca, passing him his mug of hot chocolate.

"You're unbelievable, you know that. I don't know of anyone else's partner that cares enough to ask how their day or night has been. Most women I have known are too self-absorbed to ask about the job," said Mitch, taking the cup from her.

"Really… well, you had better get used to it, babe, as I always will be interested in your job and how your day or night was. I need to know if my fiancé is happy or not," said Rebecca, smiling

"I do love you, babe. You are so good for me," said Mitch, as they walked up the stairs.

"Ditto," said Rebecca, carrying her mug of tea up the stairs with Mitch.

Chapter Twenty Six

Rebecca was awakened by a knocking at their bedroom door. Looking over at Mitch, she realised he was still asleep. Hopping out of bed to see who it was, she placed her night robe on and walked towards the door.

Paige was standing in the doorway crying.

"Mum… I'm in a lot of pain. Can you take me to the doctor's please?" said Paige, holding her stomach.

Rebecca pulled Paige into her arms for a cuddle and kissed her forehead. "Shh, it's Ok, sweetie. Let me get dressed and I will take you. Come in and sit down." Closing the door, Rebecca sat Paige down on a chair in their room and quickly got dressed.

Coming around to Mitch's side of the bed, she knelt down and lightly tapped Mitch's arm. "Mitch… Mitch."

"Hmm," said Mitch, opening one eye.

"Paige is not well. I need to take her to the hospital," said Rebecca, with a creased brow.

"What…"said Mitch, sitting up and wiping the sleep from his eyes. "I'll get dressed and… I'll meet you both out the front. I will organise the chauffeur to take you to the doctor's."

"Ok. Thanks," said Rebecca, walking back over to Paige. "Come on, sweetheart. Let's get you downstairs."

Mitch picked up the home telephone and pressed five. When it finally answered a groggy voice came over the phone.

"Yes, sir. Everything all right?" said the chauffeur, looking at his wrist watch.

"We need you to take us... Paige to the hospital. NOW," stated Mitch, authoritatively.

"Yes, sir. I will bring the car around the front," said the chauffeur, who then hung up.

Placing the home phone back in its cradle, Mitch darted for his wardrobe and pulled on some clothes.

As the limousine pulled out of the front gates, Mitch took his mobile phone out of his jacket pocket. Bringing up his contact list, he dialled the number for Paige's doctor's office, which Rebecca had given to him earlier in the day, to let the hospital know they were coming.

With Mitch and Rebecca on either side of Paige, they walked in through the sliding glass door of the doctor's office reception.

"Hello, we rang earlier about Paige Landers," said Mitch, to the receptionist.

Looking through her computer, she said, "Ah, yes...come this way." She ushered them into a waiting room, which had a hospital bed in it. "Lie down here, Paige. The doctors shouldn't be too long."

"Thank you," said Paige, pulling the white woven blanket up to her neck. As the pain got worse, she brought her knees up to her chest and winced.

Mitch and Rebecca hovered next to the bed, worrying if Paige was going to be all right. Feeling Paige's forehead, Rebecca said, "Far out, Paige you're burning up."

"Yeah, I know. I keep feeling hot and then all of sudden I am shivering," said Paige, looking up at Rebecca, her eyes distressed. "I wish the doctor would hurry up."

They only had to wait five minutes before the doctor entered the room.

"Good morning, folks," said the doctor, walking towards Paige. "So... you're not feeling too good this morning, Paige?

Paige shook her head.

"Does this hurt?" said the doctor, pressing on her stomach with his hand.

"Yes. And I keep feeling like I am burning up and then going cold," said Paige, her face pale.

Feeling her forehead, the doctor said, "Right... I think you may have an infection going on inside of you. I will order some blood tests and then we will be able to see what is happening. Ok?"

"Ok," said Paige, wincing.

"You in pain?" asked the doctor.

She nodded.

"Right... I will ask the nurse to administer some pain relief and we'll see how you go," said the doctor, writing on her notes.

"Thank you," said Paige.

He walked towards the doorway and headed for the nurse's station.

The door opened to the waiting room and Mitch and Rebecca watched the doctor walk in with a tray, which had a syringe on it.

"Hello Paige. How's the pain?" asked the doctor.

"Much better. Thank you," said Paige.

"Good. I have your blood test results... you definitely have an infection. This is quite normal considering what you have been through. No need to worry. I have some antibiotics here, which I will give you now," said the doctor, holding up the syringe. "I am going to give you two types of medication that I want you to take at home. One is for the pain relief and the other is some antibiotics. Make sure you finish all of the antibiotics tablets in the course and these pain relief ones are only for if needed. And I will see you in a couple of days unless the pain gets any worse. Ok?" He wrote out the labels for the medication.

"Ok. Thank you," said Paige, smiling.

"Thank you, doctor," said Rebecca, breathing a sigh of relief.

On the way back home Rebecca held Paige in her arms and said, "How are you feeling now, sweetie?"

"I'm Ok now, Mum. Bit tired, though," said Paige, looking down at her cast on her left arm.

"I'm glad you are feeling a little better. Don't worry, sweetheart, everything will be all right. You just need to get some rest and I am sure the medication the doctor gave you will do its magic," said Rebecca.

Paige looked up at Rebecca and said, "Mum… I don't think I can stay here without you." Her brow creased as she snuggled back into Rebecca's side.

"We will take it a day at a time, hey? See how you go," said Rebecca. She kissed Paige's forehead. "Your infection will go away, you'll see and you will start to recover soon."

"Thanks, Mum," said Paige, cuddling back into Rebecca's shoulder.

Six days went by and sure enough, Paige was beginning to feel a lot better because the healing process had kicked in and she was starting to feel like her old self again. Today had been her last visit to the doctor and he had given her the all clear to fly home to Perth

Paige and Rebecca walked out of the doctor's reception and towards the car. "So… now you can fly, have you made up your mind whether you will stay here in Seattle or come home with Mitch and me?" asked Rebecca.

"I have thought about it… and… I think that I will come home with you and Mitch. I will be back here in six weeks, anyway. It's not as if I won't see Michael again. We can talk on Skype each day. Maybe by the time I come back for the wedding I will have made up my mind to stay here. But I am not sure at the moment," said Paige.

"Ok… so can I book the plane flight home for in about a couple of days' time? Will that suit you?" said Rebecca, as they stepped into the car.

"Sure, Mum. A couple of days would be good," said Paige, looking down at her lap, as she picked the quick around her fingernails anxiously.

Rebecca nodded and watched Paige stare off into the distance, out of the car window. *Hmm, she doesn't seem too happy about her decision. This should be interesting when we arrive home, considering how close Michael and Paige have become.*

Before they knew it, it was Sunday and time for Rebecca, Mitch and Paige to go on their long journey back home to Perth. As their limousine pulled out of the driveway of the Portellico house and they waved their final goodbyes to the Portellico family, Rebecca looked over at Paige and shifted close to her. Placing her hand on Paige's, Rebecca noticed the tears streaming down Paige's cheeks, as she sat staring out of the front windscreen of the car.

"It won't be long before you see him again, sweetie," said Rebecca, handing Paige a tissue from her handbag.

With saddened eyes, Paige took the tissue from her mother, nodded and wept into Rebecca's arms.

Mitch gave Rebecca a soulful look and mouthed, 'I love you, babe.' She smiled and mouthed back, 'I love you, too.'

Frankly, I can't wait to get back home. I need some normalcy in my life at the moment. Seattle was like a dream world. I have never had money and the craziness that went along with being wealthy or even wanted it in my life. I suppose it has its good points, but it's not a world I have been brought up in and is so far from the type of person I am. In a way I am dreading our wedding day because of the paparazzi and what they represent, thought Rebecca, as she placed her arm around Paige's shoulder, pulling her in close to comfort her.

In what seemed like no time at all they were landing at the Perth Domestic Airport. Exhausted from the flights, Rebecca was glad that Mitch had organised for an Uber to collect them from the airport and drive them all home to Thornlie.

As the house came into view, Rebecca smiled and said, "Home sweet home." The tension seemed to leave her shoulders as soon as the car pulled into her driveway.

"Looks like we have visitors already," said Mitch, noticing that all the security guys, some who lived across the road with him, were waiting on the front veranda.

Standing as the car pulled to a stop, they rushed over to the car and opened the door. Mitch stepped out first and greeted his housemates, shaking their hands and patting each other on the back. Rebecca and Paige stepped out next and were welcomed with open arms by them.

Hmm, I have forgotten how nice these guys are and their funny antics. I sure did miss them all, thought Rebecca as she watched them help carry their bags into the house and joke around with Mitch.

Rebecca could see Paige was not herself as she leant up against the door frame of the lounge room looking low-spirited. "Sweetheart, why don't you go and have a shower and get into some comfortable clothes and then maybe we can have some lunch." said Rebecca, leaning into Paige and placing her arm around her.

Paige nodded, smiled briefly and numbly walked towards her bedroom with her suitcase.

With Paige being her uppermost concern, as Rebecca listened to the security guys chat, she looked over at the black metal framed clock on the wall and thought, *I wonder what is taking Paige so long in the shower. Might go see if she is all right.* As she was about to stand up and excuse herself to check on Paige, Rebecca noticed Paige coming out of the bathroom wearing her pyjamas and heading straight into her bedroom.

"Excuse me, guys. I just need to see if Paige is Ok," said Rebecca, smiling politely and standing.

Oblivious to what was going on with Paige, they nodded and carried on their conversations with Mitch.

Rebecca placed her ear against Paige's closed bedroom door and listened, only to hear her sobs. Knocking on the door, she entered her room and found Paige lying face down on her bed, crying into the mattress. Sitting on the bed, she gently rubbed Paige's back. "Come here, sweetie," said Rebecca, with her arms extended to give her a cuddle.

"I shouldn't have left him, Mum. I miss him already," said Paige, sobbing into Rebecca's shoulder.

"I know you do, sweetie. How about if we set up the computer and you can see if he is on Skype?" said Rebecca.

With a tear-stained face, Paige pulled away from their embrace. "That would be great, thanks, Mum."

Paige plugged her laptop cord into the wall and turned on her computer. With the screen eventually coming up, she dialled Michael's number into Skype. It didn't take long and he answered.

"Hi, sweet girl. It's so nice to see your face," said Michael, wiping the sleep from his eyes.

"Hello… I miss you already," said Paige, leaning against the pillows on her bedhead and placing the computer on her lap.

Rebecca left the room and let them talk.

"Is she all right, Bec?" said Mitch, as Rebecca sat next to him on the lounge.

"She is now. She is talking with Michael on Skype. I think the next six weeks are gonna be tough though," said Rebecca, her brow furrowed. "Would you guys like another cold beer or something?"

They all nodded.

"Ok. Coming up," said Rebecca, standing and walking towards the kitchen to see what she had in the way of alcoholic drinks in her fridge. Whilst she went to the kitchen, Rebecca overheard Mitch explain to the security guys about Michael and Paige and how they were now together.

With an armful of beers, Rebecca entered the lounge room and said, "Here we go," and handed the beers out.

"Babe, the guys were saying that if we need help keeping Paige busy, or cheering her up, that they could help," said Mitch, as she sat next to him on the couch.

Ever since Jackson had passed away, the security guys across the road had always treated Paige like their little sister. They wanted to see her happy again and were only too happy to help out.

"Aww, thank you. I really appreciate the offer. I will probably take you all up on that over the next six weeks," said Rebecca, looking at each of them and smiling, watching them all drink their beers. *It's a pity Mum and Dad are still away caravanning. I could really do with their support at the moment.*

"What time are you all working tonight?" asked Mitch.

Looking at his watch, Kenny said, "We all are working the same gig this afternoon, Mitch. Actually… we had better get going in a minute, because we're needed at two o'clock and we are working through until one in the morning. Drink up, gentlemen."

"Ok. Well, it was great to catch up with you all. Maybe we can catch up tomorrow for a debriefing?" said Mitch, standing and shaking each of their hands.

"I will give you a ring tomorrow morning to find out what time you are available for the debrief," said Kenny, standing and shaking Mitch's hand. Placing their empty bottles on the table, they each shook Mitch's hand and then walked towards the front doorway.

"Bye guys, and thanks for the welcome home," said Rebecca, giving each of them hug at the front door. Closing the front flywire security door, Rebecca watched them walk across the road to Mitch's house. She smiled as she walked into the kitchen and in that moment realised how much she had actually missed them. They had become like big brothers to her since Jackson had passed away.

"Will it be all right if I move my clothes and everything into here tomorrow?" asked Mitch, as he sat at the breakfast bar, waking Rebecca from her thoughts.

"I am so sorry, Mitch… I haven't even given any thought to you moving in here. With everything that has been going on with Paige, I completely forgot about it. I will have to clear out the wardrobe and drawers for you so that you can put your clothes in there," said Rebecca, feeling awkward. She paused. "I don't know how to tell you this, but here goes… I still have Jackson's clothes in there and so… I will have to take them out so you can put your clothes in there."

How am I gonna tell him that since Jackson passed away that I haven't been able to bring myself to pack up his clothes and that it was always something I kept putting off, because it upset me too much.

"God… I'm sorry, Bec. I didn't realise. Would you like me to help you with that?" said Mitch, his brow creased.

"No, but thanks for asking. It's something I need to do myself. What about if you bring your stuff over tomorrow night? I should have it cleared out by then. I feel really awful. I'm so sorry," said Rebecca, trying to hold back the tears starting to well in her eyes. The thought of saying goodbye to Jackson's stuff really was not something that she had ever wanted to do, until now. As the realisation hit her, the tears overflowed onto her cheeks.

"Don't cry, babe. I don't like to see you upset," said Mitch, taking her in his arms and holding her tight. "It must be dreadful for you to have to box up all Jackson's stuff and then for me to put my clothes in the same place. Would you prefer if I didn't move in with you yet?"

"I should have dealt with it after Jackson passed away, but I could never bring myself to pack his clothes up. And I certainly never thought I'd fall in love again; not this soon. I don't want you living across the road. Not now you are my fiancé and we are about to get married in six weeks. So the answer is, yes I want you to move in straight away. I love you, Mitch," said Rebecca, wiping her eyes, whilst she cuddled into his chest.

Mitch held Rebecca tight in his arms and kissed her hair. "I love you too, beautiful." He always made her feel safe and secure in his arms.

Rebecca opened the vanity cupboard in her bathroom to find a bar of petal scented soap to wash herself with. Searching through the long cupboard, her heart grew heavy as she soon realised that she still needed to not only pack Jackson's clothes into a box, but also his toiletries, shaver, and many other items that she had placed in the back of the bathroom cupboard after he had died. This wasn't going to be an easy day and she knew she wasn't prepared either.

The water in the shower took a few seconds to become hot and as she stepped in and closed the glass screen door behind her, the steam and hot water seemed to drown out her thoughts. With the water splashing over and cascading down her back and shoulders, she soon forgot all of her worries. Relaxed, Rebecca started to think clearly. As she finished washing her hair and body, her mindset had changed. Turning off the faucet, she hopped out the shower and dried herself off.

Picking up her dirty clothes off the bathroom floor Rebecca thought, *I might unpack my suitcase and do some clothes washing.*

"Do you have any washing, Mitch?" called out Rebecca, as she entered the bedroom to see Mitch unpacking his suitcase.

"Yep. But that's Ok, I can wash them later," said Mitch.

"I have a load to do, so I can wash yours with mine if you like," said Rebecca.

"Thanks, that would be great. I haven't had a woman wash my clothes since... well you know when. I have washed my own clothes for the past five years," said Mitch, his brow creased.

"Well… in this house we help each other with what I call the chores," said Rebecca, smiling. "And I am only too happy to wash your clothes."

"Thanks, Bec. Umm, would it be Ok for me to have a shower? It's just… I don't smell too good," said Mitch, smelling his underarm.

"Sure. You go ahead," said Rebecca. "I will go get you a clean towel from the linen cupboard."

"Thanks," said Mitch, walking towards the bathroom with his clothes.

Rebecca placed Mitch's towel on the vanity, whilst he was in the shower. "What am I going to do about Paige?" said Rebecca to Mitch as she stood next to the shower.

"Just give it a few days and see how she goes, Bec. If Paige is not all right by next weekend, I will ring my parents and plead with them to let Michael come out here until the wedding," said Mitch, washing his body.

"Hopefully you won't have to speak with your parents," said Rebecca, concern in her voice.

"I am sure things will work out," said Mitch, turning off the faucet and stepping out of the shower.

"I am sure you are right," said Rebecca. With a smirk on her face and one eyebrow raised, she handed Mitch his towel. "Hmm, I could get used to this."

"Cheeky girl," said Mitch, taking the towel from her and drying himself.

CHAPTER TWENTY SEVEN

"I might go over and start packing up my stuff into boxes, for the move over here. Will you be all right?" said Mitch, knowing Rebecca had boxes to pack as well.

"Yeah, I should be fine," said Rebecca.

He kissed her goodbye and she watched him walk across the road to his rental.

Now the washing is on I might go out to the garage to get some boxes, thought Rebecca, walking towards the kitchen and opening the pantry to retrieve the garage key. She knew she had a few empty boxes with their lids to erect in the garage so that she could pack up Jackson's clothes and personal items.

Rebecca sighed as she reluctantly made up the boxes on top of her bed. Taking one box over to Jackson's side of the wardrobe, she noticed that there was a trace of the cologne Jackson used to wear in the air. Turning the light on, she felt his presence.

"Jackson," said Rebecca, quietly. She waited for an answer. But of course there was nothing. "I know you are here. I can smell you."

She felt a cool breeze on her neck and knew instantly it was him. She looked around the wardrobe for any sign, but she didn't physically see him.

"I miss you Jackson... I know you told Paige you were happy for

Mitch and me, but could you please give me a sign, so that I know I am doing the right thing."

She felt a cool breeze again and knew that she had to start packing.

As she slowly packed Jackson's clothes into the cartons, Rebecca chatted to him about Mitch and how they were getting married. She also conveyed to Jackson about what was happening with Paige, hoping he would give her some strength. This was probably the most she had ever spoken to Jackson since he had died.

Once she had finished packing up Jackson's belongings, Rebecca felt the cool breeze dissipate. Automatically she knew he was gone.

"I will always love you, Jackson," she said out loud, looking to the roof.

One by one she carried the boxes out to the garage and stored them, hoping that one day, when she was ready, she would be able to donate them to a charity. Locking the garage doors, she turned around and pressed her back up against the wooden grain doors, looking into the sky. As her tears spilled over onto her hot cheeks, she felt saddened at the thought of what she was missing with Jackson, but at the same time, she felt happy knowing Mitch was going to be there for her now. She had never felt so alone or loved at the same time before. Wiping the tears from her face she thought, *I must keep myself busy so that I don't crack up in front of Paige, as she doesn't need to see me like this.*

Carrying in the basket from her last load of washing she hung out, Rebecca thought, *Hmm, I think I might need to do some food shopping today. Because we have been away for a while there won't be any fresh food in the fridge.* Once she made a list of what they needed, Rebecca checked in on Paige and found her sleeping soundly on top of the bed. Deciding to leave her to rest, she closed the door quietly and left a note on the kitchen bench telling her where she had gone, just in case she woke whilst she was away.

On the drive home Rebecca's hands-free mobile rang. Looking at the dash screen she noticed it was her boss. "Hello," she said as she answered.

"Welcome back. We sure have missed you," said Mark.

"Thanks. I have missed you all as well."

"So… when will you be returning to work?" asked Mark.

"Well… I would like to get everything settled at home first. So I was thinking, if it's Ok with you, that I would return to work in about two days' time," said Rebecca.

"That will work out fine with me. How is Paige going?" said Mark.

"Thanks for being so understanding. Paige is well, Mark. She still has her arm in a cast, but otherwise she is going Ok."

"Oh, that's good."

"Well, I had better go… I have just pulled into my driveway after doing some food shopping. So I will see you in a couple of days," said Rebecca, turning off the engine.

"Ok. Bye for now," said Mark.

"Bye," said Rebecca, pressing the button on her dash to end the call.

Placing her handbag on her right shoulder as she alighted from the car, Rebecca noticed Paige sitting on the front veranda.

"Hi, sweetie. Did you have a good sleep?" said Rebecca, as she walked around to the back of the car.

"Yes, Mum. I feel a bit better now," said Paige, coming over to help her carry the shopping in.

"That's great, sweetheart. Hey… I wanted to ask you; how do you feel about going back to work soon?" said Rebecca, as they walked inside with the bags.

"Sounds like a good idea, Mum. I need to keep my mind occupied, as I can see it's going to be a long six weeks. Though, I am not sure how I will go with this cast on my arm," said Paige, placing the bags on the kitchen counter top.

"Why don't you give your boss a ring and explain to him about your cast and see if he is willing to have you start back in the next couple of days?" said Rebecca, as she walked towards the front door to get the rest of the shopping from her boot.

"Ok. I will give him a ring now," said Paige, reaching for her mobile phone in her jeans pocket.

Putting the shopping away, it dawned on Rebecca that she had to cook dinner tonight. She had been spoilt rotten over the past several weeks, with the Portellico family servants making meals every day for them.

Standing in front of the freezer with the door open, she finally decided on some sirloin steak, which had been cut into strips. Placing it on the sink to thaw out, she thought, *Beef Stroganoff or Casserole, not sure?*

As Rebecca watched Paige hang up her phone she said, "How'd you go?"

"Yeah, good. I have a shift tomorrow night," said Paige, sitting at kitchen bench.

"Great. So he must have been Ok about your arm then?" said Rebecca.

"Yeah, he said to me that it was no problem and that we could work around it," said Paige.

"That's good of him. Well… I was thinking I might go have a lie down. Are you going to be all right?" said Rebecca, walking around the other side of the kitchen bench.

"Yes, Mum. I will be fine. I will wake you when it's close to dinner time," said Paige, giving her a hug.

"Ok. Thanks, sweetheart," said Rebecca, hugging her back. "Mitch should be back soon with his clothes and everything soon."

"Oh, Ok. Have a good sleep, Mum," said Paige, watching Rebecca walk down the hallway to her bedroom.

As soon as Rebecca put her head on the pillow, she was out like a light.

Her eyes opened slowly from what seemed like a deep sleep. Feeling rested, Rebecca yawned and looked over at the bedside digital clock to see it was 6.34pm. Sitting up and swinging her legs over the side of the bed, she wiped the sleep from her eyes and tried to gather her thoughts. Realising she needed a toilet break, she visited the bathroom.

Checking her appearance in the bathroom mirror, she thought, *God I look like something the cat dragged in.* After giving her face a wash with some water in the basin, she then brushed her teeth and hair. *Hmm, that's better. I need to make a start on dinner,* thought Rebecca.

Opening the door to her room, the smell of something delicious cooking hit her nostrils. As she quietly walked down the hallway and stood in the doorway of the kitchen, she watched how well Mitch and Paige were cooking dinner together. They had found the meat on the sink and decided to make dinner. It made her feel lucky to have such a thoughtful family, once again.

As Mitch turned around to get something out of the fridge he saw her standing there, smiling.

"Looks who's awake."

Walking over to her, he gave Rebecca a hug and kissed her inviting lips. "Hello, beautiful. Hope you don't mind, but Paige and I are cooking dinner tonight."

"Hi yourself, gorgeous. Thank you. That is really nice of you both," said Rebecca, looking from Mitch to Paige.

Cuddling into Mitch's shoulder, Rebecca said to Paige, "How are you going, sweetie?"

"All good at the moment, Mum. Mitch has been keeping me busy. I had to help him carry some of his stuff over," said Paige, pointing to Mitch boxes piled up in the lounge room. "Oh and then he roped me into helping him cook dinner." Paige smirked and shrugged her shoulders.

"That was nice of you, sweetie… after dinner, I can help you put all your stuff away Mitch, if you like," said Rebecca.

He nodded and said, "Sounds like a plan."

"Dinner smells nice. I am famished," said Rebecca, sniffing the air.

"We are making Beef Stroganoff with some white rice," said Paige, proudly.

"Mmm, looking forward to eating that," said Rebecca, smiling.

"Mitch brought over some wine for dinner to celebrate us being home and him moving in," said Paige, indicating to the red wine on the bench top as she walked over to the stove top.

"That was nice of you, Mitch." Rebecca kissed him on his lips.

As Paige stirred the dinner, Mitch whispered into Rebecca's ear,

"Does Ms Landers want to play later on?"

Rebecca smiled at him and nodded, whispering into his ear, "Does Sir have his tie and blindfold with him?"

With his eyebrows raised, he nodded and smiled at her. Then kissed her tenderly.

Paige turned around to see them and said, "Get a room you two!" She laughed. "Dinner is ready, actually. Table is already set and we just need the drinks now. I will finish dishing up, if you like," said Paige.

"Thanks, Paige," said Mitch, getting some glasses out the cupboard.

"I have to go into work tomorrow. I should be home for dinner though. What are you ladies up to tomorrow?" said Mitch, placing some more food on his fork.

"Actually, we both spoke with our bosses today. Paige is back at work tomorrow night. And I am back to work on Wednesday. But I have plenty to catch up on here," said Rebecca, placing her knife down and picking up her glass of wine.

"Ok. That's good. Hey Paige... are you going to Skype Michael tonight or tomorrow?" asked Mitch.

"Probably tonight," said Paige, smiling.

"Tell the family I said hello, will you," said Mitch.

"Sure will. You miss them already," said Paige, with a creased brow.

"Yes I miss them a lot, Paige. But I don't miss the lifestyle. I think that's why I like it here so much. Here is normal to me. Seattle is paparazzi, crazy, madness and I didn't like it," said Mitch, remembering just how much the paparazzi tried to find out who he was currently seeing.

"I know Mum didn't like it either," said Paige, looking at Rebecca.

"It's all right in small doses," said Rebecca.

"Well now that we have finished dinner, why don't I do the dishes and you two can go and put Mitch's stuff away. It's clogging up the lounge room," said Paige, smirking.

"Cheeky... but that sounds good to me," said Rebecca.

"Ok. Are you sure you don't need a hand in the kitchen?" said Mitch.

"No," said Paige, waving him away.

Whilst hanging his clothes, Mitch said, "Can I ask you something, Bec?"

"Sure. What is it?" said Rebecca, placing his shorts in a drawer.

"Would you mind if we put your mattress and bed head in the garage, so that I can bring my new mattress and bedhead over to sleep in? It's just... well... I feel a bit strange sleeping in another man's bed," said Mitch, feeling awkward.

"Oh God, I'm so sorry Mitch. I never even thought about that. Yes, I think that would be a great idea. Let's pull this one apart and store it in the garage and then we can go over and get your new one."

"Thanks for being so understanding, Bec. I hope you don't mind but I bought a brand new set of sheets, four new pillows and a really nice comforter set for our bed today."

"Aww, that's nice... and no I don't mind."

Once Mitch's bed and the new linen had been set up, they stood back, admiring the finished product.

"To a new beginning," said Mitch, as he pulled Rebecca in tight and kissed her lips passionately.

"You are so thoughtful. Thank you," said Rebecca.

"Sir only wants to have his way with his beautiful wife to be, on these nice clean sheets," said Mitch, smirking.

They were both startled by a knock on the door.

"Come in, sweetheart," said Rebecca.

"I just wanted to say good night and see you in the morning," said Paige, opening the door.

Rebecca hugged Paige and said, "Sleep well, my darling. See you in the morning."

"Good night, Paige," said Mitch. "See you in the morning."

"Yeah, night," said Paige, as she pulled the door closed.

As she shut the door, Mitch pulled Rebecca into his embrace and said, "I need you now. Are you ready?"

She nodded and said, "Yes, Sir," and switched off the light.

Slowly he kissed, then lapped at her neck. She felt her body quiver all over. When his teeth grazed her right ear, she moaned with pleasure.

"You won't be needing these," said Mitch, indicating to her clothes, as he stripped her down to her bra and panties, whilst slowly kissing every inch of her body.

Gently he pushed her onto the bed and she lay on top of the comforter watching him undress down to his jocks. Mitch climbed onto the bed and lay next to her, and she felt his enlarged penis press against her, whilst Mitch explored her supple body in the moonlight, which was seeping through a gap in the curtains. The warmth of his breath on her body as he trailed kisses over her made Rebecca shiver with delight. With his hand journeying up to her breast, he felt through the lacy material of her bra, her nipple harden in quick response. Hastily he unclipped her bra and discarded it to the black carpeted floor. His hot mouth sucked and bit her nipples one by one and she was tipped over the edge with unmistakable pleasure. Breathless, she orgasmed.

When their lips met, he opened her mouth fervently with a sensual kiss, allowing their tongues a brief taste. She was lost to his touch. His teasing was relentless, as he continued to pleasure her in ways she could only have imagined.

Arching her back off the bed, Rebecca moaned, "Please... I need you inside me."

"Soon," Mitch murmured.

Rebecca watched as Mitch retrieved the black blindfold out of the bedside drawer and waited in anticipation of what would happen next. Placing the blindfold over her eyes, he then took her hands and tied them to the wooden bed frame behind her.

"I'll be back in a moment," said Mitch.

She heard a door open.

Waiting eagerly for his return, she lay there wondering what Mitch was doing and why he was taking so long. All of sudden she heard the door shut and felt the bed indent as he lay next to her.

"Open your mouth," commanded Mitch.

As Rebecca opened her mouth, she felt a cool glass touch her lips.

"Drink," said Mitch, leaning into her body.

She lifted her head up off the bed and felt him tilt the glass to her lips. Taking the first sip, she realised it was wine. It was nice and cold on her throat. As she lay down, Rebecca felt his soft lips touch hers.

Mmm, his mouth tastes good, thought Rebecca, enjoying every moment.

Lifting her head off the pillow again, Rebecca sensed the cold glass touch her lips and she swallowed another mouthful of wine. With her other senses heightened, she felt Mitch slowly caress and kiss every inch of her body. When he reached her navel and quickly took off her panties, he opened her legs. Rebecca gasped with anticipation as his cold lips kissed the inside of her thigh. As she arched her body off the bed and her body quivered from his touch, she felt his tongue, still cold from the wine, stimulating and lapping at her clitoris. She was on fire. Rebecca's body shivered in anticipation of what he would do next.

"Turn over," he instructed her.

She did as she was told. Eager, she licked her lips when she heard him rip open the packet and place the condom onto his elongated shaft. As he slowly inserted his penis into her vagina from behind and moved it in and out, she adjusted to his size.

"Oh God, that feels so good. Please don't stop," said Rebecca, her breathing heavy.

As he fucked her faster and harder, she could feel another orgasm coming. She tried to stop it, but it had a mind of its own and she was shattered into a thousand pieces as she orgasmed. Rebecca then heard Mitch groan as he came and stilled over her.

Gently he pulled his cock out of her and took the blindfold off. Smiling as the sweat beaded on his top lip he untied her hands. They lay on top of the comforter of Mitch's bed exhausted, trying to catch their breath.

"Did Sir enjoy that?" said Rebecca, sweat forming on her brow.

"Mmm... I had a great time with my wife-to-be," said Mitch, as he leant over and kissed her forehead.

Pulling her into his chest, he wrapped his arms and legs around her well-toned body and they fell asleep.

CHAPTER TWENTY EIGHT

The next morning Rebecca woke feeling well rested and for the first time in what seemed like ages; she felt alive and positive about her life going forward.

As she lay on her back looking at the ceiling, she thought, *I remember before I left for Seattle that I never slept well in my bed. Every night would be the same; I would toss and turn all night long and then wake up tired in the morning.*

Turning over in bed, she reached for Mitch, but he wasn't there. She could hear the water running, so Rebecca assumed he must be having a shower before work. Looking at the digital clock next to her bed, it said 6.30am. As she lay in their new bed thinking about Mitch and what he had brought to her life so far, he walked into the room with a towel wrapped around the bottom half of his muscular body.

Oh, that chest. Adorable, thought Rebecca.

As he neared the bed he notices she is awake. "Hello, babe. Sleep well, did you?" asks Mitch.

"Hello, sweet man. I sure did, until I realised you weren't in the bed," said Rebecca.

Smiling, he sat on the bed. Leaning over her, he kisses her lips tenderly.

Mmm, toothpaste.

"You look beautiful just lying there," said Mitch, his eyebrow raised.

"I wish you didn't have to go to work today."

"I will miss you too, babe. I have a pretty full on day today. But I should be home by at least 6pm," said Mitch, tracing his hand down the side of her face.

"What do you feel like for dinner tonight?" asked Rebecca.

"I don't mind. Surprise me," said Mitch, hopping off the bed and retrieving his grey trousers and white shirt out the wardrobe to wear.

"Oh, Ok. Well, I hope you have a good day," said Rebecca, watching him get dressed.

"Thanks," said Mitch, buttoning his shirt and tucking it into his trousers. "Sorry, babe, I have to go." Mitch walked back over to the bed. "See you tonight. Have a great day." He gave her a long lasting kiss goodbye and walked towards the doorway.

"Bye, gorgeous. I love you," she shouted after him.

Hmm… I wonder what the day will bring, thought Rebecca, as she got out of bed and headed for the bathroom to have a shower.

Poking her head through the doorway to see if Paige was awake, Rebecca noticed she wasn't in her bed. The bed was unmade, clothes everywhere, and her computer was next to her pillows. Searching through the house to see if she was all right, she found Paige on the back porch steps, staring up at the sky, with tears streaming down her cheeks.

Rebecca sat next to Paige on the steps and placed her arm around her shoulders. "Come on. Let's go inside and I will make you some breakfast," said Rebecca.

Paige pulled out the stool and sat at the breakfast bar. "I miss Michael a lot and it's not until now that I realised just how much. I can't seem to get him out of my head. I go to sleep, he is on my mind. I wake up, he is on my mind. I don't know how I am going to get through the next six weeks."

"All you can do is take it a day at a time, sweetheart," said Rebecca, handing her the tissue box.

"Even though I miss Michael, I am glad to be back home. The Portellico family are lovely people, but they are not you, Mum. I would have missed you so much if I had stayed there," said Paige, wiping her nose.

"I would have missed you too, sweetheart. But now we are home, we need to get back to some sort of normality. What time do you start work today?" said Rebecca, hearing the toast pop up.

"I am working the 4pm – midnight shift," said Paige, watching Rebecca spread butter on the toast.

"I will drop you off at work this afternoon and I will organise for one of Mitch's security guys to come and collect you at midnight. Ok?" said Rebecca, placing some tea and toast in front of Paige.

"Ok. Thanks, Mum and thanks for the breakfast too," said Paige.

"You're welcome."

"What are you going to do on your last day off today, Mum?" said Paige.

"I was thinking about doing a bit of clothes washing and that was it. I might just relax all day in front of the TV or read a book. What about you, sweetie?" said Rebecca.

"I was thinking about going to see some of my friends. I haven't seen them in a while. Could I borrow your car?" said Paige.

"How do you think you may go driving with a cast on? Do you feel well enough to drive?" asked Rebecca, worried she might have an accident.

"I should be all right. Anyway, my arm doesn't hurt anymore. Can't wait to get the cast off next week," said Paige.

"Right. Will probably do you good to get out of the house, anyway. Might take your mind off Michael for a while. But I don't want you to be gone for too long," said Rebecca, watching her daughter take a sip of tea.

"Yeah thanks, Mum. Really appreciate this," said Paige, as she placed the toast up to her mouth.

Rebecca opened up the mail that had accumulated, and which the security guys across the road had collected for her whilst she was in Seattle. She paid some overdue bills online and caught up on her e-mails. As she finally sat to enjoy a cup of tea, she decided to text Mitch, to see how his day was.

'Hi Mitch, how is your day? Can't wait to see you tonight. I miss you. ILU.'
She received a message back straight away from him.

'Hey there babe, my day has been pretty full on so far. Wishing I was there with you instead of here. I miss you too. C U around 6pm. ILU. Your fiancé, Mitch.'

Rebecca smiled and thought, *I can't wait to see him later.* Placing her phone on the table, she walked into the kitchen and discarded all the junk mail into the bin, along with all the envelopes.

Opening the freezer door, Rebecca stood there trying to decide what to make for dinner tonight. She eventually decided on making some Sirloin steak with mushroom sauce, garden salad, and hot chips for her and Mitch, as Paige would be able to make her dinner at work. The rest of her day went by pretty fast, what with doing some dusting, vacuuming, sweeping the front veranda and cleaning the pool, and before she knew it, it was 3.15; time to take Paige to work.

As Rebecca prepared the garden salad for dinner, she heard a car pull into her driveway. Looking up at the clock on the kitchen wall, she wondered if it was Mitch, seeing as the time was 6.38pm. Walking towards the front door she spotted his black ute and breathed a sigh of relief. Ever since Jackson's death, she was always happy when her family came home in one piece.

"Hello, beautiful," said Mitch, when he realised Rebecca was standing at the doorway.

"Hi, babe. How was your day?" said Rebecca, smiling.

"Pretty good. Busy, but I got everything sorted out and now my business should be able to run a bit better," said Mitch, placing his muscular arms around her.

Rebecca closed her eyes and laid her head on his chest. She always felt loved whilst in his arms. "Would you like something to drink?" asked Rebecca.

"I wouldn't mind a beer, if you have one," said Mitch.

"I only have a six pack of Corona. You know… that's one of the many things that I don't know about you. What is your favourite beer?" said Rebecca.

"Hey that's the fun of getting to know me. But my favourite drink is Johnny Walker Black Label and coke, and the beer I like to drink is Pure Blonde. But I don't mind Corona. It's not a bad drop," said Mitch, looking her in the eyes.

"Are you hungry yet?" asked Rebecca, as she pulled away from Mitch's hold to retrieve the beer from the kitchen fridge.

"Sure am. I didn't get time to have lunch today," said Mitch, following her into the kitchen and noticing the salad she was making.

"I am making steak, salad and chips. I will put it on now for you," said Rebecca, opening the fridge and taking out the meat and beer.

"Mmm, sounds good, babe. Put heaps on my plate. I am famished," said Mitch, twisting off the lid from the bottle of beer.

Drinking it down fast, Mitch decided he would go have a shower, whilst Rebecca cooked their dinner.

Taking the steak off the grill, Rebecca covered it over with foil to keep it hot. Just as she set it aside, she felt two warm muscular arms wrap around her waist.

"Mmm you smell good, babe," said Rebecca, turning around to give him a kiss. It was then that she discovered that he was wearing nothing. Nothing, but the grey tie she had bought him in Seattle.

God, what a gorgeous body.

"You are such a tease, you know that? What am I going to do with you?" said Rebecca, her eyebrows raised when she saw his hardened penis.

"There are plenty of things I could think of right now," said Mitch, as he kissed her neck near her earlobe. Mitch knew how this made her libido go wild and how to turn her on.

"You have way too many clothes on Ms Landers," said Mitch, playfully.

"Sir, wants to play then, I see," said Rebecca, pulling at his tie.

Kneeling in front of her, Mitch unzipped Rebecca's Levi jeans and hoisted them down quickly. As he trailed kisses near her inner thigh, she moaned in sheer pleasure. Shifting her legs apart, she came undone as his rough tongue licked and sucked her clitoris. Picking her up, he placed her on the counter, abandoned all gentleness and entered her vagina with a sharp thrust. With her legs wrapped around him, enjoying the short, sharp burst of his cock, she felt like she was on fire, and could explode at any minute.

"Please…… I beg you…… stop. I can't handle this," and as she said it, she orgasmed and felt her body shatter into a thousand pieces.

But Mitch had not finished with her yet, fucking her harder and harder, until his body gave way to the unadulterated pleasure and he finally came.

"I have wanted to do that all day to you. Woman… what you do to me," said Mitch, as he slipped his limp cock out of her vagina and handed her a towel.

"A girl could get used to that every day," said Rebecca, smiling as she slipped off the bench.

"Now, I want my dinner, wench," said Mitch, playfully trying to pull her in close to his body.

"Wench, ha. I'll give you wench," said Rebecca, pushing him away and whipping his bum with the towel.

"Ouch," said Mitch, once again pulling her into his chest. "Cheeky wench."

"That's not what the magazines say about me," she teased. "They say I am special." Rebecca laughed.

"You sure are special. I am looking forward to marrying you and spending the rest of my life with you, Bec," said Mitch, looking into her adoring eyes.

"Me too. I can't wait to be your wife. Life sure is going to be grand," said Rebecca, cuddling into his chest and feeling the love. "Let's go have a shower."

"You sure are a great cook, Bec," said Mitch, as he ate his dinner.

"Thanks. I love to cook for you," said Rebecca. Just as she said this, the home phone rang. "Won't be a sec." She walked into the kitchen to retrieve the call. "Hello."

"Mum!" said Paige, through her tears. She sobbed into the phone.

"What's the matter, Paige?" said Rebecca, her brow creased.

"I need to come home, Mum. I can't concentrate and I have made so many mistakes tonight that my boss is not very happy with me at all. He told me to go home and come back when I had my brain functioning properly," said Paige.

"Oh sweetie… I'll leave in a minute to come and get you. Just stay at the restaurant until I get there, Ok?" said Rebecca, wondering what was going on.

"Yes, Mum. Thanks," said Paige. She hung up the phone.

As Rebecca hung up Mitch said, "What's the matter, babe? Paige all right?"

"No, she is upset again and wants to come home."

"I will lock up. You get ready and I will drive you in to collect her," said Mitch, picking up the plates and carrying them over to the sink.

"Thanks, babe."

The Mitchell Freeway was empty for a change, as they drove towards Joondalup.

"It seems your brother has made a big impression on Paige. Do you think that maybe we could Skype your parents tonight and talk to them about this?" said Rebecca.

"Yeah, sounds like a good idea. I was thinking that if they could see how upset Paige is, then maybe, just maybe, they might change their minds. But I don't want to say anything to Paige to get her hopes up," said Mitch, as she watched a motorbike speed by them.

"Thanks, Mitch. I appreciate anything you can do for my girl," said Rebecca, looking straight ahead as she watched the motorbike too. "Can't believe some drivers. Bloody idiots."

'Yeah I know. Sometimes I wish I was a copper, so that I could get these idiots off the road," said Mitch.

It was a long drive home for Mitch and Rebecca, as they listened to Paige sniff back her tears in the back seat of Rebecca's car. Her crying eventually turned into sobbing and heaving. Rebecca hated seeing her daughter like this.

"Go and have a hot shower, love, and get into your pyjamas. I will bring you in a hot drink," said Rebecca, as their car pulled into the driveway.

"Thanks, Mum," said Paige, her voice croaky, as she opened the car door.

Rebecca looked over at Mitch and said, "Thanks for driving us."

"You're welcome. You go take care of Paige and I will give Mom and Dad a ring."

"Ok, thanks."

"Knock, knock," said Rebecca, standing at Paige's door.

"Come in," sobbed Paige, wiping her tears on her cotton pyjama top.

"May I come in too?" said Mitch, carrying a laptop into her room.

"Yes," said Paige, wiping her eyes and sniffing.

"Paige... I have someone here who wants to talk to you," said Mitch, placing the laptop on her bed.

She sat up and wiped her eyes again. Her blotchy, red face was distraught until she saw who wanted to speak with her.

"Oh, Michael..." she sobbed. "I wish you were here... you are all I think about day in and day out. I even dream about you. I can't say that I have ever felt like this about a boy before. I wish I could hug you right now."

"Paige... you look terrible. How long have you been crying for? I wish I could be there for you right now. I miss you too," said Michael, with a furrowed brow.

Mitch and Rebecca left them to talk on Skype and then Mitch went to ring his parents again.

"Now, do you see how bad she is? This is just ridiculous. You have to let him come over here. I will look after him, don't worry, and he can work for me. Just until the wedding. What do you think, Mom and Dad? Please," said Mitch, his brow creased.

Helen and Grayson had seen how upset Paige looked on Skype because they were standing beside Michael when Paige was talking to him, but Paige couldn't see them as they were standing to one side. They could also hear it in her voice as well. She loved their son and would do anything to be with him again.

"Ok. But only until the wedding, no longer. Not only is Paige like this, but Michael too. It's hard as a mother to see your child upset all the time. I can see that these two love each other very much Mitch, so the answer is 'yes'. We will put Michael on a plane tomorrow with Nick. Nick was coming anyway for business, so it will work out good if they fly together," said Helen.

"Thanks Mom and Dad. You won't regret this. Text me the flight details so that I can pick them up from the airport," said Mitch, smiling.

"I will. Good night, son and take good care of your brothers whilst they are there. We will miss them," said Grayson.

"Bye. Talk to you soon. Love you both," said Mitch.

Mitch and Rebecca decided not to tell Paige because they wanted it to be a surprise for her. Michael was also sworn to secrecy as well by Helen and Grayson, but was excited about not only visiting Australia, but also being able to see his girl again.

"Mitch, tomorrow night when Paige is at work, could you please help me set up the two bedrooms for Nick and Michael? I just need some help putting the beds together that I have in the garage," said Rebecca, placing her head in the crook of Mitch's shoulder in their bedroom.

"No problem, babe. It sure will be nice having both my brothers here in Perth and staying with us," said Mitch, positioning his arm around her.

"Sure will. I had better go shopping after work tomorrow for some more food and drinks," said Rebecca, mentally thinking of meals to cook whilst Nick and Michael were visiting.

CHAPTER TWENTY NINE

The day had finally arrived and Paige was still unaware that Michael and Nick would be flying into Perth. Mitch had left early in the morning to pick them up from the airport.

With her left elbow resting on the kitchen bench, propping her up, as she sat and ate her breakfast, Paige said, "Is there anything you need help with today, Mum?"

"Umm… yeah… I could do with a hand with the food shopping, if you want to come along with me."

"Sure. Anything else?" asked Paige.

"Let me think about it and I'll let you know. I did most of the housework yesterday," said Rebecca. *You won't be asking for something to do when Michael gets here… Actually, was that Mitch's car I heard pull up?*

"Ok. I'm trying to keep busy and not think about Michael," said Paige. She had her back to the door when Mitch walked in with his two brothers.

"Look who I found hanging around the airport this morning," said Mitch, smiling.

Paige turned around to see Michael and then Nick standing there with Mitch. She screamed with joy and ran over quickly to Michael and gave him a tight hug and a long kiss.

Rebecca mouthed 'Thank you' to Mitch and smiled.

"I can't believe you are here," said Paige, cuddling into his chest. "I have missed you so much."

"I have missed you too," said Michael, cuddling her back. "It's good to see you. So… what's this talk of you not eating properly lately?" Michael pulled her chin up to meet his eyes. "We can't have that happening and now that I am here, I will look after you."

"Young love. Isn't it grand," said Nick, smiling.

"Sorry Nick… I haven't even said hello. How rude of me," said Paige, walking over and giving him a hug. "Welcome to Perth. Thanks for bringing Michael for me."

"You're welcome," said Nick.

"Hi Nick. How are you? How were the flights?" said Rebecca, walking over and giving him a hug.

"Yeah, all good, Bec. Where did you want me to put our bags?" said Nick.

"Come this way and I will show you where your rooms are," said Rebecca to Nick and Michael.

After they put their bags in their rooms, Paige took Michael out to the front porch, so they could be alone and talk.

"You guys thirsty?" asked Rebecca. "I can make a hot cuppa if you like."

"Mmm, that sounds good. Cup of coffee for me, Bec. White and one sugar," said Nick.

"Ah… I'll have a coffee too, babe," said Mitch. "Thanks."

"Ok. Why don't you two go and take a seat outside and I'll bring the drinks out," said Rebecca, filling up the kettle with cold water.

Mitch and Nick nodded.

"So… Mitch, are you living here now?" asked Nick, as he followed Mitch out to the back yard.

"Sure are, bro," said Mitch, sitting down at table under the patio.

"You know what was nice about coming into the Perth airport? No paparazzi. And no one knows us. It was so good," said Nick, his eyebrows raised as he took a seat next to Mitch.

"You are not wrong, bro. Now you know why I want to live here instead. Life is normal here. No one to bother me either," said Mitch.

"Here we go," said Rebecca, carrying the tray of hot drinks and placing them in front of Mitch and Nick.

"Thanks," they both said together.

"When do you have to start work, Nick?" said Rebecca, taking her seat at the wooden table.

"Pink is arriving Monday morning into Perth International Airport, so I have today and tomorrow off. She is only here for five days, so by next week-end I can go home; that's if you are sick of me being here," said Nick, smirking.

"Hey… you can stay as long as you like. It's nice to have you here," said Rebecca, smiling. As Mitch and Nick sat there catching up, Rebecca had a thought.

"Hey, would you guys like to do a barbeque and drinks tonight? Maybe I can invite some of our friends over as well," said Rebecca, looking from Mitch to Nick.

"Sounds like a great idea, babe. Did you need me to do or get anything?" said Mitch.

"Maybe check the outdoor setting and chairs are clean. Oh, and buy some drinks for tonight as well. I will go around to the shops and get some food for the barbeque," said Rebecca.

"Ok. Sounds like a plan," said Mitch.

"Well, I will leave you two to chat and go and make some phone calls," said Rebecca, standing and picking up her hot cup of tea.

The first person Rebecca called was her best friend, Penny.

"Hi Bec… welcome home. I was wondering when I was going to hear from you," said Penny, excited to hear from her friend of many years.

"Hi Penny. Yeah, sorry I haven't called. What with catching up with the housework, moving Mitch in, and consoling Paige, it has been pretty hectic around here," said Rebecca. "Hey, I was wondering what you are up to tonight?"

"Not a lot," said Penny.

"We are having a barbeque. Would you like to come over?"

"Umm… yeah, Ok. What time would you like me to come?" said

Penny.

"Well… if you're not doing anything right now, you could come over soon, if you want. Oh and you will get to meet Nick and Michael, you know, Mitch's brothers from Seattle that I have been talking about for the last six weeks."

"I could come over now and help with the food prep, if you like," said Penny, enthusiastic.

"Sounds good. See you soon," said Rebecca.

"I just need to have a shower and I will be over," said Penny. "Bye."

Rebecca then rang the rest of her friends to see if they too were able to come over for the barbeque.

"Looks like you have a visitor, Bec," said Nick, watching Penny's car pull into the driveway through the lounge room window. "Man, she is pretty too."

His face lit up as she walked towards the front door.

Rebecca snickered to herself, as she knew Nick would think Penny was pretty.

"Hi, Penny. Come in," said Rebecca, opening the front flywire door.

"Hi Bec," said Penny, giving her a hug.

"Penny, this is Nick. Mitch's brother from Seattle," said Rebecca, gesturing to Nick who was eagerly standing with Rebecca and Mitch at the door.

"Hi Nick. Nice to meet you. How was the flight over to Perth?" said Penny, shaking his hand.

"Hi Penny. Nice to meet you too. The flight wasn't too bad and I had Michael, our other brother, to keep me company," said Nick, smiling.

"So… Michael must be the one Paige is going with?" asked Penny.

"Yeah… the love birds are out the back catching up. We only got here a couple of hours ago and they haven't left each other's side," said Nick, his eyebrows raised and smirking.

Penny giggled. "Hi Mitch," said Penny, giving him a quick hug. "Long time, no see."

"Hi Penny. Yeah, it feels like ages since we've seen you. How are you?" said Mitch.

"I'm good. Been busy with work though. I thought I'd come early and give Bec a hand with the shopping and cooking," said Penny.

"Oh, Ok. That's nice of you," said Mitch.

"We might go and get the food now. We shouldn't be too long," said Rebecca, walking to the kitchen to get her handbag.

"God, Nick is absolutely gorgeous… hot body too… I can't wait to get to know him better," said Penny, as they pulled out of the driveway in her car.

"I knew you would like him," said Rebecca. She had spoken to Penny about Nick whilst she was in Seattle and was thrilled with their initial meeting.

"I can't believe he isn't married or doesn't have a girlfriend at least, already," said Penny, smiling, as she pulled into the Forest Lakes shopping centre car park at Thornlie.

"I think that is maybe because he is too busy working, Pen," said Rebecca, opening the car door.

"I can't wait to get to know him a bit more," said Penny, alighting from her car and locking the doors.

Rebecca smiled and nodded. *I am sure you two will hit it off,* she thought, as they walked into the shopping centre.

With the food packed into the boot of Penny's car they headed to Rebecca's house; chatting on the way about what salads they would make for the barbeque tonight. As she pulled into the drive way and turned her car off, Penny noticed Mitch and Nick sitting on the front porch. Taking her seat belt off, Penny pressed the boot open button and stepped out of the car.

Rebecca smirked as she watched Nick and Mitch walk towards the car.

"Let me do that for you," said Nick, taking the bags out of Penny's hands.

"Thanks, Nick. Not too many men around like you; such a gentleman," said Penny, taken aback by his offer.

"No problem," said Nick, walking towards the house.

Mitch and Rebecca looked at each other, smiled and rolled their eyes, leaving Penny and Nick to it so they could bring in the shopping.

"So have you two put the drinks on ice yet?" asked Rebecca, as she retrieved the cutting boards from the overhead cupboard.

"We were just about to when you ladies came back," said Nick. "Actually would you like to help me do that Penny?"

"Sure. Lead the way," said Penny. Walking out, she turned and winked at Rebecca.

"They seem to be hitting it off," said Mitch, watching them walk outside.

"It's nice to see Penny happy actually. She hasn't had a boyfriend for a long time," said Rebecca, smiling and thinking back on how Penny's life had turned out.

Since Penny had finished her university degree, and bought her pharmacy, it seemed that most of the men she had dated were too intimidated by her profession and fortune, so none of them seemed to last. Plus the fact that Penny was always busy with work, had a big impact on all her relationships, eventually ending badly.

"Seeing as Nick has asked Penny to help him, what about if I help you, if you want, babe," said Mitch, pulling Rebecca in close and placing his muscular arms around her.

"That would be great, sweet man," said Rebecca, looking into his eyes. His lips looked inviting, so she kissed him passionately.

"Why Ms Landers, I think you are trying to seduce me," said Mitch, smirking.

"You could be right there," said Rebecca, with a raised brow, feeling his hard shaft.

Through the closed door, Rebecca heard Penny and Nick calling out their names as they walked inside. Quickly dressing after their antics in the bedroom, Rebecca and Mitch walked into the kitchen and tried to look normal and calm. But it must have been showing on their faces what they had been up to.

"Where have you two love birds been hiding?" said Nick, smirking at them.

"None of your business," said Mitch.

"You two should be called Christian and Anastasia. You are just like them in *Fifty Shades of Grey*; can't keep your hands off each other," said Nick, with a raised brow.

Penny giggled.

Rebecca felt her face turn crimson red.

"Well if you can't beat them, join them, is my motto," she snickered.

"Sounds like you have read *Fifty Shades of Grey*, Nick?" said Penny, teasing him.

Nick nodded and chuckled.

"Not too many men have read those books. What did you think of them?" said Penny.

"Umm... a bit different, but not too bad," said Nick.

"I really like them. Actually I wouldn't mind being Anastasia. God, what a turn on," said Penny, blushing as she realised what she had just said out loud.

"Well, we might make the salads, hey Penny?" said Rebecca, trying to change the subject.

"Sounds good," said Penny, her face still red from embarrassment.

"We can go and check on the pool," said Mitch to Nick, indicating with his head and eyes, sideways towards the door.

"Ok," said Nick, recognising Mitch's signal.

"So what do you think of Penny?" said Mitch, as they walked outside.

"She seems really nice, bro.... hot looking, too," said Nick.

"She is single. Why don't you ask her out whilst you are here. I am sure she would enjoy your company, amongst other things, that is," said Mitch, smirking.

"You think she might want to go on a date? I wasn't sure what she thought of me," said Nick.

"Sure, dude. The body language is there, man. Take a chance," said Mitch, opening the pool gate.

When their guests started arriving, Rebecca realised that she had been so busy that she hadn't seen Penny and Nick for a while. Looking out of the kitchen window she noticed them seated out the back together. They seemed to look comfortable, having a few drinks and enjoying each other's company. It then dawned on her that she hadn't seen Paige or Michael all day either.

Knocking on Paige's closed door, Rebecca heard her say, "Come in." Michael and Paige were sitting on Paige's bed, cuddled together watching a movie.

"Hey you two… how are you both going? Did you want something to eat or drink yet?" said Rebecca.

"Not yet, Mum. We will come out later, if that's Ok. By the way, thank you for organising for Michael to come here. I will have to thank Mitch later too," said Paige, smiling.

"That's Ok, sweetie. I am glad you are happy again. Did Michael tell you he is here until we go back to Seattle for the wedding?" said Rebecca.

"Yes. I still can't believe he is here," said Paige, excitement on her face.

"Well, if you need anything, let me know. I will be out the back otherwise," said Rebecca.

"Thanks, Mum," said Paige.

"Thanks, Bec," said Michael.

"You're welcome," said Rebecca, pulling the door closed behind her. Turning around, she noticed Mitch walking down the hallway towards her.

"How are they going?"

"They're both good. They are just watching a movie in Paige's room. Paige said they would come out soon anyway. I think they are just cuddling, that's all," said Rebecca.

"It's nice to see them both happy again, isn't it?" said Mitch.

She nodded and leant in to give him a kiss on his lips. As Mitch pulled away slowly from their embrace he smiled.

"I've come in to tell you that the meat is just about cooked. I was going to ask you if you need help bringing out the salads?" said Mitch.

"Thanks, Mitch. That would be great," said Rebecca, as they walked towards the kitchen together.

It's so nice to be back home. I have really enjoyed catching up with everyone tonight, thought Rebecca, as she looked around at all her friends. *I'm so lucky to have such good friends.*

At about 1am, everyone had gone home except for Penny, who was still sitting with Nick chatting.

"Hey Penny, would you like to sleep here tonight instead of driving home?" asked Rebecca.

"Thanks, Bec. That would be good. I think I have had too much to drink anyway," said Penny, feeling the effects of the alcohol.

"I will get a pillow, sheets and blanket and leave them on the couch for you. Ok?" said Rebecca, standing. "Anyway… we are off to bed."

"Thanks, Bec," said Penny.

"See you two in the morning," said Mitch, standing.

"Yeah, good night, bro. Thanks for a great evening," said Nick.

"Good night, guys," said Penny. "Thanks for tonight."

"It's just you and I left here, Penny. Are you tired yet?" said Nick.

"A little bit. What did you have in mind?" said Penny.

"Did you want to go for a swim?" said Nick.

"Not really, Nick. I didn't bring my bikini with me, anyway," said Penny.

"Well, what about if we go inside and watch a movie and have a few more drinks," said Nick.

"Umm… yeah, Ok," said Penny, yawning. Before she knew what was happening, Nick had picked her up in his arms and was carrying her inside.

Penny giggled, as she placed one arm around the back of his shoulders. *Well this is a bit of a surprise… woo wee, he sure smells good.*

As he set her down next to the couch he said, "You look tired, Penny. It's been a long day for me too, with flying in from Seattle and all. Why don't I help you make up your bed and then I might just go and catch some shut eye," said Nick, yawning.

"Yes, I am a bit tired. Thanks for the offer of helping to make the bed, I will take you up on that," said Penny.

Once Nick helped make her bed up, he gave Penny a kiss on the cheek and said, "Good night. See you in the morning."

"Night, Nick. Sweet dreams," said Penny, sitting on the couch.

Should I have made a move, or been a gentleman? I'm certainly out of touch with relationships these days, thought Nick, as he sighed and lay on his back looking at the ceiling, with his hands under his head, in the moonlit room, feeling frustrated with himself. *I wonder what she thinks of me?*

As she lay on her side, staring straight ahead, Penny went over in her mind, all the conversations she had with Nick tonight. *I wish he had've kissed me or tried to make a move. Or was I meant to make the first move. I don't know what the protocol is these days, as I haven't dated for years. I wonder what he thinks of me.* Feeling anxious and not able to sleep, Penny decided to go to the kitchen for a glass of water.

As she leant against the sink, drinking her water in the dark, she noticed a bare-chested Nick walking toward her.

"Can't you sleep either?" says Nick quietly, standing next to her, their skin just touching.

"No. Too wired," said Penny. All of a sudden she felt nervous, because the sexual tension between them had just escalated.

Nick leant into Penny and kissed her lips tenderly. Pulling away he said, "Sorry… I probably shouldn't have done that. But I have been wanting to do it all night."

Coming back down to earth from being kissed, Penny opened her eyes and stood there in surprise. Through the moonlit window she looked into his beautiful blue eyes and put her arms around his waist. "Don't be sorry. I enjoyed it."

Nick pulled Penny in close to his body, and continued to kiss her. Feeling her need for desire through their lips, Nick picked Penny up in his arms and said, "Do you want to sleep in my bed tonight?" As soon as the words came out of his mouth, he could see from the look of shock on her face that she was not sure. "We don't have to do anything. We can just talk or sleep if you want to. I don't want to pressure you."

Penny forced a smile, gulped and said, "Thanks, Nick. You are a true gentlemen. I just don't want to rush into anything. I haven't been with a guy for a long time and you have taken me by surprise, that's all.

I would like to get to know you a bit better first."

"I can understand that," said Nick.

"Would you mind if we just lay on your bed cuddling?" said Penny.

"Sure," said Nick. He was prepared to wait for such a beauty.

Penny woke early. With the curtains open, she watched the sun come up through the window. Nick was asleep next to her. She lay there for a few minutes, just soaking up the view of his gorgeous body and handsome looks.

Opening his eyes, he yawned and said playfully, "Good morning. Like what you see?"

"Good morning. Sure do," said Penny, as she stole a kiss. "Would you like a coffee?" She tried to distract him.

Pulling her in close, he kissed her lips tenderly and said, "Yes please. White, with one sugar."

Breaking his hold and jumping out of bed quickly, she left to make the hot drinks.

Penny jumped as she felt two arms wrap around her from behind.

"What plans do you have today?" said Nick, cuddling into her back.

"I'm free all day... and night for that matter," said Penny, stirring the drinks.

"Can I treat you to lunch?" said Nick.

"Lunch would be nice. Would you like me to help you pick somewhere?" said Penny, placing the spoon in the sink and turning around.

"No that's Ok. I can find somewhere nice. I will pick you up from your house at say around two o'clock; how does that sound?" said Nick.

"Sounds good. Should I get dressed up or wear jeans?" said Penny.

"Dressy. I want to spoil you," said Nick.

"I haven't been on a date in a while. I can't wait. I am so excited," said Penny, handing him his coffee.

"Should be interesting then, as I haven't been on a date for a while, either. Too busy with work and all," said Nick. "Thanks for the coffee, beautiful."

"You're welcome," said Penny, walking over to the bench and taking a seat.

"Sounds like everyone is getting up," said Nick, sitting next to her.

"Morning… you are both up early," said Mitch, yawning.

"Morning, bro. Yeah couldn't sleep. Must be the time difference," said Nick, watching Mitch stretch his arms out towards the ceiling.

"Yeah, I would say so. Was a good night, last night," said Mitch, as he watched Rebecca walk down the hallway towards them.

"Sure was," said Penny, smiling.

"Morning everyone," said Rebecca, as she entered the kitchen. "Would anyone like a hot drink?"

"Nah, we are both fine," said Penny. "I've already made one for Nick and me."

"Yes, please, babe. I need a pick me up this morning," said Mitch, rubbing his head.

"You drink some water and then I will make you a coffee," said Rebecca, opening the fridge and getting out a bottle of water for Mitch.

"Thanks, babe," said Mitch, unscrewing the lid.

"Well… I might make a move," said Penny, standing and taking her cup over to the sink.

"Oh, Ok. You're not staying for breakfast then?" asked Rebecca.

"Nah, thanks anyway. I need to have a shower and I have a few things I want to do this morning," said Penny, smiling.

"Ok. Well maybe we might see you later," said Rebecca. She walked over to Penny and gave her a hug.

"Yeah. I will call in later," said Penny, hugging her back.

"See you later, Penny," said Mitch.

"Yeah, see ya," said Penny.

"I will see Penny out to her car," said Nick, standing.

Rebecca looked at Mitch and smirked as she watched Nick walk with Penny out to her car.

Chapter Thirty

Walking out to the back patio, smiling and feeling happy with himself, Nick found Mitch and Rebecca sitting in the morning sun having a cuppa.

"So... you and Penny, hey. What's happening there, bro?" said Mitch, testing his brother's reaction.

"We are just taking it slow at the moment. Actually I am taking her out on a date this afternoon and then somewhere nice later on," said Nick, excited.

"Word to the wise, bro... she doesn't know anything about our family yet. Not unless you told her already last night," said Mitch.

"Oh right... no, I didn't say anything about our family and I just assumed she knew. I don't think I will tell her yet. I just want to see if there is something yet, or whether it's just lust not love we have. I found out from her last night that she hasn't dated for a while because she works a lot; which is a lot like myself. Even though I could feel she wanted me last night, she held back on me, because she didn't want to rush into something. Not many girls like that around," said Nick, with a raised eyebrow.

"I am telling you now bro, Australian women are different. They won't rush into something, even if they do know you are filthy rich. They prefer love over money. Well that's what I have seen so far anyway," said

Mitch looking from Nick to Rebecca and smiling.

"You're such a sweet talker," said Rebecca, smiling. "But he is right."

"Would you be able to help me pick out somewhere nice to take her for a meal; somewhere dressy? And also to where a nice romantic view is at night time. I want to sweep her off her feet, if you know what I mean," said Nick.

"Sure… no problem," said Mitch, picking up his mobile and searching for a restaurant. "Here we go. This one is perfect. Now… somewhere romantic with a view. Well, that has to be Kings Park. It's absolutely beautiful at night time."

Taking Mitch's mobile out of his hand, Nick searched the restaurant website for the menu and looked at the photos. "This looks perfect… so you reckon Kings Park is good, hey?" said Nick, excited.

"The view is to die for at night. She will love it," said Rebecca.

"Where can I hire a black limo?" said Nick.

"I can lend you one of mine for the night and I will even throw in the chauffeur, Ok?" said Mitch.

"Hey thanks, Mitch. I didn't even know you had vehicles like that," said Nick.

"Whilst you are here in Perth, I will have to show you the business I have started up here. It's been going really good so far. I have been lucky," said Mitch.

"I would love to see what you have set up over here. I bet you have worked hard though to get it to where it is today," said Nick. "I know Mom and Dad are proud of all your achievements over here."

"Yes, I have worked hard. But it's been worth it, bro," said Mitch.

"As you probably know by now, Penny is a down-to-earth person, but she does love romance. She is the type of girl who likes flowers and a guy that opens her door. I know she really likes you already, Nick. But she is shy, so don't mistake that for her not being interested in you," said Rebecca.

"Thanks for the heads up, Bec. I appreciate it," said Nick.

"I just want to see you both happy," said Rebecca.

"Well, I might go and get ready for our date and book the restaurant. See you both later," said Nick, standing.

"Ok. See you later on. Hope you have a great time," said Rebecca, smiling.

"See you later, bro," said Mitch, shaking Nick's hand.

"What are Paige and Michael doing today?" asked Rebecca.

"Michael is taking Paige to the beach and then they will be back for dinner," said Mitch.

"What are we going to do with an empty house, gorgeous?" asked Rebecca.

"Mmm… I have something in mind. But all in good time, my love," said Mitch. She smiled at him and he pulled her in close for a sensual kiss. "Rain check for later."

"I will keep you to that promise," teased Rebecca.

The black limousine pulled into Penny's street and as her house came into view, Nick was pleasantly surprised to find a two storey brick and tile house, with beautifully manicured lawn and gardens.

When the car came to a stop in her driveway, Nick said to the driver, "Can you turn the engine off and wait for me here, driver?"

"Yes, sir" said the driver, looking at Nick in the rear view mirror.

Nick checked his reflection in the car window and then walked up to the front door. He was nervous as he rang the doorbell.

Opening the front door, dressed in her black silky dressing gown, Penny said, "Hello. Sorry, I am not ready yet. Come in. I won't be too long." She showed Nick to the lounge room/kitchen area. "Make yourself at home. There is beer in the fridge if you want one. I shouldn't be too long." She pointed toward the kitchen.

"Oh, Ok. No problem," said Nick, watching how the silk dressing gown clung to Penny's every curve, as she walked towards the carpeted stairs. Taking Penny up on her offer of a beer, Nick took one out the fridge, hoping that it might calm his nerves a bit. Whilst he waited for Penny to finish getting ready, he noticed a mantelpiece filled with picture frames of what he thought was her family and a beautiful wooden mantle clock, which had Roman numeral numbers and decided to take a closer look.

Hmm… she has good taste. That clock must be over a hundred years old, thought Nick, as he tilted the clock forward to have a look at the back of it and found the manufacturer's name. Nick had always, since a child, been a bit of a clock enthusiast and was impressed with not only its design, but also how it was still keeping time. Placing the clock back down, he then perused the photos.

"I'm ready now. Sorry I took so long," said Penny, as she walked into the lounge room.

Lost in his thoughts of the photos, Nick was startled to hear her voice. Turning around, he noticed the dress she was wearing. "Wow… you look absolutely stunning in that dress," said Nick, his eyebrows raised.

"Thanks. Worth waiting for then?" said Penny, teasing.

"You sure are," said Nick, nodding.

"So where are we off to?" said Penny.

"It's a surprise. I know you haven't been to this place before, because I asked Bec," said Nick.

"Now you have me intrigued," said Penny, smiling.

"I took you up on your offer of a beer. Thanks, but where is the bin?" said Nick, showing Penny the empty bottle.

"Here, I will put it in the bin for you. Would you like another one?" said Penny, taking the bottle from his hand.

"No thanks, Penny. Are you ready to go?" said Nick.

"I just need to get my purse and phone and then I will be ready to go," said Penny, walking over to the bench in the kitchen.

"Right," said Nick, as he walked to the front door and opened it. "Your carriage awaits, me lady." When she came to stand beside him, he bowed and smiled, as he gestured to the car waiting for her in the driveway.

"Oh wow, Nick. I have never been in a limo before. I feel spoilt," said Penny, noticing the limo for the first time in the driveway. "Thank you."

Nick shuffled across the seat and sat closely next to Penny. Placing his hand over hers, he said, "You look beautiful, Penny."

She smiled and said, "Thanks." As her heartbeat quickened, she felt her face blushing red.

"Would you like a wine whilst we drive to the restaurant?" asked Nick.

"Yes, please," said Penny. She needed to calm her nerves. Taking the glass filled with white wine from Nick, she drank it down fast.

Nick looked at her and said, "Are you nervous? It's just that you aren't saying much. And I don't think that drink even touched the sides."

She laughed and said, "Sorry. I'm not usually like this – nervous I mean," said Penny, looking into his eyes.

"Don't worry, I'm nervous too, you know. Why don't we just sit back and cuddle up and watch the view," said Nick.

"Thanks Nick. That would be great," said Penny, cuddling into him. "I'm not usually a nervous person. It's just that I haven't been out on a date with a guy for a long time and... well... to be honest with you, I haven't had much time to socialise either," said Penny, trying to relax in his arms.

"Yeah, I know what you mean; my work keeps me busy too. I can't remember the last time I have been on a date for a while either... but there's something about you Penny, I can't explain it. I am attracted to you. We just seemed to click straight away and I don't usually click with women straight away, like I have with you," said Nick, looking down at her adoringly.

Penny looked up into Nick eyes and made her move. Kissing him on his lips, she could feel his passion for her as he moaned into her mouth.

Slowly pulling away from their embrace, he said, "Maybe we can continue this later. But right now we have arrived."

Looking out the window, she said, "Mosman's Restaurant? This is where we are going for a meal? I have always wanted to come here. I have heard so many good reviews about the food and service. Oh Nick, this is so nice of you." She gave him a quick peck on the cheek.

"I'm glad you like it. Because it's something we can say we did together for the first time. Now let's go in," said Nick, opening the door and helping her alight from the car.

Nick expressed to the driver he would ring him when they needed to be picked up.

Holding Penny's hand, they walked toward the restaurant. Stepping through the glass doors, into the restaurant, Penny stood there with her mouth open admiring the room. All around the room, the view was of the beautiful Swan River through the continuous clear glass windows, which met the wooden floating floor. The tables were all set with fine white linen table cloths, silver cutlery, sparkling glasses and a white, yellow, green flower piece in the middle of each table.

When they reached the doorman, Nick said, "We have a table booked for two under the name 'Portellico'."

Looking up his computer the doorman said, "Ah, yes sir. We have your table ready that you requested. Follow me."

Looking all around as they followed the waiter through the restaurant, eventually stopping at a table that was on the edge of the room, next to the clear glass windows, Penny stood there in disbelief, as she took in the tranquil view of the sun that was going down over the Swan River. The table was set for two and very romantic indeed, with its small tea light candle.

The waiter seated them and handed them their menus, informing them of the restaurant's specials. He then returned to the doorway.

"This is the most beautiful, romantic view I have ever seen. The sun setting over the Swan River is just so breathtaking. Thank you, Nick," said Penny, looking into his eyes.

"Sure is breathtaking, isn't it? But I do know of one other view that is even lovelier; that is you, Penny," said Nick, looking at her adoringly.

Penny blushed and didn't know what to say, so she leant into Nick and just kissed him.

Just as they came up for a breath the waiter returned. "Would you like to place your orders now, or would you like a bit more time?"

"We haven't decided yet. We need a bit more time please. But we will have some white wine. Something really nice. I will let you choose," said Nick, looking up at the waiter.

"Yes, sir," said the waiter. He returned a short minute later with the wine, pouring some in a glass for Nick to taste.

Nick swirled it around the glass and then took a sip. "Mmm… nice and light. Can we have a bottle on some ice?" said Nick.

"Yes, sir. I will be back in a few minutes," said the waiter.

"Try this wine; it's really nice," said Nick, as he placed his glass near her lips.

Penny took a mouthful from the glass. "Mmm… that is nice. I am not usually a big wine drinker, but that one is really sweet." Looking at her menu, she said, "Would you like to order something we can share for entrée?"

"Sure. What did you have in mind?" said Nick.

"What about grilled tiger prawns, with spicy coconut sambal, palm sugar dressing?" said Penny.

"Mmm… that sounds good. Ok," said Nick.

"What are you going to order for your main meal, Nick?" asked Penny.

"Well, I like the 280 gram Scotch fillet with a garden salad. What about you, beautiful?" said Nick, looking from his menu to Penny.

"I was thinking of having the traditional beer-battered snapper, Mosman's hand cut chips, chunky tartare sauce and garden salad," said Penny, as she watched the waiter return with the wine in an ice bucket.

Pouring their white wine, the waiter asked, "Are you ready to order now?"

"Yes, thanks," said Nick.

Waiting for their entrée to arrive, Nick and Penny decided to go for a walk along the jetty, which was attached to the restaurant. Standing on the edge of the jetty watching the sun go down over the Swan River, they sipped their wine. As day soon became night the waiter approached them and advised that their entrée was ready.

Sitting back at their table, Penny picked one of the tiger prawns up on a fork and dipped it into the sauce. Placing it near Nick's mouth, she indicated to him to take a bite.

"Mmm… yum," said Nick, eating half. Penny enjoyed eating the other half. The sexual tension between them was starting to heat up with every bite they took.

As the entrée plate was taken away and soon replaced by their main meals, Penny said, "What profession are you in Nick?"

"I work in security," said Nick.

"Ok. What type of security?" said Penny.

"I look after singers, actors, you know that type of security," said Nick.

"Wow. You must meet some nice people," said Penny.

"Most are, but there are some, what I call 'assholes'," said Nick. "But I do enjoy the work. It's a family run business."

Penny sat there in awe of him and listened attentively as he chatted about himself.

"Enough about me, what do you do for a crust, Penny?" said Nick.

"I'm a chemist. I have my own business, in Thornlie actually, not far from Bec and Mitch's place," said Penny, proudly.

"Wow. I would never have guessed you were a chemist," said Nick, fascinated. Whilst Penny was telling Nick about her business, Nick thought, *This girl is not only beautiful but really smart as well.*

"When I was a child I was always interested in becoming a nurse or doctor. But because my family was poor, they didn't have enough money to send me to university. So, as I grew older, I saved all my money from the work I was doing and finally put myself through university. But along the way I changed to become a chemist as this interested me more. Then once I finished my studies, I decided to buy my own business," said Penny.

"You know, no wonder someone hasn't snapped you up before. You have been so busy all your life, that you haven't had time to even find a partner yet" said Nick.

"Well sort of, Nick. It's probably mostly my fault as well. I do come across to people as if I'm not interested sometimes, because I am a bit shy. So that's probably another reason why I haven't found someone. But you know, the more I am around you the more I feel comfortable. You seem to bring out the best in me," said Penny.

"I'm glad. Have you ever travelled, Penny?" said Nick.

"Never left Perth. Never had the time to travel, previously," said Penny, shrugging her shoulders.

"Are you coming to Bec and Mitch's wedding in Seattle?" said Nick.

"I wouldn't miss my best friend's wedding. So that is a yes. I am excited actually about going to the USA," said Penny.

"Great. I will be able to see you again then," said Nick.

"So how long are you in Perth for?" said Penny.

"About two weeks. It just depends on things," said Nick.

"Ok," said Penny, realising he soon would be going home.

As they were chatting the head waiter returned to their table. "Sir, madam, we will be closing soon. Would you like anything else from the kitchen?"

"No thanks," said Nick, looking at his watch and realising the night had gone by fast. He then gave the waiter his credit card to pay for the meals.

"Would you like to go for a drive somewhere?" asked Nick, as they waited for the head waiter to bring back his credit card.

"Umm… what about we go back to my place and I can make you a coffee or something?" said Penny.

"Ok, sounds good," said Nick. He rang the driver to come and collect them.

"How was everything tonight, sir?" said the head waiter.

"It was terrific. My compliments to the chef," said Nick.

Penny nodded and smiled.

"Thank you. Have a good evening sir, madam," said the head waiter, handing back Nick's credit card.

"Would you mind unlocking the door for me?" said Penny to Nick, as she fumbled with the key to the front door. Penny had drunk a bit too much wine and was feeling light headed.

"Sure," said Nick, taking the key from her and trying the lock.

"What would you like to drink, Nick?" said Penny, walking in through the front door into the kitchen.

"Coffee will be fine," said Nick, following her inside.

"Ok. White, with one sugar?" said Penny, placing her bag down on the counter and getting the cups out of the overhead cupboard.

"Yep, that's right," said Nick. He had noticed she was swaying a bit as she stood at the sink filling the kettle with water.

"Thank you for a lovely meal tonight. I thoroughly enjoyed myself," said Penny.

"You're welcome. I am glad you liked it," said Nick.

Stepping away from the fridge with the milk in her hand, Penny tripped.

"Whoops!"

As she tried to right herself, Nick caught her in his arms.

"You Ok?" said Nick, holding her upright and placing the milk on the bench.

"Thank you. Well that was a bit embarrassing," said Penny, looking down and feeling disappointed with herself.

Pulling her chin up to meet his gaze, he kissed her soft lips tenderly.

Penny felt her stomach do a back flip as she melted into his arms.

"Mmm… you smell nice," said Nick, as he gently grazed her ear with his teeth and kissed her neck.

Tilting her neck backwards, surrendering to him, her breath shuddered, as she enjoyed his touch, which awakened her libido. She had forgotten how much she craved to be desired by a man and how it felt, for many years.

Gently pushing her against the wall, his lips met hers, allowing a brief taste. With her heart racing, she surrendered to his demands.

"Undress me," Penny whispered, breathlessly. All her free will had flown out the window. "My bedroom is through there." She pointed down the hallway.

Nick picked Penny up in his muscular arms and carried her to the bedroom without a word. As he unzipped her dress, it fell to her feet and she was left standing in her bra and panties. The silhouette of her body was illuminated by the light coming through the moonlit window.

Mmm… beautiful, thought Nick.

Reaching for the buttons on his shirt, she hastily undid them and quickly discarded his shirt to the floor; allowing her to feel his muscular body. As she reached for his trouser zipper he placed his hand over hers and said, "Don't rush." He wanted to savour every moment.

Laying her on the bed, her head was in a haze as she waited in anticipation of what Nick would do next.

Tracing the shape of her body, Nick's fingers taunted her soft breast through her lacy bra. Sliding the straps down her shoulders and discarding her bra, his mouth sought the peak of her breast. Moaning, Penny arched her back off the mattress. She wanted him to be greedy.

Looking upon her in delight as he took off her last piece of clothing, Nick couldn't believe how beautiful her creamy white skin was in the moonlight. With her breathing ragged, Nick discarded his clothing. There would be no more waiting.

Penny watched in eagerness as he placed the condom on his elongated shaft. She was ready for him to take her to another level of wonderment.

Parting her legs, she released herself to him completely. Penny cried out as he entered her sex for the first time. When Nick felt her relax, he quickened the pace. She moved in rhythm with him, hungrily taking what he could offer. With his breathing ragged, Nick stopped and turned Penny over. Pulling her bottom in the air, he entered her sex from behind. She was wet and her body quivered from the frantic movements, as she held back her orgasm. Holding onto her hips as he pounded her sex with enjoyment, his body soon gave way to pleasure as he stilled over her. He felt her release soon after.

Lying on top of the quilt breathless but contented, Penny cuddled into the nook of Nick's shoulder. Kissing her forehead, Nick drew her closer into his chest. Exhausted they both fell asleep in each other's arms.

Waking, still in Nick's arms, from what seemed like a long sleep, Penny looked up to see Nick still asleep. Looking over at her bedside clock, she noticed that is was almost 3am and she was in need of a bathroom break.

Still naked from her antics with Nick, Penny walked out of the bathroom and decided to get herself a drink from the kitchen.

A she stood near the sink drinking, looking outside at the moon, she felt two arms wrap around her waist. She jumped as she hadn't realised Nick had come into the kitchen.

"I wondered where you had got to, beautiful," said Nick, kissing her neck.

"I was thirsty. Would you like a cold drink?" said Penny, leaning back into his embrace.

"Thanks, that would be nice," said Nick.

Penny pulled away from his embrace and poured him a drink. Handing Nick an orange juice, she watched as he drank it down quickly. With the moon shining through her kitchen window, she noticed his gorgeous muscular body.

Placing the glass on the sink, Nick stepped closer to Penny and enveloped her in his arms. Savouring his time with her, and enjoying her supple body, he kissed her forehead.

"Do you work out or do some sort of training?" asked Penny, as she cuddled into his chest.

"I work out daily in the gym," said Nick. Being six foot and having a great body was always welcomed by the ladies.

"You have a really nice body," said Penny, tracing the line of his ribs. As she kissed his neck and then his chest, Nick moaned and quivered from the touch of her soft fingers. Holding the bench to steady himself, it seemed her lips alone would be able to give him enough pleasure for a lifetime.

The next morning Nick was up early, getting ready for Pink's arrival into Perth. Penny was up early too, as she had work today.

"What time will you be finished working tonight, Nick?" asked Penny, brushing her hair.

"Probably around 1am babe. Sorry… it will probably be like this all week, as Pink is here until Friday night," said Nick, feeling guilty.

"So will I be able to see you this week?" said Penny, feeling like she had just been used for sex.

Nick placed his arms around her and said, "Of course you will see me. I would miss you terribly. Maybe on some of the days we can do lunch, but other days I can wake you when I get back. That's if it's all right for me to stay here, that is?"

"I would love for you to stay here, Nick. When you are free during the day, just ring me and I can meet you somewhere. I am going to miss seeing you, but I do understand, work comes first," said Penny, cuddling into his chest.

"Sorry, babe. Unfortunately it does, this time around. But next week you will have me all to yourself. I would really like to spend some more time getting to know you," said Nick, looking at his watch. "Well, I must go. See you tonight, my sweet girl. You can text me during the day if you want to."

"Bye, Nick. I miss you already," said Penny, smiling at him. "See you tonight."

After Nick left, Penny rang Rebecca to tell her about her night out. She also said that she would pop by later that afternoon after work to collect Nick's things as he was staying at her house for a while.

CHAPTER THIRTY ONE

Hearing a car pull up outside, Rebecca walked to the front door and noticed Penny had arrived and was walking towards the front door. *Oh that's right, Penny is here to pick up Nick's things. I totally forgot. Can't wait to hear about her night.*

"Hi, Penny. Come in," said Rebecca, holding the front door open.

"Hey, Bec. How was your day?" said Penny, hugging her as she walked on in.

"Pretty busy at work at the moment. But I don't want to talk about me; spill the beans," said Rebecca, anxiously smiling.

"You're not going to believe the night I had. Nick is such a great guy and he loves surprises. He comes to collect me in a limo, then takes me to a really nice restaurant called Mosman's and well, the rest you can probably guess," said Penny, talking quickly because she was excited.

"You didn't... I would never have guessed you would do that on the first date," teased Rebecca, smirking.

Penny laughed. "Thank you for setting us up. You know, I really like this guy already. In fact what's not to love? Great mind; great body, insatiable lover. I could go on forever. Bit of a bummer he has to work for the first week though," said Penny, sitting on the stool under the kitchen bench.

"You sound smitten. You must really like him," said Rebecca, excited for her best friend.

"I more than like him, Bec. The way he makes me feel when I am around him, OMG girl. I can now see how you fell in love with Mitch straight away," said Penny.

"Yeah, these Portellico men are awesome... so what was the restaurant like?" said Rebecca.

"The food was really nice and the view outside was so beautiful. We actually got there as the sun was going down over the water. Talk about breathless. I would love to go there again one day," said Penny.

"Sounds great. I am so jealous," said Rebecca, smiling.

As Penny and Rebecca were chatting, Mitch walked in the front door from work.

"Hello beautiful. I have missed you today," said Mitch as he walked into the kitchen and hugged her. Rebecca melted into his arms as he kissed her lips tenderly.

"Hello, sweet man," said Rebecca. "How was your day?"

"Busy, but good... hi, Penny. How was your date with Nick yesterday?" said Mitch.

"I had the most wonderful time, Mitch. Your brother is such a great guy. So caring and thoughtful," said Penny.

"Yeah... I rang Nick today to see how you both went and he told me all about the food and that he had a great time with you. You both have got it bad," said Mitch, teasing her. "Nick tells me he is staying at your house for the rest of the time he is here. For him to want to stay at your house with you, he must really like you."

"The feeling's mutual. I am going to miss him when he has to go back home, though. Nick is the first guy I have really liked for a while and I don't know how I will go saying goodbye," said Penny, her brow creased.

"Just enjoy your time you have together whilst he is here," said Mitch.

"Yeah... that's what I was thinking. I have told the girls at work today that I am taking some time off so that I can spend time with Nick before he has to go back. I was thinking about showing Nick around Perth, and taking him to Rottnest for a couple of days as well. Do you think he would like that, Mitch?" said Penny.

"I think he will love it. He is a very adventurous type of person," said Mitch.

"Do you think he might like Adventure World?" asked Penny.

"I reckon he would have a ball there. Why don't we all go on Saturday to Adventure World?" said Mitch.

"Sounds like a plan. I will tell Paige and Michael what we are all doing on Saturday and see if they want to come too. I have just found out another thing I didn't know about you Mitch - that you like water slides. I knew you liked theme parks, but not water slides," said Rebecca.

Mitch pulled Rebecca into him closely and said, "There will be lots of things we don't know about each other, but that will be half the fun to find out about each other over time."

I love seeing how happy these two are together, thought Penny.

"Hey, would you mind if I get Nick's stuff and put it in my car?" she said, standing.

"Sure. I'll help you pack his stuff up and carry it out," said Mitch.

Once Nick's things were packed into the car, Penny said, "Well, I might go. I'll catch up with you later on in the week about Saturday."

"Sure. No problem. Drive safely," said Rebecca, hugging her goodbye.

"See you Penny," said Mitch, waving her goodbye

The next morning Penny rang Rebecca at work.

"Hi, Bec. I rang to let you know that Nick and I will definitely be coming to Adventure World on Saturday."

"Cool. Should be good fun with the six of us going," said Rebecca, excited. "Would you like to come over for a coffee this arvo to make some plans for Saturday?"

"That would be nice. See you at 4.30, Bec," said Penny, as she hung up.

Exhausted from her stressful day back at work, Rebecca rounded her aching shoulders, which were in need of a good massage, as she was stopped at the roundabout near home. *Looking forward to seeing Penny, as I have some exciting news to chat with her about.* Pulling in the driveway of her house, Rebecca waved as she noticed Penny already waiting for her on the front porch.

"Come in, Penny," said Rebecca, stepping onto the porch.

"How was work?" said Penny, following her inside.

"Yeah, not bad. Busy, stressful. The place hasn't changed much over the years," said Rebecca, placing her handbag on the kitchen bench. "Penny, there was something I wanted to ask you."

"This looks serious," said Penny, joking around.

"Well… it is, sort of. I wanted to know if you would like be my bridesmaid in Seattle when I get married to Mitch next month," said Rebecca, smiling.

"Bridesmaid… I would love to be your bridesmaid. I was so hoping you were going to ask me," said Penny, with a smile from ear to ear. Excited, she gave Rebecca a hug. Penny and Rebecca had been friends since school and they always said they would be each other's bridesmaid.

"Cool… Nick is going to be the best man. Mitch asked him today," said Rebecca, hugging her back.

When Penny pulled away from their embrace, Rebecca could see tears in her eyes; which she thought were tears of joy.

"Yeah and that's probably the last time I will see him. Why did I agree to be set up with him, Bec? It's the biggest mistake I could have made," said Penny, as the tears spilled over onto her cheeks. "I have been so lonely for such a long time and I have fallen for this gorgeous man. What am I going to do when he leaves?"

Rebecca placed her arms around Penny, and said, "Don't worry, it will all work out. You'll see."

"Why don't you live in Seattle with Nick," said Mitch, entering the kitchen. "It's probably not something you have thought about, but if you love the guy as much as you say you do, then follow your heart. Life is too short to live without someone you love. Believe me, I know."

"You're right, it's not something I have even thought about. I really need to sit down with Nick and discuss this. Maybe we can come up with something that will work for both of us," said Penny, wiping her tears from her face. 'Thanks, Mitch."

"No problem. Hey babe… I haven't even said hello to you yet," said Mitch, as he walked over to Rebecca and gave her a kiss on the lips.

As she pulled away from his tender kiss, Rebecca said, "Hello… I missed you today too."

"I picked up the photos you took when we were in Seattle," said Mitch, taking them out of his jacket pocket and handing them to Rebecca.

"Cool. I love photos. Can I have a look too?" said Penny.

In that moment, both Mitch and Rebecca looked at each other with a serious face as realisation hit them.

Shit, the photos of his parents' house are in there and Penny will then guess that Nick is rich. What to do? thought Rebecca.

"Ah, actually, I wanted to put them in my scrap booking photo album before I show anyone. So I won't show them to you just yet Penny. Sorry. Hope you don't mind."

"No problem. I love scrap booking. They should look good when you are finished," said Penny, oblivious to what was going on.

Phew, thank God she bought the story, thought Rebecca.

"Well I had better be off. I have a lecture tonight. But if you need help with anything to do with the wedding, I am only too happy to help out," said Penny.

"Thanks Penny. And don't worry about Nick. It will sort itself out. You will see. Bye," said Rebecca, giving her a hug.

"Bye, Penny," said Mitch, as he watched her walk with Rebecca to her car.

CHAPTER THIRTY TWO

Driving home from her lecture, Penny thought about what Mitch had said to her today. Maybe she could give consideration to the thought of moving to Seattle part time, or if things worked out, maybe for good. But did she want to sell her business that she had worked so hard for? Even if she did it on a month by month basis, she would have to find someone to look after the business if she didn't sell it. There was a lot that she had to consider. Furthermore, would Nick move to Perth for good or maybe a month at a time? Would he want to give up his business that he had worked so hard for either? And something that she hadn't considered yet was, what if they broke up, then none of this would even matter? It was only early days for their relationship. Pulling into her driveway, she shifted her car in park and turned the engine off. She seemed to sit there for ages, going through events in her mind until she realised she had better get inside and have a shower before Nick came home.

With water streaming over her head and shoulders, Penny soaked up the warmth and calming feeling of the hot shower. When the shower door opened, she jumped, but to her surprise it was Nick.

"Is it all right if I hop in with you?" said Nick, smiling.

"Sure. Hurry up already and get your clothes off," said Penny, excited to see him.

"How was your day?" said Nick, discarding his clothes to the floor and stepping into the shower.

"Yeah, it was Ok," said Penny.

"You seem upset. What's the matter?" said Nick, picking up the body wash.

"Can we sit down after our shower and talk about a few things?" said Penny, her voice serious.

"Sure, babe," said Nick. Pouring some body wash in his hands, he rubbed Penny's shoulders. "How does that feel?"

"Mmm... feels nice. You have such great hands; soothing," said Penny, relaxing her shoulders, with her head pointed towards the tiled floor.

Wonder what she wants to talk about? thought Nick, his brow creased, as he continued to massage her shoulders.

With her mousy blonde hair towel dried, Penny retrieved a satin nighty and dressing gown out of her wardrobe and tried them on in front of the mirror. *Hmm, not bad.* She then headed for the kitchen to find Nick.

"Ah, there you are. I was starting to think you weren't coming out," said Nick, handing her a mug of café latte he had made, as she sat at the island bench.

"We ladies like to take a bit of time to look good for our men," said Penny, smirking.

"Well, you look lovely... I hope you like lemon cheesecake," said Nick, placing a plate in front of her with a fork.

"Yum... I love cheesecake. It's one of my favourites. Thanks Nick. That's so nice of you," said Penny, slicing into it with her fork.

"You're welcome," said Nick, smiling as he cut into his piece.

"Oh, yum. This is good cheesecake," said Penny, after she swallowed the first bite.

"Yeah, it's good all right," said Nick, swallowing his first piece, as he stood on the other side of the island bench watching her. "So... what did you want to discuss?"

Placing her fork down on the plate, she took a deep breath and said,

"What are we going to do when you have to go back home to Seattle, Nick? The longer you are here the more difficult I will find it to lose you when you go back home. Would you ever consider moving to Perth to live with me?" said Penny, feeling nervous about his answer.

Nick sat there for a moment and thought about what Penny had just asked him. "I do really care for you Penny and I would find it difficult to leave you, but that is not something I have even thought about. And it's only early days for us. Besides, I have all kinds of things that I would have to consider before making that decision. As would you if I asked you to move to Seattle with me." He walked around the island bench and sat next to her. "Also, there is something that I haven't told you yet that you will eventually find out and you may not be happy about it," said Nick, realising he had to come clean about his family.

Looking at him apprehensively, she said, "What is it, Nick? You can tell me anything. Really, I would rather know."

Nick was almost glad to get it off his chest. "The best way to tell you this is to show you something on the internet," said Nick, getting out his laptop and opening up his internet browser.

Penny looked at him with her brow furrowed and was nervous about what he was going to show her, as he placed the laptop in front of her.

"Here… type in my last name and see what comes up," said Nick, watching her reaction.

Frowning, she typed in his last name and hit enter, not thinking much would come up. As the pictures and stories appeared on the screen about Nick's family and himself, she couldn't believe what she was reading. Her prince charming was a millionaire. "Is this true on here? You're wealthy and your whole family, including Mitch are wealthy as well?" said Penny, trying to comprehend the magnitude of what she had just read. "I can understand why you didn't want to tell me."

"So you're not mad at me for not telling you?" asked Nick, with a furrowed brow.

"No, not at all. I do understand. What I don't understand is why you, who could have anyone, would fall for someone like me," said Penny, her brow furrowed.

"I am not sure I understand what you are saying," said Nick, curious.

"You know… plain Jane… come from poor family, etc." said Penny, looking him in the eyes.

"But I don't think of you that way at all. You have worked hard to get what you have, and I think if I am right, you are pretty well off now. You are no plain Jane either. You are beautiful to me. I can't believe you think about yourself like that," said Nick, now connecting the dots.

"So are you saying that even though we are from two different worlds, that you actually want to be with me?" said Penny.

"Yes. God woman, for someone so bright, you are stupid sometimes. I care for you very much and to me you are the most beautiful woman I have ever met. No matter if you have money or not, I would still love you. It's funny you know, even though we have only known each other for a few days, I feel like I have known you longer. I feel comfortable when I am around you, Penny. And for me that is a big deal… but I really don't know what to do about us living apart. Now that I have found you, I don't want to lose you, either," said Nick, giving her a hug.

"What are we going to do, Nick?" said Penny, cuddling into his chest.

"Can you leave it with me for a day and I will think about what I can do?" said Nick, looking down into her hazel eyes.

"Sure. I would even consider moving to Seattle if that is what it takes to see you," said Penny, looking up into his blue eyes.

Nick looked at her in astonishment and said, "You would consider that… just for me? Now I really know you have fallen for me."

"I think I would do just about anything for you, Nick. We may have only known each other for a few days, but I feel I would be lost without you in my life," said Penny, cuddling into his chest again. "It's funny, but if you had of told me that I was going to feel this way, I would have told you that you were mad. But now I do feel like this, I don't think I could want anything more."

"I am sure we can sort something out. Let's go to bed. It's late and we both have work tomorrow. We can talk some more about this tomorrow, anyway," said Nick.

"Yeah, I am pretty beat," said Penny.

As she cuddled into the crook of Nick's shoulder and neck, Penny thought about how happy and content she was in that moment. She realised that her life was about to change in a big way.

The next morning when Penny and Nick were leaving for work, Nick said, "I should be home early tonight so we can talk more; say around 8pm."

"Great… I will cook dinner for us. I hope you have a good day at work, my gorgeous man," said Penny.

"See you later tonight," said Nick, as he kissed her goodbye.

As Penny drove to work, she thought, *Hmm, Rebecca didn't tell me about the Portellico family wealth either. Maybe Nick swore her to secrecy too. I wondered if that means Rebecca and Mitch are going to have a really lavish wedding in Seattle. Oh, that will be something to look forward to.* She giggled to herself.

During the day Penny looked into selling her business through some brokers to see what price she would get. She also put out the feelers to her oldest staff member to see if she would be interested in looking after the place if she was to be off for some time. *It all seems doable, but I need to know what Nick wants to do first.*

Penny thought she heard a car pull up in her driveway. Taking a peak out the front window, she saw Nick being dropped off. As he waved the car goodbye, he walked up to the front door.

"Hello," said Penny, as she opened the door for him.

Nick jumped back when the door open suddenly. "Hello, I didn't realise you were there."

"Sorry… anyway, come in," said Penny.

Walking into the house, Nick said, "Mmm… what's for dinner, it smells so good." As he sniffed the air.

"I left work early today, so that I could make roast lamb with some vegetables for us," said Penny, proud of her choice. "Why don't you go have a shower and I will pour a drink for you."

"Ok. But first I want to give you something," said Nick, pulling a bunch of flowers out from behind his back.

"Oh wow… these are beautiful, Nick. Thank you so much," said

Penny, kissing him on his lips with passion.

"Beautiful flowers for a beautiful lady; that's what I was thinking," said Nick, cuddling her.

"You sure know how to spoil a girl," said Penny.

Standing at the sink, with her back to the doorway, Penny whipped the cream for the apple pie, whilst she waited for Nick to have his shower. Startled, until she realised it was Nick, she felt two arms go around her waist and his lips kiss the side of her neck. Penny felt herself melt from his touch, as he knew she loved to be kissed on her neck and earlobe.

"I have missed you today, sweet girl," said Nick.

"I missed you too, babe," said Penny.

"What's the cream for?" asked Nick.

"I have made apple pie for dessert and cream goes well with it," said Penny.

"I know something else we can do with the whipped cream, that's if we have any left after dessert," said Nick, smirking.

Penny snickered.

"You read my mind," she said, grinning.

"Would you like me to cut the roast meat up for you?" asked Nick.

"Yes thanks, that would be great. That way I can dish up the rest and make the gravy... Oh, do you like gravy?" said Penny.

"Sure do. Where do you keep your knife?" said Nick.

"There is an electric knife in that cupboard on the left," said Penny, pointing to the cupboard under the cooktop.

"Wow... this is delicious," said Nick, as he ploughed into his food. "God, you are such a great cook, woman."

"Thanks.... I love to cook. If we lived together, you would be able to taste more of my cooking. My mum taught me well," said Penny, cutting up her potato.

"Speaking of your parents, where do your mom and dad live?" said Nick, curious.

"They have retired now and live on the Gold Coast in Queensland," said Penny.

"I have heard the Gold Coast is a nice place for a holiday," said

Nick.

"Yeah, it's a really nice place. Especially if you like the beach and theme parks. Mum and Dad enjoy the lifestyle there. It's very laid back," said Penny.

"I bet you miss being able to see them," said Nick.

"Yeah, I do. But I have gotten used to them living there now," said Penny.

"Do you have any other brothers or sisters?" said Nick.

"No. I am an only child," said Penny. "I would love to have a family of my own one day. I really love children."

"Actually, me too. One day," said Nick. "Hey… I was thinking today about what we could do about our living arrangements and I have come up with an idea. If I can organise for someone to look after my business, then I can stay here in Perth until about one week before the wedding."

"Really," said Penny, excited at the prospect of getting to see and know Nick more.

"Then after the wedding, why don't you come and stay with me for about four weeks in Seattle. If you like it in Seattle then maybe you can move there, but if you don't like it then maybe I can move here to Perth. What do you think?" said Nick, looking for her reaction.

"Actually that makes sense. At least if I spend some time there, I will know if I like it or not. You know even if I hated living in Seattle, I don't think I would leave you, as I fallen hard for you, Nick. I have thought about this long and hard today and I have come to the conclusion, that wherever you are, I will be too. Life is too short to miss out on being happy with someone you love," said Penny, holding his hand across the table.

"So you have me here for another four weeks in Perth. Then we will be off to Seattle for another four weeks. By that time, we would have been together for three months," said Nick.

"Nick… I wanted to ask you something. But I am not sure you will like my question," said Penny, worried.

"What is it?" said Nick.

"If I stayed in Seattle for good with you, could we get a place of our own? As much as your parents' house is lovely and all, I would really like to live in our own special place. I know that sounds forward, because we would not have been together for too long, but I enjoy cooking and looking after you and I wouldn't be able to do that at your parents' place," said Penny, feeling awkward for even mentioning it. But she knew she needed to get it out in the open.

"I can see where you are coming from, Penny. But it wouldn't be until we got married. I don't intend on moving out until I get married. I know that sounds selfish, but I do love living at Mom and Dad's place and I would have to be sure that I am doing the right thing," said Nick.

"Ok. That's fair enough. After all we haven't been together long and I need to build trust with you. I understand. At least you're honest. At least I know where I stand and what to expect," said Penny.

"You will see what I mean when you stay there, Penny. It's not like living with your parents. I have my own space and they don't interfere in my life at all. Actually I think my mom will really love you. I have already told them both about you and how quickly I have fallen for you," said Nick, smiling.

"Really… I am looking forward to meeting them. Maybe one night we can Skype them," said Penny, getting up from the table to take their plates to the dishwasher.

Nick followed with the glasses. "Sounds like a good idea. I am sure they would like that too. Oh, and thank you for the lovely meal," said Nick.

"You're welcome. Did you feel like dessert yet, or are you still full from dinner?" said Penny.

"Yep, I definitely could fit dessert in," said Nick.

"I will dish it up now then," said Penny, opening the fridge.

As the first mouthful hit his taste buds, Nick said, "Wow… this is yummo; so good."

"Thanks," said Penny, smiling. "Glad you like it."

After dessert, Nick and Penny went into the kitchen and washed the pots and pans and all the things that couldn't fit into the dishwasher. As Penny finished wiping the last pot and put it away, Nick flicked her with the other tea towel on her bum.

"Ouch… hey… two can play that game," said Penny, flicking Nick on the legs and then his bum.

Nick laughed and said, "I haven't done the dishes for so long, that I forgot about the tea towel flicking. So much fun hey, even though it hurts."

"Sure is. But I know something better," said Penny, smirking, taking him by the hand and leading him into the bedroom.

When they reached the bed, Nick said, "How do you feel about being blindfolded?"

"Sounds interesting," said Penny, flirting.

"Ok. Take your clothes off and put this on. I will be right back," said Nick, handing her the blindfold.

When he returned, Penny was naked on the bed with just the blindfold on, as instructed. Nick stood there in awe looking at her beautiful toned body. Placing a bowl of cream on the bedside table, he took his clothes off, only leaving his boxer briefs on. "I want you to lay as still as you can whilst you have the blindfold on."

Penny nodded and waited in anticipation of what he was going to do.

Placing the bowl of cream and himself on the bed, next to her, Nick dipped his finger into the bowl of cream and then wiped the cream on her left nipple. Penny felt a cold sensation and then Nick's warm mouth on her nipple. Arching her back off the bed as he sucked it harder, she moaned.

"This is what I call dessert," said Nick, as he put some cream on her right nipple and sucked it hard. "Keep still."

She found it extremely hard to keep still. Her body was ready for him.

Placing a finger full of cream on her clitoris, Nick tormented Penny some more by licking and sucking the cream off her nub.

"Please… Nick… I don't know if I can keep still any longer," said Penny, as she had her first orgasm.

"Just a few more minutes, my love," said Nick, placing a finger full of cream onto her vagina and then licking it off slowly.

"Please… I beg you…!" Penny screamed. She had another earth

shattering orgasm.

Lying on the bed exhausted and panting from the sweet delight Nick had given her body, Nick took the blindfold off, looked into her eyes and said, "Hi sweet girl. Are you Ok?"

"Oh my God, that was too good. I think cause I couldn't move, it even felt better when I had my orgasm," said Penny, her breathing heavy.

"I do aim to please, babe," said Nick, raising his eyebrow up and down and smiling.

"And that you did," said Penny, sitting up. She noticed the bowl of whipped cream. "Ah, so that is what you were putting on me. I wondered what it was."

"You up for round two?" said Nick, teasing.

"Sure am. But I want to have some fun with you and the whipped cream and the blindfold first," said Penny, teasing him.

Nick lay down on the bed and Penny placed the blindfold on him. "Keep still," said Penny.

With tiny bits of cream on each tip of her fingers, Penny placed dabs of the cream from Nick's neck, down to his pubic hair. First she kissed his mouth, and when he kissed her back, she pulled away quickly. Teasing him, she started to kiss and suck, from the top of his chest, to near his pubic hair. His body quivered from her touch. Pulling off his boxer briefs and discarding them to the floor, she watched his hard cock spring free. Rubbing his shaft up and down with one hand, she heard him moan. Next she placed a dollop of cream on the head of his cock and started to lick it off like a popsicle. Nick arched his back off the bed and pushed his head back into the pillow, as he enjoyed the torment.

"Keep still. Don't move," said Penny.

"Mmm... I... feels wonderful," said Nick, panting.

Placing more cream on his cock, Penny started to suck it hard, pulling it in and out of her mouth, twirling her tongue around the head as well.

"Stop... I am going to come... Please," pleaded Nick. He couldn't take much more.

"Open your mouth," said Penny as she put some cream on his tongue and kissed his warm lips. Savouring the flavours, whilst lapping the cream from his mouth with her tongue, she moaned in his mouth.

When she was finished she took the blindfold off and said, "How was that?"

"God, you are good, woman. That was wonderful," said Nick. He kissed her forehead as she cuddled into his shoulder.

"Now I am ready for round two, babe," said Penny, teasing.

"You are a wicked girl, aren't you?" said Nick, sitting up and pushing her gently onto the bed. She watched as he placed a condom on his cock. Slowly he inserted his cock into her sex and pulled it in and out until he felt her become comfortable.

As he pulled his cock in and out of her sex, she kept up with him, thrusting her pelvis upwards in pleasure. Fucking her faster and faster, Penny felt it coming......*oh no, not again* and before she knew it she had come again. She was exhausted, but Nick kept fucking her harder and harder, until he stilled over her. Breathless, he lay beside her on the bed.

"That was the best damn sex I have ever had," said Nick, panting as the sheen of sweat on his body glistening in the moonlit room.

Penny cuddled into Nick's chest, exhausted from all their love-making. It wasn't long and they were both fast asleep.

CHAPTER THIRTY THREE

"Well, it's gonna be a scorcher today in Perth. The weather bureau is forecasting 30 degrees and some say it may even get higher than that. But it's going to be a great day for some of you people, here at Adventure World. Let's get this party started by playing the next song," said the radio announcer, who was situated under the trees at Adventure World today.

"How cool is this? Looks like the 94.5 radio station is set up to play music here at Adventure World today," said Rebecca, as she placed her picnic blanket down on the lawn.

"Yeah, looks like we couldn't have picked a better day," said Mitch, looking over at the stage the radio station had set up. "Ok… so what are we gonna go on first?"

"I reckon we should try the water slides. They look awesome," said Michael, taking his shirt off.

"Last there is a rotten egg," said Nick, as he stripped down to his board shorts and ran off towards the water slides. Mitch and Michael quickly ran off after Nick.

"Boys," said Penny, shaking her head. "Come on girls, let's go watch them."

Mitch, Nick and Michael all liked to race each other down the water slides to see who could finish first.

"Look at these three, would you? They are like little boys racing each other. I don't think I have seen all of them together in one spot having so much fun," said Rebecca, as she leant against the rail, watching them compete against each other down the slides.

"Come on girls... are you too chicken to race us... afraid we might beat you," said Nick, taunting them as he walked past them and back up the steps.

"Humph, cheeky shit. Let's go girls," said Penny, as she picked up a mat and walked towards the steps.

Rebecca and Paige grabbed their mats and headed up the steps with Penny.

They all had so much fun racing each other and laughed until their stomachs were sore.

"Hey you guys... do you want to try that ride?" said Paige, gesturing to the tall tower that had round tubes to fit six people in.

"That looks cool. I think we can get photos with that ride too," said Mitch, looking to where Paige was pointing.

"Sounds awesome," said Michael. "Let's go." He grasped Paige's hand and pulled her towards the ride.

With their legs feeling numb from walking all the steps to the top of the sixteen-storey slide, they all finally stepped into the tube, each grabbing a hand rail to hold on to. Once they were all in, the attendant who was holding the tube let go and down they went. The tube plummeted down the slide at a fast pace and everyone screamed as it went up the sides, then round and round, until it reached the bottom pool.

"Let's go again. That was so much fun," said Michael, as he helped carry the tube out of the pool.

"You're on," said Nick, running with Michael back towards the steps.

By the time they all had finished going on a few different tubes and rides, everyone was feeling hungry. Heading back to where their esky was under trees, the girls set up for lunch. They had prepared cold chicken and salad and rolls for lunch and the guys brought with them some water and cool drink.

Sitting on the picnic blankets, eating their lunch, they each talked about how much fun each ride was in detail and decided that they would go on some of the other rides later. Once the Mitch and Michael had finished their lunch, they decided to play some football on the grass area.

"It's great to see you enjoying yourself, sweetie. I am glad you are having a good time," said Rebecca, taking a seat on the picnic blanket next to Paige.

"I haven't had this much fun in a long time. Thanks for bringing us here today," said Paige.

"You're welcome… so… how are you and Michael getting along?" said Rebecca, as she watched Mitch tackle Michael to the ground.

"I am really enjoying having him here, Mum. He is so much fun to be around and we basically like the same things," said Paige.

"That's great, sweetie," said Rebecca.

"It seems like Nick and Penny have hit it off big time. A bit like you and Mitch," said Paige, watching Penny lying on the grass and Nick semi-lying on top of her, kissing her tenderly.

"Yeah, I can't believe how fast they have fallen for each other. I knew they would like each other," said Rebecca, looking over at them.

"Hi beautiful. Are you having a good day?" said Mitch, sitting down next to Rebecca and placing his arm around her shoulder.

Rebecca leant in to Mitch's ear and whispered, "As long as I can see your gorgeous body all day, I am happy." She smiled and looked into his blue eyes. "But in answer to your question: yes, I am having a great day." Mitch leant in and kissed her lips with a hunger that ignited a fire in her stomach.

"Get a room you two," said Michael, laughing as he sat down on the blanket next to Paige.

"Sorry," said Rebecca, embarrassed as she looking from Paige to Michael.

"Let's go get an ice cream. They have soft serve up there," said Mitch, pointing to the shop on the hill.

"Ok," said Rebecca.

"Anyone else want an ice cream?" said Mitch.

They all said 'yes'.

Before they knew it, the park was closing and the limo was there to collect them to go home.

"What about if we have a barbeque tonight," said Rebecca, as the limo pulled away from the carpark.

"Hey, that sounds like a good idea," said Mitch.

Everyone else nodded.

"We have plenty of food at home. We may need some drinks though," said Rebecca to Mitch.

"I can organise the drinks," said Mitch, holding her hand.

Arriving home, Mitch, Nick and Michael drove down to the local Dan Murphy's store and picked up some drinks, whilst Rebecca, Penny and Paige made the salads for the barbeque.

Whilst Mitch turned over the meat on the barbeque, he watched Nick, Penny, Michael and Paige in the swimming pool throwing the ball around, playing keep me off.

"Looks like they are having fun," said Rebecca, as she placed the salads on the wooden outdoor table.

"Yeah… can you watch the meat for a minute, babe?" said Mitch.

"Sure," said Rebecca, taking the tongs from him.

Mitch ran off towards the pool and jumped in, causing a huge splash over everyone, then quickly got out again. Standing on the edge of the pool, Mitch laughed because they were all cursing him as he splashed them in their faces.

Smiling, Mitch shook the water from his hair and body and walked back over to the barbeque.

"What are you laughing at?" smirked Mitch to Rebecca, as he watched her looking at the pictures she had taken of them all on her camera. Before she could answer he quickly took the camera out of her hands, picked her up and threw her in the pool. As she came up for air, everyone was laughing so hard, including Mitch who had just taken a photo of her. Rebecca chuckled, splashed Mitch and then joined in the fun of throwing the ball around in the pool.

"We must do this again before we leave to go back to Seattle. Today was so much fun," said Michael, as he collected the plates and cutlery for washing.

"I agree, bro. I have thoroughly enjoyed myself... I can't think back to when I last had so much fun," said Nick. "You know, there was something else that I enjoyed about today and that was that we didn't have paparazzi following us and spoiling the day."

"Now you know why I like it here, bro. No one to bother us. We don't have to look over our shoulders; not like when we are in Seattle," said Mitch.

"Yeah, you're not wrong. It's kind of nice not being followed. Maybe we should all move here permanently," said Michael.

"I don't think your parents would appreciate all their boys moving here. They would miss you all too much," said Paige.

"Hmm, and there is a lot more to consider than that, especially for Nick and Michael," said Mitch.

"Can you imagine what it's going to be like when we all turn up at the airport in Seattle? The paparazzi will think all their Christmases have come at once. It will surely be a frenzy," said Nick, annoyed at the thought of it all.

"I was just thinking that if they are still keeping an eye on Mom and Dad's house then they are going to be a pain on our wedding day. Are you sure you don't want to get married here, babe?" said Mitch.

"Yes, I am sure. I want to get married in Seattle," said Rebecca.

Mitch kissed Rebecca on her forehead and said, "Thank you."

"Who feels like some dessert?" asked Penny, standing.

Everyone said, 'yes'.

Penny walked inside and brought back out the apple pie and cream that she had prepared whilst the guys were out getting the drinks earlier.

"Mmm... you sure know the way to a man's heart. This woman is such a great cook," said Nick, watching Penny place the dessert on the table.

"Must be something about Aussie women. Bec and Paige are great cooks too," said Mitch.

Penny dished up the apple pie and cream. Everyone enjoyed it and complimented her on it as well, whilst Rebecca took some more photos.

"Can we all sit together? I want to get a family photo of all of us enjoying ourselves, to send to your parents. And then I want to get one of you three guys together. I am sure your parents will really love them," said Rebecca. Once all the photos were taken, she went inside and down loaded them from her camera to the computer. The one taken of Mitch and herself, she printed off and put a copy in Mitch's wallet without him knowing. She also put one in her own purse as well.

At about 11pm Nick and Penny said their goodbyes and went home and Michael and Paige decided they would watch a movie in Paige's room.

"Let's go for a swim, babe," said Mitch. It was a hot balmy night, which was good for swimming.

"Ok," said Rebecca, standing. She unwrapped the towel which was around her body and placed it on the outdoor chair.

Sitting on the steps of the pool, Rebecca watched Mitch swim some laps. On the last lap he detoured closer to the steps and grabbed hold of Rebecca's leg and pulled her further into the pool. As she came up for air, he pushed her gently up against the side of the pool with him and kissed her lips with so much passion that it ignited the fire in her stomach. Opening her mouth to his inviting tongue, she enjoyed his sensual flavours, whilst they caressed and searched each other's bodies. His shaft was hard as Rebecca released it from his shorts and stroked it for his pleasure.

"Mmm... you taste mighty fine, Mr Portellico," said Rebecca, pulling away from his lips.

"Sir would like to play," said Mitch, his eyebrow raised.

"What does Sir have in mind?" asked Rebecca.

"Well... as you have teased me so much today, I think you owe me some dessert," said Mitch.

"You just had dessert, greedy man. But I have some more waiting for you in our bedroom," teased Rebecca.

Mitch snorted, scooped Rebecca up in his arms and walked inside to their bedroom.

"Because of your teasing today, I think you deserve a spanking, Ms Landers," said Mitch, as he placed her wet body onto the bed and sat next to her.

Role play, I love this, thought Rebecca.

She looked at him nervously and asked, "What are you going to spank me with, Sir?"

Mitch held up his hand and said, "We don't have to do this if you don't want to. It's up to you, Ms Landers."

She gulped and said, "You won't hurt me will you, Sir?"

"I want to give you pleasure Ms Landers; not pain," said Mitch, sitting on the bed.

"Ok," said Rebecca, cheekily smiling.

"Bend over my knee," said Mitch, placing her on his knees. Rebecca felt him firmly put one leg behind her legs so that she couldn't get back up. Sliding her bikini bottoms down, he gently rubbed her behind, and then he slapped her bottom hard with his hand.

"Ouch. That hurts, Sir. Please… not so hard," said Rebecca, feeling the sting on her bare skin cheek. He continued the spanking until she said, "Please… I can't take any more of this. It hurts too much."

Unhooking her from his legs, she knelt on the floor, staring up at his face in the moonlit room.

Mitch held his hand out front and helped her up off the floor. "Lay on the bed."

He was gone for a few seconds and then returned with some cream to rub onto her bottom to soothe the pain. As he rubbed it in, he asked, "Are you Ok? You haven't said much."

"Ms Landers doesn't like being spanked and doesn't want to do that again."

Sitting her up on the bed, he said, "Truthfully, are you Ok, Bec?" His brow creased.

Giggling she said, "No, you didn't hurt me, silly. I was just messing with your head. You know role play. But to tell you the truth, I don't like spanking. I prefer to be blindfolded and hand cuffed."

Mitch placed his arms around her and said, "Sorry, babe. I did take that a bit far. I will go and get an ice pack from the freezer for your arse."

Placing the ice pack inside a tea towel, he quickly ran back to the bedroom and placed it on the cheek of her bottom.

"That feels better… thank you," said Rebecca, as she felt the stinging sensation had started to ease.

Mitch kissed her forehead and said, "You're welcome. I love you, Bec. Who else would put up with my silly antics?"

She turned over and looked into his eyes and said, "I enjoy your antics and they are not silly, just playful. Come on, let's go have a shower together." She pulled him by the hand and they made their way to the bathroom.

"Mmm… I love a hot shower. It always makes me feel good," said Rebecca, with her back placed under the hot water.

"Me too," said Mitch, looking into her eyes, as he pushed her wet hair way from her neck. With his hot breathed lips, he leant in, kissed and nipped at her neck and earlobes. Before she knew what was happening, Mitch had picked her up in his muscular arms and carried her into their bedroom.

Mitch gently placed Rebecca on the bed and sat next to her. "So beautiful… I can't get enough of you tonight."

"I am not complaining," said Rebecca, her eyebrow raised.

"You are so good for me, Bec… you know, you made me the most happiest guy in the world when you said you would marry me. I can't wait until we are husband and wife… if possible, my love grows for you each and every day," said Mitch, sincerely.

"I feel the same way and wish we were getting married today. I love you with all my heart and I know I want to spend the rest of my life with you," said Rebecca, looking into his adoring eyes.

As they cuddled up together on top of the doona and chatted, they comforted each other and eventually fell asleep from what was an exhausting day.

Chapter Thirty Four

Pulling out of the driveway, Rebecca's thoughts were on work. *Mondays are always busy and I know I will be working back late today, because the boss likes the cash flow and reports done. Sometimes I wish I didn't have to work. Oh well, it pays the bills, anyway.*

Looking down at the fuel gauge, Rebecca noticed it was in the red, so she decided to stop off at the Coles Express garage around the corner from her house, to fill up her car with unleaded petrol.

Standing there, waiting for bowser nozzle to click, she could see in the distance that there was a fire. Lots of smoke was billowing into the air, which looked like it was coming from over near her work.

Great... will probably be some road block in place by the time I get over near Welshpool. Luckily I have left home early today, otherwise I would be late to work, thought Rebecca, as she placed the nozzle back in the fuel bowser and screwed the fuel cap back onto her car.

Hearing the siren first and then seeing the two fire engines roar past the garage, made Rebecca go cold all over. It always made her think of the day Jackson passed away when she saw any emergency vehicles with the sirens blaring.

I hope no one is hurt, thought Rebecca, as she started her car and placed it in drive.

As Rebecca got closer to her work, the smoke got thicker and she soon realised she couldn't get down the street where her work building was because the fire department and police had blocked off the road. Deciding to park her car in the side street, she grabbed her handbag and walked the rest of the way. She didn't think her boss would be too happy about her being late, even though there was a fire close by. As she got to her work, she soon realised that it actually was her work that was on fire. Shocked, she stood there watching the firefighters trying to put the fire out.

With her hand over her nose and mouth trying to keep the smoke inhalation down, Rebecca looked around to see if she could see anyone else from work. Spotting her boss, Mark, standing across the road from the building, she ran over to him. "Oh my God, I am so sorry. How did it start?"

"I don't know how it started, Rebecca. One minute I was working in my office and the next I could smell smoke. But by the time I went to investigate the smoke, the whole back offices and warehouse were on fire. So I collected my laptop, phone and ran for my life. Even my car was engulfed in flames. I can't believe that I have lost everything. My life's work, gone down the drain," said Mark, tears flowing down his soot-blackened cheeks.

Rebecca placed her arms around him and patted his back. "As long as you are all right, that is all that matters. The building, car and your business, you can rebuild. You have insurance."

Pulling away from her, he nodded and smiled politely. "It's just hard seeing your life's work go up in flames," said Mark, running his hands through his grey hair. "But you're right, at least I have insurance... oh, it looks like the fire chief wants to talk with me. He's waving me over. I won't be a moment, Rebecca." He headed across the road.

Rebecca's brow was creased and she shook her head in disbelief, as she stood across from her work and watched the fire chief talk with her boss about the building. Sighing, she thought, *I can't believe that my work is gone. Unbelievable... hmm, I might give the boss's wife a ring to see if she can come and collect him. Shit, first things first, I need to ring the insurance company and get the ball rolling for Mark.* Rebecca took her phone out of her bag and searched the internet for the number.

As time got closer to 9am, all the staff had arrived at work to find that the building had burnt down. Everyone was in shock when they saw the burnt out building, which was now dripping with water and foam. Not knowing what to say or do with his staff, Mark had to send them all home because there was nothing anyone could do.

With the fire now completely out, just smouldering in some parts, the fire department went into the building and started a search to see what had caused the fire. Rebecca stood at the side of the road, with her boss and his wife, waiting for them to submit their findings.

Mark watched the fire chief walk towards him. It had been two long hours' wait and Mark was curious to find out why his business was now in ruins.

"So… where did it start?" asked Mark.

"We think that it started in the kitchen. Probably by the electric kettle," said the fire chief, his face blackened from the soot.

"Humph… are you sure? It's just… well, that is a new kettle," said Mark, his hands on his hips.

"This is just our preliminary findings, sir. We will know more by the end of the day," said the fire chief.

"Oh, right. So… when can we enter the building, premises?" asked Mark, looking over across the road at the smouldering building.

"Not today, sir. It's way too dangerous," said the fire chief, taking a business card out of his pocket. "Here… take this card. Ring this number tomorrow morning and they should be able to give you an update on when you can enter the building."

"Right. Thank you for all you have done here today," said Mark, shaking his hand.

"All part of the service. Is there anything else you would like to ask?" said the fire chief, shaking his hand.

"Not at the moment. I'm just devastated… it's hard to watch your whole life's work go up in flames and taken from you," said Mark, shaking his head.

Placing a hand on his shoulder, the fire chief said, "The building and workshop, you will be able to replace. But the main things is that you got out safe and sound. I am sure your wife would agree."

Nodding, Mark said, "Yes, you are right." He looked at his wife and hugged her tight.

"Well, I will leave you to it. I need to go and speak with my people and get the building fenced off," said the fire chief. "My number is on the back of the card I gave you, so please don't hesitate to ring me if you think of anything."

"Thanks," said Mark, watching him walk across the road.

"He is really nice," said Rebecca.

"Sure is," said Mark. "So... the insurance company... what did they have to say when you reported the fire and damage?"

"They said they would send someone out in the next day or so, to get the paperwork started, for the repairs or rebuild to be done. They have your number so they will ring you first," said Rebecca.

"Thanks for organising that for us, Rebecca," said Mark.

Hearing her phone ring, Rebecca took her phone out of her bag. Noticing it was Mitch calling, she said, "Excuse me. I just need to take this call." She walked away from her boss and his wife to take the call.

"Hi babe," said Mitch, as she answered.

"You're not going to believe this, but when I got to work this morning the building was on fire."

"Wow... God that is awful. Did everyone get out all right, no one hurt?" said Mitch.

"The only one at work was my boss, Mark, and yes he got out all right."

"Much damage?" asked Mitch.

"Yeah, the whole building is gone, the back workshop too, oh and the boss's car is burnt out completely. Basically, he has lost everything."

"Poor bugger. I really feel sorry for your boss. He didn't deserve that, at all," said Mitch.

"Yeah he is really shaken hey. Luckily he is insured," said Rebecca, looking at the smouldering building and then to her boss.

"Tell your boss if he needs a car, he can borrow mine until he can get another car and if I can do anything to help, let me know," said

Mitch.

"Thanks, Mitch. That's really nice of you to offer. I will let him know. Well, I had better go. I'll give you a ring later," said Rebecca, watching the anguish on her boss's face.

"Talk to you later, babe," said Mitch.

Rebecca walked over to where her boss and his wife were standing across the road from the building. "Excuse me, Mark… I was just talking with Mitch and he said to let you know, that if you need a car, you can borrow his until you can organise another one."

"Thank you. That is really nice of Mitch to offer, but I can use my wife's car until I can get another one. But thank Mitch anyway for me," said Mark, placing his hand on her shoulder.

"I will. He also said that if there is anything he can do to help, don't hesitate to ask," said Rebecca.

"Tell Mitch, I said thanks for the offer, I just might take him up on that," said Mark. "Rebecca, you may as well go home. There isn't much more you can do here. I do appreciate all the support you have given me today though and thank you for organising the insurance."

"No problem at all. If there is anything you need, don't hesitate to ring me," said Rebecca, her brow creased. "I will give you a ring later anyway to see how things are going here." She leant in and gave her boss and then his wife a hug goodbye. "Bye." She walked back to her car which was parked in the side street.

Pulling away from the kerb, Rebecca rang Mitch to see if he was free for lunch. He was busy, so she decided to go home instead. On the drive home, Rebecca sighed and thought, *I wonder if I have a job anymore and how my boss would run the business without our computer systems or a building. I am hoping that I don't lose my job as I love the work I am doing and the boss I have. Only time will tell… can't wait to get home and get out of these smoky clothes.*

Rebecca kicked her shoes off in the wardrobe and changed out of her work clothes and into her bikini. She was so hyped up from the morning's events, that she needed to go for a swim to calm herself down and knew laps in the pool would help.

One lap... two... three, counted Rebecca to herself as she touched the end of the pool, each time she did another lap. Feeling a presence and then noticing that someone was standing beside the pool watching her, she stopped midway down the pool, wiped her eyes and looked up to find Mitch standing there.

"Hey, gorgeous. I thought you had to work," said Rebecca, her breathing heavy from the laps she had done in the pool.

"Well, as I am the boss, I can get someone else to do my job and head on home to see my fiancée," said Mitch, smiling.

Rebecca swam over to the side of the pool and Mitch bent down and kissed her tenderly.

"Do you have to go back to work, or have you finished for the day?" asked Rebecca.

"I have the rest of the day off. Playing hooky with my wife to be," said Mitch, playfully. "What would you like to do for the rest of the afternoon?"

"I don't mind," said Rebecca, stepping out of the pool and placing a towel around her.

"Well... I was thinking we could go and pick out our wedding rings together today," said Mitch, as he pulled her in close.

Excited, Rebecca's eyes lit up and she raised her eyebrows. "Really...? I would love to do that."

"So let's have a shower and then we can go into the city, as there are a few nice jewellers in there," said Mitch.

"Cool," said Rebecca, hugging him tight. He smiled and kissed her forehead.

As Mitch reversed his black ute into the car park, Rebecca said, "Oh my god, Mitch... with all the excitement of purchasing a ring, I nearly forgot; can you please organise for someone to collect Paige tonight from work at midnight?"

"Sure babe. Give me a minute and I will organise it," said Mitch, turning the car off and pulling his mobile out of his pocket.

Once Mitch was off the phone Rebecca said, "Thanks so much for organising that for me."

"No problem," said Mitch.

"Actually, I will have to be home by 4.15 at the latest to take Paige to work this afternoon," said Rebecca, looking at her watch.

"Right," said Mitch. He dialled Michael's number.

"Hello," said Michael.

"Hey, can you take Paige to work at 4.15, so that she is there for 5 o'clock start?" said Mitch, looking at Rebecca and smiling.

"Sure," said Michael.

"Thanks, bro. See you later on," said Mitch, hanging up the phone.

"It sure does have its perks having your partner work in security," said Rebecca, as she watched Mitch hit end on his mobile phone screen.

Walking through the Hay Street mall, they found a few jewellers, but Rebecca was quite fussy, so she couldn't find anything she liked. Finally, they walked into Rosendorff's jewellers and as she was looking around, Rebecca found a beautiful gold band, with diamonds halfway around the ring.

"That's what I have been looking for… it will look good with my engagement ring," said Rebecca, a grin from ear to ear.

"Excuse me," said Mitch, trying to get the nearest assistant's attention.

"Yes, sir," said the assistant, walking over to Mitch and Rebecca.

"Can we try this one on?" said Mitch, pointing to the ring inside the cabinet.

She raised her eyebrows, knowing how much the rings cost. "Yes, sir. You have lovely taste, ma'am," said the assistant, unlocking the cabinet and looking from Mitch to Rebecca. "Here we go."

Rebecca looked at the ring, which was placed on a black velvet tray for her. Picking it up she slid it onto her finger with her engagement ring. Marvelling at how good they looked together, she twisted her hand this way and that, looking at the sparkle it has.

"What do you think? Do you like this one?" asked Mitch, whose patience was starting to wear thin.

"I love it," said Rebecca nodding.

"We will take this one," said Mitch, taking it off Rebecca's finger and handing it back to the assistant.

"Oh, wow, really, thank you," said Rebecca, feeling like the luckiest girl ever. She leant in and kissed his lips. "What about a ring for you, Mitch?"

"I just want something plain," said Mitch, looking from Rebecca to the assistant.

"Come with me, sir. We have some lovely ones over in the cabinet next to the window that I think you may like," said the assistant.

Mitch followed the assistant to the cabinet and looked through the glass at the selection she had. When he finally came across the one he liked the most, he said, "I will try that one on." He pointed to a plain gold band in the cabinet.

"Yes, sir. Good choice," said the assistant, as she unlocked the cabinet and handed Mitch the ring to try on.

"What do you think?" asked Mitch to Rebecca, as he moved his hand left and right.

"Wow… Mitch that is really nice on you. Do you like it?" said Rebecca, smiling.

He nods and says to the assistant, "I will take this ring as well."

"Yes, sir. So are both ring sizes Ok?" asked the assistant.

"Yes, mine is perfect," said Rebecca.

"Yes, mine is fine too," said Mitch.

"Excellent… did you want a payment plan for the rings sir, or will you be paying for them today?" asked the assistant.

"We will take them now," said Mitch, taking his phone out of his pocket so he could direct debit the money into the jeweller's account. "I just need the jeweller's bank account details."

"One moment, sir, I will get that information for you," said the assistant.

With both rings in Mitch's jacket pocket, they walked back to the car hand in hand, cuddling each other, excited about their wedding ring purchases.

"Thank you so much for my lovely wedding ring," said Rebecca, knowing what price Mitch paid for it and feeling lucky to be given such a stunning ring.

Mitch grabbed her hand and kissed it. "Beautiful ring for a beautiful lady. It looked perfect on you, babe."

"I feel spoilt actually. I wasn't even expecting to be bought such a lovely ring. I can't wait to wear it," said Rebecca, smiling as they arrived at the car. "The ring you picked out looked really good on your finger. It suited you, hey."

"Yeah, I thought so," said Mitch, unlocking the car and opening the door.

Mitch seemed deep in thought as they drove along in the peak hour traffic down the freeway. "Penny for your thoughts," said Rebecca.

"Umm… it's nothing," said Mitch.

"Tell me what you are thinking," said Rebecca, wondering why he was so quiet. She was not taking no for an answer.

The emergency lane was empty, so Mitch pulled his ute over to the side of the road, out of the traffic. As the car came to a stop and he turned the engine off, he turned to Rebecca and said, "I was thinking about the day Christine and I picked out our wedding rings and how happy we were together… I'm sorry Bec, it's probably the last thing you want to hear about."

Rebecca's brow creased and her heart melted. "I was wondering if you ever thought about Christine since we have been together. Since the day at the grave, you have not mentioned her to me, at all. I am not surprised that you remember days like that. They were happy days you two had together and no one can take that from you. I too have days when all I think of is Jackson and how much I loved him and miss him. But then I remember what I have now and that you are the most important man in my life now and how I do love you and will always love you forever."

Blinking slowly, Mitch sighed. "Yeah, it's hard some days, Bec. But then I think about how lucky I am to have you in my life and how happy I am to be around you." Mitch placed his hand on hers. "Would you like to go get a drink over there?" He pointed to a restaurant.

"Sure…" said Rebecca, as she watched Mitch start the car.

"Table for two?" said the waitress, looking from Mitch to Rebecca.

"Yes, please," said Mitch, holing Rebecca's hand. "Something with a view of the river."

"Yes, sir," said the waitress, looking down at her seating arrangement list. "Right... come this way."

They followed the waitress to a cosy table next to the window, which had a view of the water. When she stopped at the table, she asked, "Will this one be Ok, sir?"

"Yes, this is fine," said Mitch, as he pulled out a chair for Rebecca to sit on. "What would you like to drink, my love?"

"Ah... a pineapple cruiser," said Rebecca, sitting.

"We don't actually have them in stock ma'am, but I could make one up for you. It's vodka, pineapple juice and Sprite or lemonade, right?" said the waitress.

"Yes, that is correct," said Rebecca, looking at the waitress.

"And you, sir?" asked the waitress.

"I will have a Jim Beam and cola, thanks," said Mitch.

The waitress nodded and wrote the drinks down in her notepad. "I'll be back in a few minutes with your drinks," said the waitress.

"Thanks," said Rebecca, watching her walk away.

Mitch placed his hand over Rebecca's and said, "I love you, beautiful girl. Don't ever forget that. I can't wait to be your husband. You will be all mine." He looked into her blue eyes and smiled.

"You are such a sweet man," said Rebecca, she leant in and kissed his lips passionately.

As the afternoon turned into night, Mitch and Rebecca had a few more drinks and a lovely candlelit diner at the restaurant. Knowing that they had both had way too much to drink, Mitch rang for a chauffeur driven limo to come and collect them and take them home. He also organised for his security guys to collect his black ute and drop it off at home later on. Just one of the perks of owning a security business. One thing good that came out of today was that they both had discussed and agreed on how they both would never hide their feelings for their first partners they had.

CHAPTER THIRTY FIVE

Penny woke in a daze from her dreams, until her surroundings became familiar. *What day is it?* she thought to herself. *Wednesday.*

As she lay on her back, staring at the ceiling, she remembered the last two wonderful days that she and Nick had spent together, staying in a chalet on Rottnest Island. But today they were returning home.

I wonder where Nick is, thought Penny. She quickly hopped out of bed and went in search of him. Hearing his voice outside, near the front door, she decided to join him.

As Penny walked towards him, she realised he was on the phone.

Nick smiled at her as she got closer. "I will have to ring you back later to confirm details," said Nick.

Penny smiled back at him and leant on the wall near him.

"Good morning, my sweet girl," said Nick, hanging up his phone.

"Hi yourself. Come back to bed, I have missed you," said Penny, taunting him.

Nick picked Penny up in his arms and carried her inside. As he placed her down on the bed, he said, "What time do we have to book out today?"

"Around 10.30. Why?" said Penny.

Looking at his watch, Nick says, "Well its ten o'clock now. So I think we should get showered and get ready to leave."

Noticing the time on his watch, she said, "Ok. It's a pity we didn't book in for a few more days. I have really enjoyed it here with you."

"Me too. I have really enjoyed coming here. We will have to do it again one day," said Nick, kissing her forehead. "But there is something I need to tell you first. That call I was just on was Pink. She was asking if I could come to Melbourne and Sydney to be her security. Sorry babe, but it looks like I have to go to work for the next couple of days."

Saddened, Penny sighed, her demeanour become pouty. "I understand."

"I have to leave this afternoon, so I have organised my flights already. Mitch is taking me to the airport," said Nick, placing her on the bed.

"You have been busy this morning. Can I come to airport to see you off?" said Penny.

"Sure," said Nick.

That morning they checked out of the rental chalet and caught the Rottnest ferry back to Perth.

Ticket in hand and luggage checked in, Nick was ready for his flight to Melbourne.

"See you soon, bro. If you need anything done whilst you are away, don't hesitate to call," said Mitch.

"Yeah see you in a couple of days, bro. Look after my lady for me, will ya?" said Nick, shaking Mitch's hand. Mitch nodded and waited over near the exit door whilst Nick said his goodbyes to Penny.

"See you in a couple days, my sweet girl. I will miss you," said Nick, kissing her forehead.

"Bye, I miss you already and you haven't even gone yet," said Penny. She leant in and kissed his lips tenderly.

As he pulled away slowly, he waved goodbye and went through the check in area.

Penny held her tears back until Nick was no longer in sight and then she let them flow freely.

Mitch could see, when he approached Penny, that she was upset. Giving her a hug, he said, "He won't be gone long. The time will go quickly."

Hesitating before she answered, Penny said, "I know he won't be gone long. That's not what the problem is."

Mitch frowned and looked puzzled. "Huh?"

"About two years ago now, I had a friend that I saw off at the airport whose plane went down in a storm and he died. I was really close to him and so whenever I see someone I love off at the airport now, it all comes flooding back. I dread them flying because I am so scared for them," said Penny, sniffing back the tears.

"That's awful, Penny. No wonder you are upset. You shouldn't have come today and I am sure Nick wouldn't have minded saying goodbye at home instead. It might have been a lot more easier on you then," said Mitch, his brow furrowed.

"I thought I would be Ok Mitch, but obviously I'm not," said Penny, sobbing.

Mitch put his arm around Penny's waist, kissed her forehead and said, "Come on. Let's get out of here. You can come back to our house and stay with us for the night."

"Thank you, Mitch. You are so kind," said Penny, snuggling into his shoulder. "But I think I might just head off home, if that's Ok."

"No problem. If you change your mind later, come on over," said Mitch.

"Ok. I will keep that in mind," said Penny, walking towards the glass sliding doors with Mitch.

From across the airport terminal, Rebecca thought she saw Mitch. Wondering what he was doing at the airport and not knowing Nick had just flown out, she walked toward him. Having short sighted eyes, she decided to get her glasses out of her bag to confirm what she was seeing, as she thought she saw Penny too. Rebecca had been at the airport dropping her boss and his wife off, for a flight to Melbourne.

Placing her glasses on, Rebecca couldn't believe what she was witnessing. Mitch and Penny cuddling and being affectionate to each other. *Am I seeing things?* Taking her glasses off, she wiped her eyes and placed them back on her face again. As her heart rate accelerated, she became infuriated at what she was seeing and ran out of the airport to her parked car. *No... there's got to be more to it. What have they been doing behind my back?* thought Rebecca, as she sat in her car.

Tears sprang to her eyes and spilled over onto her cheeks as realisation hit her. *How could my best friend and my fiancé have betrayed me?* Sickened by what she had witnessed, she drove out of the car park of the airport and headed for home, only pulling over once to calm herself down.

As Rebecca pulled her car into the driveway of her house, she discovered Mitch's car was also there. *If he is home, I am going to confront him. How dare he do this to me?* thought Rebecca. Entering the house, Rebecca let the door slam loudly behind her, fuming as she approached Mitch.

"Hello, how was your day?" said Mitch, as he came up to her to give her a kiss.

Her nostrils flared as she pulled away from him with hatred in her eyes. She wanted him out of her house.

"You look absolutely mad about something," gulped Mitch, inching back from her.

Crossing her arms over her chest, Rebecca couldn't help herself; she blurted it out.

"Don't give me that, Mitch. I saw you and Penny hugging and kissing at the airport. How dare you do that to our relationship? You know what, I am glad I found out before we got married that you are a cheater. God... how could I have been so stupid to marry you."

With hurt in his eyes, Mitch looked at her and said, "You think you know it all, don't you. Well, you have it wrong. Nick flew out this afternoon and Penny was really upset, so I was just being a good friend and showing her some compassion, by hugging her and kissing her forehead. How dare you accuse me of playing up behind your back? Listen... don't even talk to me. I don't want to hear any more of your bullshit."

Holding his hand up, Mitch's nostrils flared as he walked off and slammed the front door behind him.

With her hand over her mouth, realisation hit Rebecca like a tonne of bricks. Feeling like she wished the earth would swallow her up. She couldn't believe what she had just accused Mitch of.

I should have known he was not that type of guy, let alone think that my best friend would do that. He has never given me any cause for concern and I know in my heart that he loves me. What have I done? God… how am I going to fix this? I have ruined everything. No trust… No relationship, thought Rebecca.

Walking out the front to apologise to Mitch, she soon realised it was too late, because his black ute was reversing out the driveway quickly. Skidding his wheels as he drove off madly down the street, she heard a car in the distance do a burn out.

Running back inside, Rebecca grabbed her phone out of her handbag and tried to ring him; but he didn't answer. She felt so ashamed of herself. Sobbing, she left him a message. "Mitch… I am so sorry for accusing you of something you didn't do. Please forgive me. I love you so much. Come back. I don't want to lose you." Pressing the end button on her phone, she felt dejected and ran into her bedroom, closing the door behind her. Throwing herself down on the pillow, she sobbed into it.

As the day became night she waited at home for Mitch to return, but he didn't. She even tried his mobile phone a few times but he didn't answer and he didn't return her calls either. At around 11.30, a blotchy-faced Rebecca decided to go to bed. Sobbing, she soon fell asleep.

Rebecca woke to the moonlight shining through the gap in her curtains, feeling dazed and in need of a drink to soothe her dry throat. Looking over at her bedside clock, it displayed a time of 2.10am. In the darkness of her bedroom she noticed Mitch sitting in a chair, with his arms folded over his chest, just staring at her. Sitting up, she said, "Mitch, are you all right? I am sorry for what I said to you today. Please forgive my arrogance."

When he didn't answer, Rebecca jumped out of bed and sat on his lap and cuddled into his chest. "Please… talk to me."

Slowly Mitch placed his arms around her, and said, "If we don't have trust in one another Bec, then we don't have anything. What you accused me of today hurt me deeply and I am still very angry at you."

Tears welled in her eyes and rolled down her cheeks. Rebecca knew she had ruined everything, but she had to try to win him back. "Do you still love me, Mitch?" said Rebecca, with a tear-stained face.

"Of course I still love you, Bec. But we have a major issue here. How could you even think that I would do that to you; knowing how much I care and love you?"

"I don't have an excuse, Mitch. I am just jealous, I suppose. We haven't been together for that long and when I saw how affectionate you were with her, I panicked and thought, well I don't know you that well, so maybe you would do something like this. I knew in my heart that you wouldn't do anything like that to me, but…" She couldn't finish her sentence, because she started to cry.

Hugging her tight, he said, "Shh… don't cry, babe."

"Oh, I am really sorry Mitch, for what I have put you through today. I love you so much. Please forgive me. I won't ever doubt you again," said Rebecca, looking into his eyes.

"Come on, let's get in bed and sleep. All will be better in the morning," said Mitch, picking her up in his arms and placing her on the bed.

She nodded.

Cuddling into Mitch's chest, Rebecca thought, *I am going to lose him and it's all my fault. I just hope he can forgive me.*

Waking early the next morning and untangling herself from Mitch's hold, Rebecca needed a toilet break. Whilst washing her hands in the bathroom basin, she thought, *I might cook Mitch breakfast.* After she washed her face, she dried it off and headed for the kitchen.

Turning the bacon over in the frypan, Rebecca jumped when she felt two hands go around her waist. "Good morning," said Mitch, pressing his body into her.

"Good morning," said Rebecca, smiling.

"Why are you up so early?" asked Mitch.

"I wanted to do something nice for you. I thought I'd bring you breakfast in bed," said Rebecca, anxiously.

"It sure does smell nice," said Mitch.

"Thanks. But after what I accused you of yesterday, I feel really shameful," said Rebecca, guilt ridden.

Turning her around on the spot, Mitch saw her tears and wiped them from her face. "Dear, sweet, beautiful girl, I love you way too much," said Mitch. He kissed her forehead. "Before you woke up last night and found me sitting in that chair in our bedroom, I was thinking that really we don't know each other that well and maybe that's my fault. So to rectify this, I thought that today, we might take a picnic lunch up to Kings Park. We could tell each other more about ourselves. You know the deep and meaningful type of stuff – like our fears, hopes, and dreams."

"I would love to do that… I can't believe you are being so good to me after the way I treated you. I don't deserve you… I love you so much, Mitch, that it frightens me in a way," said Rebecca, looking into his blue eyes.

Pulling her in close, with his arms around her waist, Mitch kissed her lips tenderly. Her world shifted as she breathed a sigh of relief. Cuddling into his chest, Rebecca could feel the love he felt for her.

Shaken out of her bliss, Rebecca heard the bacon start to hiss. "Would you like some eggs and tomatoes with your bacon?"

Mitch nodded and said, "Yes, please."

After they ate their breakfast, Mitch helped Rebecca take the dishes into the kitchen. Bending over to stack the dish washer, she felt Mitch rub up against her bottom with his hard shaft. Shutting the lid of the dishwasher, Rebecca turned around and positioned her arms around his neck. His kiss was sensual and she felt her libido start up as his teeth grazed her earlobe. Scooping her up into his arms, Mitch carried her to their bedroom, where he devoured her body from top to toe.

That afternoon Mitch drove them to Kings Park. They found a secluded peaceful, green grassy area, under a shady Jacaranda tree, to put their blanket down on. Overlooking the views of the city, they discussed their desires, dreams, hopes, fears and a great deal more over a light picnic lunch.

If they hoped, as a couple, to understand each other's needs and wants, then Mitch and Rebecca knew that they had a chance of making it as a married couple later on.

Security was what they were both looking for in the end.

CHAPTER THIRTY SIX

As the days turned into weeks, Mitch and Rebecca's wedding was getting closer. Everything was planned for and taken care of and all they had to do was to have the final fittings for the wedding dress, bridesmaids' dresses and the men's suits when they arrived in Seattle. It was all coming together nicely.

Rebecca sat on the back porch steps, mobile phone in her lap, staring out at the back yard swimming pool.

"Penny for your thoughts," said Mitch, sitting next to her on the step.

Rebecca sighed. "I've just got off the phone from speaking with my boss...I no longer have a job," said Rebecca, her brow creased.

"Shit, really. What happened?" said Mitch, placing a hand on her back.

"My boss and his wife have decided to not rebuild the business after the fire. He is going to retire instead. I am happy for him as he has worked hard all his life and deserves happiness, but I'm not sure what I am going to do now. You know, it's funny how this has all turned out. I lose my job, but I am gaining a husband. I do believe in life that things happen for a reason."

"I am sorry, Bec. I know how much you loved that job," said Mitch.

"I'm sure I won't have a problem finding another job... it's just...

well, I enjoyed the work I was doing. Anyway, I will worry about it after the wedding," said Rebecca. "How's the packing going?"

"I am nearly done. Just got to put in the last minute things tomorrow morning before we go," said Mitch. "And you?"

"Yeah, I have finished. Like you, just got the last minute things tomorrow morning," said Rebecca. "Actually, I can't believe that it's only one week before our wedding day and the six of us are flying first class to Seattle tomorrow," said Rebecca, smiling.

"Yeah, I know. Where did the last five weeks go?" said Mitch. "When I spoke with my mom last night she was saying that most of our wedding guests are arriving a few days before the wedding. She also said that she is going to organise for a limousine to collect your parents from the airport. She is looking forward to meeting them."

"Oh that's nice. She is a real sweetheart, hey. It was good of your parents to let my parents stay at their house too," said Rebecca.

"Yeah, you know Mom and Dad, they are always welcoming," said Mitch.

The day had finally arrived and the limousine Mitch had organised to drive them to the Perth Domestic Airport was pulling up to the drop off zone.

"Will here be all right, sir?" said the driver, noticing how busy it was up ahead, knowing he wouldn't be able to get a parking spot.

"Yes, here will be fine," said Mitch, looking at the driver in his rear view mirror.

Anxious, Rebecca started wondering if she had brought all the necessary documents from home that she and Mitch needed to get married. *Birth Certificate – Check. Marriage Licence – Check. Passports – Check.*

As the car came to a stop, Nick jumped out and helped the driver retrieve the luggage from the boot for the six of them. Looking around he spotted an abandoned trolley which was big enough for their six suitcases and made a bee line for it.

"Good thinking," said Mitch to Nick as he approached him with the trolley.

"Let's go," said Nick to everyone, as he placed the last bag on the trolley and started wheeling it towards the terminal check in counter.

The Perth to Sydney leg was an early morning flight and once their seats had been allocated by the steward at the check in counter and their luggage checked through, they took the escalators to the upper level to go through the x-ray machines and then onwards to find their gate.

Sitting in the lounge area, waiting for the first boarding call, Penny said, "I have never flown anywhere before and I am feeling a tad nervous… I feel like I want to be sick actually."

Nick knew from speaking with Penny previously that she would be a nervous flyer, so he had bought her some tablets from the chemist to calm her and to make her sleep on the plane. "You will be all right, babe. Don't overthink it," said Nick, holding her hand.

Rebecca overheard their conversation and said, "Come on, we will take you to the toilet and put some cold water on your face. That should make you feel better."

Penny nodded and stood up. "Thanks, Bec," said Penny, as she followed her to the toilet, with Paige.

"God, I feel like crap," said Penny, standing in front of the mirror with the water dripping off her face.

"Here," said Rebecca, opening her side pocket of her handbag. "Take one of these Rescue Remedies. They should calm you until you get on the plane."

Penny swallowed hard and said, "I couldn't stomach that at the moment, Bec. Thanks anyway."

"No problem. Well, I might go to the toilet before we board. I hate the plane toilets," said Rebecca, walking towards a toilet cubicle.

"Yeah, me too," said Penny, as she followed Paige and Rebecca to the toilet cubicle area.

Returning to the lounge area where everyone was seated, Rebecca heard over the loud speaker the first call for boarding the plane. First class passengers boarded the plane prior to anyone else.

Mitch looked up at Rebecca and smiled.

"Let's go,' said Mitch, as he took Rebecca's outreached hand.

Nick, Penny, Michael and Paige followed them towards the boarding stewardess.

Finding their allocated seats, the three guys placed everyone's hand luggage up into the overhead luggage compartments, whilst the girls sat in their seats and buckled up.

Rebecca looked across the aisle and watched Nick sit next to Penny, giving her a tablet to take and some water to wash it down.

"Put your head on my shoulder and cuddle in babe," said Nick, holding her hand.

Penny kissed Nick and said, "Thank you." She cuddled into him and closed her eyes.

By the time they were in the air Penny had fallen asleep.

"It's not long now before we arrive in Seattle," said Mitch, holding Rebecca's hand.

"It's seems like ages ago since we were there. I have missed it actually. I can't wait to see Helen and Grayson. You have such lovely parents, Mitch," said Rebecca, leaning on Mitch's shoulder.

"Yeah… I really miss them sometimes. They have been so good to me all of my life. I couldn't have asked for better parents," said Mitch.

"I was talking with Nick the other day and he told me that your parents' business is usually quiet in December, January and February. Why don't we pay for them come and stay for a holiday in Perth? We can take them on some tours and show them around Perth and maybe some other states as well, depending on how long they stay," said Rebecca.

"Hey, that sounds like a great idea. Whilst we are in Seattle I will ask them. Maybe we can surprise them with the tickets as a Christmas present. What do you think?" said Mitch, excited.

"Sounds like a plan," said Rebecca.

"No wonder I want to marry you, beautiful. You are always thinking of others and are so thoughtful," said Mitch.

Cuddling into Mitch, Rebecca said, "I love you so much, babe and I can't wait to be your wife."

"I love you too," said Mitch.

Mitch looked across the aisle at a dismayed Michael and Paige;

noticing that they seemed very quiet on the plane ride. He knew that they both had some important decisions to make once the wedding was over. *I hope whatever the decision - whether Paige stays in Seattle or Michael lives in Perth, but only if Mom and Dad agree - that it all works out for them. I don't want to see Rebecca stressed over this either. Life sure does throw you some curve balls sometimes.*

Rebecca woke to overhear the flight attendant asking everyone to put their seats in an upright position, as the plane was landing soon into Sydney airport. She wasn't looking forward to the next flight, which was to Los Angeles, because it was at thirteen hour flight, but at least they would have good seats to rest in. Moving her aching neck from side to side, Rebecca tried to loosen it up, as she had slept uncomfortably on Mitch's shoulder.

By the time they had landed and disembarked from the plane, Rebecca noticed that Penny's colour had returned to her face. Overhearing her conversation with Nick, Penny didn't seem quite so nervous about the next flight she was about to take.

Looks like those tablets Nick organised for Penny worked, thought Rebecca, as she held Mitch's hand and smiled.

Entering the Sydney Domestic Airport terminal, Mitch directed everyone to the bus that took them to the Sydney International Airport. Once they arrived and received their boarding passes, Penny, Paige and Rebecca did some duty free shopping whilst the guys had a few beers in the bar near the boarding gate.

Sitting at a table near the bar with their drinks, Mitch said, "So… you guys have some major decisions to make soon on whether to live in Seattle or in Perth. I know which one I would pick and that's Perth. No paparazzi. No one to bother you."

"Yeah, but we don't have the paparazzi follow us around as much as they did to you Mitch," said Nick.

"In fact, the only time we get annoyed by them is when we all go out for a meal or if you are in town," said Michael.

"But you both must admit, that it has been nice over the last couple of weeks, whilst you have been in Perth, not to be looking over your shoulder and to just be able to go where ever you want without worrying about anything, except enjoying yourselves," said Mitch.

"You are right there, bro. That has been nice. Just being able to do what I want, when I want, has been great. Not to mention I met the most sweetest girl ever….. and she is so good for me," said Nick, smiling.

"Well if you two need any help or someone to talk to, don't forget I am here for you both," said Mitch.

They both said, "Thanks."

"Are you getting nervous, bro, about getting married?" asked Nick.

"No… not really. I am marrying a beautiful lady that I love very much. Bit nervous about the vows though. I haven't finished writing them yet. I know what I want to say but I can't seem to put them into words," said Mitch, a bit annoyed with himself.

"Why don't you ask Dad to help you, Mitch? I'm sure he will be good at it," said Michael.

"There is always the internet. I am sure Google will be able to help you," said Nick, placing his hand on Mitch's shoulder.

"Thanks you two. I appreciate the help," said Mitch.

"So where you taking Rebecca for your honeymoon?" asked Nick.

"I have booked a flight to France. We are staying at a really nice hotel for a week and then I have booked us on a cruise back home. She doesn't know yet, so please don't tell Penny or Paige. I want it to be a surprise for Rebecca," said Mitch.

"Man, that sounds so good. I am sure you both will have a great time," said Nick.

"Sounds perfect," said Michael.

"Yeah, I thought so too," said Mitch, picking up his drink.

As the guys were finishing up their beers, the girls returned with their duty free shopping.

"Hello, beautiful," said Mitch, standing to give Rebecca a kiss on her cheek.

"Hi," said Rebecca, giving him a quick hug.

"Not long now before we are on the next flight," said Paige.

"You ladies got enough magazines or books to read on the next flight?" asked Nick.

They all nodded and said, "Yes."

"Would you ladies like a drink?" asked Mitch.

They all nodded and gave their drink orders to Mitch.

"I'll give you a hand, babe," said Rebecca to Mitch.

"Thanks, babe," said Mitch, taking her by the hand and pulling her towards the bar.

Whilst Mitch and Rebecca went to get the drinks, the other four sorted out a table and some more chairs.

Mitch handed the six boarding passes to the steward.

"Come this way," indicated the steward to first class.

Sitting down in her seat, Penny said, "Get a load of these seats. They actually fold right down so I can have a sleep. Oh and we have our own little TVs as well. How exciting." She was like a little kid let loose in a candy shop.

Laughing, Rebecca said, "Great... aren't they?"

"Thank you, Nick for talking me into flying first class. The seats are awesome," said Penny, kissing his cheek as he sat down.

"You're welcome, sweet girl. It's the only way to fly," said Nick, holding Penny's hand.

"You are so good to me. You know if someone had've told me last year that I was going to meet someone like you Nick, I would have laughed in their face. But now that I have you, I never want to be without you," said Penny, feeling lucky.

"I feel the same way, sweet girl. Don't worry, we will figure this out after the wedding," said Nick.

Looking over at Penny and Nick, Rebecca thought to herself, *Look how happy they are. I am so glad for them.*

"It's not polite to stare at people in love," whispered Mitch.

Rebecca turned to Mitch and smiled. "I am just so happy for them, Mitch. Especially Penny. She needed someone like your sweet brother to keep her happy for the rest of her life," said Rebecca.

"I know what you mean. I feel the same way. I am glad that they have found each other. I have never seen Nick so happy in all my life and he is really smitten with Penny. I think he would do just about anything for her too," said Mitch, smiling.

"You Portellico boys sure are a great catch, you know," said Rebecca, smiling at Mitch.

"Why, thank you, Ms Landers. I should be the one saying that to you. I am lucky to have found you and can't wait to marry you," said Mitch, holding her hand.

"Are you nervous about the wedding?" asked Rebecca.

"A little. But I am not nervous about marrying you, my beautiful lady. I am just excited. What about you, are you nervous?" said Mitch.

"Not in the slightest. I know in my own mind that I am marrying you because I want to be yours in every way possible. I do worry though, that I will not be enough for you though, later on," said Rebecca, looking into this eyes.

"What do you mean, 'enough for me'?" asked Mitch.

"Well, I know you love me and vice versa babe, but I am not from your world. You know, rich, powerful etc. and I don't have a bone in my body that wants for you to feel robbed of anything that you previously have had. You know what I am like Mitch, I second guess myself all the time and think I am not good enough for you," said Rebecca, nervously picking her cuticles in her lap.

"When are you going to learn beautiful, no matter if we live rich and powerful or like we live in Perth, which by the way, I love to live like that – it's a more comfortable lifestyle for me - that I will want to be with you. For me life is about being happy and I don't like it when you think that way, Ok? So please stop that. We are both equal, no matter what," said Mitch, kissing her forehead.

"You know Mitch, we have never talked about a pre-nup agreement," said Rebecca.

"Please… don't even go there, Bec. I am not asking you to do that… ever. To me that means I don't trust you and think you will run off later. And I know you are not like that. You don't even like the idea of being rich and powerful, let alone taking me for all I have," said Mitch, his brow furrowed.

"You are right about one thing Mitch, I don't want the rich and powerful life style, I don't like it. The only thing I do want is you, but sometimes, sometimes I can't help myself, I am always self-doubting. I think for me, once we are married all this nonsense will eventually stop," said Rebecca.

"I hope so. Because if you don't, Sir will have to spank you," said Mitch, smirking at her.

Laughing, she kissed him. "Mitch… can I ask you something?" said Rebecca, seriously.

"Sure. What is it?" said Mitch.

"Can we go visit Christine together before we get married?" said Rebecca, looking at Mitch, trying to gauge a reaction.

"Why do you want to go there, Bec?" said Mitch, with brow furrowed.

"I want to talk with her again, like before," said Rebecca.

"She has gone, Bec. She told me she was moving on last time we were there," said Mitch.

"Oh, right. I am sure she will hear what I have to say anyway. Plus I would love to put some more flowers on her grave," said Rebecca.

"That would be nice. Sure… we can go there if you want to," said Mitch.

"It will be good for you too, Mitch. She is still a part of the life you had together," said Rebecca.

Rebecca watched out the window of the plane for the terminal to come into view, as she heard the captain announce over the loudspeaker that they had just arrived at Los Angeles. Yawning and stretching her arms upwards, she overheard Nick telling Penny about the paparazzi.

"When we get into the terminal, there will probably be paparazzi who will recognise us and want to speak with us all. Please don't talk to them or say anything to them, as they will hound you and misrepresent everything you say. That way they won't be able to recognise your accent and say that you three are Australian either. Mitch and Bec have a happy life in Perth and we don't want to spoil that by the paparazzi finding them. So best not even to talk. Just look straight ahead and don't say anything. Sorry… I don't mean to be like this to you, but it's for the best.

You will see what I mean when we get inside. They just hound us all the time and it's annoying. Once we collect our baggage, we should be able to get into a lounge somewhere away from them," said Nick.

"Ok. You have my word," said Penny, making hand gestures that zipped her mouth. *Wow, that is pretty full on, hey.*

Disembarking from the plane, they all headed straight for the baggage carousel to collect their bags. The girls stood back whilst the guys collected the bags from the carousel. As they cleared customs and walked through the terminal doorways, Mitch noticed the flurry of reporters.

"Mitchell Portellico… Mitchell… can I get an interview with you?" said the TGM magazine guy and he wasn't the only one, there were a few reporters and photographers waiting in the wings.

God, how annoying, thought Rebecca, as she rolled her eyes and looked straight ahead.

Mitch just ignored them all. When they couldn't get Mitch to acknowledge them, they then went after Nick and Michael.

The look on Penny's face said it all. Rolling her eyes, Penny couldn't believe what she was witnessing. It was a frenzy of reports and their cameras snapping photos.

Arriving in the lounge area, specially designed so that paparazzi couldn't enter, they found some seats, and waited for their next flight.

"God, I don't believe that out there. How do you all put up with that? It's like an invasion of reporters and they don't give up asking questions, even if we don't say anything," said Penny, frustrated.

"Now you know why I like it in Perth. Here, they seem to always know where I am and they hound me 24/7. I hate it. Just to warn you, Seattle airport will be much the same. Reporters everywhere. Just don't say anything. I have already organised for a limo to collect us at the airport, so we should be able to get away from them quick smart once we get our luggage from the carousel," said Mitch.

Everyone nodded.

The next flight didn't take too long, but they all dreaded getting off the plane. As expected the paparazzi were there waiting for them. This time even trying to get the girls to talk. But the girls knew better. They looked straight ahead smiling and not even acknowledging them. By the time the guys retrieved the luggage from the carousel, it was a frenzy of reporters and cameras taking photos again. Mitch had already noticed his parents' chauffeur waiting for them outside the terminal doors.

"Let's go. Henry is waiting for us over there," said Mitch, pointing to the glass sliding doors.

With them all safely seated inside the limousine, the chauffeur put their luggage into the trunk of the car. As they drove away, the cameras were flashing through the dark tint of the car windows.

"God this is worse than the first time we were here, Mitch. What is going on? Do you think they know we are getting married already?" said Rebecca.

"Maybe. But there has been nothing in the papers according to Mom and Dad," said Mitch.

"I am glad we are having the wedding ceremony and reception at your parents' house. At least they can't get in there," said Rebecca.

"The only magazine that will be at our wedding Bec, will be one that Mom and Dad have chosen for us. It's an exclusive magazine, that only reports the truth, not rubbish, like those bastards back there. And this magazine has been told that they are not allowed to report that I am living in Perth or that you are Australian. That way, hopefully, we won't get hounded when we get back home," said Mitch.

"Life sure won't be dull whilst we are here. I just hope they don't hound us on our honeymoon," said Rebecca.

"Ah, there is no chance of that. I have made sure of it," said Mitch, smiling.

"So... where are you taking me for our honeymoon?" said Rebecca, her eyebrows raised.

"Persistent aren't you? It's a surprise and I won't tell you until our wedding night," teased Mitch.

"You sure are a teaser. But that's one of the things I love about you," said Rebecca, smiling.

Mitch laughed and said, "All in good time, my love."

Chapter Thirty Seven

On the drive to the Portellico family house, Rebecca watched Penny's face as Nick told her about some of the things she was seeing out the window of the car.

"Seattle is such a beautiful place," said Penny, rubber necking at every chance she could get.

Pulling up outside the gates of the Portellico family house, Penny's eyes lit up when the gate opened for them to drive in.

"Wow... you guys live here..? What a stunning place! This house is something like in the magazines for the rich and famous."

"Breathtakingly beautiful, isn't it? We sure are fortunate to be staying here," said Rebecca.

Henry parked the limousine at the front doors of the house and helped the ladies alight from the vehicle.

"How are you feeling?" said Nick to Penny, as they walked inside.

"A bit overwhelmed actually. I'm a bit nervous. But I can't wait to meet your parents," said Penny, fidgeting with her hands.

"Come on, let's go in. Mom and Dad are waiting for us around the back," said Mitch, grabbing Rebecca's hand and pulling her toward the front door.

"What about our bags?" said Penny.

"Don't worry, the staff will bring them in and put them in our rooms," said Nick.

"Really…" said Penny, with raised eyebrows.

"Really," said Nick, smiling.

Walking inside, looking around, Rebecca said, "I had forgotten how beautiful this place is inside."

"Me too," said Paige.

"It's just home to all of us," said Michael, shrugging his shoulders.

Penny stood there in awe with her mouth open, looking around. Placing his hand in hers, Nick smiled at her and said, "Come on. I will show you around later, but first I want you to meet my parents."

When they reached the back of the house, Helen and Grayson were waiting for them on the back patio area.

"Hello," called out Mitch.

Helen rushed over and said, "Oh… my three boys are home again." She had tears of joy in her eyes as she went over and one by one, gave them all a tight hug.

With pride in his voice, Nick introduced Penny. "Mom, Dad, this is Penny."

Helen gave Penny a hug. "It's so nice to finally meet the girl who has swept my boy off his feet. Welcome to our home, dear."

"Thanks. It's really nice of you to let me stay here. You have a beautiful home," said Penny, nervously hugging Helen.

Grayson gave Penny a hug too. "Hi Penny, I'm Grayson. It's nice to meet you finally. Don't be too intimidated by all this."

"Hi Grayson. It's nice to finally meet you too." said Penny, hugging him back.

"Would you like a wine, my dear?" said Grayson.

All too quickly Penny said, "Yes, please." She was hoping the wine might calm her nerves.

"Welcome my dears. How have you been? I have missed you both terribly," said Helen, hugging Rebecca and Paige together.

"We have missed you too, Helen. It's so nice to be back," said Rebecca, smiling.

After Grayson gave Penny her drink, he came over to Paige and Rebecca and hugged them.

"You're finally home. The place hasn't been the same without you two girls here. I have missed you both."

"We have missed you too, Grayson," said Rebecca.

Grayson then gave his three sons a hug and a handshake and told them all how much he missed them.

It sure is nice to be part of a close family, thought Rebecca.

"We are having a barbeque for dinner tonight everyone, around 7.30. How does that sound?" said Helen.

"Sounds great, Mom," said Mitch.

"How were your flights?" asked Grayson.

"Oh the flights were great. Flying first class sure has it perks. The seats are so comfortable. I think I slept most of the way," said Penny.

"The paparazzi were bad this time around though, at LA and Seattle airports," said Michael.

"So what have you all got planned for today?" said Helen.

"Not much, Mom. We were all were talking about it in the car, that we will probably chill out here today. Plus I wanted to show Penny around the house and grounds," said Nick.

"Actually I wouldn't mind having a shower, if that's Ok," said Rebecca.

"That would be nice," said Paige.

"Yeah, me too. I don't smell too good at the moment, "said Penny, smelling her armpits.

"Why don't you boys take the girls up to the showers and then we can meet down here for lunch in a few hours," suggested Helen.

"Sounds like a good idea. I'd like to get out of these stinky clothes too," said Mitch.

"Actually, Helen, could I see you in sitting room for a minute? I just wanted to speak with you about something," said Rebecca, smiling politely.

"Sure dear. Come on," said Helen, taking Rebecca by the hand.

"We won't be a minute," said Rebecca to everyone.

Helen sat on the couch and patted it, indicating for Rebecca to sit down next to her.

"Umm... something you are probably not aware of is that Michael and Paige are now together properly as a couple. If you know what I mean. Would it be Ok with you if they shared a room, or would you prefer them to have separate rooms?" said Rebecca, looking at Helen's face for a reaction.

"I had the feeling that was the case, so I have set up Michael's room so that they both can share it and yes, sleep in the same bed," said Helen.

"Thanks Helen. They have become very close since being in Perth and I don't think we will be able to separate them now. In fact I don't think Paige will leave Michael here. I have the feeling she will want to stay when I go back home. I could be wrong, but I wanted to ask you if the offer still stands for Paige to stay here with you," said Rebecca.

"Of course she can stay here, dear. Paige is part of the family, just like you are, Bec. You know I am so excited about having you as my daughter and one more won't be any different," said Helen, leaning in and giving Rebecca a hug.

"Thanks Helen. Well, it may be three of us soon. Nick and Penny are really in love with each other and I would say Penny would follow Nick anywhere and vice versa," said Rebecca.

"I have never seen Nick looking so happy. I can tell he is in love with Penny. Well dear, we had better get back to everyone to let them know their sleeping arrangements," said Helen, standing up.

"Thanks Helen, and thanks for being so understanding," said Rebecca, giving her a hug.

Walking through the house, Helen and Rebecca found everyone waiting for them near the marble staircase. "Mitch and Nick: you both know where your rooms are, so your lovely ladies can bunk with you. Paige, you can share Michael's room with him. Are you Ok with that?" said Helen.

Paige walked over to Helen and hugged her. "Thank you." She wasn't expecting to sleep in the same room as Michael.

Michael smiled at his mom and then took Paige by the hand up to his bedroom.

Watching their three sons and their partners walk up the white marble staircase to have their showers, Grayson said to Helen, "Well, that has all worked out really well, my dear."

"Did you see how happy Nick was? I haven't seen him like that for ages," said Helen.

"It must be that lovely girl, Penny. She seems very nice, Helen. No wonder he wants to eventually marry her. Actually dear, after speaking with Nick and Penny on Skype the other night, I have told them tonight that if they want to stay here instead of moving back to Perth, then they are most welcome to. But only time will tell, as they both told me that they haven't made up their minds yet on where they will live," said Grayson.

"We may find that we have Nick, Penny, Michael and Paige living here. Rebecca asked me tonight if we wouldn't mind if Paige lived here; that's if Paige wanted to stay. Apparently Michael and Paige have become inseparable," said Helen.

"It sure will be nice to have the four of them here. I don't think Mitch will ever want to move back here. He has a good life in Perth with Rebecca. But I won't completely dismiss the idea yet," said Grayson, with raised eyebrows.

"You could be right, Grayson. I just love seeing them all so happy and finally with girls that are not after their money or what comes with being a Portellico. They are all very down to earth girls and I can tell that they love our boys very much indeed," said Helen.

"Just like you and me dear. I love you very much," said Grayson, as he kissed Helen on the cheek.

Walking up the stairs, holding hands, Penny said to Nick, "I can't believe you live here. You are so lucky. And your parents are really lovely."

Nick smiled at Penny and said, "Wait till you see the rest of the house."

Opening the door to his bedroom, Penny walked in.

"God... this is like one of those expensive hotels you can stay at in Perth. This is so lovely," said Penny, walking around the huge expanse of a room and its furnishings.

"This is the bathroom," said Nick, opening the door.

"Wow… this is really nice, Nick," said Penny, looking around. "It's like something out of a magazine."

"You Australian girls are so easy to please. It's just a bathroom, no big deal, hey," said Nick, shrugging his shoulders.

"Maybe it's no big deal for you Nick, because you live like this and have had this type of lavish lifestyle all of your life. But when you come from a middle class family like mine and have had to work for everything you have, you appreciate a house like this. It just takes my breath away," said Penny, looking at Nick belittled.

"I have never thought of it like that. I suppose I do just take it for granted. You know you always make me see things in a different light when I am with you. This is one of the reasons I love you so much, Penny," said Nick, pulling her in for a hug.

"Never take what you have for granted, Nick. I never do, as you just don't know what's around the corner. Look what happened to Mitch for example, or even Bec, and how their lives have changed so much," said Penny, her brow creased.

"I would never take you for granted, Penny. I am lucky to have found you, even if I had to go halfway around the world to find you," said Nick, smiling at her.

Penny smiled and kissed his lips. "I am glad you found me. But now I really need to have a shower. Can I use your bathroom?" said Penny.

"Yes you can use our bathroom. As long as I can come with you," teased Nick.

Penny smirked and started taking off her clothes.

"Well, what you waiting for?" teased Penny.

She didn't have to ask him twice; he stripped off within seconds. Opening the glass shower door, he gestured for Penny to step into the double headed shower.

Turning on the faucet, Nick handed Penny a yellow body puff and some lovely rose perfumed body wash. "I'm all yours."

"I would hope so," teased Penny, as she placed some body wash onto the puff and washed her body, then his.

Nick enjoyed her sensual touch, as she washed his body slowly.

"Oh… it looks like I have missed a spot," said Penny, squirting some body wash into her hand and slowly rubbing it on his penis.

With every stroke, Nick felt his erection growing. She was relentless with the torment and he always loved when she caressed his cock and balls at the same time. Kneeling down in front of him, with her eyes looking up, watching his, Penny washed the soap from his penis and teased the head of his cock with the tip of her tongue.

Leaning back against the tiles of the shower, Nick moaned as he watched her put his cock into her mouth and suck it hard. Teasing him oh-so-wantonly, Penny pulled his cock in and out of her mouth rapidly, scraping her teeth ever so gently along the shaft of his cock.

Nick grabbed hold of her shoulders and pleaded with her.

"Sweet girl…. please stop…" His breathing was shallow as he tried to pull his penis out of her playful mouth.

Stopping, Penny stood back up slowly, kissing and nipping his abdomen and chest, and finally his neck.

"You sure know how to tease a man. Come here," said Nick, gently pushing Penny up against the tiles of the shower. When their lips met, he opened her mouth with his tongue and soaked up the flavours of her mouth. With so much passion and hunger, his hot mouth reached her hardened nipples.

She moaned and arched her back when his torture continued in a wayward spiral down to her pubic hair. Travelling south, kissing her pelvic area and then he found her clitoris. The feeling was so intense that she automatically orgasmed. As he licked and sucked her bulb, she panted. "Please Nick… please… I can't take much more. I am just about gone."

Turning off the shower, Nick picked her up in his arms, and carried her to their bed, where he made passionate love to her.

"Do you believe that we are allowed to stay in the same bedroom?" said Paige, once they were inside Michael's room.

"Yeah, I wasn't expecting that at all. But it makes me think, that maybe Mitch and your mom know we are sexual partners now," said Michael.

"Either way, I am glad, hey. I am over all the sneaking around. I had the feeling the other day she knew, because she asked me if I was on the pill," said Paige.

"What did you say when she asked you that?" asked Michael.

"I told her I had been to see the doctor and yes, I was now taking the pill. But I said to her that it was just in case we had sex. I didn't allude to the fact that we were having sex already," said Paige.

"Ok… hey, did you want to have a shower or bath?" said Michael.

"I think I will have a shower. I need to wash my hair as well," said Paige, touching her hair and feeling that it was greasy.

"Can I come in the shower with you?" asked Michael, his eyebrows raised and smirking at Paige.

Paige and Michael had never showered together before.

She hesitated for a second and said, "Ok. But only if you let me wash you all over," said Paige, smirking back at him with raised eyebrows.

Hopping into the shower, Paige placed her head under the large round shower head and washed her hair with the products she had brought from home. Just as she had finished, the shower door opened and Michael stepped in. His carnal eyes never left hers, when he reached for the sponge and citrus body wash, from the shelf in the shower. As he traced the curves of her body with the sponge, she moaned when his hot mouth found her nipple. Gently pushing her against the hard shower tiles, he kissed her neck, then earlobe. Paige could feel his hardened erection below touching her leg.

Taking the sponge from Michael, she poured some more body wash on to the sponge and started to wash his naked body.

"Look who has woken up from his sleep," said Paige, feeling Michael's shaft.

Turning the water off, Michael picked Paige up in his strong arms and carried her to his bed. Lying her down on the edge of the bed, he pushed her legs apart gently. Resting on her elbows, waiting in anticipation of what he was going to do to her, she watched him lick his lips. His tongue was hot when she felt him take her sex into his mouth. Swirling his tongue inside and out, licking, sucking and lapping her up as he went. She felt like she was on fire. Whimpering as he assaulted her with pure pleasure, she came in his mouth.

He rose up over her body, kissing each and every curve, and she arched her back off the bed, as his mouth met her breast. When his mouth finally met hers, their lips parted and their tongues intertwined, enjoying the taste of each other.

"Turn over," said Michael, his breathing heavy, as he rose off her.

Paige did as she was asked, then waited for him to put his condom on.

Thrusting his cock into her sex hard, she moaned with the sheer delight of how intense it felt. Fucking her fast and hard, on and on, it was relentless, until he come inside her. As he stilled over her, he felt her release as well.

Lying next to her, both of them breathless, he asked, "Are you Ok?"

"Mmm… that was too good," said Paige panting. Smiling, Paige cuddled into Michael's arms and felt so happy right at that moment.

Exhausted, but relaxed, they soon enjoyed some much need rest.

CHAPTER THIRTY EIGHT

"Hey… after we get settled, would you like to go outside and have a look at what is set up already for our wedding?" asked Mitch, packing his clothes away in the wardrobe.

"That would be great. But I think I will have a shower first. Yes, by myself. Rain check for later though," said Rebecca, excited.

Mitch smiled and nodded.

Walking hand in hand, down next to the river, which was located at the back of the Portellico property, Mitch and Rebecca smiled as they neared the huge white marquee which had the doors open either side and was set up with tables and chairs inside. Of course none of the table had been set up yet, but they could get a good idea of what it was going to look like.

"Wow… look how big this is inside. How many guest do we having coming?" said Rebecca, looking around at the enormous marquee. "It looks like there is enough room inside to seat at least two hundred guests."

"You could be right. I think there may be about that many guests coming," said Mitch, looking around.

Rebecca raised her eyebrows up and down and exhaled. As she looked out across the grounds, Rebecca spotted something in the distance. "Look at that?"

"Let's go see," said Mitch, looking in the direction she was pointing to.

As they walked from the marquee to the back of the property, Rebecca said, "I can't believe how beautiful the grounds are. All the flowers are out in bloom and mmm smell that, the grass has been freshly mowed. It certainly is going to look wonderful on our wedding day."

Nearer to the back of the house, directly in front of the lake, was a white, four posted altar that had been set up, with white chairs on the grass area. They were already set in place for the guests to watch their wedding ceremony.

"Wow... this looks fantastic. It should look really nice on our day, Mitch. I can imagine it already," said Rebecca, looking all around the grounds, excited.

Placing his arms around Rebecca's waist, Mitch smiled and then kissed her lips. Picking her up, he spun her around. When he stopped and placed her down, he said, "I can't wait to marry you. I wish it were today. I love you so much, Bec."

Leaning in, she kissed him wantonly. "I love you my, sweet man. Life sure is going to be great married to a wonderful man like you. I wish it was today too, but as they say, all good things come to those who wait."

Holding her close to his body, Mitch tried to lift Rebecca's dress hem up, so that he could get access to her body. But she pushed him away, giggling as she did.

"Would Sir like to chase me and have his way with me out here?" teased Rebecca.

"You are such a naughty girl and kinky as hell. What am I going to do with you?" said Mitch, smiling.

"You'll have to catch me first, Sir," said Rebecca, pulling away from him and laughing as she ran off.

Mitch chased Rebecca around the chairs, back and forth, trying to catch her. "You'll only make it worse for yourself if you don't let me catch you."

"That is all the fun of it, Sir. The thrill of the chase," teased Rebecca, as she tripped on the leg of a chair.

Catching her before she fell to the ground, Mitch pulled her into his arms. "Mmm... now that I have you, what will I do to you?" said Mitch, with a smirk on his face.

Rebecca fell into his arms laughing.

Picking her up in his muscular arms, Mitch carried Rebecca back into the marquee, all the while looking around to see if any grounds staff were lurking about. As he placed her down on what would be the bridal table, he proceeded to take off her blouse, then her bra, discarding them to the ground. Starting at her left nipple, his warm lips kissed and teased her body relentlessly, whilst his other hand cupped and caressed her right breast. As his lips met hers, she moaned.

"Please... I want you inside me," said Rebecca, impatiently feeling his hardened penis through his pants.

Mitch fumbled in his pockets. *Shit... I don't have any condoms on me,* he thought, as she frowned.

"What?" said Rebecca, wondering what he was doing.

"No condoms," said Mitch, frustrated.

"Don't worry, my love, I am taking a contraceptive anyway," said Rebecca.

"I hate those bloody things, anyhow," said Mitch, ripping off her panties. Lying her on the table's edge, he watched her carnal eyes as he hurriedly undid his trousers and pushed them to his ankles. Pushing her legs apart, he entered her wet sex slowly, until he could feel she was comfortable. Rebecca's body quivered with excitement as he leant over her and fastened the pace. Pushing her pelvis up to meet him every time, she all too soon could feel an orgasm coming. Panting, she tried to hold it back, but it had a mind of its own and she couldn't stop it. As Mitch quickened the pace once more, she was shaken over the precipice and then came his release.

"Mmm... well, that sure was a well spent morning," said Mitch, helping her get up off the table and pulling up his pants.

"Emphasis on spent. I am totally spent. Seeing as you didn't have a condom, I need to go to the toilet," said Rebecca, pulling up her panties. Luckily there were some portable toilets in the back yard already there for the wedding that she was able to use.

Whilst waiting for Rebecca to finish in the toilet, Mitch sat on the steps at the back of the house enjoying the view.

"You two look happy out there frolicking around," said Helen, as she sat next to Mitch on the steps and placed her arm around his shoulders.

"Mom, I am the most happiest man in the world at the moment. Bec sure is good for me," said Mitch, leaning into her and smiling.

"I am happy for you, my son," said Helen, giving him a kiss on his cheek.

"I sure do miss being home with you and Dad though. Do you think you will ever come to Perth for a visit?" said Mitch, with a raised eyebrow.

"Maybe one day, my son," said Helen.

Rebecca stood watching their display of affection to each other and realised in that moment, just how much Mitch would have missed his mom.

As she approached them, Helen looked up and said, "Hello, dear. Actually, I was coming to see you both about some pre wedding arrangements."

"Oh, Ok," said Rebecca, intrigued as she sat next to Helen on the step.

"What have you got planned for tomorrow, Rebecca?" asked Helen.

"Nothing at this stage," said Rebecca, shrugging her shoulders.

"Well… I have made arrangement for us four girls to have our nails manicured, a pedicure, waxing, facial and massage at a lovely place in the city. It will probably take about three hours. Grayson is also going to take the boys into the city to get their hair done, manicure, pedicure and a massage," said Helen smiling.

"Sounds wonderful, Helen. Thank you for organising that. I am sure the other girls are going to love it too," said Rebecca.

"Then after we have finished at the beauty salon, we are going to the bridal boutique to do the final fittings for the wedding dress and bridesmaid dresses. Grayson is going to be taking the boys to their final fittings for their suits as well. We were also thinking that at night time we could go out for dinner at the 'Grayson Restaurant'," said Helen.

Rebecca hugged Helen. "Thank you for organising all of this for us. I don't know what I would do if I didn't have you here. You're such a God-send. I am really looking forward to trying on my wedding dress," said Rebecca, excited.

"Would you ladies like me to leave so you to talk about the dresses," said Mitch.

"No. That's Ok, Mitchell. We can discuss the dresses tomorrow when it's just the girls around. Actually, I think your father is probably waiting for us in the dining room for lunch, though," said Helen, looking at her watch. "The cook has prepared roast lamb and vegetables."

"Mmm, sounds yummy," said Rebecca, standing.

"I would like to propose a toast to Mitch and Rebecca," said Grayson, once everyone had sat at the table and their glasses were filled with champagne. "Raise your glasses."

Everyone raised their glasses and Grayson said, "To Mitch and Rebecca… we are so happy you have found each other and congratulations to you both. Welcome to our family Rebecca."

"Thank you Grayson," said Rebecca smiling.

Mitch pushed his chair back and stood up. "Thanks everyone, and thanks for your kind words, Dad. I think from the first day I met this lovely lady my world changed. I knew she was the one straight away." He then sat down and kissed Rebecca on her cheek tenderly.

"I love you, sweet man. My world wouldn't be the same without you in it either," said Rebecca, looking into his eyes adoringly.

Penny wiped away a tear that had escaped down her cheek. "Oh you both are so adorable together. I am really happy for you," said Penny, as she pushed her chair back and walked over to give them both a hug.

"Thank you," said Rebecca, hugging her back. Pulling away slowly, Rebecca smiled as she watched Penny walk back to her seat.

"To celebrate I have had this made for you both," said Helen, placing a wrapped present on the table in front of them.

"Oh, Mom, Dad, you didn't have to buy us anything," said Mitch, looking at the gift in front of him.

"Nonsense. Just open it," said Helen, excited to see their reaction.

Rebecca smiled as she turned the gift upside down and ripped the sticky tape off the paper. Peeling back the paper, her eyes lit up when she saw what was inside. Looking at Mitch and then back to the engagement photo album, she said, "Wow… this is lovely. Oh and look at the wording that has been etched in gold on the front. 'Congratulations Mitch and Rebecca on your Engagement'." She traced each letter with her pointer finger and then opened the photo album. Inside were a few photos of Mitch and Rebecca in Perth together and some of them in Seattle.

"Wow… this is lovely Helen and Grayson. Thank you, we love it," said Rebecca, pushing her chair back, walking over to them and hugging them both.

"Thanks Mom and Dad. This is wonderful of you," said Mitch, standing and hugging them.

"You are both welcome," said Helen.

Grayson nodded and smiled.

"Penny, I believe from speaking with Nicholas that you are a chemist by trade," said Grayson, as he cut up his meat.

"Yes. I have my own business in Perth and I really enjoy it," said Penny, picking up her glass.

"Did you always want to be a chemist?" asked Grayson.

"When I originally started studying at university, I wanted to be a doctor. But once I started studying the chemist side of it, I seemed to like that better. Then I changed my course from becoming a doctor to being a chemist. I have never looked back. It's very rewarding too," said Penny, proud of her achievements.

"Hope you know Nick that you have a very smart lady there," said Grayson.

"Yes, I do know that about Penny, Dad. That was one of the many things about her that I love. She is quite accomplished," said Nick, kissing Penny on the cheek.

"So, Paige… at the restaurant tomorrow night did you want to hang out in the kitchen again if I can get you in?" said Grayson.

"Yes please, Mr Portellico. I would really like that. I absolutely love cooking and last time I was here they showed me a few things I hadn't seen before. It's very exciting when you are someone like me who is just becoming a chef," said Paige.

Rebecca listened to Paige talk about being chef and realised that her daughter was finally growing up into a confident woman. She knew Jackson would be so proud of her and how she had turned out. Feeling a lump in her throat as the tears formed in her eyes when she thought about Jackson, she whispered to Mitch, "I won't be a moment. Just going outside for a minute to get some fresh air."

"Everything all right?" whispered Mitch, worried. He knew she was upset about something, but he didn't know what.

"Yep," whispered Rebecca, as she held back the tears.

The river views were peaceful as Rebecca sat on the step, crying into her hands. The thought of Jackson not being around as Paige grew up, was starting to dawn on her. Remembering all the things that she and Jackson had put in place, for not only Paige's future, but their own, made her sad to think about how, that wasn't going to happen anymore. Wiping the tears from her face, she turned around to find Mitch standing behind her.

"What the matter?" said Mitch, anxiously.

"It's nothing to worry about, Mitch. I'll be Ok in a minute," said Rebecca.

"Please... tell me, Bec. I am worried," said Mitch, his brow furrowed. He sat on the step next to her.

"I know this sounds silly, but when I was inside listening to Paige chat to your dad about how she loved being a chef, I started to think of how confident she was and how much Jackson would be so proud of her. Just thinking about how he has missed out on all that and how Paige won't have him in her life to say how proud he is, well, it makes me feel sad. I'm sorry, Mitch, I can't help it, I know I am being silly," said Rebecca, sniffing.

Placing his arms around her so that she could cuddle into him for support, Mitch said, "Hey... that's not silly at all. Remember what we said in Perth about showing and explaining our feelings better? Well this is one of those times and I don't want you feeling like you can't talk to me about this either. I am here to listen, babe, whenever you need me," said Mitch.

"I love you so much, Mitch. Thank you for putting up with my silliness. I don't know what's wrong with me today. I am all out of sorts, it's not like me, hey," said Rebecca, cuddling into his chest.

"You probably just need a sleep, Bec. Why don't you go up to our room and have a nap for a while? I will be up in a little while anyway," said Mitch.

"Would you come up to bed with me so we can cuddle up for a while? Just until I go to sleep," asked Rebecca.

"Sure, beautiful. Why don't we go and let everyone know we are going for nap for a while," said Mitch.

As they entered the dining room Helen took one look at Rebecca and said, "Are you Ok, dear?"

"Yes. Just a bit out of sorts. I am going to have a lay down for a while," said Rebecca.

"Mitchell are you going with her?" said Helen, worried.

"Yes, Mom," said Mitch.

"See you both at dinner tonight then," said Helen.

They both said their goodbyes and left for the bedroom.

Lying under the blankets, Rebecca cuddled into Mitch's chest for reassurance. Confused and wrung out, she felt the tears well in her eyes once again. When they spilled over onto her cheeks, a cry escaped from her mouth.

"It's Ok. Let it out, my sweet, sweet girl," said Mitch, holding her tight.

It wasn't long before she was fast asleep in Mitch's arms.

Mitch could hear in her breathing that she was now calm and sleeping soundly. Sliding his arm out from under her, he decided to leave her to sleep for a while. Pulling the door shut quietly, he turned to find Helen coming around the corner.

"Is she asleep?" asked Helen.

"Yeah. I think she has jet lag. She couldn't stop crying. She is Ok now though, as her breathing has calmed and she is fast asleep. Poor girl, I have never seen her like this before. Not since her husband died anyway," said Mitch, his brow creased.

"I am sure she will be all right once she rests. What are you doing this afternoon, dear boy?" said Helen.

"I am going to ask Dad if he will help me with my wedding vows. I know what I want to say, but can't seem to put them into words yet. After that, I will probably go for a sleep myself as I am feeling a bit beat," said Mitch, yawning.

"Your father is down in his study. I will see you later on then," said Helen, giving him a hug. "Don't worry, she will be Ok."

"Thanks Mom," said Mitch, hugging her back.

Standing in the doorway of his dad's study, Mitch said, "Hi Dad. I was wondering if you have a minute… I need some help."

"Sure. What is it, my son?" said Grayson, gesturing for Mitch to walk in.

"I haven't written my wedding vows yet, to Bec. I know what I want to say but I can't seem to write it down so that it makes sense or even sounds good," said Mitch,

"Come over here son, and sit down," said Grayson, gesturing for Mitch to sit in the chair in front of him. "Show me what you have written so far and what you have in your head. Then we can get the laptop out and start writing something. Don't worry, we will get it sorted."

"Thanks Dad. I really appreciate your help," said Mitch.

Once Mitch showed his dad what he had written down and also explained what he wanted to say and how he felt about Rebecca, they then started to type it up. It wasn't long before they had nearly finished.

"Well son, I will leave the rest to you. Just remember it has to come from the heart and be romantic. I just have to go sort something out for the company business. I will catch up with you later, Ok?" said Grayson.

Mitch shook his dad's hand and said, "Thank for your help, Dad. I really appreciate it."

"You're welcome, son," said Grayson.

Half an hour later, Mitch had finished his vows to Bec and was proud of what he had written. Hooking the printer up to the laptop, he printed them out and then placed them in the family safe.

CHAPTER THIRTY NINE

"Penny for your thoughts," said Mitch, leaning into Rebecca at the table.

"I was thinking about the wedding," lied Rebecca. She didn't want to tell him that she was still feeling anxious. Or that all sorts of worrisome things were running through her mind. *What is wrong with me? Before I left Perth I was feeling excited about our wedding, but now, well, now I am... well, I don't know what I am.*

"Ok. How are you feeling now?" said Mitch, concerned.

"Yeah, I am Ok. I have a bit of a headache, though. Maybe I need some more sleep," said Rebecca, trying to sound convincing.

"Would you like something for your headache?" asked Mitch.

"No. That's Ok. I might just get an early night, if you don't mind," said Rebecca. *What I really want to do is go upstairs to our bedroom by myself and cry.*

Rebecca couldn't seem to shake the feelings she was having.

"Did you want some company?" asked Mitch.

"No, that's Ok. You spend some more time with your family. I am just going to go to sleep anyway," said Rebecca. *God, he must think I am some sort of bitch not wanting to spend time with him and his family. What is wrong with me?*

"Ok. I won't be too long anyway. I am pretty tired myself," said Mitch, giving her a hug.

Once she had said her good nights to everyone, Rebecca left the dining room and walked upstairs to their bedroom.

It was dark in the room when she entered and only the moon was shining through onto the walls. Walking over to the window, looking out across the back yard, she was excited to see their wedding altar and chairs set up. In a few more days she would be Mitch's wife: Mrs Rebecca Portellico.

Should I be this happy? Do I deserve to be this happy? thought Rebecca, as she watched the lake water shimmer.

With her mind racing and going over everything in detail, she started to think about Jackson once more. They had met at an early stage in their lives and fell in love straight away.

I remember our wedding day. We were so in love and with all the happiness that we thought would last forever. Little did we know that it would be taken away from us so soon in our life, thought Rebecca, as the tears sprang back into her eyes and spilled over onto her cheeks.

Sliding down the wall, she crouched on the floor. Placing her hands over her face she sobbed. As she looked up at the ceiling, she asked God, "Why?". She wasn't even sure she was doing the right thing by getting married so soon after Jackson's death.

With her head face down on her knees, she heard the door shut quietly. Wiping her eyes and face on the sleeve of her top, she watched Mitch cross the room to their bed. Noticing she wasn't lying in the bed, he looked around the room and once his eyes adjusted to the light, he spotted her sitting next to the window on the floor.

Rushing over and kneeling in front of her, he asked, "Babe, are you Ok?"

"I am afraid, Mitch... I am so afraid that once I marry you and my life is happy again, that I will lose you, like I lost Jackson. I don't ever want to feel that pain again, ever. But as the wedding nears, my fears have become more frequent in my thoughts," said Rebecca, through her tears.

"You won't lose me, Bec. Maybe from old age," said Mitch, joking. "What about if I run you a hot bath with some of that lovely berry bath solution you like. It may help soothe you for a while."

She nodded. "That sounds nice."

"Come on, let's get you out of these clothes and into the bath," said Mitch, standing and holding out his hand.

Lying in the warm bath, cuddled into each other, Mitch wondered how he was going to approach the subject of help. But he knew he had to ask the question.

"Bec... do you think you may be depressed and in need of someone, besides all of us, to talk to about how you are feeling?"

Turning around to face him, she said, "I don't know... I never did speak with anyone when Jackson passed away. I just tried to deal with things in my own way... maybe it's time I did. Do you know someone like a shrink, I can see, Mitch?"

"Actually, I do. I can make an appointment for you tomorrow, if you like," said Mitch, stroking the side of her head.

"Thank you. You must think that I am a crazy woman or something. I wouldn't blame you if you didn't want to marry me," said Rebecca, with her head down and tears welling in her eyes again.

Mitch lifted Rebecca's chin up with his hand, until their eyes met. "I don't think of you that way at all, Bec. You've had a lot to deal with in the last twelve months and obviously you need to speak with a counsellor about this. I love you and yes, I still want to marry you. So please stop trying to push me away, Ok? Because it won't work. I love you too much," said Mitch, sincerely.

"Sorry," said Rebecca, cuddling into his chest.

The next morning Mitch got up early to see if he could get Rebecca booked in to see a counsellor. Luckily there was an opening at 7am at a clinic not too far away from the Portellico home.

"Rebecca Landers," called the red headed female counsellor, looking around the room.

"Yes," said Rebecca, as she heard her name called. Rebecca gave Mitch a quick peck on the lips and then followed the counsellor down the hallway into her room.

Closing the door, the counsellor held out her hand to shake Rebecca's.

"Hi Rebecca. My name is Carol. Take a seat," she said, gesturing to a beige leather lounge chair located in the middle of the room. "What can I do for you today?" She sat in another beige leather lounge chair, opposite to Rebecca, that had a coffee table in front of it, with her pad and pen.

Anxious, Rebecca sat in the leather chair, placing her handbag on the carpet. Smiling politely, she looked at Carol and started to tell her about the last eighteen months of her life and how she was currently feeling.

Carol listened carefully to Rebecca, occasionally nodding and asking some questions, only writing sometimes on her notepad. The session was quite informative and helpful, but the hour seamed to go fast for Rebecca and before she knew it, her time was nearly up.

"So you are happy for me to discuss your visit today with Mitch?" asked Carol.

"Yes, that's fine," said Rebecca. *Wonder what Mitch will think.*

"Ok. I will go and get him," said Carol, standing and walking towards the doorway.

Rebecca stayed seated until Mitch and Carol returned to her office.

"Take a seat next to Rebecca, Mitch," said Carol, gesturing to the leather lounge chair, as she shut the door to her office.

Mitch nodded at Carol and smiled at Rebecca as he sat next to her and placed his hand in hers.

Carol sat on the leather chair opposite Mitch and Rebecca and placed her notepad on the table between them. "Mitch, as you know, Rebecca has been through, and has had to deal with a lot in the last eighteen months. What with her two brain operations, which by the way, she is still healing from, her husband passing away suddenly, losing her job, her daughter's accident and now a feeling of guilt for being happy, that is a lot for any human being to come to terms with... but I think what she is most scared of is the unknown. So what she needs from you, Mitch, is reassurance."

"Right," said Mitch, looking from Carol to Rebecca and smiling.

"Also with the wedding looming, Rebecca has been stressed with all the planning. So… what I am going to do is prescribe some medication for Rebecca that will help calm her anxiety," said Carol.

"Thanks doc, that all makes sense. Appreciate the help," said Mitch, looking from Carol to Rebecca. "I think once we are married and are on our honeymoon then everything will fall into place."

"I am sure it will," said Carol, looking from Mitch to Rebecca. Standing, she walked over to her desk and unlocked her bottom drawer. Pulling it open she looked through the drawer and pulled out a packet of tablets for Rebecca. "Right, here we go." She handed the long packet over to Rebecca.

"Thanks," said Rebecca, placing it in her handbag.

"Well… it seems our time is up," said Carol, looking at her watch. "If the medication doesn't work and you are still feeling like this in a couple of days, don't hesitate to come back and see me. Ok? Good luck with your wedding. Take care of yourself."

"I will. Thank you," said Rebecca, standing and shaking her hand.

"Thanks, Carol," said Mitch, standing and shaking her hand.

Rebecca stared straight ahead out the front windscreen of the car and went over in her mind everything that she and the counsellor had discussed this morning.

"You Ok?" asked Mitch, as he gripped the steering wheel tight.

"Yeah, I'm fine. Thank you for taking me to see the counsellor, Mitch. After talking with her I can now see that I should have gone to see someone when Jackson passed away. I didn't realise how much I had bottled up and stored away to get through his death. She did suggest before you came into the room, that I come back again, or go see someone when I get back home. She said the tablets were only a short term fix for me," said Rebecca, looking at Mitch's profile.

"I'm just glad she was able to help you, that's all," said Mitch, pulling into the driveway of the Portellico home.

"Please don't tell anyone about me taking these tablets, will you? I am a bit embarrassed," said Rebecca.

"I won't, babe. But you do need to remember to take them three times a day," said Mitch, parking the car around the back of the house.

"I won't forget," said Rebecca, taking her seat belt off and stepping out of the car. "Can we make some breakfast when we get inside? I am famished."

"Sure. What would you like?" said Mitch, opening the door to the kitchen for her.

"Just some toast with a cup of tea, will be fine," said Rebecca, walking in. Placing her unzipped bag on the island bench, she took her tablets out of the foil packaging and walked over to the cupboard to retrieve a glass.

"There is some cold water in the fridge if you want it," said Mitch, placing the bread in the toaster.

"Tap water is fine," said Rebecca, placing her glass under the spout. "Would you like a hand?"

"Nah… I'm good. You sit down," said Mitch, getting some plates and mugs out of the top cupboard.

"Ok," said Rebecca, as she sat down at the island bench and took her medication. As she waited for Mitch to make her toast and a cup of tea, she thought, *I wonder how long before these tablets start to work.*

"Here you go," said Mitch, placing a cup of tea and dry toast in front of Rebecca.

"Thanks, Mitch," said Rebecca, placing her knife into the butter and spreading it on her toast. "You know I am starting to feel a bit better. I don't feel so anxious either."

Her shoulders felt like a huge weight had been lifted from them.

"I am glad you are feeling better, beautiful. Just remember I am here for you always, my sweet girl," said Mitch, caressing her face. Mitch leant in and kissed her gently on her lips.

Pulling away slowly, Rebecca said, "Thank you. What would I do without you? You are so good to me."

"And you for me, my love," said Mitch, looking into her eyes adoringly. "Don't worry, it will all sort itself out, you'll see."

"I'm sure it will. What time is it" said Rebecca, trying to look at Mitch's wristwatch.

"It's nine o'clock," said Mitch, realising they needed to hurry up.

"We had better hurry and finish up our breakfast as I think Mom and Dad and the others will be wondering if we are still coming."

"Oh shit, yeah. With everything going on, I totally forgot about that," said Rebecca.

Entering the sitting room, Rebecca and Mitch found everyone talking about how exciting their day was going to be. "Right, we are all here now. You both ready to go?" said Helen, to Mitch and Rebecca.

"Yep. We are both ready," said Rebecca. Truth be told, she was extremely excited about the whole day that Helen had planned for her.

"See you later, beautiful. Text me if you need me," said Mitch, giving Rebecca a tight hug and kissing her tenderly on the lips.

"I will miss you, my sweet man. Have a good day, and enjoy yourself," said Rebecca.

The others gave their partners a kiss goodbye as well and then they were all off in two separate cars.

Driving along, Penny and Paige, who sat next to each other, looked through some magazines and were quite chatty about things that they each liked.

Helen leant into Rebecca and said quietly, "How are you dear? Did the counsellor help at all this morning?"

"The session with her really helped and she gave me some tablets to take for my anxiety. I am feeling a lot better at the moment. I have put a reminder on my phone to take my tablets. But I do need to take them with food. Please don't tell anyone I went to see the counsellor or that I am on medication, Helen… I feel a little bit embarrassed," said Rebecca, in a low voice, with a creased brow.

"My lips are sealed, dear. I won't discuss it with anyone, not even Grayson. You can count on me," whispered Helen.

Giving Helen a hug, Rebecca said, "Thank you."

"Hey Mum… you feeling better today?" asked Paige, looking over at Rebecca.

"Yes, sweetheart. I was just feeling a bit off yesterday, that's all. But I am all right today. Must have been a bug or something," lied Rebecca.

"I'm glad you're better. I would have hated going to the beauty salon without you today," said Paige, smiling.

"Thanks, sweetheart. That means a lot," said Rebecca.

The limousine pulled up next to the kerb outside the beauty salon and straight away Rebecca noticed that there was a men's suit place next door. "You all go in. I won't be a moment. I want to get Mitch something special," said Rebecca, pointing to the shop.

"Ok, dear. But don't be too long," said Helen, as she alighted from the car.

Entering the men's suit shop, Rebecca straight away spotted what she wanted to buy for Mitch next to the front counter. "I will take this one," said Rebecca, pointing to a beautiful teal coloured tie with an imprint embedded into it, to the store owner. "It's a present for my fiancé."

"Mmm, nice choice ma'am. I am sure he will love it," said the store owner, taking it off the rack and placing it into a long grey gift box for her.

Happy with her purchase, she thanked the store owner and proceeded next door to the beauty salon.

"Come sit over here, dear," gestured Helen, as she saw Rebecca walk through the doorway.

Rebecca smiled and headed for the manicure chairs. As she took her seat the Asian lady asked, "Are you having manicure and painted in French polish style too?"

"Yes, please. That sounds awesome," said Rebecca, looking to Helen for approval.

"We are all having the same, dear," said Helen to Rebecca. "Will look elegant with your dresses."

As each of them finished getting their French polish done, their assistants then showed them over to the pedicure chairs & basins and asked them to choose a colour for their toe nails. They each chose a different colour for their toe nails to be painted. Once they were finished, they each had waxing of their desired areas done in a private room and a shoulder massage as well. Finally there were the facials. By the time Rebecca had finished all the beauty treatments, she felt so relaxed.

Whilst Rebecca waited on the black leather couch, which was located in the front of the shop, for everyone to finish their beauty treatments, she decided to flick through some of the magazines. Hearing the bell go on the front door of the shop, she looked up to see Mitch standing in front of her.

"Hi, beautiful. How's your day?" said Mitch, smiling.

"Hi…. I have had the most perfect day so far. This was a really great idea of your mom's coming here. So what are you doing here?" said Rebecca, standing up and giving him a hug.

"I only have a few minutes, as the guys are waiting for me in the car. I came to give you this. I saw it in the jewellers' today and thought this would look really nice on you," said Mitch, handing her a long velvet blue box.

Rebecca couldn't wait to open it. Excited, she said, "Thank you. God, you are so thoughtful." Opening the box, her eyes lit up. It was a fine link, gold bracelet. "Oh, wow Mitch. This is beautiful. Can I wear it now?"

Mitch nodded and took the bracelet out of the box, placed it on her wrist and did up the clip.

Rebecca held her wrist out and twisted it left and right, watching the bracelet sparkle under the fluoro lights. Enjoying its loveliness, she said, "Thank you, Mitch. I really love it. You sure are spoiling me."

"You're welcome, my sweet, beautiful girl. It's just nice to see the smile on your face," said Mitch, leaning down to give her a warm hug.

"I bought you something today too. It's not as good or as expensive as your present, Mitch. But I thought it would look really nice on you," said Rebecca, taking the box out of her handbag and handing it to him.

"That's nice of you to buy me something. See, great minds do think alike," said Mitch, smiling. Taking the cover off the box, he saw the tie. "Wow this is really nice, Bec. I love the colour and how it has a print embedded on it. Maybe I can wear it tonight at dinner."

"Mmm, I thought it would look good on you. It matches your eyes," said Rebecca, holding the tie up to him.

"Thank you so much, babe… but… sorry, I must go as the guys are waiting," said Mitch, looking through the glass window of the shop.

Rebecca could see Nick with his head out the window of the limo saying, "Hurry up, bro."

"You had better go. Looks like they are getting anxious. I will see you later at home anyway. And thank you for my beautiful present," said Rebecca.

"Thank you too, babe. See you later," said Mitch, as he gave her a quick kiss on the lips and was off out the store.

Sitting back down on the couch, Rebecca watched his car pull away from the kerb. Looking at her stunning gold bracelet, she couldn't believe how lucky she was to receive something so beautiful.

"Was that Mitchell I just saw?" asked Helen, as she walked towards Rebecca, with Penny and Paige.

"Yes. Look what he bought me," said Rebecca, proudly showing off her bracelet to the three women. "I couldn't believe it. I looked up and he was standing there to give it to me. He is such a generous, sweet man."

"That's my son for you, always surprising. Oh, that is beautiful, dear," said Helen, watching it sparkle in the salon lighting.

"Wow, that is beautiful, Mum," said Paige.

"You have one awesome man there, Bec," said Penny. "Would have cost him a fortune."

"I sure feel lucky to have Mitch in my life," said Rebecca, looking from Penny to Paige, then Helen.

"Did you give him the gift you bought him this morning?" asked Penny.

"Yeah… he loved it," said Rebecca, smiling.

"Well ladies… who's hungry after all this pampering?" asked Helen, as she took her credit card out of her purse and paid the assistant.

"Me… I'm starving," said Rebecca.

Penny and Paige both nodded.

Whilst everyone chatted around the table, Rebecca took the opportunity to get her second tablet for the day out of her handbag and quickly swallow it down with some water. As she placed her glass down on the table, Rebecca watched the three of them chat and laugh. *I feel so lucky to have such good family and friends in my life.*

"So… have we all had enough to eat?" asked Helen.

"Yes, thanks, Helen," said Rebecca.

Paige and Penny both said, "Yes".

"Well, let's head on over to the bridal boutique and get you ladies fitted," said Helen.

I can't wait to see my dress and try it on. I am really anxious as to how it will look on me, though, thought Rebecca.

"Great, I'll get the driver to bring the car around," said Helen, taking her mobile out of her handbag.

"Good Afternoon. Portellico wedding isn't it?" asked the store owner.

"Yes. How are you Sienna?" said Helen.

"Well, thank you for asking. So who is the bride-to-be?" said Sienna, smiling.

"This is Rebecca, the bride. And these two lovely ladies are Penny and Paige, the bridesmaids," said Helen.

"Nice to meet you all, ladies. Come this way, my dears. I have your beautiful dresses all ready for you," said Sienna, taking Rebecca by the hand.

Following Sienna through a side door, they were escorted to a large antique white room, with damask floral motif pattern wallpaper at the bottom, separated by a thick, white wooden railing, which had three fitting rooms with white curtains around the outside walls. In the centre of the room, facing the fitting rooms, was an L-shaped, light grey velour lounge, with a silver ice bucket which had champagne on ice and some fluted glasses on a square marble table. Next to the fitting rooms was a long rack that had all their dresses hanging from it. Up the other end of the lavish fitting room were three ceiling to floor length mirrors, each mirror showing a different angle of your reflection and a square white boxed platform.

"You are first, Rebecca," said Sienna, walking over to the rack and taking her dress out of the white bag. "Take a seat ladies, and pour yourselves a glass of champagne."

"Thank you, Sienna," said Helen, walking over to the lounge with Paige and Penny.

Anxious, Rebecca smiled and waited in anticipation to see what her dress looked like. When Sienna presented it to her, a lump formed in her throat. She hadn't seen anything this beautiful in all her life, except for in the bridal magazines.

"What do you think, Rebecca?" said Sienna, noticing the delight on Rebecca's face. Sienna had actually designed the dress herself for Rebecca.

Rebecca didn't answer at first, instead she stood there admiring the dress. "Wow... it is absolutely beautiful. I can't wait to try it on," said Rebecca, feeling the fabric and tracing her fingers over the lace patterns.

"Let's go into that fitting room on the left and I will help you try it on," said Sienna, carrying Rebecca's dress over to the fitting room.

Sienna closed the curtain on the fitting room and took the wedding dress off the padded coat hanger, whilst Rebecca undressed down to her bra and panties. Holding the dress open in front of Rebecca, Sienna said, "Hold onto me for support and step into the dress, my dear."

She did as instructed, pulling it up over her muscular body and then took her bra off.

Rebecca watched in the mirror as Sienna laced up the back bodice of her strapless, white satin and lace wedding corset gown.

"Ok, how does that feel?" asked Sienna, kneeling on the floor and smoothing out the free flowing full length skirt, for Rebecca to see the length.

"Not sure. The bodice feels good and makes me look slim, but the seam at the top of the bodice is bulging a bit," said Rebecca, pointing to the side of the bodice.

"Ah... let's pin that in and see what you think," said Sienna, picking up the pin cushion. "Ok, how about now?"

"That's better. I love how the love heart style shaped bodice sits. It actually accentuates my breasts. And the white jewels on the lace, they look awesome," said Rebecca, twirling this way and that, in front of the mirror to see how it fitted her. *It's turned out exactly how I had imagined it.*

When Rebecca stepped out of the change room, the girls gathered around her and had a look. "Well… what do you think ladies?" said Rebecca, twirling around slowly.

"Oh, don't you look just gorgeous, dear. That dress is stunning on you. My boy sure will love this dress," said Helen, smiling.

"Wow… you look pretty Mum," said Paige, at first standing back and looking the dress over and then hugging Rebecca.

The tears of joy spilled over onto Penny's cheeks. "You look absolutely beautiful in that dress, Bec. Mitch will love it. You look like a princess."

"Can you step up onto this?" asked Sienna, indicating to a square white boxed platform.

Rebecca pulled the full length skirt up off the floor and walked over to the platform.

"Wow… look at the back of your dress," said Paige, watching Rebecca step up onto the platform.

"Stunning, isn't it?" said Rebecca, turning around and releasing her skirt to the ground.

"Right… let's see how these look on you," said Sienna, carrying over a tiara and veil to Rebecca. Standing on the platform she positioned the tiara and veil onto Rebecca's head, then once again smoothed out the full length skirt of her gown. Taking some dressmaking pins out of her pocket, Sienna knelt on the floor and hemmed the dress's length.

"How does that feel?"

Rebecca took a long look at herself in the three mirrors. Smiling, as she moved from side to side, she said, "Looks perfect." *I feel like a queen. Very beautiful. Everything has turned out better than I thought or hoped for.*

"Good. What we will do now is take your gown off and then I can give your dress to the machinist to make the final alterations," said Sienna, gesturing to the fitting room.

"Ok. What about the corset I ordered?" asked Rebecca.

Sienna walked over to the long dress rack. "Ah, yes. Here it is. Let's get you out of that dress and try this on," said Sienna, taking it out of the bag.

The strapless corset, which Rebecca had ordered for under her wedding dress was black, white and a light blue, with lots of lace and satin. It also had suspenders to attach her stockings to.

"That will drive Mitch absolutely crazy when he takes your wedding dress off, Bec," said Penny, her brow raised as she watched Rebecca step out of the fitting room.

"That's the point. I want him to love what he sees when he takes my wedding dress off," said Rebecca, standing in front of the three mirrors twisting left and right to see how well it fitted her body.

"So you're happy with how this fits, Rebecca?" asked Sienna, standing at the side.

"Yes, it's good," said Rebecca, smiling.

"Great. Why don't you get dressed and then we can see what the bridesmaids' dresses look like on Paige and Penny?" said Sienna, gesturing for Rebecca to walk back over to the fitting room.

Rebecca watched Penny and Paige parade in front of her and Helen in their backless, opal dark blue, knee length dresses. "They look stunning, girls. I love the double spaghetti straps and the how the dress drops from under the breast line, yet drawing attention to the V-neckline. They look very flattering on you both," said Rebecca, as she looked from Paige to Penny.

"How do they feel, ladies?" said Sienna, with her dressmaking pins in hand.

"I love it," said Paige, twisting from side to side in the mirror.

"Perfect fit," said Penny, looking in the mirror.

"Great. I will get you to take them off and you can try on your dress next Helen, if you like," said Sienna.

After the fittings were all done and the four girls were standing back at the front counter with Sienna, Rebecca said, "When are the dresses and everything going to be dropped off at the Portellico house?"

"I will drop them off on the morning of the wedding and will stay around to help you get the back corset straps done up on your dress as well," said Sienna.

"Oh, thank you. I was wondering how we were going to navigate that. It looks very tricky," said Rebecca, taking her credit card out of her wallet.

"So, I will see you around 10 on your wedding day," said Sienna, showing the final tally to Rebecca.

As the limo pulled into the driveway of the Portellico house, the first thing the girls noticed as they got closer to the house, were the washboard stomachs, muscular arms and really cute tight buttocks of the three Portellico brothers, Mitch, Nick and Michael, who were wearing faded denim jeans, on the lawn area playing touch rugby. Grayson was watching from the sidelines, nearer to the house, as a referee.

As the car came to a stop and the women stepped out from the limousine, Helen said, "I might go and organise some drinks."

"Good idea," said Penny, watching her man.

"Would you like a hand?" asked Rebecca, as she looked from Mitch to Helen.

"No, I should be all right, dear. But thank you for asking. It looks like Grayson has put a table and chairs in the shade so that you girls could sit outside and watch the guys play touch rugby." said Helen, gesturing to the side of the house. "Give me your bags and I will take them inside with me."

"Oh, Ok. Great idea," said Penny, just about drooling over Nick.

They each handed their handbags to Helen, not even noticing when she walked inside.

Helen giggled to herself as she walked inside.

Not even noticing that the women had returned home, Mitch, Nick and Michael continued with their game until they were exhausted from the heat of the day.

"Boys!" shouted Helen, as she walked towards them carrying a tray of ice cold lemonade drinks.

"When did they get back?" said Nick, now noticing the girls sitting on the side lines, and his mother with the tray of drinks.

"Not sure…hey, that was so much fun. I haven't played touch rugby in such a long time. I miss it," said Mitch, his breathing heavy.

"Yeah, me too. That was great fun," said Nick, trying to get his breath back.

"Hey… you two always cheat, so I always lose. But yeah, it was so much fun. I miss this too," said Michael, bending forward and resting his hands on his knees. "Looks like Mom has brought us out some cold drinks, let's go."

"Well boys and girls, we have about one and a half hours before we have to be at the restaurant. So I might go start getting ready," said Helen, standing.

"I will come with you," said Grayson, standing.

Everyone else followed Grayson and Helen inside.

"How was your day, dear?" asked Grayson, placing his hand in Helen's.

"I had a wonderful day with the girls. What about you, my love?" said Helen, as she walked towards the front doors of the house with Grayson.

"Yeah, we had lots of fun. Wasn't it wonderful watching them playing touch rugby out there? It was like the old days, when they used to have so much fun," said Grayson.

"Sure was, my dear," said Helen, as they walked up the marble stairs to their bedroom.

Walking behind them, Rebecca overheard Grayson and Helen talk about their sons. *Hmm, they must miss Mitch so much and how it used to be when the three Portellico boys were home. God, imagine if Nick and Michael moved to Perth too.*

CHAPTER FORTY

Being a fairly new restaurant, Grayson's had become pretty popular with the paparazzi lately. The Portellico chauffeur always knew to pull up around the back of the restaurant, so that the family could go in through the back door without too much fuss from the paparazzi.

Alighting from the car, Rebecca noticed out the corner of her eye a photographer, who continued to snap their photos as they entered through the back door.

Bastards just don't give up, she thought to herself.

The doorman, who seemed to know the Portellico family well, approached them and said, "Right this way Mr and Mrs Portellico. I have the table ready for you all."

"Thank you," said Grayson.

Once everyone was seated, the doorman summoned over the waiter. "This is Ray, your waiter for tonight. He will be happy to take your orders."

"Thank you," said Grayson, nodding.

Ray proceeded to give everyone their menus and fill up the water glasses. "Would anyone care for some drinks?" asked Ray.

After looking through the drinks menu, everyone placed their orders and Ray walked over to the bar to have their drinks made up.

"Hello, my dear friend. It's nice to see you here again," said George, the owner, to Grayson. "How have you been?"

"Hello. I am well, thank you. What about yourself?" said Grayson, standing and shaking his hand.

"I have been really well, my friend. Have they taken your orders yet?" said George.

"No. But that's Ok. We all haven't decided what we want as yet." said Grayson. "There is so much beautiful food to choose from, my friend."

The waiter returned to the table with their drinks and carefully placed them on the table.

"Ray, please make this table your number one priority tonight. These are my good friends," said George.

"Yes sir," said Ray, bowing slightly with his head and smiling.

Looking at Paige, George said, "Dear, would you like to come back into the kitchen again to have a look around?"

"I would love to. Thank you," said Paige, as she stood up and followed him back to the kitchen.

"Great. I will see you later, my friend," said George.

"That was really nice for George to ask Paige again," said Rebecca to Grayson.

"Sure was," said Grayson, picking up his glass.

Whilst everyone waited for their meals to come out, Mitch leant in and said quietly into Rebecca's ear, "Would you like to dance, beautiful?"

"Love to," said Rebecca, pushing her chair backwards and standing with Mitch.

Mitch enveloped Rebecca in his arms and she laid her head on his shoulder as they danced slowly to the music.

"I love you, my sweet man," said Rebecca, her heart melting as she cuddled into his arms.

He smiled and they continued to dance without words for a few more songs.

Snapping them back into reality, Nick tapped Mitch on his shoulder and said, "Your meals have just arrived, bro."

"Thanks, Nick," said Mitch, as he followed Nick back to the table with Rebecca.

"How was your dinner, babe?" said Rebecca, placing her knife and fork in the centre of her plate.

"Was really good. Love the food here at Grayson's," said Mitch, rubbing his stomach. "Hey... I was thinking... would you like to go somewhere special after dinner? Just the two of us?"

"Sure," said Rebecca.

"What you cats up to tonight?" said Nick, listening to their conversations.

"Just going to take my beautiful fiancée somewhere special," said Mitch, looking from Nick to Rebecca.

"What about you? What are you both up to tonight?" asked Mitch.

"Well... I was thinking of taking Penny to see some of the local sights. They're much prettier at night," said Nick, placing his hand on Penny's. She smiled at him.

"Sounds good," said Mitch.

"Helen, could I ask you a favour?" said Rebecca, leaning into her arm.

"What is it, dear?" said Helen, smiling.

"Would it be all right if Paige goes home with you, as Mitch asked me to go somewhere special with him?" said Rebecca.

"Sure. No problem at all," said Helen, placing her hand over Rebecca's.

Listening to the conversation, Paige said, "Actually Mum, I was going to ask if it would be Ok, if Michael and I go to see a movie tonight after dinner."

"I can't see that being a problem sweetheart. But how are you going to get there and back home again?" said Rebecca.

Helen spoke up and said, "Grayson and I could drop them both off at the movie and we could send the car back later to pick them up, if you like."

"Thanks, Helen. That is nice of you," said Rebecca.

"My pleasure, dear," said Helen, patting Rebecca's hand.

"Well it looks like that is all sorted then, Paige," said Rebecca.

"Thanks, Mum and Helen," said Paige, smiling at them both.

"Where are we going?" asked Rebecca, cuddling into Mitch's side, as the car pulled away from the back of the restaurant.

"You'll have to wait and see," teased Mitch.

He smiled and kissed the side of her forehead. Closing her eyes, Rebecca smiled and continued to enjoy the ride with her man.

"Will here be Ok, Mr Portellico?" asked the driver, looking into the rear view mirror at Mitch, as he pulled the car near to the kerb.

Mitch looked out the tinted window and said, "Yes, this is fine."

Rebecca sat up straight and looked around at her surroundings through the windows. When her door opened and the fresh air hit her lungs, she asked, "Where are we?"

"This is called Kerry Park, ma'am," said the driver, holding his hand out for Rebecca to take it.

Stepping out of the car, Rebecca smiled and said, "Wow... look at the view of Seattle city from here, Mitch. Isn't it beautiful? Looks like hundreds of jewels shining all at once."

"I thought you would like the view and being a good night, weather-wise, I thought we might go for walk and soak up each other and the view," said Mitch, placing his hand in hers.

Rebecca smiled and walked across the green manicured lawn, over to the metal railing with Mitch. "I would like that."

The night air was still as Mitch and Rebecca walked hand in hand down the pathway. Looking across the calm water Rebecca noticed the Seattle city skyline had now become breath-takingly beautiful, with colours of red, orange, purple and yellow lights all twinkling in the distance.

"Thank you for bringing me here tonight. It sure is such a beautiful view," said Rebecca, sitting on the bench with Mitch.

"From where I am sitting the view is absolutely stunning," said Mitch, looking into her eyes.

Rebecca smiled. "Why thank you, kind Sir."

Mitch leant in and kissed her neck tenderly. Pushing her long brown hair away, his teeth gently grazed her earlobe. Rebecca's body quivered from his touch. When their lips finally met, the passion ignited a fire in her stomach that needed extinguishing.

Mitch smiled and whispered in her ear, "I want you", as he placed Rebecca's hand on his erection and leant into it.

Raising her eyebrows up then down, she smirked and placed his hand on her bare leg, slowly raising it up to her panty line. "Me too."

Placing his hand over hers, he took over from there. Teasing her through the sensation of touch, stimulating her clitoris with his fingers through Rebecca's satin panties. As her breathing increased, her body felt like she was on fire. Moaning into his mouth as their lips parted, she continued to fondle his hardened shaft eagerly. Mitch knew where this was taking them.

"Woman… what you do to me," said Mitch, his breathing heavy.

Taking his mobile phone out of his jacket pocket, his eyes on Rebecca the whole time, Mitch rang the driver. "Come pick us up."

"Yes, sir. I am still parked where I dropped you off," said the driver.

"Right," said Mitch, looking up ahead and spotting the limousine. Pressing the end button on his phone he turned to Rebecca and said, "Where would you like to go, my beautiful girl?"

"Surprise me," said Rebecca, as she leant in and kissed his neck.

The driver smiled, nodded and opened the door for them to step in.

"I won't be a moment, my sweet girl," said Mitch, gesturing to Rebecca to hop into the car.

She smiled and took her seat in the limousine.

Mitch took his mobile phone out of his jacket pocket and dialled a familiar number. After instructing the person on what his requirements were for the night, he hung up the phone and stepped back into the car.

As the car pulled away from the Kerry Park viewpoint, Mitch instructed the driver to take them to the Salmon Bay Marina.

When the car pulled into the carpark of the Marina and parked, Rebecca said, "What are we doing here?"

"My family has a yacht here," said Mitch, opening the door and helping Rebecca out of the car. Leaning in he whispered, "So Sir thought it would be a more romantic place for you and I to make love here."

"Mmm… could be interesting, Sir," teased Rebecca, as she walked hand in hand with Mitch towards the water, which had all sorts of yachts moored at a long wooden jetty. Noticing a grey headed man, who was standing next to a white and dark blue yacht with the name Portellico written on the side of it, which had lights on inside, she smiled with wonderment.

"Good evening Mr Portellico, ma'am," said the grey headed man.

"Is everything in order as I requested, Frank?" asked Mitch.

"Yes, sir. All ready for you," said Frank.

"Thank you. We won't be needing you for the rest of the night, so you can go. Oh and thank you for coming at such short notice," said Mitch, shaking his hand.

"Yes, sir… you are welcome," said Frank, shaking his hand. "Goodnight sir, ma'am." He smiled and walked towards the car park.

Stepping onto the boat, Mitch held his hands out for Rebecca to join him. As she boarded the boat, he pulled her closely into him, smiled and said, "Come on, I will show you around."

Taking her by the hand, Mitch eagerly showed Rebecca around the sixty metre, two storey yacht. When they reached the lower deck, which had four king-size bedrooms, each with their own private bathrooms, and a huge dark oak, stainless steel galley, which were all situated off a long dark oak hallway, they came to a stop in front of a doorway which entered into a lavish bedroom.

Much to Rebecca's surprise as the door opened, there were red rose petals laid on top of the white bed spread. "Aww… so beautiful, Mitch and the room's perfume smells pretty."

"Glad you like it," said Mitch, pulling her into the room further.

Rebecca's eyes did a three-sixty, as she looked all around at the lavish room's dark oak wood wall panelling in between the square windows and its white and grey tone carpet and furnishings.

Wow… not at all what I expected to see tonight, thought Rebecca, as her eyes lit up in delight.

Before she could express her gratitude, Mitch pulled her by the hand into the bathroom which adjoined the bedroom. As soon as he opened the door, Rebecca noticed a huge white bath, that had been filled with water and some bubbles. The bathroom was decorated with small tea candles, which smelt like citrus, and with the lights off it looked romantic.

He has thought of everything, thought Rebecca, as she looked around the lavish white, black and grey marble bathroom tones.

"I want to get you out of that dress and see your beautiful body," said Mitch, from behind her. Unzipping her dress, he slipped it off over her head and placed her dress over a chair, which was next to the vanity. "Sit on the edge of the bath."

Rebecca did as she was instructed.

Kneeling in front of her, Mitch unfastened Rebecca's shoes and then placed them next to her dress. Her breathing increased as she sat on the edge waiting in anticipation of what he would do next.

Eagerly she watched as he slowly took his clothes and shoes off and placed them on the chair with her dress. The sight of his muscular body made her take a deep breath as he approached her. Bending over, Mitch placed his lips over Rebecca's whilst pulling her up to stand. His breath was warm as their lips parted and their tongues intertwined. Losing herself to this sweet man was easy.

As she slowly pulled away from his tempting lips, she ran the tip of her tongue across his left nipple and pulled it ever so gently, with her teeth.

Mitch tipped his head backwards and moaned with the pleasure of her touch. His breathing grew rapid, as she continued her torture by pulling his hard shaft up and down in fast jerky motions with her hand.

As Rebecca's underwear was pulled off quickly, Mitch picked her up in his arms and they both slipped into the hot, but soothing water. The bubbles rose up to Rebecca's nipples as she sat facing Mitch, whilst he lay back in the bath

"Sit on me… I need to fuck you," said Mitch, looking into her eyes carnally.

Feeling for his hard penis under the water, she lowered herself onto his cock. Rising up, then down over his elongated shaft, Rebecca's breath became heavy and she felt an orgasm coming.

"Oh my…"

Holding onto his shoulders, with her chin pointing towards the ceiling, she came undone in his arms in seconds, and so did Mitch. Exhausted and panting, with her forehead on his shoulder, she tried to catch her breath.

"You sure know how to keep me happy, beautiful lady," said Mitch, breathing heavily.

"I could say the same about you," said Rebecca, sitting up and smiling, as she looked into his blue eyes.

"Would you like to stay here and cuddle up for a while?" asked Mitch.

"Good idea," said Rebecca, as she lay in between his legs, leaning into his chest, the water keeping them warm. "Is there anything to eat or drink on board?"

"Sure is. Give me a minute to catch my breath and then we can hop out and I can get you something?" said Mitch.

"No rush… I am happy to lay here for a while," said Rebecca, turning on her side and placing her head on his shoulder, wrapping her right arm around his waist.

Dressed in white bath robes that they had found in the bathroom cupboards, Mitch and Rebecca made their way down to the galley of the boat. Opening the fridge door, Rebecca found a plate of cold meats, cheeses, red grapes, avocado, olives and a beetroot dip on the middle shelf.

"Mmm, this looks yummy," said Rebecca, taking the plate out of the fridge and placing it on the black marble benchtop. "Looks like we have some crackers here too for the dip."

"Cool… so what would you like to drink? We have a white wine or pink champagne," said Mitch, holding up both bottles from the fridge door.

"What about a glass of both?" said Rebecca, not being able to make up her mind.

"Ok," said Mitch, smiling.

Whilst Mitch was pouring one glass of each type of drink, Rebecca took the biscuits out of the packet and placed them onto the plate with the other food. They then decided to take the food and drinks back to the bedroom and relax.

"Mmm, it smells nice in here, doesn't it?" said Rebecca, sniffing the air as they entered the bedroom.

"It sure does," said Mitch.

Placing the food on the bed and the drinks down on the little tables next to the bed, they sat upright, cuddling with the pillows gathered up behind them.

"I love you, my sweet man. I am glad you are my forever," said Rebecca, looking back at Mitch as she pulled the plate of food toward them.

"I love you too, my beautiful girl. We only have two more days and then we are husband and wife," said Mitch, smiling.

"I know, I am looking forward to our wedding day. Mitch... I wanted to ask you something," said Rebecca, anxiously.

"What is it, babe?" said Mitch, picking up his glass.

"I was wondering... well... when we get back to Perth, can we purchase a home of our own? You know, something you and I can call our own," said Rebecca.

Mitch smiled at Rebecca, leant in and kissed her lips gently. "I was hoping you would want to."

"I want a home that we can call our house, where we become one," said Rebecca, looking into his eyes.

"Would you like a house or an apartment?" asked Mitch, placing the glass near his lips.

"I don't know. I haven't really thought about it. But if it was an apartment, it would have to be the size of a house, as I don't like small places. And it has to have a swimming pool," said Rebecca, thinking about all the things she would like in a new place. Rebecca had rented all her life and was now in a position to afford to buy a place she could share with Mitch.

"When we get back to Perth, we can look around if you want to. I look forward to finding something together," said Mitch, placing his glass down on the small table.

"Thank you," said Rebecca, hugging him. As they lay there cuddling into each other, Mitch and Rebecca discussed what type of house or apartment they both liked and how excited they were about their future together.

"Thank you for a wonderful evening, Mitch."

"You're welcome, sweet girl," said Mitch.

A few hours later, Mitch and Rebecca asked their driver to come and collect them and take them back to the Portellico home. Rebecca needed to get some rest because she had a big day tomorrow, with her parents coming in from Perth.

Chapter Forty One

With her heart beating fast, Rebecca waited impatiently in the back seat of the limousine, whilst the driver waited near the baggage carousel at the Seattle airport terminal, holding a sign up in front of him, with Rebecca's parents' last name on it. She had decided to surprise them by coming to collect them with the driver.

Looking through the tinted glass window of the car, she watched them coming out of the airport terminal doors with the driver and their luggage. Jumping out of the car with excitement, she ran over to them.

"I am so glad you are here, Mum and Dad," said Rebecca, with tears of joy in her eyes.

"We are happy to see you too, sweetheart. And it's not long now before your big day," said Wendy, hugging Rebecca.

"Can I get a hug now?" said Keith, teasing them.

"Hello, Dad. I sure have missed you," said Rebecca, hugging him tight.

"Let me look at you." He stood back and took in Rebecca's appearance. "You haven't changed a bit; still as beautiful as ever."

They all hadn't seen one another for a while, because Rebecca's parents had been touring Australia in their caravan for the past eighteen months, only coming back for visits now and then.

Rebecca smiled.

"Aww, thanks Dad. Come on let's get in," said Rebecca, gesturing for her parents to step into the limousine.

"Wow... this sure is nice of Helen and Grayson to send a limo to collect us. And it was a nice surprise to see you here as well," said Wendy, sitting next to Rebecca, holding her hand.

"You wait till you meet them Mum. Helen and Grayson are such really nice, down to earth people. The whole family is like that," said Rebecca, smiling. "Did you both have good flights?"

"We sure did, love. The funniest thing happened when we got to the Sydney airport, though. We had originally booked economy flights all the way here, but when we booked in at the check in counter, our flights had been upgraded to first class. When I told the lady there must be a mistake; she said, 'No mistake' and that the fare had been paid for by Mitch Portellico. We couldn't believe our luck. That man of yours is something special, dear. He sure is a keeper... oh, and the first class seats, wow, we couldn't believe what a comfortable journey we had all the way here. Talk about spoilt. We will have to thank Mitch when we meet him. I can't wait to meet him, Bec. He seems very lovely, indeed," said Wendy, leaning into Rebecca's shoulder.

"You sure have a good man there, Bec," said Keith, glad Rebecca had found a man who not only clearly cared for Rebecca, but her parents too.

Wendy and Keith had never met Mitch prior, because he was never around when they come to visit Rebecca at her home. This was because Mitch was always working and also because he lived across the road. But they knew Mitch was a good friend of Rebecca's and had helped her immensely since Jackson's death.

"I am so glad you are here, Dad. I have missed you and the talks we used to have," said Rebecca, smiling.

"I have missed you too, Bec," said Keith, patting her hand.

"How is Paige going, dear?" asked Wendy.

"She is going good, Mum. Actually she has fallen for Mitch's brother Michael. They are so in love and I am happy for her; she deserves some happiness," said Rebecca.

"Oh, right. That was quick," said Wendy.

"Yeah, I suppose so," said Rebecca, her eyebrows raised.

Arriving at the Portellico home, both Wendy and Keith were in awe of how lovely the house looked on the outside.

"Wow… this sure is nice, dear. I bet the inside is even better," said Wendy, staring out of the front window.

"Look at those manicured gardens. I bet they have a full time gardener," said Keith, looking out of the side window of the car.

When the car pulled up at the front door, the driver quickly got out and opened the door. He held his hand out to Wendy and Rebecca, so they could alight from the car.

"Thank you," said Wendy to the driver, as she took his helping hand.

"Don't worry about your bags Mum and Dad, the driver will take them up to your room. Come on, I want you to come and meet Mitch," said Rebecca, walking toward the front door with her parents.

Mitch was waiting for them at the front door as soon as they entered the house.

"Mum, Dad, this is Mitch," said Rebecca, proudly standing next to Mitch.

Mitch held out his hand for Keith to shake it. "It's nice to finally meet you both," said Mitch, looking from Keith to Wendy. "How were your flights?"

Wendy gave Mitch a hug and said, "It's very nice to meet you too, Mitch. And thank you for upgrading our flights. That was very nice of you. The first class seats are really comfortable."

"Yes, thank you, son. Was nice of you to do that for us," said Keith, smiling.

"It's the only way to fly. At least by the time you get here you still feel pretty good. It's a pity though that they don't have showers in first class," said Mitch, smiling.

"Oh, that would be funny, dear," chuckled Wendy.

"Your parents have a lovely home here, Mitch," said Keith, looking all around.

"Mmm...they sure do. But they have worked hard to have this type of house too," stated Mitch. "Speaking of which, they are waiting for us out the back. So why don't we go through?" Mitch indicated the way.

Mitch placed his hand in Rebecca's and led them through the house to the back patio area. As Wendy and Keith walked through the house they couldn't believe how grand the house was inside and were in awe of the decor and its surroundings.

"Mom, Dad... Wendy and Keith are here," said Mitch, reaching the patio area, with Rebecca.

Helen and Grayson looked over to see the four of them standing in the doorway. Standing Helen said, "Oh, it's so lovely to finally meet you both." She hugged them both, one at a time.

Grayson pushed his chair back and walked over to Keith and Wendy to shake their hands.

"Welcome to Seattle. Did you have a good flight?"

"Yes, we did have a good flight. Thanks to your lovely son who upgraded us to first class," said Keith.

Grayson looked at Mitch and smiled. "That's Mitch for you – always thinking of others first. He was even like that as a child, so thoughtful."

"Would you both like to freshen up, or could we tempt you with a few drinks out here under the patio?" asked Helen.

"I would really love a shower first," said Wendy. "Then a few drinks sound terrific later on."

"Sounds like a good idea," said Keith, smelling his armpit.

"Come on, I will show you both to your room where you can freshen up and then we can have some drinks later," said Helen, placing her arm through Wendy's and leading her back inside.

"You have such a beautiful house, Helen," said Wendy, as they neared the top of the staircase.

"Thank you, Wendy," said Helen, walking into the bedroom Wendy and Keith were staying in. "There are fresh towels in the bathroom and these will get changed daily for you." She pointed in the direction of the bathroom that was adjoining their bedroom. "Now... I will leave you both to freshen up and we will see you downstairs later for lunch.

Grayson is cooking a barbeque for us all. Oh, I forgot to ask, what do you both like to drink in the way of alcohol?" said Helen.

"Keith likes a beer and I like wine. But we don't want you to go to any trouble. We will just have whatever you have," said Wendy.

"It's no trouble, my dear. Just want to make you feel comfortable whilst you are here," said Helen, smiling.

"Thanks Helen. That's very thoughtful of you," said Wendy, giving her a hug.

"Well, I will let you get settled in and see you both in a little while downstairs," said Helen, walking towards the doorway.

"Ok. Thanks, Helen," said Keith.

After Helen left, Wendy walked over to the bathroom doorway and took a look inside. "Do you believe the bedroom and bathroom we have? Sure is lavish. Talk about spoilt rotten."

"Yes, it sure is extravagant. I might have a shower first if you don't mind, dear," said Keith, walking into the bathroom. "You could swing a cat in here, Wendy."

"Yeah, I know," snickered Wendy, following Keith into the bathroom. "Hey that shower would fit the two of us; what do you reckon?" said Wendy.

"Only one way to find out," said Keith, taking his smelly clothes off. They both undressed and hopped into the shower.

"Mmm… smell this body wash, Keith. It smells like berries," said Wendy, sniffing the body wash bottle and then placing it in front of Keith's nose.

Keith leant into Wendy, raised an eyebrow and said, "Mind if I wash you, sweet lady?"

"I thought you would never ask," said Wendy, brazenly. Wendy and Keith had a loving, wonderful marriage and they still enjoyed the sensual side of it.

"Hopefully we can find the patio area, Keith," said Wendy, as she pulled the door closed to their bedroom.

"Humph, yeah," said Keith, as he walked towards the staircase with Wendy.

Paige closed the door to Michael's room and spotted her grandparents.

"Nanny, Grandad, you're here!" shouted Paige, as she rushed over to give them a hug. "I have missed you so much. And I have so much to tell you."

"We have missed you as well, dear child. My, you have grown. You're now a young lady, not a child anymore," said Wendy, holding her at arm's length and looking her up and down.

"Oh don't embarrass the girl, Wendy," said Keith.

As they were talking Michael walked up the staircase. "Hello, I'm Michael, Paige's boyfriend."

"Hello, dear boy. It's nice to meet you," said Wendy, giving him a hug.

Keith held out his hand and shook Michael's hand.

"Good to meet you my boy. Rebecca has told us a lot about you. It's nice to put a face to your name."

"Thanks. It's nice to meet you both too," said Michael, looking from Keith to Wendy and then to Paige.

"Well, we were just about to go outside to sit with your parents, Michael. Can you show us the way? The house is so big that I think we would get lost," said Wendy.

"You'll get used it. After a day or so, you'll know your way around," said Michael, smiling. Michael took Paige's hand in his and led the way outside to the patio area.

Joining everyone under the patio area, Paige introduced Nick to her grandparents and of course they already knew Rebecca's best friend, Penny.

"Come sit down, Wendy and Keith. Grayson has nearly finished cooking lunch for us all," said Helen, carrying the drinks over to the table.

"Thanks Helen. Is there anything you would like some help with?" said Wendy.

"No, that's Ok. But thanks for asking," said Helen, passing Wendy a glass of wine and Keith a tall glass of beer.

Watching the chatter between the parents, Mitch whispered in Rebecca's ear, "Looks like our parents are getting on really well. You'd think they were old friends the way they are talking."

"Yeah, I'm glad, Mitch. It's nice to see them all enjoying each other's company," said Rebecca.

"How are you feeling, my sweet girl?" said Mitch, kissing the side of Rebecca's head.

"Actually, I am feeling that good I could scream it out loud. I haven't felt this good in ages. The tablets must be doing their job," whispered Rebecca.

"That's great," said Mitch, smiling.

"So… what are we doing tonight, Mom?" said Nick, looking across the table to Helen.

"I was thinking we could all go out to dinner at the Space Needle Restaurant. I can book it for 7.30 and we can take two limousines," said Helen, looking around the table.

"I have heard of the Space Needle Restaurant, it's a revolving restaurant and is meant to have a very nice atmosphere and food," said Wendy.

"Yes, that's right. It has the most gorgeous view at night. I thought you all would enjoy it. Oh and Paige, the manager there said you could come and have a look in the kitchen, if you wanted to," said Helen.

"Really… that would be awesome. Thanks for organising that for me, Mrs Portellico," said Paige, excitedly.

"You're welcome, dear," said Helen, patting her hand.

"Lunch is ready, everyone. Just help yourselves," said Grayson, pointing to the food on the table next to the barbeque.

"Wow, this is a great spread, Grayson," said Keith, looking over the food he had cooked.

"Thanks, Keith. Would anyone like a drink of anything?" said Grayson, looking around the table.

They all gave their orders of what they wanted to drink to Grayson and then helped themselves to the lovely spread of salads and cooked meat Grayson and Helen had prepared for lunch.

With plates cleared away and only their empty drink glasses left on the table, Grayson said, "Wendy and Keith, would you like to have a look around the house and grounds?"

"That would be great," said Keith.

"I would love to," said Wendy.

"Come on then," said Grayson, standing with Helen. "See you all later on kids."

Grayson and Keith walked together chatting in front of Helen and Wendy, who walked arm in arm towards the lake at the back of the property.

"It seems your parents and our parents are getting on like a house on fire," said Nick to Rebecca.

"Yeah. It's like they are old friends who have known each other for years," said Rebecca, with raised eyebrows.

"So… as your wedding day is tomorrow, what's happening when we get back home tonight? Are the girls sleeping in one room and the boys in another? It's meant to be bad luck if the bride and groom see each other before the wedding," said Penny.

"I hadn't actually thought about that," said Rebecca.

"Me either," said Mitch. "I'll talk with Mom later and see what we can come up with, Ok?"

"Thanks, babe," said Rebecca.

Penny and Nick nodded in agreeance.

"I would say Mom and Dad will be gone for a while with your parents. Would you like to go and see Christine still?" whispered Mitch to Rebecca.

"Yes, I would like that, Mitch," whispered Rebecca.

"Nick, will you let Mom and Dad and Bec's parents know that we had to go out for a while and that we will see them later on tonight," said Mitch, getting up from the table.

"Sure, bro. No problem," said Nick, nodding.

"See you all later on," said Rebecca, looking around the table as she stood up.

Arriving at the cemetery, and parking across the road from Christine's gravesite, Rebecca said, "Do you mind staying in the car so I can talk with Christine?"

"No, that's Ok," said Mitch, taking his seat belt off.

"Thank you. I won't be too long," said Rebecca, leaning in and kissing his cheek.

Rebecca bent down in front of the gravesite to pick up the dead flowers that she and Mitch had left last time they were there and replaced them with the new floral arrangement they had bought today on the way to the cemetery. Once she returned from placing the dead flowers in the bin, Rebecca sat with her legs tucked to the side, on the grass in front of the gravesite and started to chat with Christine about how she had fallen in love with Mitch and that they were really happy together. She also told her that they were getting married tomorrow. As Rebecca prattled on and looked around the cemetery, she thought she saw Christine standing next to an oak tree, near the gravesite. Rebecca had only seen a picture of Christine once, so she wasn't a hundred percent sure it was her. Standing, Rebecca wiped her eyes, making sure of what she was seeing. As her eyes opened again, she noticed Christine had moved from the oak tree to now standing in front of her. Startled, she took a step back, then regained her composure and smiled politely at Christine.

Christine placed her hand out in front of her and smiled at Rebecca. Her brown hair was moving gently in the cool breeze. Rebecca watched Christine's lips move, but she couldn't hear a word Christine was saying.

"Sorry, I can't hear what you are saying," said Rebecca, her brow furrowed.

Christine nodded to her in acknowledgement.

This was the first time Rebecca had ever seen a ghost. She wasn't scared, instead she felt calmness.

With Jackson I have always felt his presence near me, but never have I seen him, so why am I able to see Christine? thought Rebecca, swallowing hard.

As Rebecca looked from the headstone to Christine, she noticed a shape of a man who was shimmering in and out, until finally the person became clear to her. It was Jackson. Blinking and trying to make sense of what was happening, her heartbeat quickened and tears filled her eyes.

"Jackson… what are you doing here with Christine?" said Rebecca, surprised. Looking at him she noticed he had on the same outfit that she had chosen for him at the funeral.

You look so handsome. I just want to hold and hug you tight, thought Rebecca, as she looked from Jackson to Mitch, who was still sitting in the car.

"Hello, beautiful," said Jackson, his smile melting her heart.

"How did you know I was here?" said Rebecca, with a furrowed brow.

"Christine found me and brought me here. It's hard to explain, but she was the one that found me," said Jackson.

"Thank you, Christine. You don't know how much this means to me," said Rebecca, who had always wanted to say goodbye to her husband.

She nodded her head in acknowledgement.

"Becky, I don't have long here… I wanted to tell you that I am happy you have found love again and are getting married. Mitch is a terrific choice. Did Paige tell you she saw me?" said Jackson, smiling.

"Yes, she did tell me. But I wasn't sure if she just dreamt it or not," said Rebecca.

"It was so good seeing Paige and she helped me find my brother," said Jackson, his shimmering shape fading, as he looked from Rebecca to Christine, who was behind him.

Rebecca watched as Christine's lips moved again, but again, she couldn't hear what Christine was saying.

"Sorry Becky, I have to go now. But I am sure we will see each other again one day. Say hello to Paige for me. Take care of yourself and enjoy your time with Mitch. Bye for now."

"Wait…" said Rebecca, her arm stretched out front. But it was too late. He had disappeared. *Jackson…* Tears welled in her eyes and overflowed down her cheeks as she sat on the grass contemplating what had just happened.

Rebecca felt a warm hand touch her shoulder.

"Are you all right?" asked Mitch, standing next to her.

Startled by his touch, she turned and stood up. When she realised it was Mitch, her sobbing increased as she cuddled into his chest.

"Shh… everything will be all right," said Mitch, stroking her hair.

"Jackson was just here with Christine," said Rebecca, through her tears.

"Yes, I know. Christine just told me," said Mitch, with his arms around her.

"I miss him a real lot, Mitch. I had forgotten how much, until today," said Rebecca, wiping her tears.

"Are you going to be Ok?" said Mitch, looking into her eyes.

Nodding, she said, "Yes."

"How about I take you back to the car?" said Mitch.

"Ok," said Rebecca, turning around to the grave site. "Bye, Christine and thank you."

Christine nodded her head in acknowledgement and smiled.

"I will be back in a minute, my love," said Mitch to Christine, as he placed his arm around Rebecca's waist and walked towards the car.

"I won't be long. I just need to say goodbye," said Mitch, opening the car door.

"How long have you been able to see and speak with Christine?" asked Rebecca, intrigued.

Mitch gulped hard. "Umm… probably from the day of her funeral. I remember thinking I was seeing things at first and thought I was going mad from my grief. But after the funeral, when I came to visit her gravesite every day, I always found her waiting for me. At first it was comforting, but then as time went on, I became depressed, knowing that I would never truly be able to be with her again. And it wasn't until I spoke with my dad, that I realised there was more to life than visiting my dead wife every day. So that's when he and I decided to start up a security business in Perth." Mitch sighed and raked his fingers through his hair.

Rebecca nodded and said, "That must have been hard leaving Christine?"

"Yeah, it was. I didn't even say goodbye. I just ran as far as I could get to try and dull the pain. You know what it's like. You must have felt the same when Jackson passed away suddenly?" said Mitch, his brow creased.

"Yeah, I think I would have done just about anything to dull that pain. One thing that kept me going though, was the fact that I felt his presence in the house most of the time. It always gave me great comfort thinking he was there still. God, when I saw Jackson just now, it was so overwhelming," said Rebecca, remembering what Jackson had said to her today. "What a day!"

"Yeah, you said it… will you be all right here by yourself whilst I go say goodbye to Christine?" said Mitch.

"I'll be Ok. Take your time," said Rebecca, climbing into the car seat.

Mitch gave her a kiss on her forehead and shut the door.

Approaching the gravesite, Mitch saw Christine floating by the grave and waiting to speak with him.

"So… Bec told you about us. Are you Ok with that?" said Mitch.

"I am happy that you have found true love again, Mitch. Bec is such a lovely person and will be a good wife for you. I just want to tell you one thing though. And that is to never take anything you have or love for granted, Mitch. Bec is your second chance in life. So please always remember she is your number one priority, now you are marrying her," said Christine, sincerely.

"I will remember that, my love. And thank you for being so understanding," said Mitch.

"Well… I have to go now, Mitch. But there is one thing I wanted to tell you before I leave. You are going to make a great father, and soon," said Christine and then she faded away.

Mitch stood at the gravesite with his mouth open, not believing what Christine had just told him.

I am going to be a father… how… when… is Bec pregnant, or will she fall pregnant later?

A huge grin came over his face, but Mitch knew he couldn't say anything to anyone, as they probably wouldn't believe that a ghost told him that he was going to be a father. He had always wanted to have children, but didn't think it would be possible now.

As he stood there contemplating his future, Mitch felt a pair of arms wrap around his waist. Turning around he saw Bec standing there.

"You look happy. What are you grinning about?" said Rebecca.

"You wouldn't believe me if I told you," said Mitch.

"Try me."

"You sure you want to hear this?" asked Mitch.

"Yes, what is it. Now I'm intrigued."

"Christine just told me that I was going to be a great father one day, and soon," said Mitch, with raised eyebrows.

Rebecca looked at Mitch anxiously and said, "What... why would she tell you that?"

"I don't know. But I have always wanted kids, Bec," said Mitch.

Rebecca stood there in shock for a moment, remembering something from about twenty two years ago.

"What are you thinking about?" said Mitch, looking at her puzzled face.

"Christine might be right. I was thinking about when I fell pregnant with Paige and how anxious I was. It's a lot like now. But I can't be. I am sure it was depression this time around. I am a bit overdue for my monthly though. But I just put it down to being excited about the wedding and everything else," said Rebecca, looking worried.

"So you mean you might be," said Mitch, excited.

"Maybe... I am not sure unless we go get a blood test done," said Rebecca.

"Come on. I will take you to our family doctor," said Mitch, as he pulled her toward the car.

Arriving at the doctors', Mitch and Rebecca had to wait about thirty minutes before Mitch's family doctor could see them.

"Ms Landers," called the doctor, as he looked around the room.

Rebecca placed her bag over her shoulder and stood up, following him into his office with Mitch.

"Hello... what can I do for you today, Ms Landers?" said the doctor.

"I want to check to see if I am pregnant," said Rebecca, as she sat in front of him.

"How many weeks late are you?" asked the doctor.

"Only a few," said Rebecca, shrugging.

"Ok. We will do an initial pee test first," said the doctor, reaching in his cupboard behind his desk for the test. "You just need to pee into this cup for me and then I can test it." He handed Rebecca a plastic cup, with a yellow lid. "The toilets are just out the door and to the left in the hallway, my dear."

"Right… Ok," said Rebecca, taking the cup from him and walking towards the closed door.

A few minutes later, Rebecca returned with the sample for the doctor to check.

Taking a white plastic coated paper stick out of the pregnancy test packet, he placed it into the plastic cup. Waiting for a few seconds he then gave Rebecca and Mitch the results. "Well… well, this says you are pregnant. But to be sure, we will need to do a blood test," said the doctor, smiling.

Mitch and Rebecca looked at each other and smiled. Standing, Mitch picked Rebecca up off her seat and whizzed her around the room, whilst shouting, "Yahoo!".

"I don't want to be the party pooper, Mitch, and I know you are excited, but you need to put Rebecca down. We need to wait for the blood results to come back first to confirm the pregnancy," said the doctor.

"Ok," said Mitch, placing Rebecca back on ground.

"Doctor, I have been taking these tablets for anxiety. Are they still Ok to take if I am pregnant?" said Rebecca, handing him the bottle of pills.

The doctor took a look at the tablets and said, "Yes dear, these tablets are safe to take whilst pregnant. But until we get your blood results back I don't want you having alcohol or any other drugs besides these as these will harm the baby if you are pregnant."

"Yes, doctor. But how long before we get the results back from the blood test?" said Rebecca.

"It usually takes a week. But I could probably tell you both in a couple of days if I have it rushed through," said the doctor.

"Tomorrow we are getting married and then we will be on our honeymoon. Can you please ring us with the results as soon as you get them? I will give you our mobile numbers before we leave," said Mitch, anxiously.

"Yes, Mitch. Oh, and congratulations on the wedding tomorrow," said the doctor.

"Thanks, doc," said Mitch.

"Right, let's get this blood test done," said the doctor, picking up his desk phone to organise the nurse to come and do a blood test on Rebecca. "If you are pregnant, when you get back from your honeymoon I want to see you straight away so we can talk about the pregnancy," said the doctor.

"Yes, sir," said Rebecca, her heart racing.

On the drive back to the Portellico house Rebecca aimlessly stared out of the front window of the car.

I might be pregnant. Unbelievable... thought Rebecca, excited at the prospect of becoming a mother again.

Placing her hand over Mitch's hand, which was on the gear stick, she said, "I don't know whether I can contain myself tonight, Mitch. I am so excited. I never thought I would ever have children again."

"I know. I feel the same way. I don't know how I am going to hide this stupid grin on my face and not be able to say anything to anyone tonight," said Mitch, watching the road and then looking back and forth to Rebecca.

"We are just going to have to put on our best poker face tonight, babe. The next couple of days are going to be the longest days of my life. I can't wait to find out for sure," said Rebecca.

"Me too," said Mitch, smiling.

"You know what, Mitch, I don't care about superstition. I don't want to sleep apart from you tonight," said Rebecca.

"Me neither. What we could do, is after breakfast tomorrow, we just won't see each other until the wedding ceremony. I am sure the girls and my brothers will make sure of that," said Mitch.

"Sounds like a good idea. Can you tell them all at dinner tonight?" said Rebecca, anxiously.

"Sure, beautiful. Anything for you. Bec, you might be a mom again and I might be a father. God, I am excited!" said Mitch, smiling.

CHAPTER FORTY TWO

"Penny for your thoughts," said Rebecca, leaning into Mitch as the limousine drove through the city.

"I was thinking about our big day tomorrow and just how much I love you, sweet lady," said Mitch, turning to face her.

"Me too," said Rebecca, placing her head on his shoulder and smiling.

"I'm looking forward to seeing what the Sky City Space Needle Restaurant is like. Apparently the view is to die for," said Penny, excited.

"Me too. I had a look online today at the menu and it looks really yummy. And we have to try the ice-cream with topping that is on a bed of ice. It looks fantastic," said Paige.

"Mmm, that sounds yummy. I might try that myself," said Rebecca, as their car pulled up next to the Space Needle.

When the elevator door opened and they stepped inside the restaurant, the first thing Rebecca noticed was the uninterrupted view through the continuous glass windows all around the restaurant. The view was breathtaking of the city below them, with all its jewel-like lights. All the tables were set out with white linen table cloths, with silvery cutlery. The restaurant was pretty full tonight, so luckily Helen had reserved a table.

Showing them to their round table, the waitress seated everyone and explained about the menu for tonight and then took their drink orders.

"I noticed you didn't order alcohol. You not feeling well, Bec?" asked Penny, concerned.

"I am all right. It's just… I don't want to wake up with a sore head tomorrow," said Rebecca, quickly, without thinking.

"Come on… one won't hurt you," said Nick, teasing.

"Give it a rest, Nick. The lady said, she didn't want a drink," said Mitch, annoyed at Nick's persistence.

Mitch mistakenly put his hand on Rebecca's belly and started to rub it. When she realised what he was doing, she pushed his hand away.

I hope no one saw him rubbing my stomach. We don't want people jumping to conclusions yet, thought Rebecca.

When Rebecca looked up, Penny and Nick were both smiling at her, but they never said a word. Rebecca felt her face blush red and just smiled back at them.

Nick looked at Mitch and mouthed, "Sorry, bro."

Mitch nodded back.

"Are you two at all nervous about tomorrow…? It's just that you both look so calm," said Wendy.

"I think the reason we are so calm Mum, is that we are not nervous about tomorrow, at all. In fact, we are so excited that we can't wait. I am especially looking forward to the honeymoon. Mitch won't tell me where he is taking me yet. It's a surprise," said Rebecca, looking from Wendy to Mitch.

"Oh, how romantic, dear," said Wendy, smiling.

"What would you like to do about the sleeping arrangements tonight Mitch and Bec?" said Helen.

"Nothing, Mom. We have spoken with each other this afternoon and we don't want to be apart for a night. We decided that after breakfast tomorrow, we will then go off separately with the guys and girls, and get ready," said Mitch, indicating to the bridesmaids and groomsmen.

"Actually, I was thinking that the girls could probably set up and get ready in our room, and then us guys could get ready in Nick's room, if that's Ok with you, Nick?"

"Sounds like you have it all worked out, son," said Helen, smiling.

"No problem, bro. But I won't be letting you out of my sight. We don't want you taking a sneak peek at the bride before the wedding. Now that would be bad luck," said Nick, teasing.

"Would you both like breakfast in bed tomorrow morning? I can have the kitchen make you something really special," said Helen, looking from Mitch to Rebecca.

"That sounds really nice, Helen. Thank you," said Rebecca.

"Thanks, Mom," said Mitch.

"Have a look outside, everyone. Isn't it beautiful?" interrupted Paige.

"Ma'am, you have one of the most perfect views in Seattle," said the owner, standing next to their table.

"Freddy... how are you?" said Grayson, getting up out of his chair to shake his hand.

"I am well, Grayson. And yourself, old friend?" said Freddy, hugging Grayson.

"I am really good, my friend. My son, Mitch is getting married tomorrow, so we decided to come here for their last dinner tonight as singles," said Grayson, indicating to Mitch and Rebecca.

"Wow... you are one lucky guy, Mitch. Your bride-to-be is beautiful," said Freddy, gesturing to Rebecca.

"Thank you," said Mitch, placing his arm around Rebecca and looking at Freddy.

Rebecca smiled politely, as her face turned red from embarrassment.

"So... who is the lovely woman that wants to see my kitchen?" asked Freddy, looking around the table.

"That would be me," said Paige, holding her hand in the air.

"Come with me, my dear and I will show you our famous kitchen. Maybe you might want to work here one day," said Freddy.

Paige raised her eyebrows and said, "Thank you. I may take you up on that, one day." Pushing her chair back and standing, she followed Freddy into his kitchen.

Twenty minutes later Freddy returned to their table with Paige.

"Thank you for the tour, Freddy. I will let you know in a few days about the apprenticeship offer, if that's Ok," said Paige, shaking his hand.

"I will hold it for one week for you, my dear. Is that long enough to make your decision?" said Freddy.

"Yes, sir," said Paige, smiling.

"Well it looks like all your meals have arrived. So enjoy and I will see you all later," said Freddy.

"Did he just offer you a full time apprenticeship, Paige?" asked Rebecca.

"Yes… I couldn't believe he even asked me. Would you mind if I took it and lived in Seattle, Mum? I know I would miss you, but this is a once in a lifetime job offer and I would be mad to say, no. Plus, I then get to stay here with Michael, whom I really don't want to leave, anyway," said Paige, excited, her brow creased.

"Whatever you decide sweetheart, is fine with me. I just want to see you happy, that's all," said Rebecca.

Paige walked over to Grayson and gave him a kiss on his cheek, and a hug. "Thank you. I know it was you who told him I was looking for a job and he said you recommended me. That was so nice of you."

"You're welcome, my dear and I know you will do me proud. I am happy you are going to be staying with us," said Grayson, hugging her back. "Helen will have to take you into the consulate to organise your working visa and a permanent resident visa as well, dear, next week."

"Yes and we will have to find out what you need to wear to work and go buy them next week as well," said Helen.

"Thank you both for doing all this for Paige," said Rebecca.

"You're welcome," they both said together.

"Actually, as you are still here next week, Wendy and Penny, would you like to come shopping with Paige and I? And maybe we can go and have lunch somewhere as well," said Helen.

"Oh, that sounds good. I'd love to," said Wendy, excited.

"That would be great. Thanks Helen," said Penny, smiling.

"Do you play golf, Keith?" asked Grayson.

"Sure do," said Keith.

"Well, what about if we play a round of golf when the women go shopping next week?" said Grayson.

"Sounds like a great idea to me, Grayson," said Keith.

"You two boys working next week or have the week off?" said Grayson, to Michael and Nick.

"We both have the week off, Dad. Why's that?" said Nick.

"Would you like to play a round of golf with us two old boys," said Grayson.

"Mmm… what you reckon Michael; we could whip the old boys at a round of golf?" teased Nick.

"I'll be in that, "said Michael, smirking.

"I think us old boys could show you both a thing or two. But it sounds like a plan," said Grayson, smirking.

With the dinner plates cleared away and everyone's desserts now sitting in front of them, except for Penny, Paige and Rebecca, Helen said, "What did you ladies order?"

"I think we all ordered the same thing," said Rebecca, looking from Helen to the waitress carrying their desserts on a tray towards them. "We ordered the ice-cream on ice."

Paige and Penny nodded in agreeance.

"Oh right," said Helen, picking up her dessert spoon.

"Wow… look at that," said Paige, her eyebrows raised, as she watched the waitress place the dessert in front of them and then pour hot water onto the ice, which was under a bowl of ice-cream. The ice started to steam and it looked effective as the vapours spilling out over the side of the dish. Paige had never seen anything like it in her life and was very impressed.

"Cool," said Penny, watching the vapours spill out over the side of the dish.

Rebecca smiled and said, "Awesome."

"Well… who is ready to go home?" asked Grayson, looking around the table.

Everyone nodded and said, "Yes." With their meals devoured and the overwhelming view enjoyed by all, everyone was ready to go home. Standing, they all walked over to the elevator, whilst Grayson paid for the dinner at the counter.

"How was your night?" asked Freddy, as he joined them all at the elevator.

"Was just wonderful, Freddy. Thank you for a lovely evening," said Nick.

Everyone agreed.

"I am glad you enjoyed it. Well… here is your elevator. Have a good night," said Freddy, slightly bowing his head, gesturing to the elevator door opening.

"Good night, my friend," said Grayson, coming to stand beside Freddy.

"Yes, good night. See you again soon," said Freddy, shaking his hand, then watching them all step into the elevator.

As the Space Needle elevator doors pinged and then opened, Rebecca noticed that the two limousines were still waiting for them as they stepped out. With her eyebrows raised, she smiled to herself and thought, *Am I ever going to get used to this type of lifestyle? Chauffeurs and limousines.*

On the ride home to the Portellicos' home, everyone in the limousine was quiet and frequently silently yawning. They all were pretty full from dinner and generally tired. Tomorrow was going to be a big day and they all had to get up early, so as soon as they arrived home everyone said their good nights and went to their bedrooms.

With his arm outstretched for Rebecca to cuddle into the nook of his shoulder, Mitch placed his hand on her stomach and said, "I hope there is a little person growing in here."

"I would love to have your child, Mitch. And you will make a great father, too," said Rebecca, cuddling into him, under the covers

Mitch smiled. "You think so… how do you know?"

"Because you are such a great person already and what comes with being the most wonderful and generous person, is being a great father as well. Believe me, I know," said Rebecca, looking up into his eyes.

"Thank you. I love you, my soon wife to be," said Mitch, lowering his head to kiss her forehead.

As they lay their discussing parenthood and their upcoming wedding, their voices soon drifted and they both fell to sleep in each other's arms.

CHAPTER FORTY THREE

Still entwined in each other's arms, Rebecca and Mitch were woken by a knock on their bedroom door.

"Can we come in?" asked Helen, opening the door a little bit and peeping around the corner.

"Yes, Mom. Come in," said Mitch, yawning and wiping his eyes.

"Sorry, dears. Did we wake you?" said Helen, noticing Rebecca and Mitch still under the covers.

"That's Ok," said Rebecca, sitting up and wiping the sleep from her eyes. Taking a deep breath in, Rebecca's senses came alive as she watched Helen and her mum walk towards their bed, carrying a tray each, with a special breakfast they had prepared for their wedding day. "Mmm, something sure smells good."

Mitch and Rebecca both propped their pillows up against the bedhead and flattened out the sheets, so that the trays of food Helen and Wendy were carrying could be placed down on the bed.

"Wow, thank you, both," said Mitch, looking down at his tray of food.

"Thank you. This is really nice of you," said Rebecca, looking from Helen to Wendy.

"You are welcome," said Helen, smiling.

"My pleasure. How did you sleep?" said Wendy, smiling.

"Like a log. What time is it?" said Rebecca, yawning.

"It's 8 o'clock, dear," said Helen, looking at her wristwatch.

"Thank you for waking us. I was dead to the world when you knocked on the door," said Mitch.

"You're welcome. Well, we will leave you both to enjoy your breakfast. Good luck for today, my boy," said Helen, leaning in and giving Mitch a hug.

"Enjoy the day, sweetheart. Hope you like the breakfast," said Wendy, leaning in and giving Rebecca a hug.

Helen and Wendy then swapped sides of the bed and gave Mitch and Rebecca a hug and then left them to enjoy their breakfast.

Mitch and Rebecca smiled at each other and pulled the covers off their food.

"Mmm, smells so good," said Rebecca, eyeing the Spanish style omelette, bacon, toast, tomatoes, mushrooms and cup of tea on her tray. Noticing a little folded over note on her tray, she opened it and read it to herself. *A special breakfast for two special people. Happy Wedding Day. Lots of love always, Mums.*

"How sweet," said Rebecca, handing it to Mitch.

"Yeah. They are both so thoughtful, hey," said Mitch, after he read the note and handed it back to Rebecca. "Look at all this food." He picked up his knife and fork and started to devour his breakfast.

Rebecca smiled, placed the note on her bedside table and took a sip of her tea.

As Mitch ate the last bit of his breakfast, he said, "Well… I suppose I had better leave you to get ready. Don't be late to the altar, my love."

"Until this afternoon, my gorgeous man, stay safe," said Rebecca, smiling.

Mitch leant in and kissed her lips tenderly. As he pulled away slowly, he looked into Rebecca's eyes, caressed her face with his hand and smiled. "Bye, my love." Picking up his tray, he got out of bed and placed it on the ground, then left for Nick's room.

Stepping out of the shower, Rebecca heard a knock at her bedroom door. "Come in," she shouted.

"Can we come in, pretty lady?" asked Penny, peeping around the bathroom door.

"Come in ladies, come in," said Rebecca to Paige and Penny as she clipped up her strapless bra.

"Your big day is finally here. Are you excited?" said Penny, smiling.

"Sure am," said Rebecca, placing her bathrobe on. She then heard a knock at the door.

"I'll get it," said Paige, walking over to the doorway. It was the hairdresser and her staff to do their hair and make-up. "Come in, ladies."

And so the day began.

The morning seemed to fly by fast for Rebecca, Penny and Paige and they enjoyed all the pampering and attention the makeup and hair stylists had given them.

"Well… our job is done. We will leave you to get ready," said the head stylist to Rebecca.

"Thank you, ladies. I am really happy with how our hair and makeup look," said Rebecca, who along with Penny and Paige were still dressed in their bathrobes.

"You're welcome. Congratulations and I hope the rest of your day goes just as smooth," said the head stylist, as she picked up her black carry case and walked towards the doorway with the other stylist.

"Thank you," said Rebecca, as she watched the door open and stylist walk out, whilst the bridal boutique owner walked in the door to help Rebecca into her wedding dress and tiara and veil.

Before she knew it, they were all finished and ready to walk down the aisle. Penny had even made sure that Rebecca had something, blue, borrowed and new for her special day.

Paige stood behind her mum and watched how she looked in the mirror. "You look beautiful, Mum."

"Thanks, sweetie," said Rebecca, turning around to give her daughter a hug.

"Yeah, wait till Mitch gets a look at you," said Penny, coming to stand next to them.

"I hope he likes it," said Rebecca, anxiously. She jumped when she heard the sound of someone knocking at the door.

"Can I come in?" said Keith, opening the door.

"Come in, Dad," said Rebecca, smiling.

As he walked into the bedroom and spotted Rebecca for the first time, tears welled in his eyes and a huge smile came over his face. "Wow… you look absolutely stunning, Rebecca," said Keith.

"Thank you, Dad. You don't look half bad yourself," said Rebecca, looking at how handsome her Dad was in his black suit and teal blue tie. Smiling, she gave him a hug.

"Mitch sure will be happy to see you. Are you just about ready to go?" said Keith.

"I think so," said Rebecca, looking to Paige and Penny for an answer.

"You have everything you need," said Penny, giving Rebecca a hug.

"We will wait for you downstairs, Mum," said Paige, giving her mum a hug too.

"Thank you for all your help today, Paige and Penny. I don't know what I would have done without you both," said Rebecca hugging them both at once. "You both look beautiful."

The music started to play as Penny, Paige, Rebecca and her dad stood at the end of the aisle. As Penny and Paige walked slowly down the aisle first, Keith placed his arm through Rebecca's and they started their journey up towards the altar too.

"Don't let go of me, Dad. I might fall," whispered Rebecca, as she watched everyone stand.

He smiled at his daughter and patted her hand.

"Breathe in and out slowly. You will be Ok," said Keith, calmly.

Looking up at Mitch, who was standing with Nick, Michael and the celebrant, Rebecca noticed a huge smile come over Mitch's face and could feel his heart melting when their eyes connected.

God, he looks so handsome in his suit, thought Rebecca, as she met his smile and stood in front of him.

When Rebecca's dad gave her hand to Mitch, the celebrant said,

"Who gives this woman?"

"I do," said Keith. Rebecca smiled and Keith kissed her cheek. He then took his seat next to Wendy in the front row.

Mitch leant into Rebecca and whispered, "You look beautiful in that gown. I am the luckiest man alive today."

She smiled at him and said, "Back at ya, babe." They turned towards the celebrant, both ready to say their vows to one another.

"You can now kiss your bride," said the celebrant, looking at Mitch.

Mitch nodded and lifted the veil from Rebecca's face and kissed her passionately. Everyone applauded and cheered when the celebrant introduced them as Mr and Mrs Portellico.

After some initial photos and signing of the wedding certificate, Mitch and Rebecca were congratulated by their family and friends.

As Rebecca and Mitch watched and waited for some individual photos to be taken of both their families in the beautifully manicured gardens at the back of the property, Rebecca's thoughts were interrupted by Penny handing a glass of water over to her and a glass of champagne over for Mitch to drink.

"Thank you," said Rebecca, as it dawned on her that Penny may know her secret. "You know, don't you? Listen we aren't sure yet. So please don't say anything."

Penny looked from Rebecca to Mitch, nodded and said, "Your secret's safe with me. When do you find out for sure?"

"On our honeymoon," said Mitch, quietly.

"I am so excited for you both," said Penny, smiling.

"What are you all whispering about?" said Nick, his eyebrows raised.

Rebecca felt her face turn red, as she looked from Nick to Mitch.

"That's for us to know and you to find out," teased Penny.

"Cheeky girl. I will just have to get it out of you later," said Nick, placing his arm around Penny and smiling.

Once the photos were done, it was time for Mitch and Rebecca to sit down for an interview with two reporters and their photographers, whom they had agreed with to give a story and photos to. Each one lasted only twenty minutes. When they were finished, it was time to enjoy their reception.

"Can I get your attention, everyone... please be up standing... I would like to introduce Mr and Mrs Mitchell Portellico," said the Master of Ceremonies, who stood on the edge of the wooden dance floor with his microphone in hand.

All eyes turned towards the entrance and watched on as Rebecca and Mitch walked into the marquee, which had white chiffon ceiling drapes with bright white lighting intertwined hanging from the ceiling, followed by Nick, Penny, Michael and Paige. Everyone clapped and cheered, as they pushed their seats back and stood up to welcome the married couple to their reception.

The bridal party were shown to their white linen draped seats at the bridal table, which had a floral arrangement at the back of each chair holding the linen in place.

"Please take your seat, everyone," said the Master of Ceremonies over the microphone to the guests. He then explained about the format for tonight.

Mitch leant into Rebecca and whispered into her ear, "I love you, beautiful lady."

Rebecca looked into his blue eyes and smiled. "I love you too, my sweet man." Leaning in, she kissed his lips tenderly, lingered and then pulled away slowly. "I am the most happiest girl alive today. Now I am yours to do with as your heart desires."

"Mmm... that sounds good. I will take you up on that tonight when we arrive at our destination," teased Mitch, as he raised his eyebrows.

The waitress stood in front of them and cleared her throat to get their attention. "Excuse me Mr and Mr Portellico, would the happy couple like a drink of something?"

"My lovely wife will have a cold non-alcoholic drink and I will have a pink champagne, please," said Mitch.

"Would you like some ice with your drinks, sir?" asked the waitress.

"Yes, please. Oh and how long before the food comes out, as we are both hungry?" asked Mitch.

"I could get you both a plate of something now, if you like, so that you didn't have to wait, sir," said the waitress.

"That would be great. I am famished," said Rebecca.

"Give me ten minutes and I will have something for you both," said the waitress, placing her notepad and pen back in her apron. She then headed for the house.

"I can't believe how beautifully this has been set up, Mitch," said Rebecca, looking around the marquee at the white linen covered round tables, each one with a opal dark blue, green and white floral arrangement centrepiece and an elegant set up of cutlery and glassware. Each seat had a large opal dark blue bow fastened to the back, holding the white linen in place.

"I know… it's just how we pictured it. Perfect," said Mitch, looking around the marquee. He then spotted the wedding cake, which was situated to the right of the room in the middle, just near the entrance. "Did you see the wedding cake?"

"Yeah… I love it. I saw it when we walked in," said Rebecca, picturing the lace ribbon design white marzipan, with opal dark blue ribboned, floral wedding cake.

"Here comes our food," said Mitch, noticing the waitress walking towards them.

"And our drinks, too," said Rebecca, watching the waiter walk towards them with a two chilled, long fluted champagne glasses.

"Here we go," said the waitress, placing a large plate in front of Mitch and Rebecca, which had grapes, asparagus, cheese, sliced meats, eggs, olives and biscuits on it.

"Thank you. That is fine," said Mitch to the waiter and waitress. The waiter nodded and walked away.

"Is there anything else I can get you, sir, ma'am?" asked the waitress.

"No…" said Mitch.

The waitress nodded and walked away towards the house.

Mitch picked up the grapes and held them above Rebecca's mouth. Teasing her, he placed them near to her lips and then pulled them away quickly as she tried to take a bite. Giggling, she eventually reached up and plucked one off the bunch with her teeth. As she swallowed the grape and watched Mitch place a grape into his mouth, Rebecca giggled once more and picked up a piece of asparagus off the plate. Teasing him, she placed it into her mouth and pulled it in and out, sucking as she went.

"You are one bad girl, aren't you? Stop that," said Mitch, laughing and looking around. "Oops, here come our mothers."

"That was nice of the waitress to bring you some food, dears. Were you both hungry?" said Helen, now standing in front of the table.

"Yes. I think it must be all the photos and interviews we did. Has made us really thirsty and hungry," said Mitch, picking up his glass of champagne.

"I noticed you are not drinking, my dear. Are you all right?" said Helen.

"Just a slight stomach upset, Helen. I should be fine," said Rebecca, feeling her stomach.

"That's a shame, dear. I have brought you something I thought you might like to drink today. You remember the wine you liked when you first arrived here a few months ago?" said Helen.

"Oh that was thoughtful of you, Helen. Thank you," said Rebecca.

"Your phone is buzzing, dear," said Helen, looking at Rebecca's mobile, which was on the table.

"Oh. Thank you. Excuse me," said Rebecca, standing and accepting the call. "Hello." She walked away from the table.

"Hello, Mrs Portellico, this is doctor's office. We are just ringing you with the results of your blood test for pregnancy," said the receptionist.

"That was quick. The doctor told us it would be a few days before we knew the results," said Rebecca, trying not to hold her breath because she was nervous and excited at the same time.

"Well… the doctor got the pathology to rush it through so that you would both know the results before you go on your honeymoon. You are definitely pregnant, Mrs Portellico. The doctor has asked if you could please make sure you book an appointment to see him when you come back from your honeymoon," said the receptionist.

"Really… umm, oh yes, I will," said Rebecca, her eyebrows raised. Out the corner of her eye, she could see Mitch grinning from ear to ear and impatient for an answer.

"Thank you for ringing," said Rebecca, as she pressed end on her phone and walked back over to the bridal table.

Mitch knew it was the doctor's office calling, as he was listening to the phone call and at the same time trying to distract Helen and Wendy.

"So what did they say," asked Mitch, anxiously.

Nodding, Rebecca said, "Yes."

With Helen and Wendy still standing in front of them, Mitch said, "Would you two ladies please excuse us for a minute? I need to have a private chat with Bec, if that's Ok?"

"Is everything all right, dear?" asked Helen.

"Yes. Everything is fine, Mom," said Mitch, standing.

"Ok," said Helen. Both Helen and Wendy looked at them curiously, placed their arms through each other's and walked back to their table.

"We are going to be parents, babe," said Rebecca quietly, hugging Mitch and smiling.

"So you are definitely pregnant?" said Mitch, pulling away from their embrace and smiling.

Nodding, she said, "Yes."

"I feel like screaming from the top of my lungs our good news. Do you mind if I announce it to everyone, or did you want to wait?" said Mitch, excitedly.

"I am so excited now; tell everyone. I don't mind," said Rebecca, feeling like she was on cloud nine.

Mitch picked up his glass and started tapping it with a fork to get everyone's attention. The guests then quietened in the room.

"Everyone we have just had some wonderful news given to us and we wanted to share it with you. Bec and I are going to have a baby. Bec is pregnant," said Mitch, grinning from ear to ear, as she looked around the room.

As soon as Mitch announced their good news, Rebecca looked over at Paige to see what her reaction was. When their eyes met, Paige gave Rebecca the thumbs up signal and was smiling, mouthing, 'Congratulations.'

Rebecca smiled and mouthed back to Paige, 'Thank you.'

Every person in the room erupted and cheered. There were even some "yee-has" and clapping for the happy couple.

Mitch leant in and kissed Rebecca on the lips and said, "Do you believe, my beautiful girl, you are going to be a mom again and I am going to be a father. I can't wait, Bec."

"I have always wanted more children and now… well, now I am going to be a mum again. I can't believe it, hey," said Rebecca, as she hugged Mitch tightly. "Thank you."

Rebecca's mum and dad rushed over to Mitch and Rebecca.

"No wonder you weren't drinking, my dear. I am so happy for you both," said Wendy. She congratulated them both with a hug.

Rebecca's Dad, Keith, shook Mitch's hand and gave him a hug and said, "Thank you. I am going to now be a grandfather for the second time. I am so excited for you both."

Paige wasn't far behind them, either. "Wow… I am so excited for you both. Hey, and now I will have a brother or a sister! Cool."

Rebecca hugged Paige tightly and said, "I love you, sweetheart. I am so glad you will have a brother or sister too."

Grayson and Helen rushed over to Mitch and Rebecca and Helen said, excitedly, "I am going to be a Grandma. I can't wait. Oh, I am so happy for you both. Congratulations." She hugged them both tightly.

Grayson shook Mitch's hand and said, "Congratulations, son. Well done."

When Mitch looked up, there were many of the guests waiting in a line to congratulate him and Rebecca as well.

Rebecca watched as Nick and Penny walked towards her, Penny with her arms out front for a hug. "I am so happy for you. I can't wait for it to be born so I can spoil it rotten."

"How did you know I was pregnant?" asked Rebecca, as she pulled away from her embrace.

"Nick and I saw Mitch rub your tummy at dinner the other night and we just put two and two together, and figured you must be. Plus when you didn't drink, that was a dead give-away, my friend," said Penny, smiling.

Smiling, Nick gave Rebecca a tight hug and said, "Thank you for making my brother happy. He has always wanted kids and never thought it would ever happen." Turning to Mitch, he smiled and shook his hand. "Congrats, bro. I bet today is the best day of your life at the moment, hey?"

"You got it in one, bro. I got to marry the girl of my dreams and now I am going to be a father. I just can't believe it," said Mitch, smiling and shaking his hand back.

The day soon turned into night for Mitch and Rebecca and by the time the meals had been consumed, the wedding cake had been cut and the bridal waltz had finished, and they had spent time with each of their guests, the reception was nearing an end and it was time to leave.

"You ready to go?" asked Mitch, placing his hand out front.

"Sure am," said Rebecca, taking his hand and standing. "Looks like your mom has got it all sorted." She watched Helen organise all the guests to form a guard of honour send-off.

"Aww, that's nice. Come on," said Mitch, pulling Rebecca towards their guests who had lined up with their arms raised above their heads to form an arch.

As they walked through the guard of honour send-off and said their goodbyes to all of their family and friends, Rebecca noticed both their parents and Paige, waiting for them at the end of the line.

Paige smiled and hugged Rebecca. "Bye, Mum. Have a great time on your honeymoon," said Paige, as the tears of happiness formed in her eyes.

"Thank you for today, sweetheart. We'll be back before you know it. Oh and good luck with the new job whilst I'm away. Just lean on Helen and she will help you sort out your visa application and everything. Ok?" said Rebecca. Pulling away from their embrace, she looked into Paige's eyes and noticed the tears welling. "If you need me whilst I am away, please call. Ok?"

"Thanks, Mum. I am sure I will be fine," said Paige, wiping her eyes.

"Here, dear," said Helen, handing Paige a tissue.

"Thank you," said Paige, sniffing her tears back.

"Have a good time on your honeymoon," said Helen, to Rebecca and Mitch. "Don't worry, we will look after Paige for you, dear."

"Thanks, Helen," said Rebecca, leaning in to give her a hug.

"Good luck, son," said Grayson, to Mitch as he leant in to give him a hug.

"Thanks, Dad," said Mitch, hugging him back. He then turned around and gave his mom a hug too.

"Thanks for everything you both have done for our wedding and reception. I couldn't have asked for a better day," said Rebecca, as she hugged Grayson.

"Oh, you are welcome, Bec," said Grayson, as he hugged her back. "Enjoy your honeymoon."

"Looks like your ride is here," said Wendy, smiling.

Mitch and Rebecca turned around to see a white limousine pulling up in front of them. The driver then came around and opened the door up for them to step in.

"Bye… enjoy yourselves," said Wendy, as she stood in front of Rebecca and Mitch and gave them both a hug at the same time.

Keith then joined them and shook Mitch's hand. "Take care of my girl."

"I will, sir," said Mitch, shaking his hand. "She is in safe hands."

"Bye. Have a great time sweetheart," said Keith, looking into Rebecca's eyes and then hugging her tight.

"Thanks, Dad," said Rebecca, hugging him back.

"Well… we had better go," said Mitch to Rebecca, as he gestured to the car. "Bye, everyone."

All of their guests clapped and cheered as they stepped into the car. As the driver closed the door, Rebecca and Mitch both noticed their parents and family were standing in a straight line waving them off.

Penny smiled as the limousine drove away, and she noticed the white lettering signage on the back window of the car, which said, 'Just Married'.

"Well, Mrs Portellico, I can now tell you where we are going for our honeymoon," said Mitch, as he placed his hand in Rebecca's and cuddled into her.

"As long as I am with you, my sweet man, my world is complete," said Rebecca, looking into his adoring eyes.

"First, we are going to a hotel to get changed out of these clothes and into something a bit more comfortable. Then we take a plane to France," said Mitch, watching her reaction and smiling.

"What… you're taking me to France? Oh Mitch, thank you," said Rebecca, hugging him.

"But that's not all. We are in France for a week and then we are taking a slow boat cruise back to Seattle; where we will stop off at numerous destinations along the way. By the time we get home, we will have been gone for two weeks," said Mitch.

"Oh Mitch, that sounds really wonderful. Thank you, so much," said Rebecca, leaning in. As their lips met, her heart melted and her body felt warm all over. "What time is our flight to France?"

"Not for another four hours. So we have plenty of time at the hotel. I can have my way with you then, Mrs Portellico," said Mitch, with a raised eyebrow and smirking.

"Mmm… is that right. I look forward to that," said Rebecca, smirking.

I wonder what he will think of my corset when he takes my dress off, thought Rebecca, as she snuggled into him.

CHAPTER FORTY FOUR

The elevator pinged when it stopped at their floor and the doors opened. With swiftness, Mitch picked Rebecca up in his muscular arms and carried her to their suite door and over the threshold.

"Ever the romantic, aren't you, my sweet husband?" said Rebecca. She leant in and kissed him on his lips tenderly.

Entering the room, Rebecca noticed that the lights were dimmed low and there was an ice bucket with ice and cold drinks chilling next to the small bar fridge. Mitch carried her into the sweet scented bedroom, where Rebecca's face lit up when she saw that the bed was filled with red and pink rose petals.

"Oh wow, Mitch, this is beautiful," said Rebecca, surprised.

Without saying a word, Mitch set her down on her feet in front of the bed and turned her around so that he could undo the wedding dress. As the last strap was unfastened and her dress fell to the ground and she stepped out of it, Mitch stood there with his mouth open in awe of her beautiful corset and figure.

"Do you like what I chose for you, my gorgeous husband?" said Rebecca, waving her hand down her figure.

"Man... that is stunning on your beautiful body," said Mitch, with raised eyebrows, wanting to devour her body.

"Why thank you, Sir," teasing Rebecca, smiling, as she slipped her shoes off.

Mitch picked Rebecca up in his arms and gently lay her on the queen size bed, quickly undressed and lay his warm body next to hers. With his hard shaft touching her thigh, she instantly became wet when he grazed her earlobe with his teeth. As his lips sucked and kissed her neck, she moaned when her libido kicked into overdrive. When he reached the tops of her corset engorged breasts, she felt like her body was going to explode into a million pieces from his touch. Once he had her corset unfastened and off, he lapped at her right nipple, teasing it with his tongue and nipping at it with his teeth ever so gently. She arched her back and quivered when he then did the same to her left nipple.

"Mmm... did you bathe in something really nice this morning? You taste good, babe," asked Mitch, as he excitedly kissed her stomach and moved towards her pubic region.

"Yes," she said, panting. She couldn't talk. His teasing was overwhelming her senses.

Pulling her gently over to the edge of the bed, Mitch knelt in front of her knees and pushed her legs apart. Eagerly he lapped at Rebecca's clitoris, in anticipation of her orgasm she was about to have.

She lay breathless as he joined her back on the bed. But his relentless torture wasn't over yet. Rolling Rebecca over onto her stomach, he pulled her arse into the air. With her legs spread, he rammed his enlarged cock into her wet sex with vigour. Overwhelmed, she cried out loud when she felt his enlarged shaft enter her vagina and quicken his pace.

Rebecca felt slightly out of breath as he fucked her faster and harder. "Please... don't... stop." She could feel another orgasm coming. She tried to stop it, but it had a mind of its own. As she orgasmed, she heard him groan as he came inside her.

Breathless, they lay in each other's arms sated on top of the doona, but feeling overwhelmed by the pleasure they had just given each other.

"I can't believe you are finally mine, forever. God, I love you so much. Your wedding vows to me today were really wonderful and heartfelt, Mitch. I will cherish them forever," said Rebecca, laying on Mitch's chest and looking up into his eyes.

"I meant every word of them, my sweet wife. Today was just so perfect in every way," said Mitch, leaning down and kissing her forehead. "Would you like a drink, babe?"

"Yes, please."

As Mitch untangled himself from their cuddle, he picked Rebecca up in his arms and carried her into the bathroom. Entering the dim lit room, she first noticed the tea light candles all around the room and then the big white oval shaped bath which was filled with water, rose petals and bubbles. The smell in the room was divine to her over-heightened senses.

"Wow. This is lovely," said Rebecca, hugging Mitch. "Thank you."

"You're welcome," said Mitch, placing her into the bath. "I'll be back in a minute. Just going to get our drinks."

The water was a bit hot at first, but once her body adjusted to the temperature, it was just right.

"Here you go, my love," said Mitch, handing her a crystal glass.

"Thank you," said Rebecca, watching him step into the hot water with his drink. Resting his back up against one end, he sat with his legs stretched out, nearly touching the other end and Rebecca took her place between his legs, pressing her body into his chest. They lay there for a few minutes together, drinking their cold drinks and soaking in each other's touch.

"Aww, that feels nice," said Rebecca, pushing her feet into the jets as the pump started up.

"Mmm… feels nice on my back too," said Mitch, leaning into the back of the bath. He had turned on the heater to keep the water warm for them.

"This is nice and relaxing, babe," said Rebecca, snuggling into his chest.

"I'm glad. I wanted it to be perfect for you," said Mitch, placing his glass on the bath ledge, wrapping his arms around her waist and kissing her neck. Placing his hand onto her stomach, he rubbed it gently. "We have a little person growing in there."

"You are going to make a wonderful father," said Rebecca, smiling. "It's exciting, isn't it?"

"Sure is. I am looking forward to becoming a father," said Mitch.

"How long before we need to leave, Mitch?" asked Rebecca. She was excited about flying to France.

"Umm, probably about another half an hour before we need to get ready."

"Ok," said Rebecca, as she closed her eyes to soak up the ambience of the room and Mitch's muscular body.

Standing in line to board the plane, Rebecca looked at her watch and started to yawn. It was now four in the morning and both she and Mitch were really tired from their long day of nuptials.

Hmm, twelve hour flight to France. I think once the captain turns off the seat belt sign I might lay the seat down and get some rest. So exhausted… thought Rebecca, as she sat in her first class seat.

Rebecca woke to Mitch saying, "Hey… sleepyhead, wake up."

"What time is it?" mumbled Rebecca, as she yawned and placed her chair in the upright position.

"It's about two hours before we land. They are just starting to serve breakfast. Would you like some?" said Mitch.

"Yes, please," said Rebecca, wiping the sleep from her eyes.

"How do you feel this morning?" asked Mitch.

"Good. How did you sleep?" said Rebecca, placing her hand in his.

"I slept like a log," said Mitch, stretching his legs out front.

"That's good… I might go to the toilet," said Rebecca, unfastening her seat belt.

As usual, the line for the toilet was long. So, by the time Rebecca got back to her seat, breakfast had already been served.

"Mmm, this looks good. I'm famished," said Rebecca, eyeing the food on her tray.

Mitch nodded and watched her devour her breakfast in record time.

"You hungry or something?" asked Mitch, as he watched Rebecca finish the last bite.

Rebecca nodded.

"Would you like some of mine? I'm not that hungry," said Mitch.

"Sure," said Rebecca.

"You sure have a big appetite this morning," said Mitch, with a raised eyebrow.

"This is what I am like when I am pregnant. Just so hungry all the time," stated Rebecca.

"Well, we don't want you ending up like the Goodyear blimp, do we?" said Mitch, smirking.

Elbowing him in the arm, she said, "Funny, aren't you."

"Just kidding," said Mitch, smiling.

"Ladies and Gentleman, if you haven't done so already, can you please place your seats in an upright position and fasten your seat belts, as we will be landing in Charles de Gaulle airport shortly," said the steward, over the PA system.

Rebecca watched the cabin crew walk throughout the plane and make sure things were ready for landing. Placing her hand in Mitch's, she looked into his eyes and smiled.

Once the plane landed, they collected their luggage from the carousel and proceeded through to customs. About one hour later they were on their way in a limousine to the hotel Mitch had booked.

"Wow, look at those old buildings, Mitch. Aren't they beautiful?" said Rebecca, craning her neck as she looked out the window as they drove along.

"Some of the architecture is remarkable, isn't it?" said Mitch, looking out the window.

"I can't wait to see the rest of France," said Rebecca, noticing the car was stopping outside a cream building that had red awnings over each window, with small planter boxes on each balcony. "Is this where we are staying?"

"Yes," nodded Mitch, as he watched the driver open his door. "Come on."

Stepping out, he thanked the driver and tipped him.

"Thank you, sir," said the driver, noticing the one hundred Euro note in his hand. "Will you be needing anything else, sir?"

"No. Only our luggage," said Mitch, placing his hand out front to help Rebecca out of the car.

"Very good, sir. I will organise for the bellboy to carry them in for you," said the driver, walking around to the boot of the car.

Rebecca's eyes roamed from side to side as they entered the lavish hotel, which was built in the early 1920's and had an architectural style of art deco, through the revolving glass doors. With its cream painted walls, cream and black square marble tiles and recessed round ceiling, which had a glass chandelier hanging from the centre, Rebecca couldn't believe how extravagant the hotel was as she followed Mitch, past the round pillars, towards the long wooden reception desk.

Arriving at the reception desk to book in, the lady at the counter, who had a French accent said, "Welcome to the Hotel Plaza Athenee Paris. How can I help you today, sir?"

"We have a honeymoon suite booked under Mr and Mrs Portellico," said Mitch.

She then looked up her computer and said, "Ah, yes. The Signature Eiffel Suite. We have your room ready for you sir, madam." Booking them in she handed Mitch the keys to their room and organised for a bellboy to bring the luggage up to their room with them.

"Here we go, Mr and Mrs Portellico, this is your room," said the bellboy, holding the door open for Mitch and Rebecca.

Mitch picked Rebecca up in his arms and carried her into the room. As the bellboy held the door open, Rebecca noticed he had a smile on his face and guessed he knew they were a newly married couple on their honeymoon.

Mitch placed Rebecca down gently on her feet and asked the bellboy to show them around the spacious room and explain how everything in the room at the hotel worked. Before the bellboy left Mitch gave him a customary tip.

"I hope you have a lovely honeymoon Mr and Mrs Portellico. And if there is anything I can get or do for you, please don't hesitate to ask," said the bellboy, his eyebrows raised as he looked at his one hundred Euro bill tip.

"Thank you," said Mitch, walking back to the open doorway with the bellboy.

Closing the door, Mitch walked over to the window and pulled opened the curtains. "Have a look at this, Bec," said Mitch.

"Wow… look at the view, Mitch. Isn't it wonderful? When are we going sight-seeing?" said Rebecca, as she looked out the window, excited.

"Any time you want to. All I have to do is make a phone call and we can go straight away," said Mitch.

"Cool. I think I would like to unpack my bag first and then have a shower to freshen up. Oh and maybe a bit of fun with my husband too," said Rebecca, smirking.

"Mmm… the last part sounds good to me, babe," said Mitch, smirking with a raised eyebrow.

Rebecca giggled and walked into the bedroom. As she unzipped her suitcase she heard a knock at the door.

"Room service," they called from the other side of the door.

"I'll get it," said Mitch, remembering he had ordered lunch for them as part of their first day in Paris.

As Mitch opened the door, the waiter pushed the food trolley into the room. The wonderful smells of what was under the covers wafted through the room and it made Rebecca feel hungry.

"Mmm… that smells delicious. What have you ordered?" said Rebecca, walking into the lounge room.

Mitch took the covers off the food and there was pasta carbonara, lamb casserole, sweet curry chicken with rice, and a tossed salad. For dessert there was crème brulee.

"Wow… thank you for ordering this for us," said Rebecca.

"Well, I know you like all these dishes and so do I. I can't wait to try them," said Mitch. He then tipped the waiter and showed him to the door.

After choosing what they wanted to eat from each dish, Mitch and Rebecca decided to sit outside on the balcony and eat their meals, because it had a view of the Eiffel Tower and Paris.

"This is nice and relaxing, isn't it? Thank you for bringing me here," said Rebecca, looking around at the view. She had to pinch herself, because she still couldn't believe she was in Paris.

Mitch smiled at her and said, "You deserve to be spoilt, beautiful girl. I enjoy seeing how happy you are. After lunch would you like to go and do some sight-seeing or shopping?"

"I would like to do some sight-seeing. What about you? What would you like to do?" said Rebecca, placing some food on her fork.

"I wouldn't mind taking you shopping. But if you want to do some sight-seeing; that's Ok with me too," said Mitch, picking up his glass.

"Ok. Sight-seeing it is then," said Rebecca, smiling.

"I will need to ring reception and see if we can book something," said Mitch, placing his fork and knife in the middle of his empty plate.

"Ok." She watched Mitch walk inside and use the hotel phone, next to their bed, to book the sight-seeing tour with reception. Rebecca couldn't wait to see some of Paris. Besides Seattle, this was only her second time overseas and she sure was excited.

"They said they can pick us up at 2pm from the front of the hotel," Mitch called out, interrupting Rebecca from her thoughts of things she would like to see and do whilst in France. "I just need to go down to the reception and pay for the tickets. I won't be a minute. Why don't you get ready whilst I am gone?"

"Ok," said Rebecca, walking inside. As she came to stand in front of him, she leant in and kissed his lips tenderly. "Don't be long."

Rebecca quickly had her shower and got dressed, whilst she waited for Mitch to return. As she sat on the couch, with her handbag, ready, she looked at her watch.

Hmm… 1.55pm. Mitch better hurry up otherwise we will be late, thought Rebecca, anxiously looking at the doorway to their hotel room.

When her watch hit 2 o'clock, she started to get worried. *I might ring reception*, thought Rebecca, as she walked over to the bedside table and picked up the phone.

"Hello. This is Mrs Portellico. Is that reception?"

"Yes, ma'am. What can I do for you this afternoon?" said the receptionist.

"Well… my husband, Mr Portellico, is he still in reception paying for our sight-seeing tour? Or has he left?" asked Rebecca, worry in her voice.

"One moment ma'am, I will check with the other staff here," said the receptionist.

Rebecca waited on hold for a minute before the receptionist returned to the phone conversation.

"Mrs Portellico, we haven't seen your husband this afternoon. Our staff remember him ringing to book the car, but he hasn't come down yet to pay. Are you sure he is not in another part of the hotel?" said the receptionist.

"I'm not sure. When he left the room about forty minutes ago, he was going to reception to pay for the tour, so I was expecting him to return by now. The tour was booked for 2pm," said Rebecca, anxiously. "Wait, does your hotel have cameras so that you can see if he is here or has left?"

"Yes, ma'am, we do. Can you leave this with me and I will go see our security team and see if Mr Portellico is still in the hotel or whether he has left, for some reason," said the receptionist.

"Ok. But it's not like him to leave me here and as I said before, he only said he was coming down to reception to book the tour and was coming straight back. Will I wait in my room or come down to reception to see you?" said Rebecca, impatiently tapping her nails on the bedside table.

"Wait in your room, ma'am. Just in case he comes back. You never know, he may have left to buy you something. It's quite common in Paris for men to do that. He maybe just stuck in traffic. But we will check out the camera footage and let you know," said the receptionist.

"Ok. Thank you." After hanging up the phone, Rebecca sat on the bed trying to figure out where Mitch might have gone. *It's not like Mitch to leave without saying a word. I am really worried*, thought Rebecca.

When the room phone rang, Rebecca just about jumped out of her skin.

"Hello?" said Rebecca.

"Mrs Portellico, this is the hotel security calling. Could we please ask you to come down to reception?"

"Yes. I will be there in a few minutes," said Rebecca hanging up the phone. Grabbing her handbag, mobile phone, and door key, she quickly headed for the elevator.

As the elevator door opened, Rebecca quickly ran towards the reception area. Noticing a lot of people, including the police, standing at the counter talking, Rebecca introduced herself to the receptionist.

"Hello, Mrs Portellico. We have some news for you. But I will let the police detective tell you all the details," said the receptionist, indicating to the police officer. "Excuse me gentlemen, this is Mrs Portellico."

"Good afternoon, Mrs Portellico. I am Detective Aubertin. Please... come with us into the hotel office, as we need to discuss some details with you." His French accent was apparent.

"What is this about? Do you know where my husband is?" said Rebecca, worried. She felt nauseous in her stomach and had the sneaking suspicion something had happened to Mitch.

"Follow me please, Mrs Portellico," said Detective Aubertin.

Entering the office, Rebecca was asked to sit down in front of a desk.

"Mrs Portellico, we have some rather disturbing news. The hotel security has viewed the camera footage and it looks like your husband has been abducted. This happened near your room at the elevator door. He put up a struggle, but it looks like he was overpowered. We haven't viewed all the hotel footage yet from different angles, but we will and try to see if we can find out who it is that has taken him. We have also put out an alert to all police about your husband. Please don't worry, we are sure we will find him," said Detective Aubertin.

Shaking, Rebecca couldn't hold back her tears, as they spilled over onto her cheeks.

"What... why would someone take him? We have only just arrived today, so how did anyone know he was here?" said Rebecca, through her tears.

Handing her a tissue, Detective Aubertin said, "At this stage we are not sure ma'am. I am currently waiting for all the footage to be viewed and we should know soon."

Knocking at the door, a grey headed man with a security uniform asked if he could enter the room.

"Come in... what did you find?" said Detective Aubertin.

Handing the detective a piece of paper, the security guy said, "There are the two photos we have been able to get from the camera footage in the hotel."

Taking a good look at the photos, Detective Aubertin said, "Thank you, Paul." Placing the photos in front of Rebecca on the desk, he asked, "Mrs Portellico, do you recognise these two people?"

Picking the photos up, she studied them. "This one here... is this a female? She looks familiar... I am just trying to remember where I know her face from. But the other man... I don't know him at all," said Rebecca, anxiously, looking at Detective Aubertin.

"Take another look, Mrs Portellico. Where do you remember her from? Think... this is very important," said Detective Aubertin.

Nervous, but wanting to help, she tried to remember. It then dawned on her where she had seen this woman. "I think her name is Claudia and she works for TGM magazine in the USA. I remember her hounding us at the airport for an interview."

"Are you sure?" said Detective Aubertin.

"Yes," said Rebecca, looking at the photos again. "But I still don't know who the other person is."

"Ok. Well, this is a start anyway," said Detective Aubertin. Taking his phone out of his pocket, he placed a call to his police station. "Sergeant Taut, I want you to see if you can get us an up to date photo of a woman who works at the TGM magazine. Her name is Claudia. We don't know her last name, but I am sure you can look into this for us and find out her whereabouts."

Why would she have abducted Mitch? I don't understand, Rebecca thought to herself.

Hanging up his phone, Detective Aubertin said, "We should know more in a few minutes, Mrs Portellico. Would you like to make some phone calls to family?"

"Once we find out more information; yes I will ring them. But in the meantime, what can I do to help?" said Rebecca.

"There is nothing you can do at the moment," said Detective

Aubertin.

"Mrs Portellico, would you like a cup of tea?" said the hotel receptionist, who was sitting on the right.

"Yes, please," said Rebecca. All of a sudden Rebecca felt bile coming up to her throat and she then passed out.

Chapter Forty Five

"Bec... Bec... wake up, sleepyhead." Through her subconscious, Rebecca could hear someone calling her name out. With a fuzzy head, she opened her eyes, and to her surprise, Mitch was sitting next to her on the bed. Sitting up quickly, Rebecca threw her arms around him and said, "Oh Mitch, I am so glad you are all right."

"Hmm... are you Ok?" said Mitch, frowning, as he hugged her back.

Looking around the room, Rebecca wiped the sleep from her eyes and realised it was daytime outside. "Where have you been, Mitch?" said Rebecca, with creased brow.

"Down to reception to pay for the tour. Did you miss me?" said Mitch, teasing her.

"What...?" said Rebecca, looking Mitch in the eyes and feeling totally confused.

"I have only been gone for twenty minutes and when I returned you were asleep," said Mitch, smiling.

Feeling her head, it dawned on her. *Stupid brain...*

"You're not going to believe this. But when you went down to pay for the tour, I must have fallen asleep. Whilst I was asleep, I dreamt you had been abducted by Claudia from the TGM magazine and the police were now searching for you. How bizarre is that. God... am I glad that was only a dream and not real," said Rebecca, hugging him.

"Really…you're silly, hey. How are you feeling, anyway," said Mitch, his eyebrows raised.

"Except for the unreal dream, yeah good," said Rebecca, tracing his facial features.

"Well, we have about five minutes before we have to be in reception, so how about you get ready and we can go," said Mitch.

"Ok," said Rebecca, getting up off the bed in a daze.

When will my brain ever stop these vivid dreams I have. They always seem so real. When I spoke to the neurosurgeon the other day, he said that it wasn't normal, but surmised that these types of dreams would eventually stop as my brain healed. I am looking forward to that day, thought Rebecca, as she brushed her hair in front of the bathroom mirror.

Collecting them from the hotel, the driver took Mitch and Rebecca to the Arc De Triomphe and the Louvre Museum. As the day became night, the last stop was the Eiffel Tower. To her surprise Mitch had book dinner at the Eiffel Tower Restaurant, Le Jules Verne.

Walking through the restaurant over to their small romantic table near the window, which had the legs of the Eiffel Tower displayed through the glass, Rebecca noticed as she sat down, that they had the most spectacular view of Paris. Being up so high, the buildings and street lights at night looked like a million jewels all shining at once with brilliance. Once they were settled in their bronze coloured leather chairs, the waiter took their orders and headed for the kitchen.

"What a great view. Paris is really beautiful at night. I have had such a wonderful day, thanks to you Mitch," said Rebecca, placing her hand over his.

"Me too. The view sure is beautiful up here on the second floor," said Mitch, looking into her blue eyes. But he wasn't looking at the view outside, he was looking and referring to Rebecca.

"Thank you," said Rebecca, blushing. "Did you have a good day?"

"Sure did, my love. Especially because I got to spend it with my lovely wife," said Mitch. "What would you like to do tomorrow, Bec?"

"Actually, I was having a look at some brochures earlier and I wouldn't mind taking a cruise on the Seine, it looks really good. What do you think?" said Rebecca, taking the brochure out of her bag and showing it to Mitch.

"Ok," said Mitch, taking the brochure from her and checking it out. "Looks great, babe. I will give them a ring now and see if we can book it for tomorrow."

"Cool," said Rebecca, watching Mitch take his phone out of his jacket pocket. She then poured a glass of water for them both.

Wow… look at this view. One side the Seine River and the other of Paris. Oh so beautiful, thought Rebecca, as she looked out the window of the restaurant, whilst she waited for Mitch to finish his call.

"Luckily, they had a cancellation and we can go tomorrow," said Mitch, hanging up his phone.

"Awesome. Thanks for booking the cruise," said Rebecca.

"That's all good. We are on the 11am – 12.30pm cruise," said Mitch.

"Sounds great, Mitch. Hopefully it's a good tour," said Rebecca, as she picked up her glass of water.

Returning to the table with their meals and then their drinks, the waiter asked, "Was there anything else you both would like?"

"No, thank you," said Mitch.

Rebecca shook her head.

"Enjoy your meals," said the waiter, looking from Mitch to Rebecca.

"Thank you," said Rebecca, smiling politely.

"Was there anything in particular that you wanted to see or do whilst we were here, Bec?" asked Mitch, picking up his drink.

"I would love to do Disneyland. Oh and I would love to get on a Segway and have a look around. There is just so much I want to see, but I don't think there is any way possible that we will be able to fit it all in. I wouldn't even mind going to London for a day. We are really close to London aren't we?" said Rebecca, cutting her food up.

"Yes, we are close to London. You tell me what you want to see or do and I will arrange it for you," said Mitch, placing some food on his fork.

"Thanks, Mitch. You are so good to me… but I do feel kind of funny though, spending all this money. I must admit, I am still not used to this type of lifestyle and what it can offer. Don't get me wrong, I am enjoying myself and I appreciate it, but I would have been happy doing something less expensive too," said Rebecca, with her brow creased.

"I don't want you to worry about any of that, hey. Money is not that important, and I too would have been happy somewhere less expensive. But I wanted to give you a honeymoon that you deserve, my sweet girl. I know you feel that it's not right that I won't let you contribute to our holiday, money-wise, but what you have to understand is that I am a millionaire and can afford it and these sorts of expenses are nothing to me," said Mitch, reaching for her hand.

"Yes, I understand all that Mitch, but what you don't understand about me, because we haven't known each other long enough yet, is that I like to pay my own way and it does not feel right to me sponging off you. I know it doesn't feel like that to you, but I do have principles that I like to live by. So in saying this, can we compromise? Can you let me pay for some things at least?" said Rebecca, as she looked from her hand to his face.

"You know this is one of the reasons I wanted to marry you as I knew from day one that you loved me for me and not my money and what it could provide. So… Ok, from tomorrow I will let you pay for whatever you want to pay for. You just have to say, otherwise I will pay. I love you, my sweet, beautiful wife," said Mitch, leaning in to kiss her.

Looking into his adorable eyes, she kissed him on his lips ever so passionately. "Thank you. I love you too, my sweet, sweet man."

The waiter returned to their table and asked, "Excuse me sir, madam… would you like some dessert or coffee?"

"No, thank you," said Rebecca.

"No, thank you. Could you please arrange for the bill?" said Mitch.

"Yes, sir," said the waiter, slightly bowing.

Arriving back at their hotel room, Mitch and Rebecca had a look through the room service menu and decided to order a lemon cheesecake slice, vanilla custard, a crème brulee and two coffees which were to be delivered to their room about ten o'clock.

As it was only nine o'clock and they still had an hour to kill, Mitch said, "Would you like to go for a swim in the heated pool, downstairs?"

"Sure. That sounds great, actually," said Rebecca. "I'll just go and get into my bikini."

"Yeah, me too… board shorts, that is," said Mitch, smiling.

As it was late, there was no one in the swimming pool area when they arrived, so they had it all to themselves.

"You look hot in that new bikini. So hot that Sir would like to take you out of it," teased Mitch, as he watched Rebecca walk down the steps and into the pool water.

"Well, you will have to catch me first," said Rebecca, swimming away from him, giggling.

Mitch dove into the pool and it wasn't long before he caught up to her.

"Why Mrs Portellico, you are one teasing woman and now I have caught you, you won't be able to get away from me that easily again," said Mitch, smirking, as he placed an arm either side of her against the pool.

"Well maybe Mrs Portellico doesn't want to get away from you now," teased Rebecca, as she rubbed her hand against his shaft, through his board shorts.

Mitch pulled Rebecca into his body and kissed her lips lustfully. Pulling away slowly, he looked into her eyes and then moved to her neck. As his lips sucked and kissed her neck and then her earlobe, Rebecca's body quivered in excitement. Pulling her left breast out of her bikini top, he placed his warm mouth over it and started to suck her hardened nipple gently.

"Aww, God that feels so good. Please don't stop," said Rebecca, rubbing his hard erection against her vagina.

Mitch whispered into her ear as he sucked it, "Here or our room?"

"Here. I want you now," mumbled Rebecca, her breathing heavy.

Slowly he tugged Rebecca's bikini bottoms down and as she stepped out of them, she watched them float away. Picking her up in his arms, he walked to the end of the pool and placed Rebecca on the steps. She watched in anticipation, as he pulled his swimmers off and sat on the step next to her. Her heart was hammering as she watched his erection sit straight up out of the water. No longer able to contain herself, she quickly jumped onto his lap and inserted his smooth penis into her wet vagina. Mitch placed his hands on her hips and he pulled his cock in and out of her sex rapidly. As he took her bikini top off completely, Rebecca's body quivered whilst he caressed one breast and sucked, nipped at the other. As she continued to move up and down his cock, in sync with him, she could feel her orgasm coming. Moaning, Rebecca felt the unadulterated pleasure he provided her as he sucked hard and then pulled her nipple with his teeth. Her mind and body fell apart in his arms. Panting and feeling exhaustion, Mitch then came undone.

Sated, Mitch and Rebecca sat there for a few minutes with their arms wrapped around each other trying to calm their breathing, before they remembered that they were out in public and needed to get dressed.

Mitch snickered and smiled as he helped Rebecca put her bikini top and bottoms back on, and then his own swimmers.

"That was so good, babe," said Rebecca, sitting on the pool steps.

"Mmm... I didn't want it to stop," said Mitch, looking into her eyes.

Rebecca snickered and smiled. "Me either."

"We had better get going as dessert will be in our room soon," said Mitch, standing.

"Give me five minutes. I just want to go for a swim," said Rebecca.

"Ok," said Mitch, sitting down on the edge of the pool, with his legs in the water.

"You looked like you really enjoy that," said Mitch, handing Rebecca a towel as she hopped out the pool.

"I used to compete in my younger days and I was really good at it too. Won a lot of medals in breaststroke. I still love to swim, it makes me feel good all over. Even having a shower; the water makes my body come alive," said Rebecca, wiping the water from her face.

"Serious... you used to compete in swimming? I would never have guessed that. See I found out another thing about you again today," said Mitch, smiling.

"Did you play any sport when you were younger, Mitch?" asked Rebecca, wiping the water off her body.

"I used to play touch rugby, not professionally. But I used to love to play each week when I was younger. I played it up until I was about twenty two years of age," said Mitch, remembering back to when he was younger and how much he loved to play.

"Why did you give it up when you like it so much?" asked Rebecca, wrapping the towel around her body.

Mitch looked at Rebecca and raised his eyebrows.

"That's when I met Christine. I suppose in hindsight now, I should have kept playing. But she took up a lot of my time and well, it was either her or rugby and I chose her."

"Oh, right… I would never want you to do that for me, Mitch. If you ever want to play a sport or enjoy something, please don't ever give it up for me. Life is too short," said Rebecca, leaning in to give Mitch a hug.

"Thank you, sweet girl. But no matter what, you and our baby are my number one priority now," said Mitch, gently patting her stomach.

"I have seen how happy you are when you play touch rugby, Mitch, and you should look into playing it again when we get back home. If you enjoy it, why not," said Rebecca.

"Are you sure? Touch rugby takes up a lot of time and that's time I won't be spending with you, Bec," said Mitch.

"Yes, I am sure. You should have something that you like to do, that's besides spending time with me," said Rebecca. Mitch pulled her chin up to his and kissed Rebecca's lips, ever so gently.

"Most women wouldn't agree to that, but I suppose you are not most women, are you?" said Mitch.

Shaking her head, Rebecca said, "No."

Mitch picked Rebecca up in his arms and she cuddled into his chest as he carried her back to their room.

CHAPTER FORTY SIX

"Did you enjoy the tour?" asked Rebecca, as she walked hand in hand with Mitch along the jetty.

"I had a great time and wasn't the person on the microphone very informative? He even told me things I didn't know," said Mitch.

"Yeah, I thought he was so good too. So… what would you like to do this afternoon?" asked Rebecca, as they walked next to the railing along the Seine River.

"Truthfully… I would like to take you shopping. I want to buy you some nice clothes for you to wear whilst you are pregnant. Especially since soon your belly will be growing," said Mitch, patting her stomach.

"Ok. I would love to," said Rebecca. Secretly, she was excited too.

Mitch pulled his phone out of his pocket and organised for a car to come and pick them up and take them shopping.

After a full afternoon of shopping at the factory outlets and two busy shopping centres, it was time to go back to their hotel. When their driver finally stopped at their hotel entrance, the doorman opened the car door and helped Mitch and Rebecca in with all the parcels and bags they had from the shopping they had done. Both had bought themselves some nice clothes, and Rebecca even bought Mitch another tie to add to his collection.

Mitch opened the door to their room, then let the doorman walk on through with their parcels and bags, and place them on their bed. As the doorman walked back toward the doorway, Mitch tipped him.

"Thank you, sir. Is there anything else I can get for you both?" said the doorman.

"No, thank you," said Mitch.

"Good night then," said the doorman, as he shut the door behind him.

"Thank you for buying me all these lovely clothes today, Mitch," said Rebecca, placing her arms around his waist.

"You are most welcome, my beautiful girl. I enjoyed seeing your face light up each time you found something you liked," said Mitch, hugging her.

"I hate to say this, but it was so nice to go shopping and not have to look at the price tag and think, 'can I afford that or not?'," said Rebecca, smiling.

"You see, having money can be fun sometimes, can't it?" said Mitch, pulling away slowly and looking into her eyes.

Nodding, Rebecca said, "Yes… Mitch… would you mind if we stay in tonight instead of going out. I am just a bit tired. I think it's all the fresh air and the shopping we did today. I feel pretty exhausted, hey."

"Sure. That's no problem. I was wondering if you were tired?" said Mitch.

"I feel a bit worn out. But otherwise I feel great. Married life sure agrees with me, my sweet man."

Mitch kissed Rebecca's forehead and said, "Why don't you go have a lie down for a while. I can wake you up later for dinner."

"Sounds good, but only if I can cuddle into you. It will make me sleep easier," said Rebecca.

"Come on then," said Mitch, taking her by the hand and pulling her towards the bed. Taking the parcels and bags off the bed and placing them on the floor, he then lay on the bed with her.

"Hey, beautiful… are you going to sleep all night? I am getting a bit lonely here by myself," said Mitch, sitting on the side of the bed and running his hand down the side of Rebecca's face.

Rebecca slowly pulled herself up into a sitting position and yawned. "What time is it?"

"It's 7.30. Would you like to help me order some dinner from the room service menu?" said Mitch.

Smiling at him, Rebecca cuddled into his shoulder and said, "I feel like I have been run over by a truck. I feel so tired."

"Would you like me to run you a nice soothing bath with some bubbles?" said Mitch, kissing the side of her head.

"Sounds nice, babe," said Rebecca, yawning.

Leaving Rebecca to gather her thoughts and get undressed, Mitch walked into the bathroom and ran a bath for her. Once the bath was filled up, he returned to the bedroom. Picking her up in his muscular arms, he carried Rebecca into the bathroom and placed her in the warm water.

With her head resting against the back of the bath, she said, "Mmm… this is really nice, Mitch. Thank you for running the bath for me."

"How are you feeling, babe?" said Mitch, sitting on the ledge of the bath.

"Better, thank you. This water is rejuvenating my skin and seems to be giving me some energy back. I reckon if you hadn't of woken me I could have slept all night. Sorry, babe… you must have been lonely and bored with no company," said Rebecca.

"Well… I wasn't totally bored. I did make some phone calls whilst you were sleeping. I caught up on how my business was doing in Perth. I also rang Nick to see how Paige was going," said Mitch.

Rebecca sat up straight and said, "Is she Ok?" She always worried about Paige.

"Lay back down," said Mitch, pushing her gently back up against the bath. "Yes, Paige is Ok. She has applied for a working visa and is just waiting to hear back on that, so that she can start working at the Space Needle. But all in all she is going really good."

"Phew… thank you for checking on her for me, Mitch. That was really nice of you."

"You're welcome. Oh and the best news of all is that Nick told me

Penny is going to move to Seattle permanently to be with him. They are going to live at the Portellico family home until they are married and then buy their own home. Nick was over the moon about it. If there is one person that deserves to be happy, it's Nick, and Penny certainly makes him very happy."

"Wow... that is big news. I am so happy for them both," said Rebecca, smiling as she envisaged Nick and Penny together. "Hey... I am starting to feel better now. What are we having for dinner?"

"I'll just go and get the menu," said Mitch.

When Mitch returned to the bathroom, Rebecca asked, "Would you like to get in with me?"

Mitch looked at Rebecca and said, "If I get in I will want my way with you, my beautiful wife and I don't want to tire you out any more than you already are."

"What... you can't even get in for a cuddle?" teased Rebecca.

"You don't have to ask me twice," said Mitch, smiling and taking his clothes off and getting in behind her with the menu. "So what do you feel like for dinner?" He placed the menu in front of her.

"Mmm... let me see. I feel like some chunky vegetable soup and bread. Oh and maybe a toasted steak and salad sandwich," said Rebecca.

"Wow, you are hungry, aren't you?" said Mitch, with a raised eyebrow.

"Yep. So what are you going to have, Mitch?" said Rebecca.

"I might have the same, that sounds good actually," said Mitch, looking over her shoulder.

Hopping out of the bath and drying themselves off, Mitch rang room service to place their orders. After about thirty minutes, the food was served in their room and they ended up eating it in bed.

"This is really nice soup and I love the crusty bread," said Rebecca.

"Sure is. Hey... what would you like to do tomorrow?" said Mitch.

"I would like to spend the day holding you and enjoying your company, Mitch, as newlyweds. I know that sounds lazy, but that's how I feel."

"You know that sounds perfect. I would love to just spend a day enjoying your company and making love. And, if my memory serves me correct you know how to give out great massages," said Mitch, smiling.

"I love massages, too," said Rebecca, smirking.

"Ok, fair enough… so what about if we go and see Moulin Rouge tomorrow night," said Mitch.

"I would love to see that and maybe some dinner as well," said Rebecca.

"The pamphlet I saw downstairs actually says the show comes with a meal, so that will work out well. Once we finish dinner I will ring reception and book it for us," said Mitch.

"Thanks Mitch," said Rebecca, giving him a hug.

The rest of the night they lazed in bed talking about different things until they drifted off to sleep.

The next day, Mitch and Rebecca lazed in bed until mid-morning and enjoyed each other's company. After breakfast they went for a swim in the hotel's outdoor swimming pool, located on the top floor of the hotel, and sun-baked on the deckchairs. When it was time for lunch, Mitch and Rebecca looked up a local Italian restaurant on the internet, which they could walk to, and soaked up the ambience of what Paris had to offer. The rest of the afternoon was spent snoozing and cuddling on the bed, back at the hotel.

Rebecca woke at four o'clock feeing well rested. Still naked from their antics earlier, she turned over in bed and noticed that Mitch was sound asleep.

He must be tired, thought Rebecca, lying there watching him breathe peacefully. As she contemplated what she could do whilst he slept, she couldn't help herself, she leant in and kissed his lips.

Mitch opened his eyes to see Rebecca smiling at him. "What are you up to Mrs Portellico?"

"Nothing," said Rebecca, smirking.

"I think you are up to something," said Mitch, his eyebrows raised, as he turned on his side and rested his head on his hand.

"Well… nothing a sweet afternoon delight won't fix, anyway," teased Rebecca.

"I think I can accommodate that request," said Mitch, smirking.

"Mrs Portellico, you sure know how to please me," said Mitch, panting, as he lay next to Rebecca, with his arm stretched out for her to cuddle into him.

"I was about to say the same thing," said Rebecca, breathlessly, as she cuddled into the crook of his neck. "So out of breath."

"Yeah, me too," said Mitch, wiping the sweat off his top lip. "So... when will you start to show?" Mitch rubbing Rebecca's flat stomach.

"Pretty soon. You will probably start to see a bump and then by three months you should be able to see a lot more of me. Why do you ask?"

"Just wondering when I will have more of you to kiss and love, that's all," said Mitch, smiling as cuddled into Rebecca.

Rebecca breathed a heavy sigh and looked up at the ceiling. "Yeah... I won't have a nice body then. I will be all baby fat."

"I don't mind. I will love you even more," said Mitch, as he then kissed the side of her head.

"You always know what to say. God, is it possible to love you more every day?" said Rebecca, sitting up.

"The feeling is mutual, my sweet wife. You know we are going to have a great life together and having children will make it even better," said Mitch, as he sat up.

"Are there any names you like for a boy or girl?"

"I haven't really thought about that yet. I will have to look on the internet to see what names I like. Then again, we can do that together, as it has to be something we both like," said Mitch, getting up off the bed and walking towards the bathroom. "Let's have a shower and we can get ready for Moulin Rouge. I have ordered a car to collect us at 6.30pm, as the show starts at 7.30pm."

"Sounds like a good idea," said Rebecca, walking over to the wardrobe.

The night was still early by the time the Moulin Rouge dinner and stage show had finished, so Mitch organised for a car to take them for a nice relaxing scenic tour of Paris.

"Did you enjoy the show?" asked Mitch, holding Rebecca's hand, as they cuddled in the back seat of the car.

"Sure did... I loved the storyline. It had me mesmerised," said Rebecca, cuddling into Mitch. "Did you enjoy it?"

"Yeah, I did. The meal was good too," said Mitch, remembering the delicious gravy on his tender piece of steak.

"Paris sure is a pretty place," said Rebecca, looking out the window at the night lights of Paris.

"Paris is beautiful at night. Would you like to go anywhere in particular?" said Mitch, as he watched the driver approach the Arc de Triomphe.

"I've heard the Louvre Museum is good to view at night... oh, wow, Mitch, look at that. The Arc de Triomphe is so beautiful, the way it's lit up."

"Sure is," said Mitch, looking in the direction she was pointing to, up ahead. "Driver... can you take us to some of the monuments of Pairs, like to Louvre Museum and anything else you think we may like?"

"Yes, sir. You both sit back and I will drive around to some of the sights," said the driver, looking in the rear view mirror at Mitch and Rebecca.

Mitch and Rebecca both nodded and smiled, as they looked back at the driver in the rear view mirror.

The driver ended up taking them to the Eiffel Tower, Champ de Mars, Trocadero, Louvre Pyramid, and the Tour Montparnasse Skyscraper, where they went up to the 56th floor observation deck to view the city of Paris.

As they stepped back into the car, after buying some pastries and lattes from a well-known café in Paris called Stohrer, Mitch said to the driver, "Can you take us back to the Hotel Plaza Athenee Paris."

"Yes, Sir. You and your lovely wife sit back and enjoy the ride to the hotel," said the driver, in a Parisian accent.

"What would you like to do when we get back to the hotel?" asked Mitch to Rebecca.

Looking at Mitch sheepishly, Rebecca said, "I thought I'd save my pastry for later and have you for my dessert tonight, Mr Portellico."

"Did you now... I see you are back to your naughty self again. But,

I think I can accommodate you there," teased Mitch.

As the car pulled up out the front of their hotel, Rebecca said to the driver, as she looked into the rear view mirror, "Thank you for a wonderful night. I thoroughly enjoyed all the places you drove us to."

"You are welcome Mrs Portellico. I am glad you enjoyed it," said the driver, smiling as he turned the engine off. Quickly opening his door, he exited the vehicle and ran around to open their door.

As Mitch and Rebecca stepped out of the car, Mitch tipped the driver.

"Thank you, Mr Portellico," said the driver, smiling when he noticed the five hundred Euros in his hand.

Mitch pressed the floor number inside the elevator and watched the doors close. Noticing Rebecca's cheeky smile in the reflection of the elevator walls looking back at him, Mitch gently pushed Rebecca back against the wall and kissed her neck. As his hands wandered up her dress and found her clitoris, his teeth grazed her right earlobe. Rebecca took a deep breath in and a quivered breath out as his pleasing hands teased her vagina. Rubbing his hardened penis through his pants, she wanted her way with him in the elevator, but she knew she had to wait. When they reached their floor and the elevator doors pinged open, they were both panting. As Rebecca straightened herself up, Mitch retrieved the hotel key card from his pocket and they made a dash for their room, giggling as they went.

"You sure know how to turn a girl on, Mr Portellico," teased Rebecca, once they were inside their hotel room.

"That's the plan, Mrs Portellico," said Mitch, with a raised eyebrow, his heart rate accelerated by her beauty. Impatiently, he drew her towards him and eagerly pulled her dress off over her head and discarded it to the ground. Rebecca then took off her bra and panties, whilst she watched Mitch undress. By the time they reached the bedroom, there were clothes and shoes strewn from the doorway to the bed. When they were finally on the bed, Mitch made love to Rebecca and pleased her in every way.

Could our honeymoon get any better than this? Rebecca thought to herself, as she lay in Mitch's arms, before going to sleep.

Mitch turned over in bed and reached for Rebecca, only to realise she wasn't in bed any longer. As his hand felt around the bed, he turned towards the bathroom doorway and noticed a light shining into the room through a crack in the doorway. In the background he could hear Rebecca retching. *Bec.*

"Bec... are you Ok? Can I get you anything?"

"A glass of water would be nice, Mitch," said Rebecca, in a muffled voice.

Mitch quickly hopped out of bed and ran over to the small kitchenette fridge, retrieved a glass of water and headed to the bathroom.

With the glass of water in hand, he opened the bathroom door, only to find Rebecca lying on the cold bathroom floor curled in a ball.

"Bec," said Mitch, as he kneeled on the floor in front of her and helped her sit up. "Here sweet girl. Drink this water."

"Thank you," said Rebecca, taking the glass from Mitch. Taking a sip, she felt the coolness of the water soothe her throat. "I'm not sure, but I think I may have morning sickness. I feel really nauseous." She rubbed her stomach gently.

"What about if I run you a nice warm bath, babe; would that help?" asked Mitch, his brow furrowed.

"Yes, please." Rebecca quickly placed the glass on the hard tiled floor and leant over the toilet to be sick again.

Once Mitch had run the bath, which he had put some lavender lotion in it for her, he helped Rebecca up off the floor, took her bathrobe off and placed her in the bath. As she lay back against the end of the bath with her eyes closed, Mitch placed a cold compress on her forehead.

"Oh, thank you. That feels nice on my forehead... I'm sorry, Mitch... this mustn't be very nice for you to see. It should pass soon. I don't usually stay sick all day; that's if this is morning sickness," said Rebecca.

"Don't be silly. It's Ok... sit up and I will wash your back and give you a neck and shoulder massage. Hopefully this may help," said Mitch.

As he massaged Rebecca's neck and shoulders she felt herself relax.

"That feels good Mitch, and it's helping. Thank you," said Rebecca, rolling her head from side to side.

"That's good… here… have some more water," said Mitch, handing her the glass and watching her take a sip. He then continued to massage her neck and shoulders. "Lay back and I will massage your temples."

Handing the glass back to Mitch, Rebecca pressed her back against the head of the bath and closed her eyes as he massaged her temples.

"Thank you, Mitch, it's helping. I am starting to feel a bit better."

After a few minutes, Mitch asked, "What about if I put you in the shower and you can position your head under the water and see if that helps?"

Rebecca nodded, and said "Ok."

Mitch placed his hands out front and helped Rebecca stand and step out of the bath and into the shower.

With her eyes closed and her forehead pointed towards the floor, Rebecca placed her head and the back of her neck under the warm water for a few minutes. As the tension started to release from her and the nauseated feeling seemed to diminish, she said, "Mmm, that feels nice."

"That's good," said Mitch, holding the glass door of the shower open.

"Thank you, Mitch. I think I should be all right now," said Rebecca, as she opened her eyes and turned around, reaching for the body wash.

"Can I get you anything?" asked Mitch, watching her pour the body wash onto the loofah and start to wash herself.

"No, thanks. But thanks for asking," said Rebecca, washing the bubbles off and turning off the faucet. While she was drying herself off, she noticed that a little bump had already started to appear on her stomach. "Mitch… can you see this? I have a little bump." Rebecca smiled and pointed to her stomach area.

"I can see it. Wow… that's our son or daughter growing in there," said Mitch, his eyebrows raised. "I didn't think I would be so excited about seeing a little bump, but I am…are you still feeling Ok?"

"Yeah. I am fine now," said Rebecca, placing the white fluffy towel on the rail.

"Can I feel our bump?"

She smiled and pulled him closer, taking his hand and placing it on her stomach.

Rubbing it around in circles, he then bent down and kissed her belly.

Sure is a nice feeling, thought Mitch, as he stood up. Kissing her forehead, he said, "I am the happiest man alive."

Tears welled in his eyes and flowed down onto his cheeks.

Wiping the tears from his cheeks, Rebecca then cuddled into his chest. "I love you," said Rebecca.

"And I you, my beautiful wife," said Mitch, placing his arms around her. "Would you like anything to eat this morning, Bec, or just water for the time being?"

"Maybe some toast might be good. It may help keep my stomach calmer, and maybe a cup of tea. I think from now on I need to start eating and drinking sensibly. It might help with the morning sickness. I remember when I was pregnant with Paige that if I ate and drank sensibly then I didn't get too much morning sickness," said Rebecca.

"Would you like to go to London today, or do something else?" asked Rebecca, spreading some butter on her toast.

"Yeah, I would love to go see London. But are you going to be Ok travelling?" said Mitch, as he looked into her blue eyes.

"I feel fine at the moment, so yeah, I think so," said Rebecca, shrugging.

"Ok… I will ring after breakfast and organise the flights," said Mitch, cutting his bacon. "Tomorrow is our last day in Paris, so what would you like to do?"

"Not sure… surprise me," said Rebecca, smiling.

Mitch smiled and nodded. "Hmm, I think I know just the thing."

Rebecca smiled as she took a bite of her toast.

"I will pull over here, sir, madam," said the driver, pulling the car over next to the London Eye.

"That will be fine," said Mitch, looking at the driver in the rear vision mirror.

Placing the car in park, the driver hopped out of the car and quickly opened the back door for Mitch and Rebecca to alight from the limousine. "You should be able to catch the hop on, hop off bus at the front of the London Eye, Mr Portellico." He pointed towards the bus stop.

"Right. Thank you," said Mitch to the driver.

"Would you like me to wait here?" asked the driver, in an English accent.

"No. That will be all for the moment. I think we may catch a ferry back to Paris," said Mitch, looking from the driver to Rebecca.

"Ok. Here's my card. If you change your mind, please give me a call and I will come and pick you up from wherever you are in London, anytime," said the driver, handing Mitch his business card.

"Thanks," said Mitch, taking the card and placing it in his pants pocket. "Bye for now… come on Bec, let's go see if we can get on the London Eye."

"Can't wait to see the view from up there," said Rebecca, smiling as she pointed to the top of the Ferris wheel.

By the time the day had turned into night, Mitch and Rebecca had seen most of London via the hop on, hop off bus tour and with a lot of walking they saw sites which included, Westminster Abbey, National History Museum, Buckingham Palace, Regents Canal, Portobello Markets and many more monuments.

As Mitch and Rebecca arrived at the terminal to catch the ferry that would take them from London to Paris, they checked the timetable in the window of the building, only to find that they had missed the last ferry.

"Looks like we might be needing that driver again," said Rebecca, as she placed her hand over her mouth and yawned.

Mitch nodded and pulled his phone out of his pocket, along with the business card that the driver had given him earlier in the day and rang the driver to confirm a pick up point and arrival time.

"As luck had it, he was in the area. He will be here in five minutes to collect us," said Mitch to Rebecca, as he pressed end on his phone and placed it back in his pants pocket. As they both sat on a bench seat near to the roadway, Mitch placed his arm around Rebecca's shoulder and pulled her in close.

"Thank you for a great day," said Rebecca, as she placed her head on Mitch's shoulder and cuddled into him.

"You're welcome. We sure saw a lot today. That was a good idea catching the hop on, hop off bus tour," said Mitch, as she kept an eye out for the driver.

"Yeah... you know I have always wanted to see London, but never thought I'd get here," said Rebecca, as she felt the cool night wind touch her face. "It's starting to get a bit chilly."

"The car will be here soon enough and we will be warm then," said Mitch, noticing the cool night air. "This looks like him now, actually."

Mitch and Rebecca watched the limousine's headlights pull close to the kerb and the driver's familiar face come into view. Standing, Mitch helped Rebecca up and then opened the car door for her to hop in. As she stepped into the car and scooted over, so that Mitch could get in next to her, Rebecca looked into the rear view mirror at the driver and smiled.

"Good evening, Mr and Mrs Portellico. How was your sight-seeing today?" said the driver.

"It was awesome," said Rebecca.

"Great..." said the driver, his eyebrows raised. "Your accent, are you from Australia?"

"Yes... Perth," said Rebecca, as she snuggled into Mitch.

"Perth... I haven't been there yet. I have been to Sydney though. Very busy, a lot like here," said the driver.

"Yeah, Sydney is busy. Perth is a bit more relaxed though," said Rebecca, smiling politely.

"Could you take us to the airport, driver?" asked Mitch.

"Yes, sir. Is the car warm enough for you both?" said the driver.

"Lovely, thanks," said Rebecca, cuddling into Mitch. "It was starting to get chilly out there."

"Yes, that is something that London has going for it, unfortunately. The cool breeze here sneaks up on you at night time. Well, sit back and enjoy the ride to airport," said the driver, as he placed the car in gear and they pulled away from the kerb.

Rebecca yawned and closed her eyes as she placed her head on Mitch's shoulder and relaxed.

We have got another big day tomorrow, so I might suggest to Bec that we go to bed early tonight, thought Mitch, as he silently yawned. Looking down at Rebecca, he noticed she had fallen asleep. Kissing the side of her head, Mitch then gently rested his head on hers and closed his eyes, until they arrived at the airport.

The next day, Mitch organised for a limousine to collect them from the hotel reception at 11.30am.

As Rebecca took her seat in the car, she asked, "So… where are we going today?"

"It's a surprise," teased Mitch, smiling at her.

Rebecca smiled at him and cuddled into Mitch's shoulder. As she looked through the front windscreen of the car, she thought, *I wonder where we are going. Paris is always so picturesque.*

"What's this place called?" said Rebecca, excited as car slowed and she looked out the side window, noticing the beautiful park and grounds.

"It's called Parc Des Buttes–Chaumont and we are going to have a lovely romantic picnic lunch here," said Mitch, smiling.

"Really… what a lovely surprise," said Rebecca. She then gave Mitch a kiss on his right cheek.

Opening the door, the driver placed his hand out in front and helped Rebecca alight from the car. He then went to the trunk of the car and retrieved a blanket and a cane basket.

"Would you like me to set this up for you sir?" said the driver.

"No, that won't be necessary. We will do that. Can you come back later to collect us, say around 4pm?" said Mitch, taking the blanket and basket from him.

"Yes, sir," said the driver. He then returned to the car and drove off.

"Come on, let's go and find a nice spot to have some lunch," said Mitch, holding Rebecca's hand.

Walking through the park, they found a lovely spot with a beautiful view of the gardens and fountains where they could relax and have their lunch. Mitch set the blanket out so Rebecca could sit down and then he got the lunch out of the cane basket. He had organised for some grapes, Colby tasty cheese, French roll bread, dip & biscuits, asparagus, fresh cuts of meats, chicken and some white wine for Mitch and sparkling non-alcoholic drink for Rebecca.

"Yum, this all looks so good. I am looking forward to eating it," said Rebecca, eyeing the array of food.

"You like?" asked Mitch, smiling.

She nodded and said, "What's not to like... thank you."

"You're welcome," said Mitch, handing Rebecca her drink.

"Thanks," said Rebecca, taking the glass from Mitch.

"Here's to us," said Mitch, as he clinked her glass with his.

Rebecca smiled and took a sip of her drink. *He is so sweet.*

Just when Rebecca thought that her day couldn't any better, she watched Mitch pull a blue velvet box out of his pocket and hand it to her. "I bought these in the hotel jewellery store yesterday for you," said Mitch, watching her response.

Placing her glass on the blanket, Rebecca smiled and opened the box quickly. To her surprise, inside was a lovely pair of gold tear-drop diamond earrings. "Wow... these are beautiful, Mitch. I can't believe you bought these for me. Thank you so much," said Rebecca, her eyes open wide with excitement. She couldn't take her eyes off how exquisite they looked. Leaning in, she smiled and hugged Mitch.

"Would you like to wear them now?" asked Mitch, enjoying how happy they made her feel.

"Yes, please. Can you help me put them in?" said Rebecca. Taking them out the box, he placed each one in her earlobes. Rebecca checked through her handbag and found a little mirror in the side pocket. Looking from left to right, she watched how they sparkled in the sunlight. "These are really lovely, Mitch. Thank you."

"I saw these yesterday at the hotel jewellers and couldn't resist. I knew they would look stunning on you and they do. You are so beautiful, Bec," said Mitch.

Leaning in, she kissed his lips passionately. Pulling away slowly, she looked into his eyes and said, "I love you so much, my sweet man. I don't think I could be any happier than I am today in your arms."

"It's a nice feeling isn't it? The feeling of being in love with someone," said Mitch, holding her in his arms.

Rebecca nodded, and leant in to kiss him again.

The rest of the afternoon they spent indulging themselves with the food and cuddling up on a blanket, enjoying each other's company in the warmth of the afternoon sun.

The day zoomed by quickly for Mitch and Rebecca and soon enough it was time to board the cruise ship. Rebecca had asked Mitch earlier in the day if they could board early so that they could check out all the activities and restaurants on board. Once the cruise attendant took their luggage and placed them on a baggage trolley, which would be brought to their cabin later, Mitch was given the keys to their room. After booking in Mitch and Rebecca decided to head to their cabin first, before looking around the ship.

"Can't wait to see our room," said Rebecca, excitedly, as they walked down a long wooden and glass panelled, wide corridor, with plush dark blue carpet, which had beautiful round patterns in the middle.

"Me too," said Mitch, as he stopped in front of a doorway and placed the card into the door to open it. Holding the door open for Rebecca, he watched her face light up as she walked in.

The vast room had antique white coloured walls, dark brown and cream zigzag carpet, with a light grey and black toned coloured quilt on the bed in the cabin, were of exquisite taste. As Rebecca sat on the long, black velour foot stool at the end of the queen size bed, she looked through the sheer light grey and white curtains and noticed an outside balcony with oak coloured wooden decking, which had a table and two chairs, overlooking the ocean. Looking around at Mitch she smiled and said, "Wow, this is exquisite. I love it."

"Sure is nice," said Mitch, looking all around the room, as he sat on the plush beige toned arm chair, across from the black glass looking bedside draws, which had clear glass stands lamps with black shades. Hearing a knock at their door, Mitch walked over to the door and looked through the peep hole, only to see the cabin steward standing on the other side with their luggage.

"Come in," said Mitch, opening the door for the steward.

The steward nodded and wheel their luggage into the room, placing them near the black glass doored wardrobe provided. "Is there anything I can get you this evening, sir?" asked the steward.

"Ah, no. I think we are pretty right at the moment," said Mitch, taking a fifty Euro out of his pocket and handing it to the steward.

"Oh, thank you, sir," said the steward, smiling. "Well… if that is all, I will leave you to it. I will be back later to turn down your bed."

"Oh, that's not necessary tonight," said Mitch, smirking.

"Right. Well, have a good night then sir, madam," said the steward, looking from Mitch to Rebecca and then walking towards the doorway, closing the door behind him.

"Wow, we get our beds turned down. Now that's fancy," said Rebecca.

Mitch chuckled. "So how has your day been so far, Mrs Portellico?" said Mitch.

"It's been a perfect day, thanks to you, my wonderful husband," said Rebecca, as she walked over to Mitch.

"Are you hungry for dinner yet?" asked Mitch.

"No. But I know something else I am hungry for," teased Rebecca.

"Well… I think I can accommodate you, Mrs Portellico," said Mitch, smirking at Rebecca.

"You won't be needing these then, will you?" said Rebecca, removing his clothes, one by one. Gently, she pushed Mitch onto the bed. "Mmm, what an awesome sight. My husband lying here naked for me to do anything I want to him."

"Your will is my command. Do with me what you want," teased Mitch, as he placed his arms out straight on either side of him.

Rebecca, walked over to her suitcase, unzipped it and took out a pair of handcuffs and a blindfold. Twirling them around on her pointer finger as she walked back over to Mitch, she asked, "Does Sir want to play role reversal tonight?"

"That could be interesting. And yes, Sir would like to play," said Mitch, smirking.

Rebecca smiled as she sat on the bed and placed the handcuffs on his wrists, shackling him to the bedhead. She then placed the blindfold over his eyes. "No peeking, now."

As she stood up and undid her buttons, taking her clothes off so as she was completely naked, Rebecca could see Mitch trying to sense what was going on. Smirking, she walked over to the fridge, retrieved some ice blocks out of the freezer, placed a few in a glass and walked back over to the bed and sat down next to Mitch. Placing the ice blocks near his lips, she said, "Suck on this."

Mitch opened his lips and as the ice entered his mouth he felt the coolness first hit his lips and then his tongue. A few seconds later, Rebecca pulled it quickly out of his mouth and started to rub it on his body. Beginning from his left nipple, she continued down to his pelvis with the ice block, licking the same spots the ice had been, but stopping at his pubic hair trail.

With the ice starting to melt, Rebecca licked, sucked and mischievously kissed the same spots, as Mitch's body slightly arched off the bed in the pleasure. Feeling Mitch's body quiver, she kissed his neck and grazed her teeth lightly over his right earlobe. Looking down his torso she could see his erection was growing. Taking hold of his penis in her hand, she started to move her hand up and down his shaft. When her wet tongue licked and sucked the head of his cock, Mitch arched his back off the bed once more, moaning with pleasure as she pulled the full length of his cock in and out of her mouth and started to twirl her tongue around the head. "No more... please... I can't take anymore."

"Soon, my sweet man," said Rebecca, knowing he was on the precipice. But still she continued with the onslaught.

"Please, Bec... please... stop," pleaded Mitch, his breathing ragged.

Rebecca took off Mitch's blindfold and watched him try to focus. "How was that? Did Sir enjoy himself?" said Rebecca, unshackling him from the handcuffs attached to the bedhead.

"Oh my God... that was extreme pleasure and I loved it," said Mitch, his penis standing firm and needing her desperately. He then realised she was naked. "But now, it's my turn to give you some pleasure. Lay down."

Pushing her legs apart, he put his cock into her sex and fucked

Rebecca fast and hard, just how she liked it. "You are so wet, woman. Turn over," instructed Mitch, as he pulled his cock out of her vagina.

She did as she was told.

His relentless torture didn't finish there. As he pulled his cock in and out of her sex, she moaned at the pleasure he provided. "Oh... God... Mitch, that... feels... so... good. Please don't stop... faster."

He seemed to go on and on, until a breathless Rebecca orgasmed, tipping him over the precipice; he stilled over her back. As he took his semi-limp penis out of her vagina, Rebecca collapsed on the bed in sheer exhaustion.

Cuddled up into each other's arms, they heard the ship's horn blast and they both laughed.

"That's hilarious," said Rebecca, giggling.

Mitch snickered and said "How appropriate." He kissed the side of her head and then rested his cheek on her head. "Let's go have a shower and go get some dinner. I am famished after all that love-making."

"Me too," said Rebecca. "I could eat a horse."

Luckily her morning sickness had subsided for the time being.

After eating their meals, Mitch and Rebecca took a walk around the ship, collecting a few pamphlets on the way, so they could see what there was to do and see on-board. At around 11.30pm they went back to their cabin, where they had dessert delivered to their room and discussed what they were going to do tomorrow, and the rest of the week on-board the ship.

The rest of the week seemed to go by fast for both Mitch and Rebecca on their honeymoon. They tried massages from head to toe, manicures, pedicures, and facials. Most days they swam and sun tanned out on the deck, whilst watching others splashing around them. They also watched a few concerts and water acrobats on-board the ship. With the ship having seven restaurants, they tried each one at least once. The ship even had a dessert shop, where they could choose from a huge selection of any cakes or desserts from anywhere around the world. Some of the sporting events, like volleyball in the pool, were fun and they did some rock climbing as well.

As each port came around to get off, they did some sight-seeing and also bought gifts for everyone back home, at each place they went. Mitch and Rebecca thoroughly enjoyed the cruise and were sorry that it was coming to an end, as it also meant their honeymoon was coming to an end too.

CHAPTER FORTY SEVEN

With their bags lagging behind them as they walked down the tunnelled gangway from the ship, Rebecca spotted Penny and Nick waiting for them. Smiling, Rebecca was excited to see them and couldn't wait to tell them about their honeymoon.

"Hi, Bec! Wow, don't you look good, all relaxed and tanned from your holiday," said Penny, hugging Rebecca.

"Hi, Penny. Thanks. I have missed you," said Rebecca, hugging her back.

Nick and Mitch shook hands and gave each other a brotherly hug. "Good to have you back home, bro."

"Thanks. It's good to be home. How have you been?" asked Mitch.

"Yeah good, bro. Looks like you both had a good time. You both look nice and relaxed. How was the honeymoon?" said Nick, looking from Mitch to Rebecca.

"It was out of this world. I had so much fun and my sweet husband spoilt me rotten," said Rebecca, cuddling into Mitch's side.

"Well, let's get you both home. Everyone is dying to see you and find out how your honeymoon was," said Nick.

Sitting next to Rebecca in the limousine as it pulled away from the kerb, Penny asked, "How's the pregnancy going? Any morning sickness yet?"

"Actually, I have only had one day so far of morning sickness and it was only for an hour or so. Mitch helped me through it. I worked out by eating healthy and not having any spicy foods, that I didn't get it again. I think I have been lucky so far. Some days I have been sapped of energy though. But otherwise really well, hey. How are Paige and Michael going?"

"Like a house on fire. They are in love, for sure. You know Paige applied for her working visa, don't you?" said Penny.

"Yeah, I know. I sure will miss her," said Rebecca, her brow furrowed and sadness in her voice.

"Actually, I have some news of my own. I have chosen to stay here with Nick. I am going to return to Perth with you guys, but once I have sold my business and have my affairs in order, I am moving to Seattle," said Penny, excited.

"Wow… that is big news! I am sure going to miss you too, Penny. But I am happy for you as well," said Rebecca.

"I will miss you, too. One good thing though, is that I can keep an eye on Paige for you, if you like," said Penny.

"I am sure Paige will be all right. Thanks for the offer though," said Rebecca. "So did Mum and Dad get off Ok?"

"Yeah, they flew home yesterday. Helen and Grayson took them to the airport and I think that your mum and dad said that they will be coming back soon, as they all got along really well," said Penny.

"I'm glad. It's was nice to see my mum and dad. I don't get to see them much these days because they are always off caravanning," said Rebecca, smiling.

"Yeah, you must miss them," said Penny.

Opening the front door to the Portellico family home, Mitch and Rebecca noticed a banner that had been erected inside the foyer saying, 'Welcome Home Mitch and Rebecca.'

"Aww… that is so lovely," said Rebecca, looking up at the banner.

"I am glad to be home. I do miss how welcoming my parents always are," said Mitch.

"Everyone is out on the back patio area, so why don't we all head out there?" suggested Nick.

"Ok," said Mitch, taking Rebecca by the hand.

When Paige saw her mum for the first time in two weeks, she came running over and gave her the biggest hug.

"I have missed you, Mum," said Paige.

"I have missed you too, sweetheart," said Rebecca, hugging her tightly.

Everyone came over and gave Mitch and Rebecca a hug and asked about their honeymoon and how Rebecca's pregnancy was going. As usual Grayson had cooked a barbeque and as it was such a beautiful day outside, they all decided to eat their lunch out under the patio area.

"I sure am going to miss you both when you return to Perth in a couple of days. Can't you stay a bit longer?" said Helen, sadly.

"Sorry Mom, we can't stay any longer. My business is suffering whilst I am away. So we have to go back to Perth," said Mitch, placing his arm around his mom's shoulders.

"I wish you would both move to Seattle. We would love to have you both here. Especially now you are pregnant, Bec," said Helen, looking from Mitch to Rebecca.

Feeling guilty and totally caught up in the moment, Rebecca looked at Mitch and said, "It's up to Mitch where we live. I would live anywhere you are. I know you moved away from Seattle for a few reasons. One of them being the paparazzi and I don't blame you, I don't like them either because of how intrusive they are in our life. But as I said, it's up to you where you want to live."

Placing his hand over Rebecca's, and looking her in the eyes, Mitch said, "I didn't know you wouldn't mind living here, beautiful. I always thought you only wanted to live in Perth. So... if I changed my mind one day, are you saying that you would move to Seattle with me?"

"I would follow you anywhere, my sweet man; you know that," said Rebecca, lovingly.

"Maybe we need to sit down tonight and really discuss what we want to do now. Really weigh up the pros and cons," said Mitch.

"Sounds like a good idea, babe. I will be happy whatever we choose.

Just as long as I am with you," said Rebecca.

"Sounds like you two have a lot to discuss. You are always welcome here. But if you want a place of your own we can help you with that as well," said Grayson, looking from Helen, to Mitch then Rebecca.

"Thanks, Dad. Of course, I do have a home here in Seattle of my own. It's just… well… that is where Christine and I lived. Since she passed away I haven't been there. Too many memories. But I don't know how I would go now I am married to Bec… and also I don't know if you would like it, Bec. Anyway, we are getting ahead of ourselves here. We can discuss this later on tonight," said Mitch, watching Rebecca's reaction.

Rebecca nodded and politely smiled.

"Not putting any pressure on you, but it would be nice to have you both here," said Paige, from across the table.

"Yeah. I do hope you reconsider. But we all understand if you want to go back to Perth," said Penny.

"I would love to be able to spend time with my grandchild," said Helen.

"You know Mitch you could always sell your business in Perth and only just have your business here to run. That's if you both stay in Seattle," said Grayson, trying to convince him.

"Come on everyone, I think you all are putting way too much pressure on them both. Just let them weigh it up. They will make a decision that suits them, not what we all want," said Nick, looking around the table.

"You are right, Nick. Sorry, Mitch and Rebecca. But we sure will miss you," said Helen, sadly.

"How is your new job going, sweetheart? Do you like it? What's the boss like? Have you told your old boss you are not coming back yet?" asked Rebecca to Paige, trying to change the subject.

"Slow down, Mum. Take a breather," said Paige. "Yes, I have rung my old boss and he wasn't very happy about me leaving, but has forwarded my paperwork to my new boss so that I can continue my apprenticeship. He actually wrote me a very nice reference as well and told me he would miss my lovely smile. But he did congratulate me on getting the job and said he was happy for me. My new boss is such a great teacher and yes, I love it. The meals they are teaching me to cook are way better than what I have been making at my old job. I am so lucky to be given this chance. My new boss says that I am doing well and he likes what he has seen so far. Oh, and after the three month probationary period, he said, if he likes me then he would continue my apprenticeship."

"Oh honey, I am so glad for you. Everything is working out nicely for you here. You found the man of your dreams and a great job. You can't ask for more than that," said Rebecca, remembering all the stages Paige had gone through in her short life so far and how far she had come, especially since Jackson had passed away. Rebecca was extremely proud of her daughter.

"Yeah, I have been really lucky so far," said Paige, smiling.

"You have been really quiet since we have been back. How are you Michael?" said Rebecca.

"I'm going good, Bec. Just tired. Worked late last night. I am over the moon about Paige staying here in Seattle," said Michael, placing his hand over Paige's and then looking at Rebecca.

"If we decide to go back to Perth Michael, there is one thing I want you to promise me and that is that you will look after Paige's happiness. Please don't ever let her down. She has given up a lot to stay here with you," said Rebecca, frankly.

"I know Paige has given up a lot to stay here with me and I do really appreciate that. You can count on me, Bec. I love Paige very much and would do anything for her happiness. She means the world to me," said Michael, looking from Rebecca to Paige.

Rebecca hugged Michael and said, "Thank you."

"Would you like to go upstairs for a rest, babe?" said Mitch quietly, noticing Rebecca yawning.

"Mmm… that might be a good idea. I am starting to get tired," said Rebecca.

Mitch then stood up and said out loud, "Hope you don't mind, but we are going to have a rest for a while. We will catch up with you all later on tonight for dinner. By the way, what are we doing for dinner tonight, Mom?"

"We are having dinner at home tonight, son. The cook is making a lovely dinner for us," said Helen.

"That sounds great. Thanks, Mom," said Mitch, pushing his chair in.

"See you all later on," said Rebecca, yawning.

Walking up the stairs to their room, Rebecca said, "I might have a bath before I lay down."

"Oh, Ok. After you hop in I will come and sit by the bath if you want and we can talk," said Mitch.

"Why don't you hop in with me instead? We can just cuddle up and talk, if that's Ok," said Rebecca.

"Ok. I'd like that," said Mitch.

Mitch wrapped his arms around Rebecca, resting his head on hers, and they lay there for a few moments enjoying each other's embrace.

"What are your thoughts on moving to Seattle permanently, or would you prefer to stay in Perth?" asked Mitch.

"I suppose for me I have grown up in Perth and that's all I know. I had a great job there, but not any longer, oh and lots of friends that I would miss, as well. But in saying that, I do love Seattle, because it's a lot like Perth. Plus Paige is here, and Penny. I get along really well with your parents too. Actually I have become so close to them that I would miss them if we stayed in Perth. I was even contemplating the other day asking them if I could call them Mom and Dad, as I love them so much. Your mom is really loving and she has helped me a lot since I have known her, and your dad, he is such a wonderful person. What about you babe, how do you feel about all this?" asked Rebecca, seriously.

"Well, I love Perth and I have my own business there, which has helped me have the lifestyle I have now, but Seattle is my home for sure. I just don't like the paparazzi, that's all. But in saying that, I would not make my decision based on them. I do miss my family a lot, but I enjoy my independence as well," said Mitch.

"So really, why do we live in Perth, besides for your business and a few friends? What is keeping us there?" stated Rebecca.

"I suppose it's the lifestyle. We live in a comfortable middle class family area and it's actually nice and quiet. I know we have actually discussed that we would like to move to a place of our own one day, but do you reckon we would pick an area the same or something a bit more up market?" said Mitch.

"I would like a bit more up market. But still in the suburbs," said Rebecca.

"We could have that sort of house and area in Seattle too, Bec," said Mitch, stating the obvious.

"Would you miss having your own business in Perth, with lots of independence?" asked Rebecca.

"I still have my own business in Seattle at the moment and I could talk with Dad about my independence and how much I like it. I really like making my own decisions in Perth. It actually feels good to be in control of one's own life, for a change. What about you, if you moved here do you think you would still work once bubby is born?" asked Mitch.

"I don't know the answer to that question. When I had Paige, we had no choice because we didn't have much money, so I had to go back to work. But I do enjoy working, it keeps me sane and I enjoy the kind of work I do, as well," said Rebecca.

"Hmm… I want to run something past you to see what you think… if we can find a nice family home here in Seattle and I can run my own business without my Dad's control, then, do you think we would be happy here, like we are in Perth?" said Mitch.

"We could be… but only time would tell. We could always try it for a year and see how we go. But I wouldn't sell your business in Perth, just in case we don't settle here in Seattle. Also, I can do your books and accounts for your business from home and look after bubby at the same time," said Rebecca.

"What about if we go look at my house tomorrow and also some other ones as well. You know, just to see if you and I like the feel of living here," said Mitch.

"Ok. That sounds like a good idea. I can usually tell if a place is like home to me straight away. So are you saying if we find a place we like, that we may move here permanently for one year, to see if we can settle in Seattle," said Rebecca.

"Yeah, I suppose I am saying that. But I only want to do the move to Seattle and am happy to do that, if you are. This can't be a one sided decision. I need your honest opinion. I need to know what you like and it can't be just because I am here. You need to consider where you would like to live the most," said Mitch.

"You know Mitch, I think I already know where I want to live, but I think I am just scared of the unknown."

"I think that I'm a bit anxious of the unknown, too. But we have to move forward and make a life for ourselves, Bec. Let's just have a look on the internet tonight to see what houses are available and then go have a look at them tomorrow. That might make up our minds for us," said Mitch.

"Sounds like a good plan. You know you are just so level-headed when it comes to planning our future," said Rebecca, turning around in the bath.

Mitch smiled. "How you feeling? Would you like to get out of the bath?" asked Mitch.

"Yeah… we are shrivelling up here," said Rebecca, looking at her wrinkled hands. "But I only want to get into bed and cuddle up to you Mitch. I always feel so safe in your arms."

Mitch smiled and said, "I love to cuddle up to you too, beautiful. It makes me feel good inside. I feel I could conquer the world when you are with me. Come on, let's get out then."

Awakened by a knock at their door, Rebecca said, "Come in."

"Are you both coming down for dinner?" asked Paige, as she popped her head around the door.

"Sure, sweetheart. What time is it?" said Rebecca, just realising it was dark in the room, as she picked up her phone to find out the time.

"It's 7.20," said Paige.

"Right… we must have fallen asleep. We will get dressed and be down in about 15 minutes. Ok?" said Rebecca.

"Ok. I will let everyone know. See you down there," said Paige, closing the door behind her.

Entering the dining room, Rebecca said, "Mmm, something sure smells good. Makes me feel hungry."

Mitch smiled and said, "You are always hungry. But it does smell good."

When Mitch and Rebecca sat down at the table, Helen stood up and pulled a parcel out from under the table and brought it over to them. As Helen gave it to Rebecca, she said, "Your mom and I made this for your baby whilst you were on your honeymoon."

Rebecca stood up and gave Helen a hug. "Aww, thank you. That was really nice of you and Mum to do that for our baby."

Opening up the parcel, Rebecca found a white knitted cot blanket, a bonnet, booties, and mittens. "Oh aren't these just beautiful, Mitch? Thank you so much, Helen. They are perfect. Oh and they are so soft as well. Feel that on your skin, Mitch," said Rebecca, handing them to Mitch. "So, you and Mum knitted all these whilst we were gone. You both are really lovely. I can't thank you enough."

Tears sprang to her eyes.

Helen hugged Rebecca and said, "Don't cry, dear. You will make me cry. I love you so much, Bec. You are like my own daughter and I just wanted to do something for my grandchild. So that he or she will know that I love them. Your mother felt the same way."

"I will have to ring Mum tomorrow and thank her," said Rebecca, wiping her tears away.

"Thank you, Mom. That was really nice of you to knit all these for our baby. I love you," said Mitch, standing and giving her a hug.

That night, after dinner, Mitch went in search for his Dad and found him in the study. "Can I have a word, Dad?"

"Come in, son. Take a seat," said Grayson, standing. "What can I do for you, Mitch?'

"Would it be all right if we use the limousine and the chauffeur all day tomorrow?" asked Mitch, as he sat across from his father on the couch.

"Sure, son. What are you and Bec going to be doing tomorrow?" asked Grayson, sitting on the couch.

"Bec and I are going to have a look at a few houses. Just to see if there is anything we like and could feel comfortable living in. But please don't tell anyone else what we are doing. We don't want to get everyone's hopes up to think that we may settle here. We just want to see what's out there and if we can replicate what we have in Perth," said Mitch.

"Ok, son, my lips are sealed. But can I add one house to the list of options?" said Grayson.

"We don't want to live here, Dad. This is yours and Mom's house and we want to have our own house to live in," said Mitch.

"It's not here, son. It's about two blocks from here. I know it's on the market and it's a lovely place with a great view. And it's far enough away from us that you will have your independence. I will give you the address anyway. Just have a look and see what you think," said Grayson.

"Thanks, Dad, I appreciate the help. Talking about independence … if I moved back here and ran my business again, could I ask you to step back from it and let me run it on my own? I have been doing really well with my own security business in Perth, so I am ready to do it here now as well, that's if we decide to stay," said Mitch.

"Yes, you have been doing really well in Perth and I can see from the business figures that you have made a good profit from it. So I do think you are ready to be given the independence to run your own business here as well. I won't interfere, son, but if you need help I am only too happy to advise you," said Grayson.

"Thanks, Dad. I really do want to make a go of it here for myself and my family," said Mitch, standing and shaking his hand. "Don't get me wrong, Dad, I still want you involved, it's just I want to be the one making the decisions."

"I totally understand, Mitch. And I don't think I am ready to give up work, just yet," said Grayson, smiling.

That night Mitch and Rebecca searched the internet for some homes they could look at and booked the appointments with the real estate companies. Mitch even showed Rebecca the house his Dad was talking about and he showed her some pictures of his house he used to live in, with Christine.

"Well… I think we had better get some shut-eye early tonight because we have a long day tomorrow looking at all these houses," said Mitch.

"Good idea. I am starting to get excited though. Especially as we may find something we really like and feel we can settle into," said Rebecca, turning the computer off and placing it on the bedside drawers.

"Come here," said Mitch, laying down and holding out his arm for Rebecca to cuddle into his shoulder.

That night Rebecca and Mitch both dreamed about looking at houses.

The next morning Mitch and Rebecca woke to the alarm going off at 8.30. Once they were ready, they went down for breakfast. As they were eating breakfast Grayson entered the dining room and said, "Good morning."

"Good morning," they both said together.

"Don't forget to take some photos of the homes you are looking at today, so that you can reflect later on what you liked the most about each one. It will help to choose one later on," said Grayson.

"Thanks, Dad. That's a good idea," said Mitch.

"The limousine and the chauffeur are waiting for you both out the front, so why don't you take some tea or coffee and food with you and get going before everyone else wakes and asks what are you both doing today. If they ask me I will just say that you both went out early but didn't say where you were going," said Grayson.

"Thanks, Dad," said Mitch, standing. "We might just get something on the way, hey."

"Sounds good to me. See you later on today, Grayson," said Rebecca, as they walked towards the front door.

"Good luck. See you both this evening," said Grayson

The first house they went to was Mitch's house. It was a lovely weatherboard house that was situated on the water's edge. Very similar to a boat house, but larger. Rebecca noticed Mitch was shaking a little as he took the key out of his pocket to open the door. He seemed extremely uncomfortable.

Pushing the door open, he stood in the doorway and said, "I don't think I can live here. Way too many memories. Sorry babe, this was a waste of time."

"It's not a waste of time. This place was special to you once. Come on, let's lock up and go," said Rebecca, holding his hand.

He nodded and they walked back to the car.

They ended up going to see eight other places that day. Each house had its own special appeal to it, but didn't feel like home to them both. There was only one more place to look at before they headed back to the Portellico family house. It was the place Grayson had told Mitch about.

Pulling up to the house, Rebecca's mind went from tired and sick of looking at houses, to excited.

"Wow, isn't this beautiful," said Rebecca, as she looked through the window of the car.

"The outside definitely looks like it needs a bit of work, though," said Mitch. He was fed up with looking at any more houses.

The real estate woman was standing at the front door, when they alighted from the car.

"Good evening Mr and Mrs Portellico. How are you both this evening?" She held out her hand to shake both of theirs.

"Good, thank you," said Mitch, shaking her hand.

"Hello," said Rebecca, shaking her hand.

"Come on inside and I will show you around."

They followed her inside.

"The house looks like it needs a bit of work?" said Mitch, as he stood inside the foyer, holding Rebecca's hand.

Not making any reference to what Mitch had just said, she said, "It is a two storey house, eight bedrooms, and each has its own full size bathroom. It has a large kitchen and scullery, dining room, sitting room, large marble staircase, and as you can see, a beautiful chandelier hanging in the huge foyer. Oh and the patio area out the back has a view that is breathtaking. It overlooks the river and you can see the Seattle skyline. The gardens out the back of the house are beautifully manicured and there is a grand style children's playground, with swings, a fort, and seesaw."

"It sounds good. Do you mind if we have a look around by ourselves?" asked Mitch.

"Take your time Mr and Mrs Portellico. I will wait for you in the kitchen."

"Thanks," said Rebecca, as she followed Mitch upstairs.

As they reached the top of the stairs, Rebecca walked over to a tall window and looked outside to the back areas. "I could see our children playing there." said Rebecca, looking at the playground.

"Yeah, it's a really good playground," said Mitch, standing beside her. "I think the inside needs a bit of work though. Some remodelling. I wonder what the asking price is?"

"Hmm, I bet it is expensive, especially in this area," said Rebecca, trying not to get her hopes up.

Walking through the house, they came upon the real estate lady in the kitchen. "What is the asking price of the house?" said Mitch.

"The owners want a quick sale, Mr Portellico; they are only asking 1.5 million, when really it's worth 3.5 million at the moment."

"Yes, but it needs a lot of work done to it to get it back up to scratch," said Mitch, looking around.

"What do you think is a fair price, Mr Portellico?"

"I would offer 1 million only. I think it will cost that again to get it up to scratch – liveable," said Mitch.

"So... would you like to put in an offer today, Mr Portellico?"

"I will speak with my wife first and then let you know," said Mitch.

"Ok. I will leave you to have a chat. I will be outside once you are ready."

Taking a walk up the stairs again to the second floor, they found what would be a master bedroom. "What do you think of the house?" said Mitch.

"The view of the river and the manicured gardens from here is beautiful. I know the house needs some work done to it, but it has so much potential and character. I feel I could settle here," said Rebecca, standing at the window looking out.

"So out of all the houses today that we have seen, which house have you liked the most?" said Mitch.

"This one is my favourite. I feel like I could bring up a family here. I have been walking around trying to get a feel for each room and imagining what furniture could be where in each room. For example, there is a study room in the house and the way the room is positioned in the house, it could be a room for you to work from, or me to do your accounts work from. I love the house," said Rebecca.

"So would you like to buy this house, or should we keep looking?" said Mitch.

"I really like this house, Mitch. I would buy this house if I could afford it. A girl can always dream, anyway," said Rebecca.

"Well, I would like to make your dreams come true," said Mitch, looking at Rebecca for an answer.

Rebecca gave a heavy sigh and said, "As much as I love this house Mitch, we can't afford 1 million dollars. I only have about 800 thousand in my bank account, and………."

"Stop… I don't want to hear that. If you like this house then we will buy this one. Don't worry about the money side of it. As I told you before, I have plenty of money and a million is nothing to me," said Mitch, pulling her in close and placing his arms around her waist.

"You really mean it? But hang on, you haven't even said if you like the house. This has to be a home you love too, Mitch. You can't just buy it because I like it the best," stated Rebecca.

Leaning into Rebecca, he kissed her lips tenderly and said, "I love you, beautiful. You are always thinking about what I would like, not just yourself. But in answer to your question… yes, I really love this house. It has a lot of potential and I can see once it has been renovated it will look good. You know, one of the things I like about this house as well, is that we can choose together the colour of the paint, the carpets, tiling etc. It's something we can share and build together, instead of like some of the other homes we visited today, where we just moved in and it didn't have a piece of us embedded into it," said Mitch.

"You're right about that. Can we go and see the real estate lady and give her our offer?" said Rebecca.

"Yep, come on," said Mitch, taking her by the hand and walking down the stairs.

As the real estate agent rang the owners to speak with them about the offer, Mitch and Rebecca went for a walk inside the house to talk about some of the renovations they could do, and colours they both liked.

After about ten minutes the real estate agent found them and said "I have spoken with the owners and they have told me they are prepared to come down to 1.2 million only. They won't go down any further, as they will be losing too much money."

They both looked at each other and Mitch could see the disappointment in Rebecca's face, as he knew she really did love the house.

"Ok. We will take it at that price," said Mitch, smiling.

"Terrific. Come into the sitting room and we can fill out some paperwork for the purchase of the house and property," said the real estate lady.

"Thank you for buying the house. I just love it and I can see we will be happy here. I am so excited," said Rebecca, hugging Mitch as they walked towards the sitting room.

Once all the paperwork was filled in and signed off, the real estate agent said, "It will take approximately twenty eight days before the house will be in your names. Then, once it in in your names, you can start the renovations."

"Thank you" said Mitch, shaking her hand.

"Yes, thank you," said Rebecca, shaking her hand.

"Congratulations. I am sure the house will be lovely once you finish the renovations. I would love to come back and evaluate it for you, once it's done."

"I am sure we can organise that," said Mitch, as the three of them walked towards the front door.

As their car drove out of the driveway, Mitch and Rebecca looked back at the house and started to dream about living there and how great it was going to be.

Cuddling into Mitch, Rebecca said, "I love you. I am so excited about our new home. I can't wait to move in now. But you know what this means, don't you? We are staying in Seattle. Are you ready for that, because I sure am. Now we have our home, I am committed to going back to Perth to pack up and move back here."

Mitch smiled at her and said, "Me too. I can't wait to move back here with you in our new home, together as our own little family."

He kissed the side of her head and snuggled into her side.

By the time they arrived back to the Portellico family home it was six o'clock. Walking inside they found Helen and Grayson in the sitting room, relaxing and reading.

"Hi, Mom and Dad," said Mitch, as he walked in hand in hand with Rebecca.

"Hi, son. How was your day?" said Grayson.

"Really good. Actually we have a surprise for you both," said Mitch, sounding excited.

"What is it? Don't keep us in suspense, dear," said Helen, impatiently.

"We bought a house in Seattle today, which means we are going to be moving back here to live," said Mitch, smiling and watching their reactions.

Helen screamed with joy and said, "I am so glad for you both! It's going to be so nice having you both living here and now I will get to see my grandchild grow up."

Tears of joy ran down her face.

Grayson walked over to them and said, "Congratulations. Sure will be great to have you back home again, my son."

"The house we bought needs some renovations, so we were going to ask you if it would be Ok if we stayed here until it's finished?" said Mitch.

"Of course you can stay here until it's finished. You are always welcome here, you know that," said Helen.

"So which house did you buy, son?" said Grayson.

"The one you told us about Dad. We only paid 1.2 million for it, but it's really worth 3.5 million. But it needs repainting, new carpets, new tiling, and other renovations to bring it to life again. But you know what, when Bec and I walked in, we knew straight away that it was our new home. We just felt settled and that the house felt like a home to us," said Mitch, looking from his Dad to his Mom and then Rebecca.

"I'm so glad, son. Actually I know of some architects and design experts that can help you with the renovations, when you are ready," said Grayson.

"So are you still flying back to Perth tomorrow?" said Helen.

"Yes. We still have to pack up our houses. Plus I have to put someone in charge of my business in Perth. I am not going to sell it just yet. So I would say we won't be back in Seattle for two to three months at least," said Mitch.

"I can't wait to tell Paige and Penny that we are staying in Seattle," said Rebecca.

"You don't have to dear, they are standing behind you and have heard every word you have said," said Helen.

Penny and Paige came rushing over to Mitch and Rebecca, hugging them tightly and telling them they were glad they were going to stay in Seattle.

"Hey… it's going to be like old times, bro, with you here. I am so glad you are moving back," said Nick, hugging Mitch and slapping his back.

"Yeah, I sure have missed being here and I didn't realise until we came back home, just how much I had missed it," said Mitch.

The rest of the night was spent talking about Mitch and Rebecca's new house and the plans they had for it. Also, their plans for the future.

Chapter Forty Eight

Mitch looked out of the small aeroplane window onto the tarmac. "Will be good to be back in Perth. But we have a lot to do before we can come back to Seattle."

"Yeah, I sure have missed home. I am looking forward to living in Seattle, though. Life won't be dull, that's for sure," said Rebecca, clicking her seat belt into the buckle.

"You know, I haven't even stopped to think about how much life is about to change for you and for Paige as well. How are you feeling about moving?" said Mitch, holding Rebecca's hand.

"When I think back to how my life was two years ago; well, it was very different. I was happily married to Jackson then. If you had've told me how much my life was about to change, I wouldn't have believed you. I never thought I would leave Perth and be moving to Seattle either. Don't get me wrong, I love you very much Mitch and I am happy to be moving to Seattle and start a new life with you. I just never envisaged it, that's all," said Rebecca, looking into Mitch's eyes.

"I know how you feel, my love. I felt the same when I left Seattle to start my security business in Perth. It was very daunting. I didn't have any friends or family there and really, when I think back to then, I was running from my past. I just wanted to forget the pain I was feeling. I remember meeting you and Jackson for the first time and becoming good friends, though. When I think about that day, it was the start of getting to know you, and then, well you know the rest," said Mitch, holding her hand tight.

"Yeah, it's funny how things have turned out for us. It's like the universe pulled us together. I am looking forward to spending the rest of my life with you, Mitch. You make me so happy and fulfilled, hey," said Rebecca, cuddling into his side.

"I feel the same way. That reminds me, I need to advertise for a manager to look after my security business in Perth when we get back. Hopefully I can find a trustworthy person to take it on for me," said Mitch.

"Well, we just won't leave Perth until you do find someone you can trust. It's not worth leaving your business with someone who will not be as good as you are with it. We have to be a hundred percent sure that when we leave we have everything under control. I am sure you will find a good manager. Things will work out, I am positive. I will have to ring the real estate agent when we get back as well to cancel the lease on the house we are living in. Plus we will have to get some quotes on what it will cost to ship our furniture and everything else via sea freight to Seattle. We sure are going to be busy."

"I'll look after the shipment of both of our furniture and all our other things, as I know someone who will do it cheap for us. And I know I can trust this person to get our stuff there in one piece and not damaged. Also, I will have to talk with my old housemates to see if they want to take over the lease, as currently it's still in my name," said Mitch, his brow furrowed.

Before they knew it, the plane was landing at Perth Domestic Airport. Mitch had organised for a car to collect them at the airport and take them home. Cuddling into Mitch in the back of the car, Rebecca fell asleep.

"Babe, we're here," said Mitch, as the car pulled into the driveway of Rebecca's house.

Waking, Rebecca looked out of the front window to see her home. "Ok," said Rebecca, sitting up straight.

Once they were inside, Rebecca opened up all the doors and windows to let some fresh air into the house. It was a bit musty from being locked up for so long. After they put away their luggage and its contents, they decided to have a much needed shower and sleep for a few hours.

Mitch woke and wondered what time it was. The bedside clock told him 2pm, so he decided he would go and get a drink of water. As Rebecca was still asleep, he thought he would hook onto the internet and advertise the security business management job. Once that was done, he rang his friend about taking their furniture and other belongings to Seattle in about six weeks.

Hearing a knock at the door, he peered through the front window to see who was there. It was Kenny from across the road, who Mitch employed at his security business.

Opening the door, Mitch said, "Hey, Kenny. How's it going?"

"Hey, man. Good, thanks. How about you?" said Kenny, opening the flywire and shaking Mitch's hand.

"Yeah, going good, Kenny. Come in," said Mitch, holding the door open.

Walking into the lounge room, Mitch indicated for Kenny to take a seat on the couch.

"So how's the business going?" said Mitch.

"It's been hectic without you man. Glad you are back," said Kenny. "Oh, here's yours and Rebecca's mail."

He handed it to Mitch.

"Thanks for collecting the mail whilst we were away. It's much appreciated. Umm… I have some news to tell you, Kenny. Bec and I are going to move to Seattle, permanently," said Mitch, watching Kenny's reaction.

"Wow… that's a big move, man. What are you going to do with the business here?" said Kenny, running his fingers through his thick blonde hair.

"Actually, just before you came over I advertised on the internet for a manager. I just need someone to look after the business and all the staff for me whilst we are in Seattle," said Mitch.

"I might know someone who may be interested. I'll let him know your number and you can meet him and see what you think. He is managing another business at the moment, but not happy with the job, so he wants to make a change. I reckon he would be trustworthy," said Kenny.

"Thanks Kenny, that would be great. I'll talk to him and see how we go. Hey do reckon either yourself or one of the other guys would want to take over the lease of the house?" asked Mitch.

"I will talk to the guys tonight and we will sort something out. One of us will take it over. I will let you know, so that we can go and change the paperwork at the real estate office," said Kenny.

"That would be good, Kenny. Just one less thing to worry about. Thanks," said Mitch.

"So where is Bec?" asked Kenny.

"She is asleep, exhausted from the plane trip. Guess what?" said Mitch.

"What," said Kenny. *God, what other bombshell is he going to drop on me?*

"I am going to be a Dad. Bec is about two months pregnant. We found out on the night of our wedding," said Mitch.

"You sly dog. I am so happy for you, Mitch. That's such good news," said Kenny, shaking Mitch's hand.

"Yeah we are pretty rapt," said Mitch.

"So how long before you both move to Seattle?" asked Kenny, anxious.

"Probably about six to eight weeks," said Mitch.

"Sure am going to miss you, man," said Kenny.

"Yeah, and I will miss you all too," said Mitch. "Would you like a drink?"

"Nah. I had better get going, mate. I just thought I'd come over and give you your mail and see how you are doing," said Kenny, getting up out of his seat.

"Thanks, Kenny. I'll catch up with you later, anyway," said Mitch, shaking his hand.

After Kenny left, Mitch returned to the bedroom to see if Rebecca was still asleep. As he approached the bed she stirred. Lying down next to Rebecca, facing her, he ran his hand over her cheek.

As she opened her eyes, he said, "Hi, sleepyhead. I was wondering when you were going to wake up."

Rebecca smiled at him and cuddled into his chest.

"Hi, my gorgeous man. I was just dreaming about you. That's probably why I didn't wake; I was enjoying myself way too much," smirked Rebecca.

"Mmm, I see, and what were we doing in your dream, babe?" said Mitch.

"Playing and enjoying each other," said Rebecca.

"You are one naughty girl, aren't you?" said Mitch, teasing her.

It had now been four weeks since Mitch and Rebecca returned home and everything was starting to fall into place for their move to Seattle. They were now finally living in a hotel suite as the lease had run out on the house they were in, and their belongings and furniture were on a ship to Seattle.

Mitch had found a really reliable business manager and his lease to his place had been taken over by Kenny.

The day before they left Perth all their good friends ended up throwing a huge going away party for them to say goodbye. Rebecca sure was sad to be leaving such good friends and a city that she loved, but also looked forward to a new adventure.

Before they knew it, Mitch and Rebecca had arrived back in Seattle and it was only a couple of months before they could move into their own home.

Today was the appointment at the doctor's to have a check-up and an ultrasound done. Rebecca had hit the four month mark and her belly, much to her dismay, was getting huge.

Once the doctor had checked Rebecca's blood pressure and done a urine test, he said, "Let's get you up on the table and we can do the ultrasound now. You should be able to hear your baby's heartbeat today."

Mitch and Rebecca looked at each other and smiled, as the doctor turned the monitor around so that they could see their baby.

Pouring some gel out of the tube onto her stomach, he then placed the ultrasound probe onto Rebecca's stomach. Looking at the monitor, he frowned and twisted his lips sideways. "Can't be… just one moment, I need to check this before I say anything."

Mitch and Rebecca looked at each other nervously and Mitch held Rebecca's hand firmly. Waiting anxiously and watching the doctor continue the ultrasound and double checking what he was looking at made them feel tense.

"You are having two babies. Yes, there are definitely two babies in there; two heartbeats," said the doctor, smiling.

"Pardon… did I just hear you correctly? You said we are having two babies?" said Mitch, with a creased forehead.

"Yes. Listen, there are two heartbeats," said the doctor, turning the sound up on the monitor.

Rebecca was still in shock and hadn't said anything.

"Are you Ok, babe?" said Mitch holding her hand and looking at Rebecca's face.

"I am shocked. I don't believe it. But it would explain why I am so hungry and tired all the damn time. Unbelievable. Do you know what sex they are?" said Rebecca.

"Yes. Are you sure you both want to know?" said the doctor, looking at them apprehensively.

They both nodded.

Pointing to the screen, he said, "The one on the left is a boy and the one on the right is a girl. And they are both really healthy."

"I don't believe it," said Rebecca, anxious, but excited at the same time.

"Oh God, double trouble," said Mitch, laughing.

"Do twins run on either side of your families?" asked the doctor.

Mitch and Rebecca both nodded.

"But I didn't think I would ever be able to carry twins. This is unbelievable," said Rebecca.

"Rebecca, I will need to see you at least every second week because you are carrying twins. As you get further along, I will need to see you even more regularly. I must warn you though, that most twins are born through caesarean. Not through a normal delivery, so please prepare yourself for that, just in case," said the doctor, seriously.

"Oh, Ok. Can we get a picture of them both?" said Rebecca.

"Yes. I will print one out for you now," said the doctor.

On the way home in the car, Mitch and Rebecca were both quiet, as the realisation of having twins sunk in.

"I am sure going to have my hands full with two babies," said Rebecca, placing her hand on her stomach.

"Mmm… it probably won't be easy for a while. But we have plenty of family here who will want to help," said Mitch.

Rebecca cuddled into Mitch's side and said, "I still can't even believe this is happening. Talk about an automatic family."

Arriving at the Portellico family home, Mitch and Rebecca couldn't wait to get inside to let everyone know their exciting news.

Mitch yelled out, "Mom, Dad, you home? We have some exciting news!"

Helen and Grayson came rushing out of the sitting room and Helen said, "What is it, son?"

Rebecca handed them the ultrasound photo and said, "Look carefully and you will see why we are excited."

"Two babies. There are two babies! Wow… unbelievable. Do you know what sex they are?" said Helen, excited.

"Boy and girl. Aren't we the luckiest couple around?" said Mitch.

"Well you sure are going to have your hands full, but we are here to help," said Helen.

"Congratulations," said Grayson, hugging Mitch and Rebecca together.

"Two grandchildren… I won't be able to contain myself. I am going to spoil them rotten. Oh, wait till your parents find out, dear. They are going to be over the moon," said Helen.

She hugged Mitch and Rebecca tight.

"Do you reckon you will have one nursery in the new house dear or two?" asked Helen.

"God, I haven't even thought about that at all," said Rebecca. "I suppose now is the time to get the renovators to change things in the house?"

"Don't stress about that now, babe. We can work it out later," said Mitch, as he put his arm around her waist.

"Would you two like to go out tonight to celebrate, or stay home and celebrate?" said Helen.

"My gorgeous man needs a night out as he has been working so hard lately, plus putting up with me. So if Mitch agrees, can we go out to celebrate?" said Rebecca.

"Sounds like a great idea to me," said Mitch, smiling.

"Well, it's settled then. What about Grayson's Restaurant, does that sound all right?" said Helen.

"That sounds fine, Mom. I think everyone is home tonight as well. Will be nice to go out and celebrate our news with everyone," said Mitch.

As the last glass of champagne was poured by the waitress at the restaurant, Grayson stood at the end of the long square table, cleared his throat and tapped on his glass with his knife. As he looked around at each of his family's faces, the table quietened, and he said, "I would like to propose a toast… to our ever growing family; may we be blessed with good health, happiness, and a love that always shines through."

Everyone raised their glasses and said "Hear, hear."

Rebecca took a sip of her water and placed the glass on the table. Smiling, she looked around the table, and realised that she had finally found security in her friends, her family and her new home.

CATCH UP ON ALL THE LATEST NEWS AND UPDATES FROM SUSAN HODDY

For the latest news on Susan Hoddy visit:-

Facebook: Susan Hoddy - Author

Twitter: @susan_hoddy

Instagram: susanhoddy

Website: www.susanhoddy.com

If you would like a group or book club reading done of some chapters and/or a book signing in your store, please contact Susan via her website to organise an appointment.

ACKNOWLEDGEMENTS

It never gets any easier, and in some ways this book was the hardest book for me to write. But even though it's been hard, I have thoroughly enjoyed writing it.

This book would not be here, resting in your hands, or on your e-reader if it weren't for the following people. I owe all of them my deepest gratitude.

My fiancé, Michael Houston and my daughter, Samantha Hoddy. You have always given me time and space to write my books and have been interested in what I am writing. I could not have written this without your continued advice, support and love. I feel truly blessed to have you both in my life. Thank you, Michael and Sam.

My long time, and good friend, Sue Nichols, who spent countless hours proof reading my manuscript, and has given me some honest feedback. My readers will definitely thank you for all the spelling and grammatical errors you found. Thank you again, Sue.

Several friends, family members, and associates, all of whom have read my manuscript and given me feedback on what they wanted to see in the storyline and book cover. Many thanks to you all.

My book cover designer, Beti Bup from The Book Cover Designer, who worked tirelessly to provide me with a truly breathtaking cover design. Thank you, Beti Bup.

Susan Hoddy is a young-adult fiction writer, best known for her Lepidoptera Vampire Series. Susan was born in Perth, Western Australia in 1966, and enjoys a good chinwag with family and friends, cups of tea, day-dreaming and writing.

Susan has always worked in many facets of an office during her life, but in 2012 she decided life was too short and wanted to make a start on her passion, which was writing. After acquiring her novel writing diploma from the Australian College of Journalism, she continues to create worlds where fantasy and romance exist, with her books.

In 2019 Susan won two book awards for Attraction and Awakened in the Lepidoptera Vampire Series from New Apple Literary Fifth Annual Indic Book Awards.

'Attraction: The Lepidoptera Vampire Series – Book One' was chosen as the "Official Selection" in the **YOUNG ADULT GENERAL FICTION** category.

'Awakened: The Lepidoptera Vampire Series – Book Two' was chosen as the solo "Medalist Winner" in the **YOUNG ADULT GENERAL FICTION** category.

www.ingramcontent.com/pod-product-compliance
Lightning Source LLC
Chambersburg PA
CBHW020456020726
47493CB00001B/54